NOTHING CAN
POSSIBLY GO WRONG

P9-CML-189

NOTHING CAN POSSIBLY GO WRONG

PRUDENCE SHEN & FAITH ERIN HICKS

:01

First Second
New York

First Second
New York

Story copyright © 2013 by Prudence Shen
Adaptation and illustrations copyright © 2013 by Faith Erin Hicks

Published by First Second
First Second is an imprint of Roaring Brook Press,
a division of Holtzbrinck Publishing Holdings Limited Partnership
175 Fifth Avenue, New York, New York 10010
All rights reserved

Cataloging-in-Publication Data is on file at the Library of Congress.

978-1-59643-659-6

First Second books are available for special promotions and premiums.
For details, contact: Director of Special Markets, Holtzbrinck Publishers.

First edition 2013
Book design by Colleen AF Venable
Printed in the United States of America

10 9 8 7 6 5 4 3 2 1

For my parents,
even though they never bought me a robot

—P. S.

For all the girl geeks

—F. E. H.

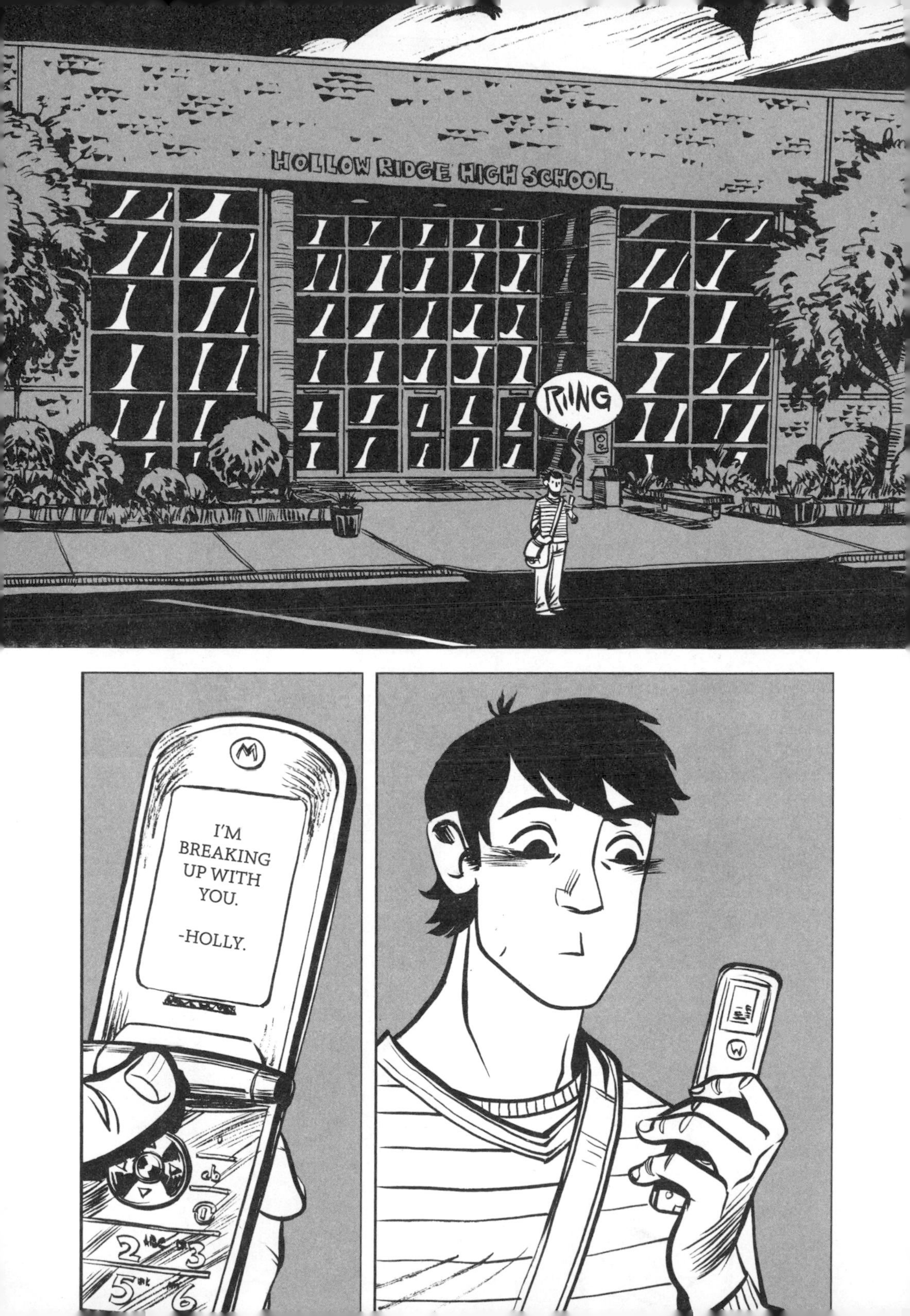
HOLLOW RIDGE HIGH SCHOOL
RIING
I'M BREAKING UP WITH YOU.
-HOLLY.

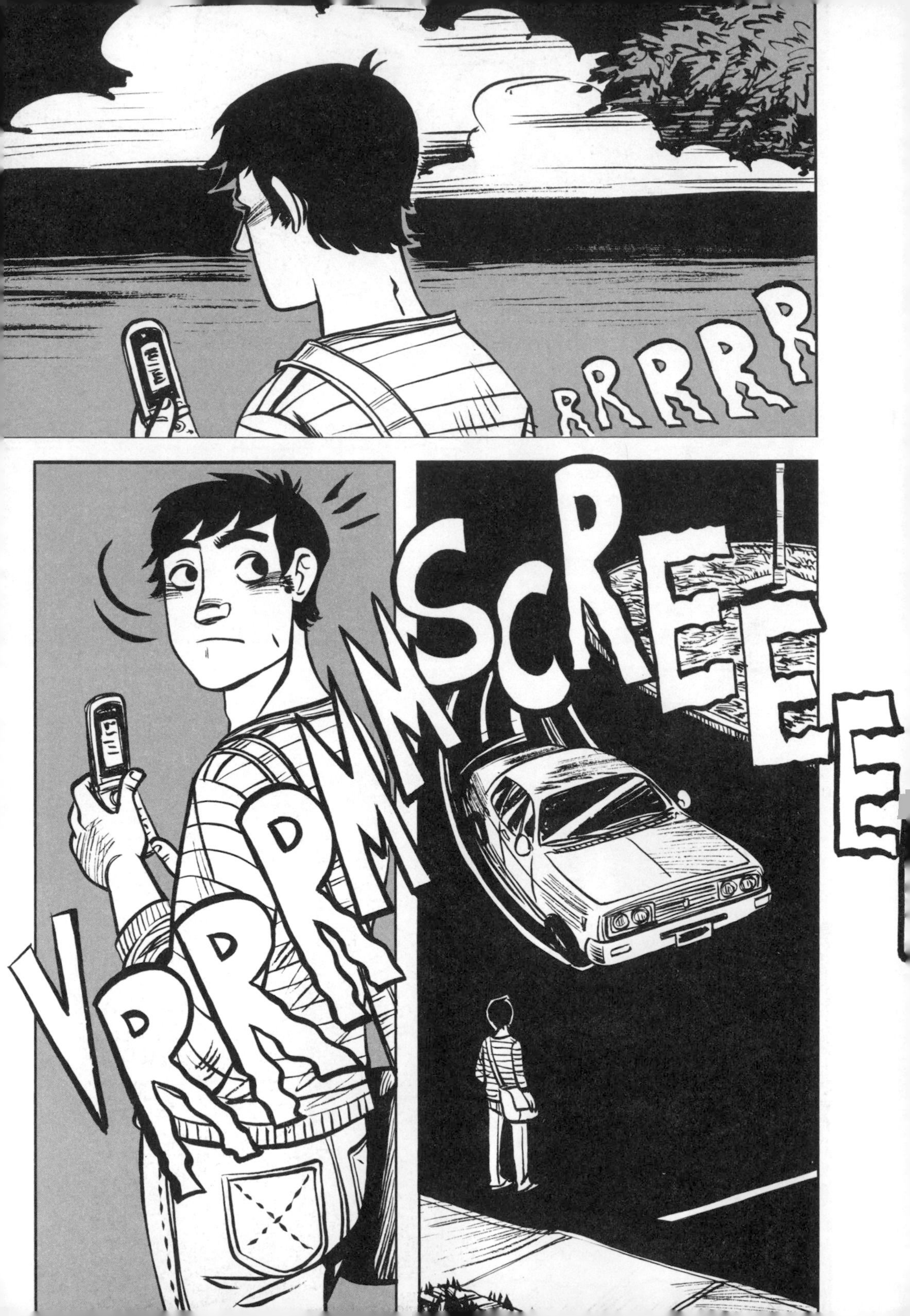
RRRRRR
VRRRRMM
SCREEEE

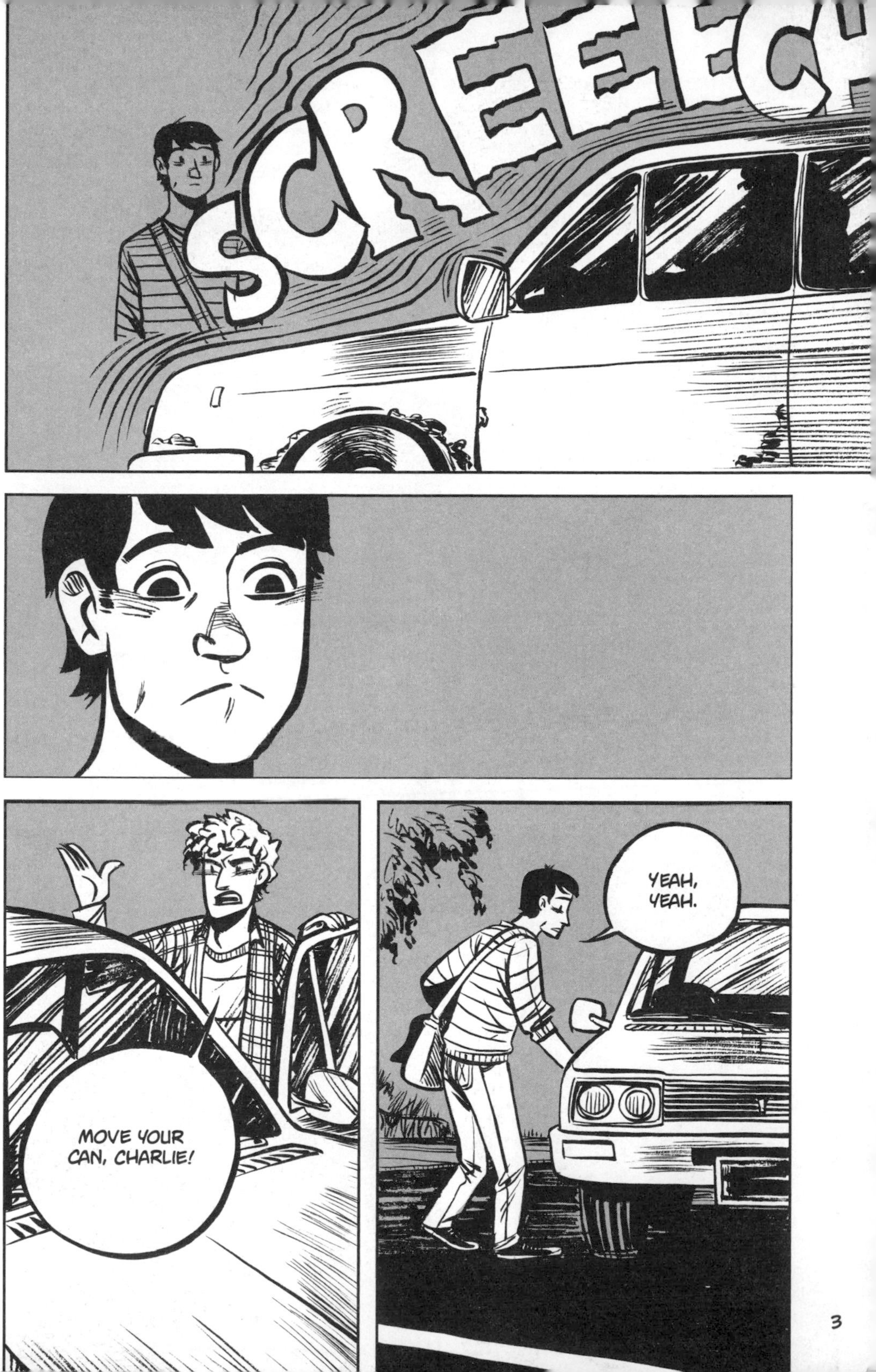
SCREEECH
MOVE YOUR CAN, CHARLIE!
YEAH, YEAH.

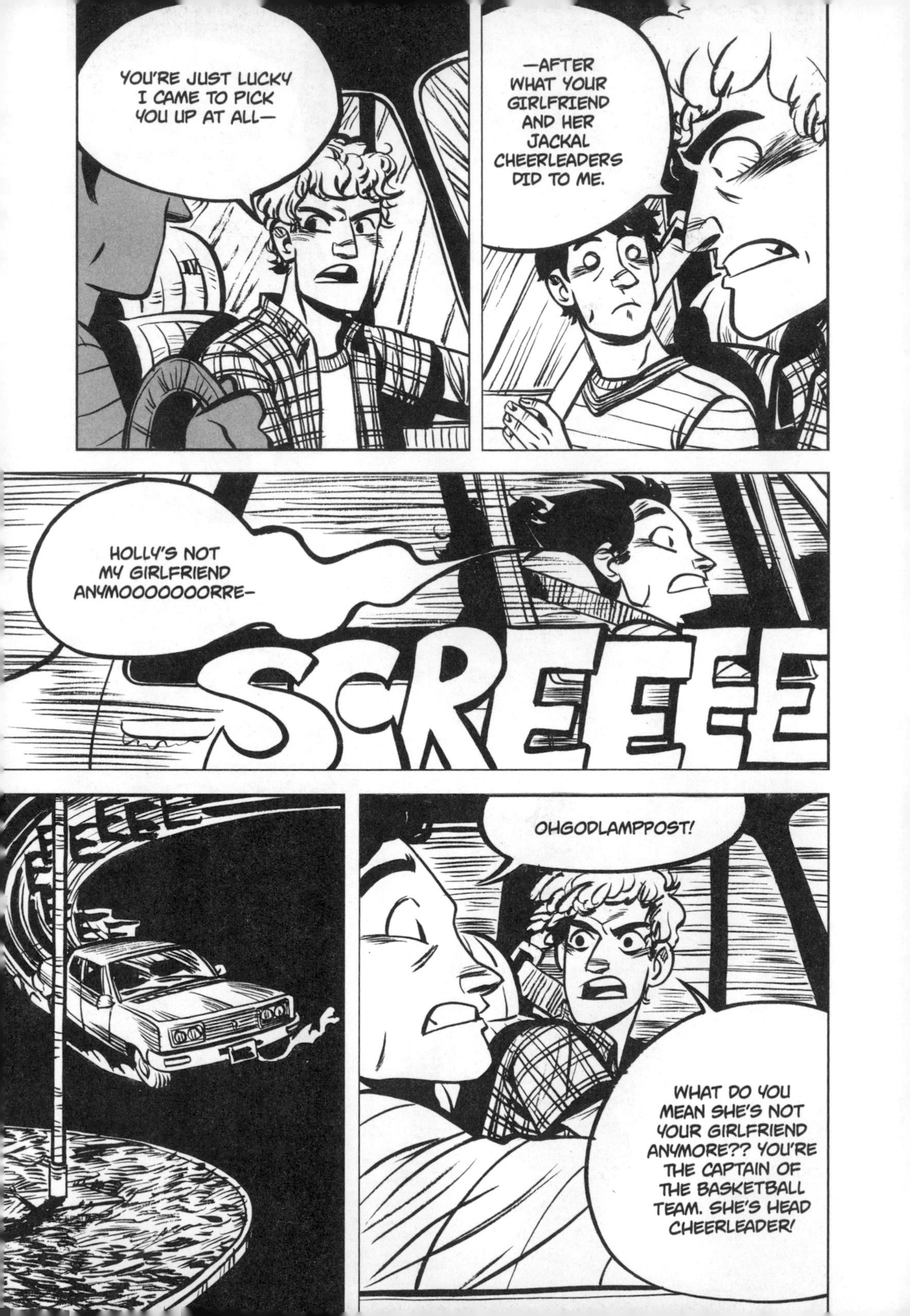
YOU'RE JUST LUCKY I CAME TO PICK YOU UP AT ALL—
—AFTER WHAT YOUR GIRLFRIEND AND HER JACKAL CHEERLEADERS DID TO ME.
HOLLY'S NOT MY GIRLFRIEND ANYMOOOOOOORRE-
SCREEEE
EEEEE
OHGODLAMPPOST!
WHAT DO YOU MEAN SHE'S NOT YOUR GIRLFRIEND ANYMORE?? YOU'RE THE CAPTAIN OF THE BASKETBALL TEAM. SHE'S HEAD CHEERLEADER!

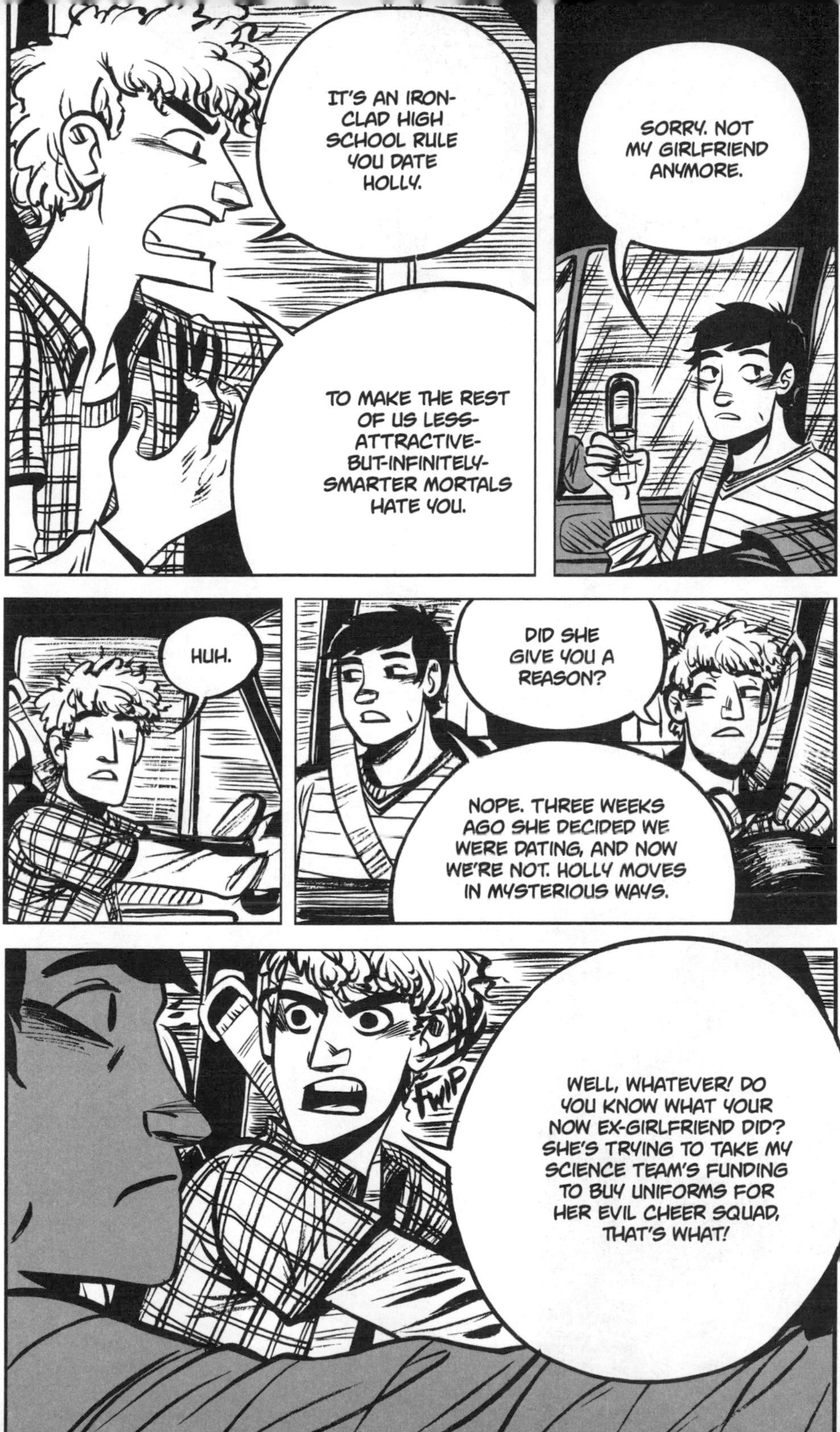
IT'S AN IRON-CLAD HIGH SCHOOL RULE YOU DATE HOLLY.
TO MAKE THE REST OF US LESS-ATTRACTIVE-BUT-INFINITELY-SMARTER MORTALS HATE YOU.
SORRY. NOT MY GIRLFRIEND ANYMORE.
HUH.
DID SHE GIVE YOU A REASON?
NOPE. THREE WEEKS AGO SHE DECIDED WE WERE DATING, AND NOW WE'RE NOT. HOLLY MOVES IN MYSTERIOUS WAYS.
FWIP
WELL, WHATEVER! DO YOU KNOW WHAT YOUR NOW EX-GIRLFRIEND DID? SHE'S TRYING TO TAKE MY SCIENCE TEAM'S FUNDING TO BUY UNIFORMS FOR HER EVIL CHEER SQUAD, THAT'S WHAT!

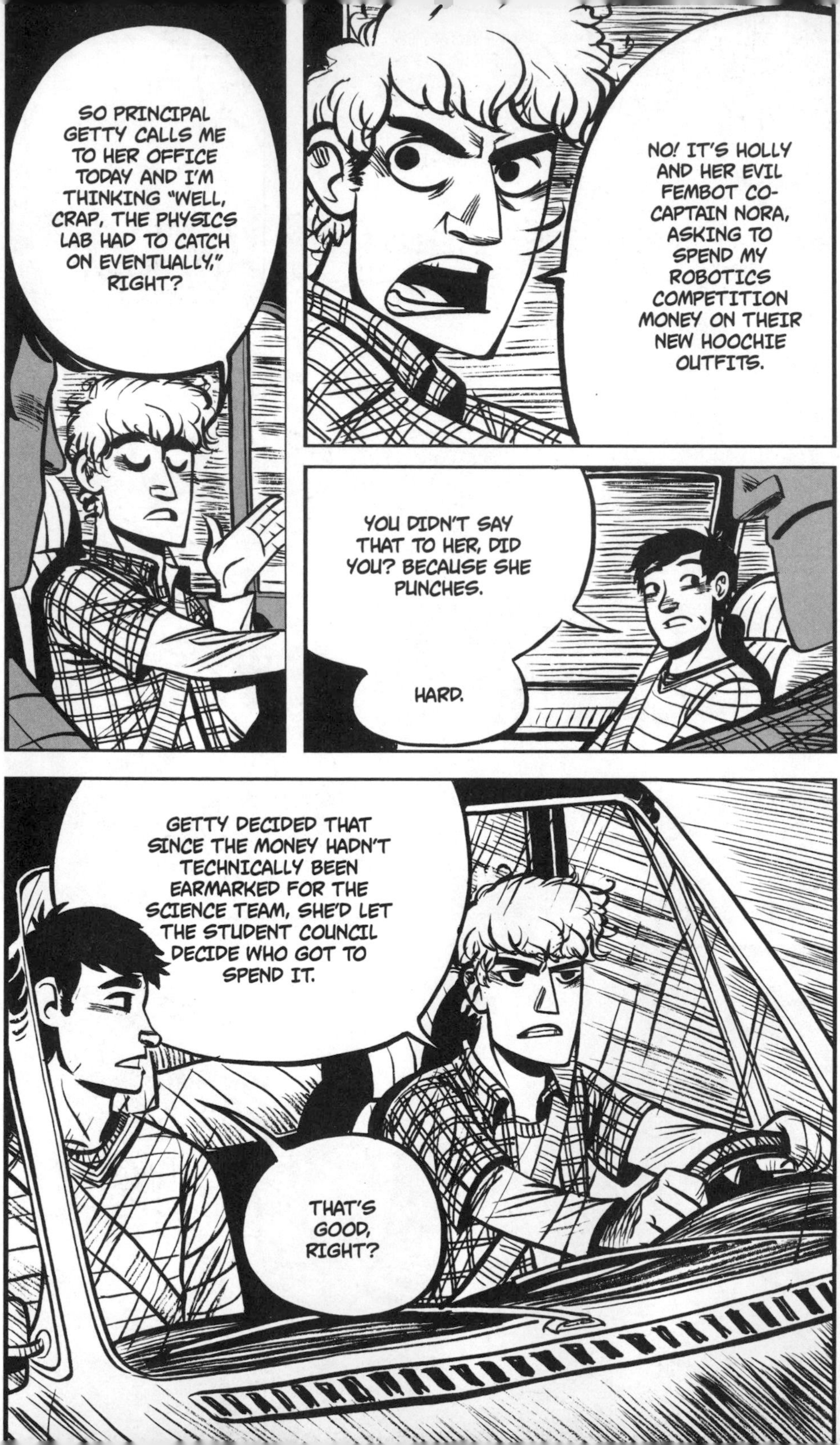
SO PRINCIPAL GETTY CALLS ME TO HER OFFICE TODAY AND I'M THINKING "WELL, CRAP, THE PHYSICS LAB HAD TO CATCH ON EVENTUALLY," RIGHT?
NO! IT'S HOLLY AND HER EVIL FEMBOT CO-CAPTAIN NORA, ASKING TO SPEND MY ROBOTICS COMPETITION MONEY ON THEIR NEW HOOCHIE OUTFITS.
YOU DIDN'T SAY THAT TO HER, DID YOU? BECAUSE SHE PUNCHES.
HARD.
GETTY DECIDED THAT SINCE THE MONEY HADN'T TECHNICALLY BEEN EARMARKED FOR THE SCIENCE TEAM, SHE'D LET THE STUDENT COUNCIL DECIDE WHO GOT TO SPEND IT.
THAT'S GOOD, RIGHT?

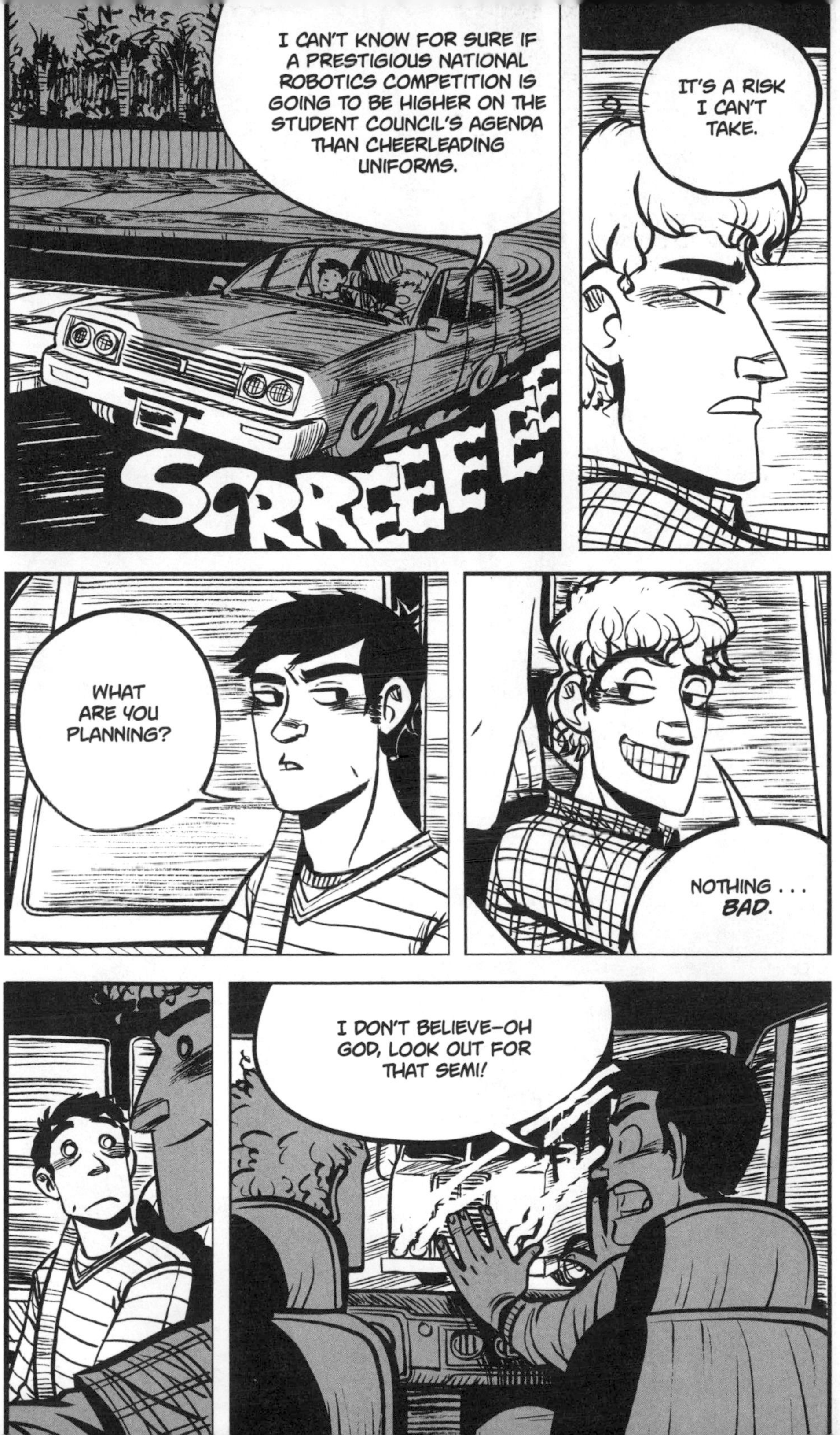
I CAN'T KNOW FOR SURE IF A PRESTIGIOUS NATIONAL ROBOTICS COMPETITION IS GOING TO BE HIGHER ON THE STUDENT COUNCIL'S AGENDA THAN CHEERLEADING UNIFORMS.
SCRREEEE
IT'S A RISK I CAN'T TAKE.
WHAT ARE YOU PLANNING?
NOTHING . . . *BAD*.
I DON'T BELIEVE–OH GOD, LOOK OUT FOR THAT SEMI!

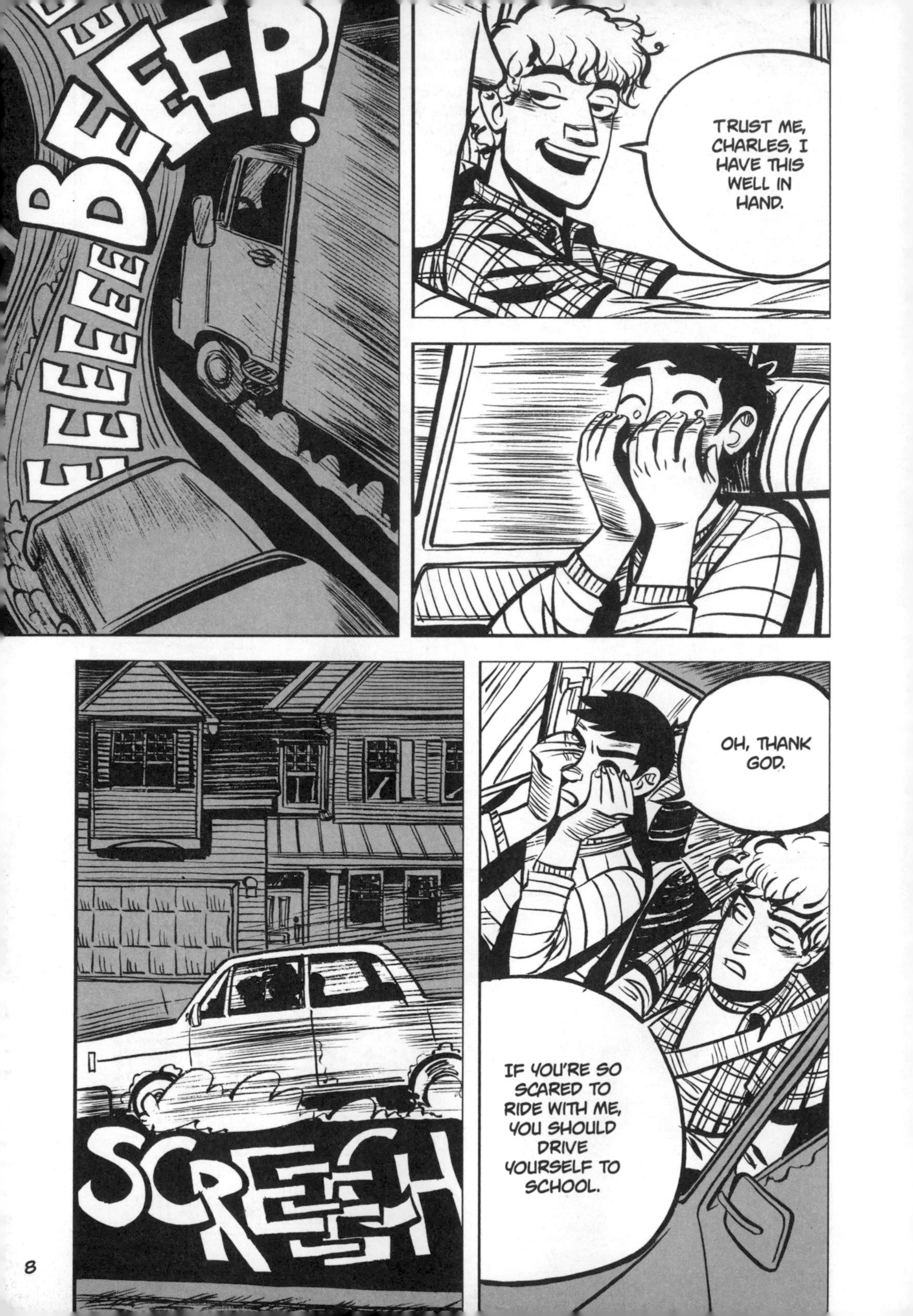
BEEEEEEEEEEEEEP!
TRUST ME, CHARLES, I HAVE THIS WELL IN HAND.
SCREEEEECH
OH, THANK GOD.
IF YOU'RE SO SCARED TO RIDE WITH ME, YOU SHOULD DRIVE YOURSELF TO SCHOOL.

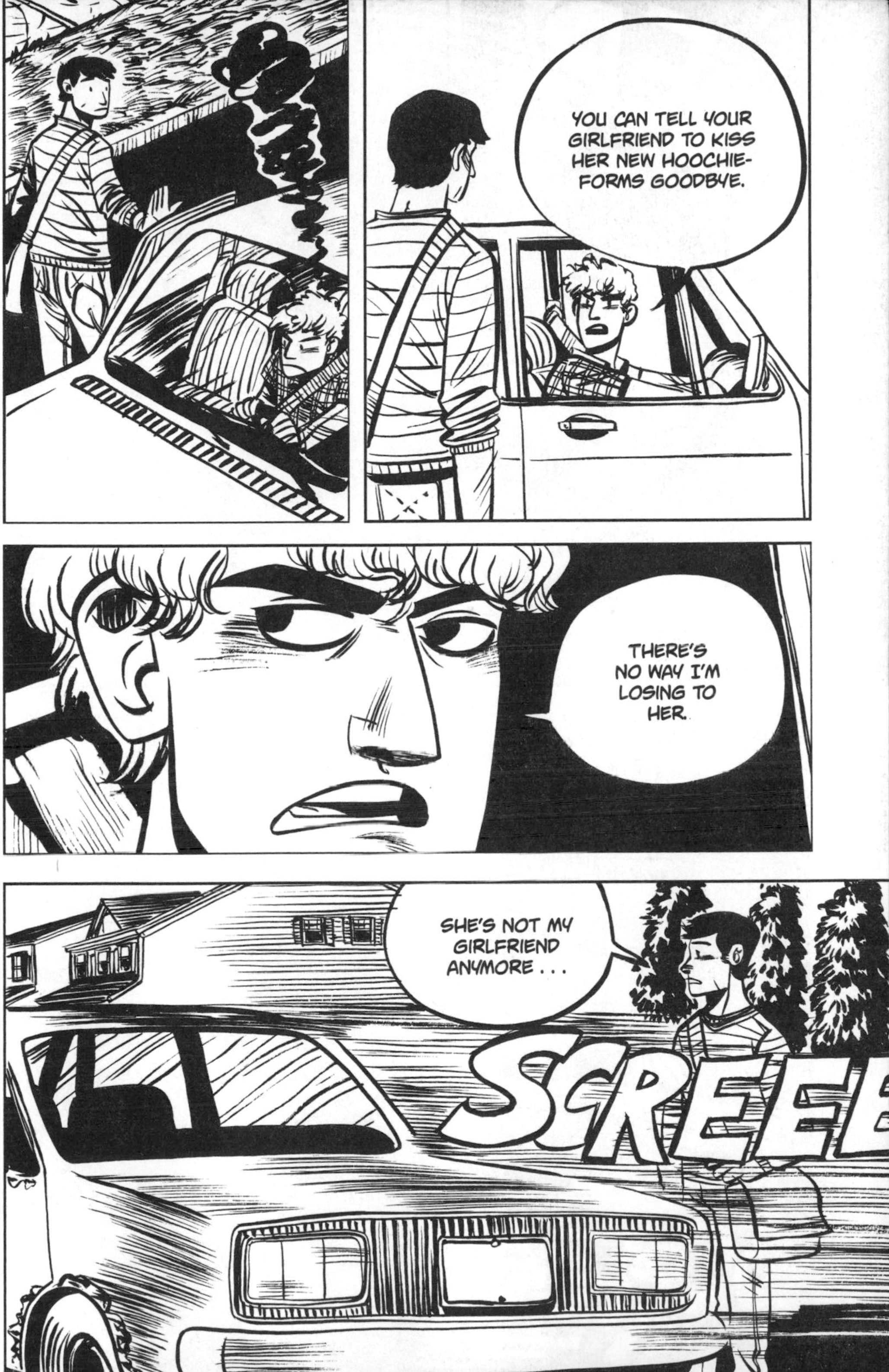
YOU CAN TELL YOUR GIRLFRIEND TO KISS HER NEW HOOCHIE-FORMS GOODBYE.
THERE'S NO WAY I'M LOSING TO HER.
SHE'S NOT MY GIRLFRIEND ANYMORE . . .
SCREEE

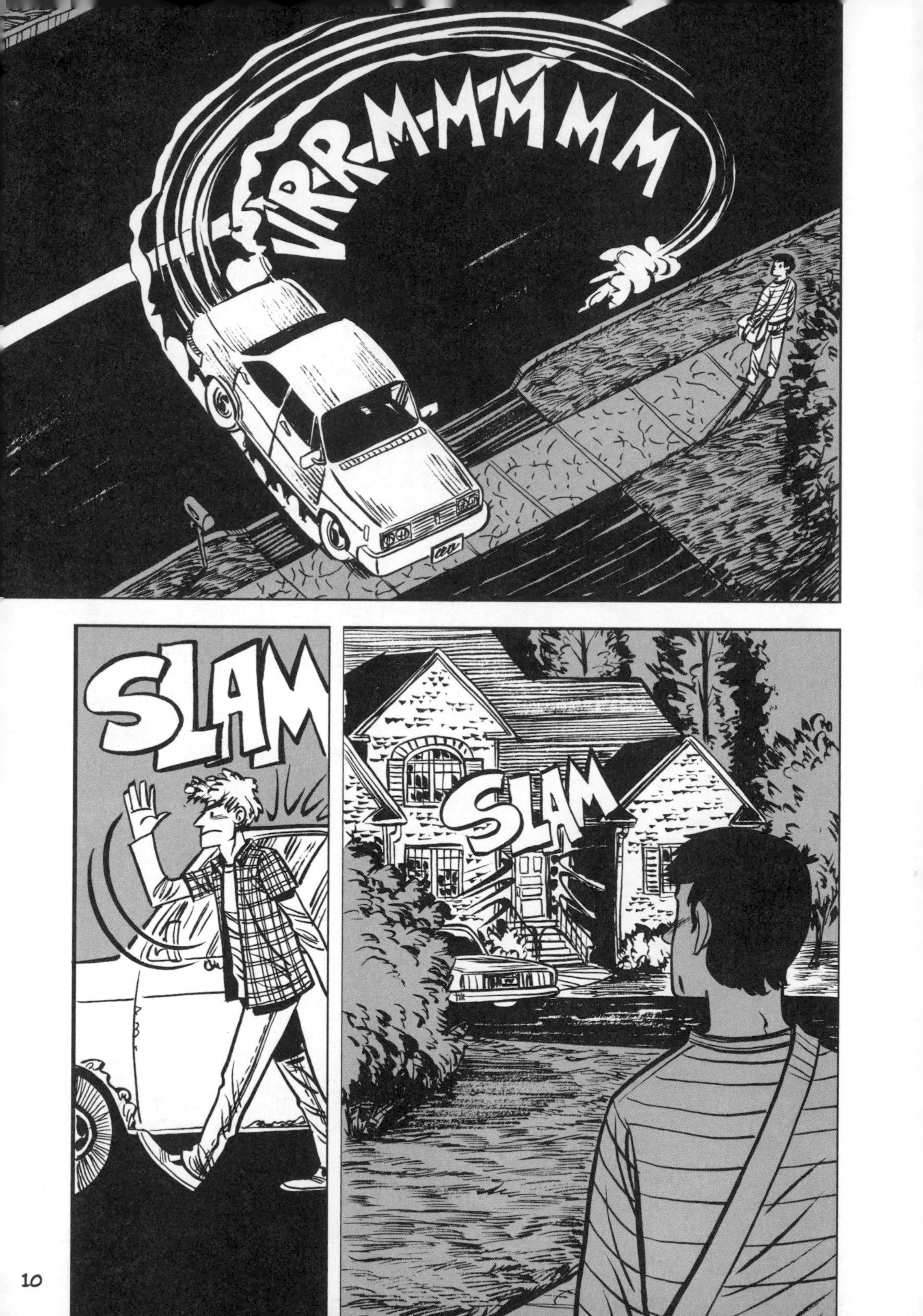
VRR-M-M-M-M M M
SLAM
SLAM

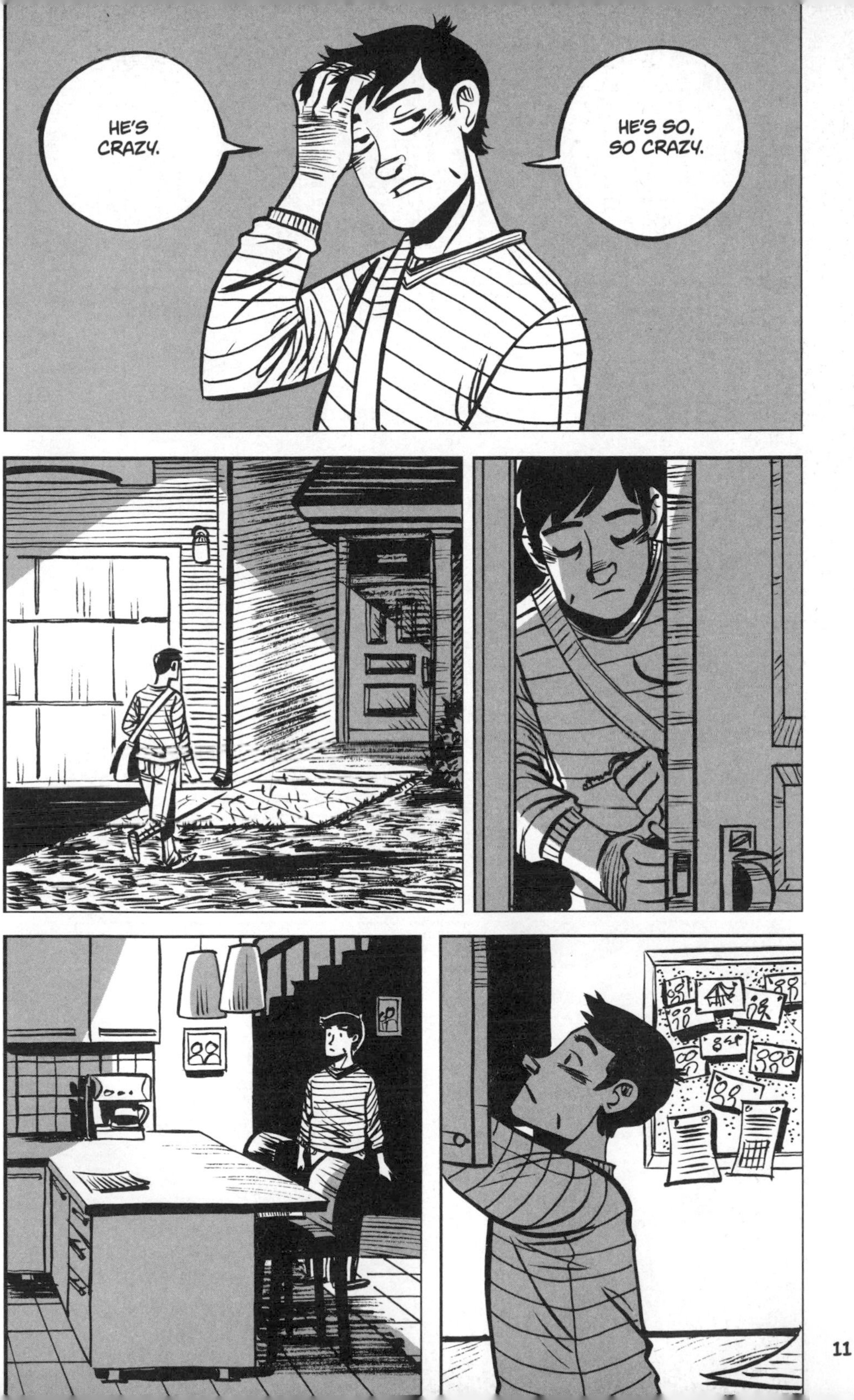
HE'S
CRAZY.
HE'S SO,
SO CRAZY.

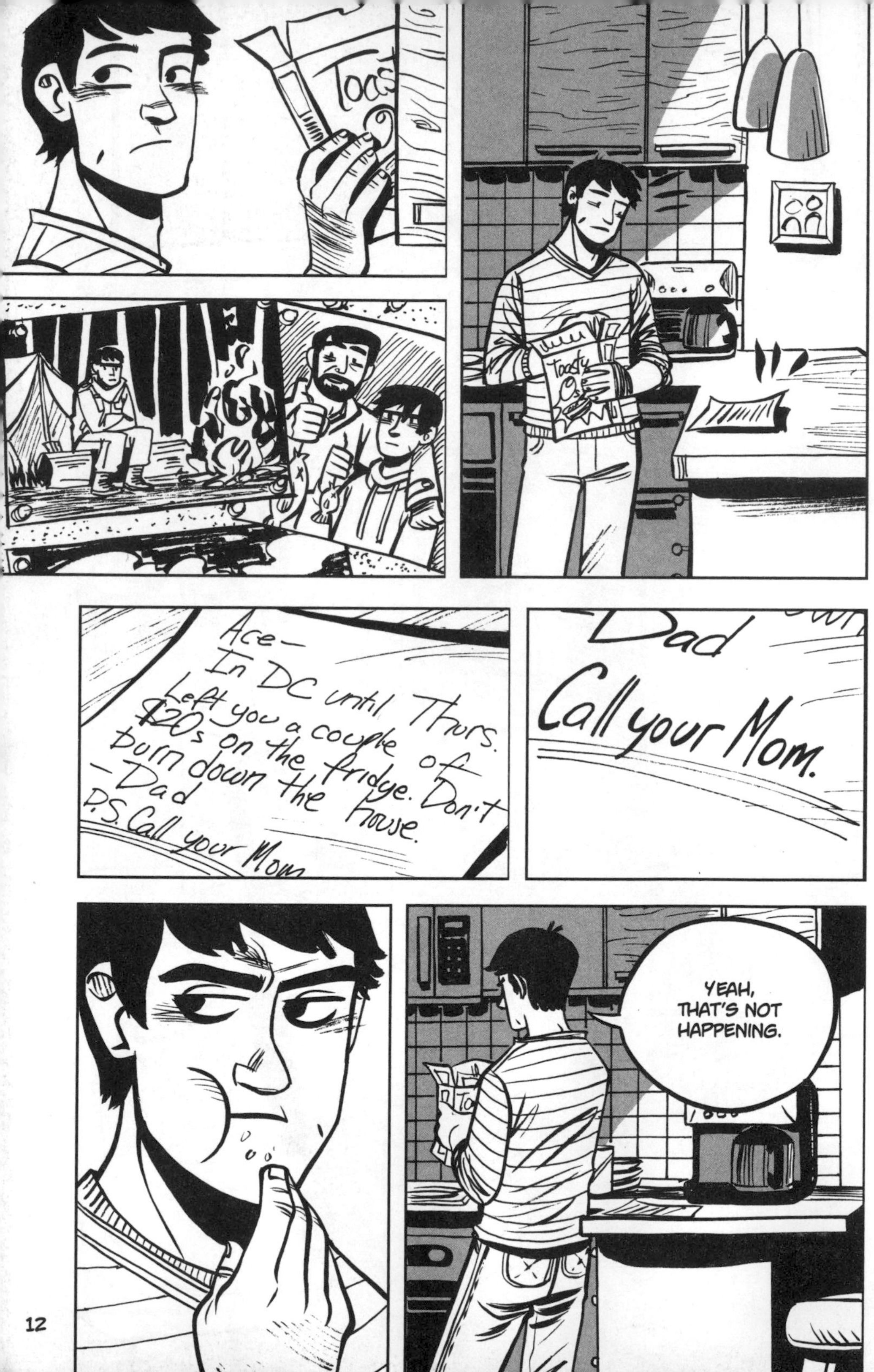
Toasty O's
Ace—
In DC until Thurs.
Left you a couple of
$20s on the fridge. Don't
burn down the house.
—Dad
P.S. Call your Mom
Dad
Call your Mom.
YEAH, THAT'S NOT HAPPENING.

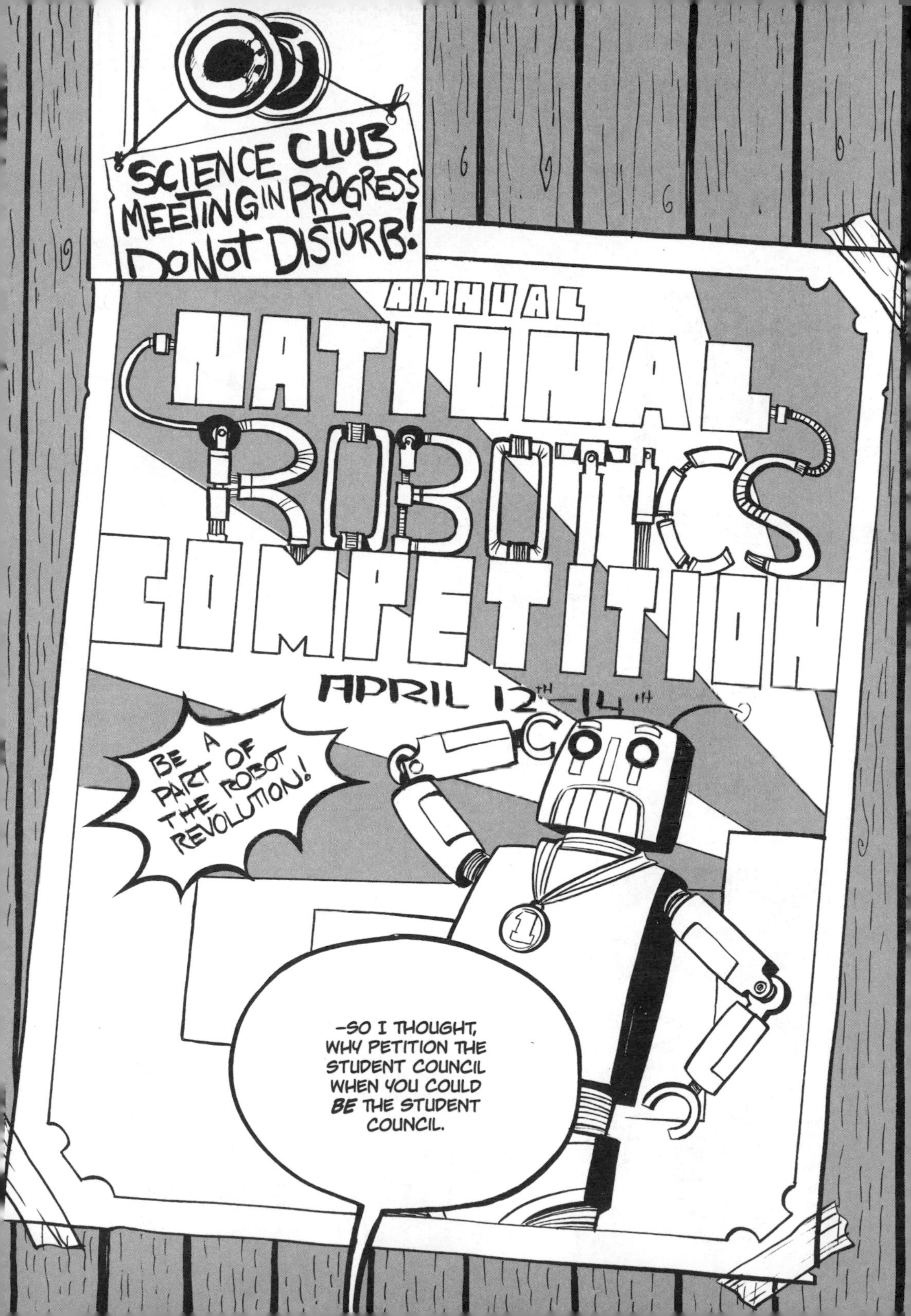
SCIENCE CLUB MEETING IN PROGRESS DO NOT DISTURB!
ANNUAL
NATIONAL ROBOTICS COMPETITION
APRIL 12TH–14TH
BE A PART OF THE ROBOT REVOLUTION!
–SO I THOUGHT, WHY PETITION THE STUDENT COUNCIL WHEN YOU COULD *BE* THE STUDENT COUNCIL.

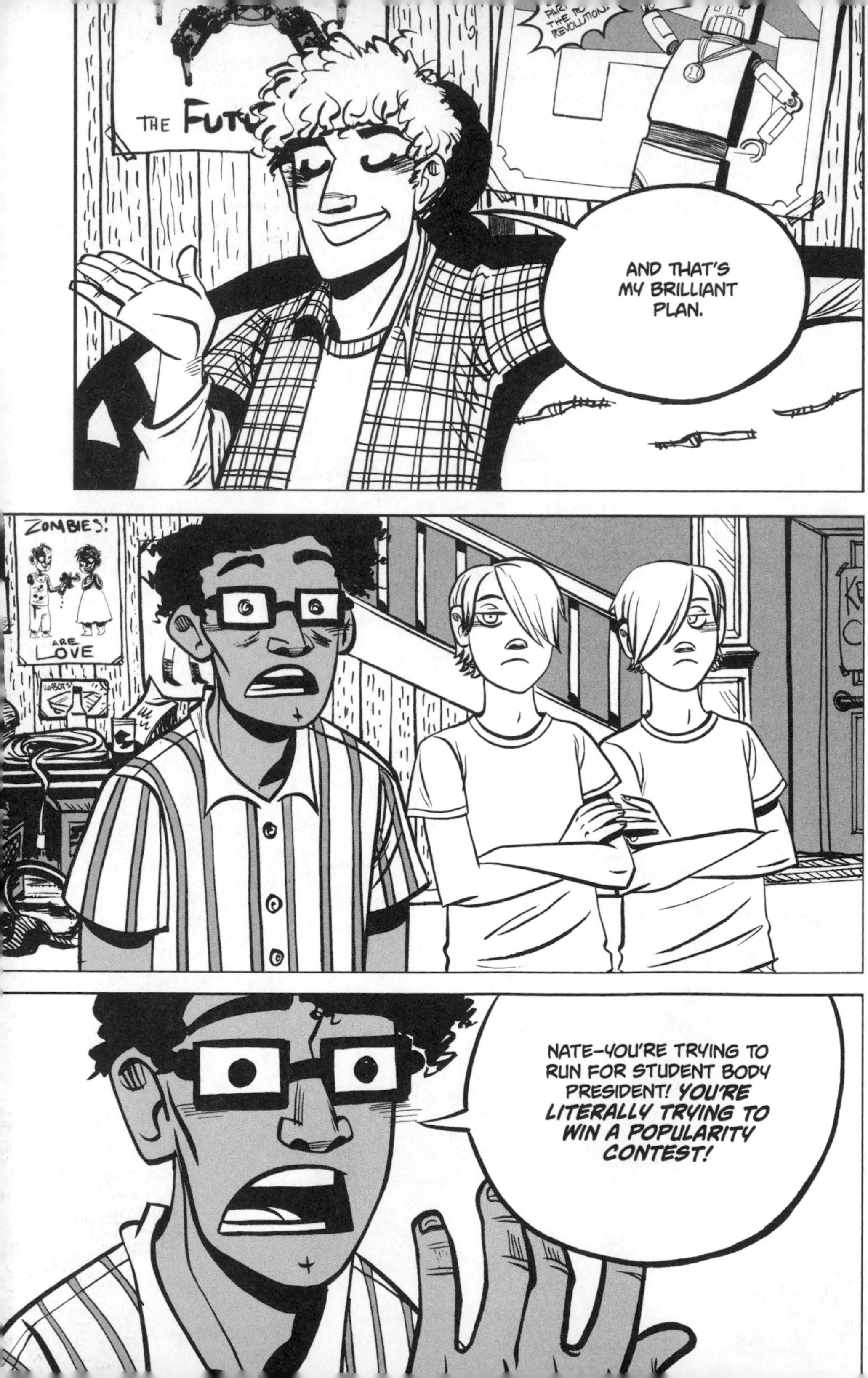
AND THAT'S MY BRILLIANT PLAN.
ZOMBIES!
ARE LOVE
NATE–YOU'RE TRYING TO RUN FOR STUDENT BODY PRESIDENT! *YOU'RE LITERALLY TRYING TO WIN A POPULARITY CONTEST!*

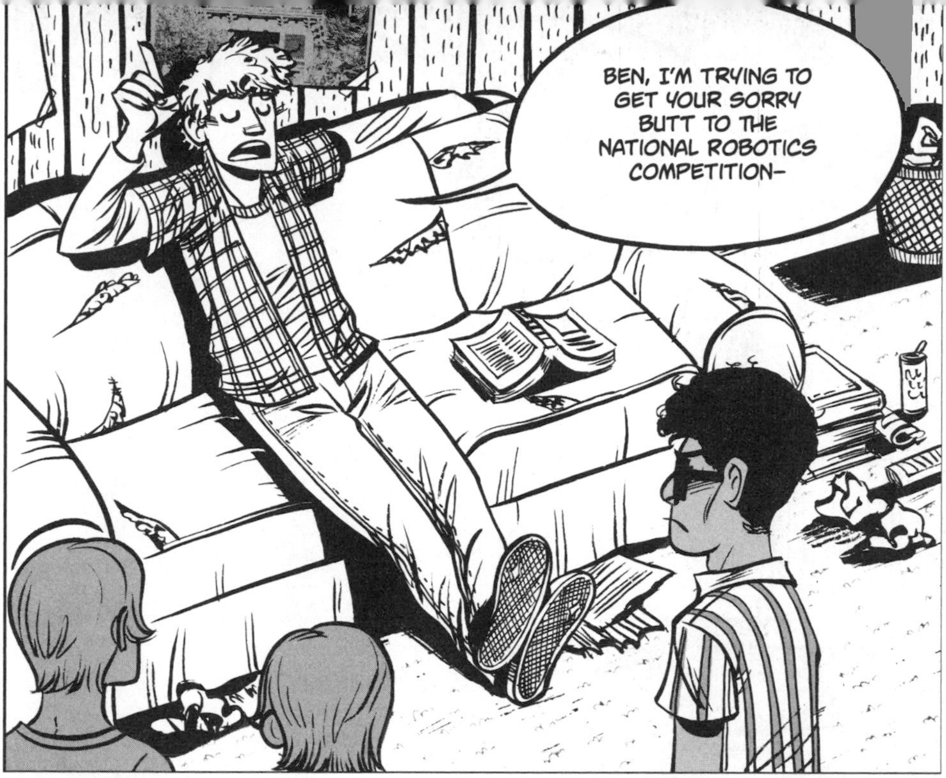
BEN, I'M TRYING TO GET YOUR SORRY BUTT TO THE NATIONAL ROBOTICS COMPETITION–

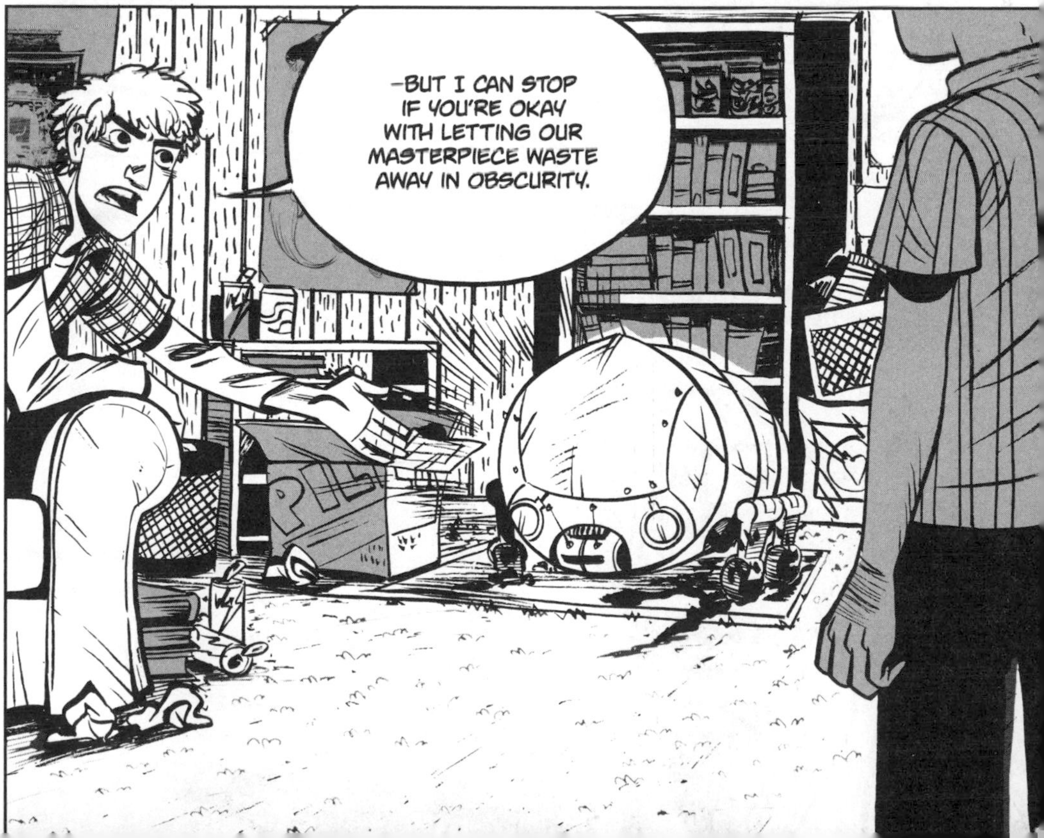
–BUT I CAN STOP IF YOU'RE OKAY WITH LETTING OUR MASTERPIECE WASTE AWAY IN OBSCURITY.

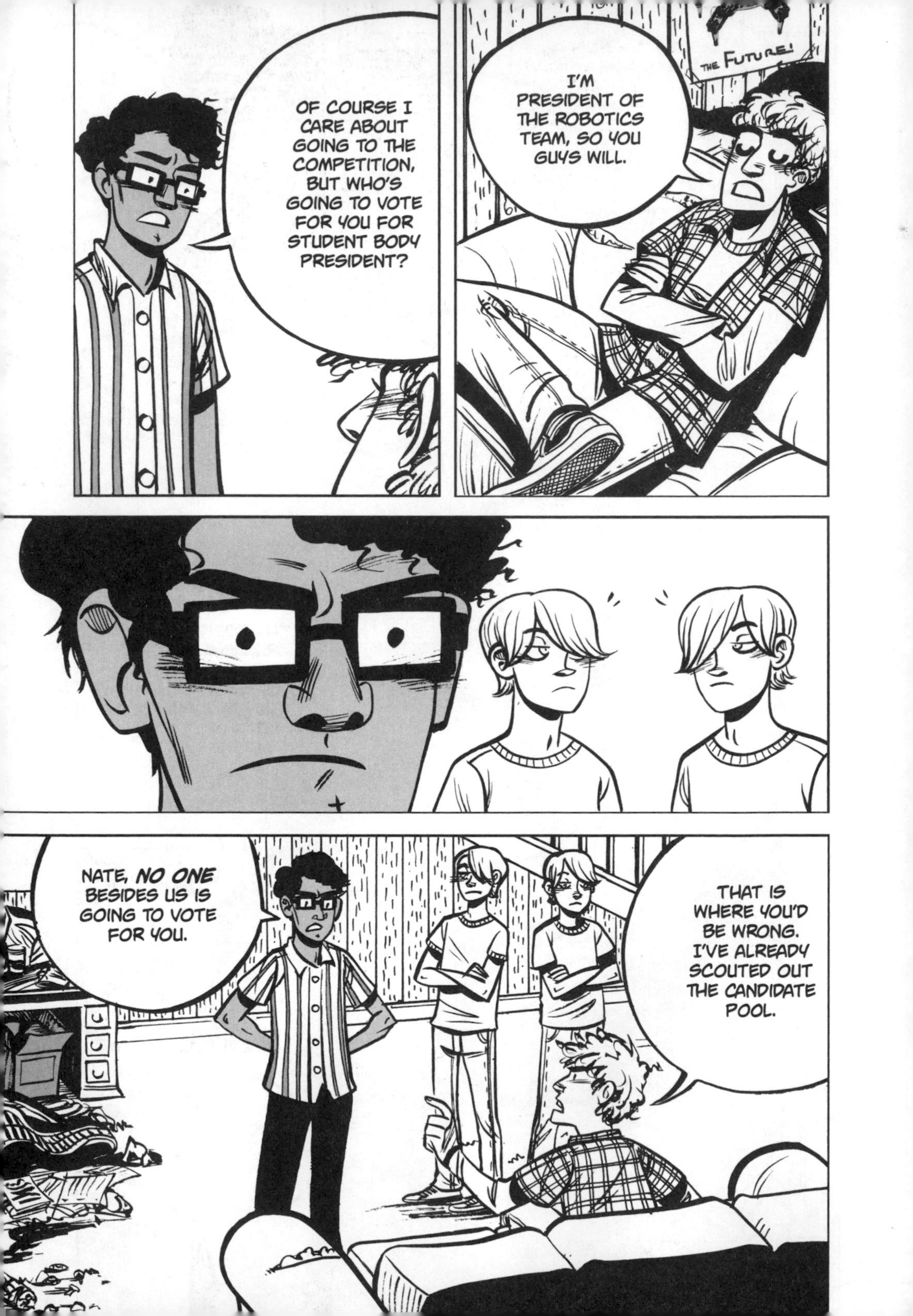
OF COURSE I CARE ABOUT GOING TO THE COMPETITION, BUT WHO'S GOING TO VOTE FOR YOU FOR STUDENT BODY PRESIDENT?
THE FUTURE!
I'M PRESIDENT OF THE ROBOTICS TEAM, SO YOU GUYS WILL.
NATE, *NO ONE* BESIDES US IS GOING TO VOTE FOR YOU.
THAT IS WHERE YOU'D BE WRONG. I'VE ALREADY SCOUTED OUT THE CANDIDATE POOL.

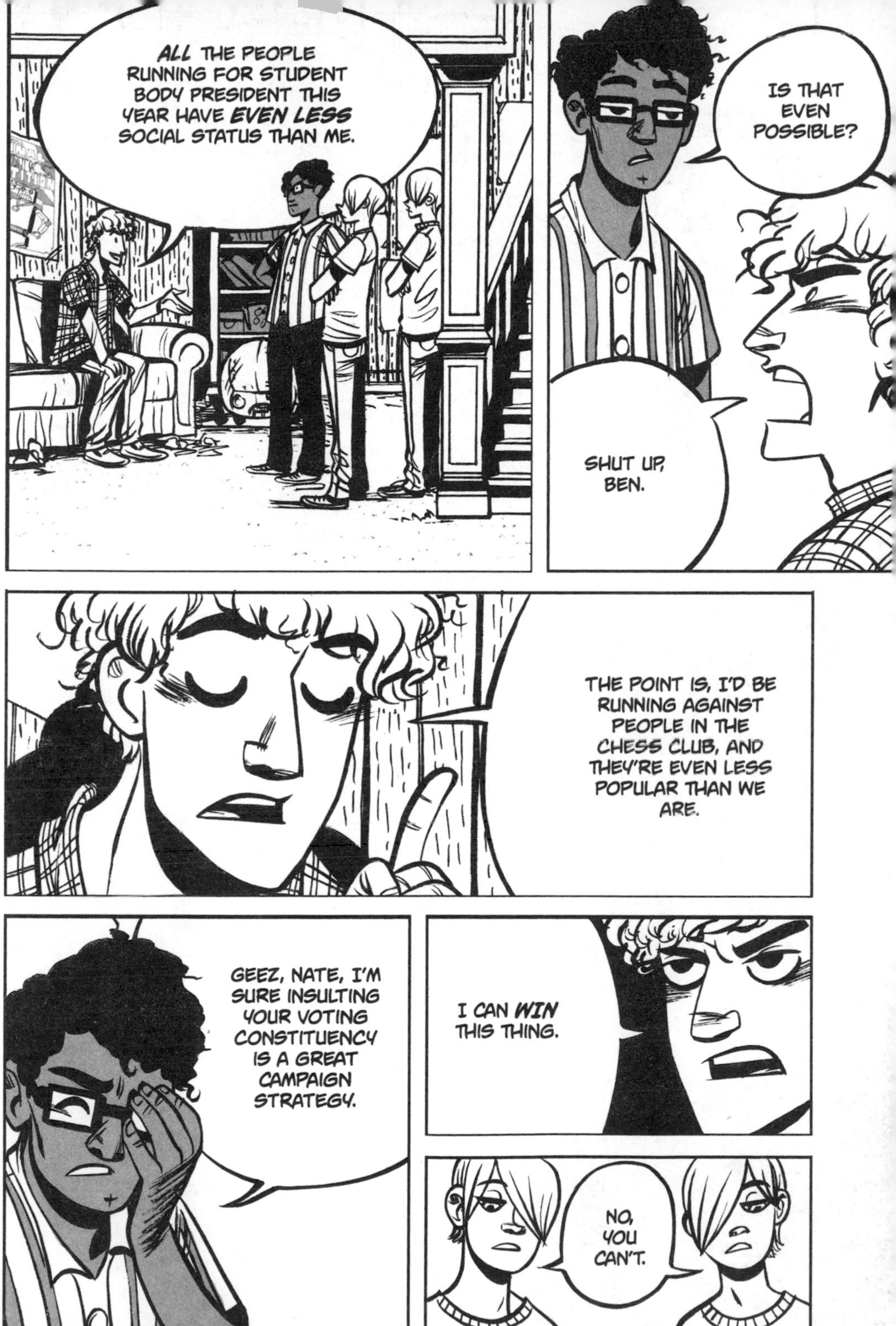
ALL THE PEOPLE RUNNING FOR STUDENT BODY PRESIDENT THIS YEAR HAVE EVEN LESS SOCIAL STATUS THAN ME.
IS THAT EVEN POSSIBLE?
SHUT UP, BEN.
THE POINT IS, I'D BE RUNNING AGAINST PEOPLE IN THE CHESS CLUB, AND THEY'RE EVEN LESS POPULAR THAN WE ARE.
GEEZ, NATE, I'M SURE INSULTING YOUR VOTING CONSTITUENCY IS A GREAT CAMPAIGN STRATEGY.
I CAN WIN THIS THING.
NO, YOU CAN'T.

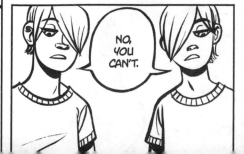

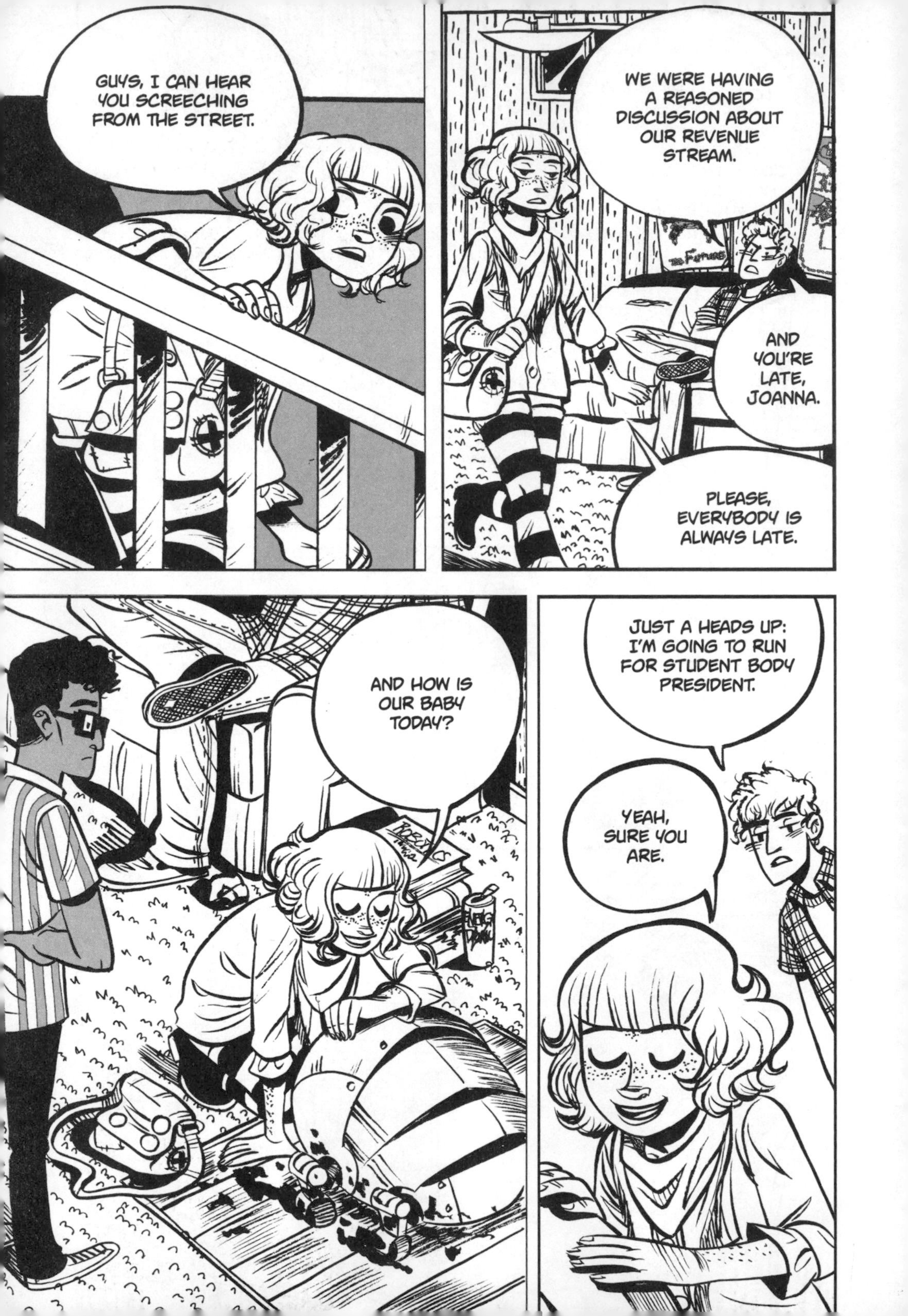
GUYS, I CAN HEAR YOU SCREECHING FROM THE STREET.
WE WERE HAVING A REASONED DISCUSSION ABOUT OUR REVENUE STREAM.
AND YOU'RE LATE, JOANNA.
PLEASE, EVERYBODY IS ALWAYS LATE.
AND HOW IS OUR BABY TODAY?
JUST A HEADS UP: I'M GOING TO RUN FOR STUDENT BODY PRESIDENT.
YEAH, SURE YOU ARE.

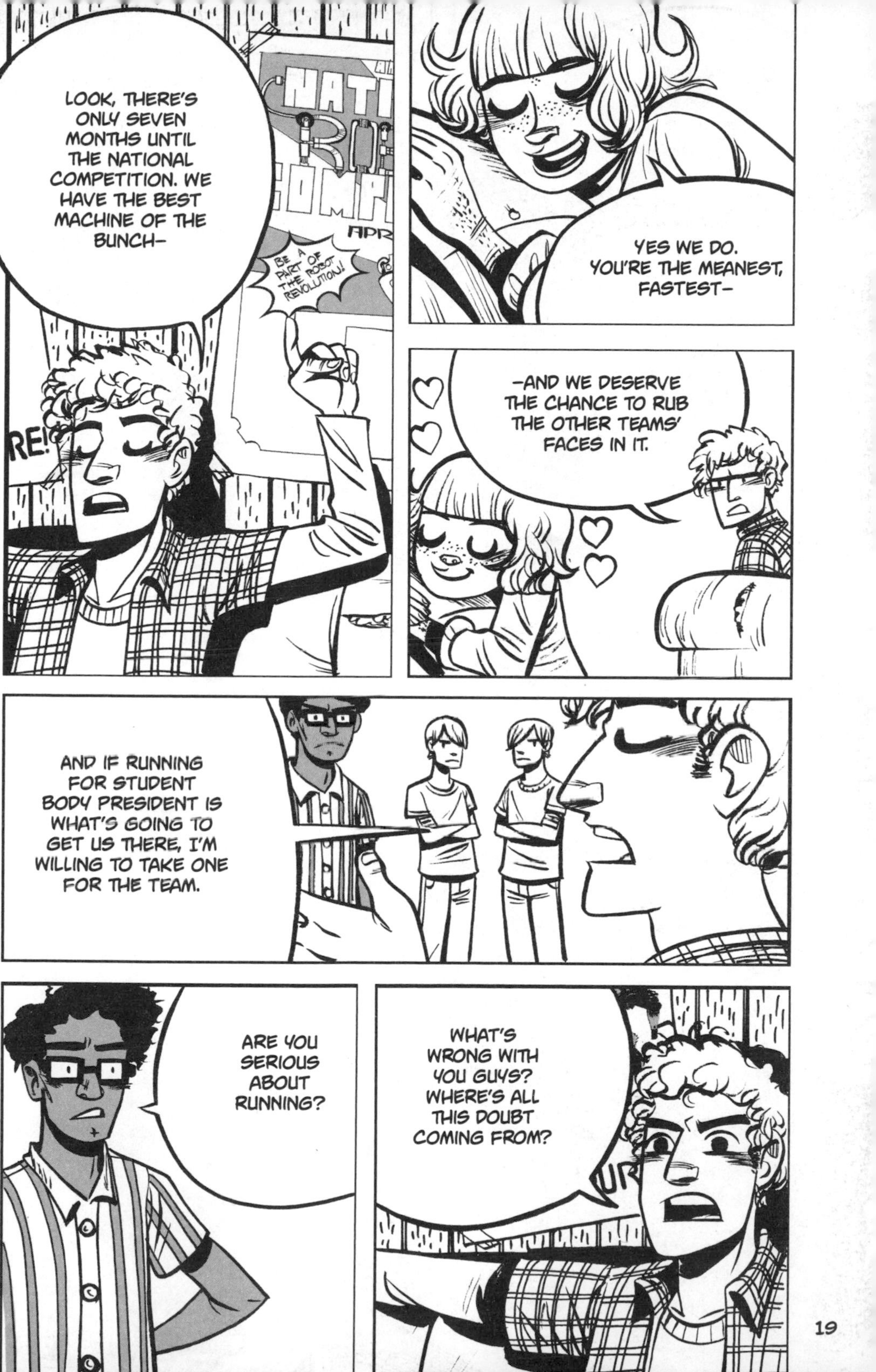
NATI
RO
COMP
APR
BE A PART OF THE ROBOT REVOLUTION!
LOOK, THERE'S ONLY SEVEN MONTHS UNTIL THE NATIONAL COMPETITION. WE HAVE THE BEST MACHINE OF THE BUNCH–
YES WE DO. YOU'RE THE MEANEST, FASTEST–
–AND WE DESERVE THE CHANCE TO RUB THE OTHER TEAMS' FACES IN IT.
AND IF RUNNING FOR STUDENT BODY PRESIDENT IS WHAT'S GOING TO GET US THERE, I'M WILLING TO TAKE ONE FOR THE TEAM.
ARE YOU SERIOUS ABOUT RUNNING?
WHAT'S WRONG WITH YOU GUYS? WHERE'S ALL THIS DOUBT COMING FROM?

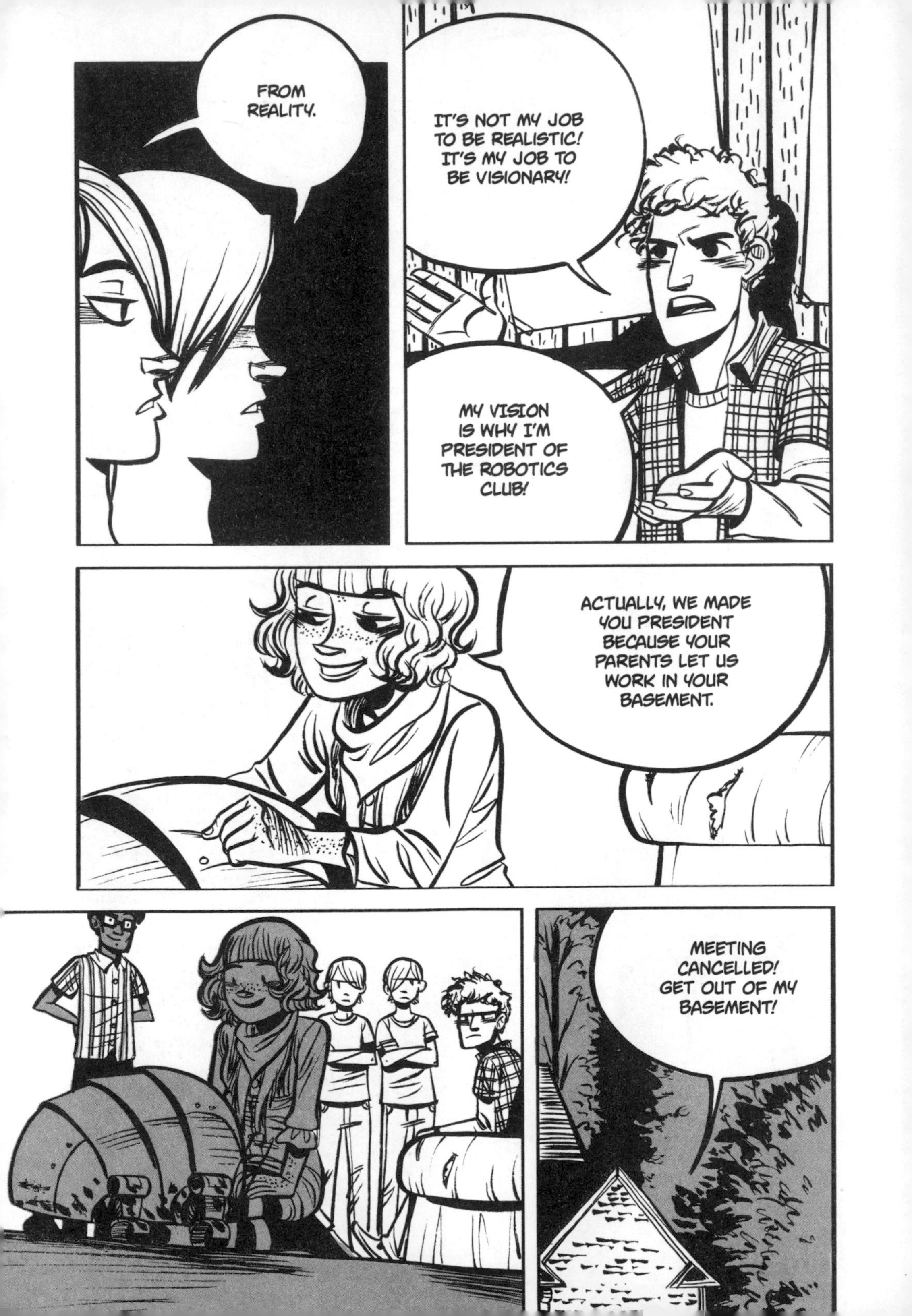
FROM REALITY.
IT'S NOT MY JOB TO BE REALISTIC! IT'S MY JOB TO BE VISIONARY!
MY VISION IS WHY I'M PRESIDENT OF THE ROBOTICS CLUB!
ACTUALLY, WE MADE YOU PRESIDENT BECAUSE YOUR PARENTS LET US WORK IN YOUR BASEMENT.
MEETING CANCELLED! GET OUT OF MY BASEMENT!

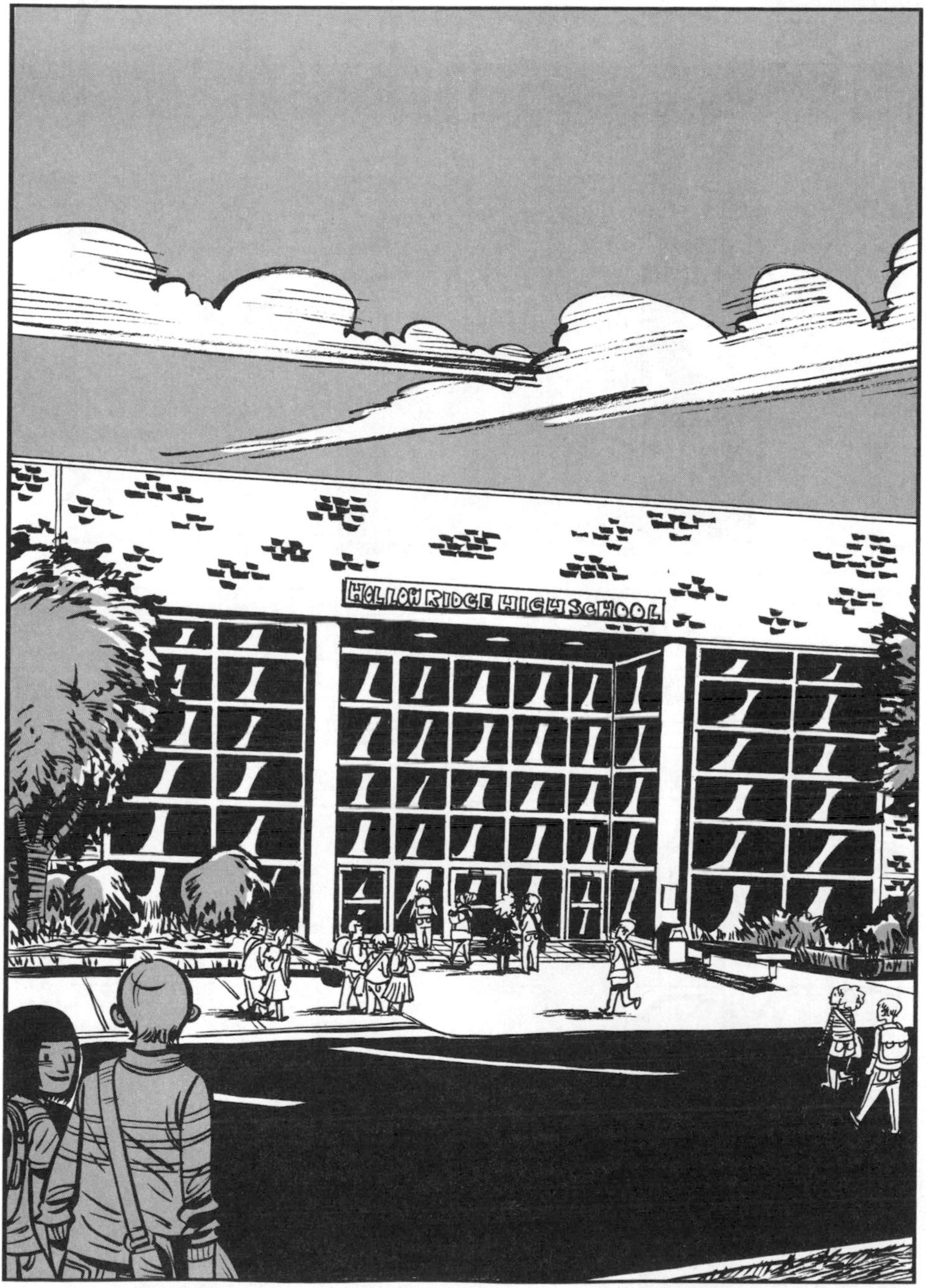
HOLLOW RIDGE HIGH SCHOOL

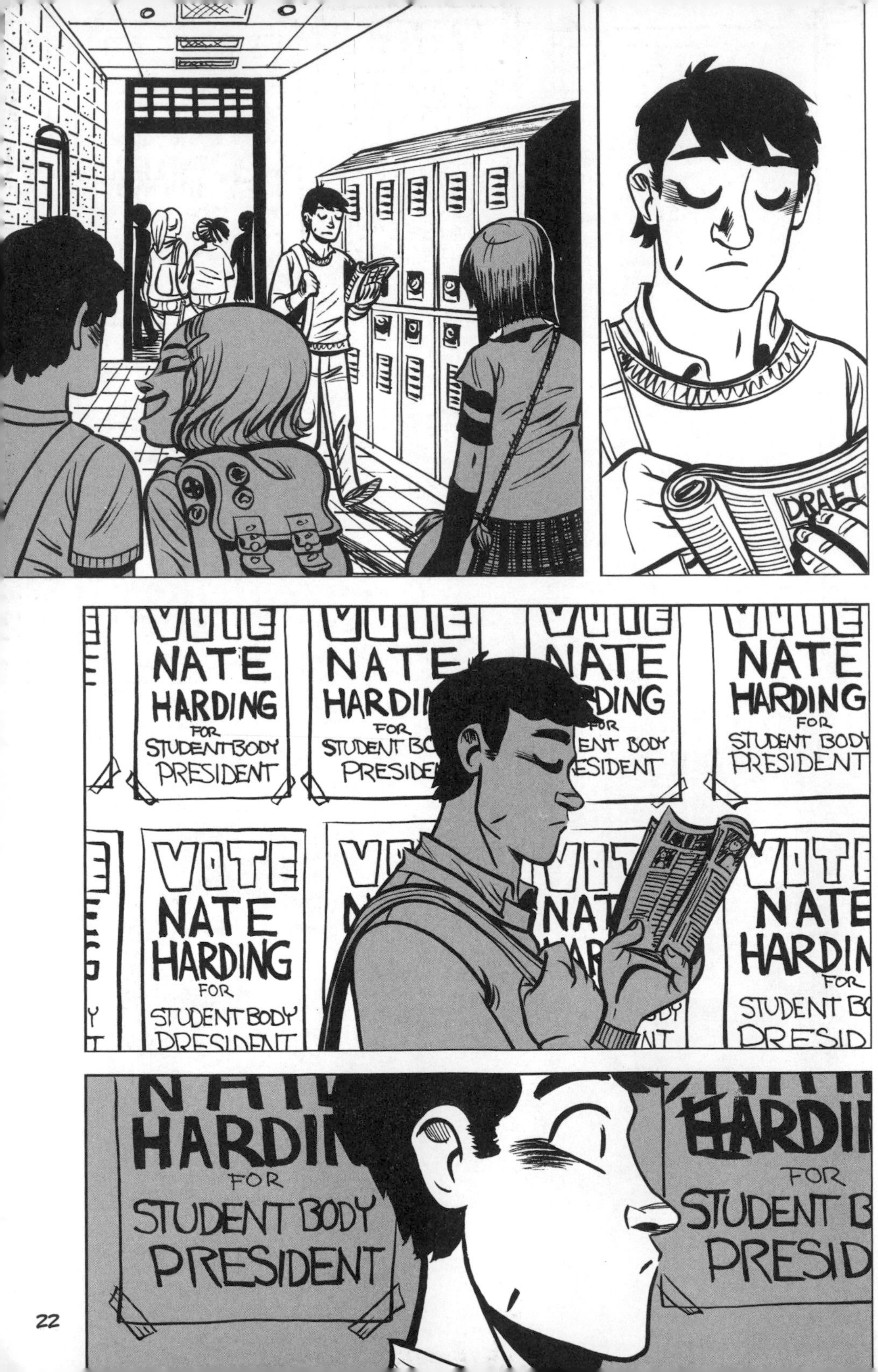
VOTE
NATE
HARDING
FOR
STUDENT BODY
PRESIDENT

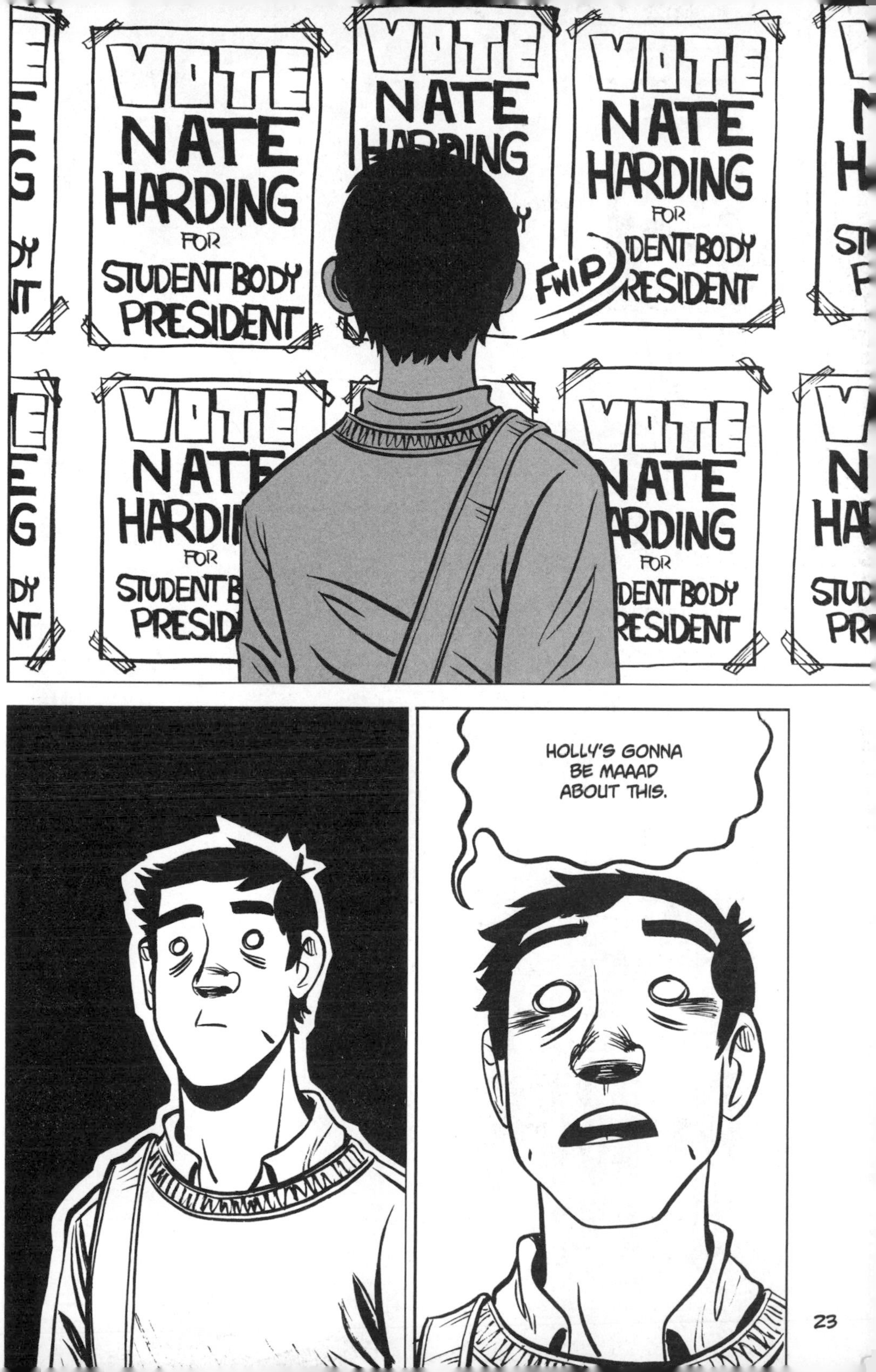
VOTE NATE HARDING FOR STUDENT BODY PRESIDENT
FWIP
HOLLY'S GONNA BE MAAAD ABOUT THIS.

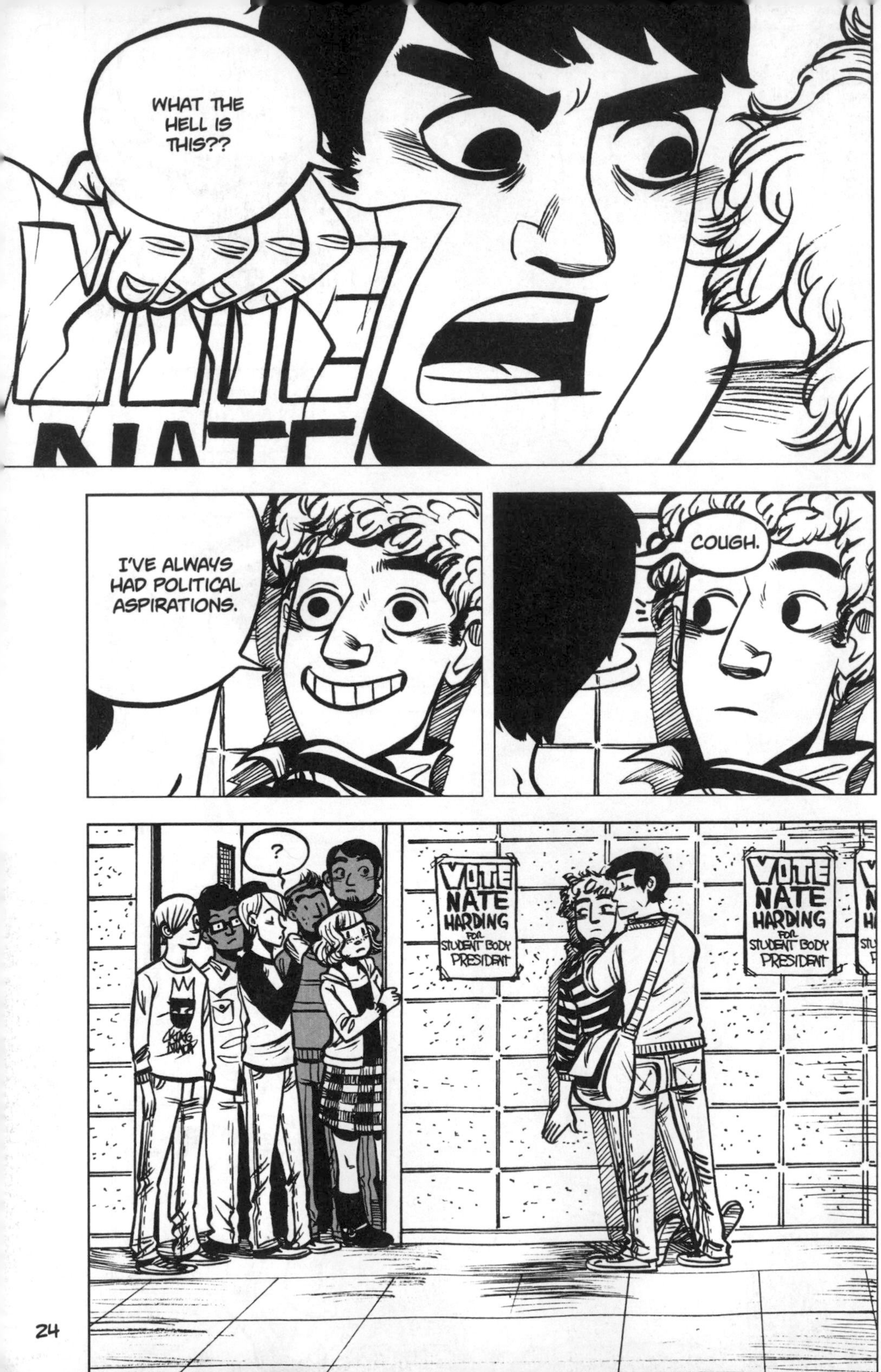
WHAT THE HELL IS THIS??
NATE
I'VE ALWAYS HAD POLITICAL ASPIRATIONS.
COUGH.
?
VOTE NATE HARDING FOR STUDENT BODY PRESIDENT
VOTE NATE HARDING FOR STUDENT BODY PRESIDENT

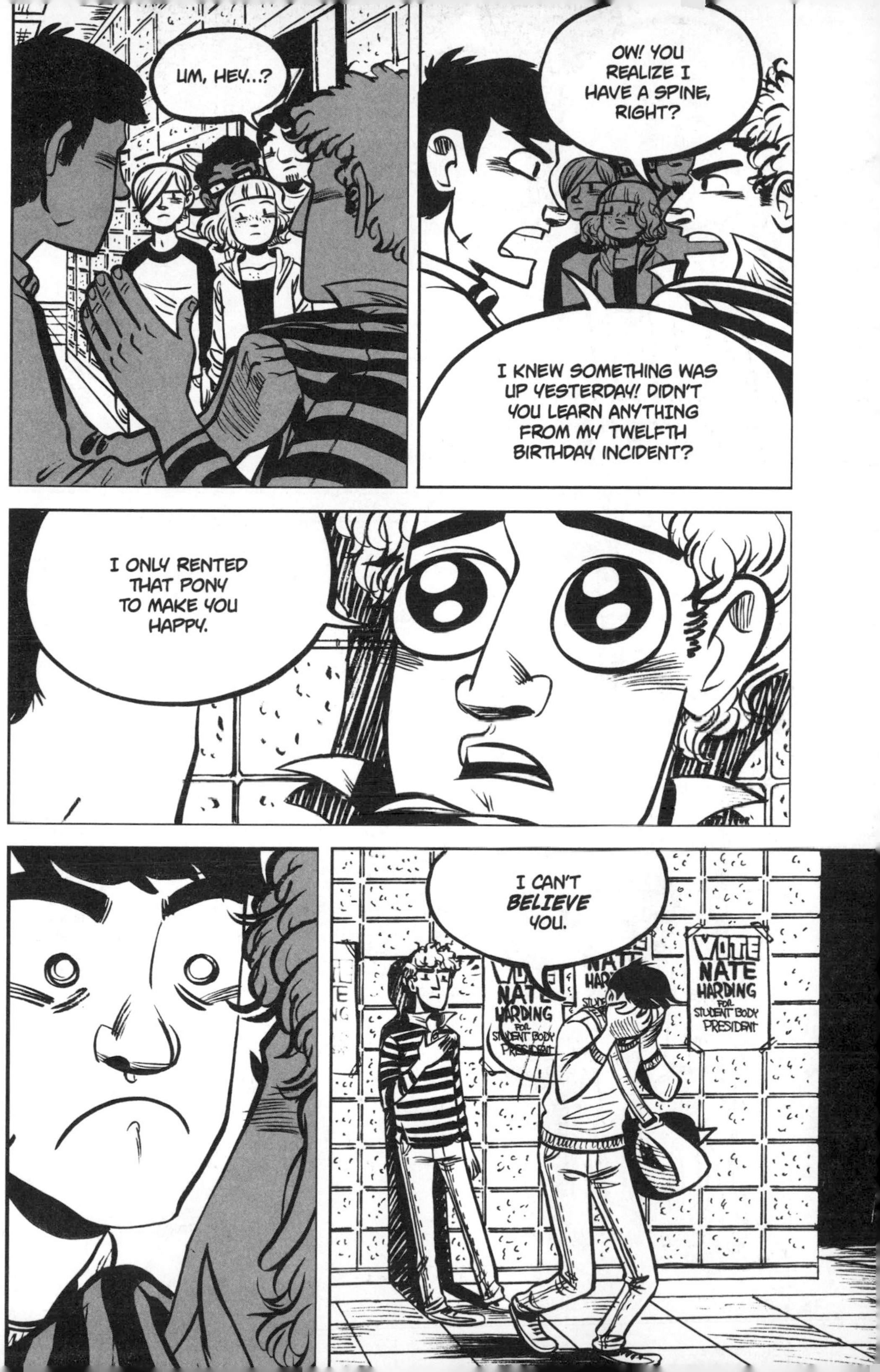
UM, HEY...?
OW! YOU REALIZE I HAVE A SPINE, RIGHT?
I KNEW SOMETHING WAS UP YESTERDAY! DIDN'T YOU LEARN ANYTHING FROM MY TWELFTH BIRTHDAY INCIDENT?
I ONLY RENTED THAT PONY TO MAKE YOU HAPPY.
I CAN'T *BELIEVE* YOU.
VOTE NATE HARDING FOR STUDENT BODY PRESIDENT
VOTE NATE HARDING FOR STUDENT BODY PRESIDENT

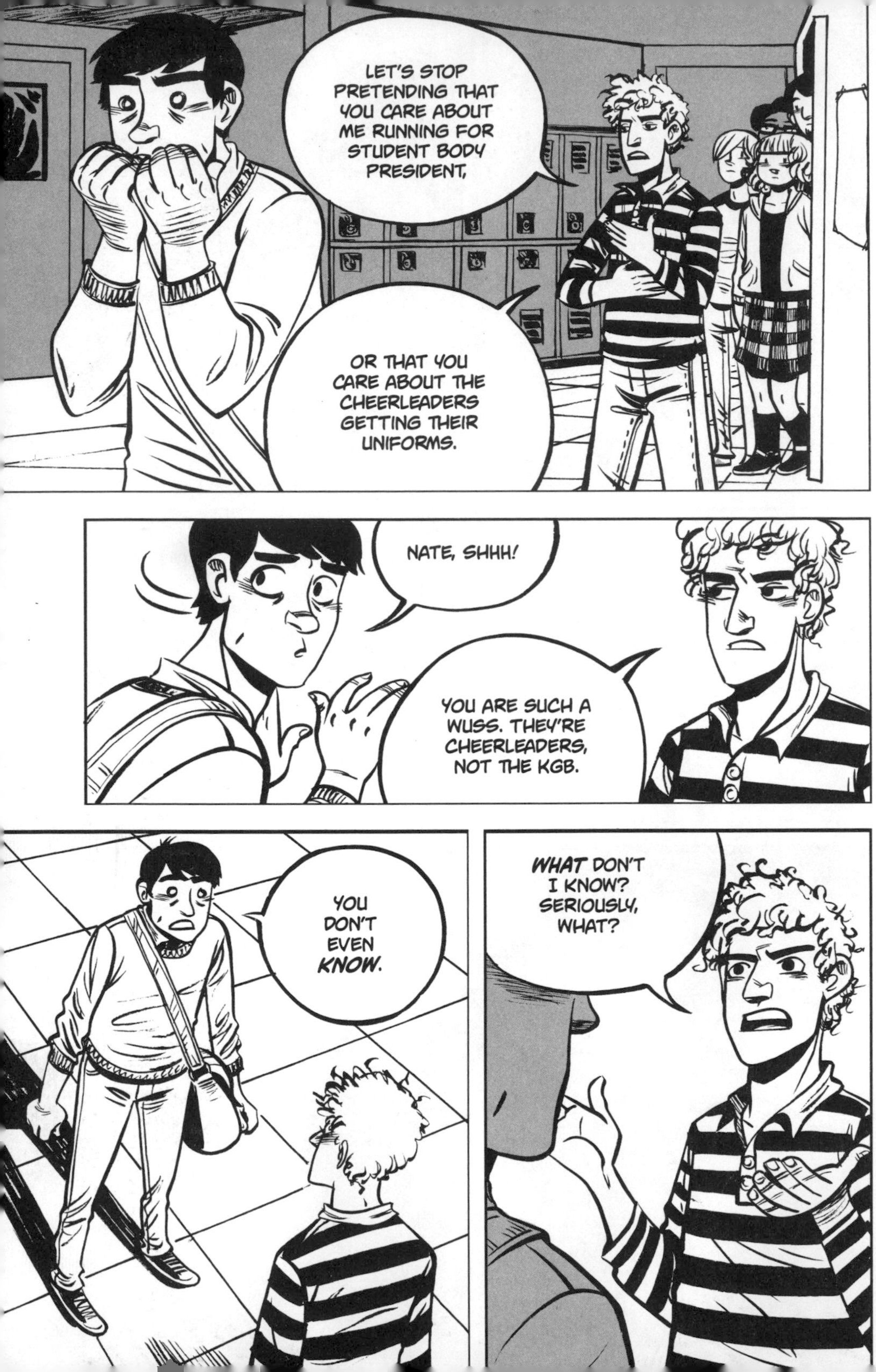
LET'S STOP PRETENDING THAT YOU CARE ABOUT ME RUNNING FOR STUDENT BODY PRESIDENT,
OR THAT YOU CARE ABOUT THE CHEERLEADERS GETTING THEIR UNIFORMS.
NATE, SHHH!
YOU ARE SUCH A WUSS. THEY'RE CHEERLEADERS, NOT THE KGB.
YOU DON'T EVEN *KNOW*.
WHAT DON'T I KNOW? SERIOUSLY, WHAT?

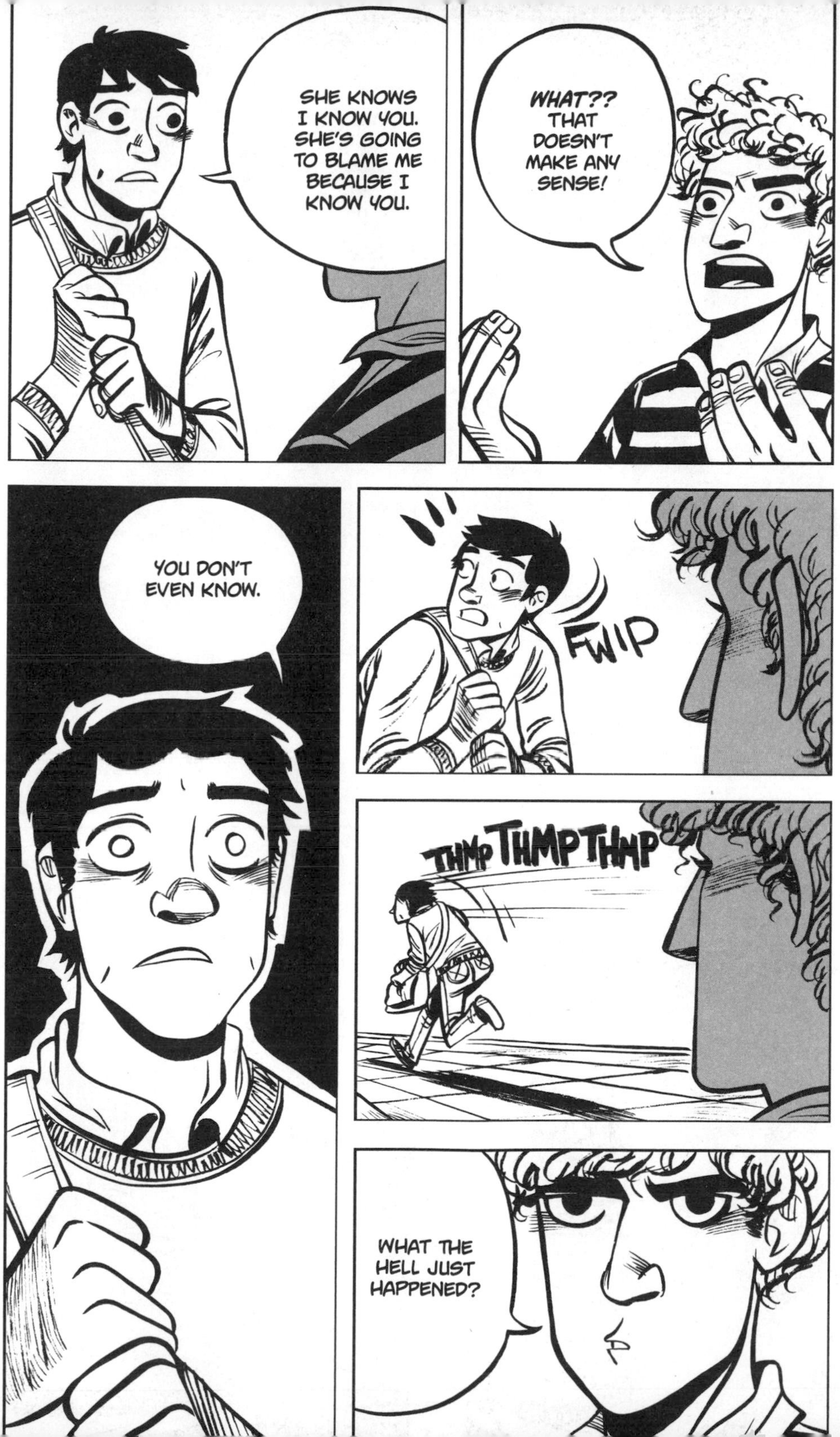
SHE KNOWS I KNOW YOU. SHE'S GOING TO BLAME ME BECAUSE I KNOW YOU.
WHAT?? THAT DOESN'T MAKE ANY SENSE!
YOU DON'T EVEN KNOW.
FWIP
THMP THMP THMP
WHAT THE HELL JUST HAPPENED?

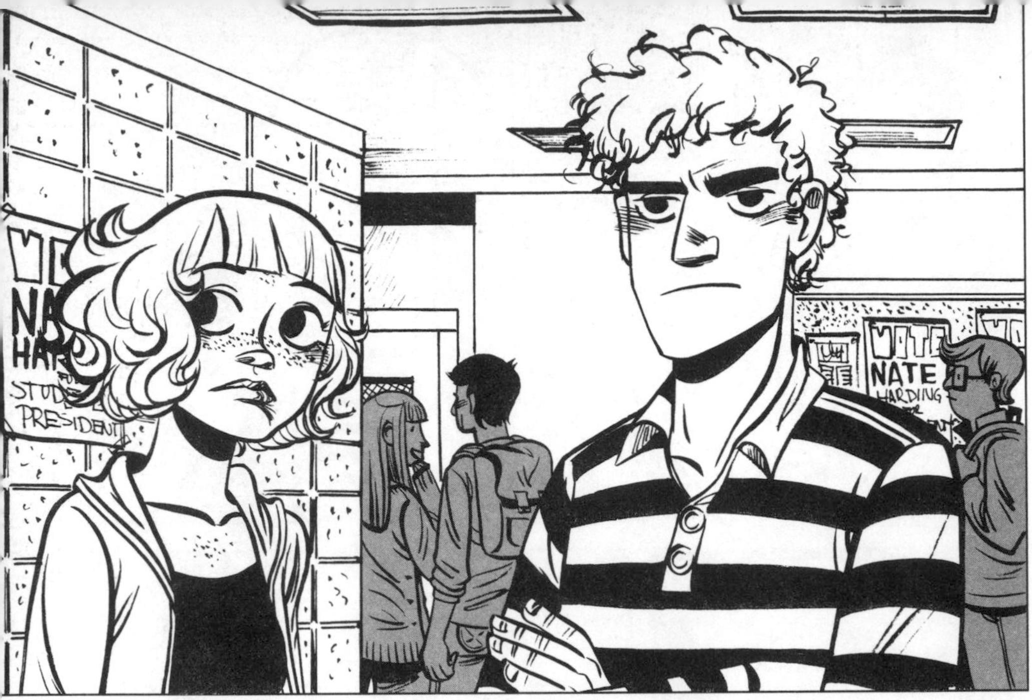
NATE
HARDING

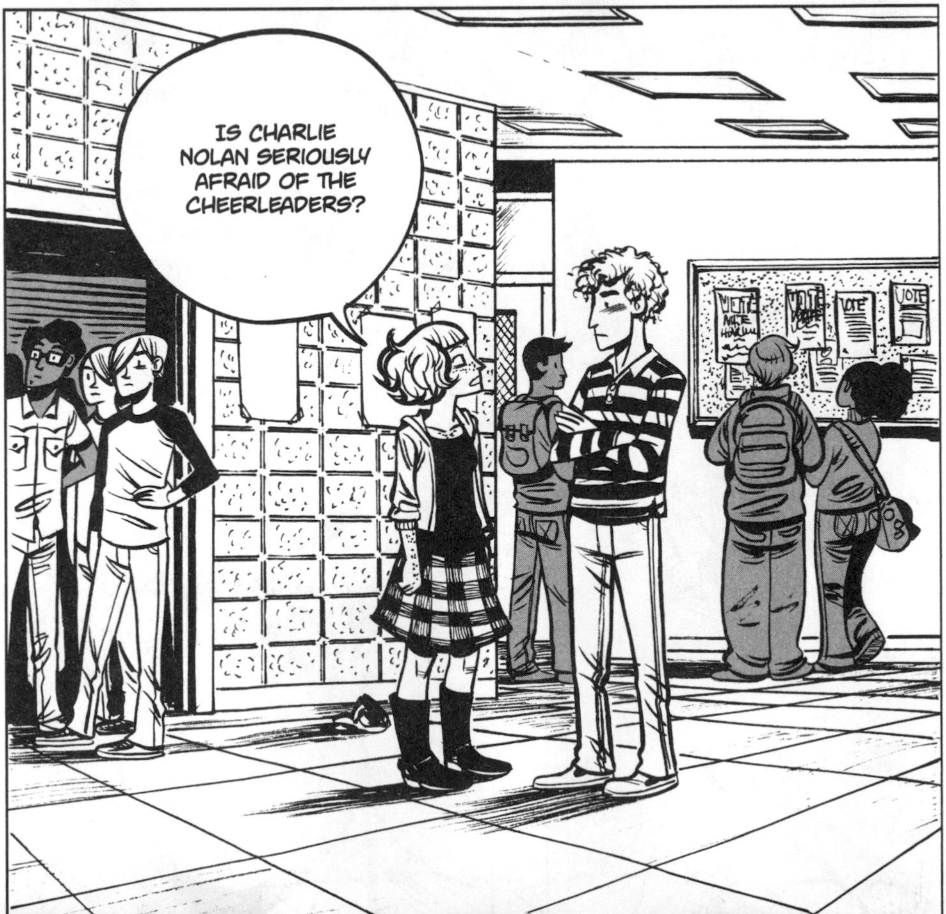
IS CHARLIE NOLAN SERIOUSLY AFRAID OF THE CHEERLEADERS?

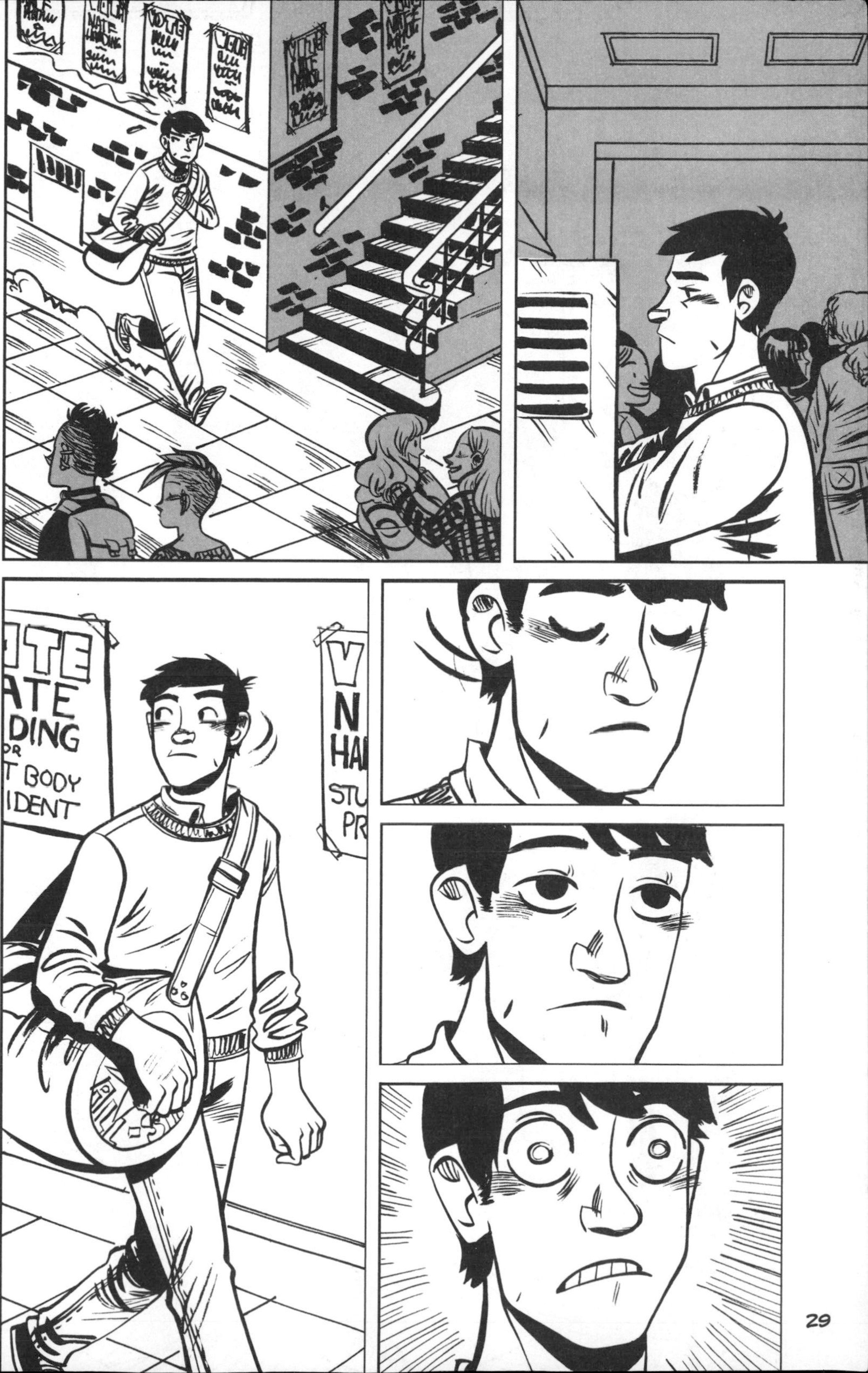
VOTE
NATE HARDING
VOTE
UTE
ATE
DING
T BODY
IDENT
V
N
HA
STU
PR

BOYS' LOCKER ROOM

VOTE NATE HARDING BODY STUDENT PRES

VOTE NATE H...

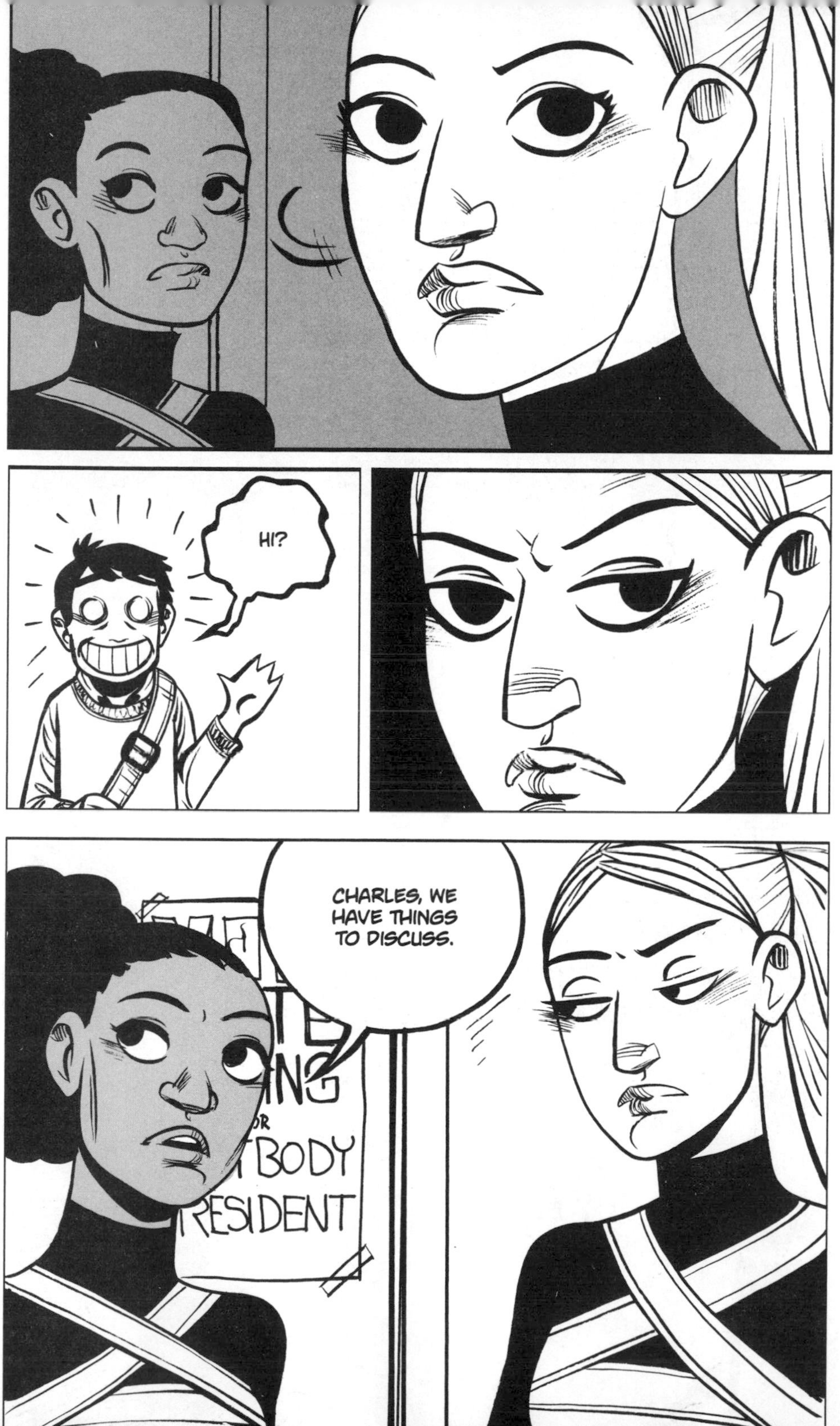
HI?
CHARLES, WE HAVE THINGS TO DISCUSS.

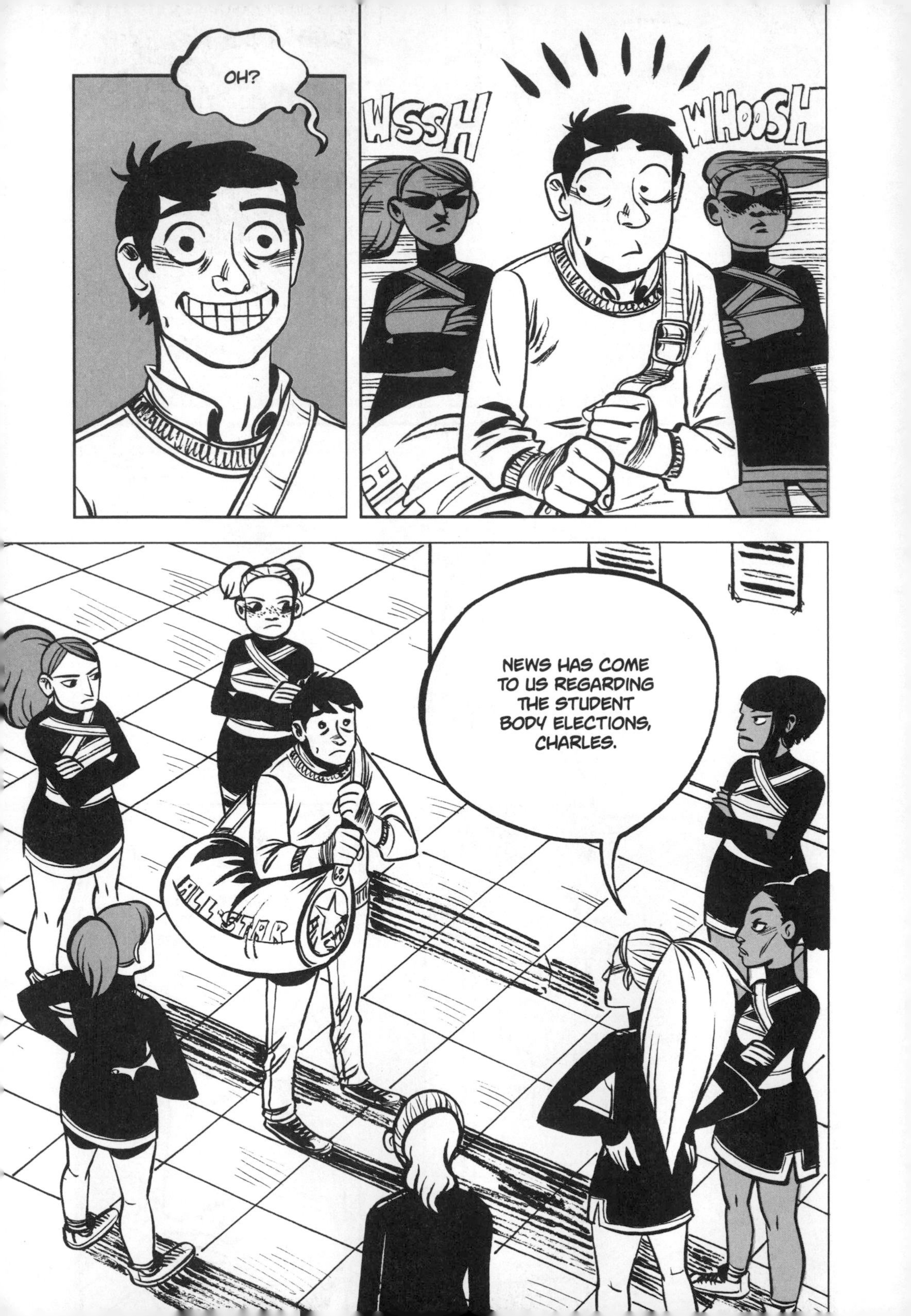
OH?
WSSH
WHOOSH
NEWS HAS COME TO US REGARDING THE STUDENT BODY ELECTIONS, CHARLES.
ALL STAR

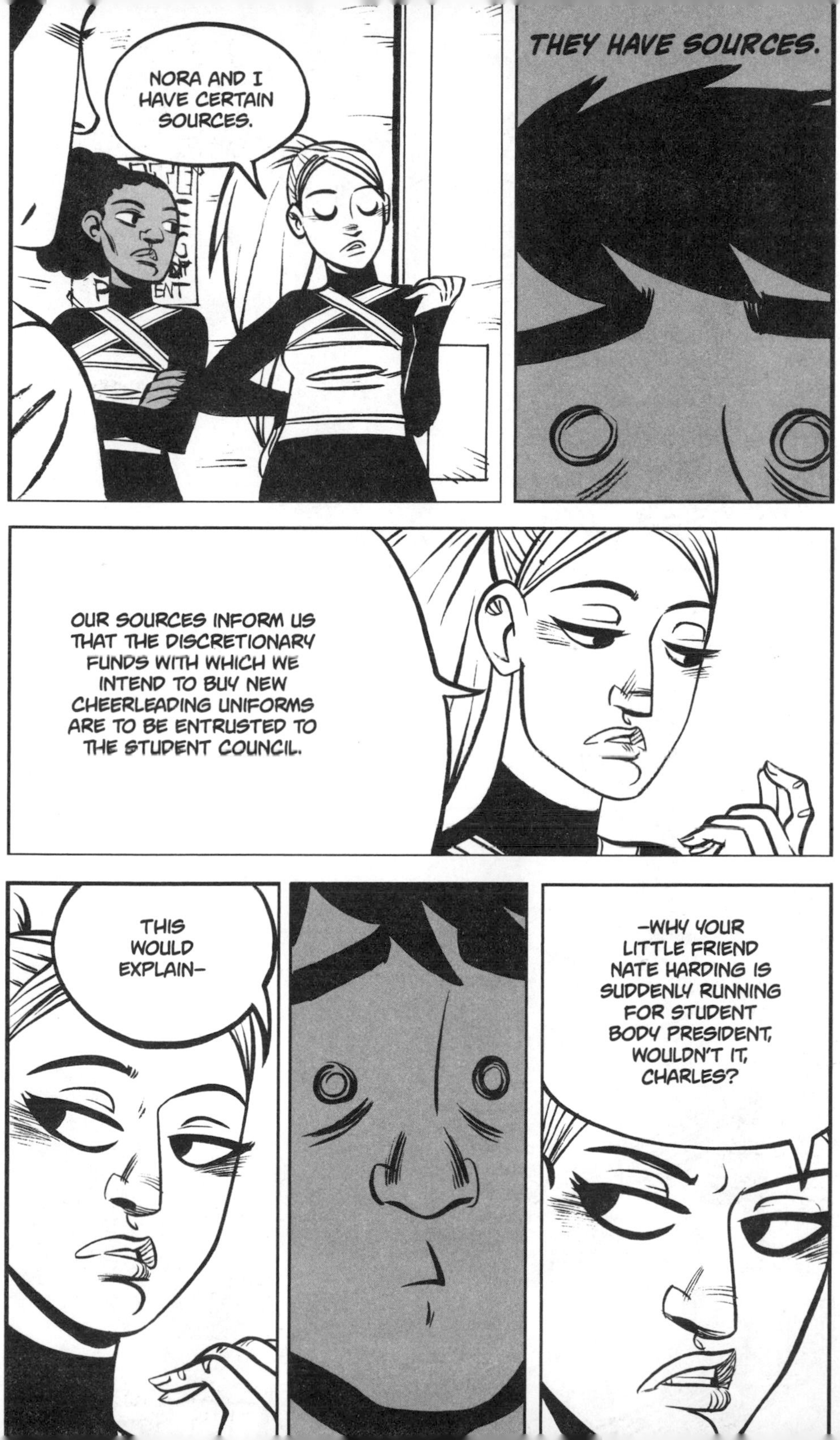
NORA AND I HAVE CERTAIN SOURCES.
THEY HAVE SOURCES.
OUR SOURCES INFORM US THAT THE DISCRETIONARY FUNDS WITH WHICH WE INTEND TO BUY NEW CHEERLEADING UNIFORMS ARE TO BE ENTRUSTED TO THE STUDENT COUNCIL.
THIS WOULD EXPLAIN-
-WHY YOUR LITTLE FRIEND NATE HARDING IS SUDDENLY RUNNING FOR STUDENT BODY PRESIDENT, WOULDN'T IT, CHARLES?

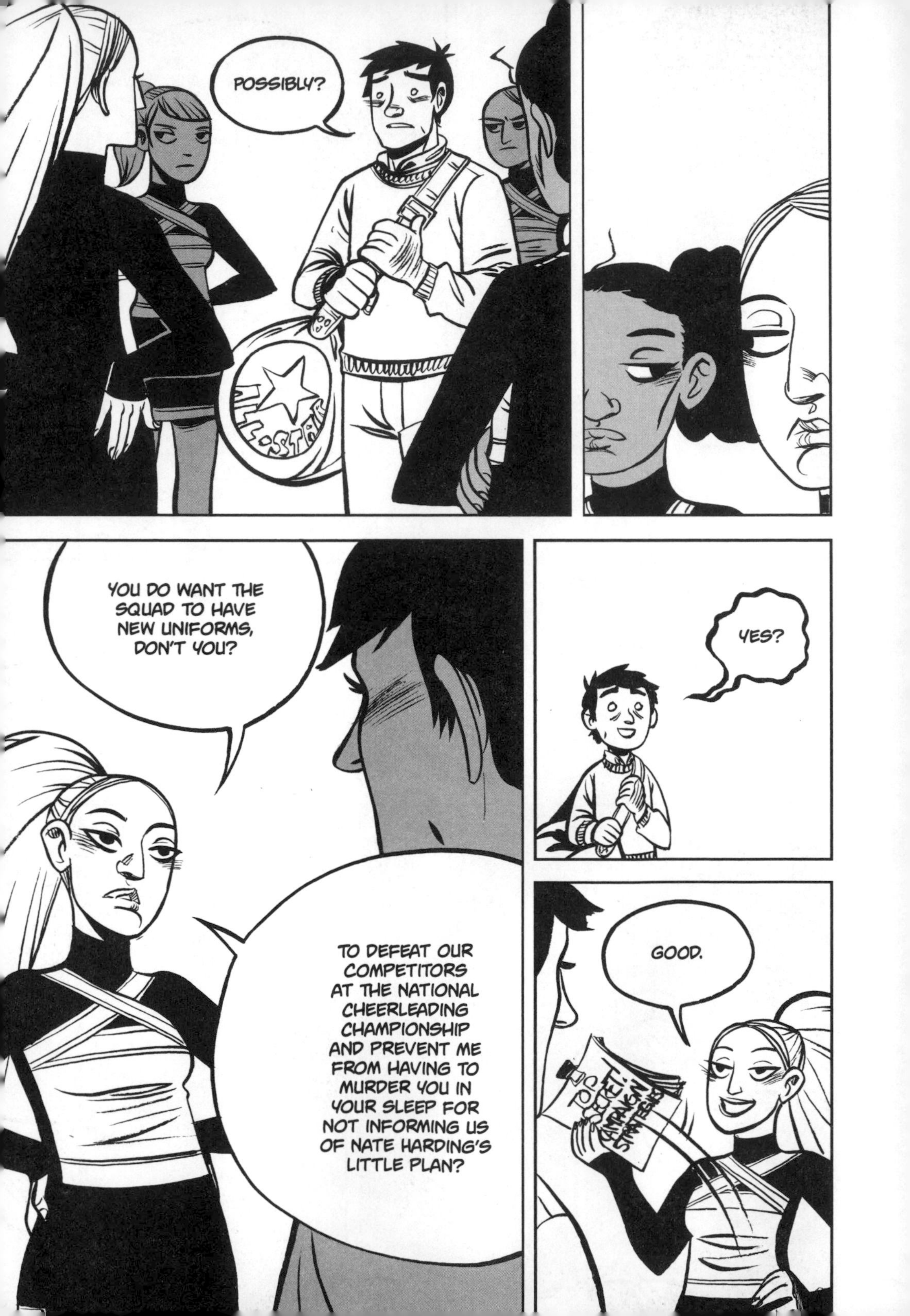
POSSIBLY?
ALL-STAR
YOU DO WANT THE SQUAD TO HAVE NEW UNIFORMS, DON'T YOU?
YES?
TO DEFEAT OUR COMPETITORS AT THE NATIONAL CHEERLEADING CHAMPIONSHIP AND PREVENT ME FROM HAVING TO MURDER YOU IN YOUR SLEEP FOR NOT INFORMING US OF NATE HARDING'S LITTLE PLAN?
GOOD.

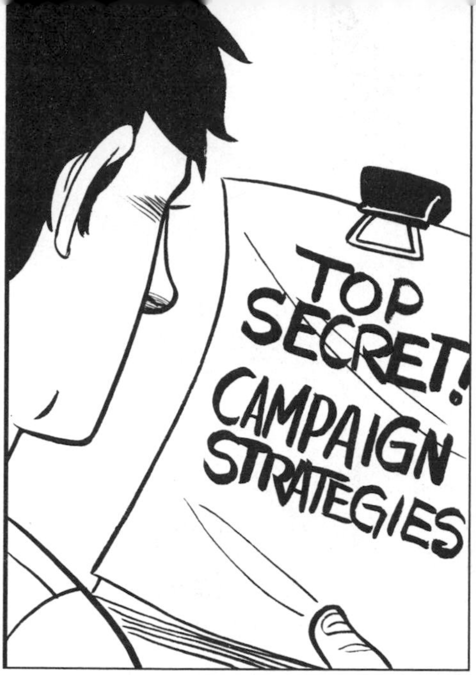
TOP SECRET!
CAMPAIGN STRATEGIES

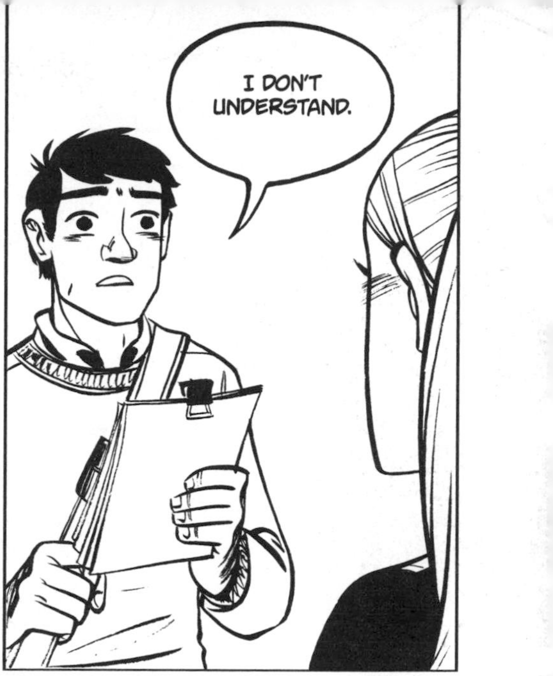
I DON'T UNDERSTAND.

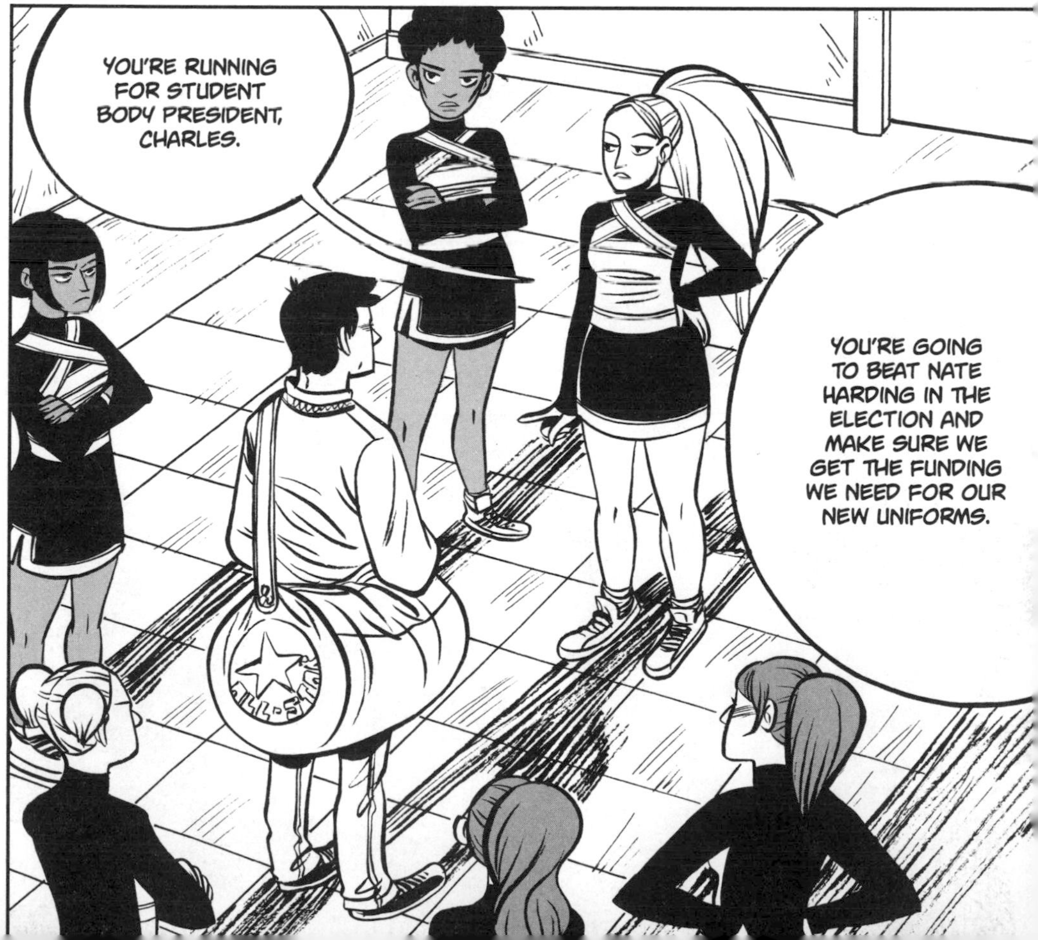
YOU'RE RUNNING FOR STUDENT BODY PRESIDENT, CHARLES.
YOU'RE GOING TO BEAT NATE HARDING IN THE ELECTION AND MAKE SURE WE GET THE FUNDING WE NEED FOR OUR NEW UNIFORMS.

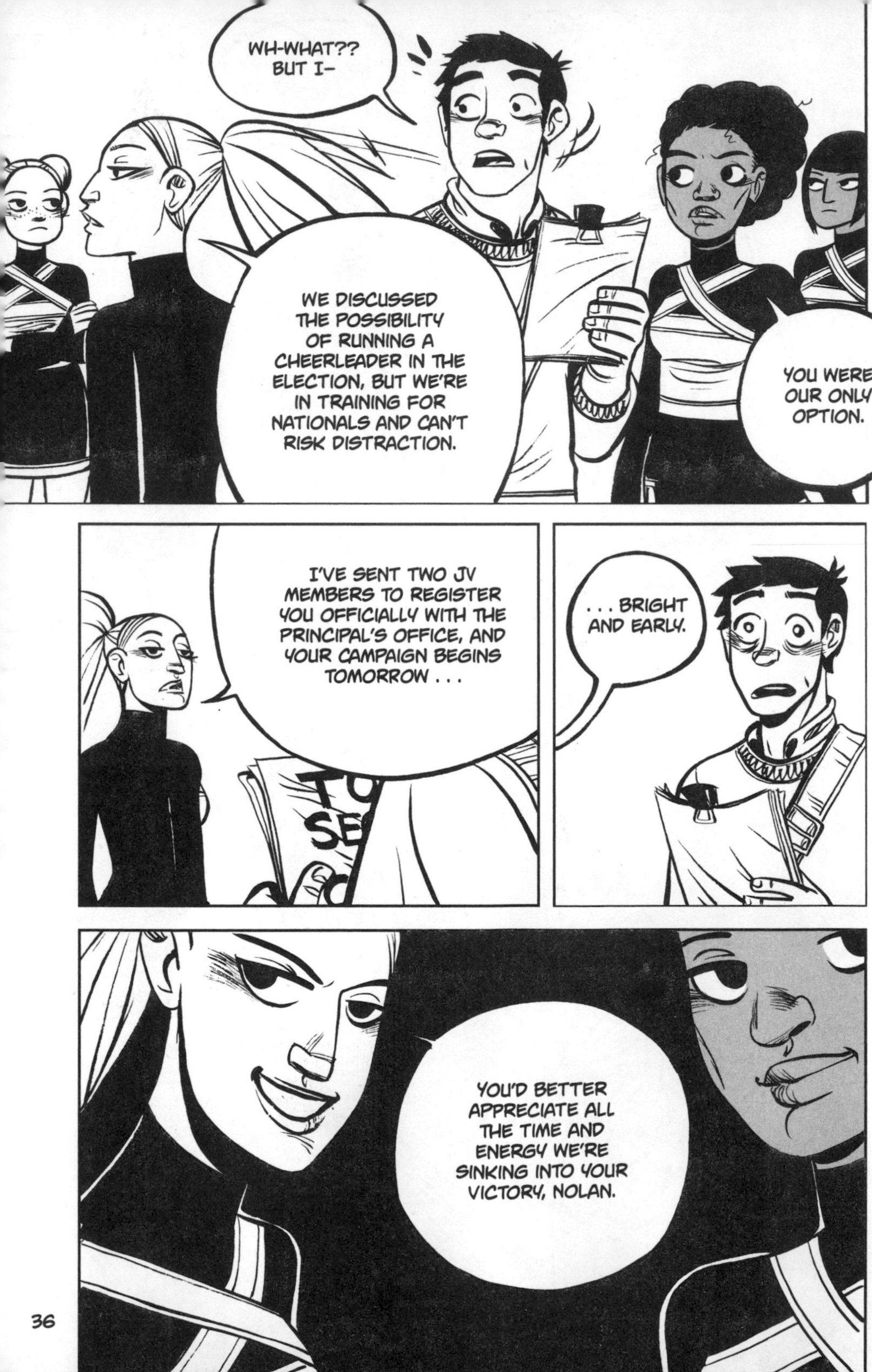

WH-WHAT?? BUT I–
WE DISCUSSED THE POSSIBILITY OF RUNNING A CHEERLEADER IN THE ELECTION, BUT WE'RE IN TRAINING FOR NATIONALS AND CAN'T RISK DISTRACTION.
YOU WERE OUR ONLY OPTION.
I'VE SENT TWO JV MEMBERS TO REGISTER YOU OFFICIALLY WITH THE PRINCIPAL'S OFFICE, AND YOUR CAMPAIGN BEGINS TOMORROW . . .
. . . BRIGHT AND EARLY.
YOU'D BETTER APPRECIATE ALL THE TIME AND ENERGY WE'RE SINKING INTO YOUR VICTORY, NOLAN.

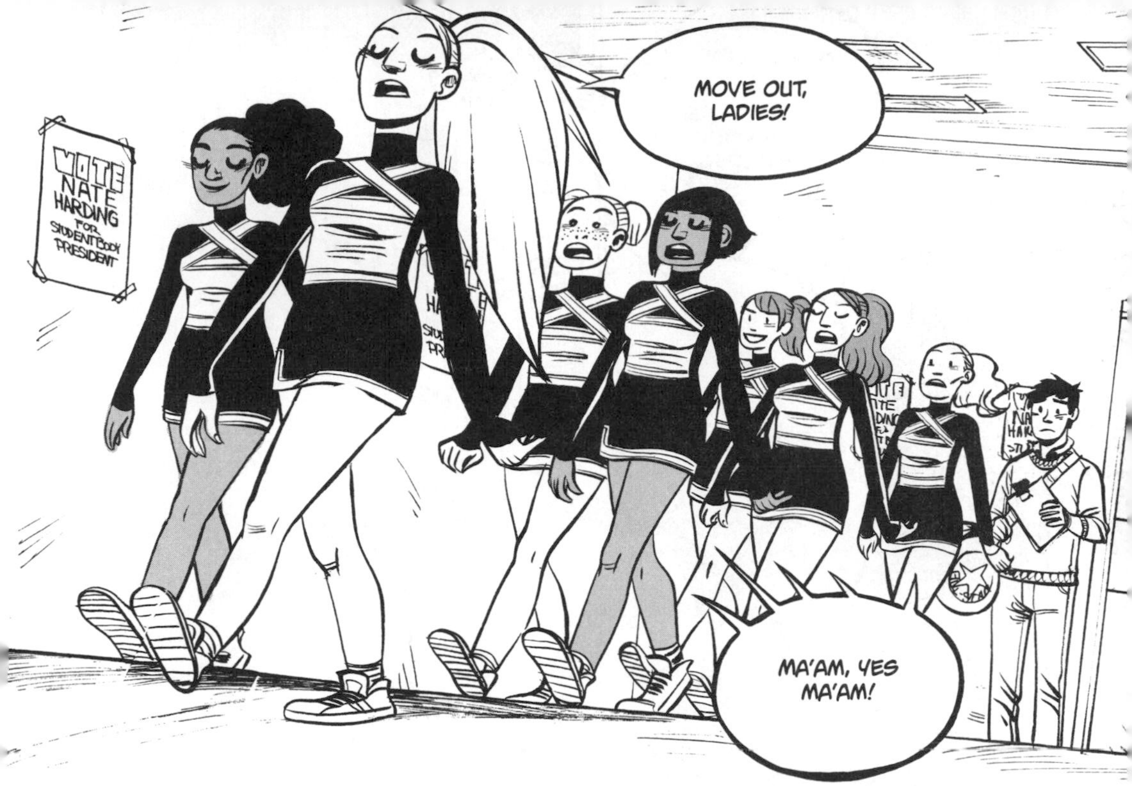
VOTE NATE HARDING FOR STUDENT BODY PRESIDENT
MOVE OUT, LADIES!
MA'AM, YES MA'AM!

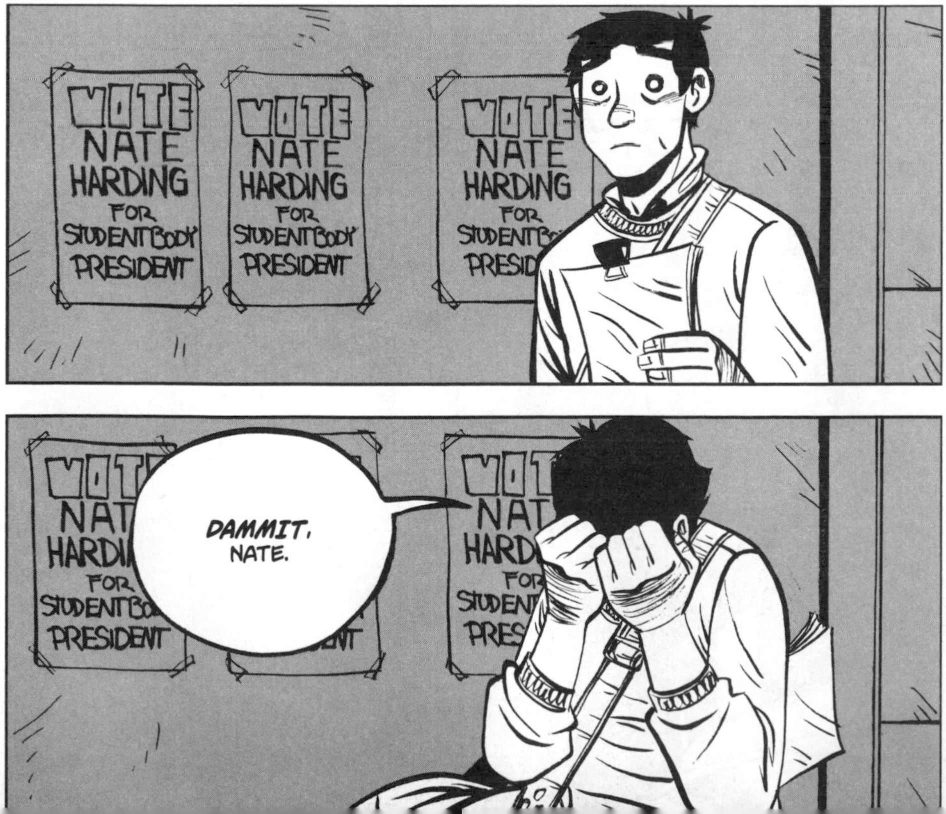
VOTE NATE HARDING FOR STUDENT BODY PRESIDENT
DAMMIT, NATE.

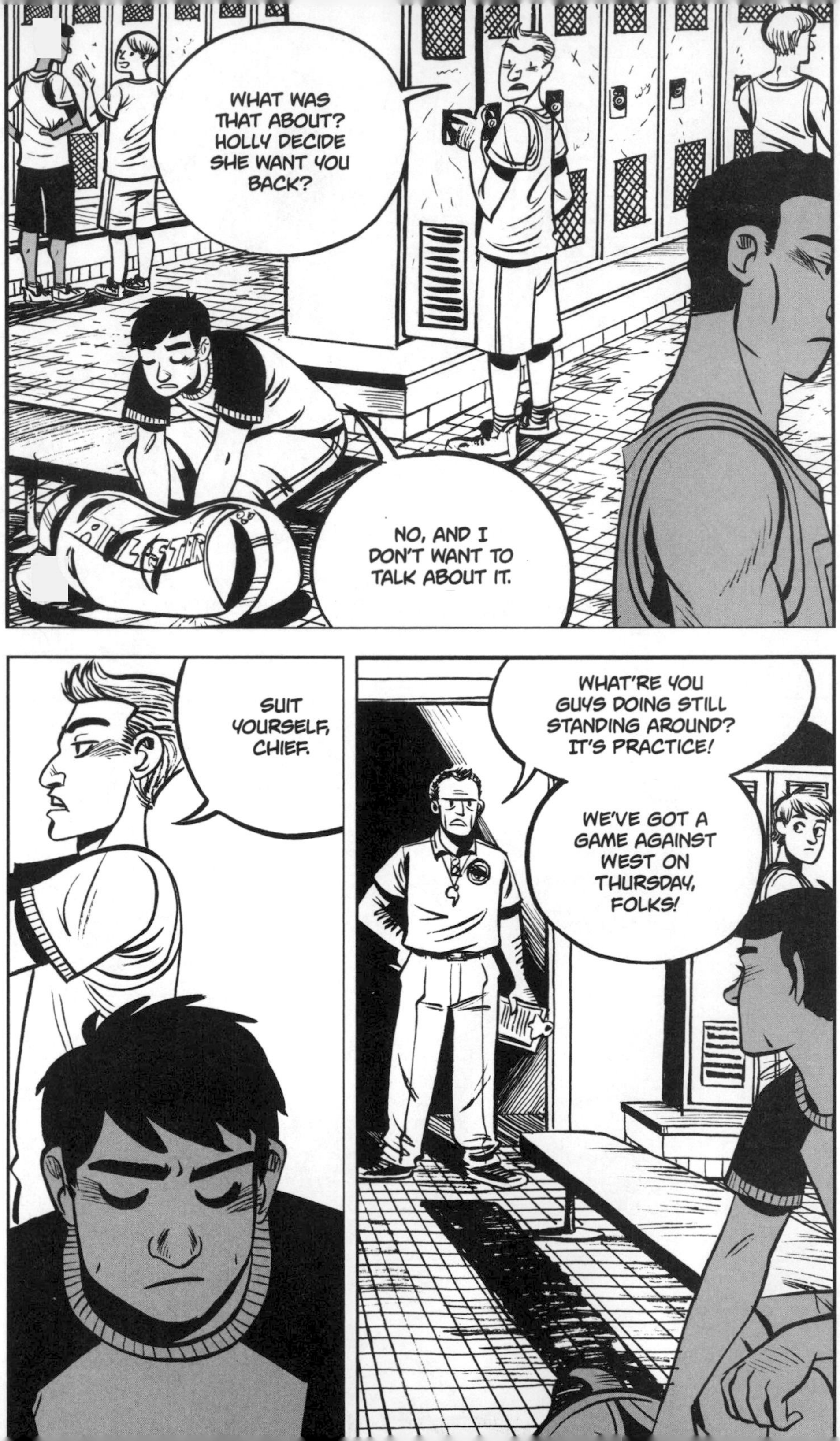
WHAT WAS THAT ABOUT? HOLLY DECIDE SHE WANT YOU BACK?
NO, AND I DON'T WANT TO TALK ABOUT IT.
SUIT YOURSELF, CHIEF.
WHAT'RE YOU GUYS DOING STILL STANDING AROUND? IT'S PRACTICE!
WE'VE GOT A GAME AGAINST WEST ON THURSDAY, FOLKS!

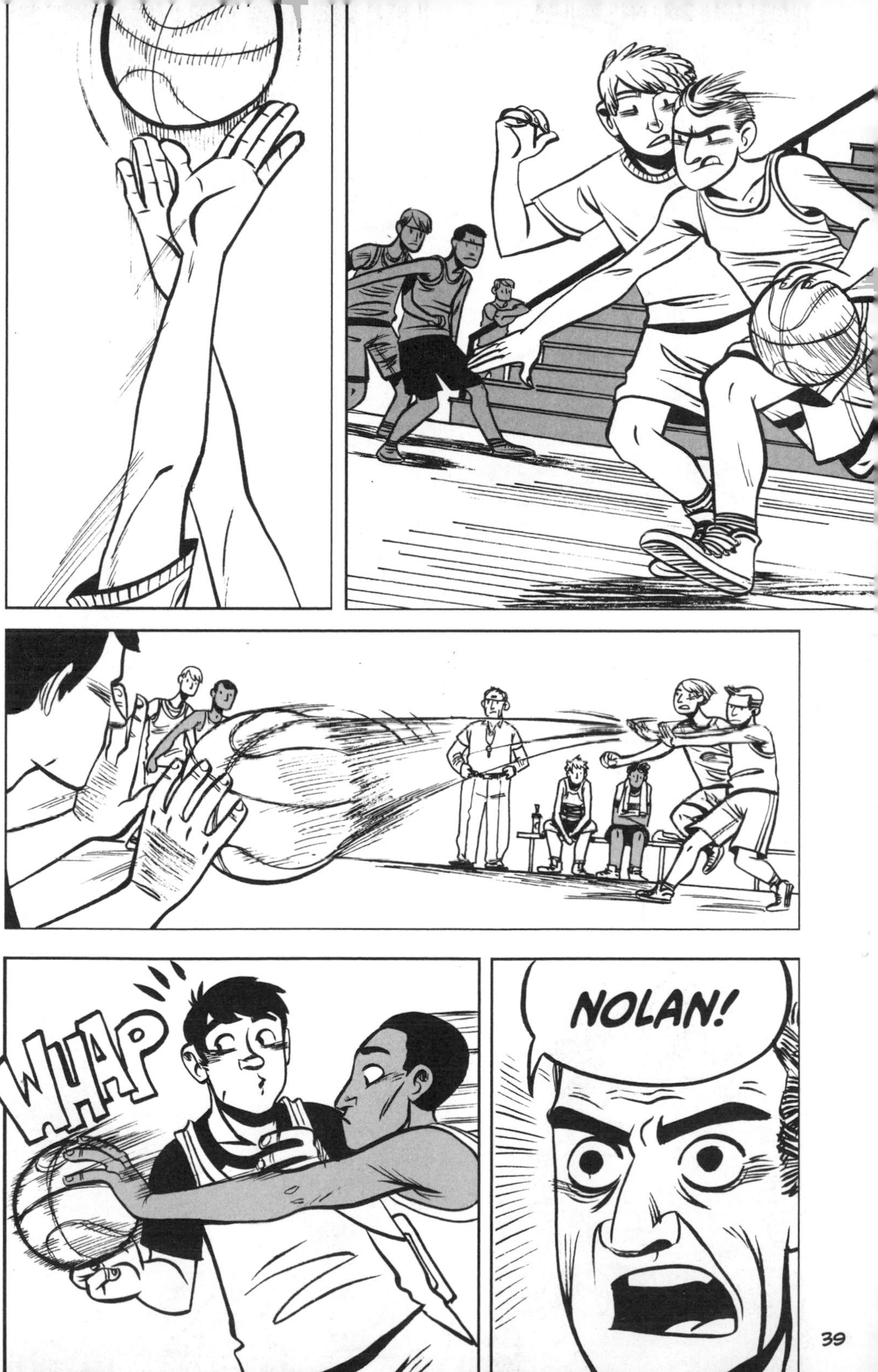
WHAP
NOLAN!

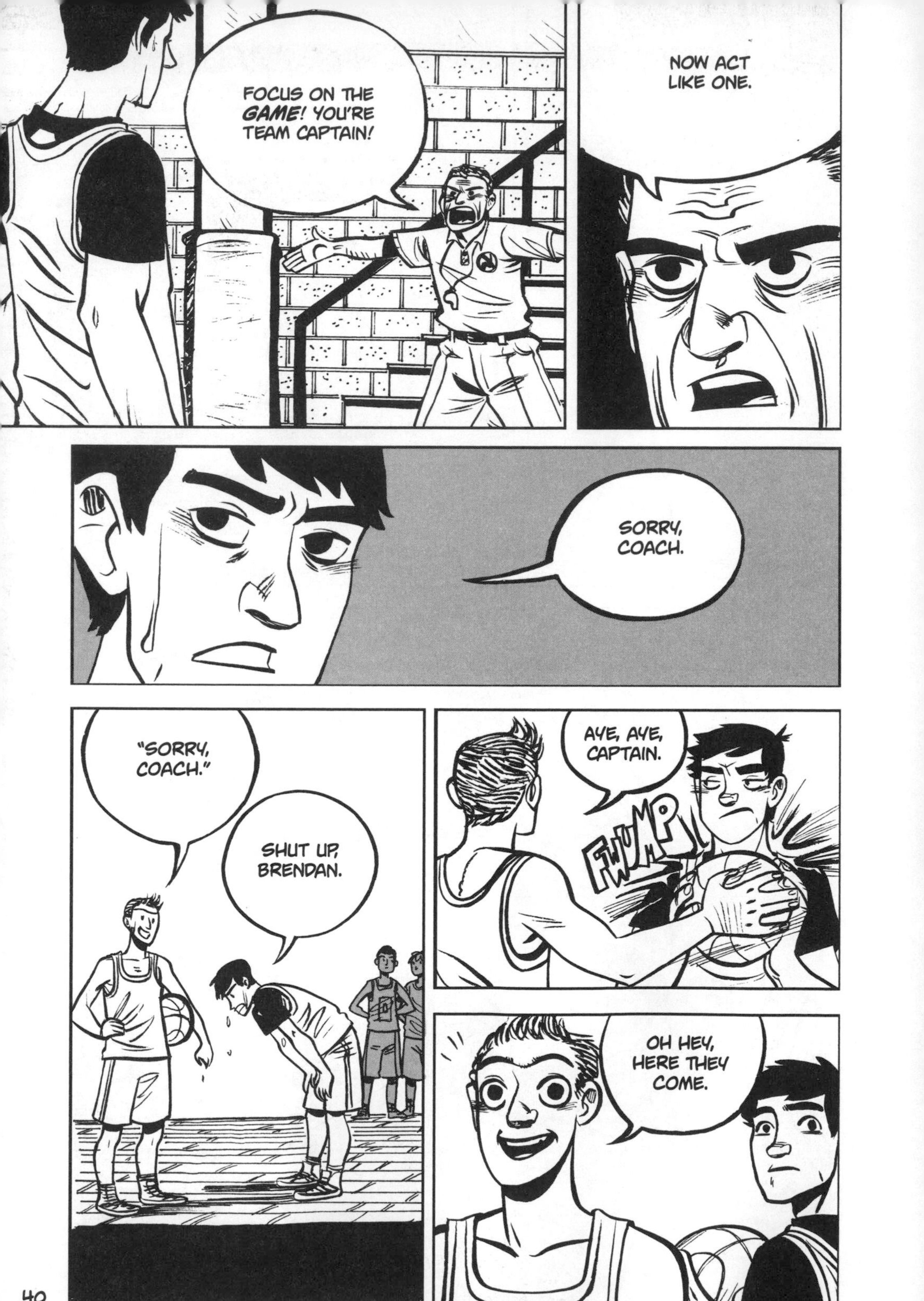
FOCUS ON THE *GAME*! YOU'RE TEAM CAPTAIN!
NOW ACT LIKE ONE.
SORRY, COACH.
"SORRY, COACH."
SHUT UP, BRENDAN.
AYE, AYE, CAPTAIN.
FWUMP
OH HEY, HERE THEY COME.

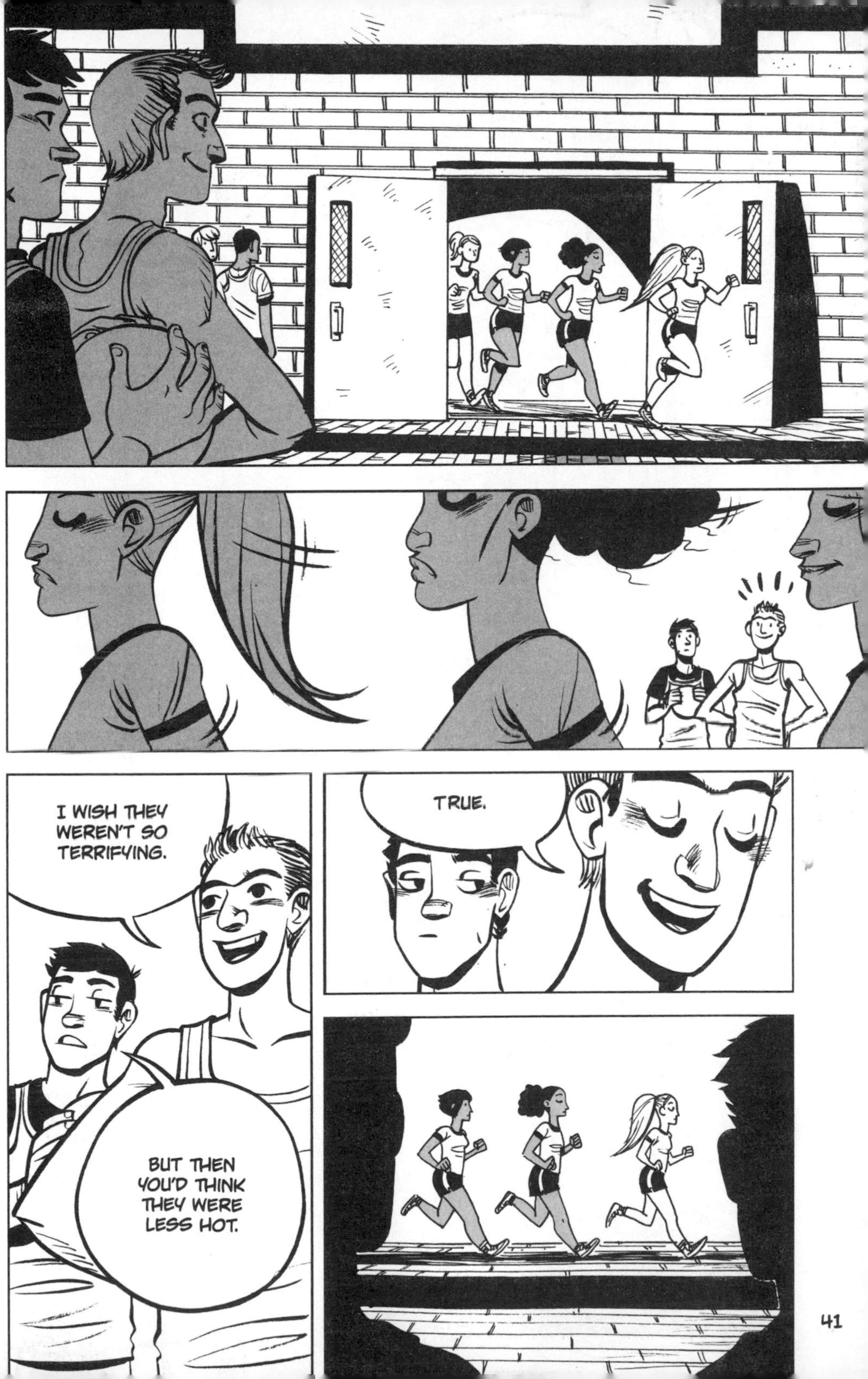
I WISH THEY WEREN'T SO TERRIFYING.
BUT THEN YOU'D THINK THEY WERE LESS HOT.
TRUE.

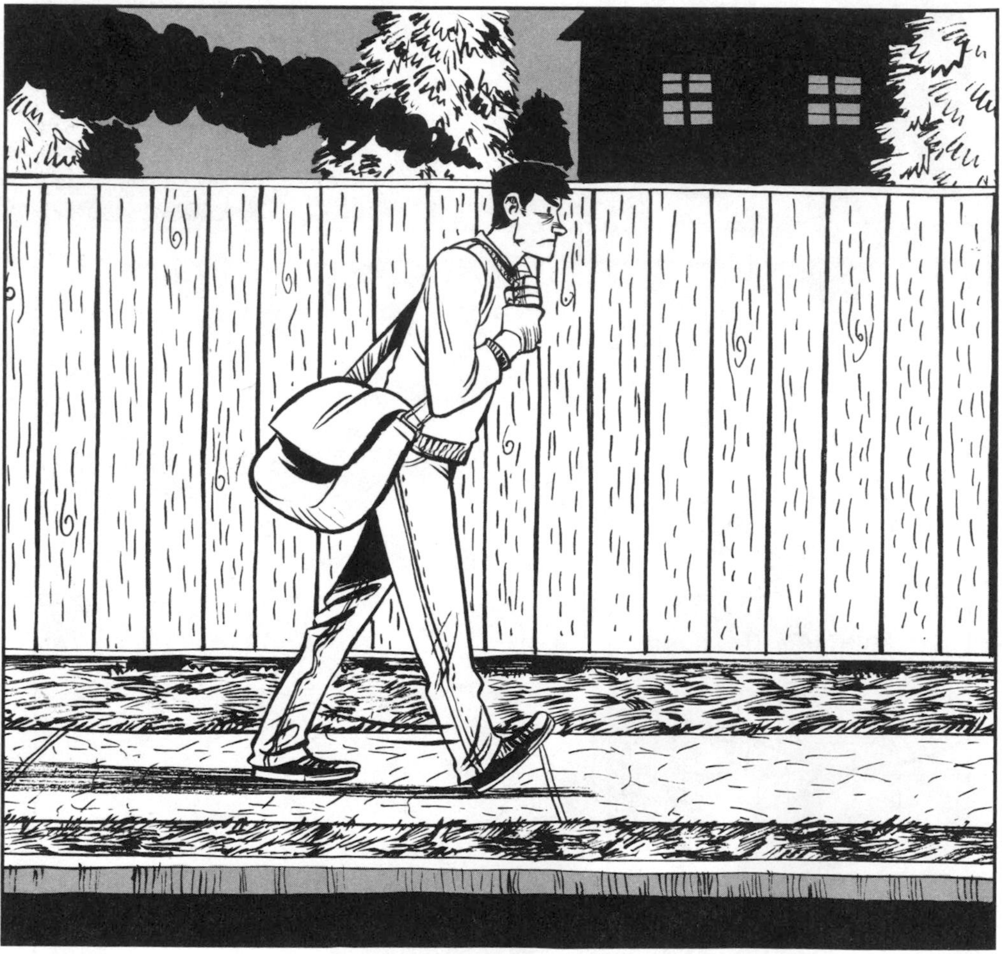

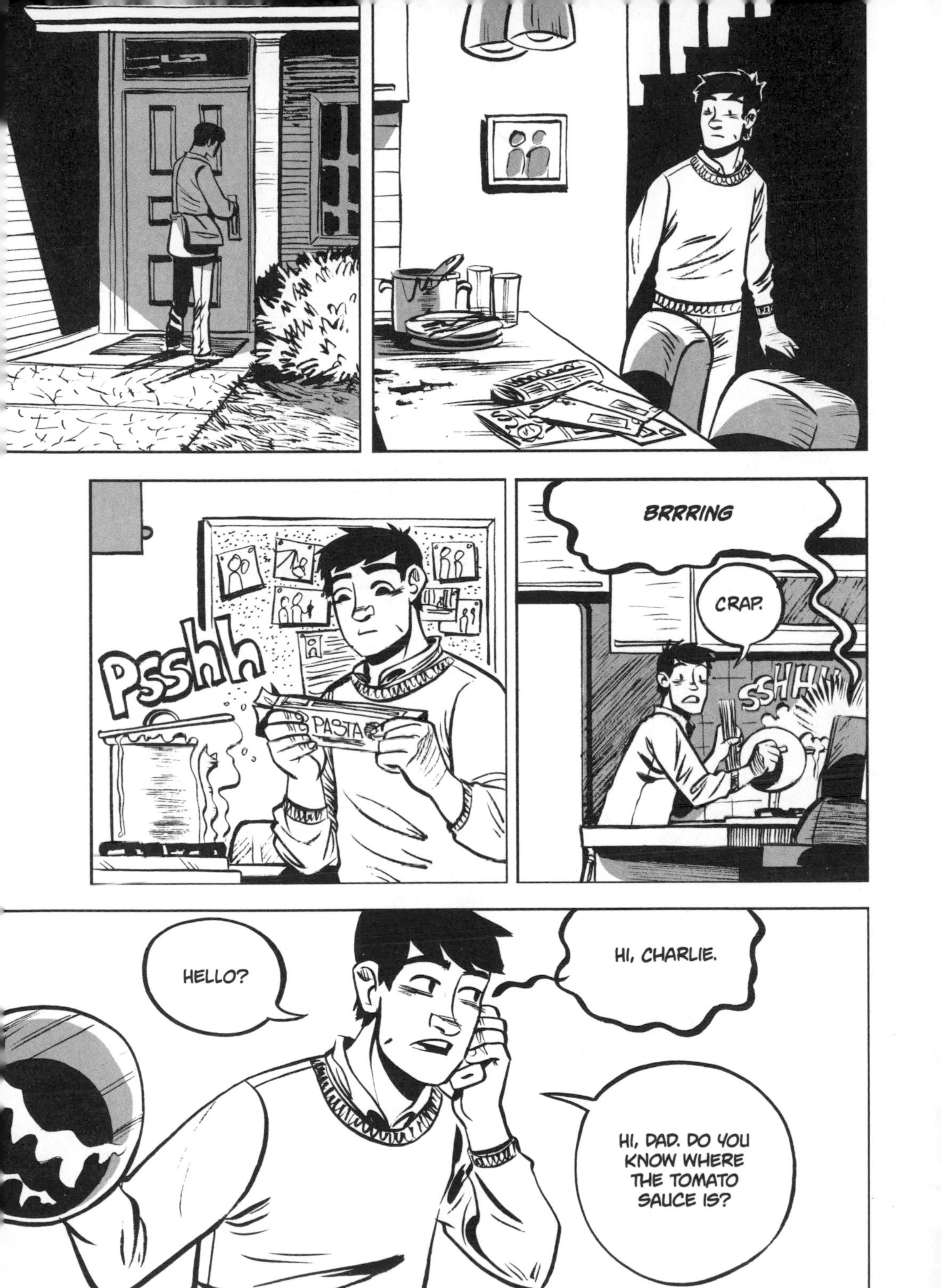
Psshh
PASTA
BRRRING
CRAP.
SSHH
HELLO?
HI, CHARLIE.
HI, DAD. DO YOU KNOW WHERE THE TOMATO SAUCE IS?

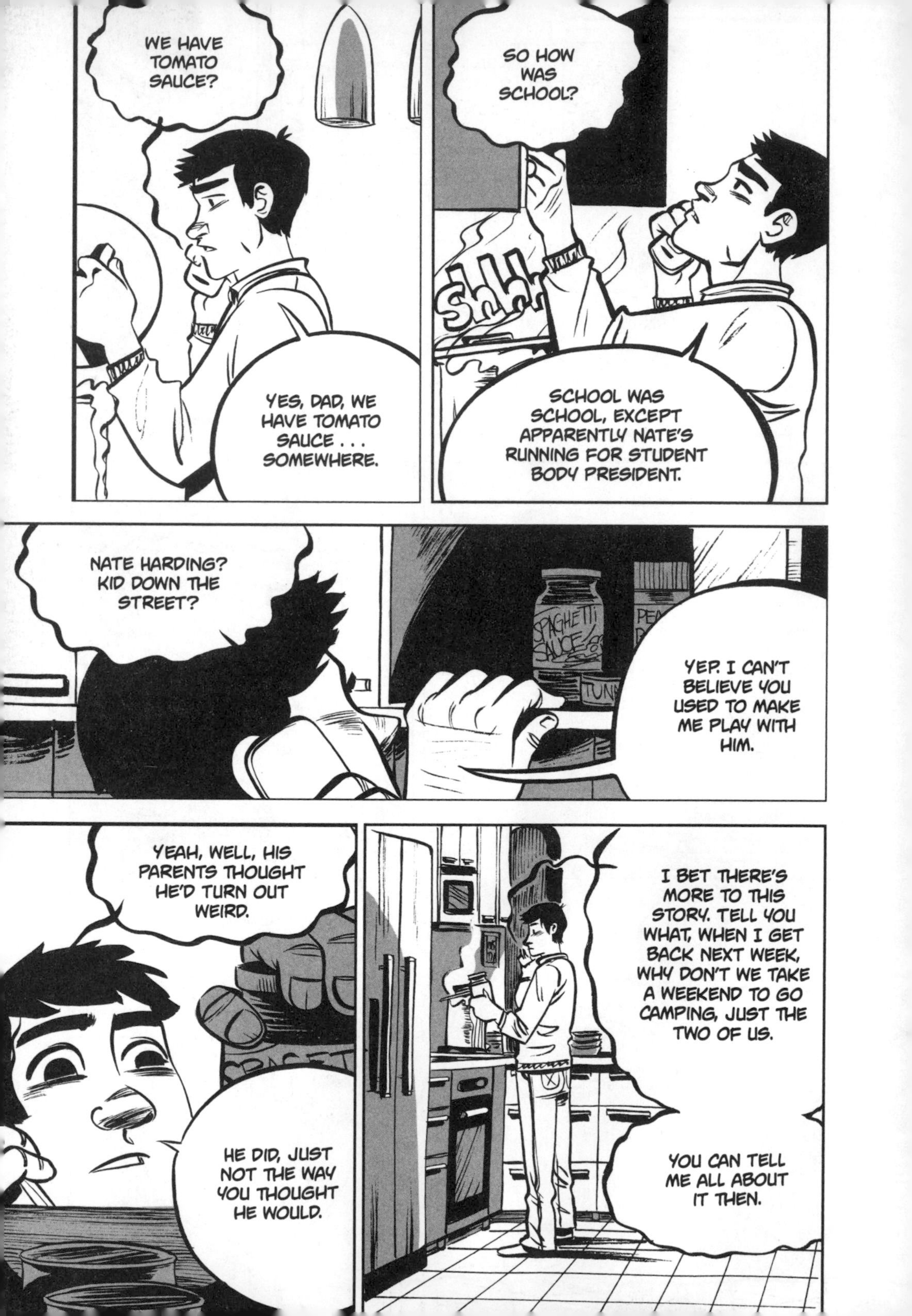
WE HAVE TOMATO SAUCE?
YES, DAD, WE HAVE TOMATO SAUCE . . . SOMEWHERE.
SO HOW WAS SCHOOL?
Shhh
SCHOOL WAS SCHOOL, EXCEPT APPARENTLY NATE'S RUNNING FOR STUDENT BODY PRESIDENT.
NATE HARDING? KID DOWN THE STREET?
SPAGHETTI SAUCE
YEP. I CAN'T BELIEVE YOU USED TO MAKE ME PLAY WITH HIM.
YEAH, WELL, HIS PARENTS THOUGHT HE'D TURN OUT WEIRD.
HE DID, JUST NOT THE WAY YOU THOUGHT HE WOULD.
I BET THERE'S MORE TO THIS STORY. TELL YOU WHAT, WHEN I GET BACK NEXT WEEK, WHY DON'T WE TAKE A WEEKEND TO GO CAMPING, JUST THE TWO OF US.
YOU CAN TELL ME ALL ABOUT IT THEN.

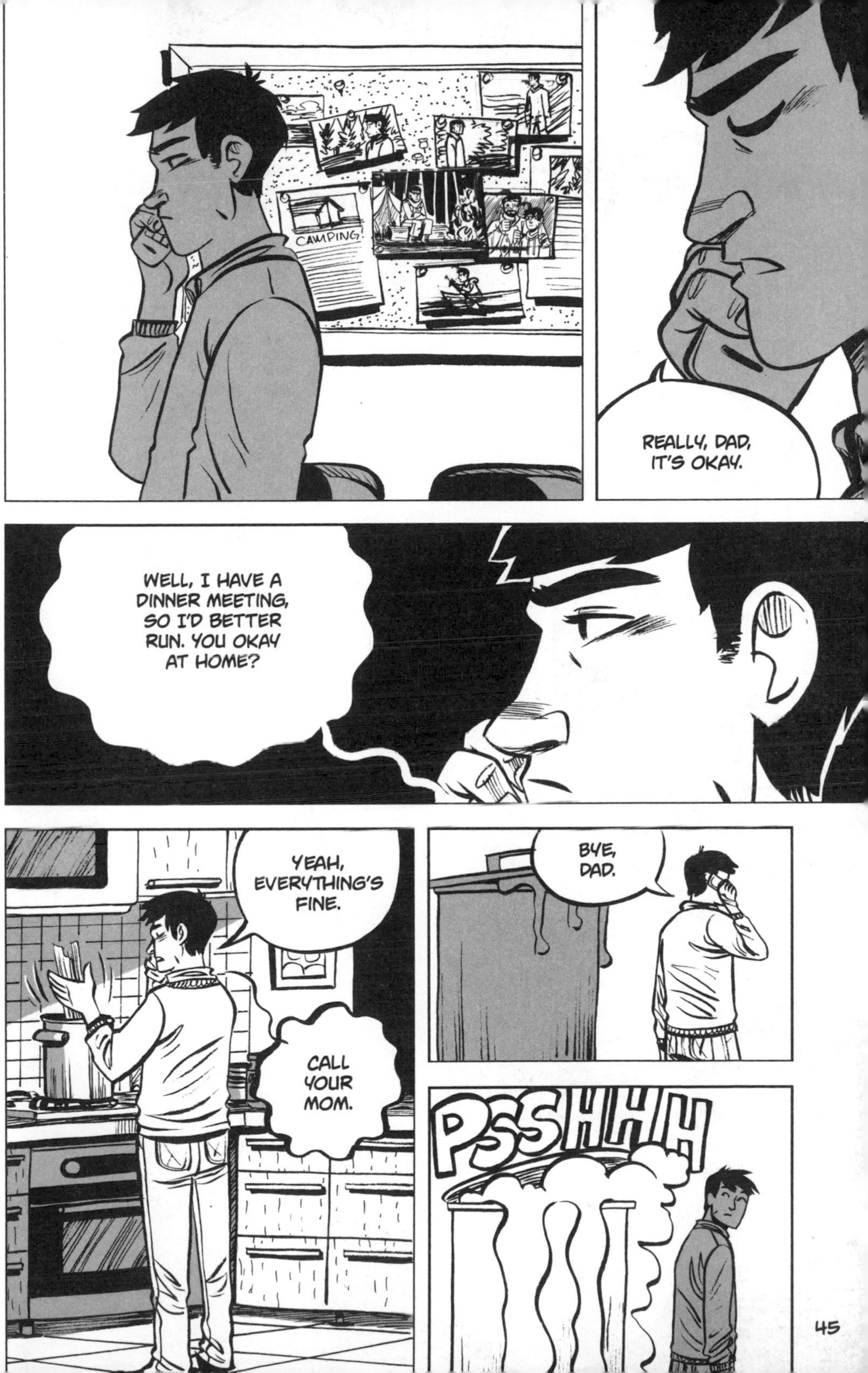

CAMPING!
REALLY, DAD, IT'S OKAY.
WELL, I HAVE A DINNER MEETING, SO I'D BETTER RUN. YOU OKAY AT HOME?
YEAH, EVERYTHING'S FINE.
CALL YOUR MOM.
BYE, DAD.
PSSHHH

NATE & CHARLIE'S PLAYDATE

I'M HERE AGAINST MY WILL.

IS YOUR DAD TRYING TO LIGHT THE BARBEQUE BY RUBBING TWO STICKS TOGETHER?

YEAH. HE'S OUTDOORSY.

WHERE'S YOUR MOM?

SHE'S IN CALIFORNIA.

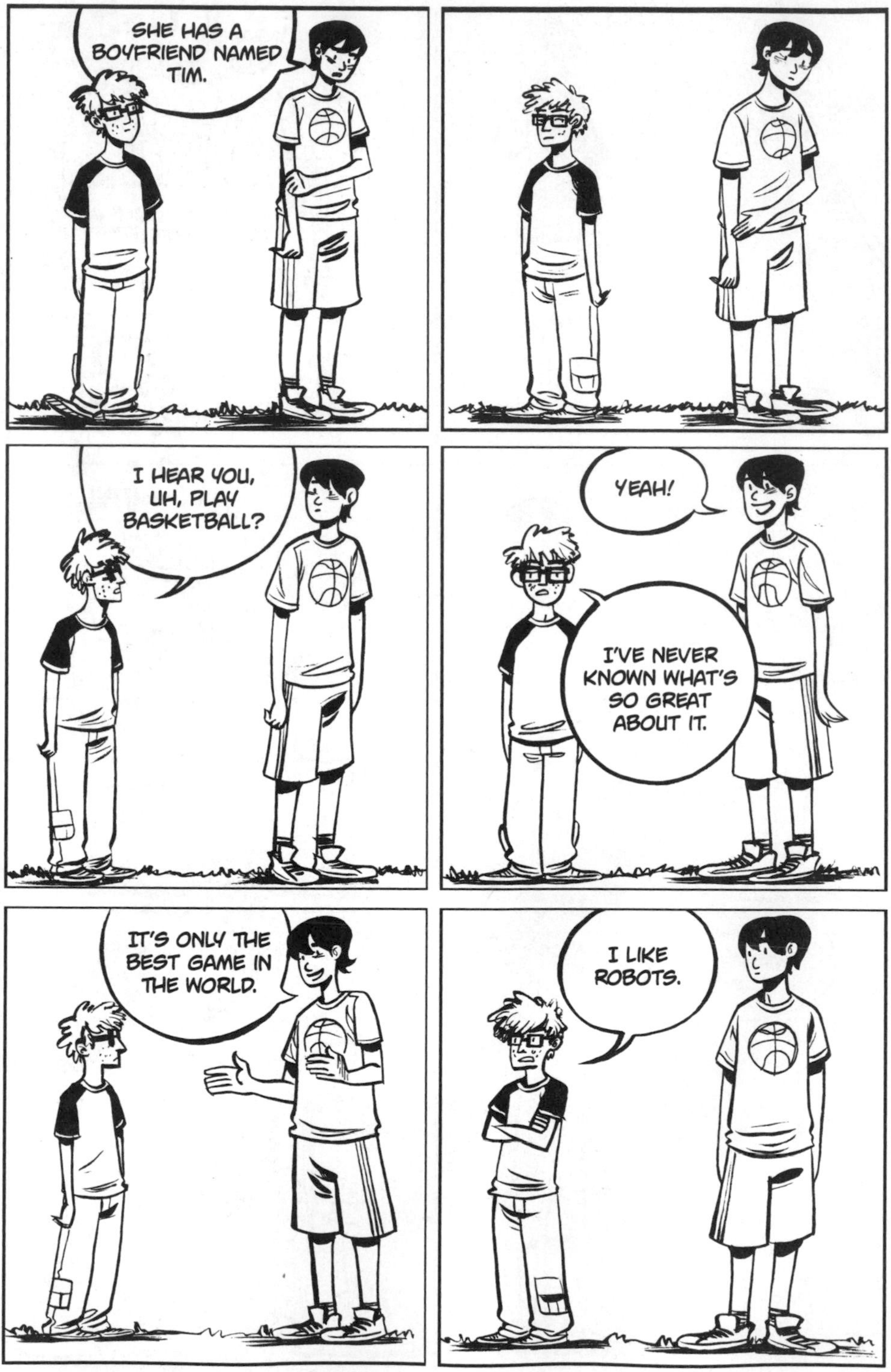
SHE HAS A BOYFRIEND NAMED TIM.
I HEAR YOU, UH, PLAY BASKETBALL?
YEAH!
I'VE NEVER KNOWN WHAT'S SO GREAT ABOUT IT.
IT'S ONLY THE BEST GAME IN THE WORLD.
I LIKE ROBOTS.

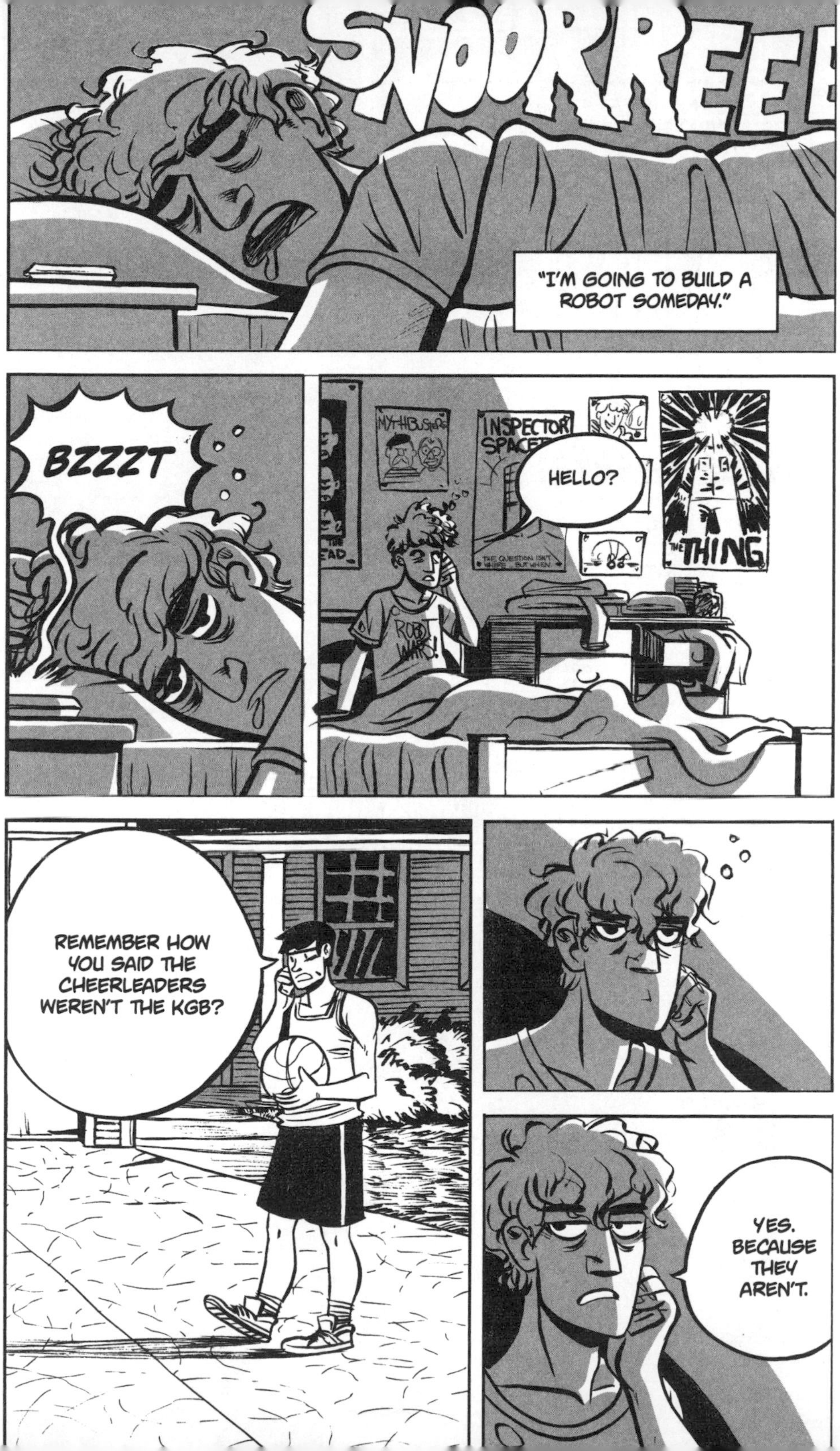
SNOORREEE
"I'M GOING TO BUILD A ROBOT SOMEDAY."
BZZZT
MYTHBUSTERS
INSPECTOR SPACETIME
HELLO?
THE THING
ROBOT WARS!
REMEMBER HOW YOU SAID THE CHEERLEADERS WEREN'T THE KGB?
YES. BECAUSE THEY AREN'T.

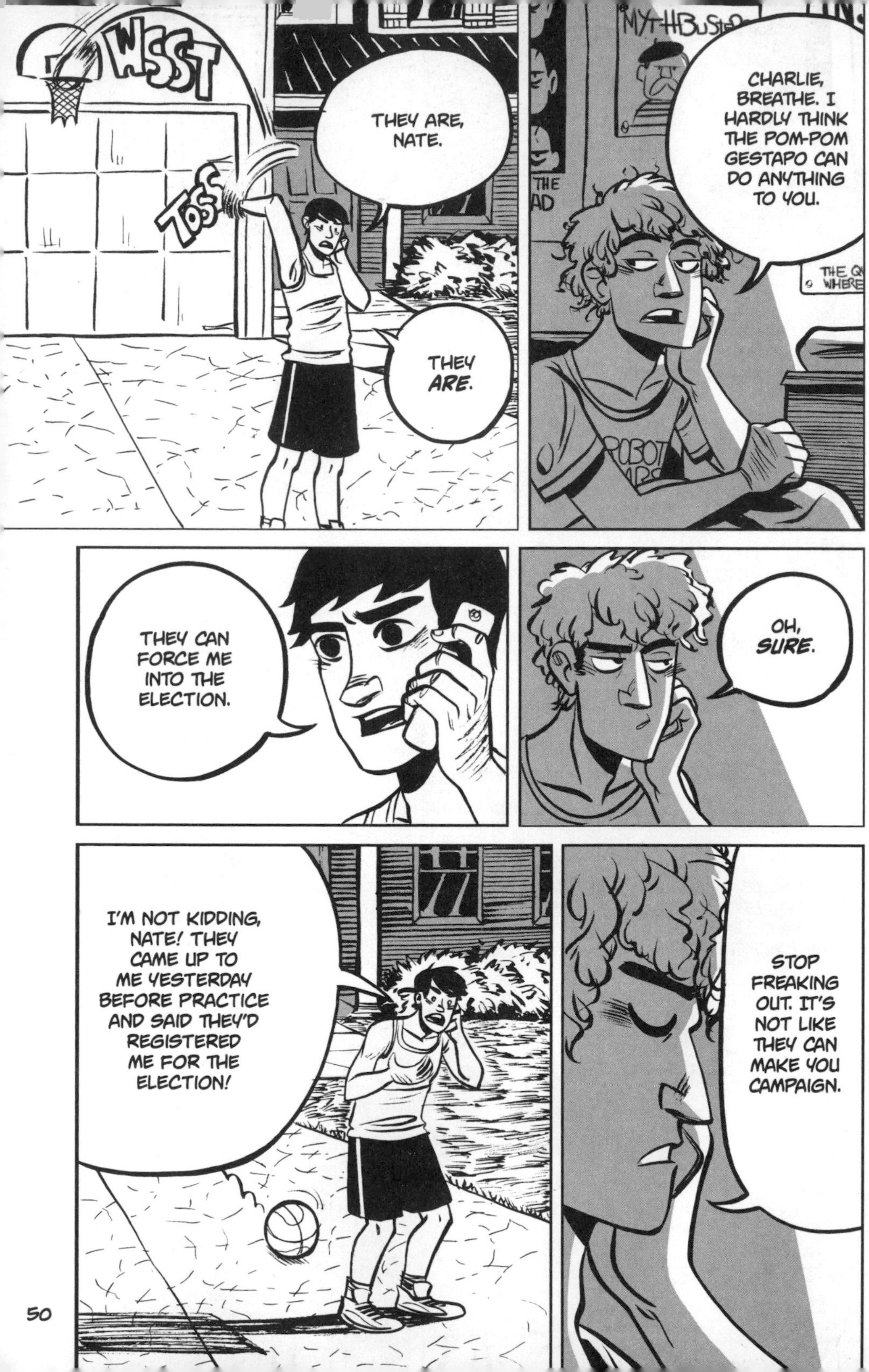
WSST
TOSS
THEY ARE, NATE.
THEY *ARE.*
CHARLIE, BREATHE. I HARDLY THINK THE POM-POM GESTAPO CAN DO ANYTHING TO YOU.
THEY CAN FORCE ME INTO THE ELECTION.
OH, *SURE.*
I'M NOT KIDDING, NATE! THEY CAME UP TO ME YESTERDAY BEFORE PRACTICE AND SAID THEY'D REGISTERED ME FOR THE ELECTION!
STOP FREAKING OUT. IT'S NOT LIKE THEY CAN MAKE YOU CAMPAIGN.

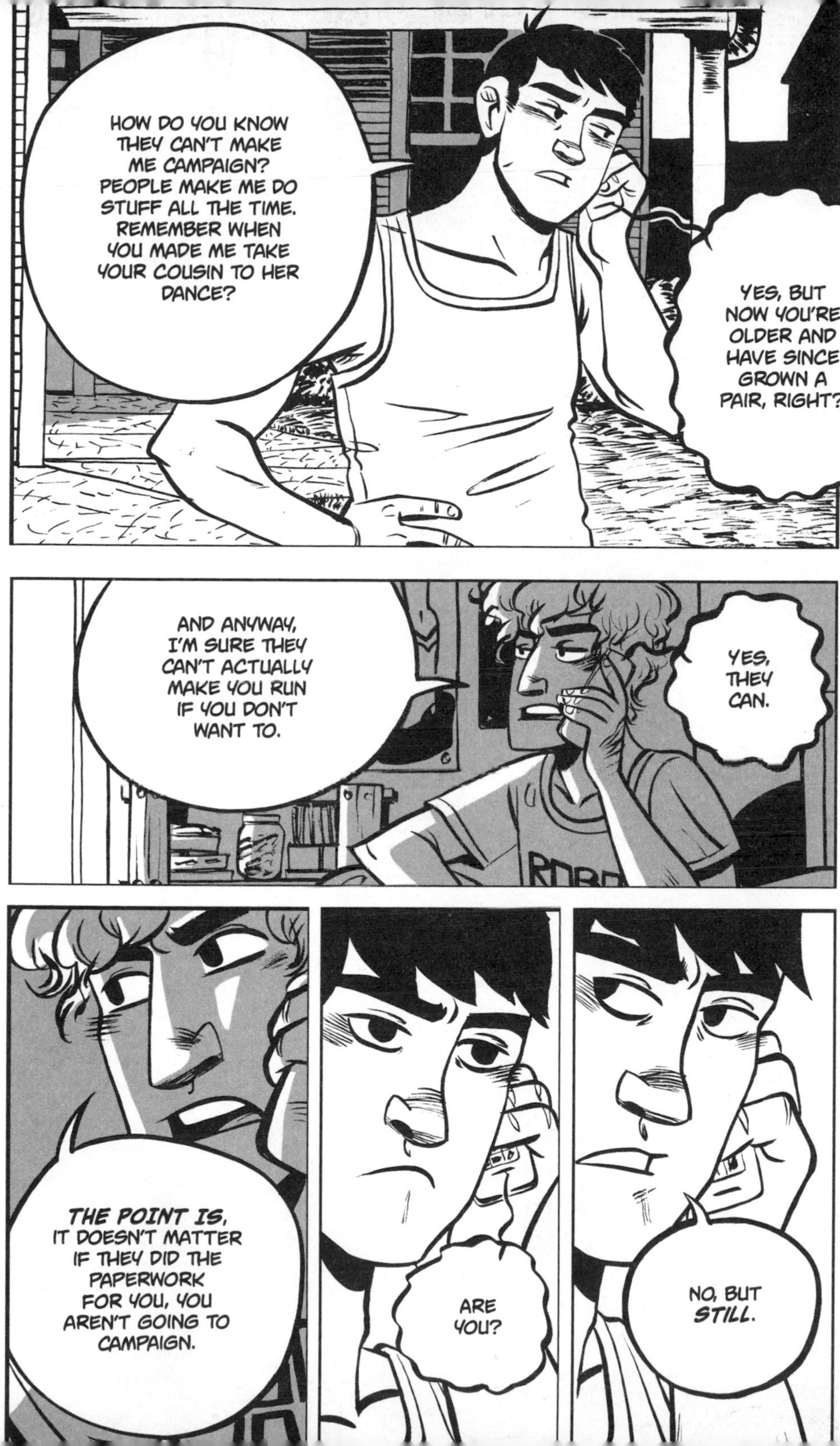
HOW DO YOU KNOW THEY CAN'T MAKE ME CAMPAIGN? PEOPLE MAKE ME DO STUFF ALL THE TIME. REMEMBER WHEN YOU MADE ME TAKE YOUR COUSIN TO HER DANCE?
YES, BUT NOW YOU'RE OLDER AND HAVE SINCE GROWN A PAIR, RIGHT?
AND ANYWAY, I'M SURE THEY CAN'T ACTUALLY MAKE YOU RUN IF YOU DON'T WANT TO.
YES, THEY CAN.
THE POINT IS, IT DOESN'T MATTER IF THEY DID THE PAPERWORK FOR YOU, YOU AREN'T GOING TO CAMPAIGN.
ARE YOU?
NO, BUT STILL.

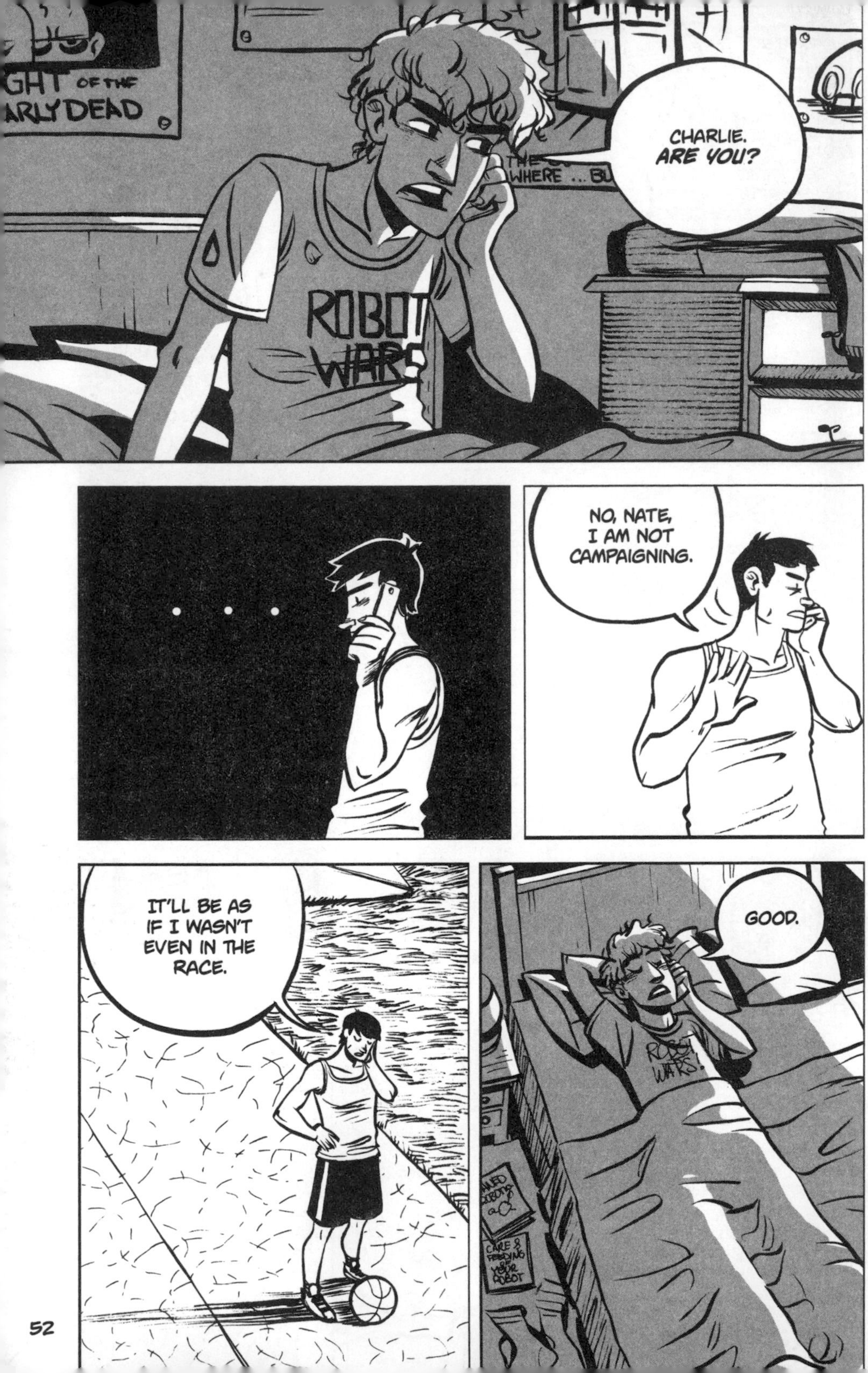
CHARLIE.
ARE YOU?
ROBOT WARS
. . .
NO, NATE, I AM NOT CAMPAIGNING.
IT'LL BE AS IF I WASN'T EVEN IN THE RACE.
GOOD.
ROBOT WARS!
CARE & FEEDING OF YOUR ROBOT

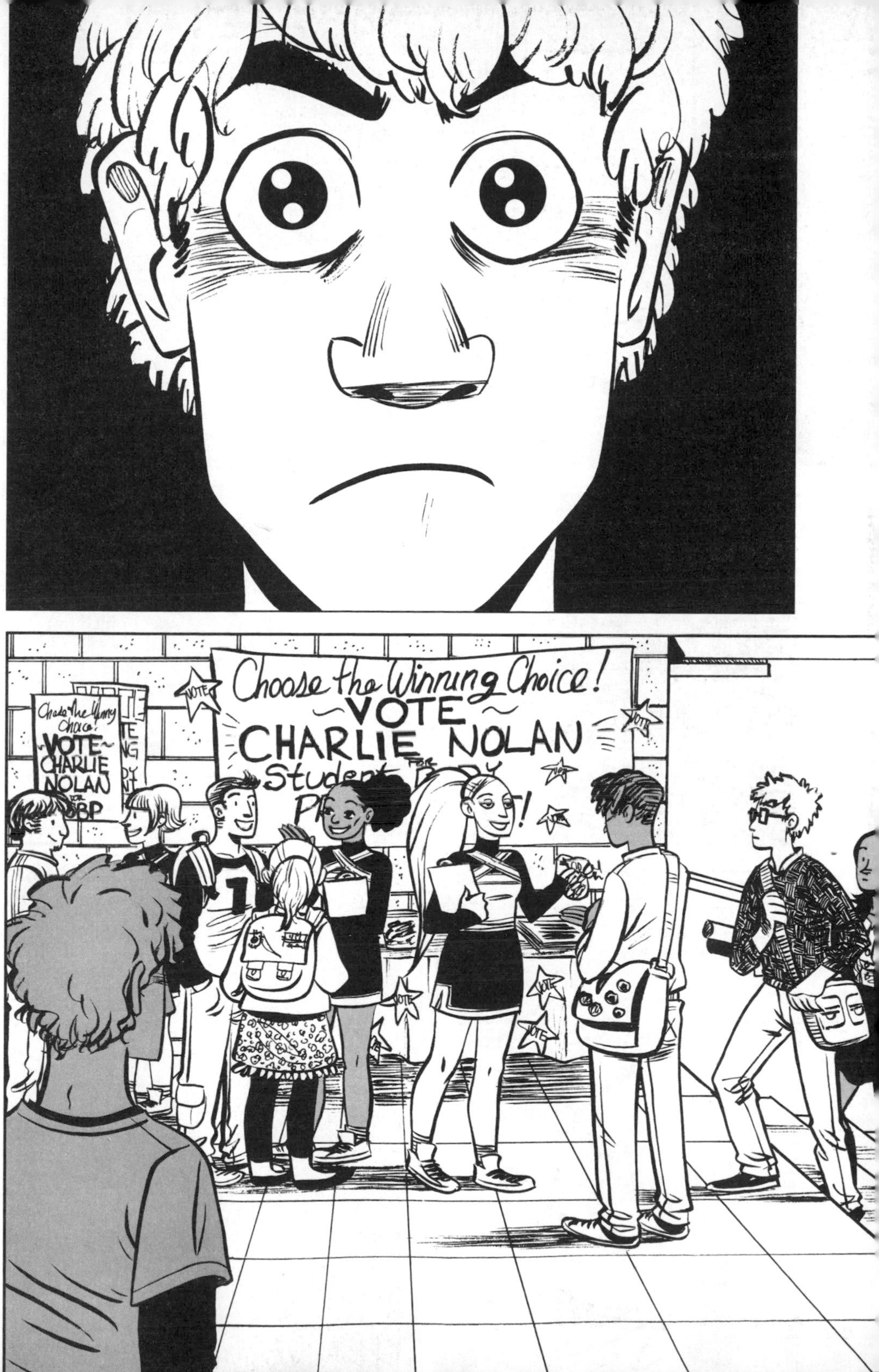
Choose the Winning Choice!
VOTE
CHARLIE NOLAN
Choose the Winning Choice!
VOTE
CHARLIE
NOLAN
FOR

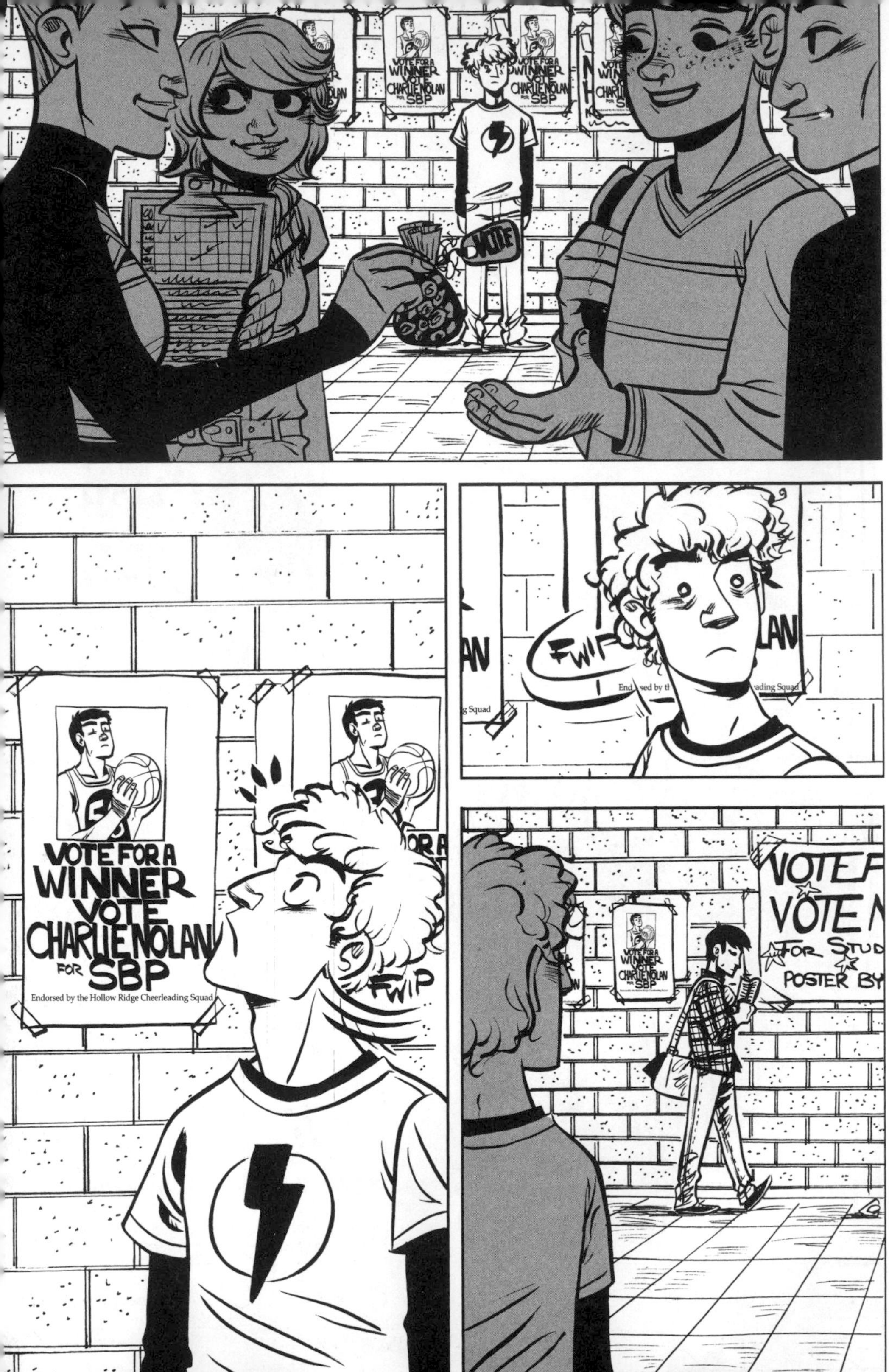
VOTE
VOTE FOR A WINNER VOTE CHARLIE NOLAN FOR SBP
Endorsed by the Hollow Ridge Cheerleading Squad
FWIP
FWIP
VOTE F
VOTE N
FOR STUD
POSTER BY

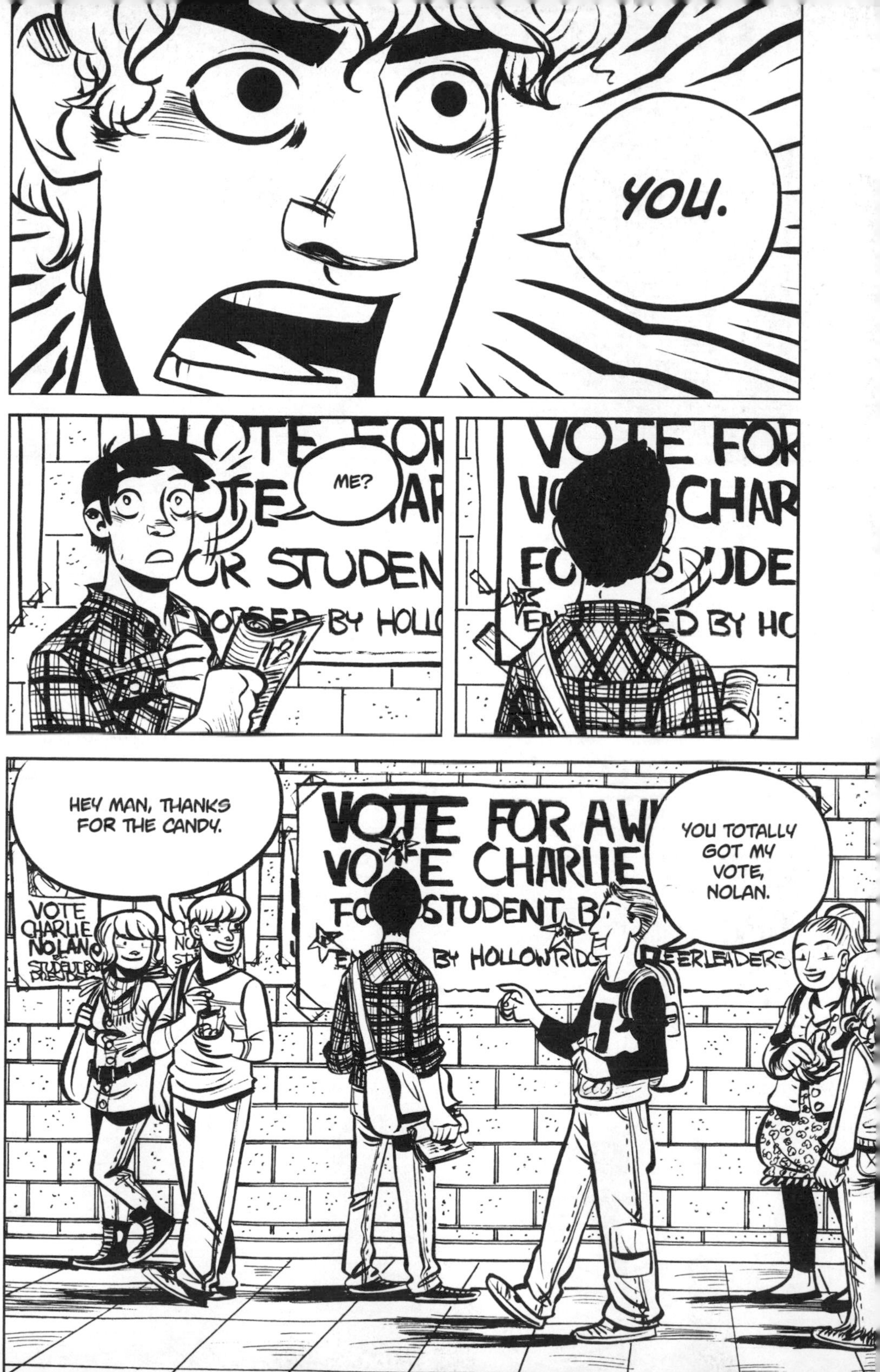
YOU.
ME?
HEY MAN, THANKS FOR THE CANDY.
YOU TOTALLY GOT MY VOTE, NOLAN.

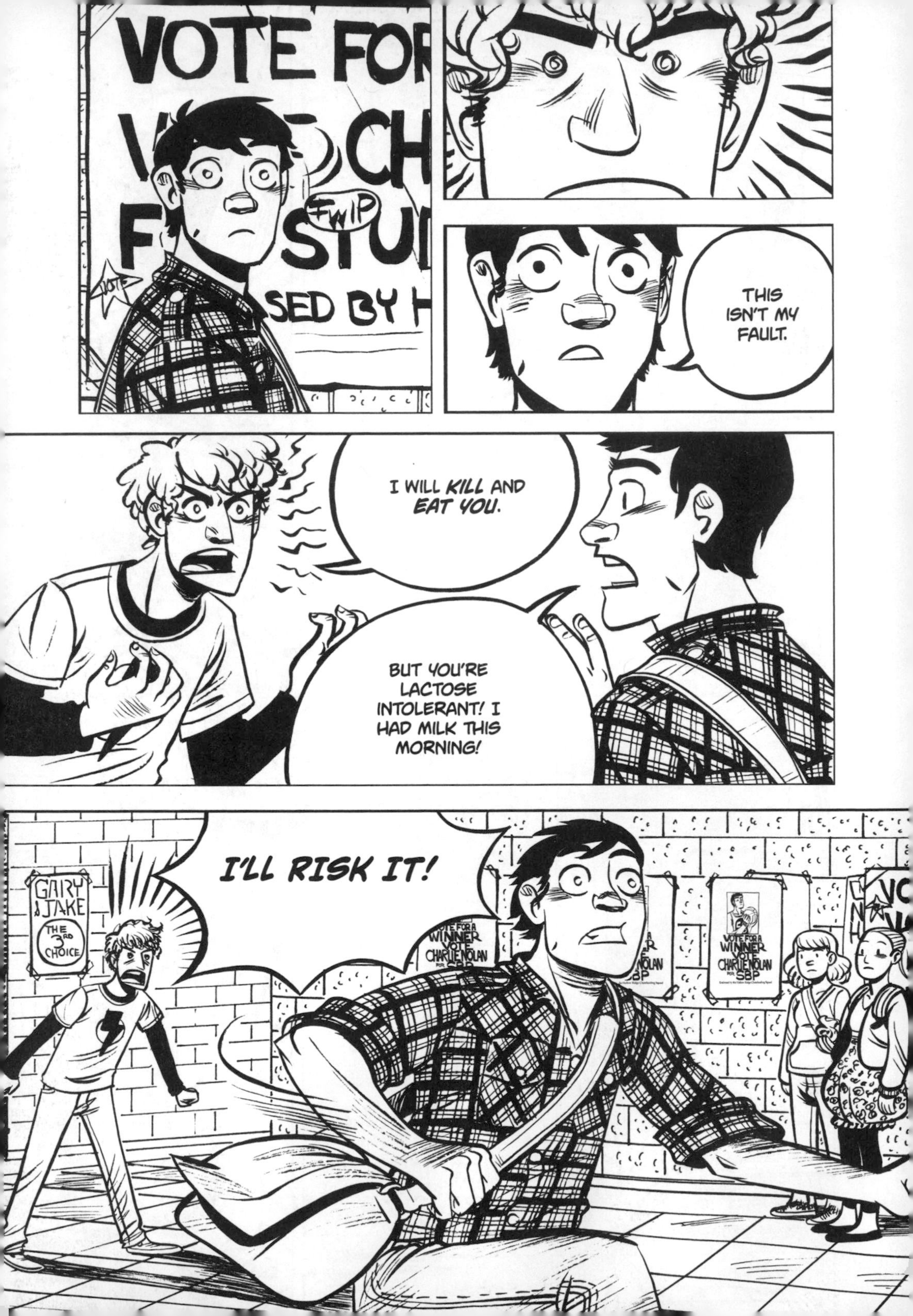
VOTE FOR
FWIP
THIS ISN'T MY FAULT.
I WILL KILL AND EAT YOU.
BUT YOU'RE LACTOSE INTOLERANT! I HAD MILK THIS MORNING!
I'LL RISK IT!
GARY & JAKE THE 3RD CHOICE
VOTE FOR A WINNER VOTE CHARLIE NOLAN FOR SBP

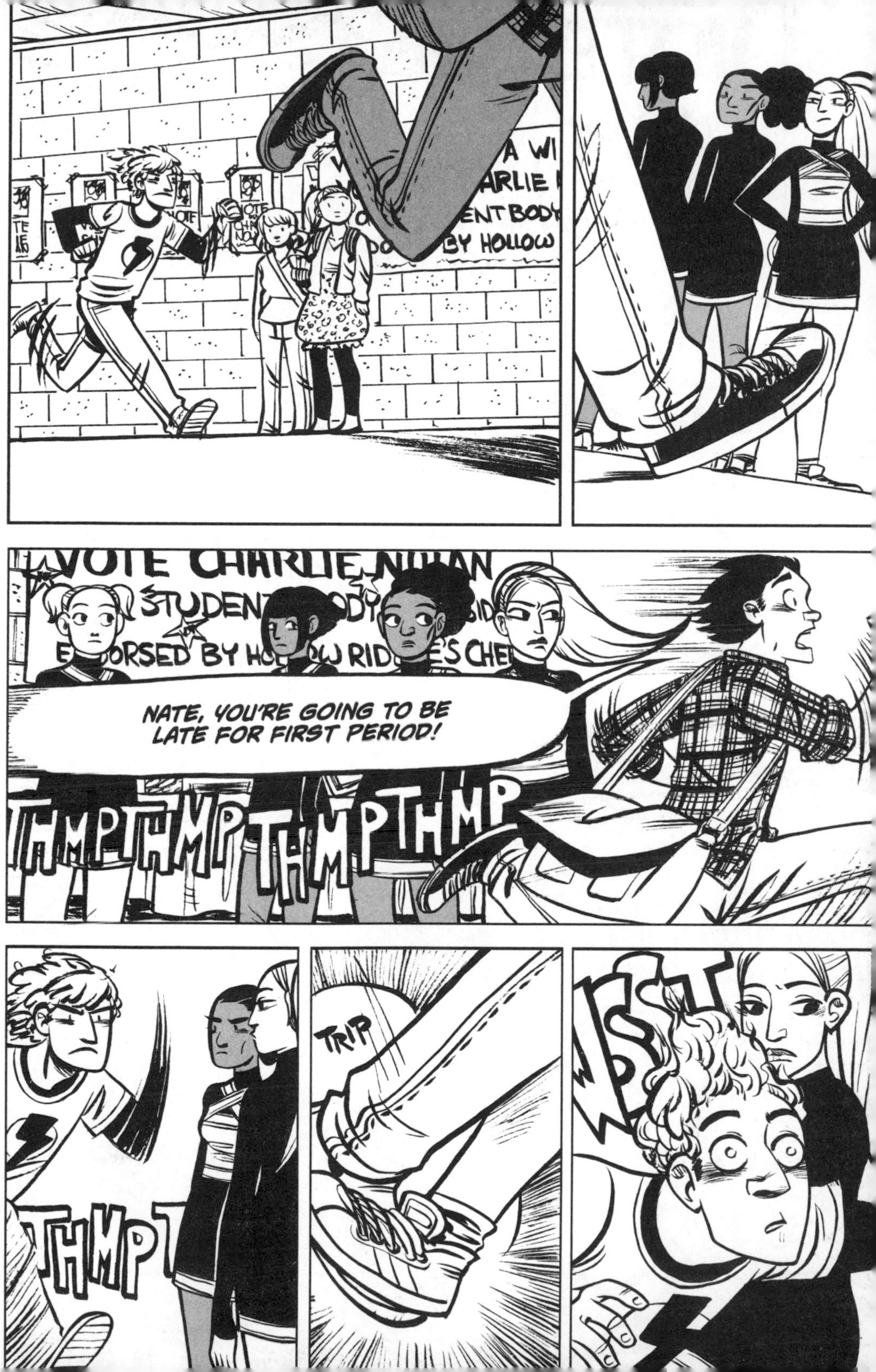
NATE, YOU'RE GOING TO BE LATE FOR FIRST PERIOD!
THMP THMP THMP THMP
THMP
TRIP

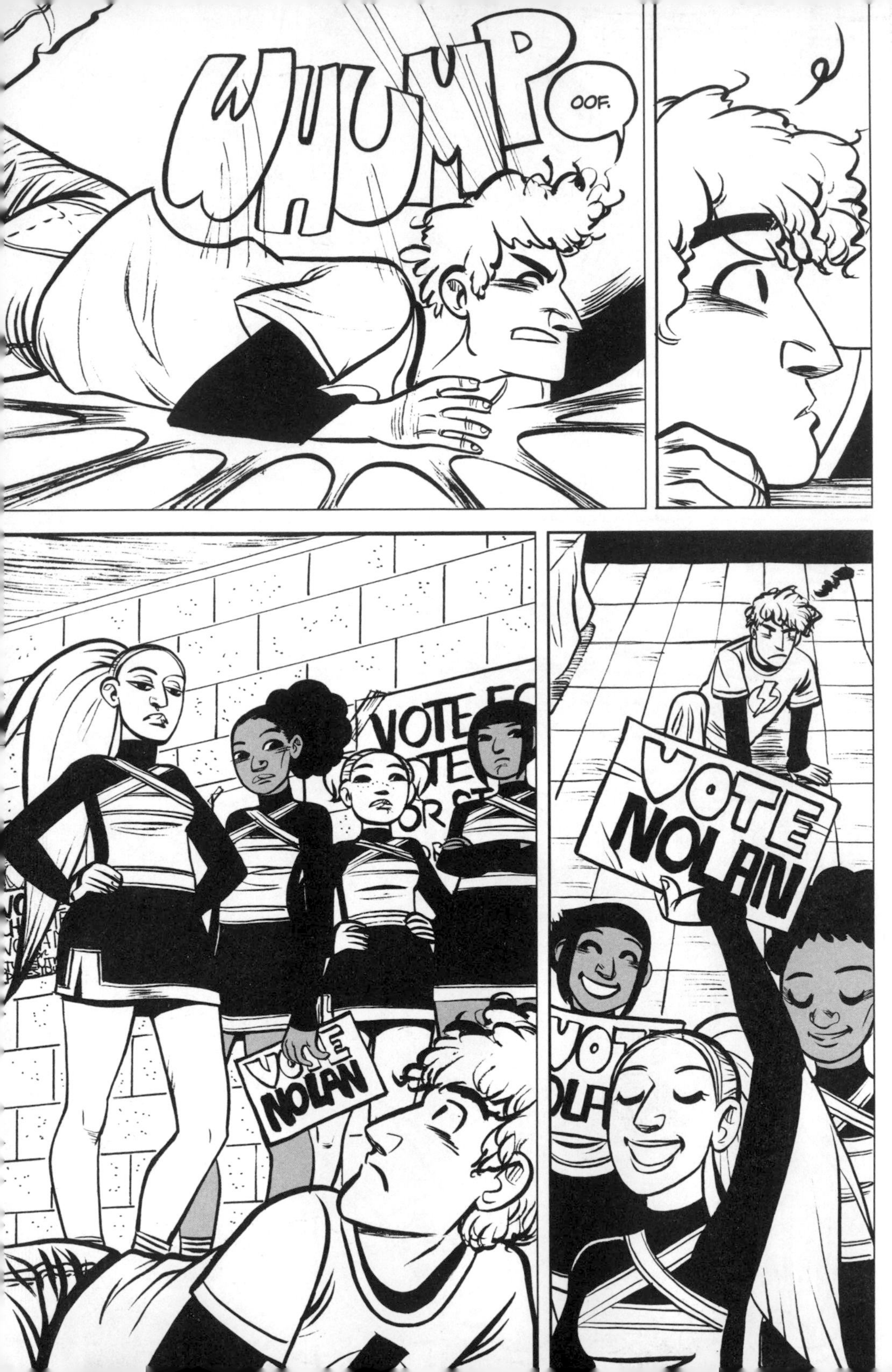
WHUMP
OOF.
NOLAN
VOTE NOLAN

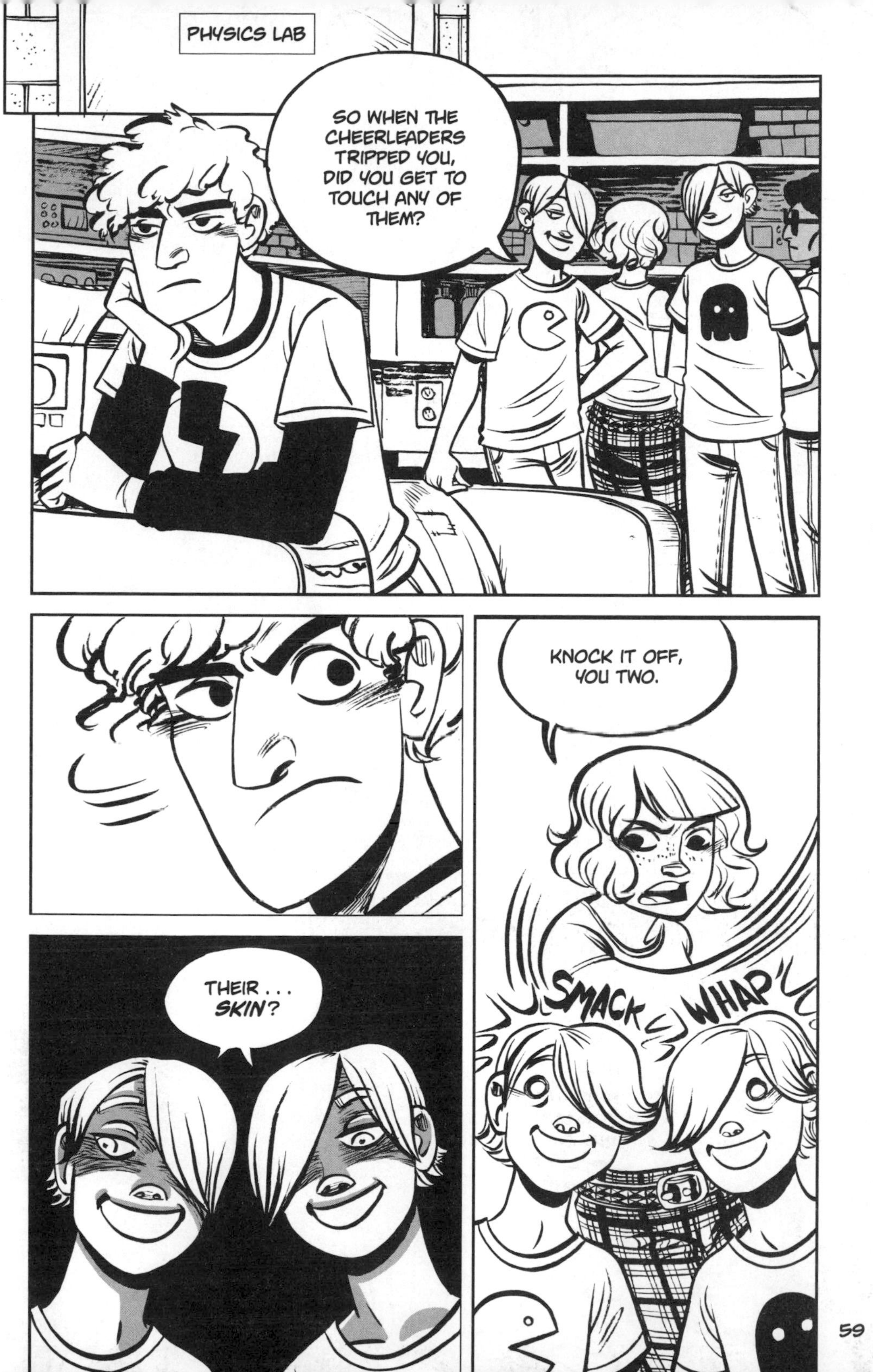

PHYSICS LAB
SO WHEN THE CHEERLEADERS TRIPPED YOU, DID YOU GET TO TOUCH ANY OF THEM?
THEIR . . . SKIN?
KNOCK IT OFF, YOU TWO.
SMACK
WHAP

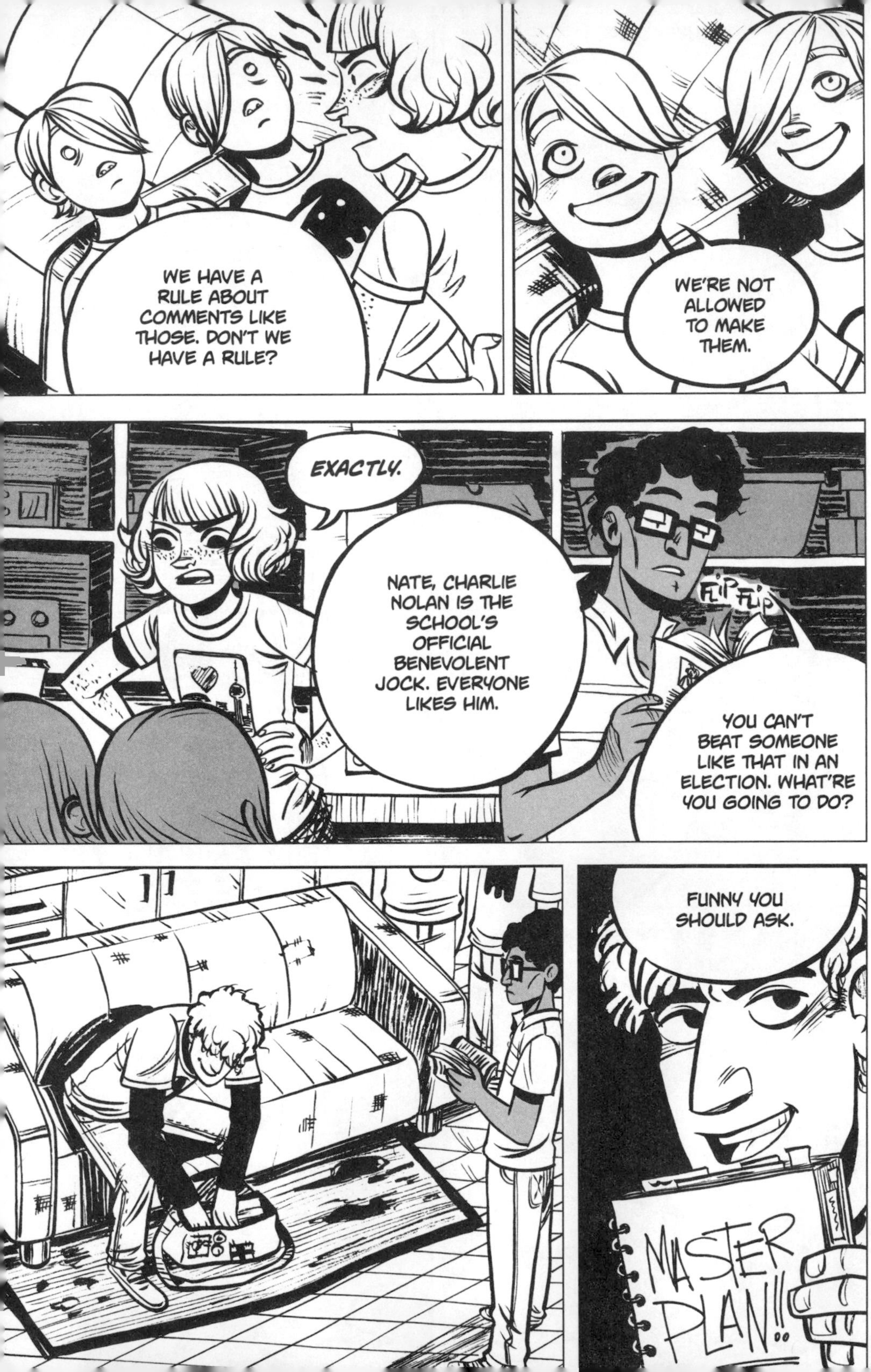
WE HAVE A RULE ABOUT COMMENTS LIKE THOSE. DON'T WE HAVE A RULE?
WE'RE NOT ALLOWED TO MAKE THEM.
EXACTLY.
NATE, CHARLIE NOLAN IS THE SCHOOL'S OFFICIAL BENEVOLENT JOCK. EVERYONE LIKES HIM.
FLIP FLIP
YOU CAN'T BEAT SOMEONE LIKE THAT IN AN ELECTION. WHAT'RE YOU GOING TO DO?
FUNNY YOU SHOULD ASK.
MASTER PLAN!!

NEXT DAY

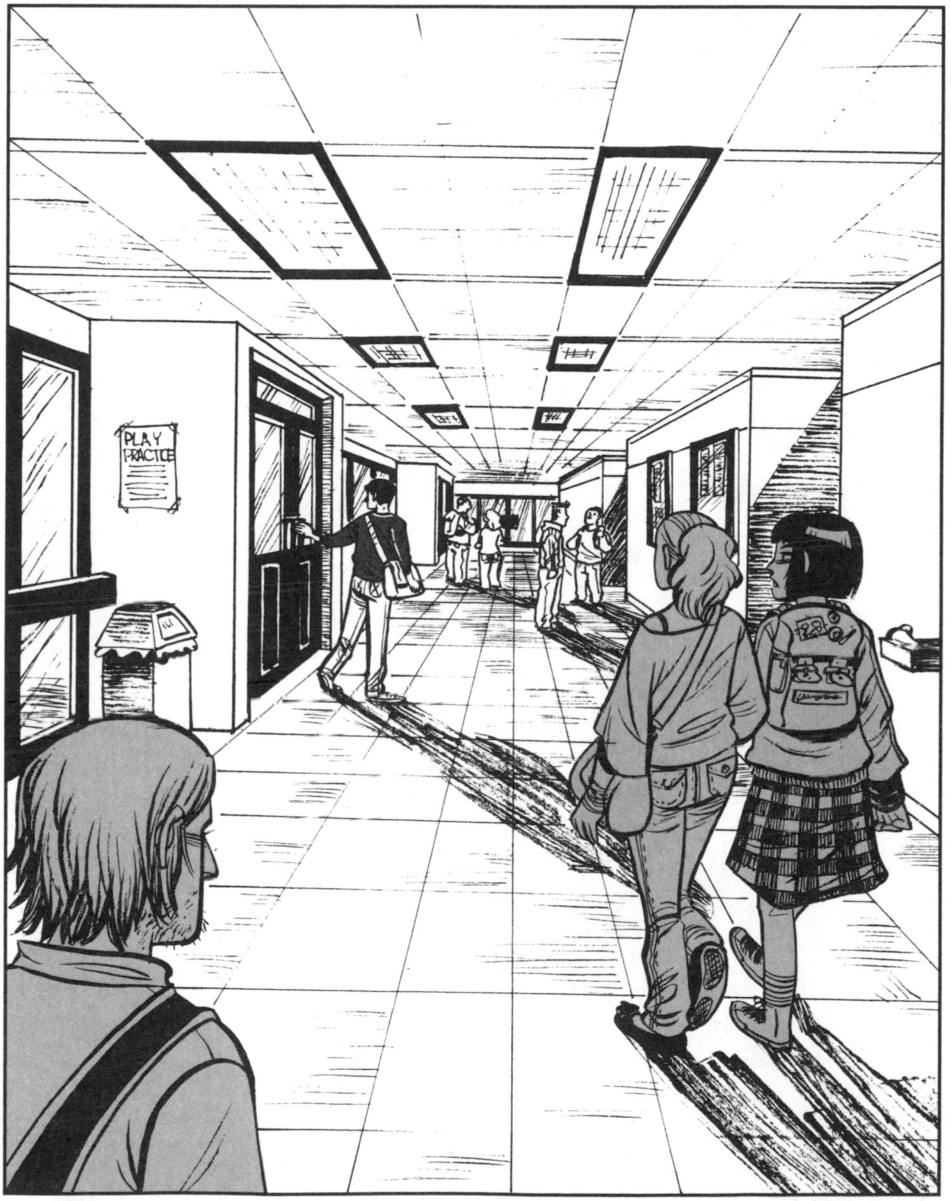
PLAY PRACTICE

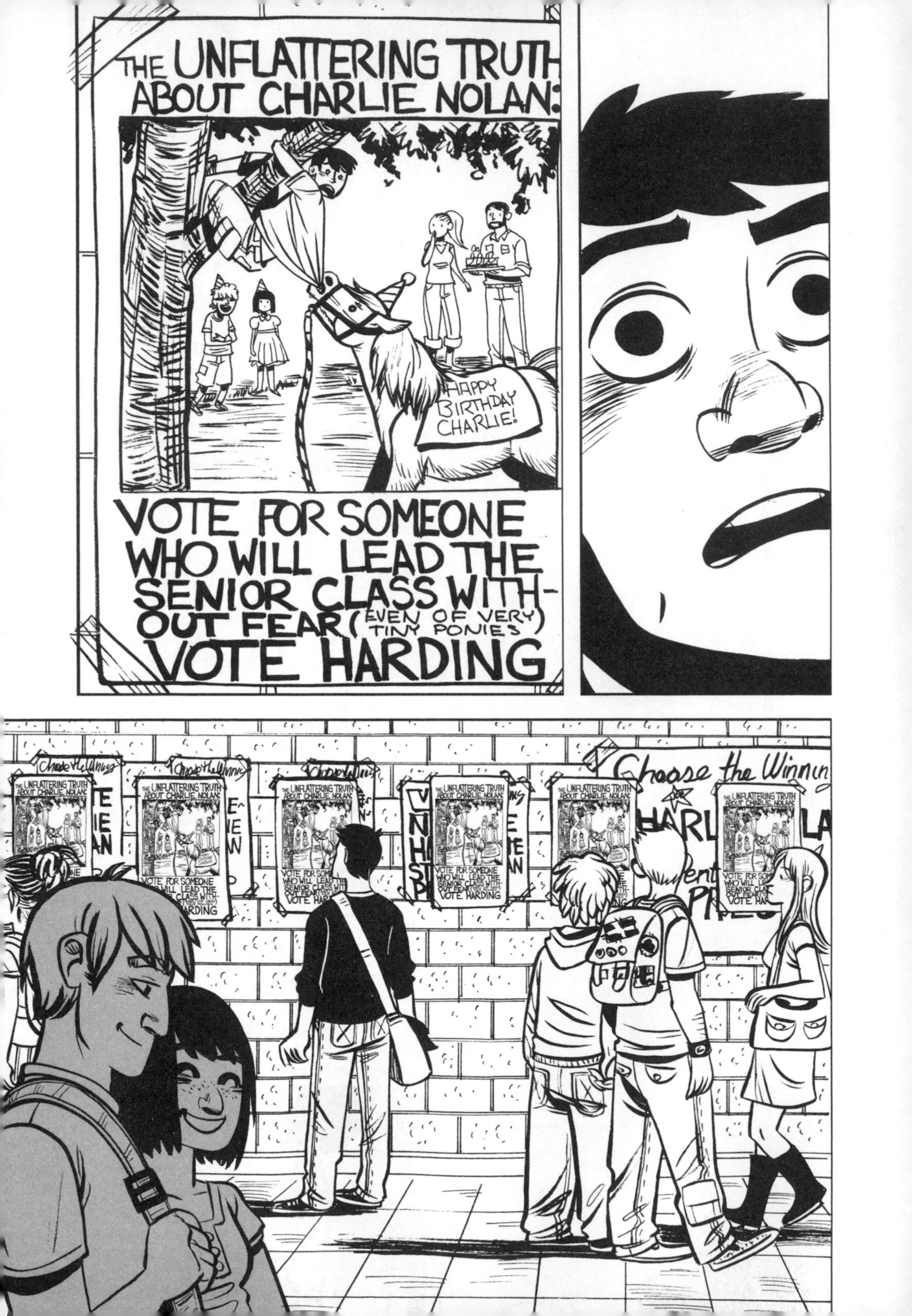
THE UNFLATTERING TRUTH ABOUT CHARLIE NOLAN:
HAPPY BIRTHDAY CHARLIE!
VOTE FOR SOMEONE WHO WILL LEAD THE SENIOR CLASS WITHOUT FEAR (EVEN OF VERY TINY PONIES)
VOTE HARDING
Choose the Winnin
CHARL LA

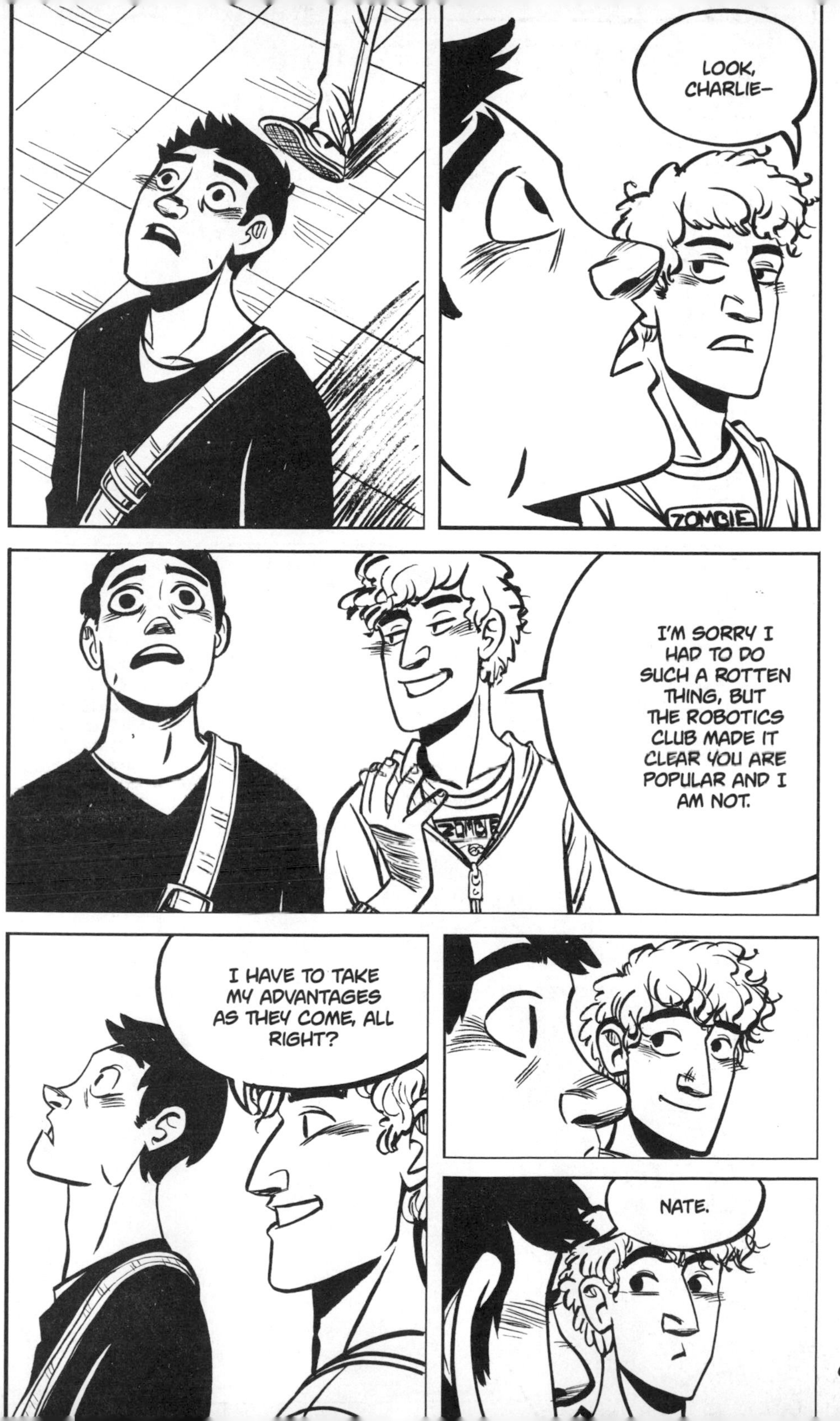

LOOK, CHARLIE-
ZOMBIE
I'M SORRY I HAD TO DO SUCH A ROTTEN THING, BUT THE ROBOTICS CLUB MADE IT CLEAR YOU ARE POPULAR AND I AM NOT.
I HAVE TO TAKE MY ADVANTAGES AS THEY COME, ALL RIGHT?
NATE.

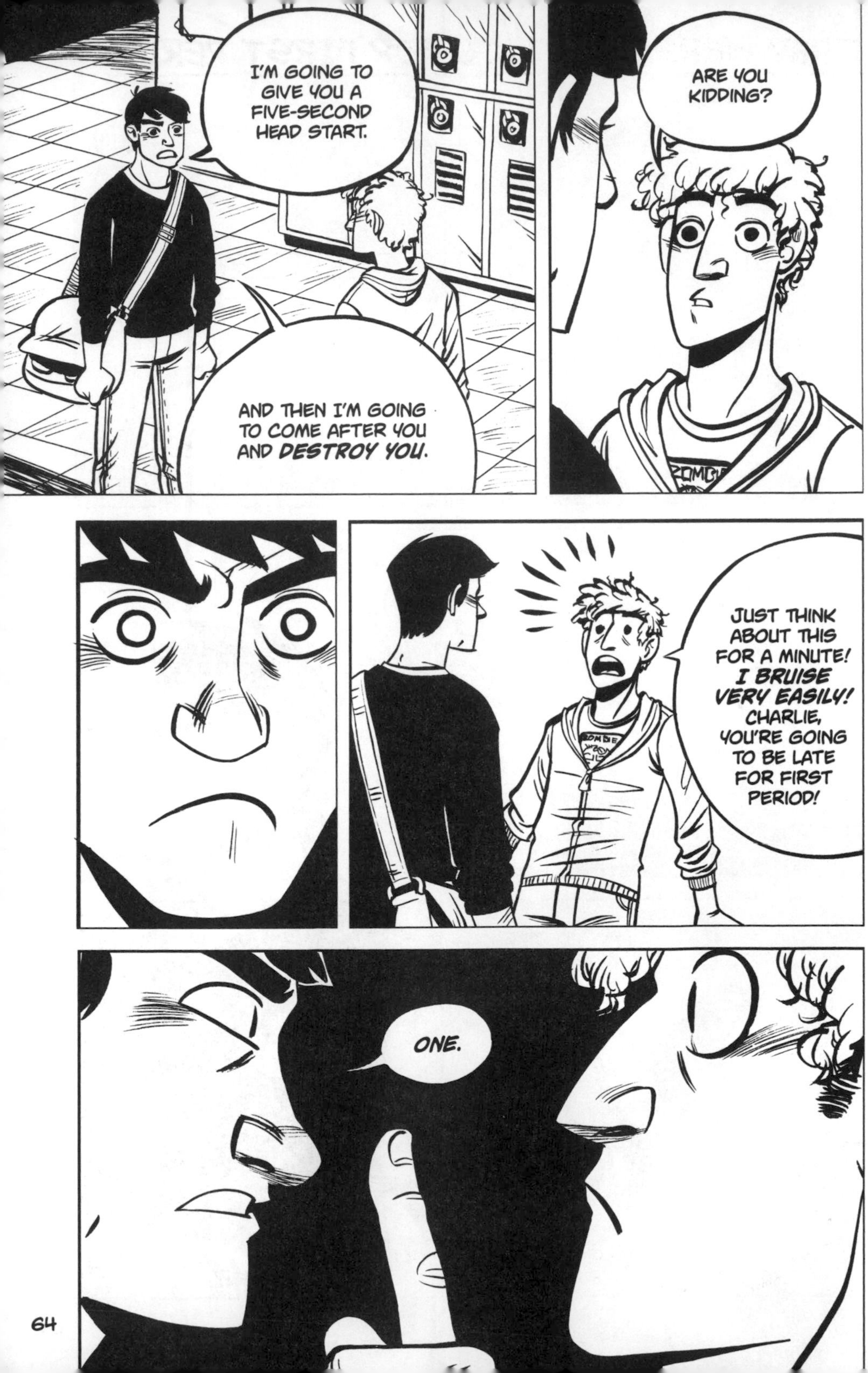
I'M GOING TO GIVE YOU A FIVE-SECOND HEAD START.
AND THEN I'M GOING TO COME AFTER YOU AND DESTROY YOU.
ARE YOU KIDDING?
JUST THINK ABOUT THIS FOR A MINUTE! I BRUISE VERY EASILY! CHARLIE, YOU'RE GOING TO BE LATE FOR FIRST PERIOD!
ONE.

THEY WERE BOTH LATE FOR FIRST PERIOD.

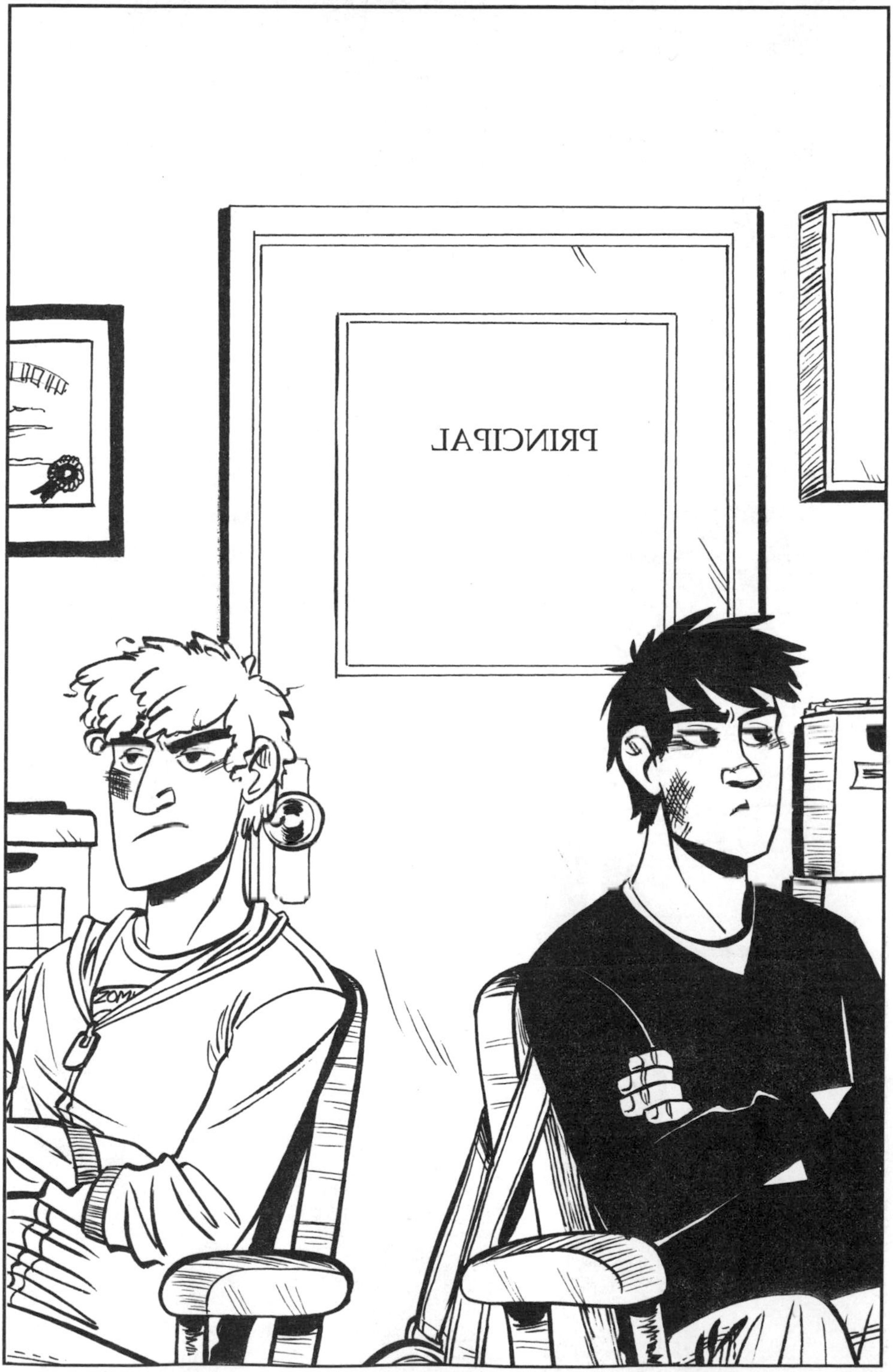
PRINCIPAL

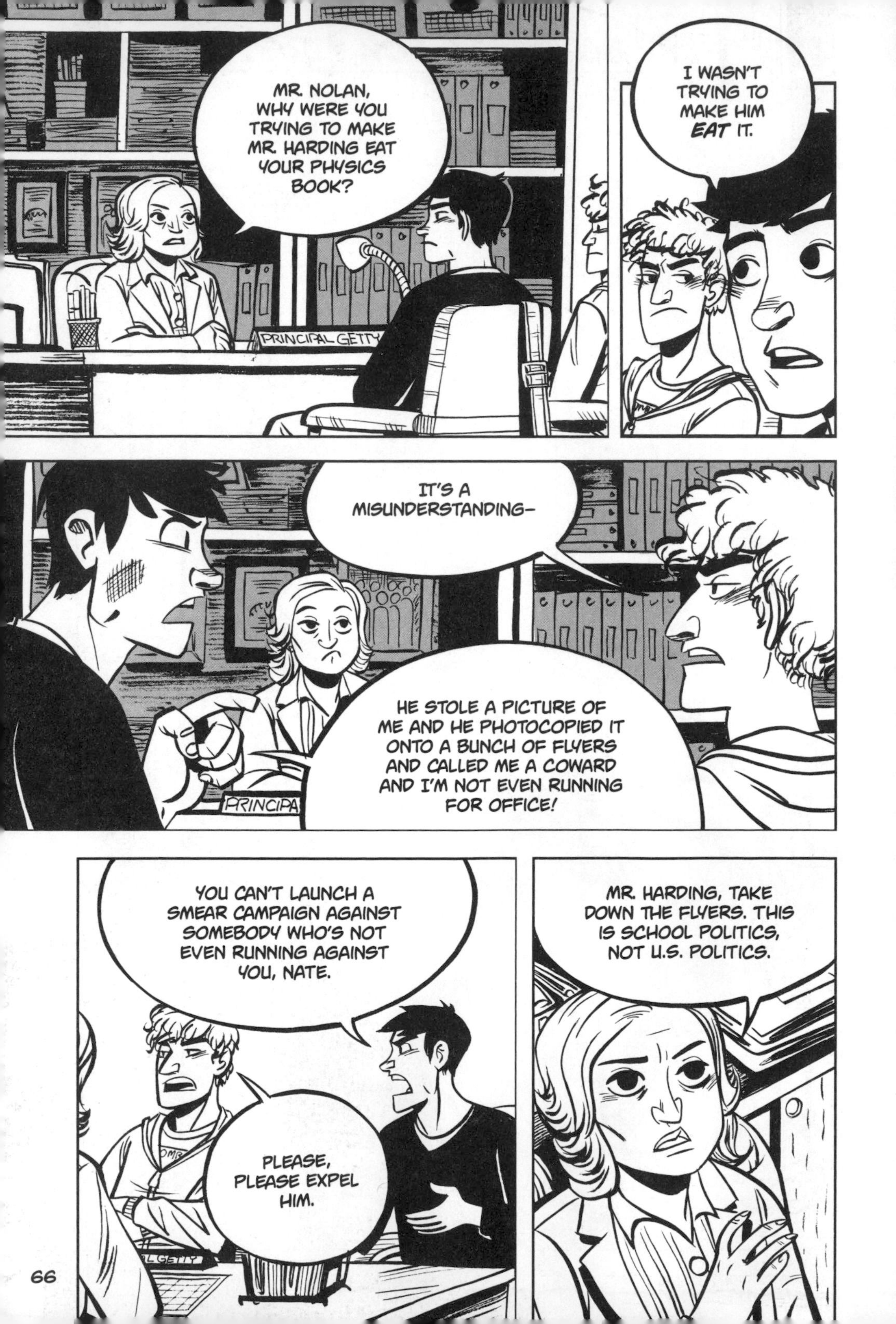
MR. NOLAN, WHY WERE YOU TRYING TO MAKE MR. HARDING EAT YOUR PHYSICS BOOK?
PRINCIPAL GETTY
I WASN'T TRYING TO MAKE HIM *EAT* IT.
IT'S A MISUNDERSTANDING–
HE STOLE A PICTURE OF ME AND HE PHOTOCOPIED IT ONTO A BUNCH OF FLYERS AND CALLED ME A COWARD AND I'M NOT EVEN RUNNING FOR OFFICE!
PRINCIPA
YOU CAN'T LAUNCH A SMEAR CAMPAIGN AGAINST SOMEBODY WHO'S NOT EVEN RUNNING AGAINST YOU, NATE.
PLEASE, PLEASE EXPEL HIM.
MR. HARDING, TAKE DOWN THE FLYERS. THIS IS SCHOOL POLITICS, NOT U.S. POLITICS.

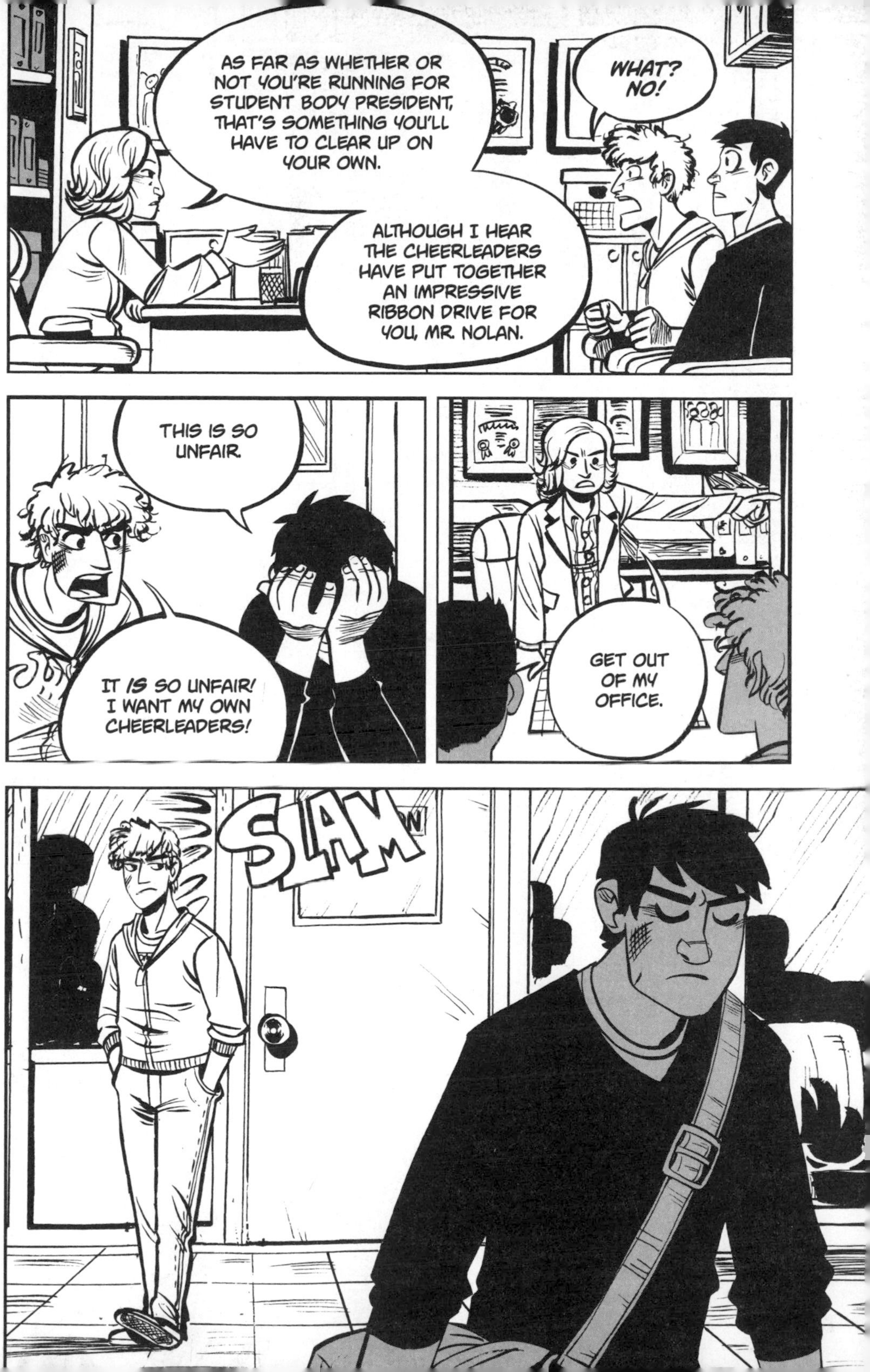
AS FAR AS WHETHER OR NOT YOU'RE RUNNING FOR STUDENT BODY PRESIDENT, THAT'S SOMETHING YOU'LL HAVE TO CLEAR UP ON YOUR OWN.
WHAT? NO!
ALTHOUGH I HEAR THE CHEERLEADERS HAVE PUT TOGETHER AN IMPRESSIVE RIBBON DRIVE FOR YOU, MR. NOLAN.
THIS IS SO UNFAIR.
IT *IS* SO UNFAIR! I WANT MY OWN CHEERLEADERS!
GET OUT OF MY OFFICE.
SLAM

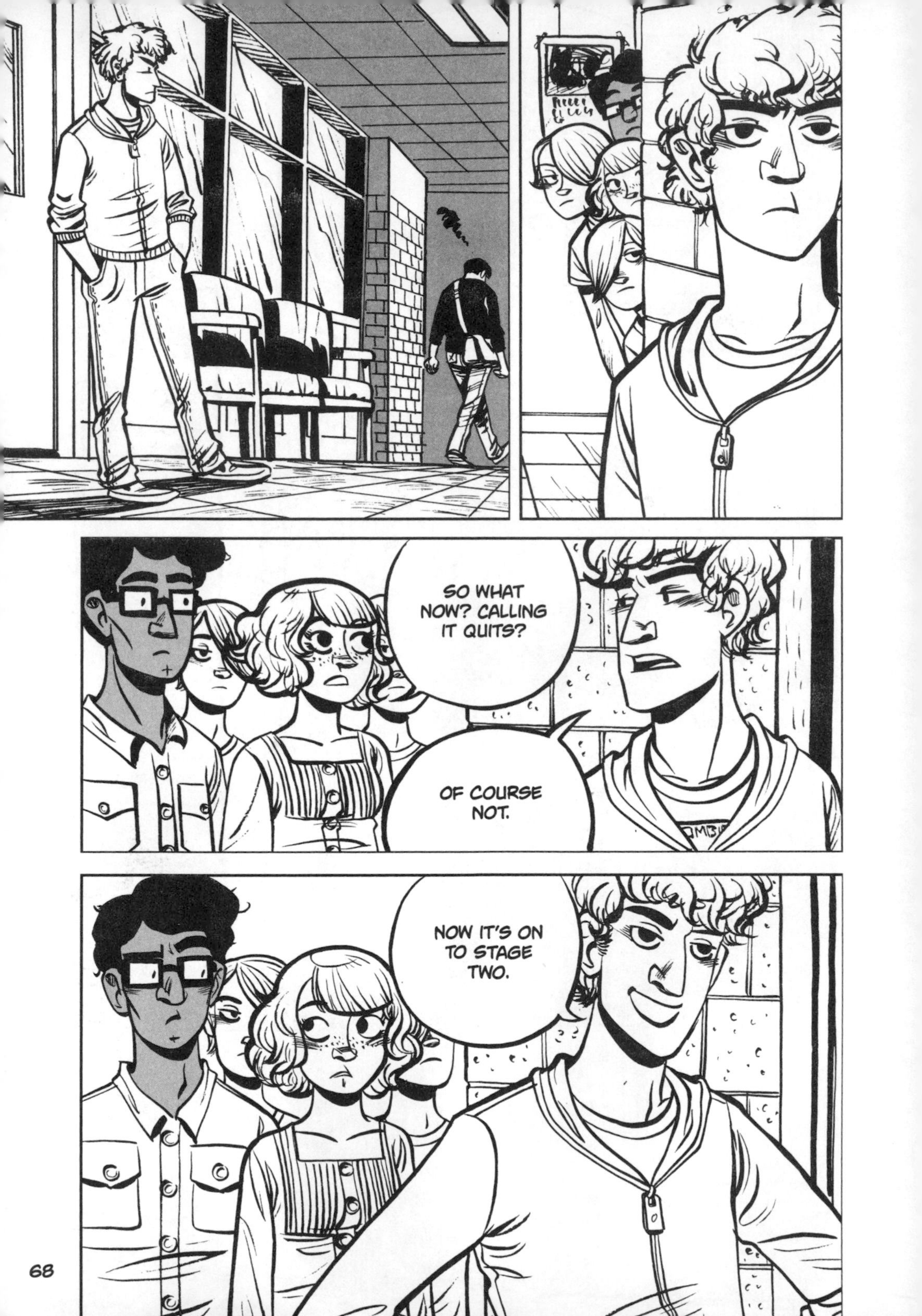
SO WHAT NOW? CALLING IT QUITS?
OF COURSE NOT.
NOW IT'S ON TO STAGE TWO.

GAME DAY

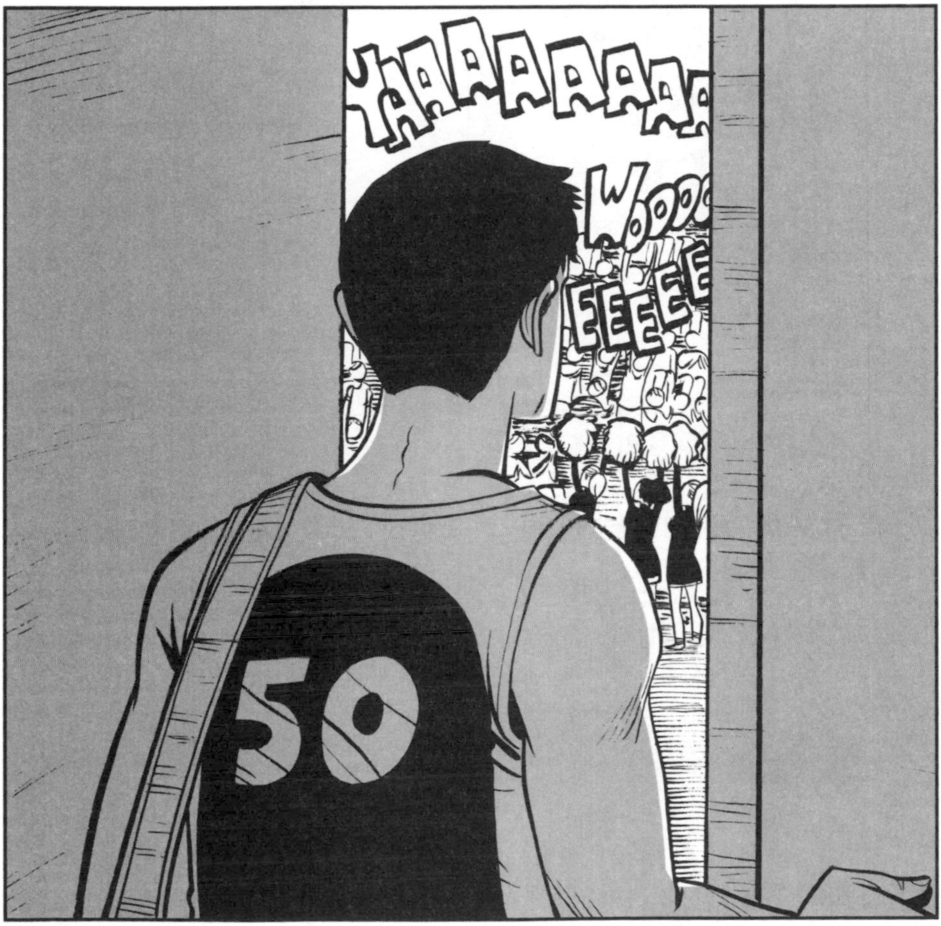
YAAAAAAAA
WOOOO
EEEEE

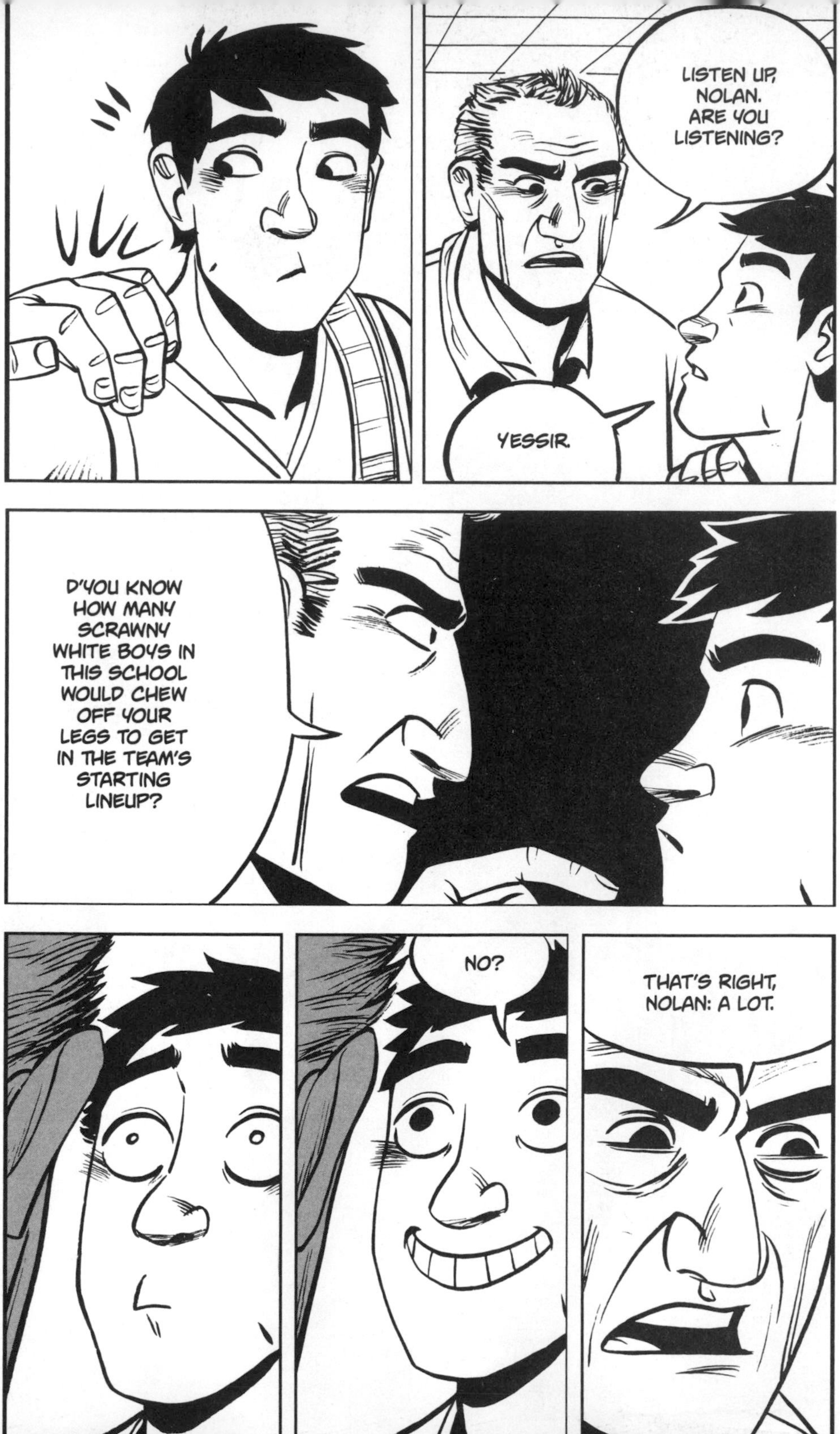
LISTEN UP, NOLAN. ARE YOU LISTENING?
YESSIR.
D'YOU KNOW HOW MANY SCRAWNY WHITE BOYS IN THIS SCHOOL WOULD CHEW OFF YOUR LEGS TO GET IN THE TEAM'S STARTING LINEUP?
NO?
THAT'S RIGHT, NOLAN: A LOT.

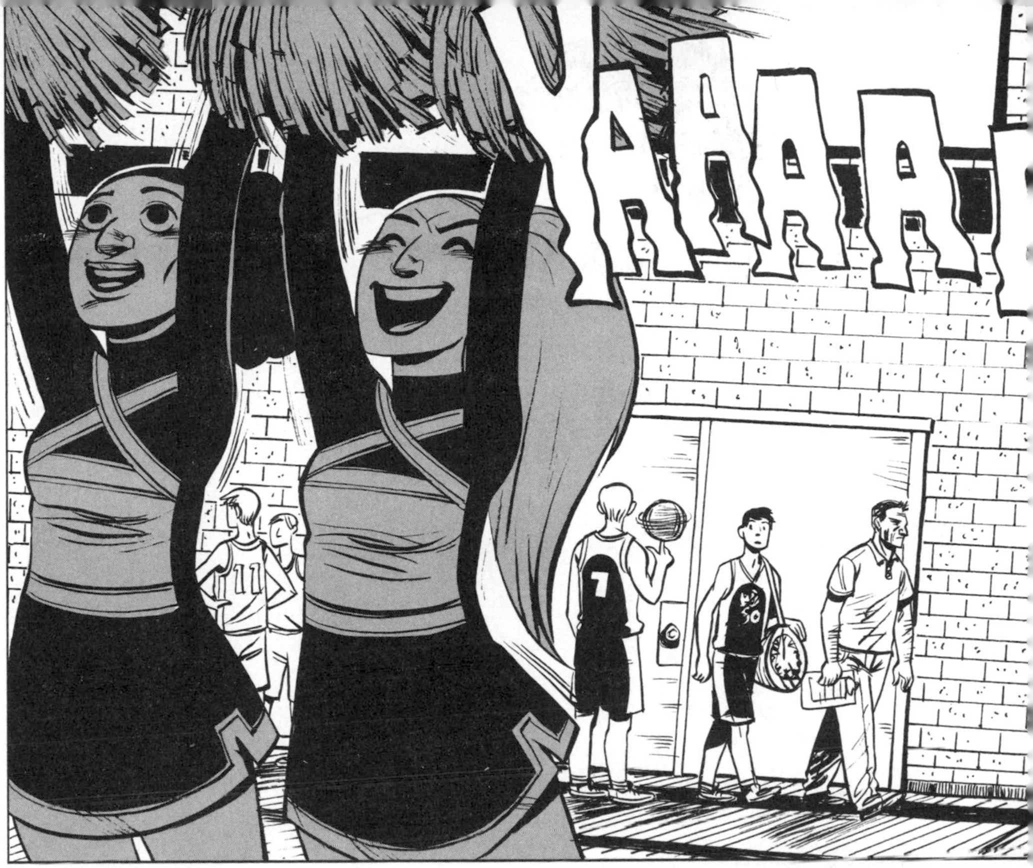
YAAAA

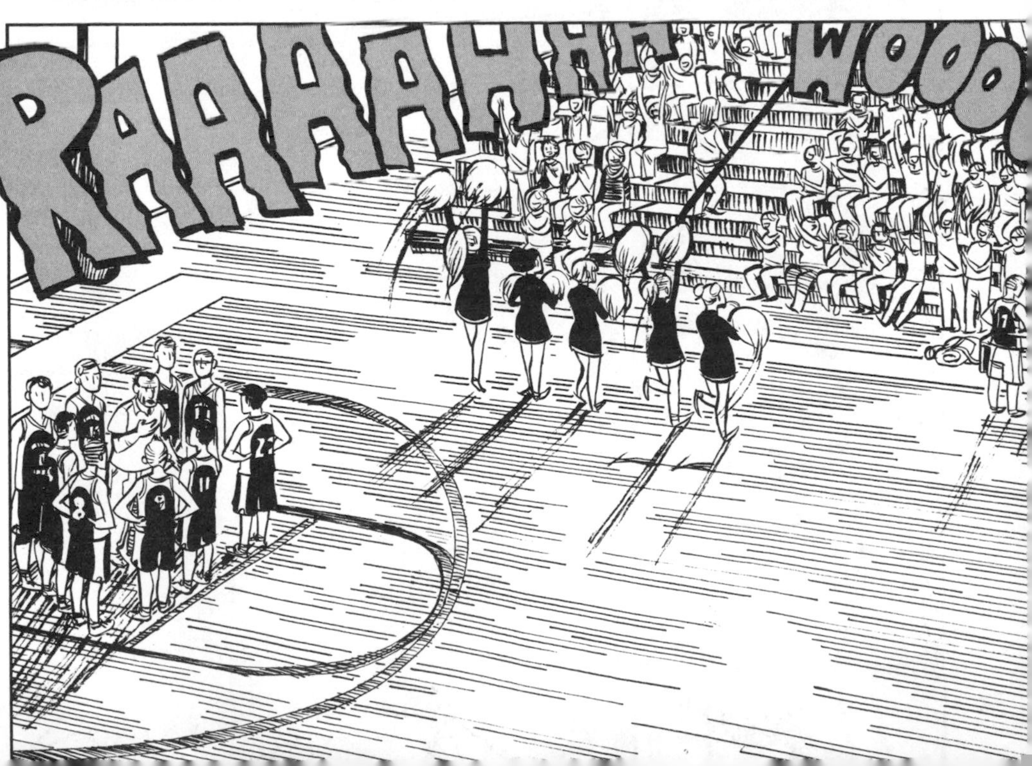
RAAAAHH
WOOO

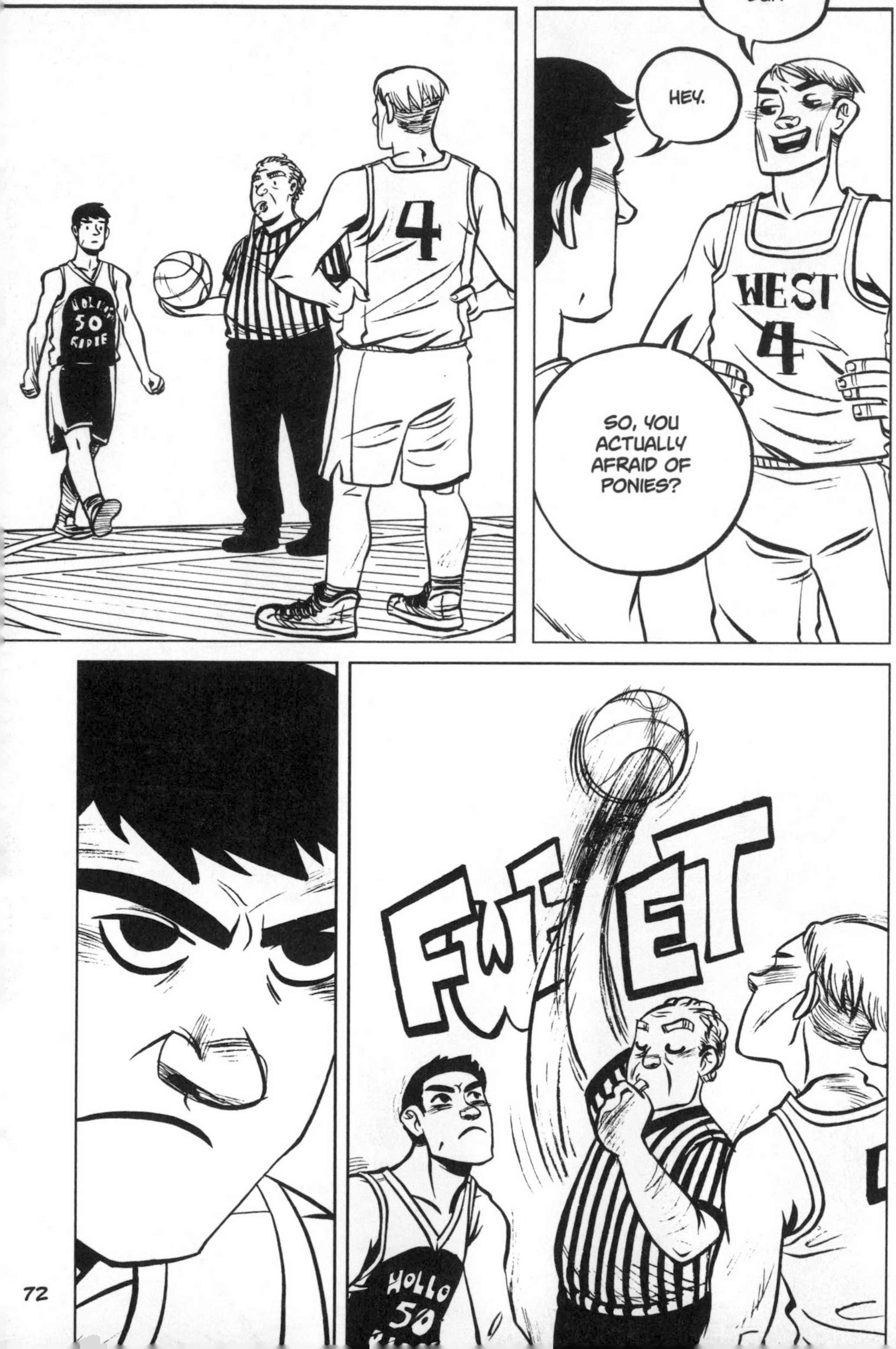
'SUP.
HEY.
WEST
4
SO, YOU ACTUALLY AFRAID OF PONIES?
HOLLO
50

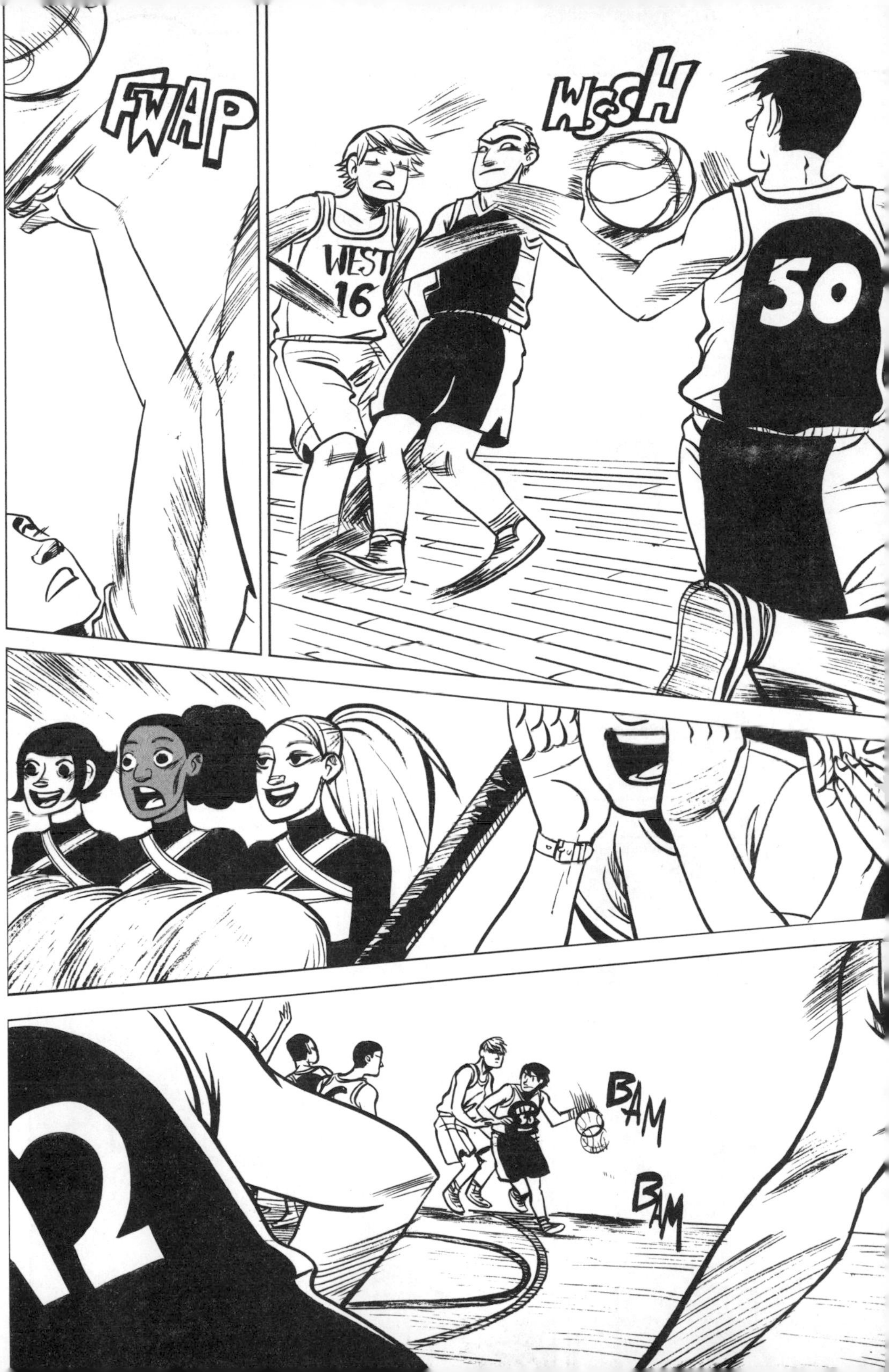
FWAP
WSSH
WEST
16
50
BAM
BAM
12

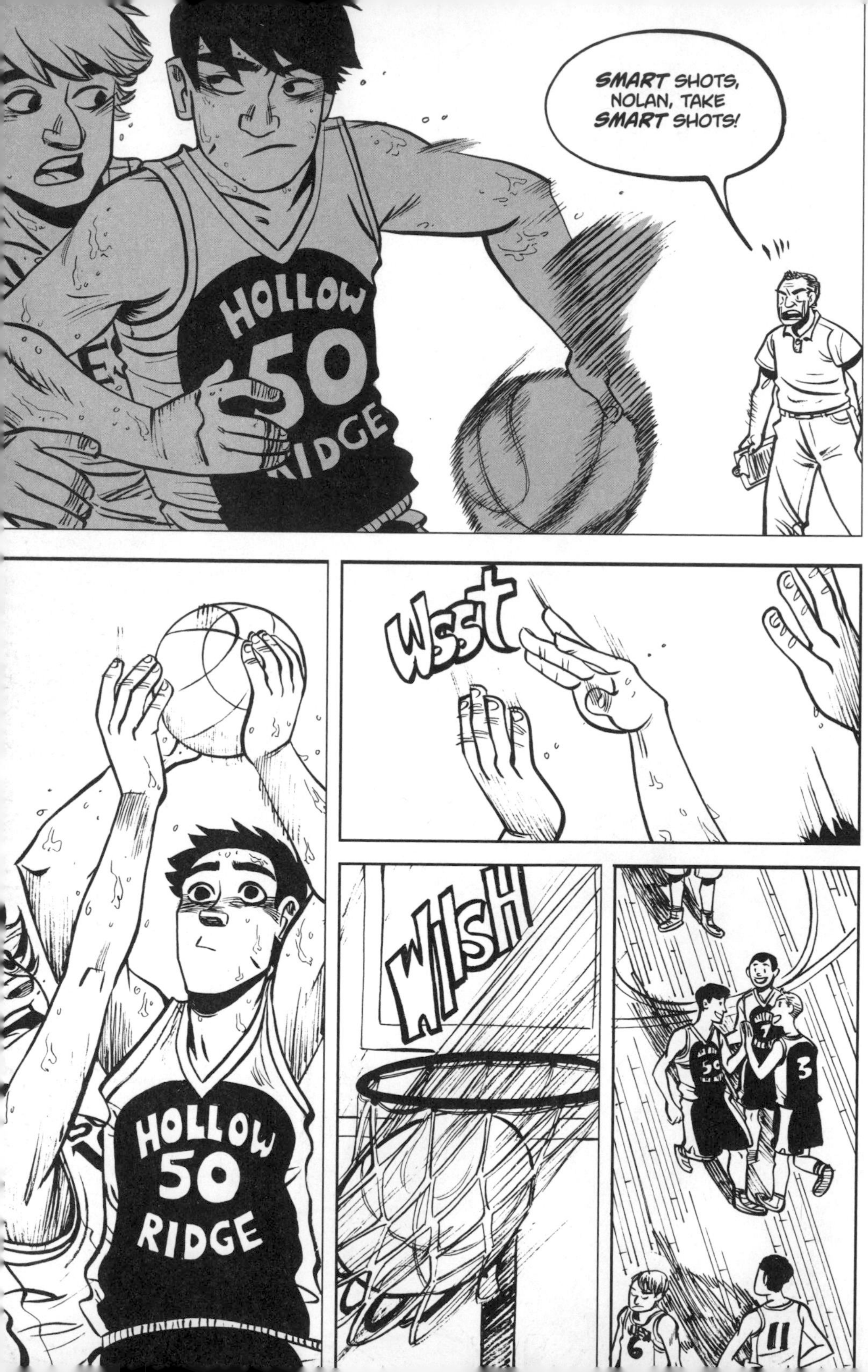
SMART SHOTS, NOLAN, TAKE SMART SHOTS!
HOLLOW 50 RIDGE
WSST
HOLLOW 50 RIDGE
WISH

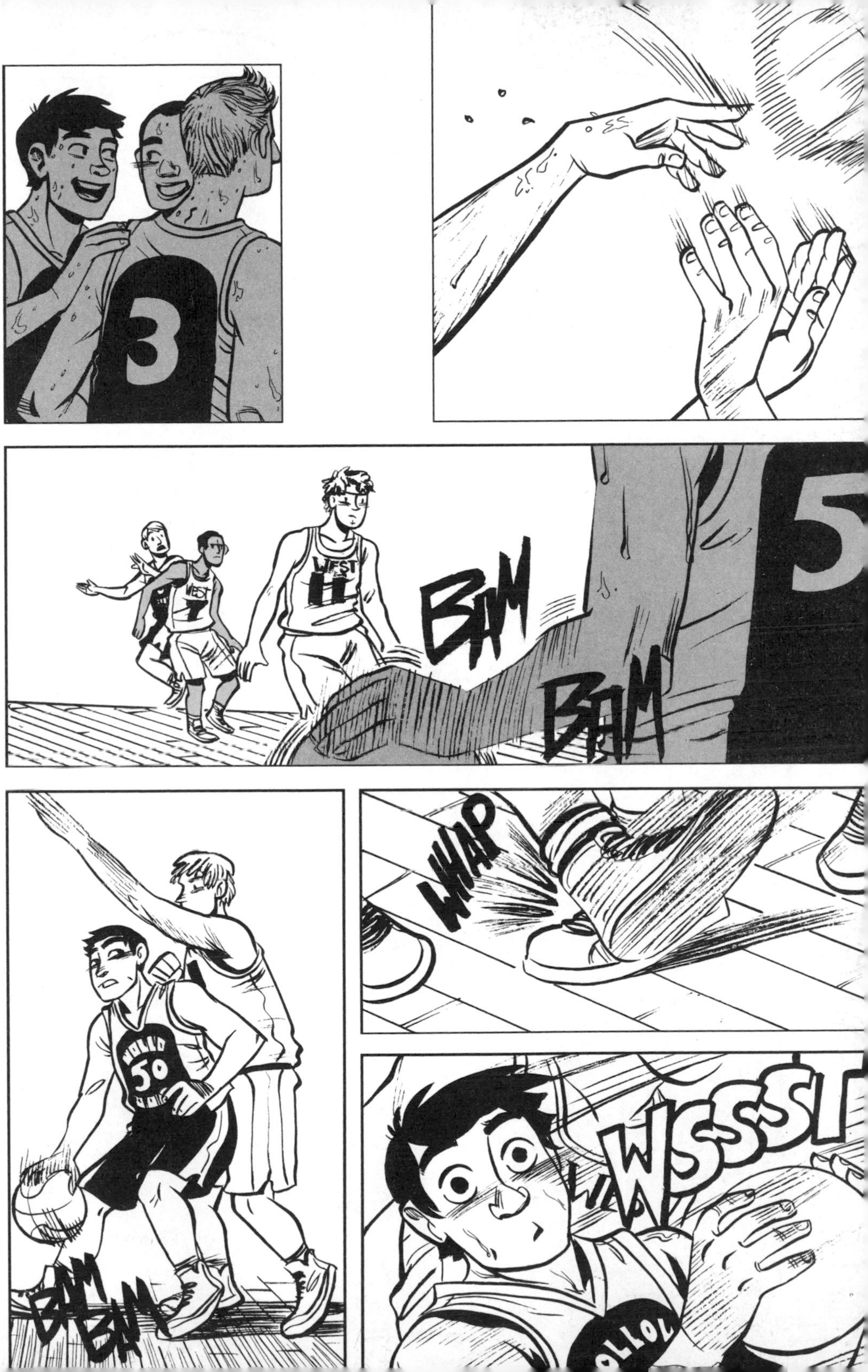
BAM
BAM
WEST
WEST
WHAP
BAM
BAM
WSSST

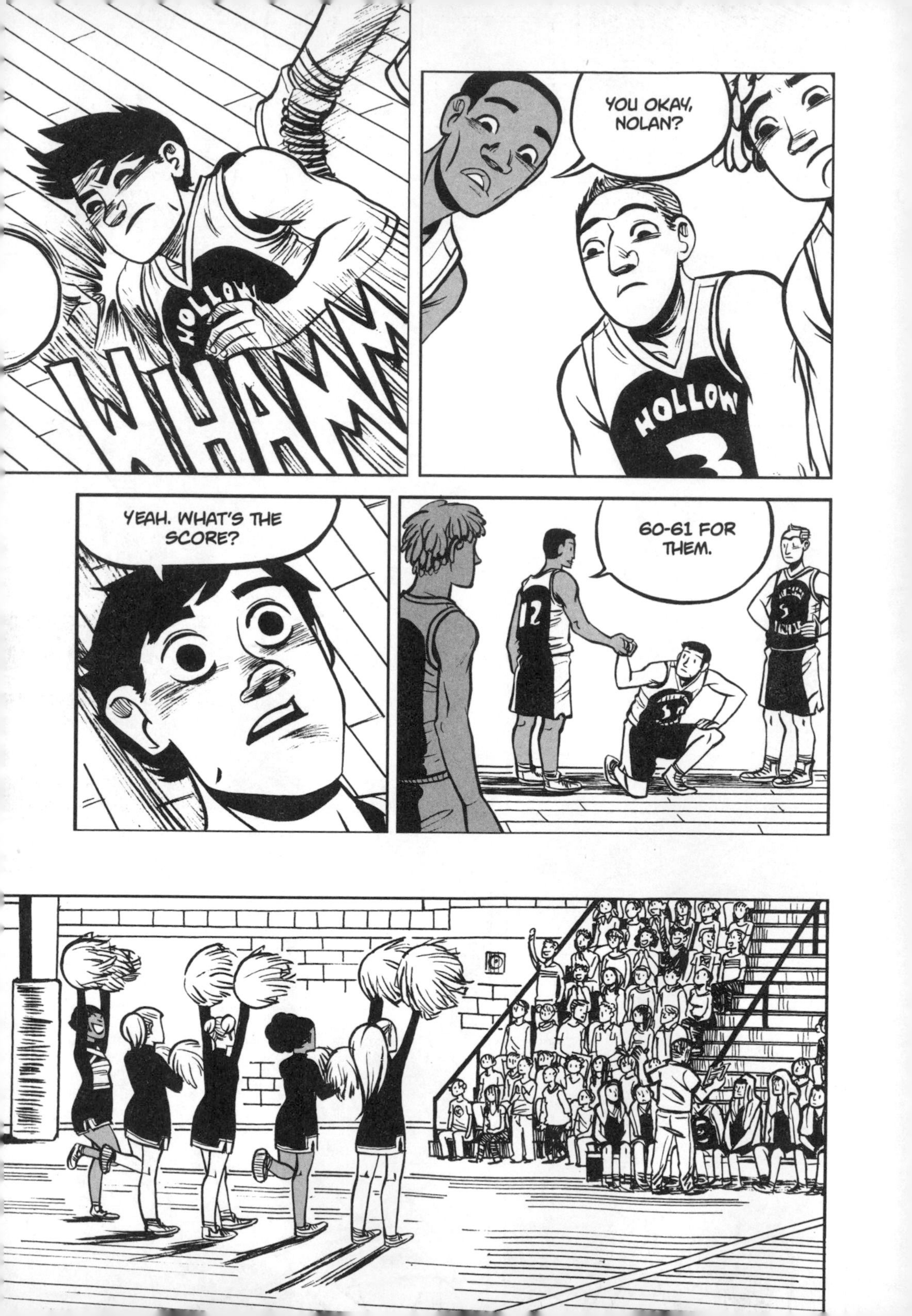
WHAM
YOU OKAY, NOLAN?
HOLLOW
YEAH. WHAT'S THE SCORE?
60-61 FOR THEM.

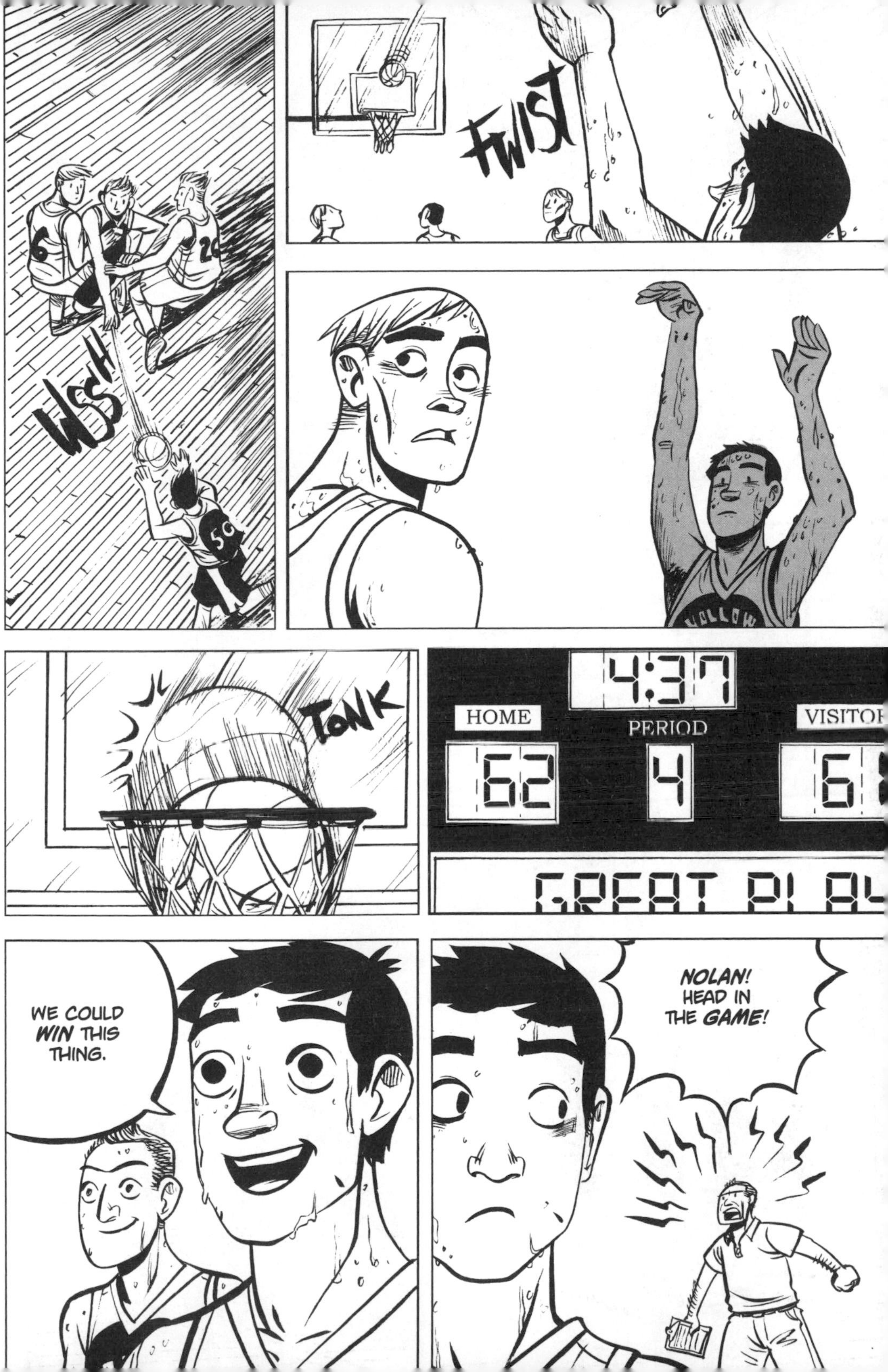
WSSH
FWIST
TONK
4:37
HOME
PERIOD
VISITOR
62
4
GREAT PLAY
WE COULD WIN THIS THING.
NOLAN! HEAD IN THE GAME!

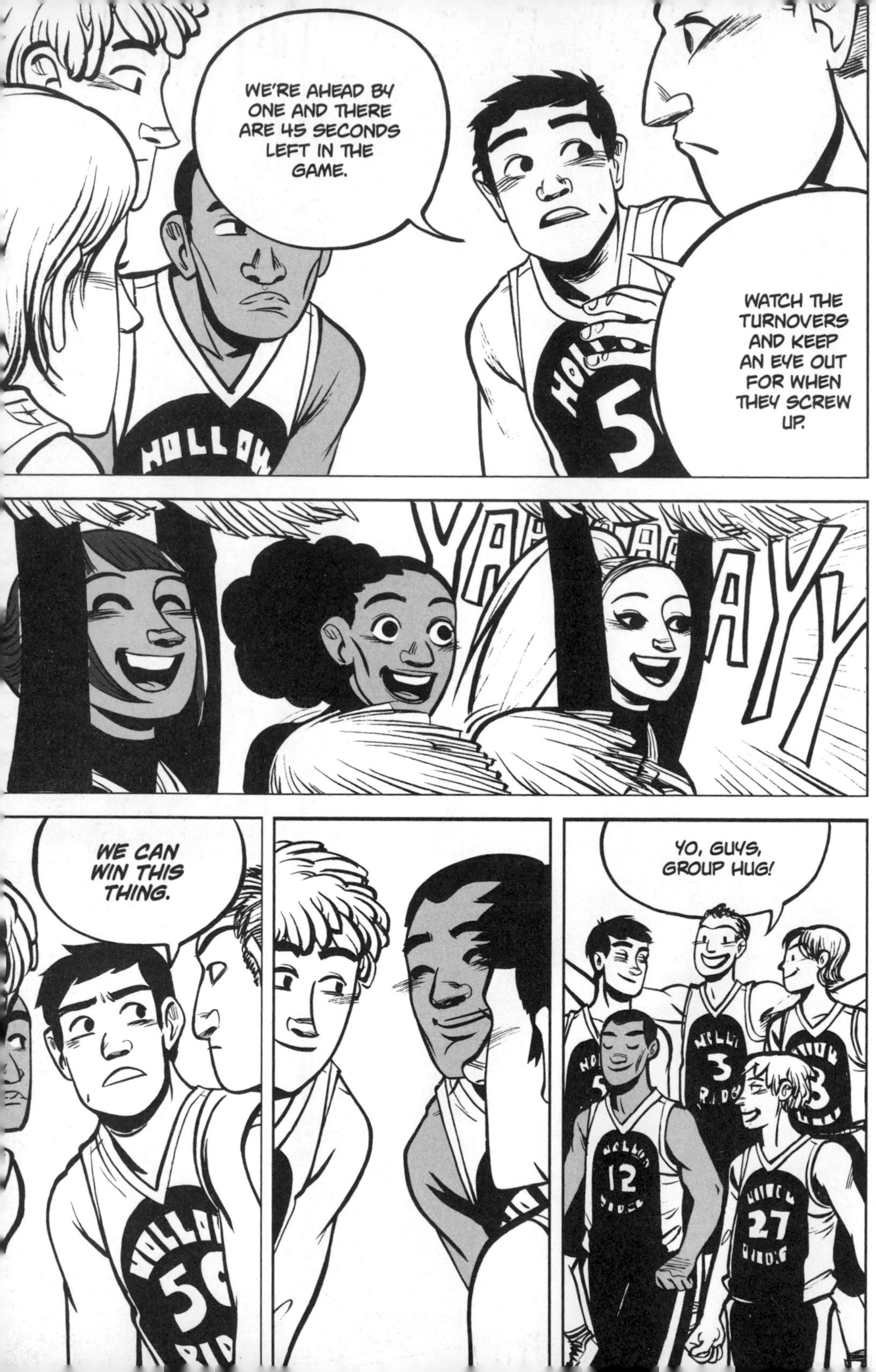
WE'RE AHEAD BY ONE AND THERE ARE 45 SECONDS LEFT IN THE GAME.
WATCH THE TURNOVERS AND KEEP AN EYE OUT FOR WHEN THEY SCREW UP.
YAAAAAYY
WE CAN WIN THIS THING.
YO, GUYS, GROUP HUG!

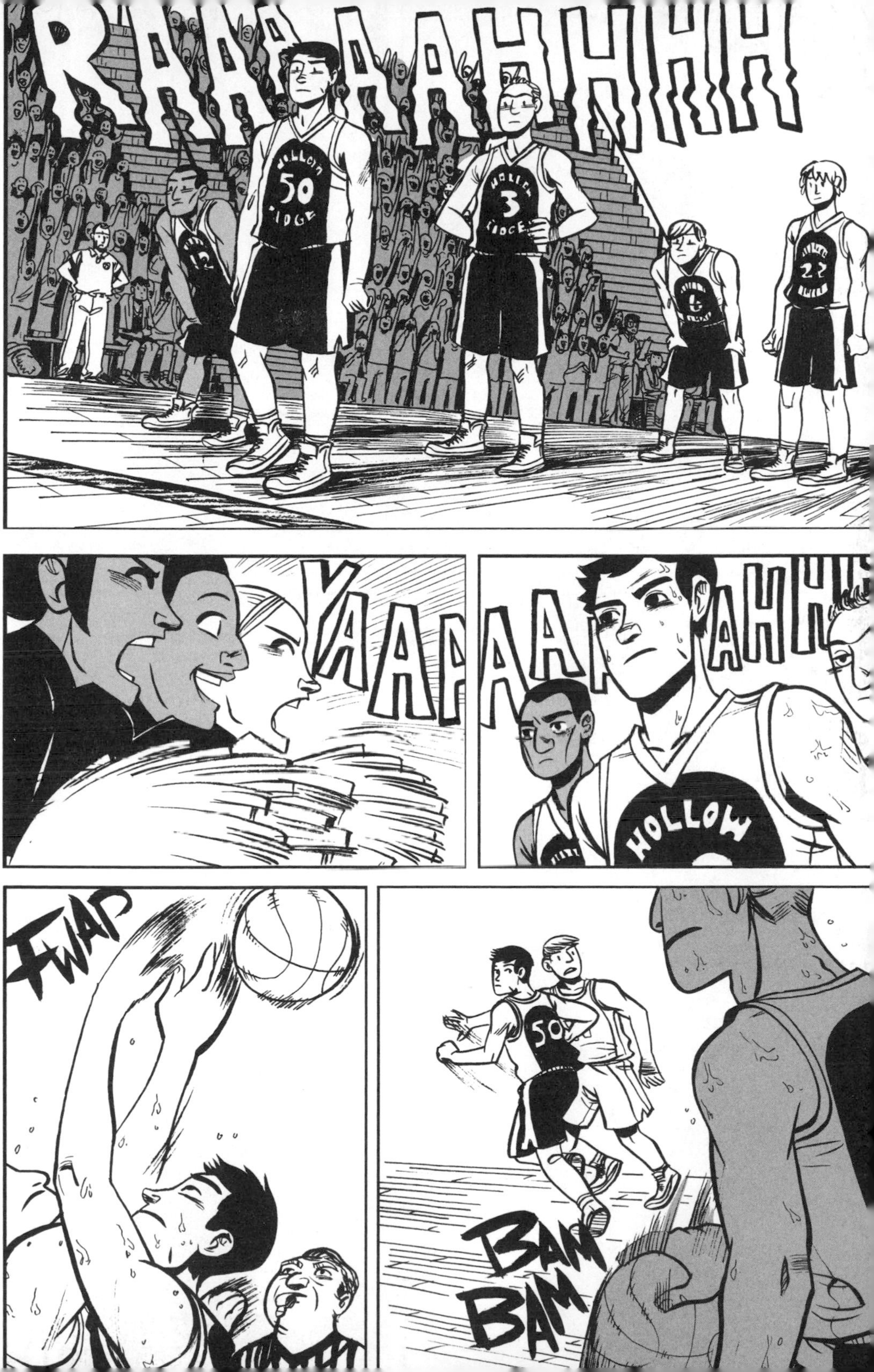
RAAAAAHHHH
50 HOLLOW RIDGE
3 HOLLOW RIDGE
YAAAAAAAHHH
HOLLOW
FWAP
BAM
BAM

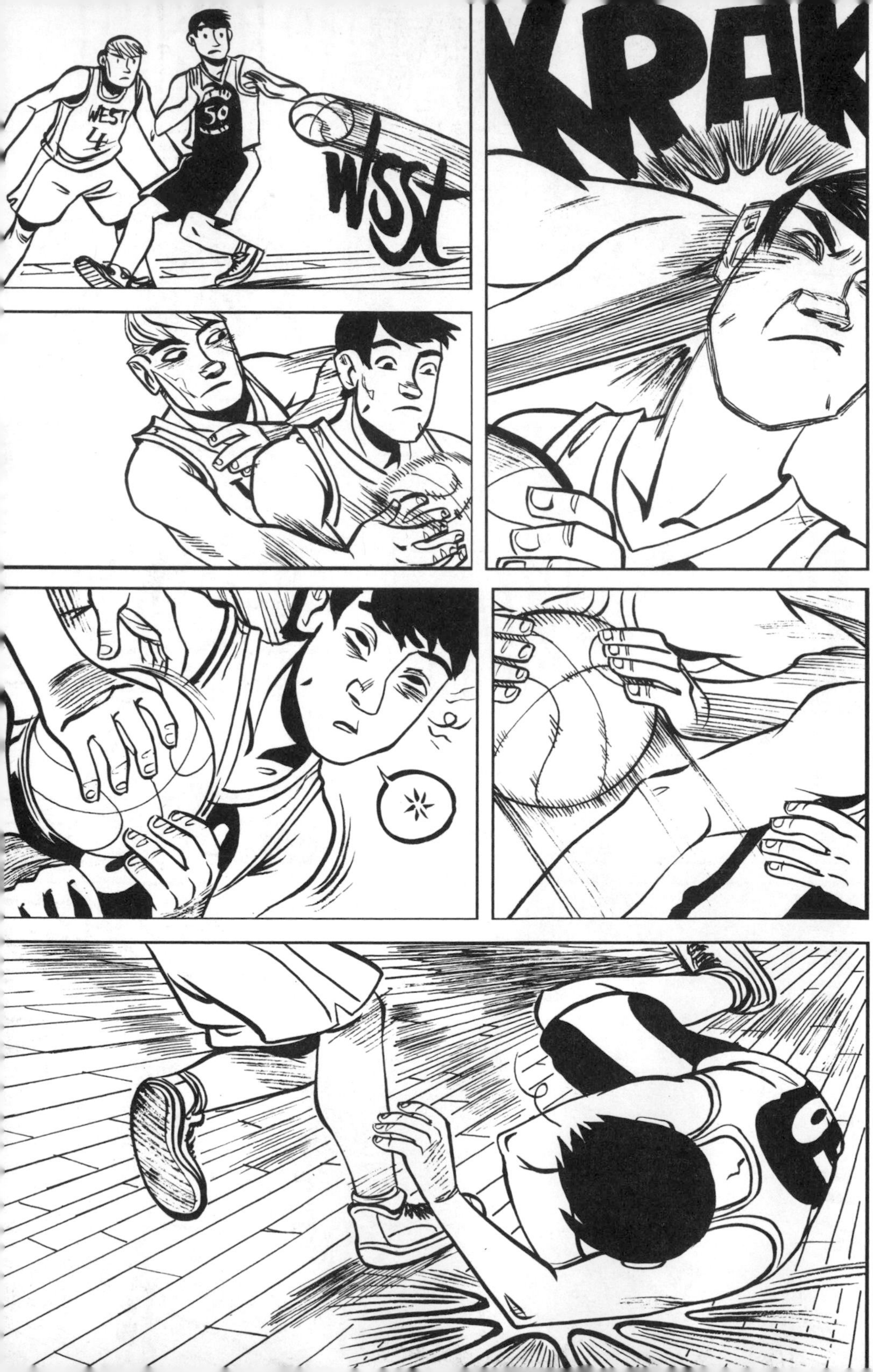
WEST
4
50
wsst
KRAK

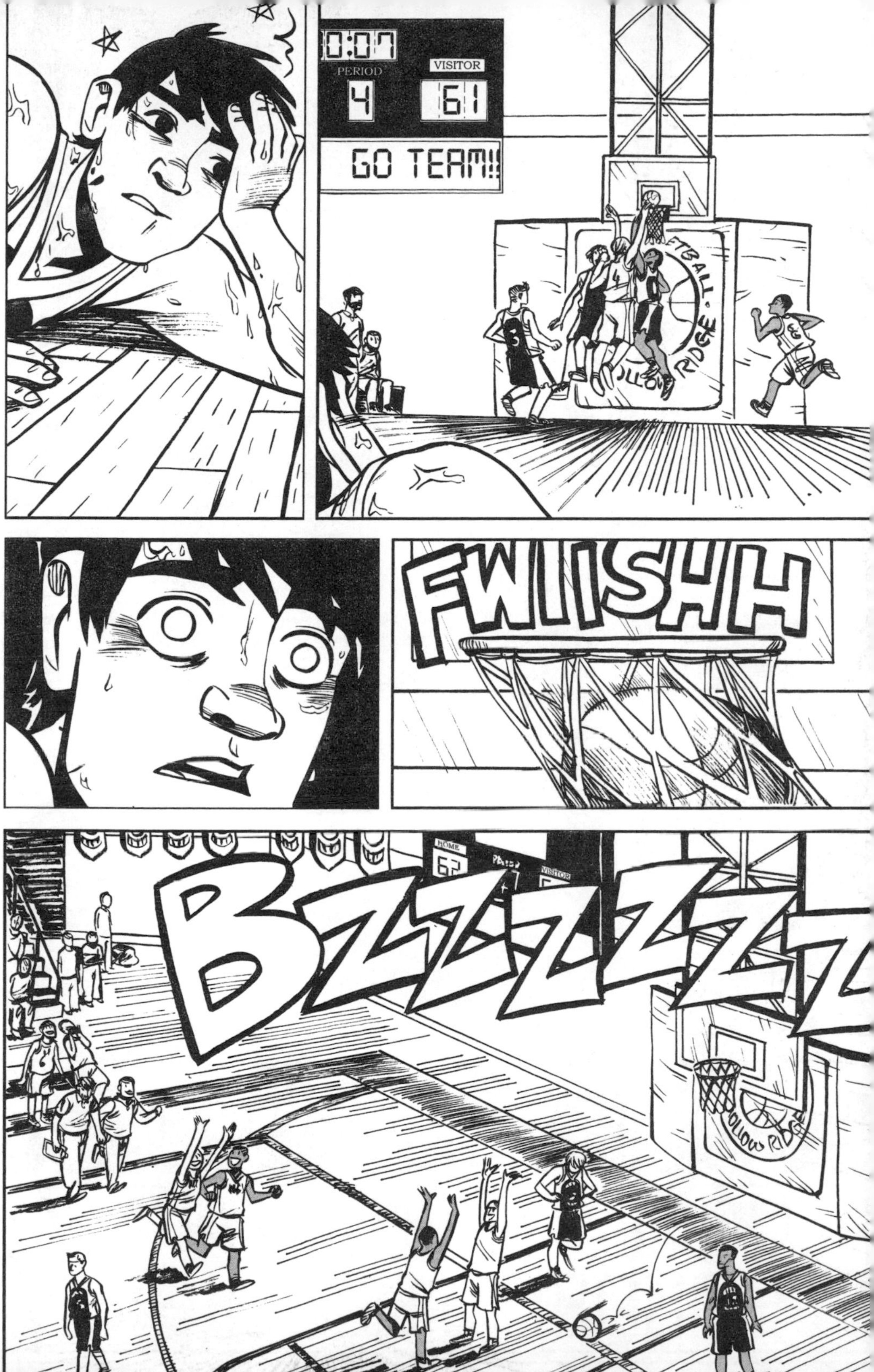

0:07
PERIOD
VISITOR
4
61
GO TEAM!!
FWISHH
BZZZZZ

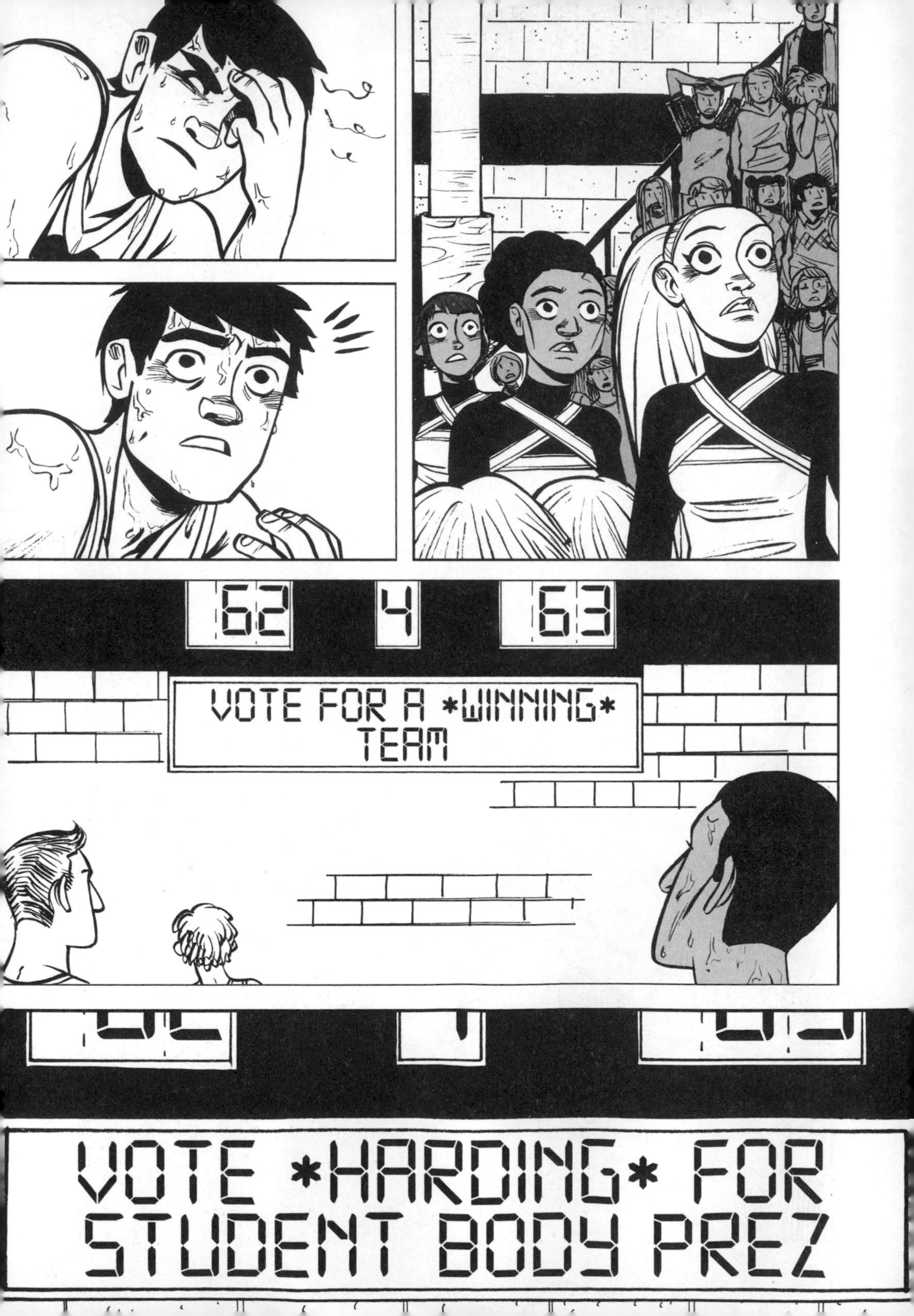
62
4
63
VOTE FOR A *WINNING* TEAM
VOTE *HARDING* FOR STUDENT BODY PREZ

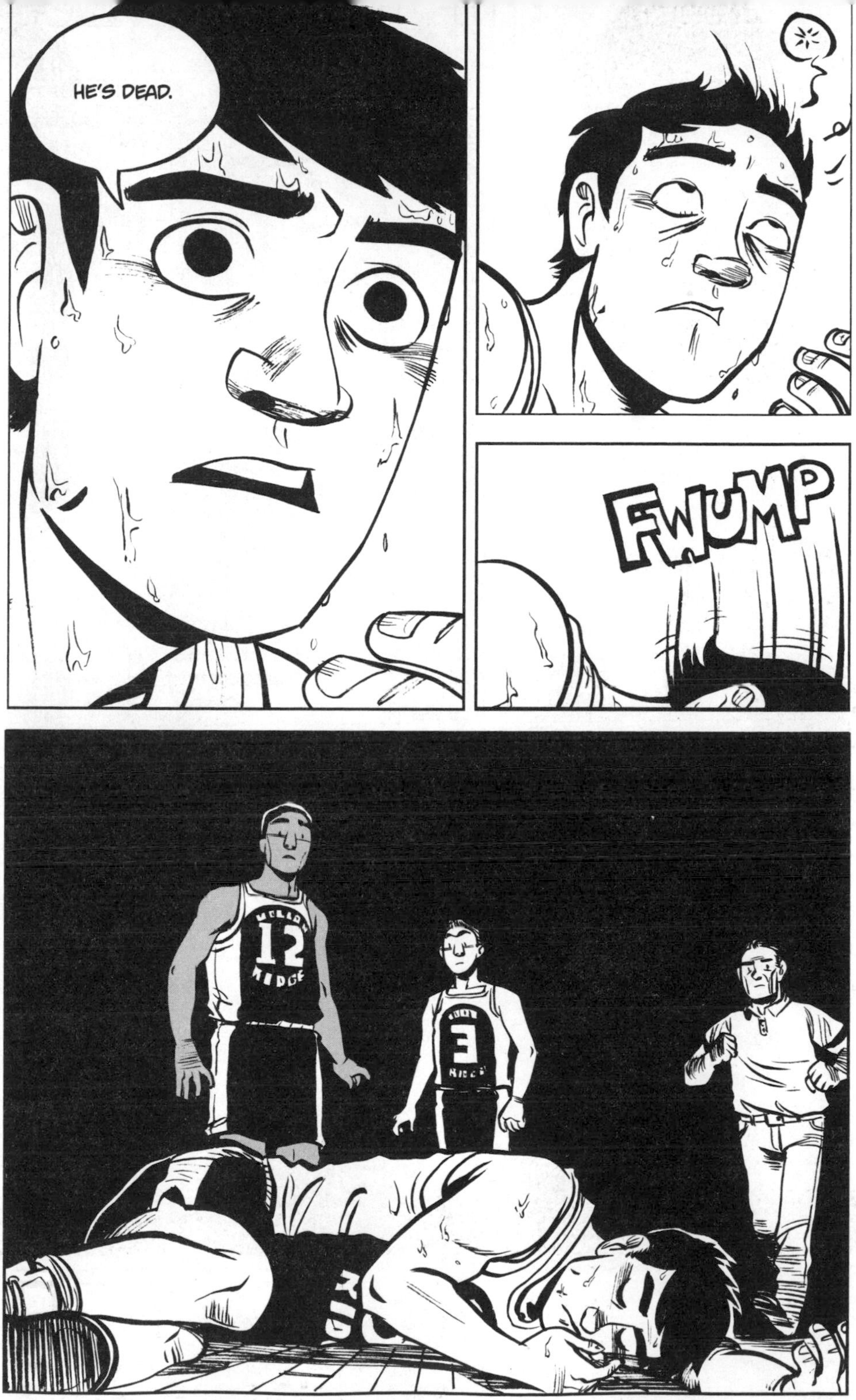
HE'S DEAD.
FWUMP

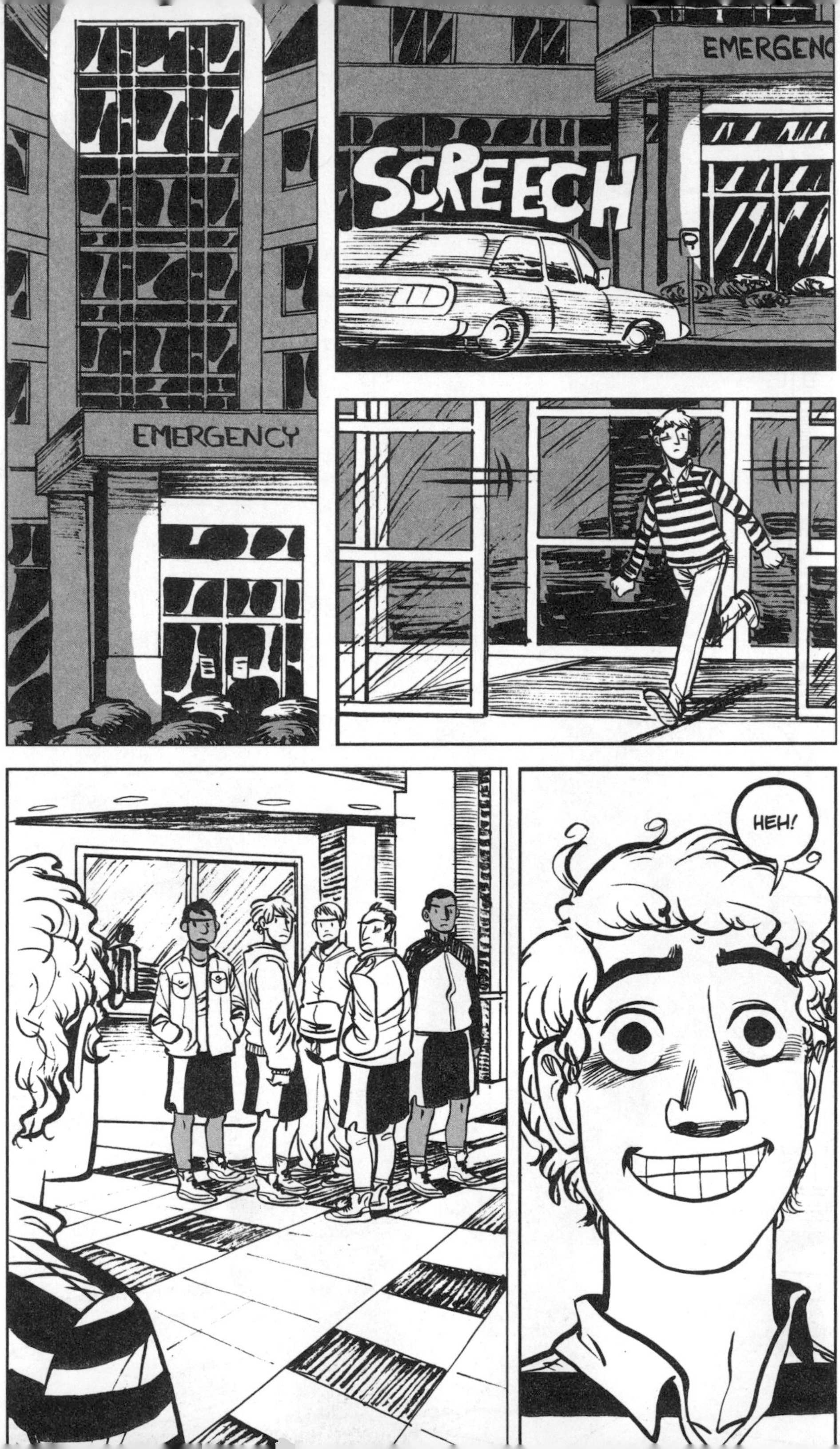
EMERGENCY
EMERGENC
SCREECH
EMERGENCY
HEH!

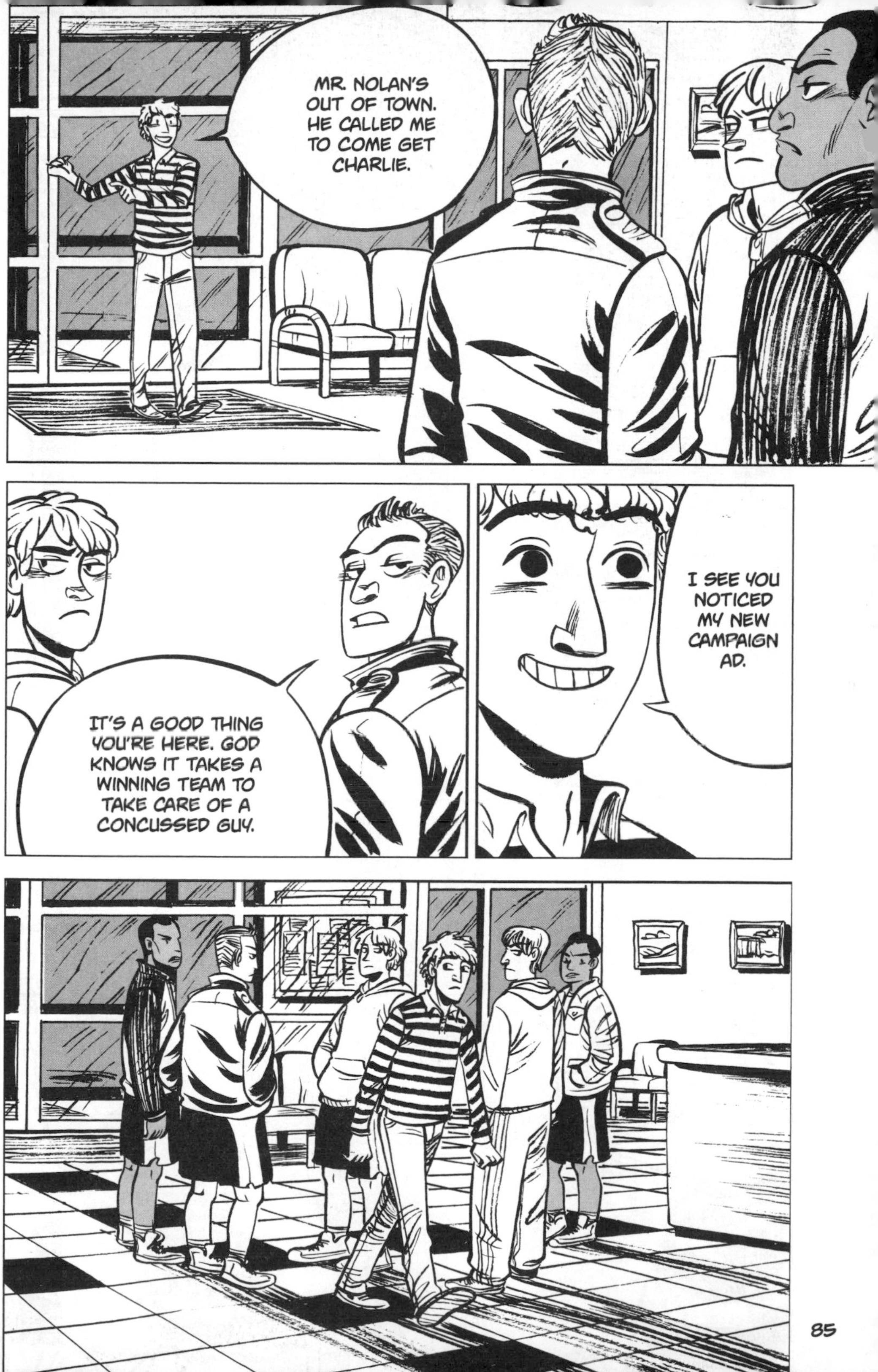
MR. NOLAN'S OUT OF TOWN. HE CALLED ME TO COME GET CHARLIE.
IT'S A GOOD THING YOU'RE HERE. GOD KNOWS IT TAKES A WINNING TEAM TO TAKE CARE OF A CONCUSSED GUY.
I SEE YOU NOTICED MY NEW CAMPAIGN AD.

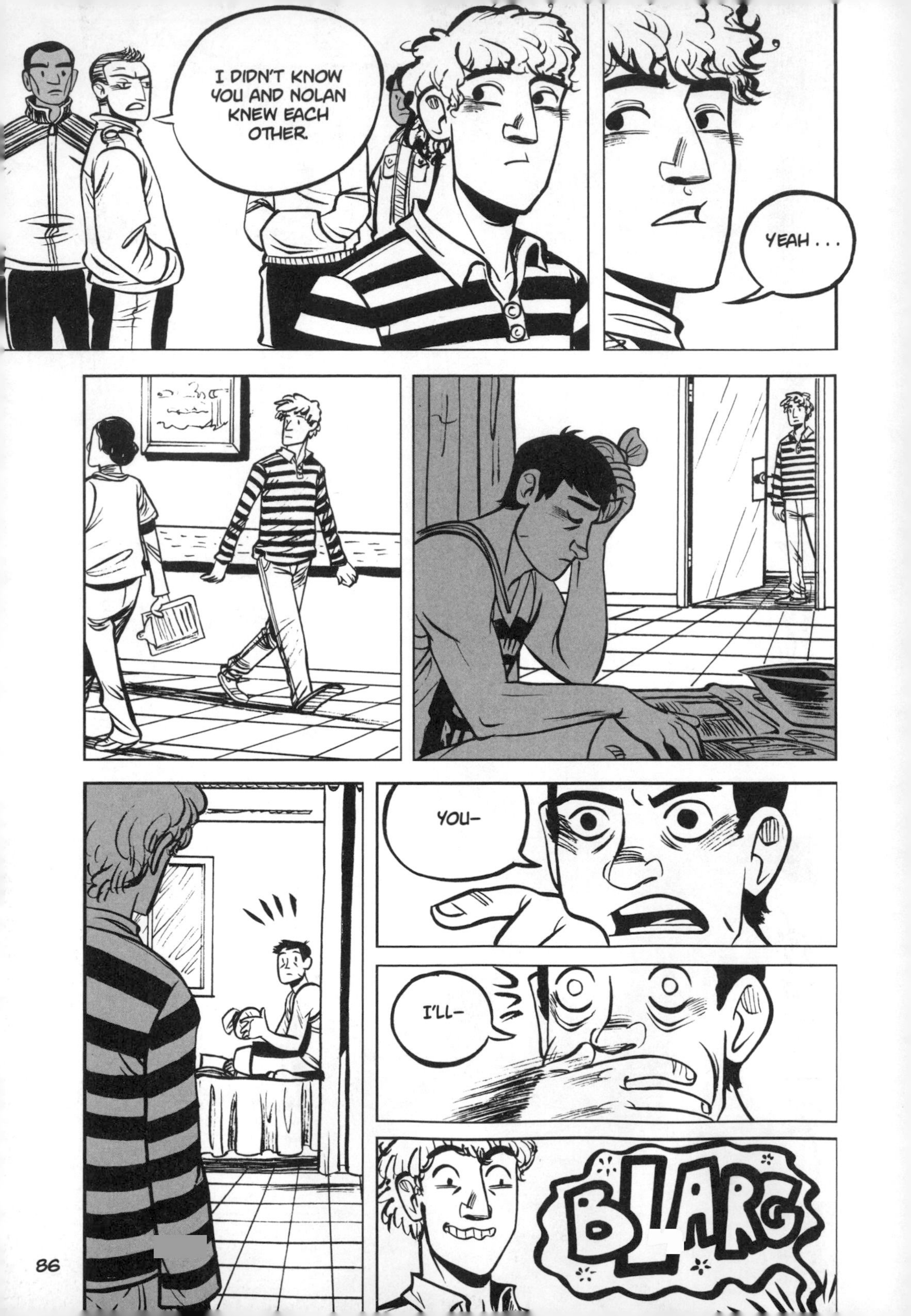
I DIDN'T KNOW YOU AND NOLAN KNEW EACH OTHER.
YEAH . . .
YOU-
I'LL-
BLARG

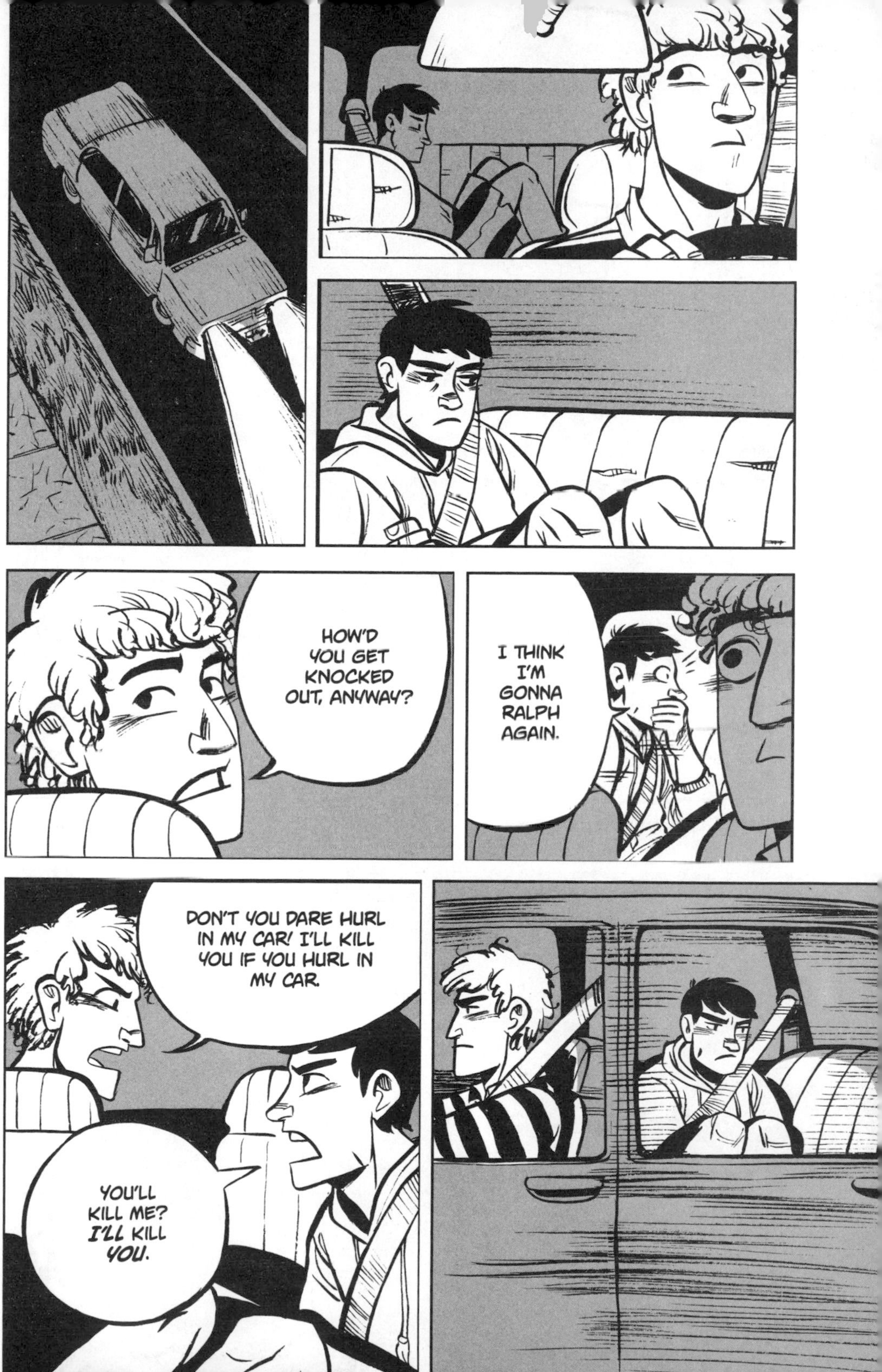
HOW'D YOU GET KNOCKED OUT, ANYWAY?
I THINK I'M GONNA RALPH AGAIN.
DON'T YOU DARE HURL IN MY CAR! I'LL KILL YOU IF YOU HURL IN MY CAR.
YOU'LL KILL ME? I'LL KILL YOU.

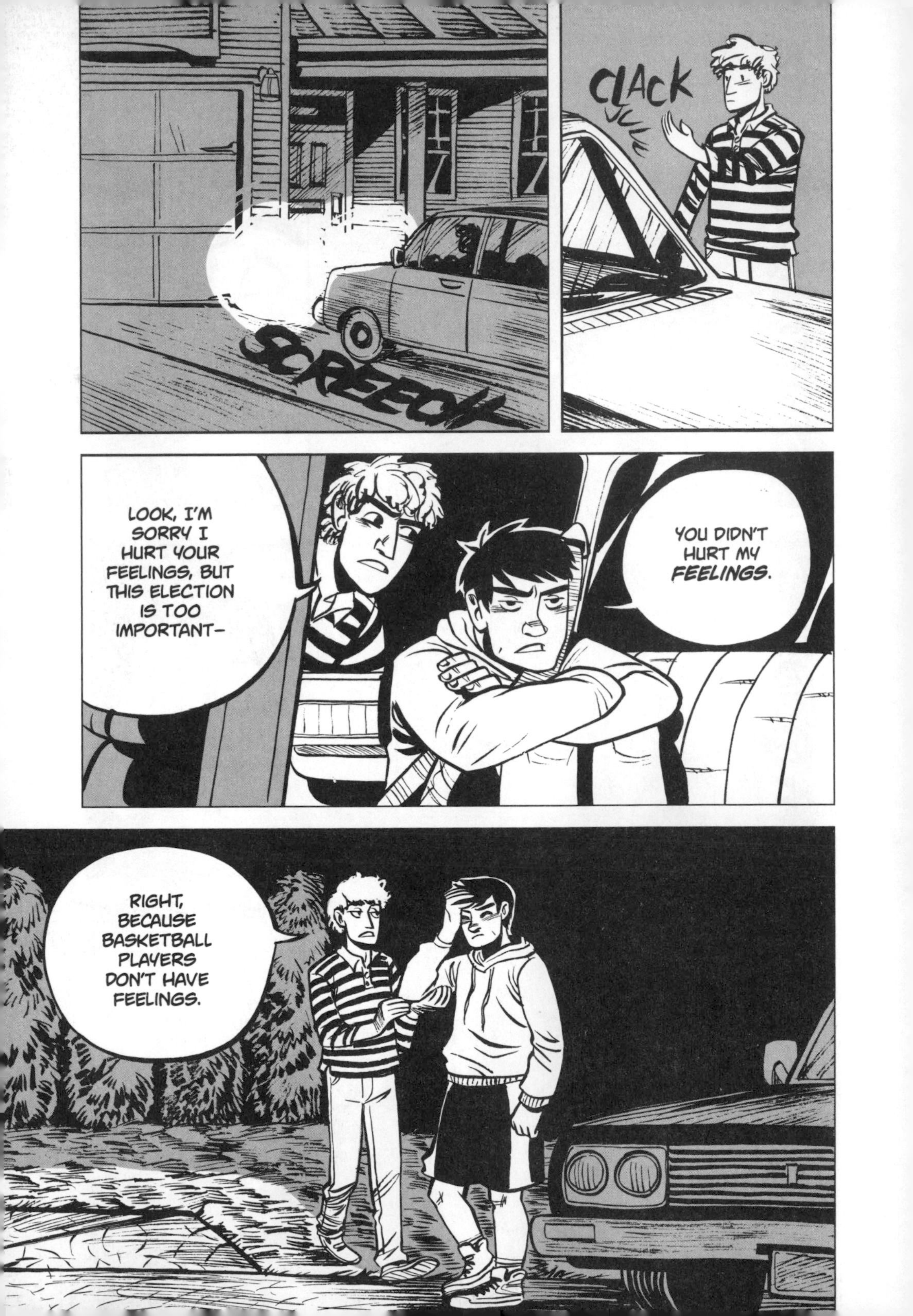
SCREECH
CLACK
LOOK, I'M SORRY I HURT YOUR FEELINGS, BUT THIS ELECTION IS TOO IMPORTANT-
YOU DIDN'T HURT MY FEELINGS.
RIGHT, BECAUSE BASKETBALL PLAYERS DON'T HAVE FEELINGS.

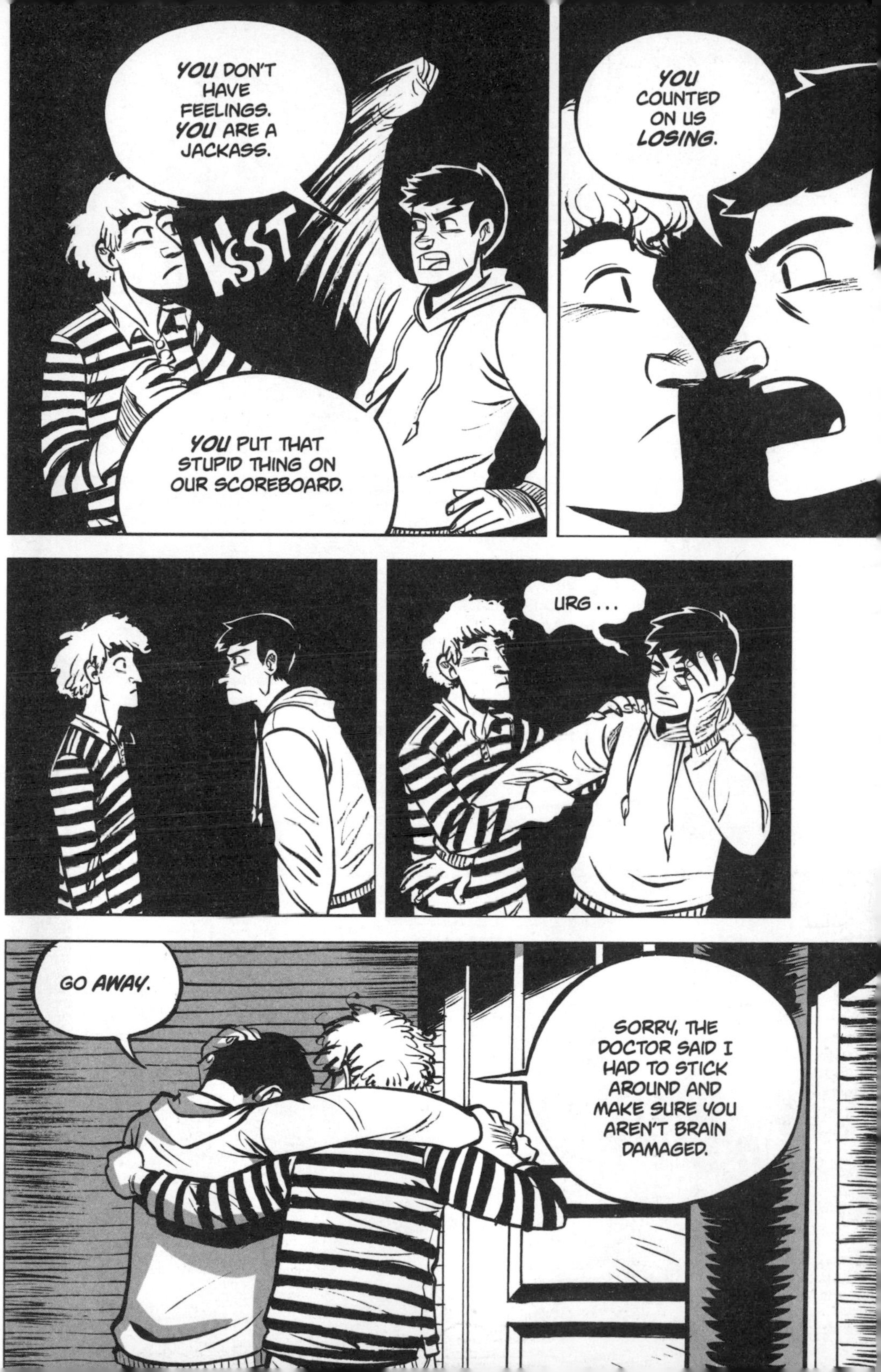
YOU DON'T HAVE FEELINGS. YOU ARE A JACKASS.
KSST
YOU PUT THAT STUPID THING ON OUR SCOREBOARD.
YOU COUNTED ON US LOSING.
URG . . .
GO AWAY.
SORRY, THE DOCTOR SAID I HAD TO STICK AROUND AND MAKE SURE YOU AREN'T BRAIN DAMAGED.

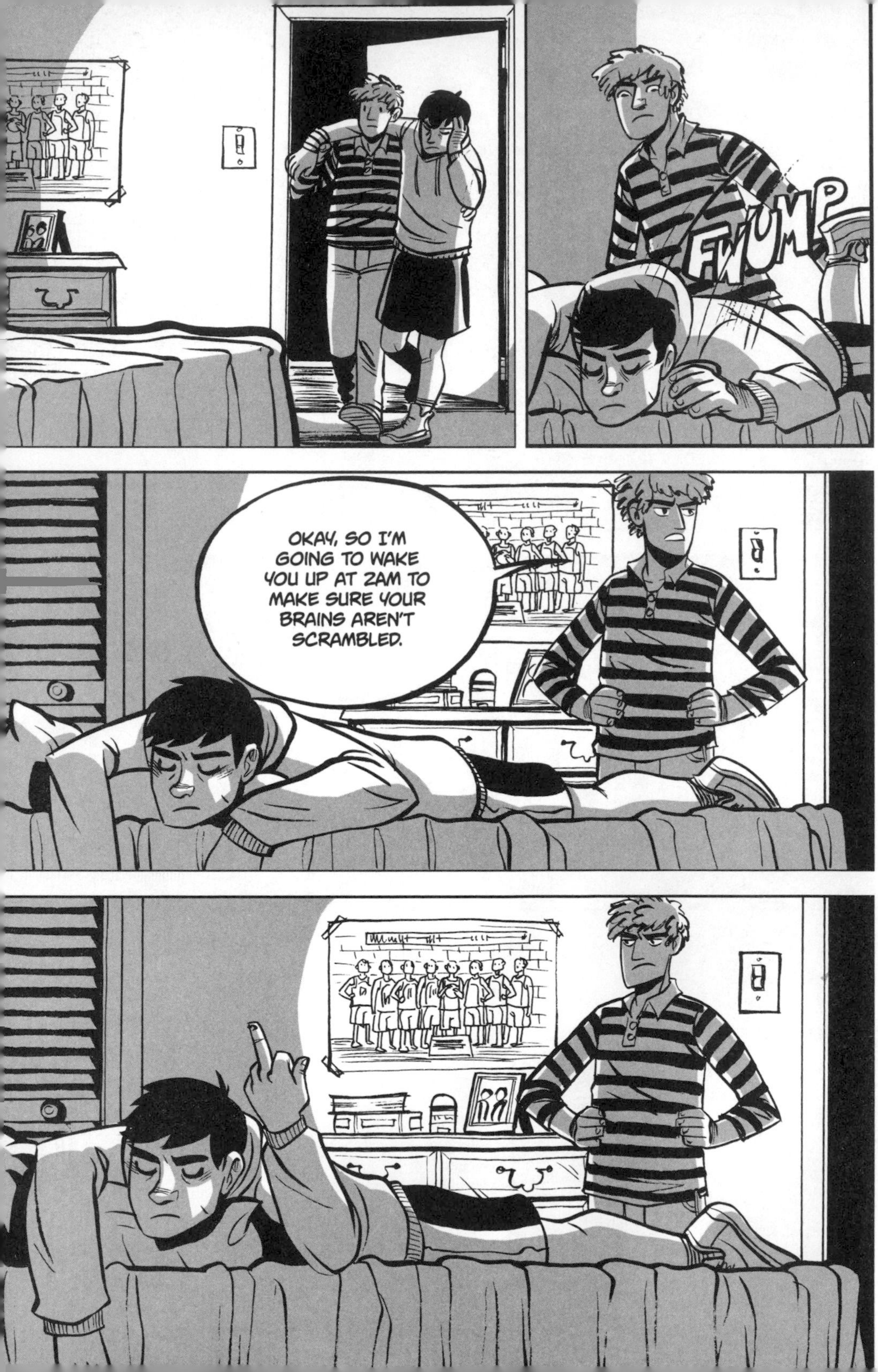
FWUMP
OKAY, SO I'M GOING TO WAKE YOU UP AT 2AM TO MAKE SURE YOUR BRAINS AREN'T SCRAMBLED.

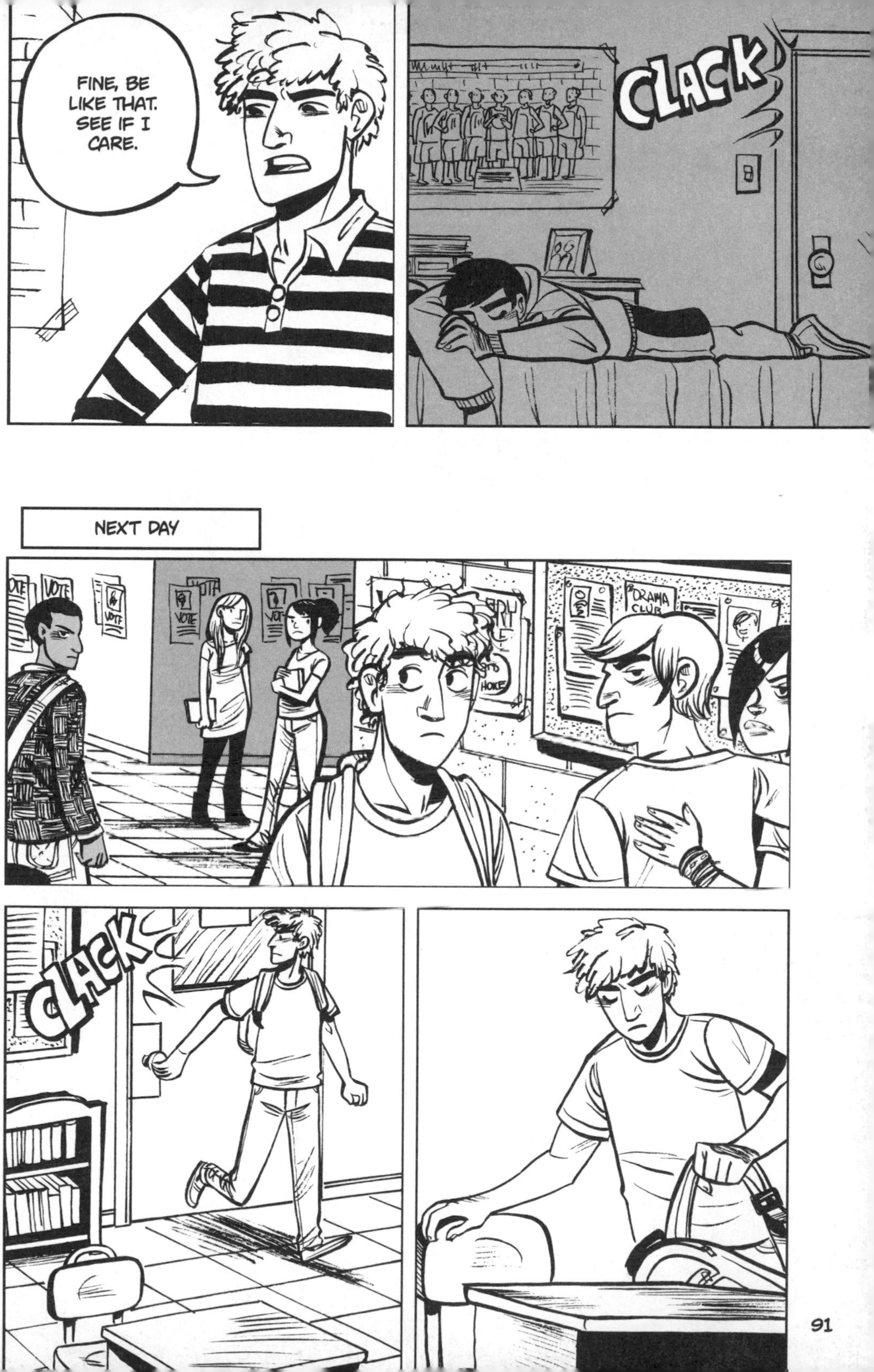
FINE, BE LIKE THAT. SEE IF I CARE.
CLACK
NEXT DAY
VOTE
DRAMA CLUB
CLACK

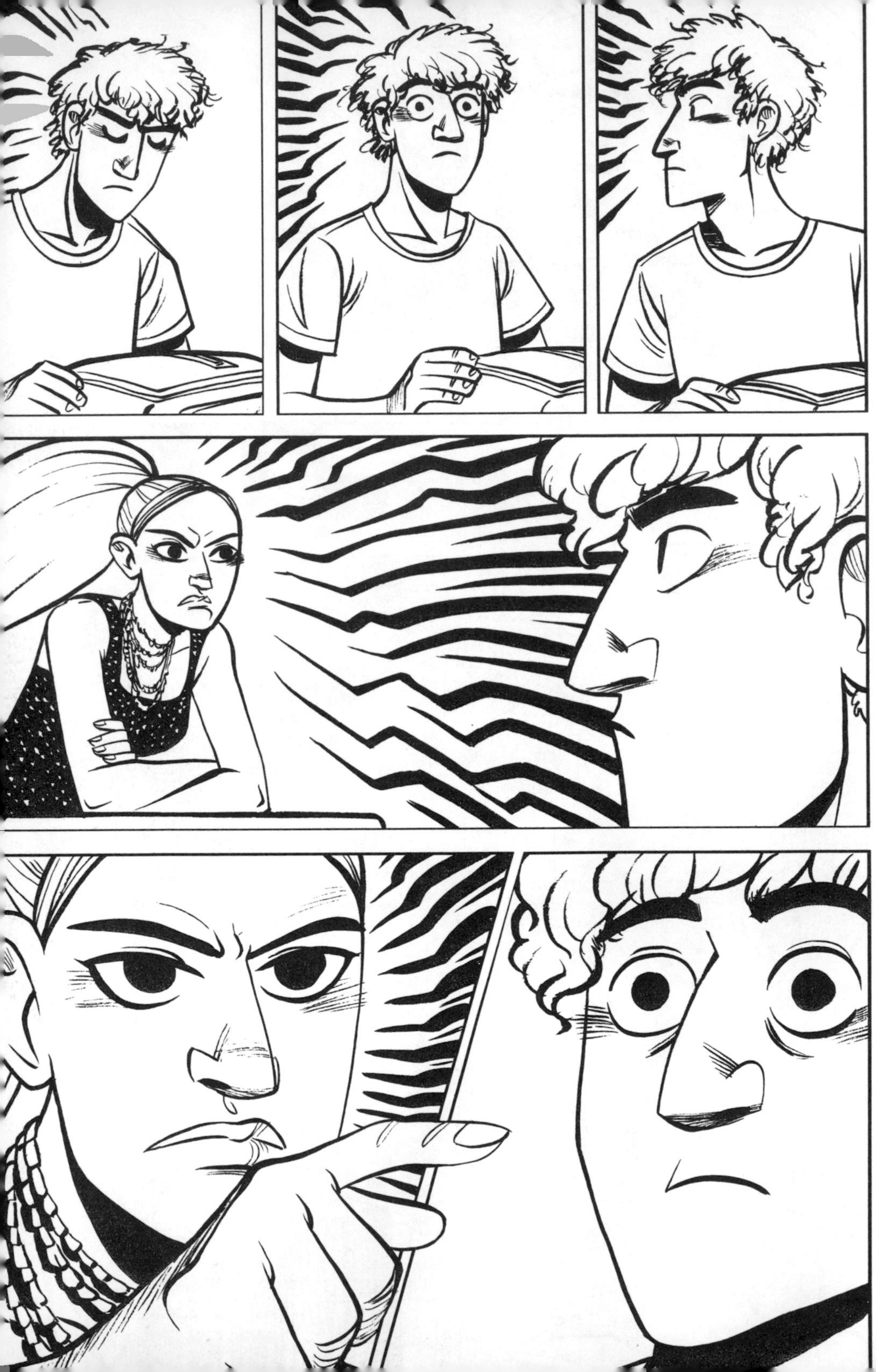

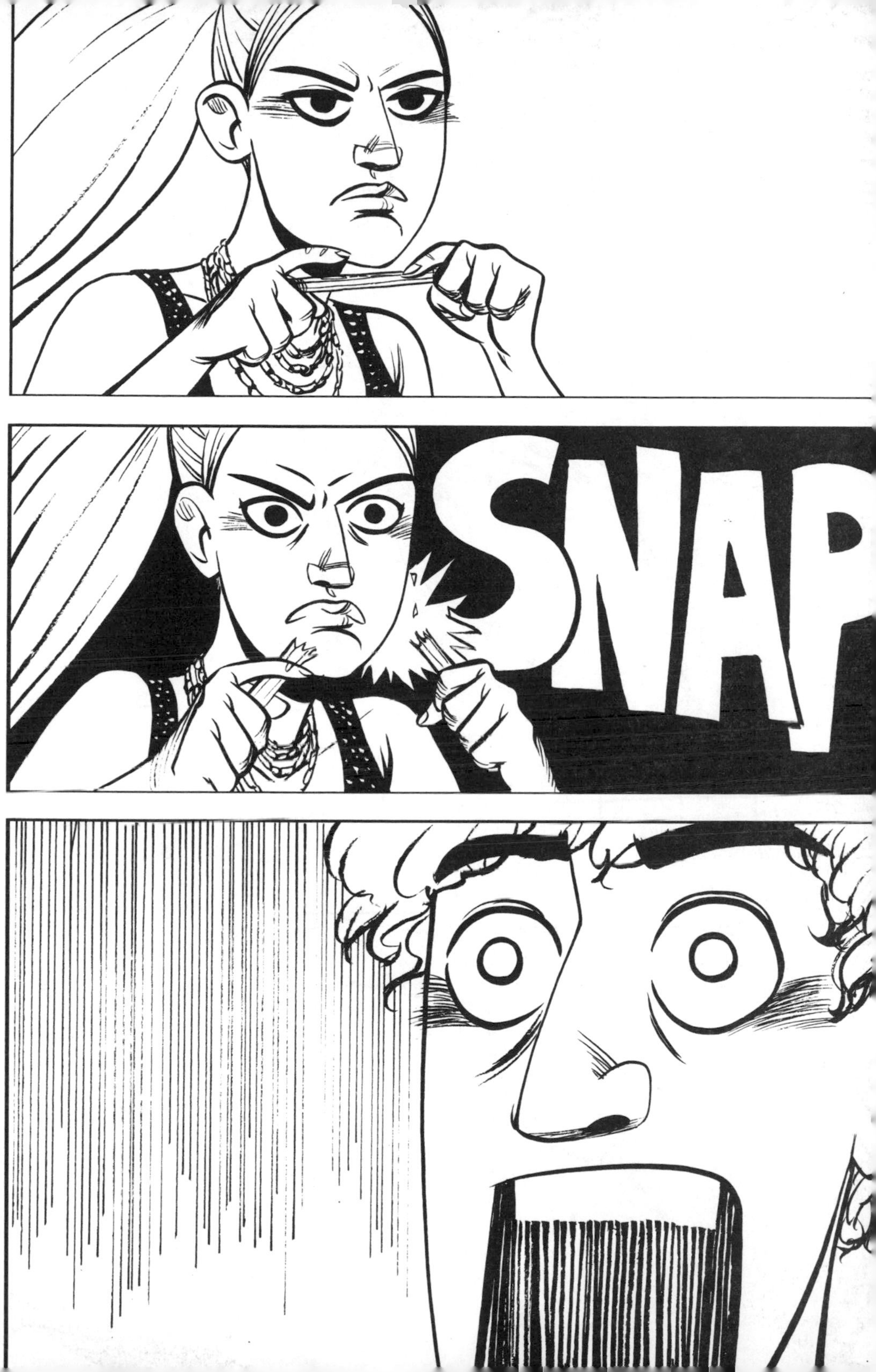
SNAP

HIDEOUS WRONGS COMMITTED AGAINST MY PERSON:

	BASKETBALL PLAYERS	CHEERLEADERS	PEOPLE SUCKING UP TO THEM
SHOVED INTO LOCKERS	5	1	2(!!)
TRIPPED IN HALLWAY	1	4	3 (possibly some unintentional, but I DOUBT IT!!!!)

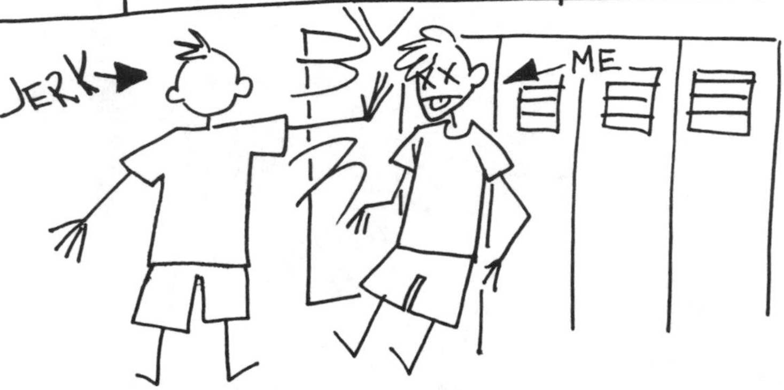
JERK
ME

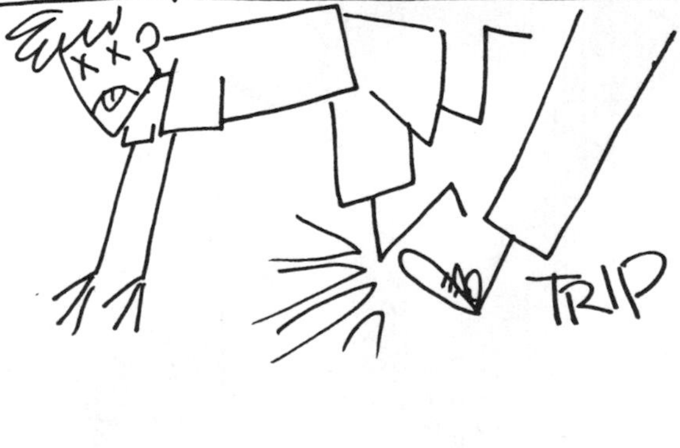
TRIP

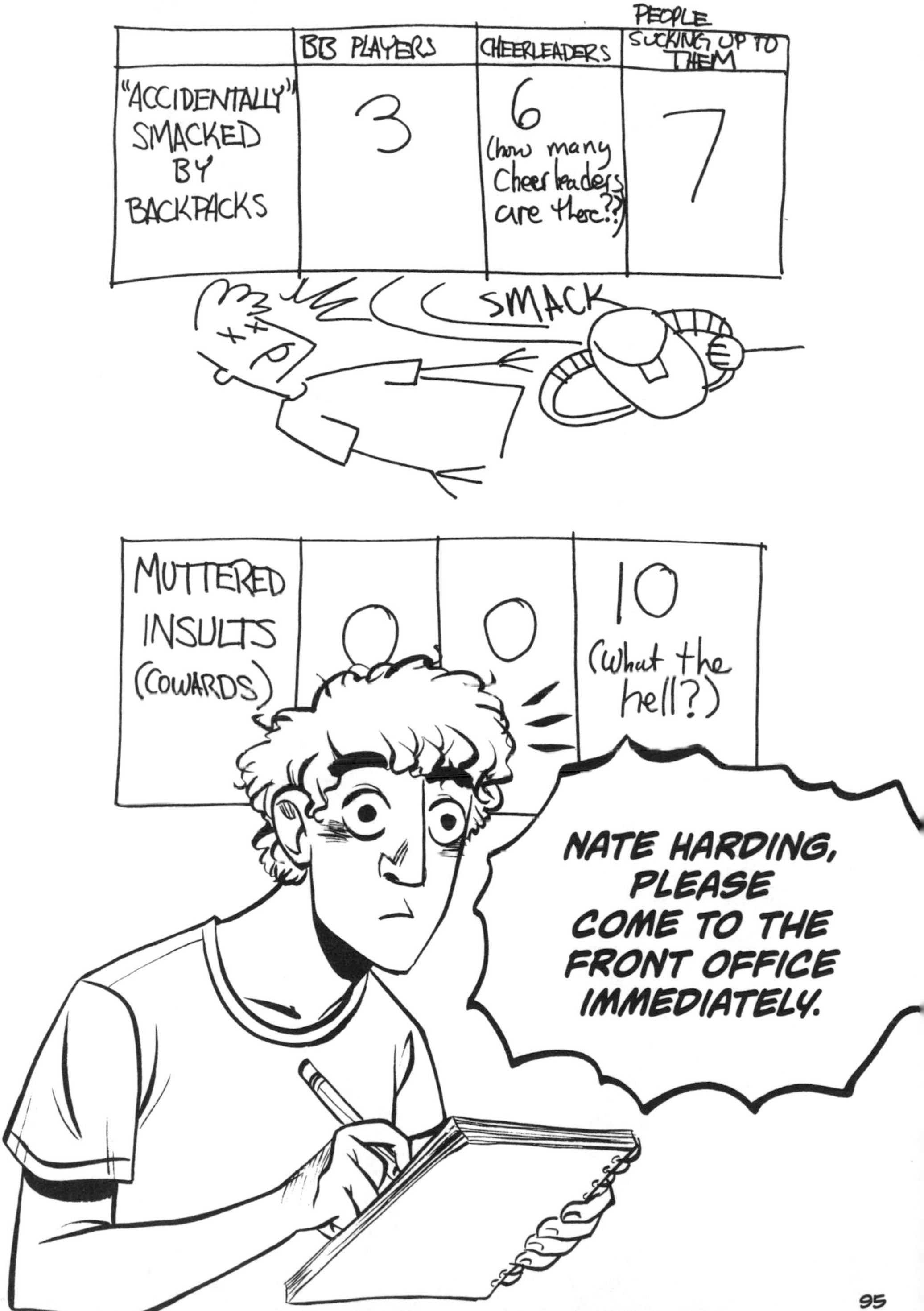
BB PLAYERS
CHEERLEADERS
PEOPLE SUCKING UP TO THEM
"ACCIDENTALLY" SMACKED BY BACKPACKS
3
6 (how many Cheerleaders are there??)
7
SMACK
MUTTERED INSULTS (COWARDS)
0
0
10 (what the hell?)
NATE HARDING, PLEASE COME TO THE FRONT OFFICE IMMEDIATELY.

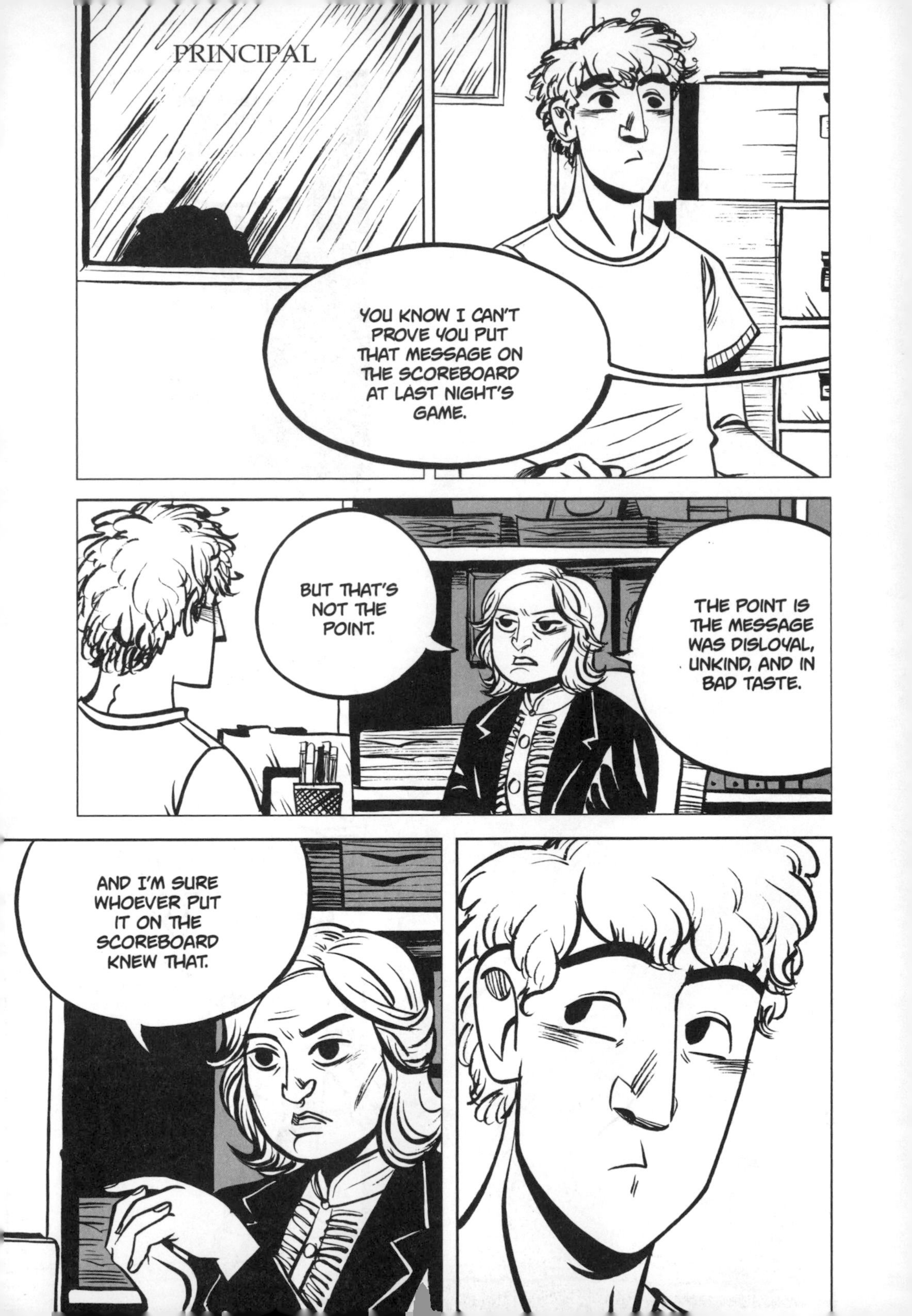
PRINCIPAL
YOU KNOW I CAN'T PROVE YOU PUT THAT MESSAGE ON THE SCOREBOARD AT LAST NIGHT'S GAME.
BUT THAT'S NOT THE POINT.
THE POINT IS THE MESSAGE WAS DISLOYAL, UNKIND, AND IN BAD TASTE.
AND I'M SURE WHOEVER PUT IT ON THE SCOREBOARD KNEW THAT.

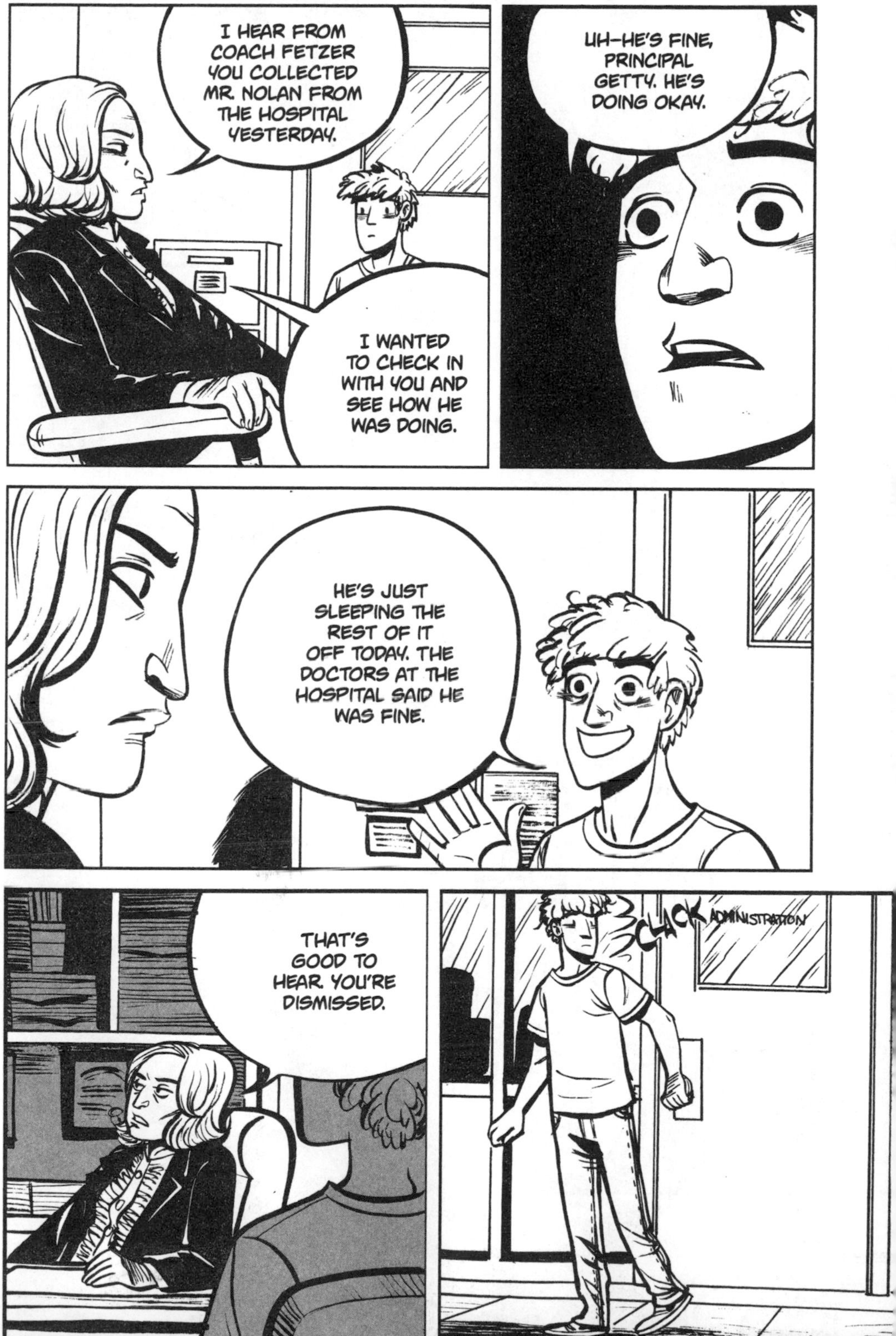
I HEAR FROM COACH FETZER YOU COLLECTED MR. NOLAN FROM THE HOSPITAL YESTERDAY.
I WANTED TO CHECK IN WITH YOU AND SEE HOW HE WAS DOING.
UH—HE'S FINE, PRINCIPAL GETTY. HE'S DOING OKAY.
HE'S JUST SLEEPING THE REST OF IT OFF TODAY. THE DOCTORS AT THE HOSPITAL SAID HE WAS FINE.
THAT'S GOOD TO HEAR. YOU'RE DISMISSED.
CLACK
ADMINISTRATION

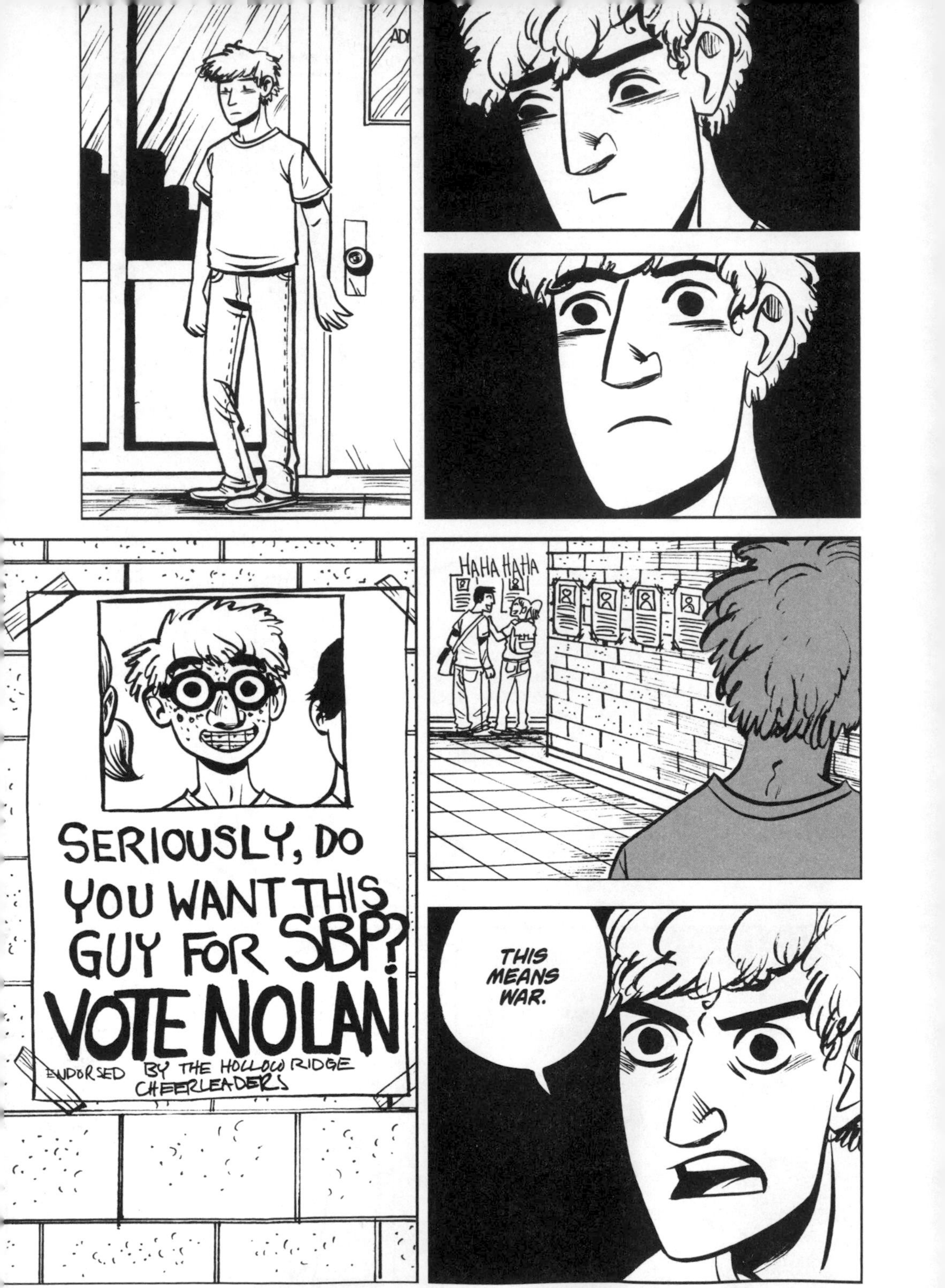
HAHA HAHA
SERIOUSLY, DO YOU WANT THIS GUY FOR SBP?
VOTE NOLAN
ENDORSED BY THE HOLLOW RIDGE CHEERLEADERS
THIS MEANS WAR.

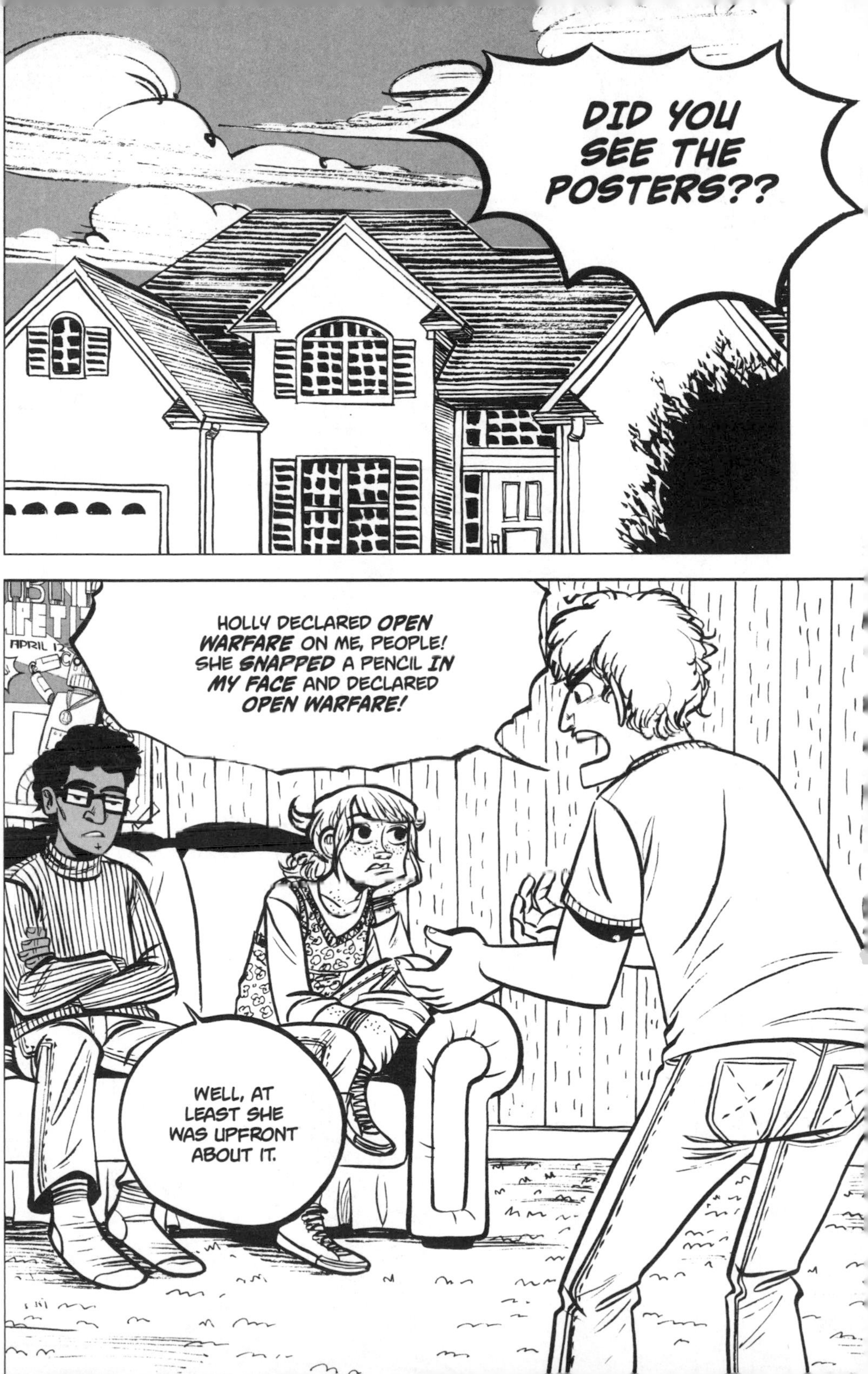
DID YOU SEE THE POSTERS??
HOLLY DECLARED OPEN WARFARE ON ME, PEOPLE! SHE SNAPPED A PENCIL IN MY FACE AND DECLARED OPEN WARFARE!
WELL, AT LEAST SHE WAS UPFRONT ABOUT IT.

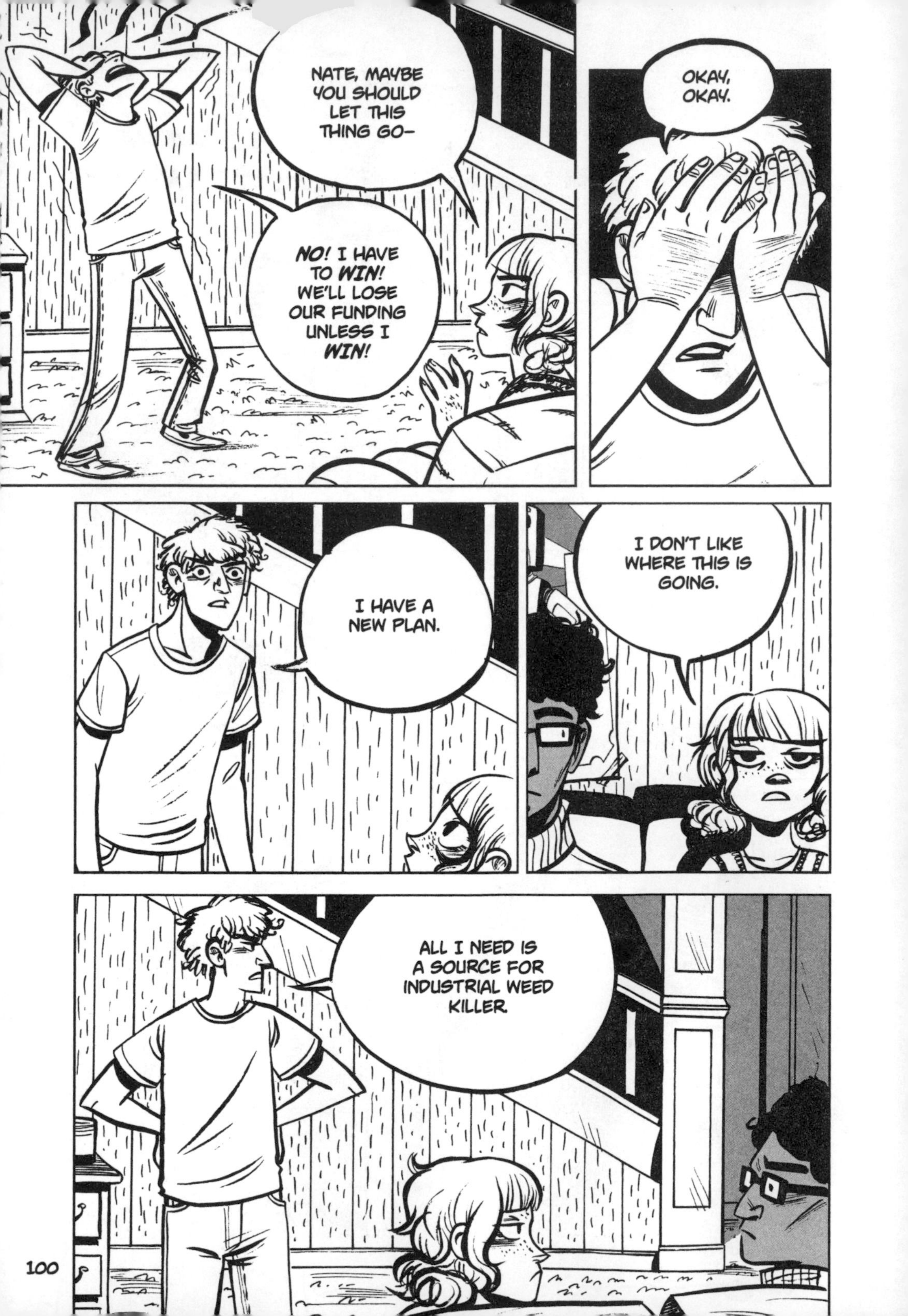
NATE, MAYBE YOU SHOULD LET THIS THING GO–
NO! I HAVE TO WIN! WE'LL LOSE OUR FUNDING UNLESS I WIN!
OKAY, OKAY.
I HAVE A NEW PLAN.
I DON'T LIKE WHERE THIS IS GOING.
ALL I NEED IS A SOURCE FOR INDUSTRIAL WEED KILLER.

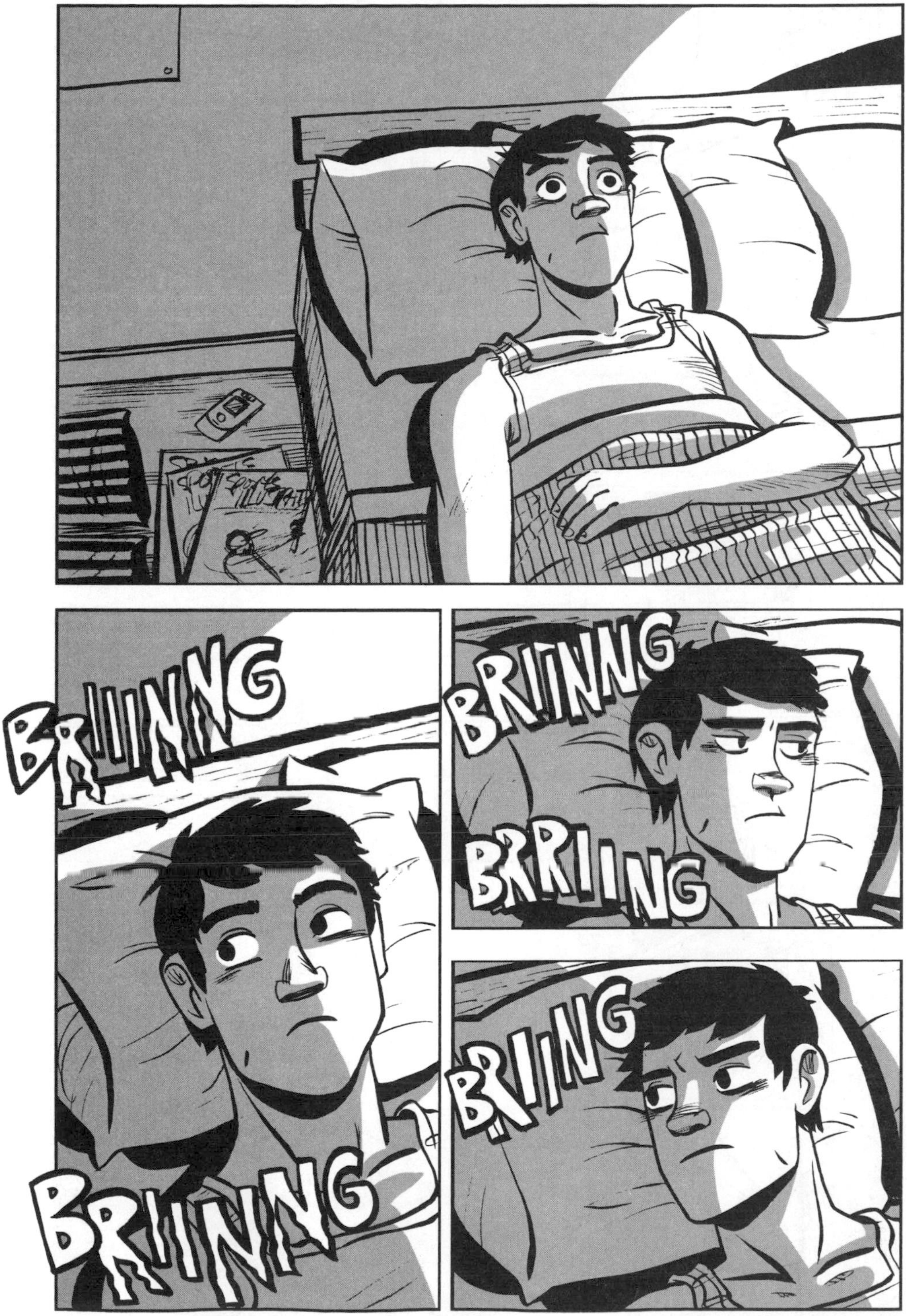
BRIIINNG
BRIINNG
BRIINNG
BRRIING
BRIING

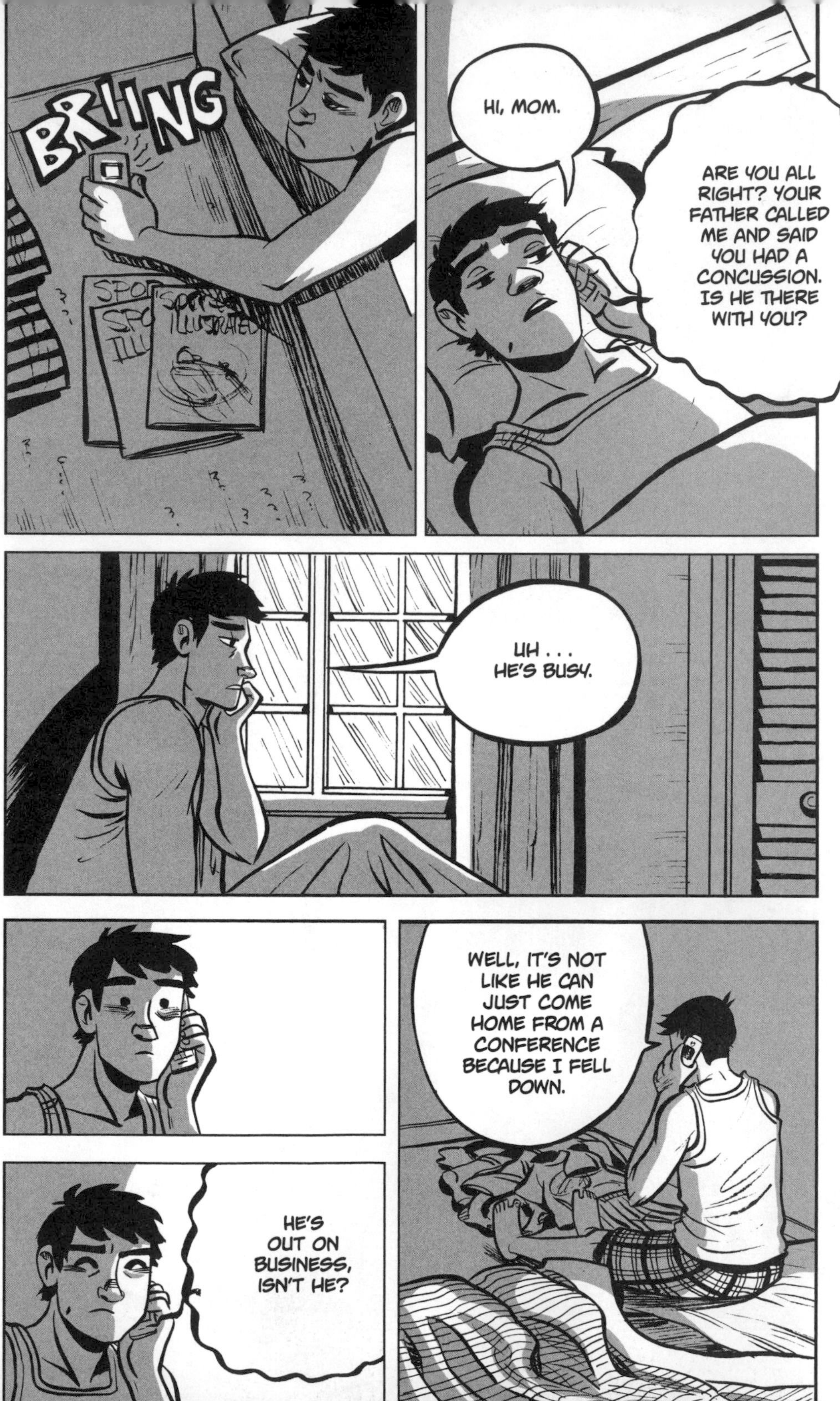
BRIING
HI, MOM.
ARE YOU ALL RIGHT? YOUR FATHER CALLED ME AND SAID YOU HAD A CONCUSSION. IS HE THERE WITH YOU?
UH . . . HE'S BUSY.
WELL, IT'S NOT LIKE HE CAN JUST COME HOME FROM A CONFERENCE BECAUSE I FELL DOWN.
HE'S OUT ON BUSINESS, ISN'T HE?

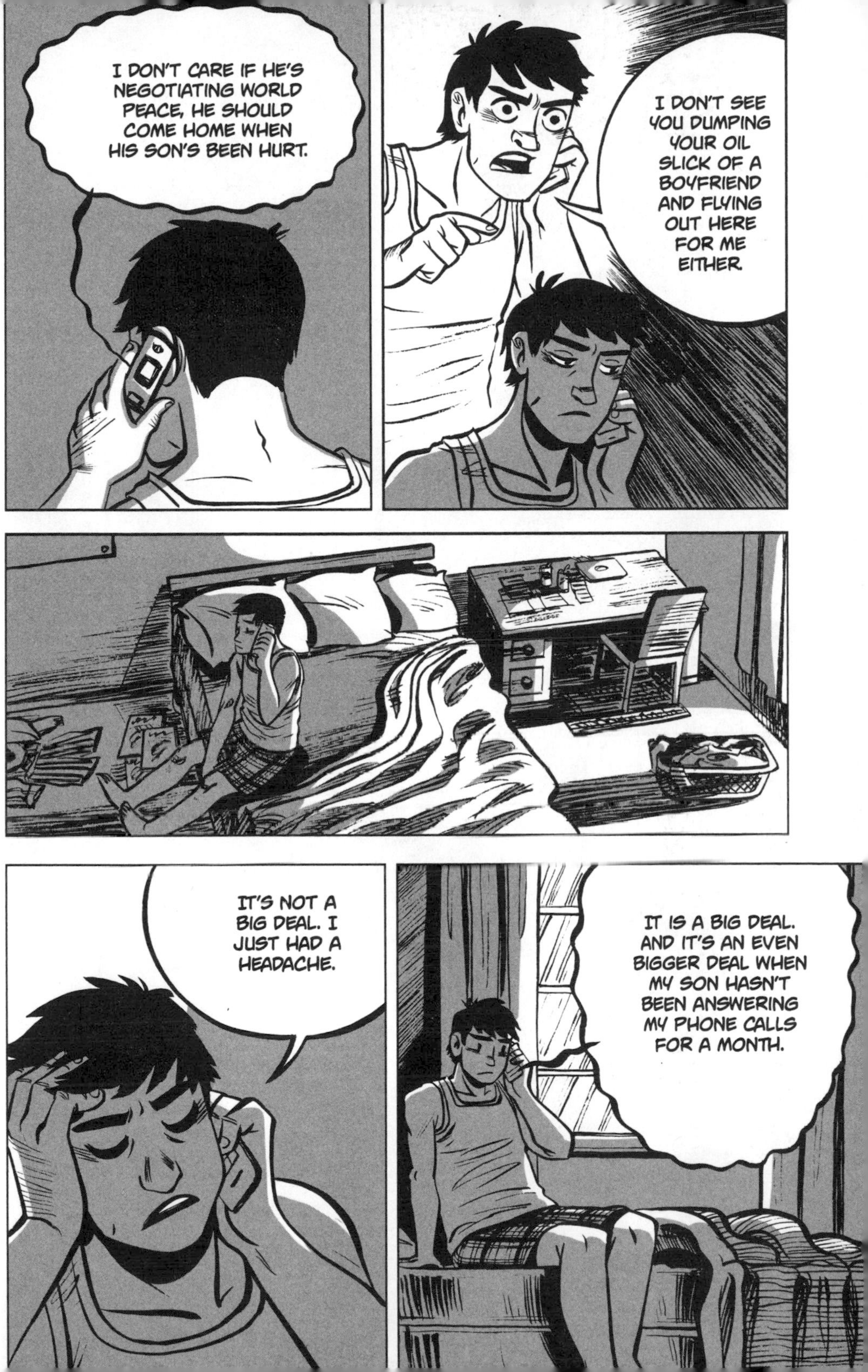
I DON'T CARE IF HE'S NEGOTIATING WORLD PEACE, HE SHOULD COME HOME WHEN HIS SON'S BEEN HURT.
I DON'T SEE YOU DUMPING YOUR OIL SLICK OF A BOYFRIEND AND FLYING OUT HERE FOR ME EITHER.
IT'S NOT A BIG DEAL. I JUST HAD A HEADACHE.
IT IS A BIG DEAL. AND IT'S AN EVEN BIGGER DEAL WHEN MY SON HASN'T BEEN ANSWERING MY PHONE CALLS FOR A MONTH.

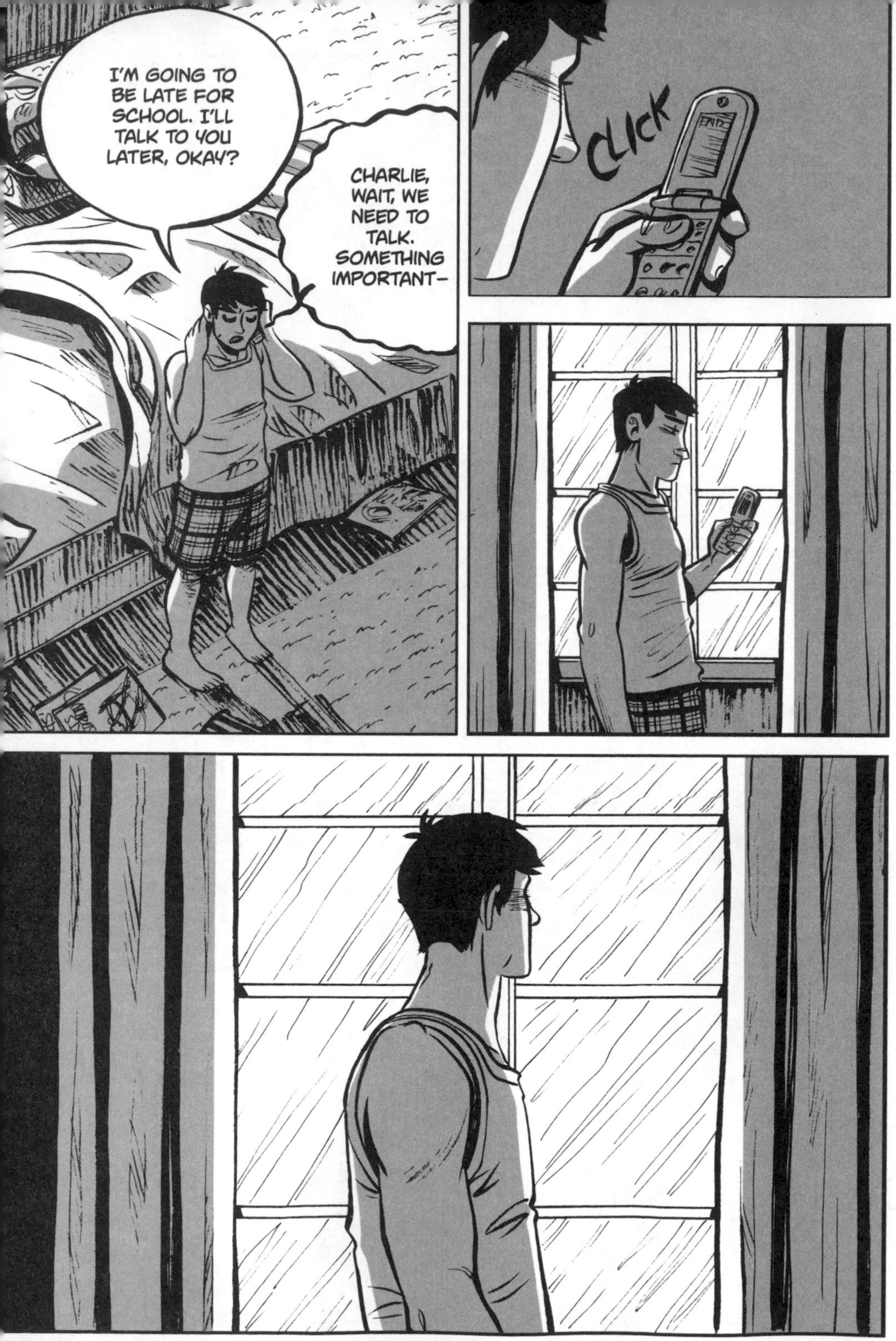

I'M GOING TO BE LATE FOR SCHOOL. I'LL TALK TO YOU LATER, OKAY?
CHARLIE, WAIT, WE NEED TO TALK. SOMETHING IMPORTANT–
CLICK

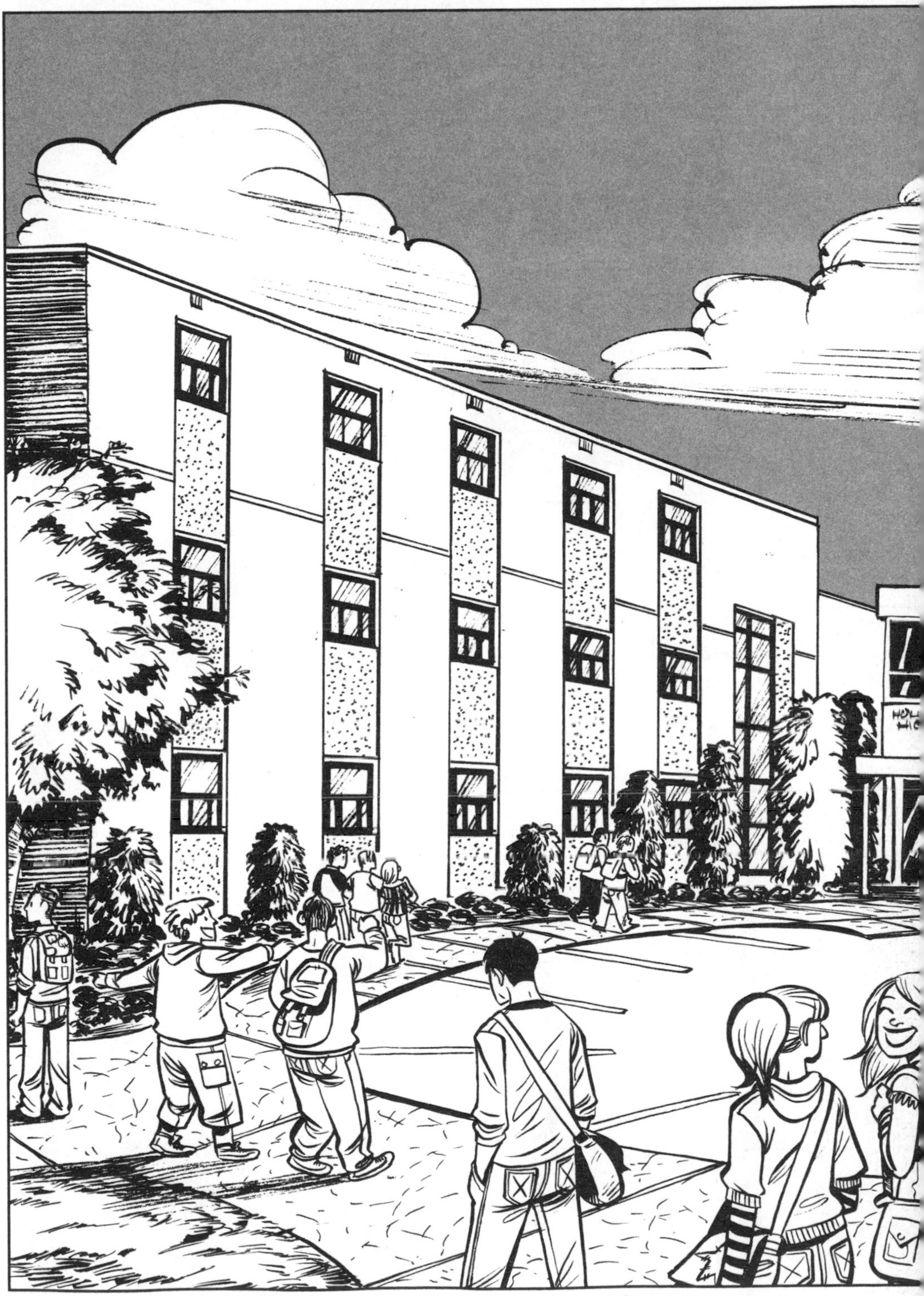

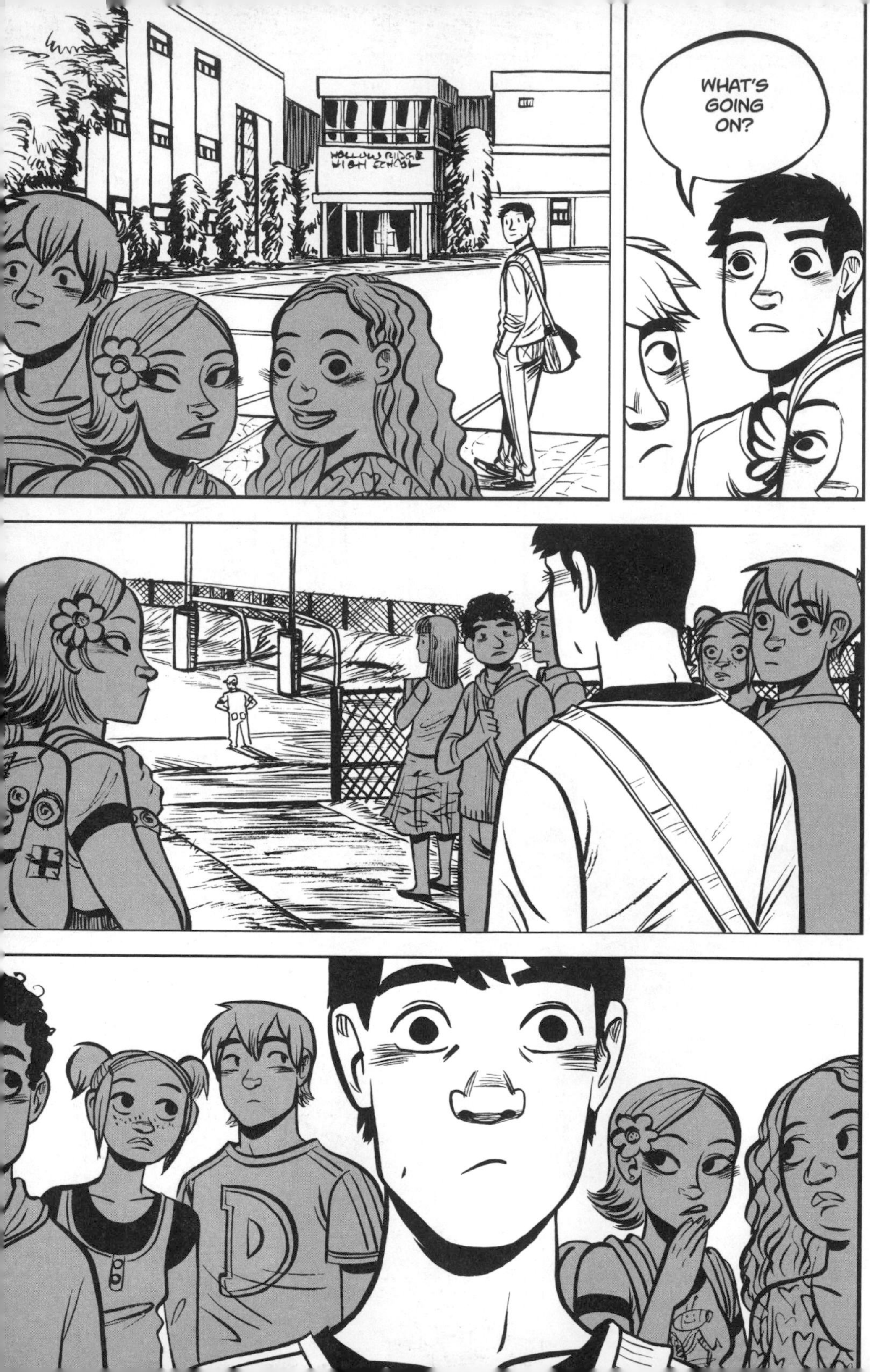
HOLLOW RIDGE HIGH SCHOOL
WHAT'S GOING ON?

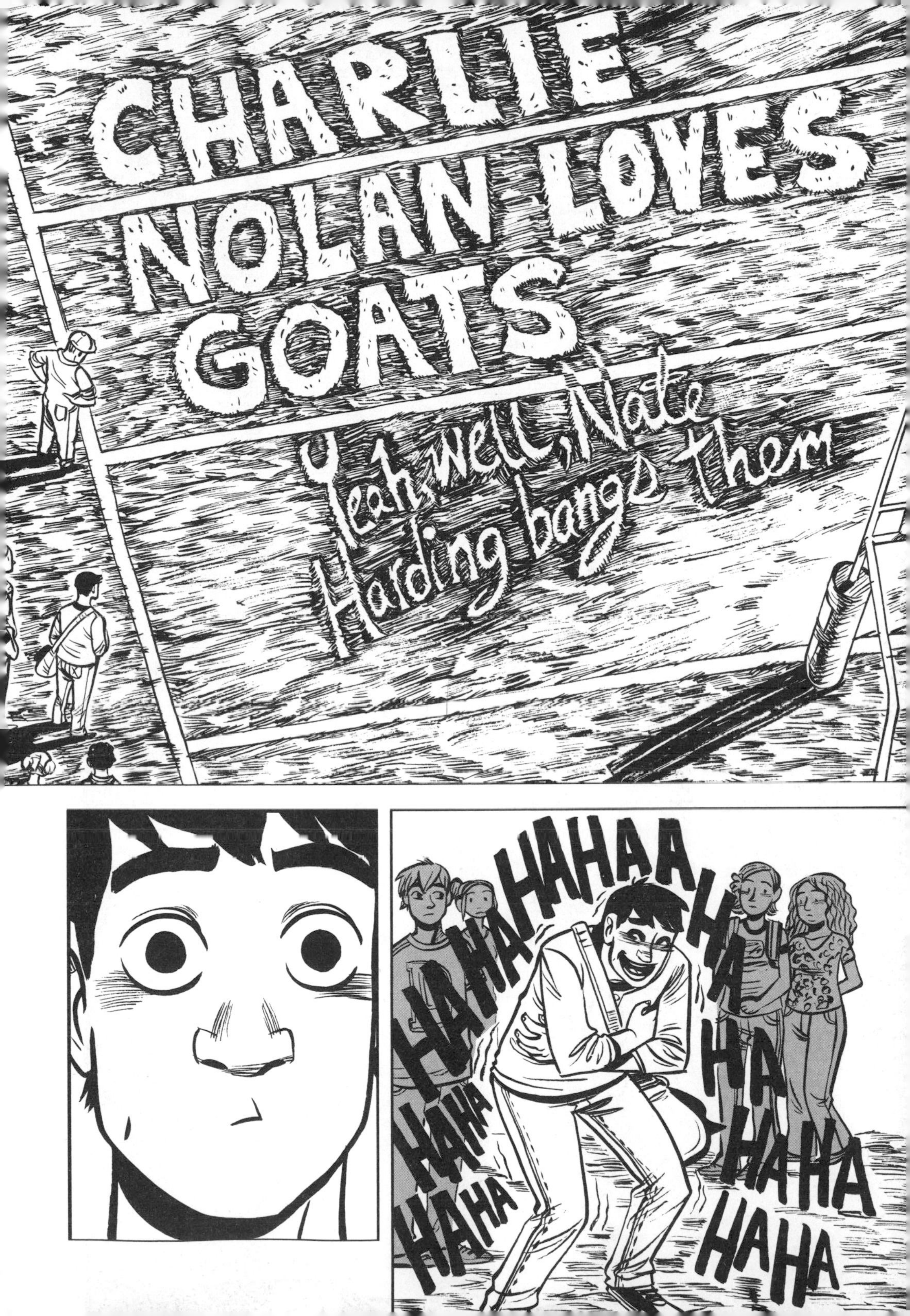

CHARLIE NOLAN LOVES GOATS
Yeah, well, Nate Harding bangs them
HAHAHAHAA
HAHA
HAHA
HAHA
HAHA
HAHA
HAHA
HAHA

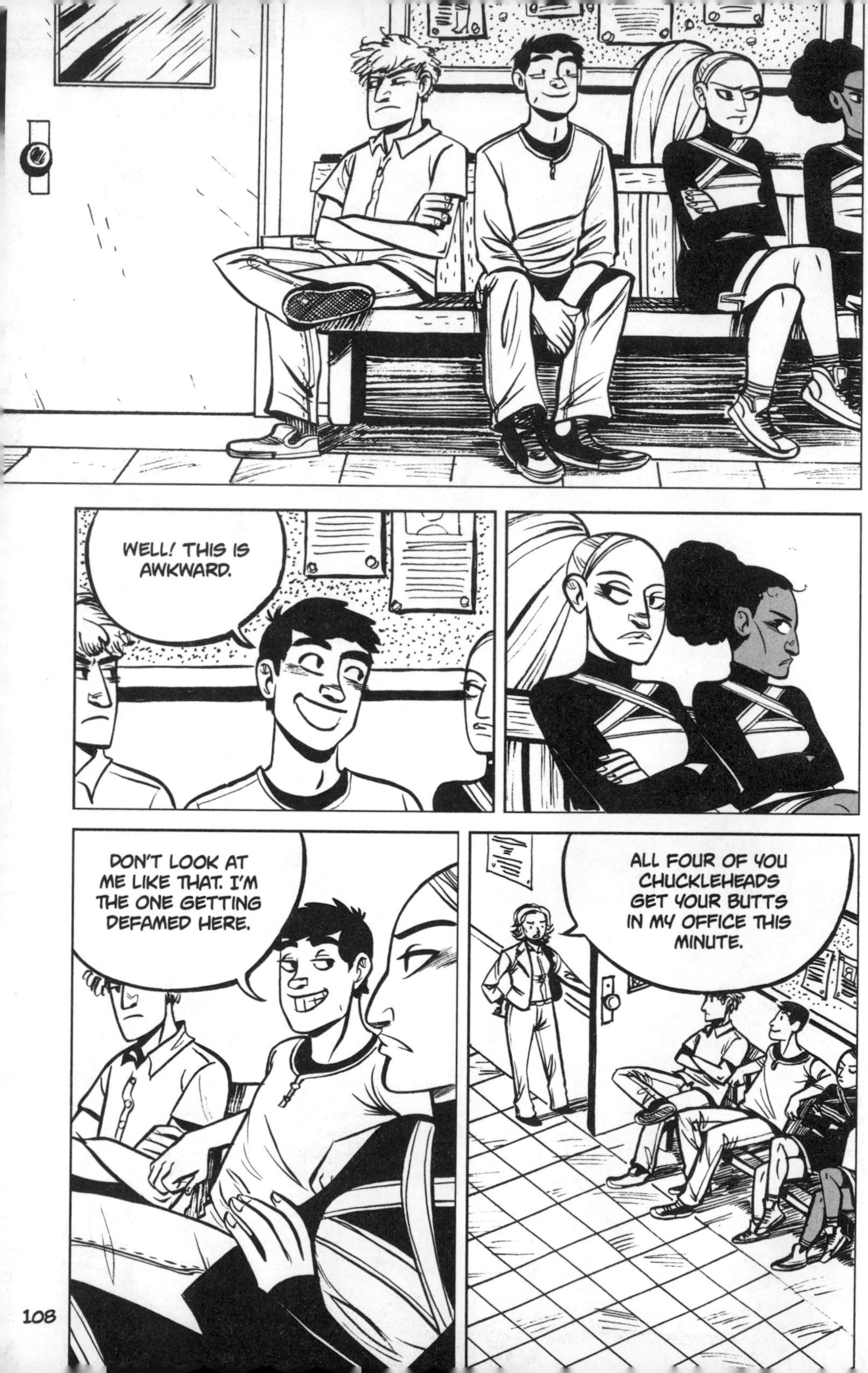

WELL! THIS IS AWKWARD.
DON'T LOOK AT ME LIKE THAT. I'M THE ONE GETTING DEFAMED HERE.
ALL FOUR OF YOU CHUCKLEHEADS GET YOUR BUTTS IN MY OFFICE THIS MINUTE.

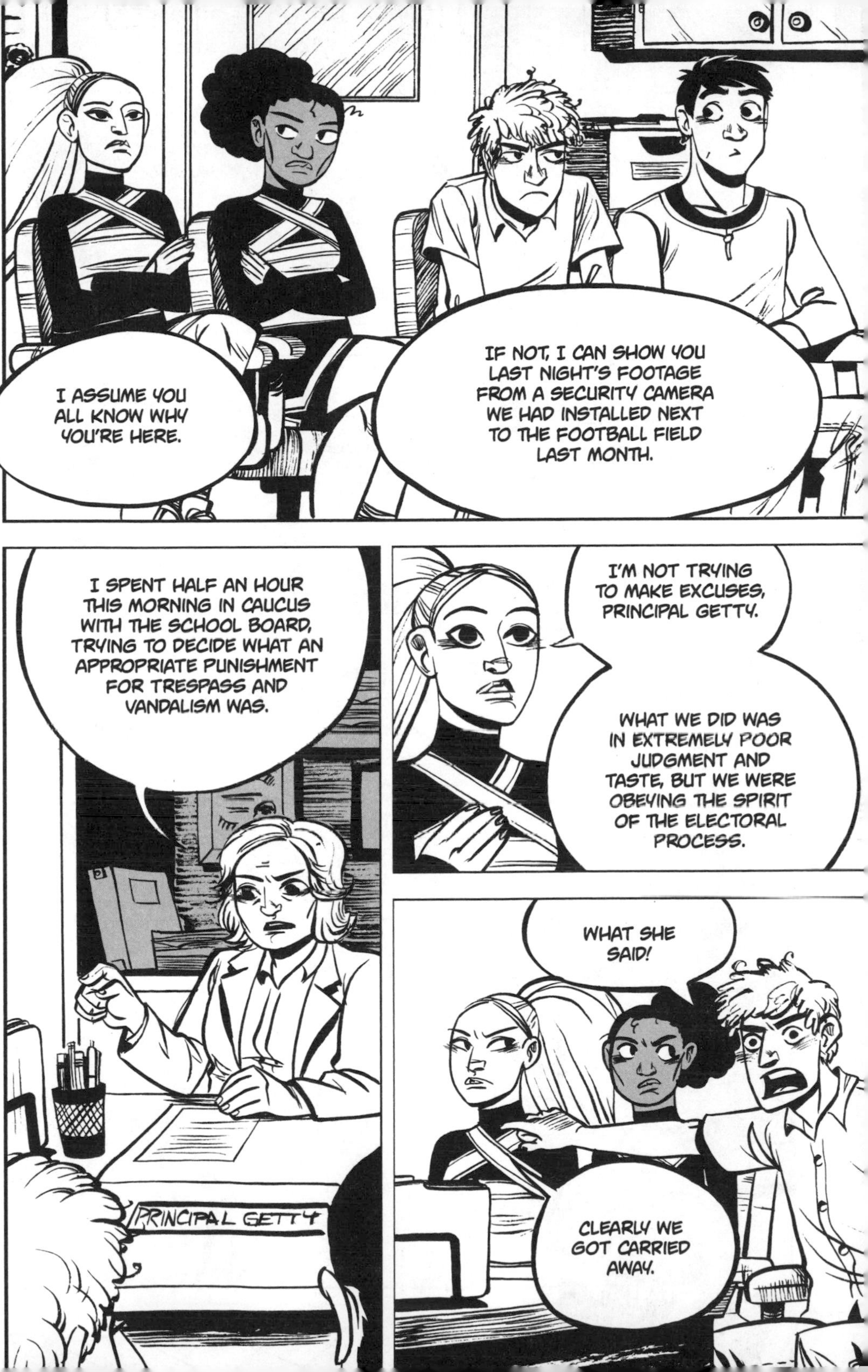
I ASSUME YOU ALL KNOW WHY YOU'RE HERE.
IF NOT, I CAN SHOW YOU LAST NIGHT'S FOOTAGE FROM A SECURITY CAMERA WE HAD INSTALLED NEXT TO THE FOOTBALL FIELD LAST MONTH.
I SPENT HALF AN HOUR THIS MORNING IN CAUCUS WITH THE SCHOOL BOARD, TRYING TO DECIDE WHAT AN APPROPRIATE PUNISHMENT FOR TRESPASS AND VANDALISM WAS.
PRINCIPAL GETTY
I'M NOT TRYING TO MAKE EXCUSES, PRINCIPAL GETTY.
WHAT WE DID WAS IN EXTREMELY POOR JUDGMENT AND TASTE, BUT WE WERE OBEYING THE SPIRIT OF THE ELECTORAL PROCESS.
WHAT SHE SAID!
CLEARLY WE GOT CARRIED AWAY.

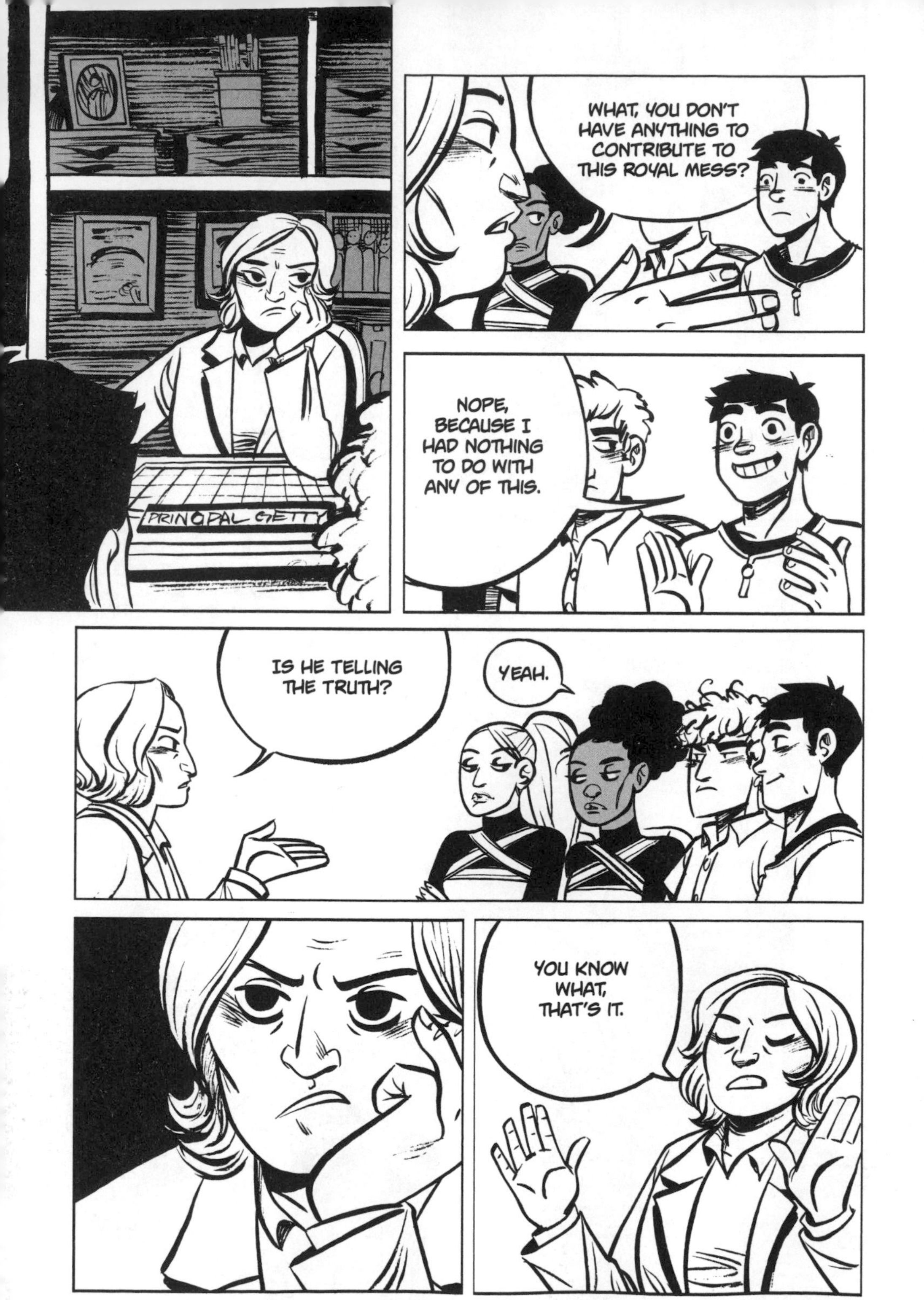
PRINCIPAL GETTY
WHAT, YOU DON'T HAVE ANYTHING TO CONTRIBUTE TO THIS ROYAL MESS?
NOPE, BECAUSE I HAD NOTHING TO DO WITH ANY OF THIS.
IS HE TELLING THE TRUTH?
YEAH.
YOU KNOW WHAT, THAT'S IT.

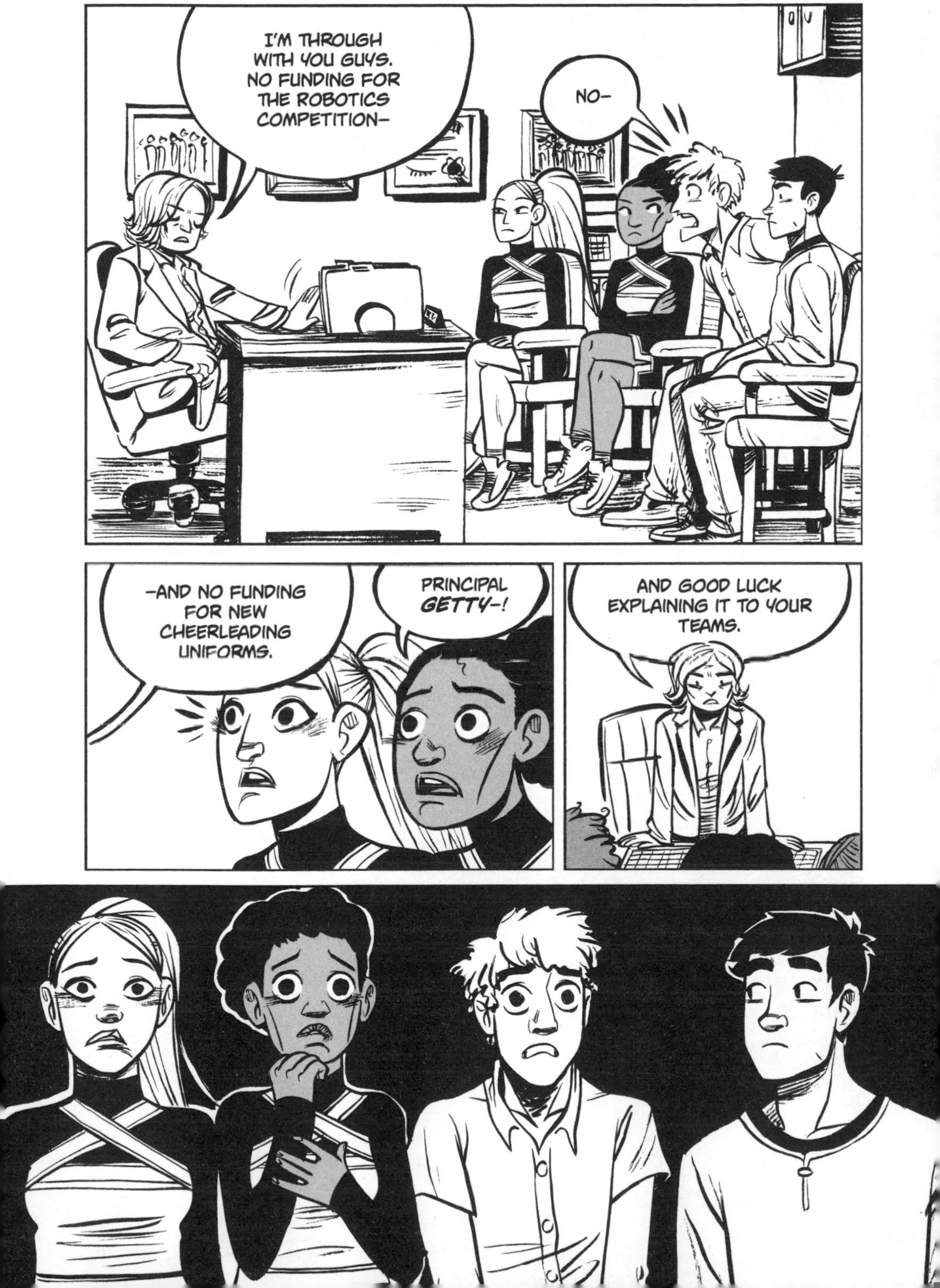
I'M THROUGH WITH YOU GUYS. NO FUNDING FOR THE ROBOTICS COMPETITION–
NO–
–AND NO FUNDING FOR NEW CHEERLEADING UNIFORMS.
PRINCIPAL *GETTY*–!
AND GOOD LUCK EXPLAINING IT TO YOUR TEAMS.

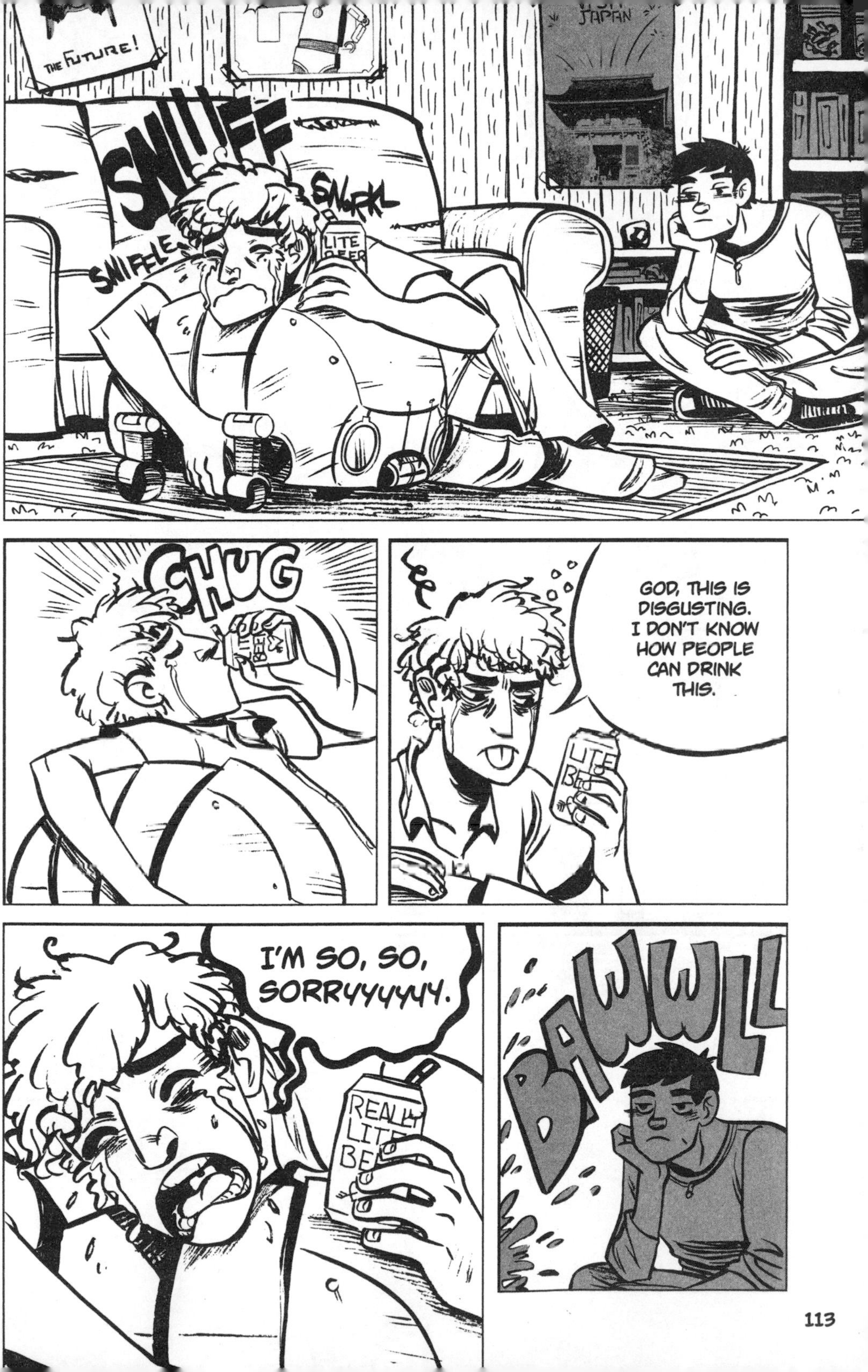
THE FUTURE!
JAPAN
SNIFF
SNORKL
SNIFFLE
LITE BEER
CHUG
GOD, THIS IS DISGUSTING. I DON'T KNOW HOW PEOPLE CAN DRINK THIS.
I'M SO, SO, SORRYYYYYY.
REALLY LITE BE
BAWWLL

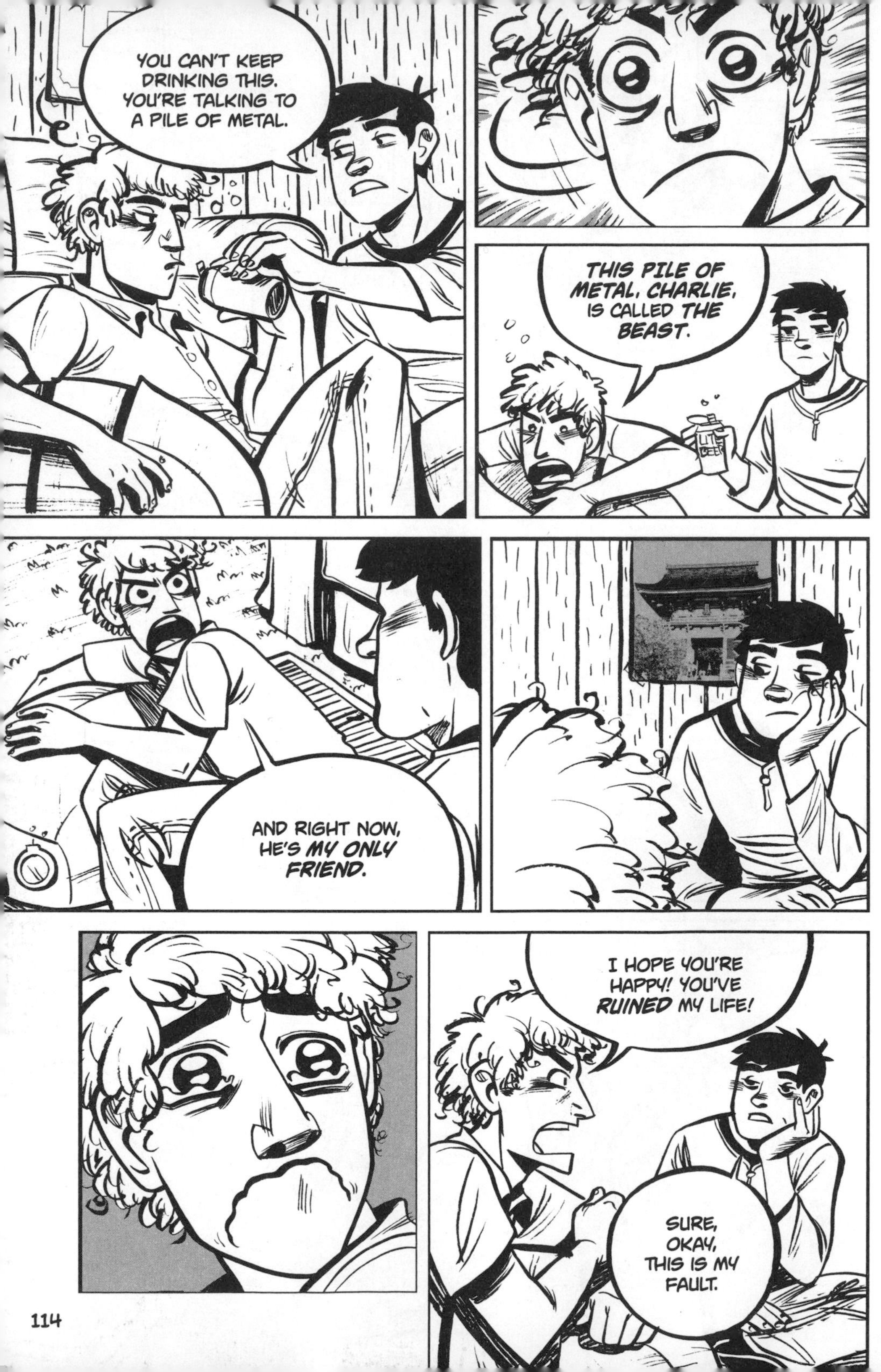
YOU CAN'T KEEP DRINKING THIS. YOU'RE TALKING TO A PILE OF METAL.
THIS PILE OF METAL, CHARLIE, IS CALLED THE BEAST.
LITE BEER
AND RIGHT NOW, HE'S MY ONLY FRIEND.
I HOPE YOU'RE HAPPY! YOU'VE RUINED MY LIFE!
SURE, OKAY, THIS IS MY FAULT.

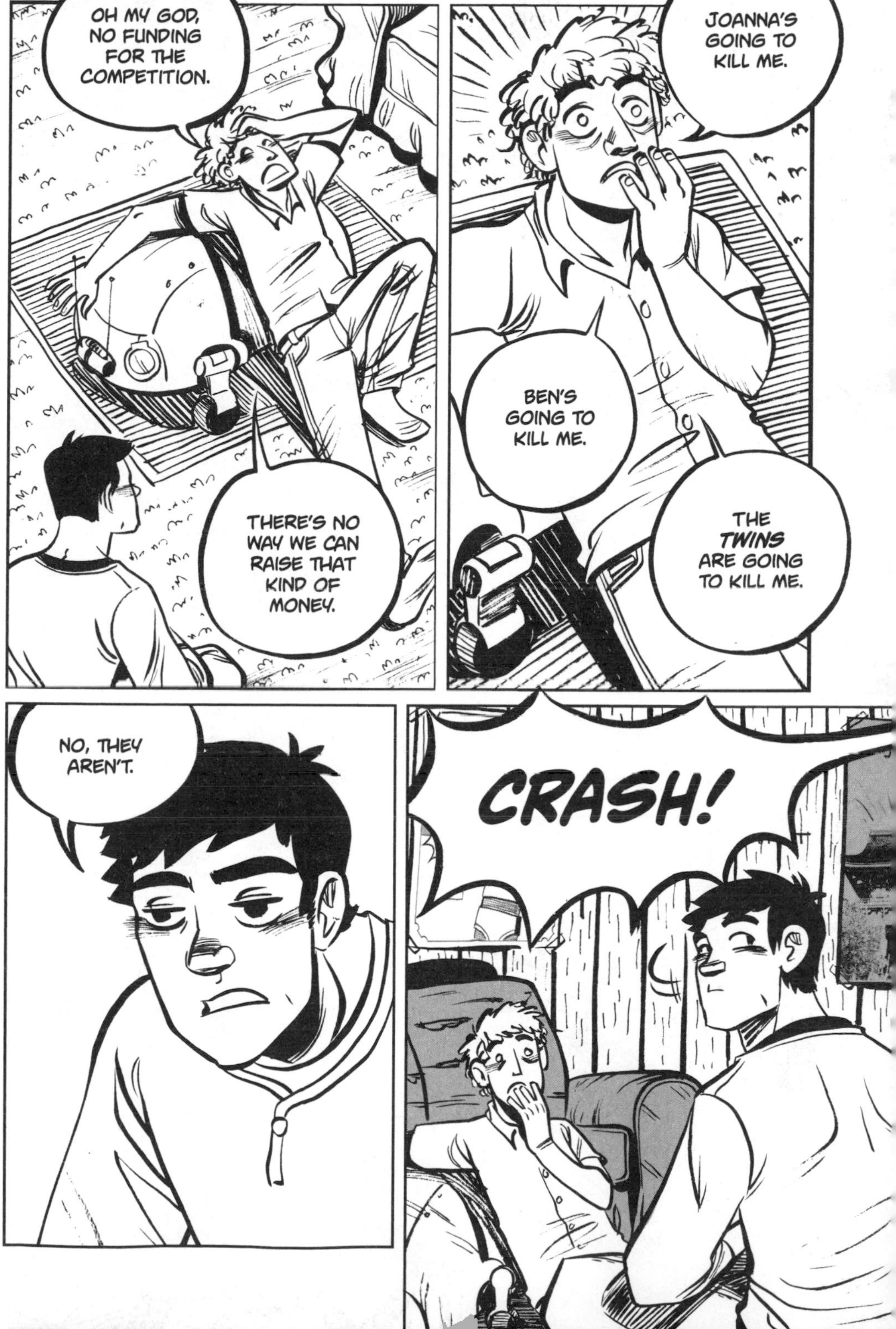
OH MY GOD, NO FUNDING FOR THE COMPETITION.
THERE'S NO WAY WE CAN RAISE THAT KIND OF MONEY.
JOANNA'S GOING TO KILL ME.
BEN'S GOING TO KILL ME.
THE *TWINS* ARE GOING TO KILL ME.
NO, THEY AREN'T.
CRASH!

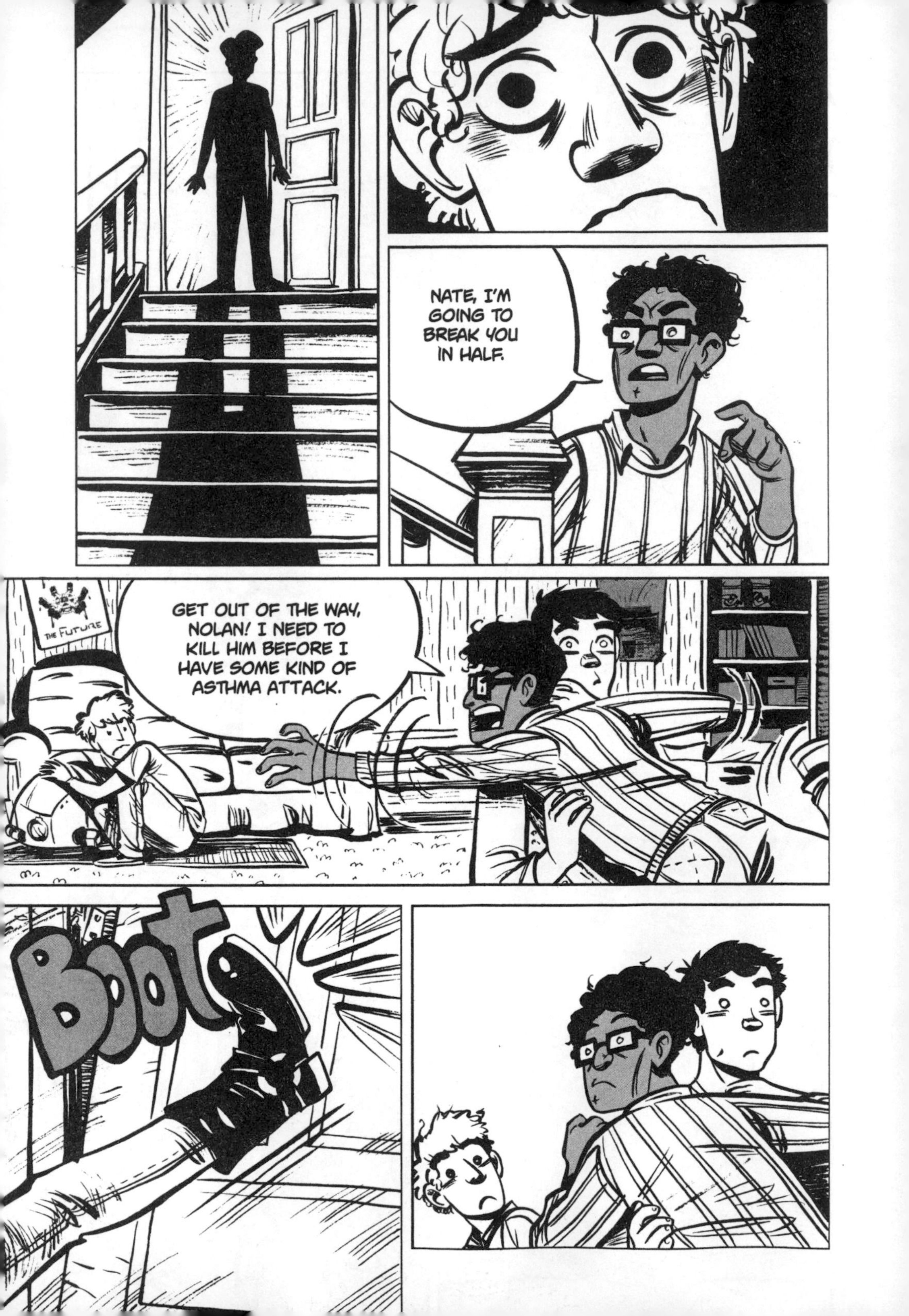
NATE, I'M GOING TO BREAK YOU IN HALF.
THE FUTURE
GET OUT OF THE WAY, NOLAN! I NEED TO KILL HIM BEFORE I HAVE SOME KIND OF ASTHMA ATTACK.
BOOT

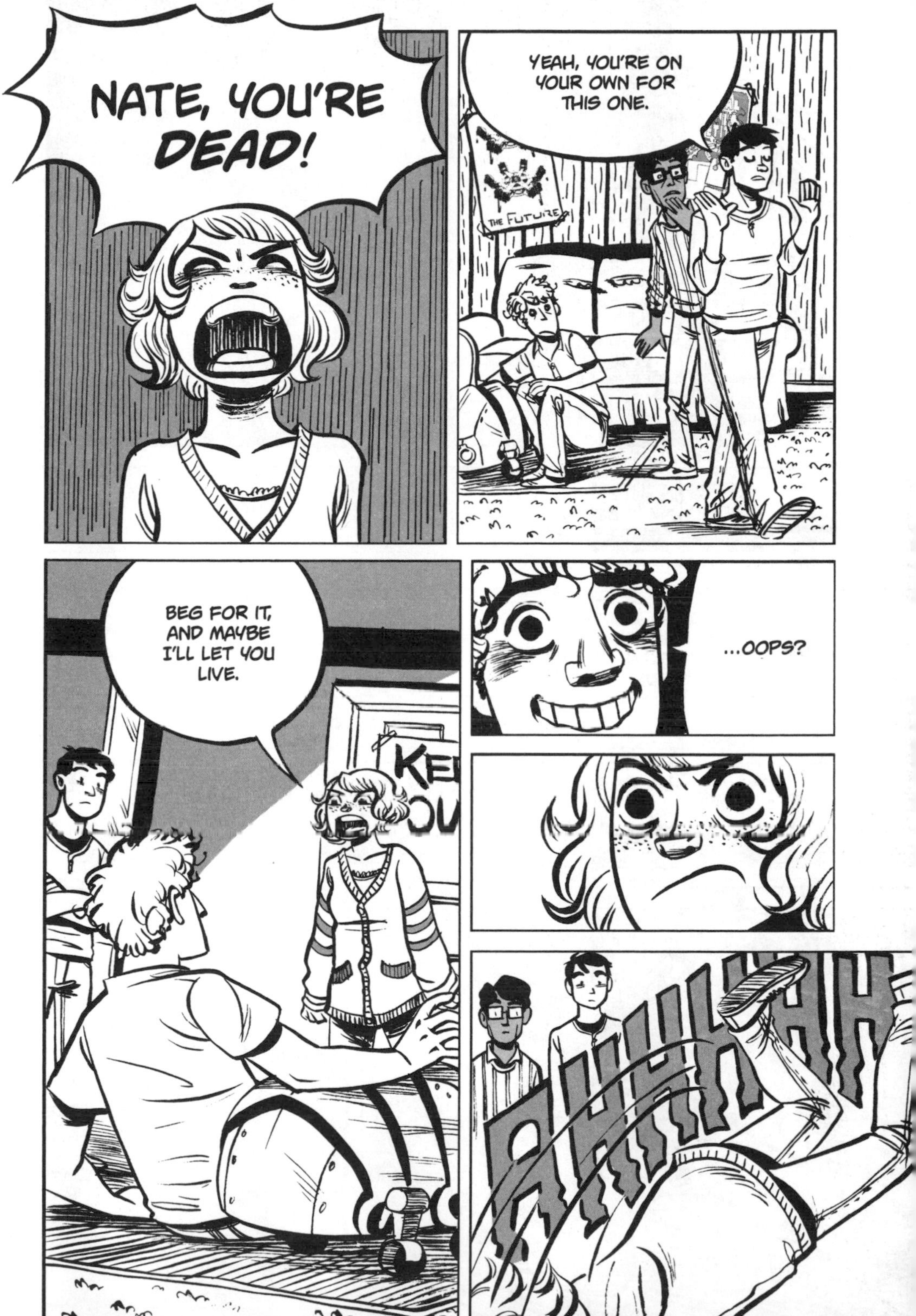
NATE, YOU'RE *DEAD!*
YEAH, YOU'RE ON YOUR OWN FOR THIS ONE.
THE FUTURE
BEG FOR IT, AND MAYBE I'LL LET YOU LIVE.
...OOPS?

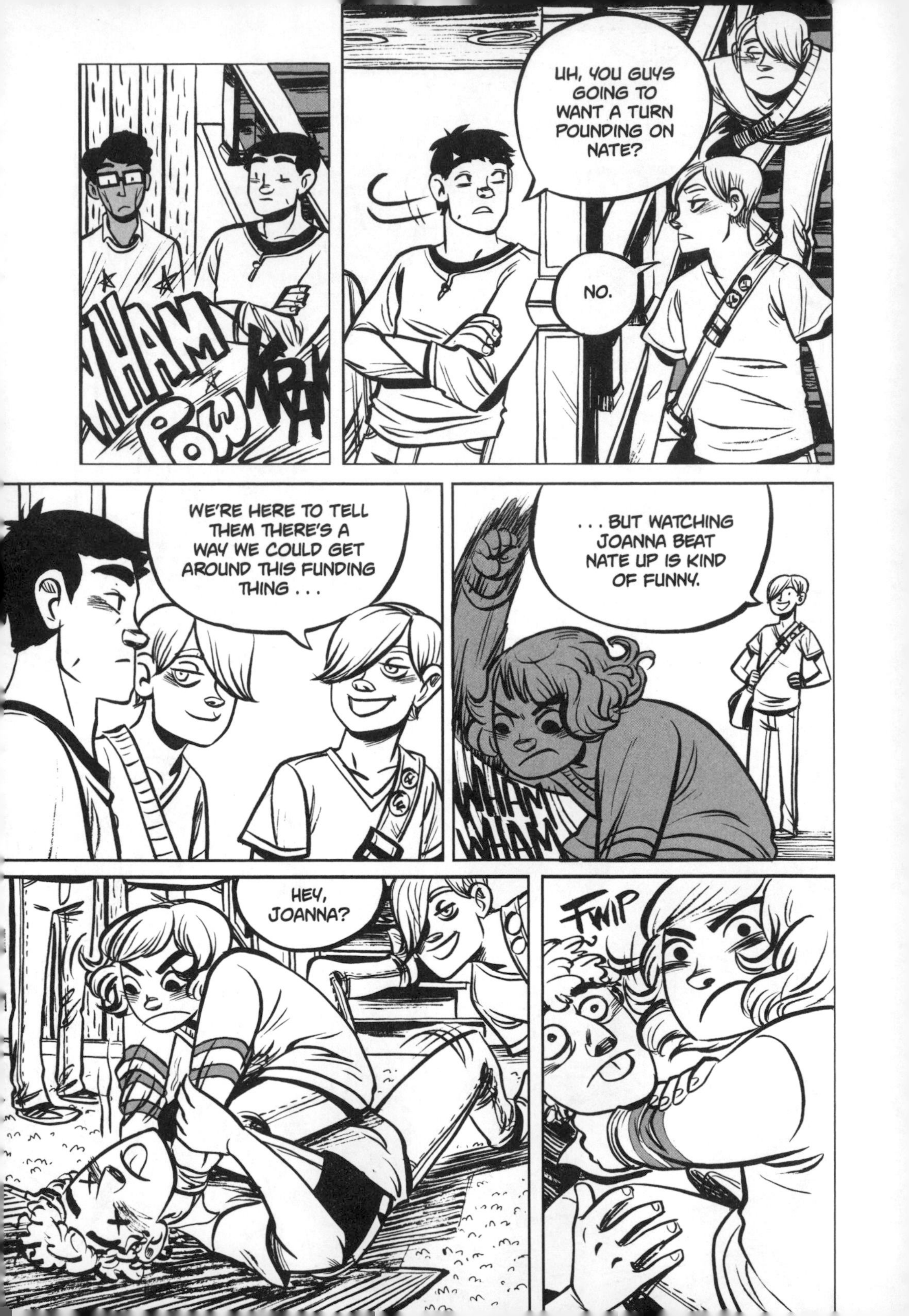
WHAM
POW
KRAK
UH, YOU GUYS GOING TO WANT A TURN POUNDING ON NATE?
NO.
WE'RE HERE TO TELL THEM THERE'S A WAY WE COULD GET AROUND THIS FUNDING THING . . .
. . . BUT WATCHING JOANNA BEAT NATE UP IS KIND OF FUNNY.
WHAM
WHAM
HEY, JOANNA?
FWIP

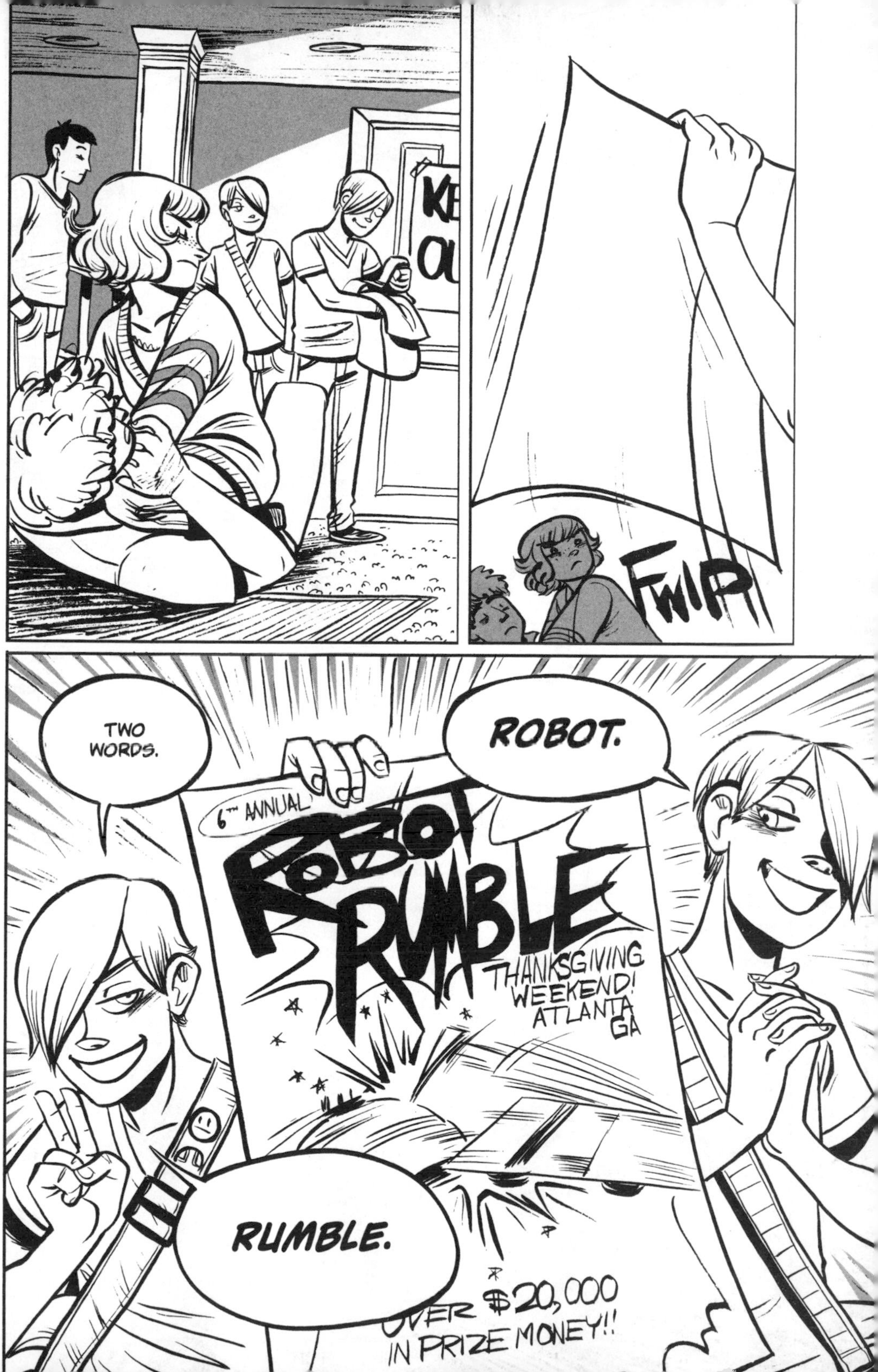
FWIP
TWO WORDS.
ROBOT.
6TH ANNUAL
ROBOT RUMBLE
THANKSGIVING WEEKEND! ATLANTA GA
RUMBLE.
OVER $20,000 IN PRIZE MONEY!!

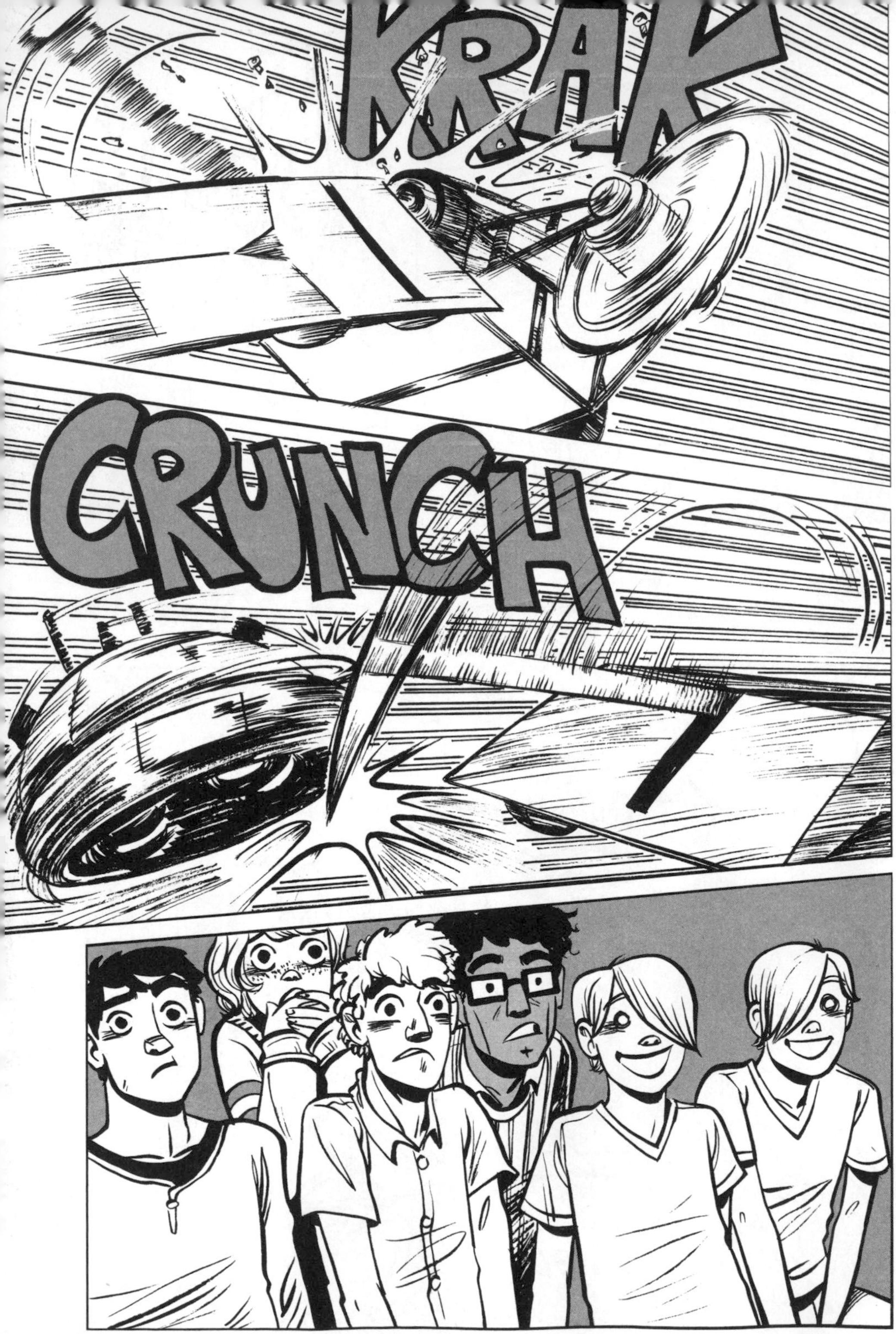
KRAK
CRUNCH

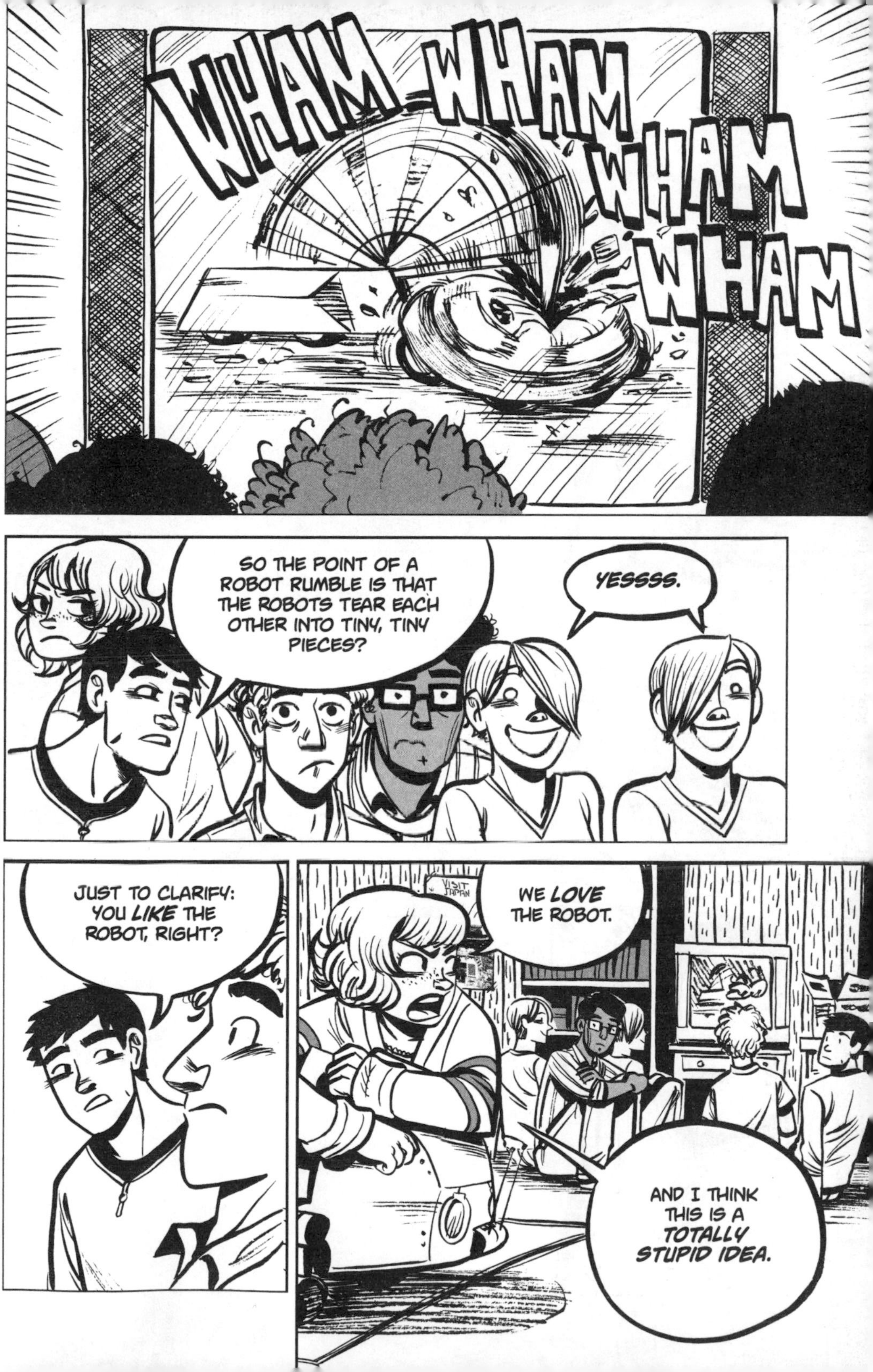
WHAM WHAM WHAM WHAM
SO THE POINT OF A ROBOT RUMBLE IS THAT THE ROBOTS TEAR EACH OTHER INTO TINY, TINY PIECES?
YESSSS.
JUST TO CLARIFY: YOU *LIKE* THE ROBOT, RIGHT?
VISIT JAPAN
WE *LOVE* THE ROBOT.
AND I THINK THIS IS A *TOTALLY STUPID IDEA.*

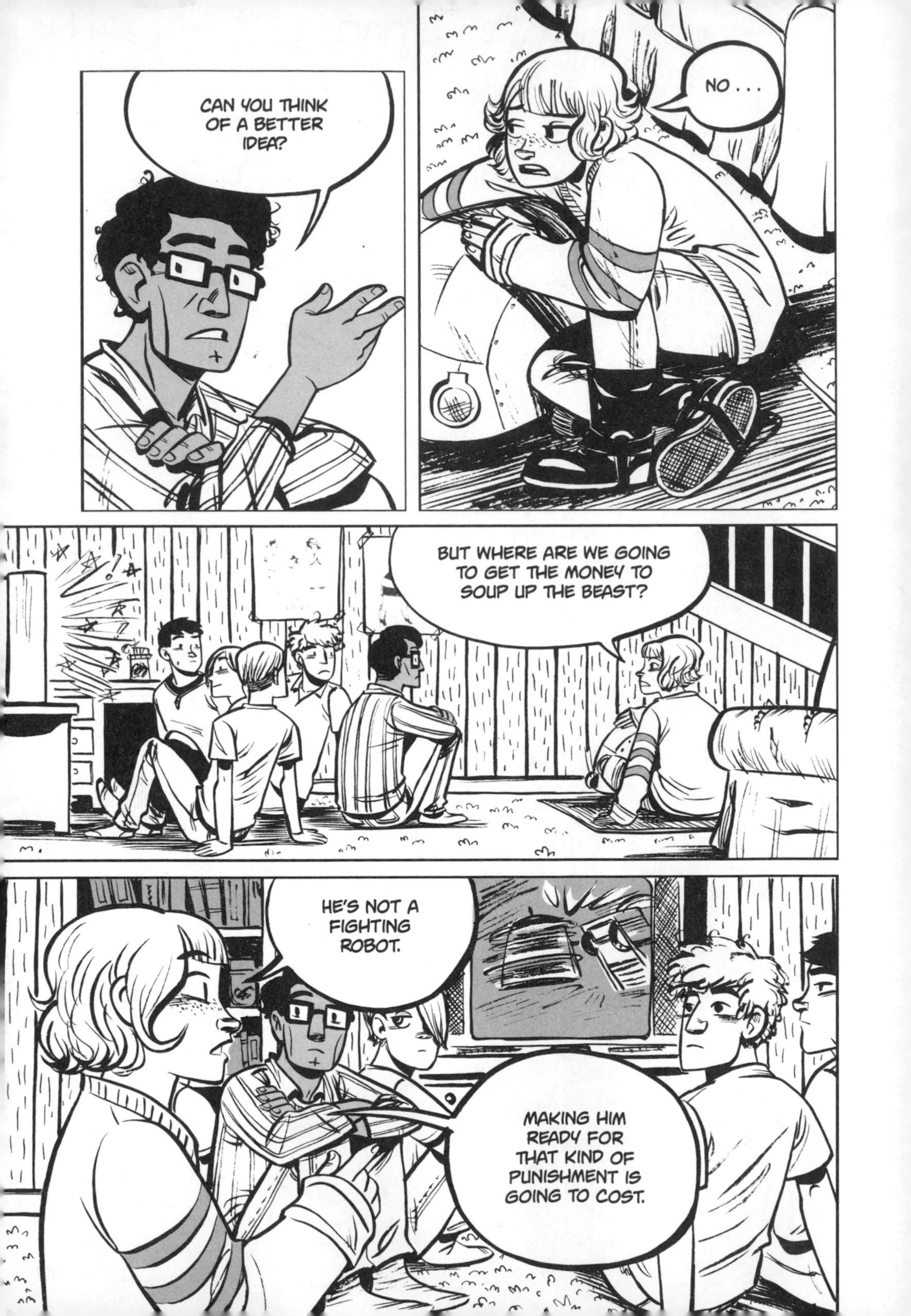
CAN YOU THINK OF A BETTER IDEA?
NO . . .
BUT WHERE ARE WE GOING TO GET THE MONEY TO SOUP UP THE BEAST?
HE'S NOT A FIGHTING ROBOT.
MAKING HIM READY FOR THAT KIND OF PUNISHMENT IS GOING TO COST.

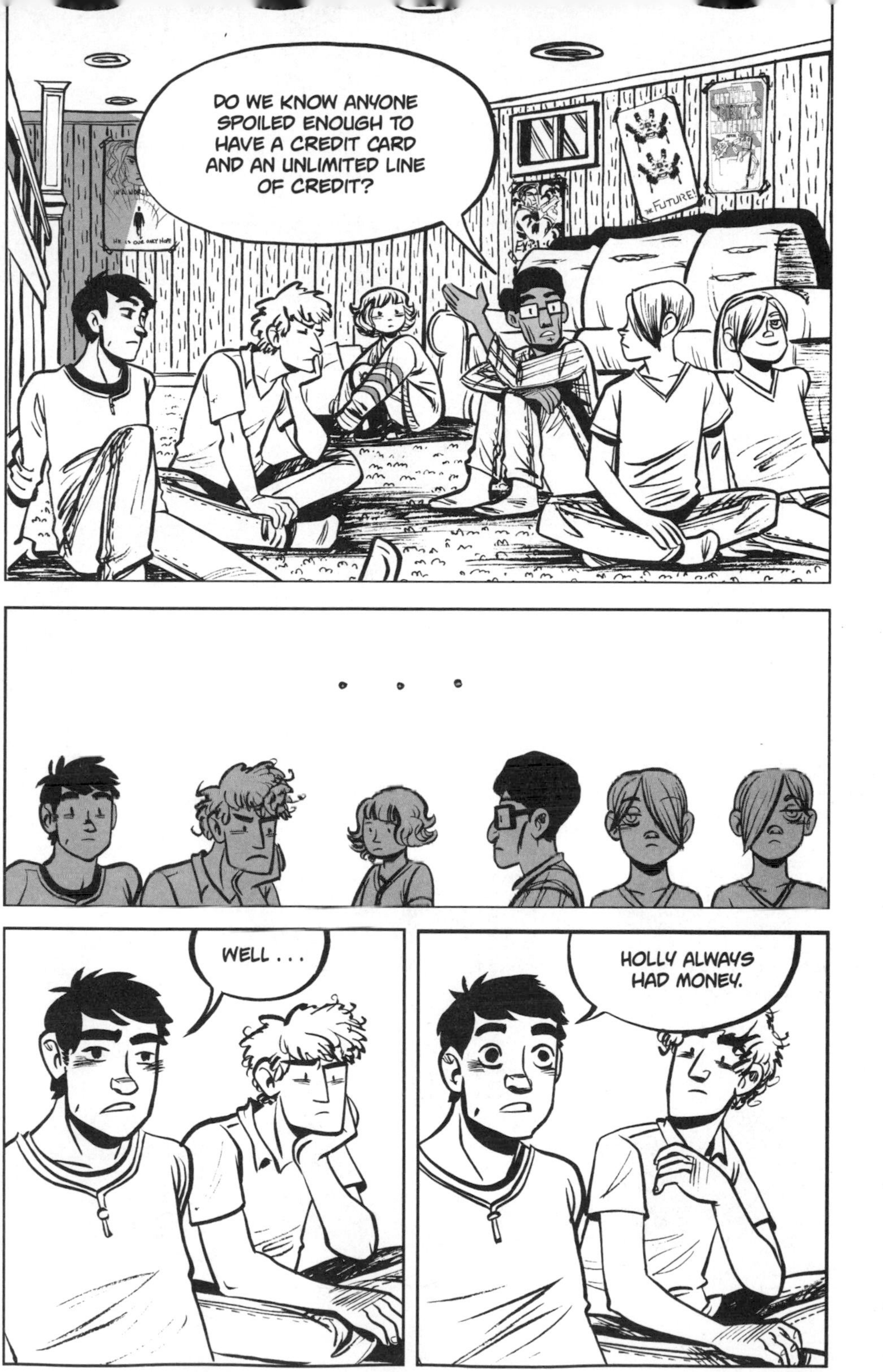
DO WE KNOW ANYONE SPOILED ENOUGH TO HAVE A CREDIT CARD AND AN UNLIMITED LINE OF CREDIT?
. . .
WELL . . .
HOLLY ALWAYS HAD MONEY.

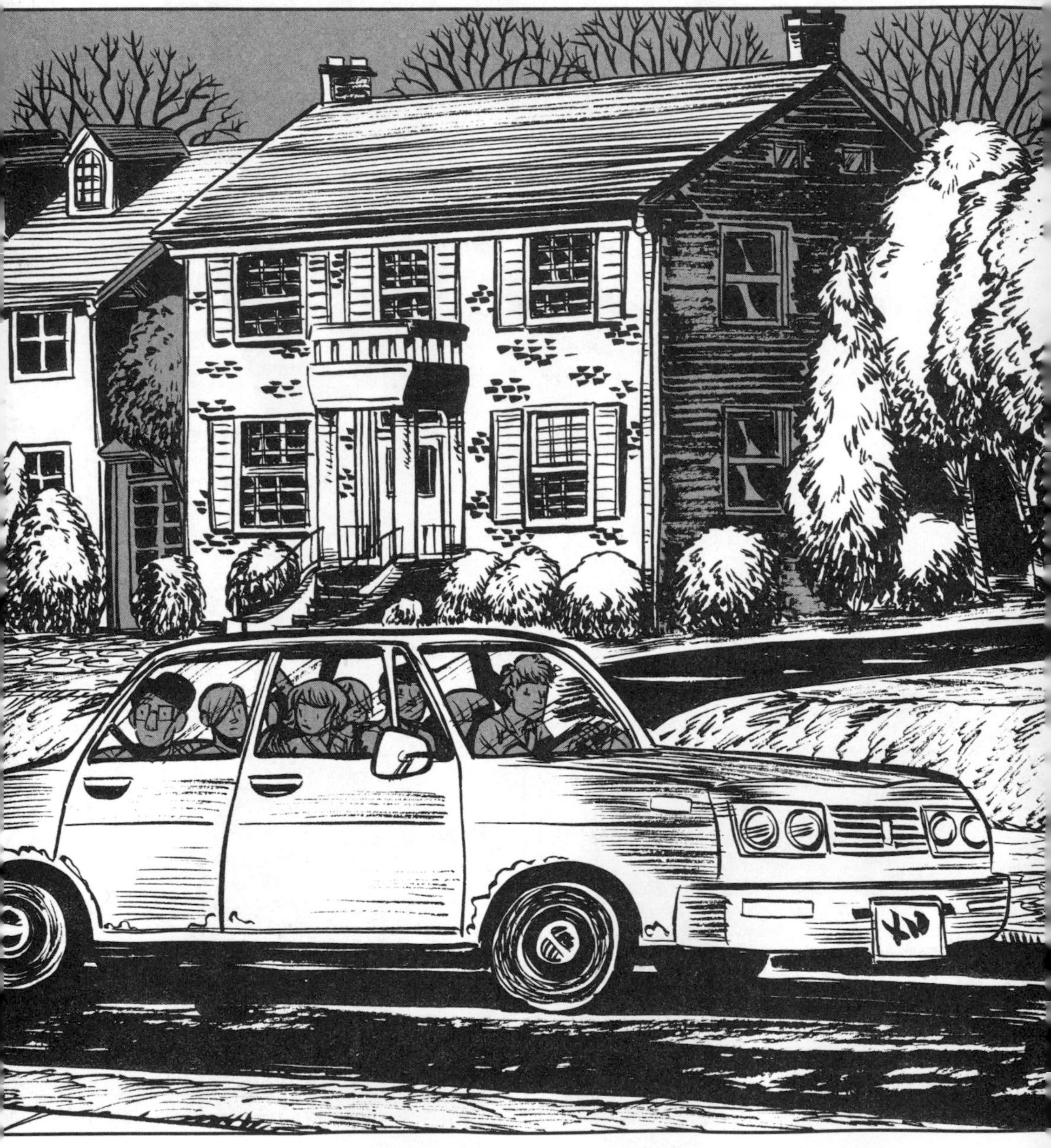

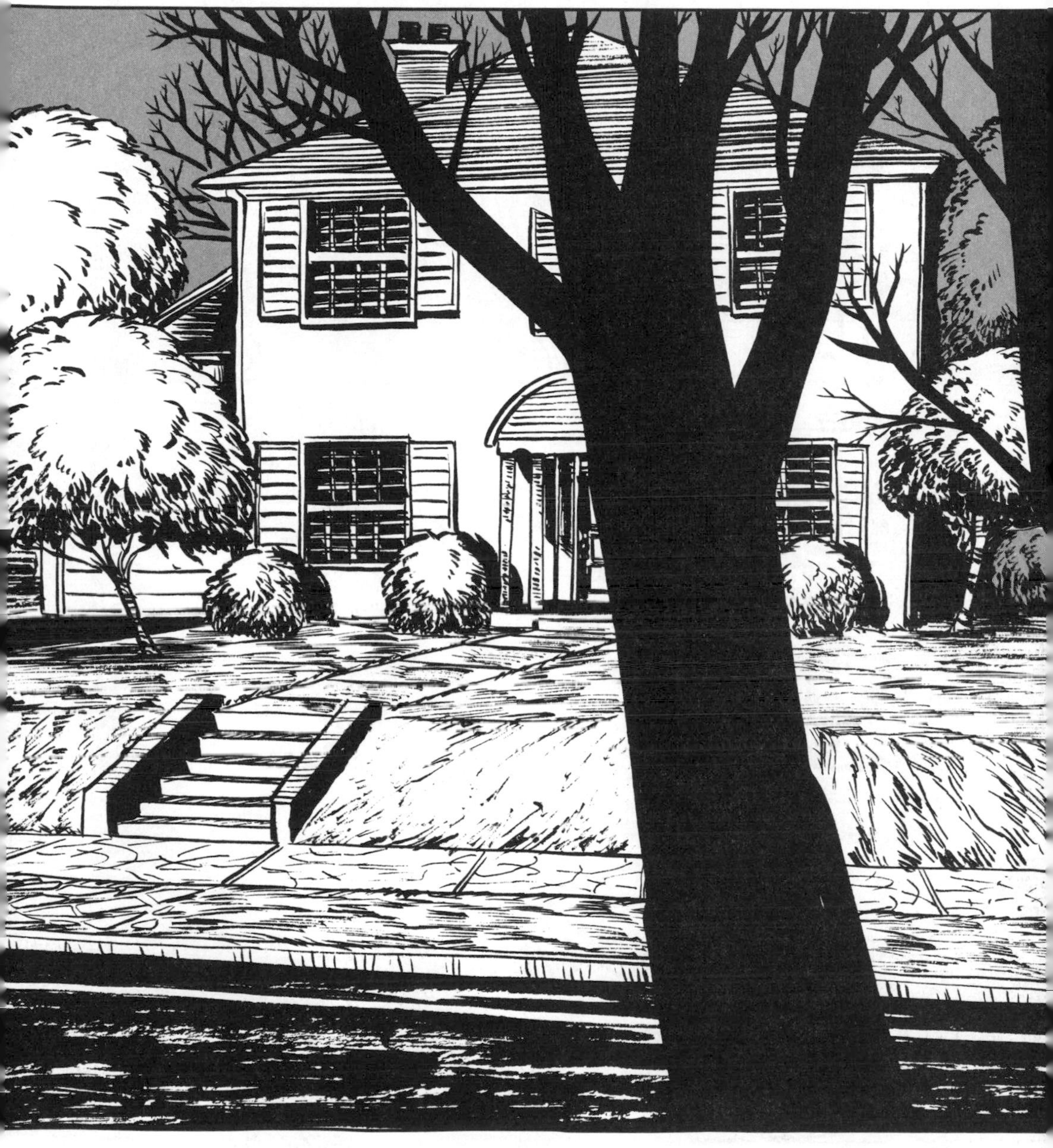

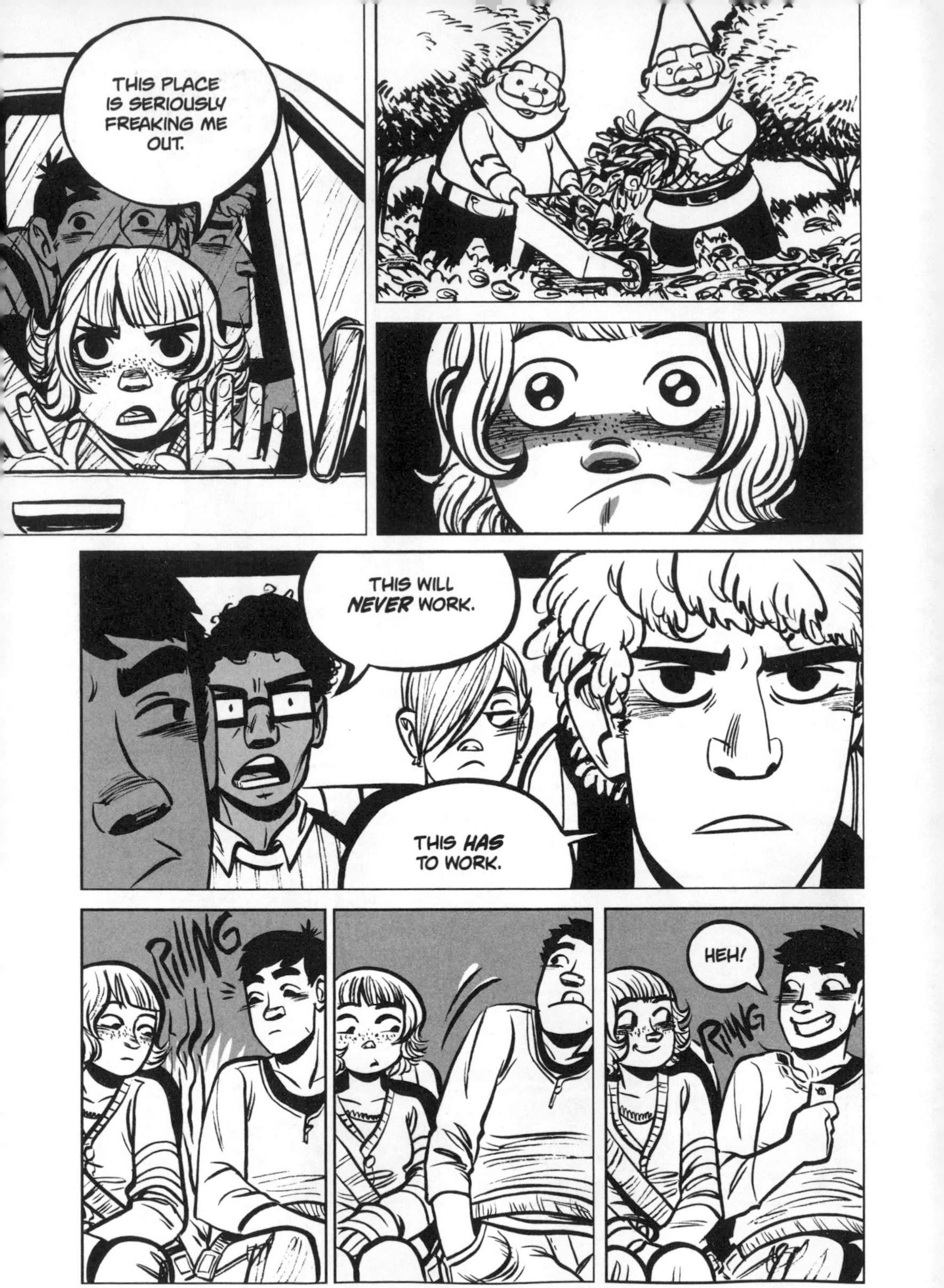
THIS PLACE IS SERIOUSLY FREAKING ME OUT.
THIS WILL NEVER WORK.
THIS HAS TO WORK.
RIIING
HEH!
RIIING

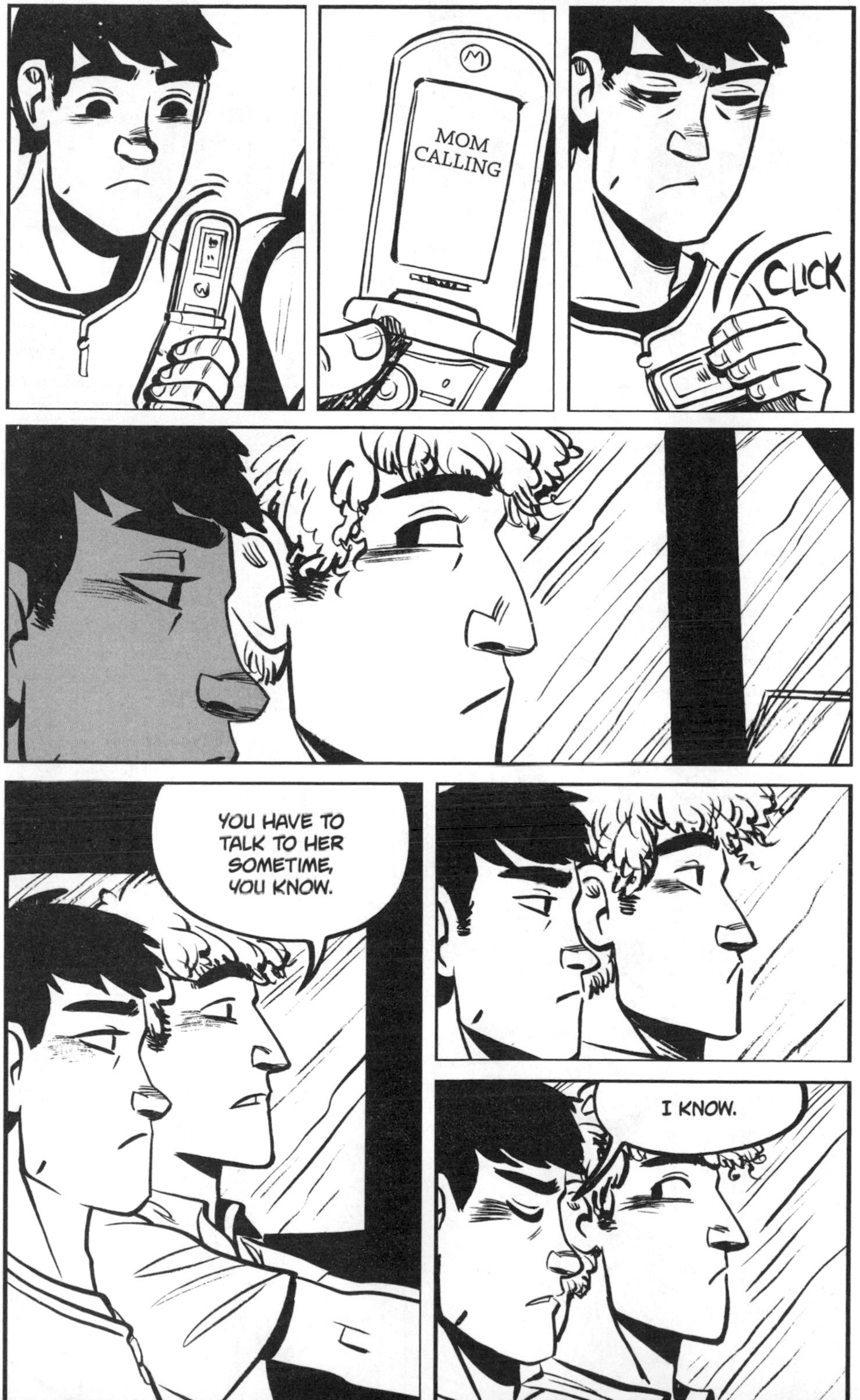
MOM CALLING
CLICK
YOU HAVE TO TALK TO HER SOMETIME, YOU KNOW.
I KNOW.

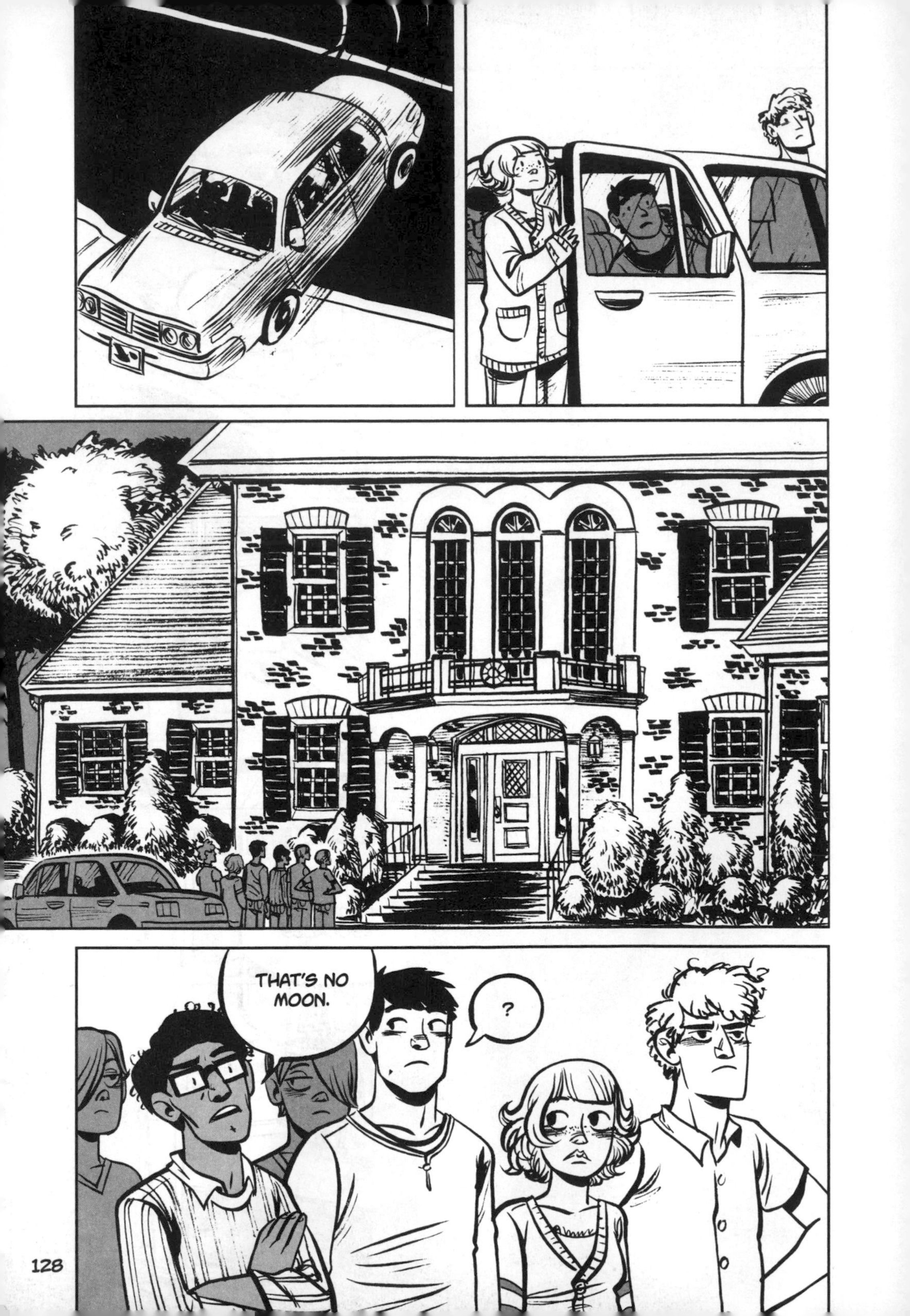
THAT'S NO MOON.
?

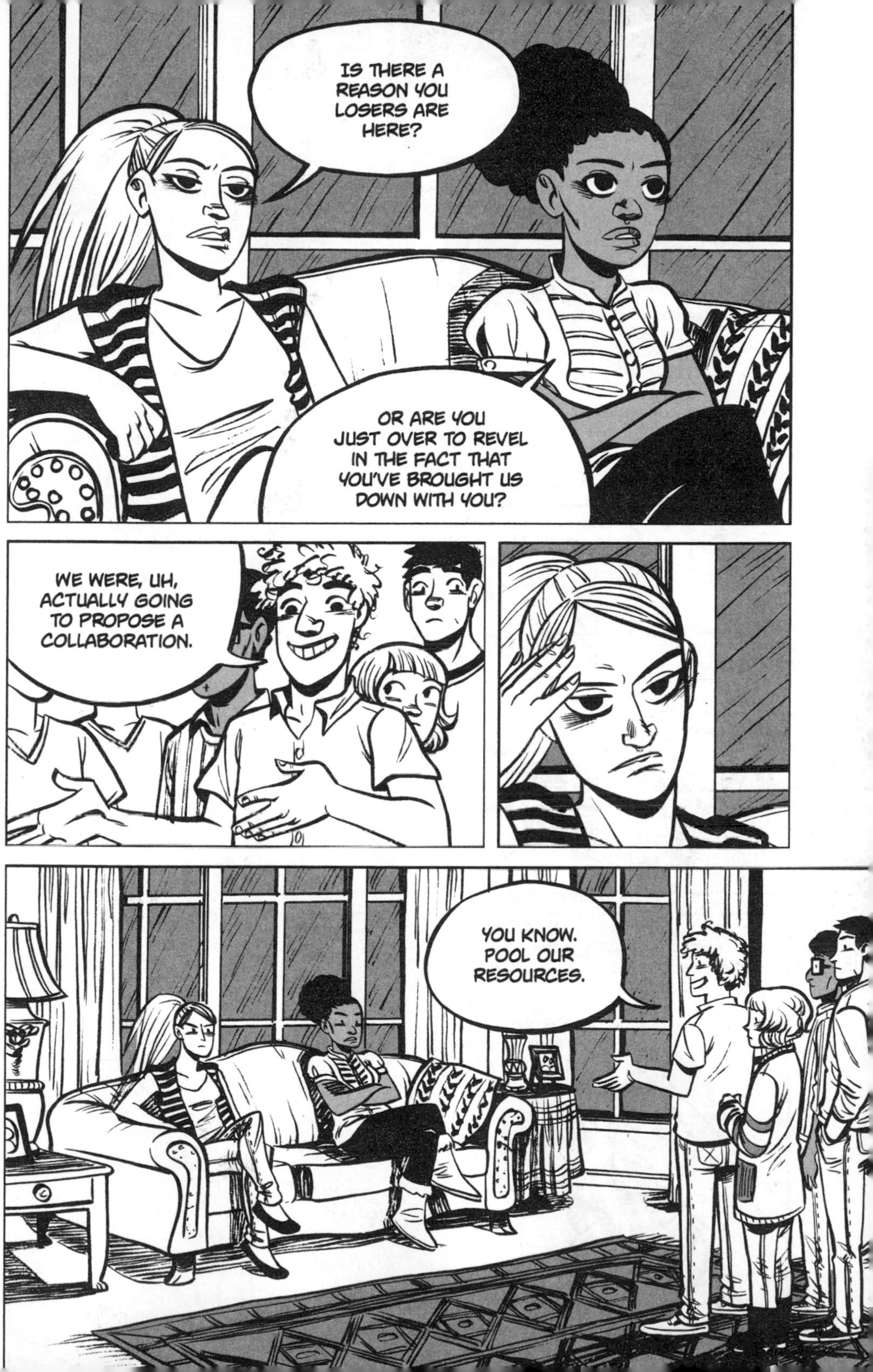
IS THERE A REASON YOU LOSERS ARE HERE?
OR ARE YOU JUST OVER TO REVEL IN THE FACT THAT YOU'VE BROUGHT US DOWN WITH YOU?
WE WERE, UH, ACTUALLY GOING TO PROPOSE A COLLABORATION.
YOU KNOW. POOL OUR RESOURCES.

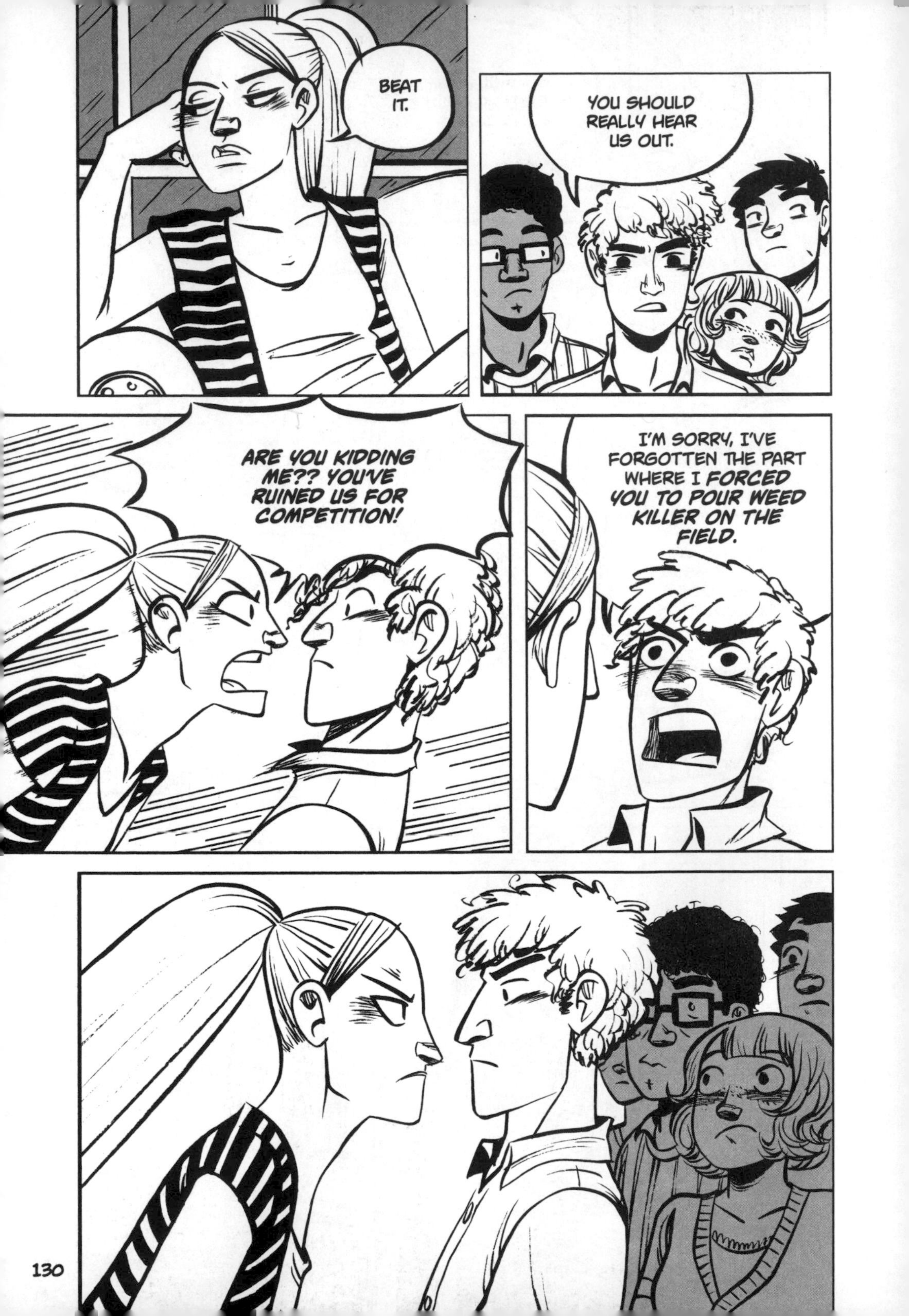
BEAT IT.
YOU SHOULD REALLY HEAR US OUT.
ARE YOU KIDDING ME?? YOU'VE RUINED US FOR COMPETITION!
I'M SORRY, I'VE FORGOTTEN THE PART WHERE I FORCED YOU TO POUR WEED KILLER ON THE FIELD.

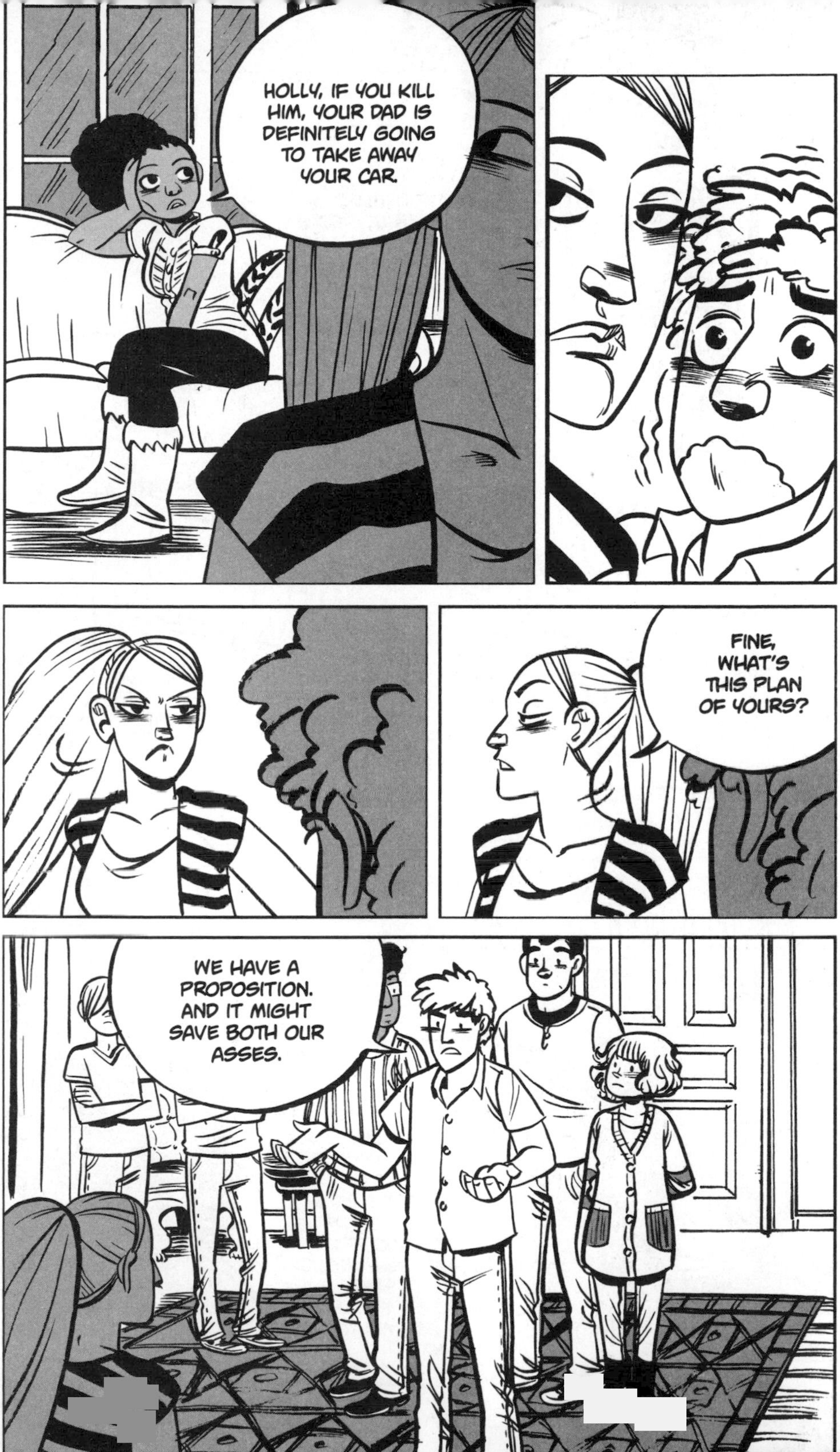
HOLLY, IF YOU KILL HIM, YOUR DAD IS DEFINITELY GOING TO TAKE AWAY YOUR CAR.
FINE, WHAT'S THIS PLAN OF YOURS?
WE HAVE A PROPOSITION. AND IT MIGHT SAVE BOTH OUR ASSES.

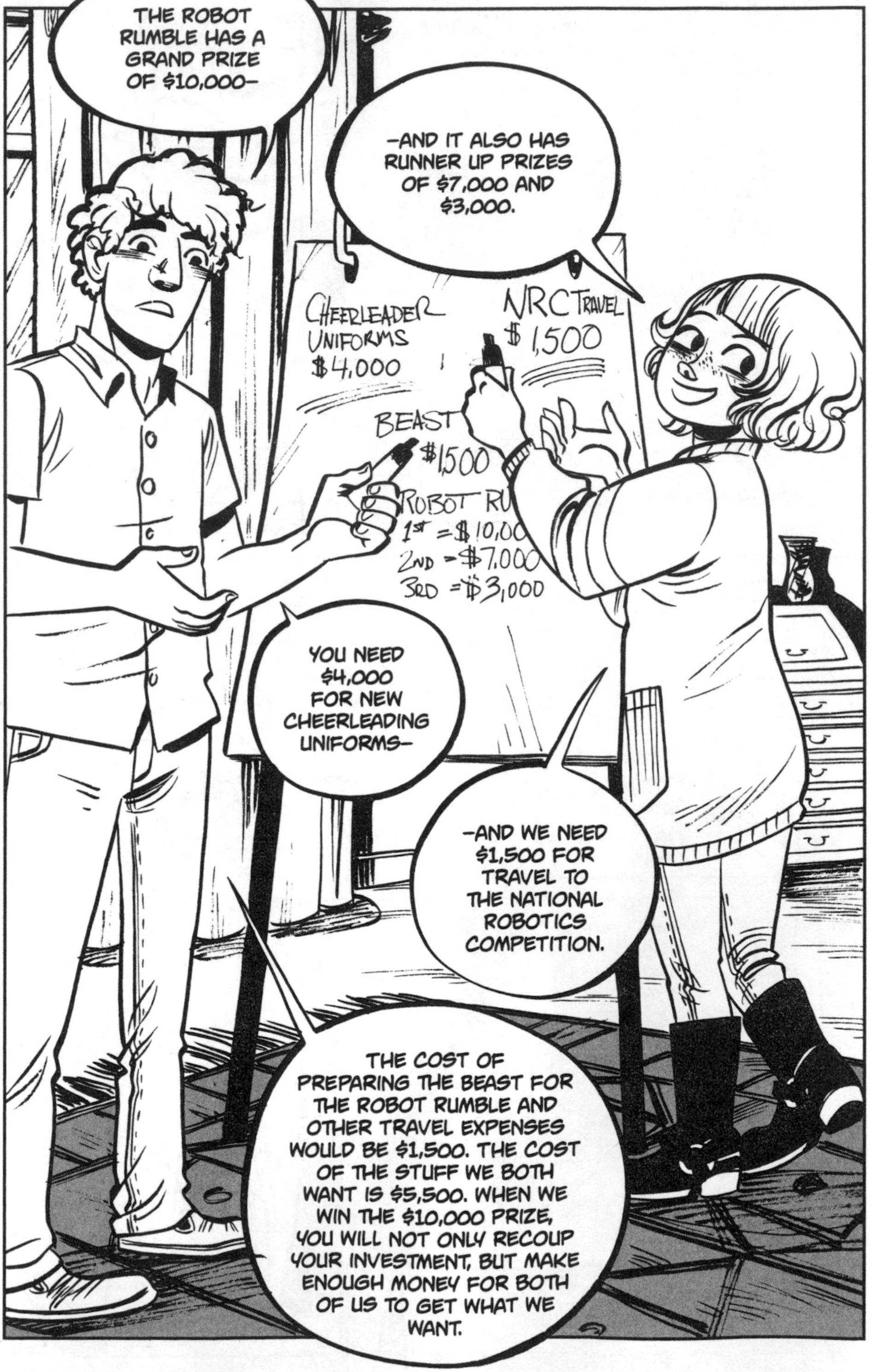
THE ROBOT RUMBLE HAS A GRAND PRIZE OF $10,000–
–AND IT ALSO HAS RUNNER UP PRIZES OF $7,000 AND $3,000.
CHEERLEADER UNIFORMS $4,000
NRC TRAVEL $1,500
BEAST $1500
ROBOT RU
1ST = $10,00
2ND = $7,000
3RD = $3,000
YOU NEED $4,000 FOR NEW CHEERLEADING UNIFORMS–
–AND WE NEED $1,500 FOR TRAVEL TO THE NATIONAL ROBOTICS COMPETITION.
THE COST OF PREPARING THE BEAST FOR THE ROBOT RUMBLE AND OTHER TRAVEL EXPENSES WOULD BE $1,500. THE COST OF THE STUFF WE BOTH WANT IS $5,500. WHEN WE WIN THE $10,000 PRIZE, YOU WILL NOT ONLY RECOUP YOUR INVESTMENT, BUT MAKE ENOUGH MONEY FOR BOTH OF US TO GET WHAT WE WANT.

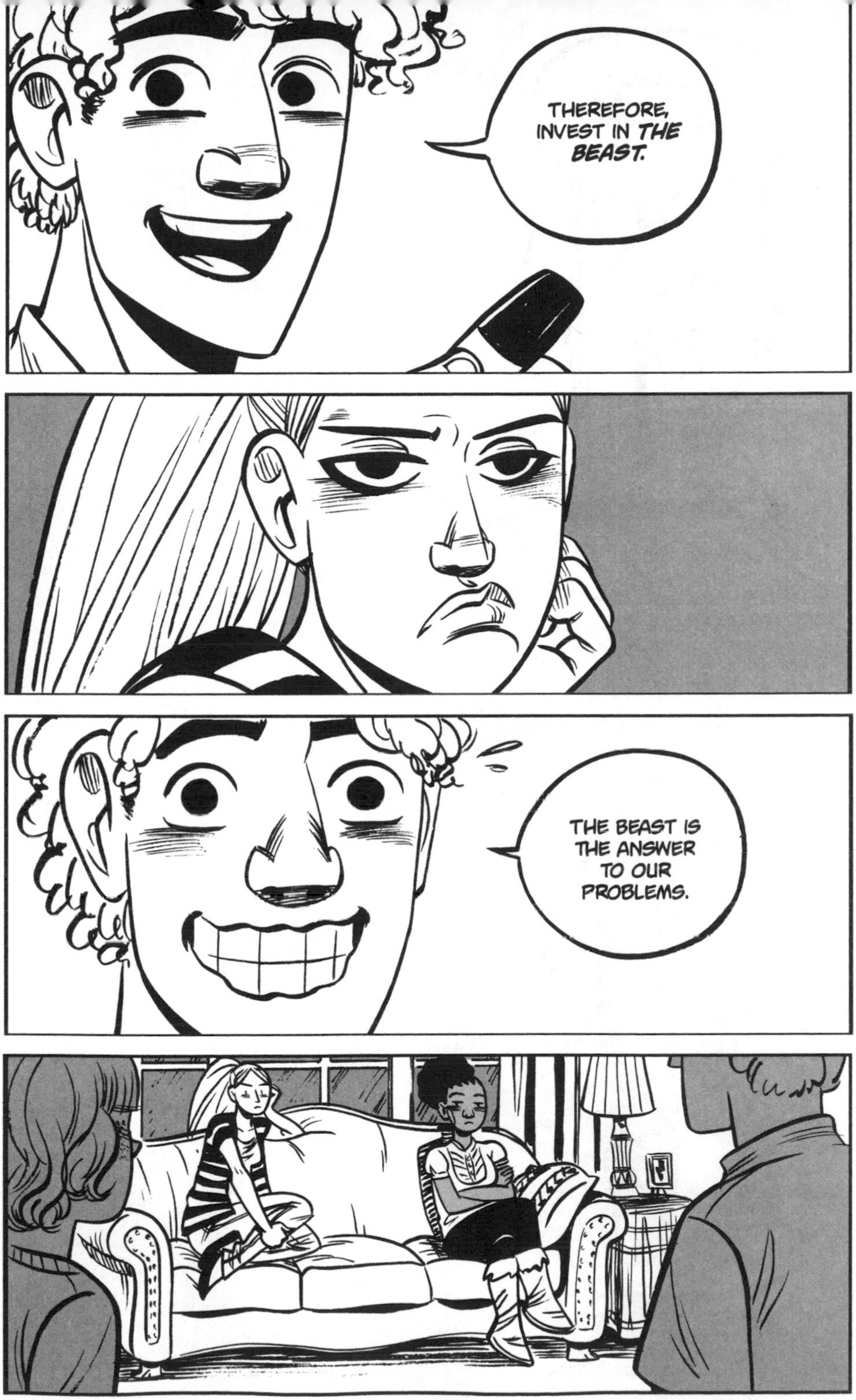
THEREFORE, INVEST IN *THE BEAST.*
THE BEAST IS THE ANSWER TO OUR PROBLEMS.

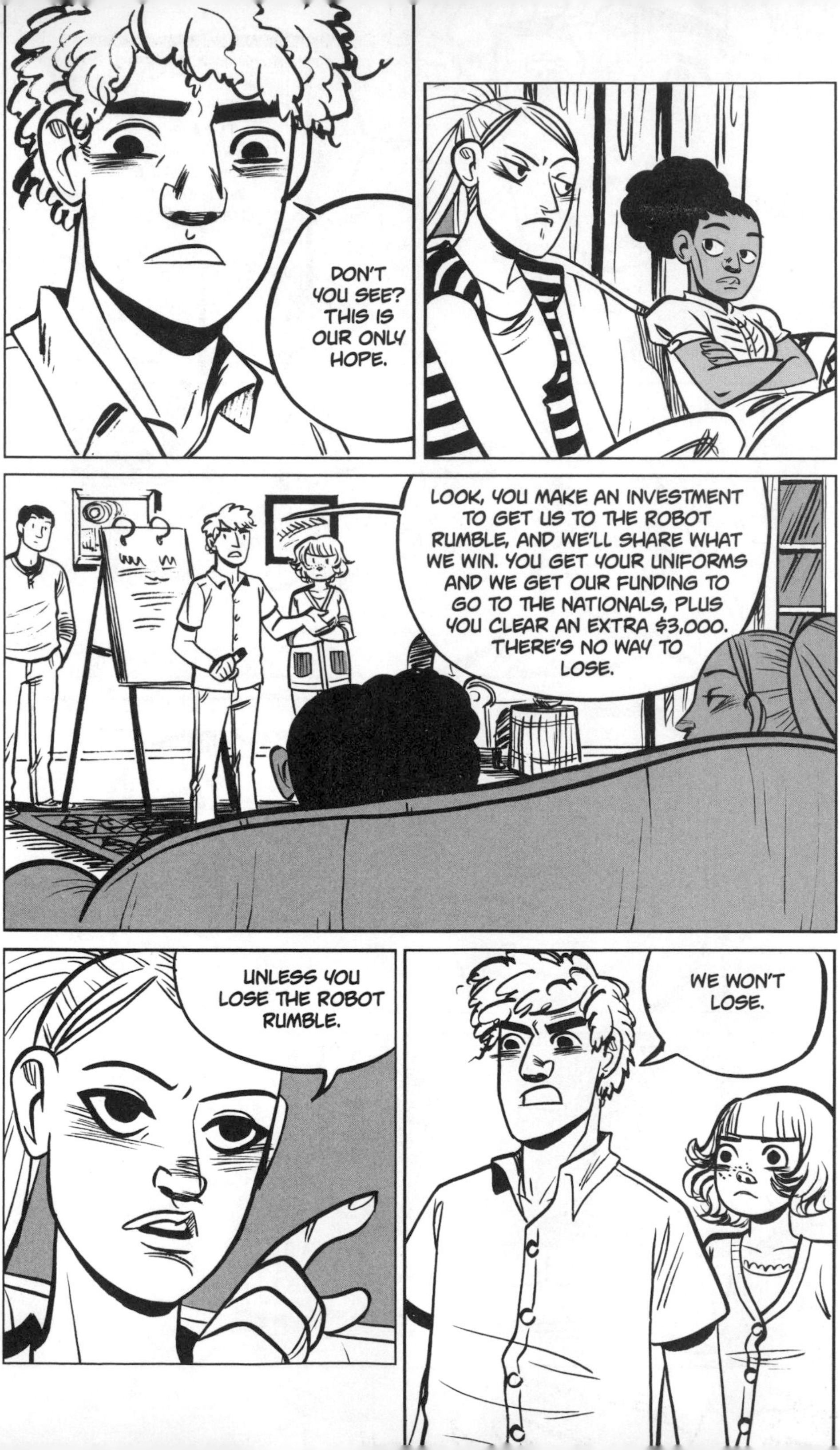
DON'T YOU SEE? THIS IS OUR ONLY HOPE.
LOOK, YOU MAKE AN INVESTMENT TO GET US TO THE ROBOT RUMBLE, AND WE'LL SHARE WHAT WE WIN. YOU GET YOUR UNIFORMS AND WE GET OUR FUNDING TO GO TO THE NATIONALS, PLUS YOU CLEAR AN EXTRA $3,000. THERE'S NO WAY TO LOSE.
UNLESS YOU LOSE THE ROBOT RUMBLE.
WE WON'T LOSE.

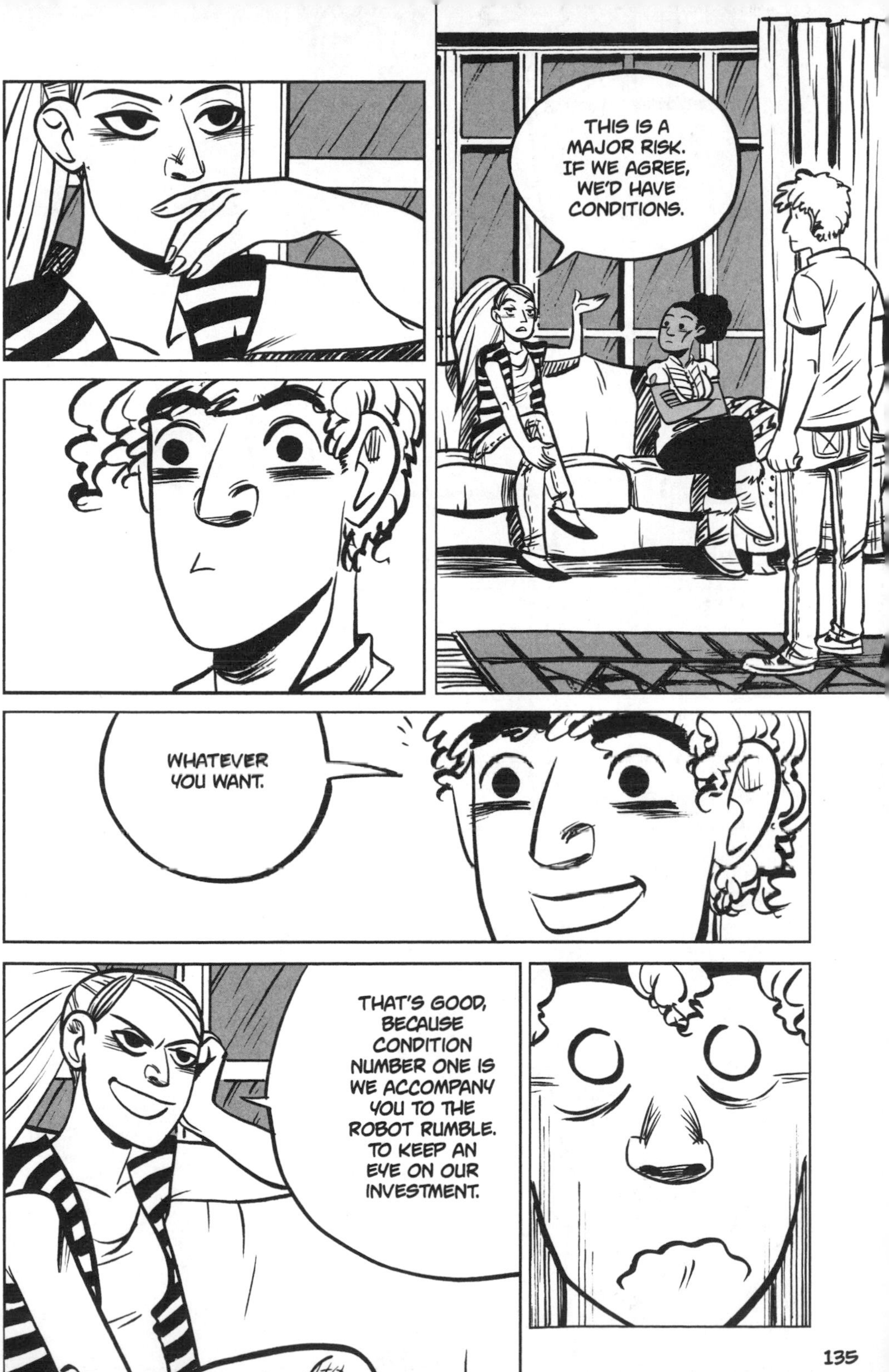
THIS IS A MAJOR RISK. IF WE AGREE, WE'D HAVE CONDITIONS.
WHATEVER YOU WANT.
THAT'S GOOD, BECAUSE CONDITION NUMBER ONE IS WE ACCOMPANY YOU TO THE ROBOT RUMBLE. TO KEEP AN EYE ON OUR INVESTMENT.

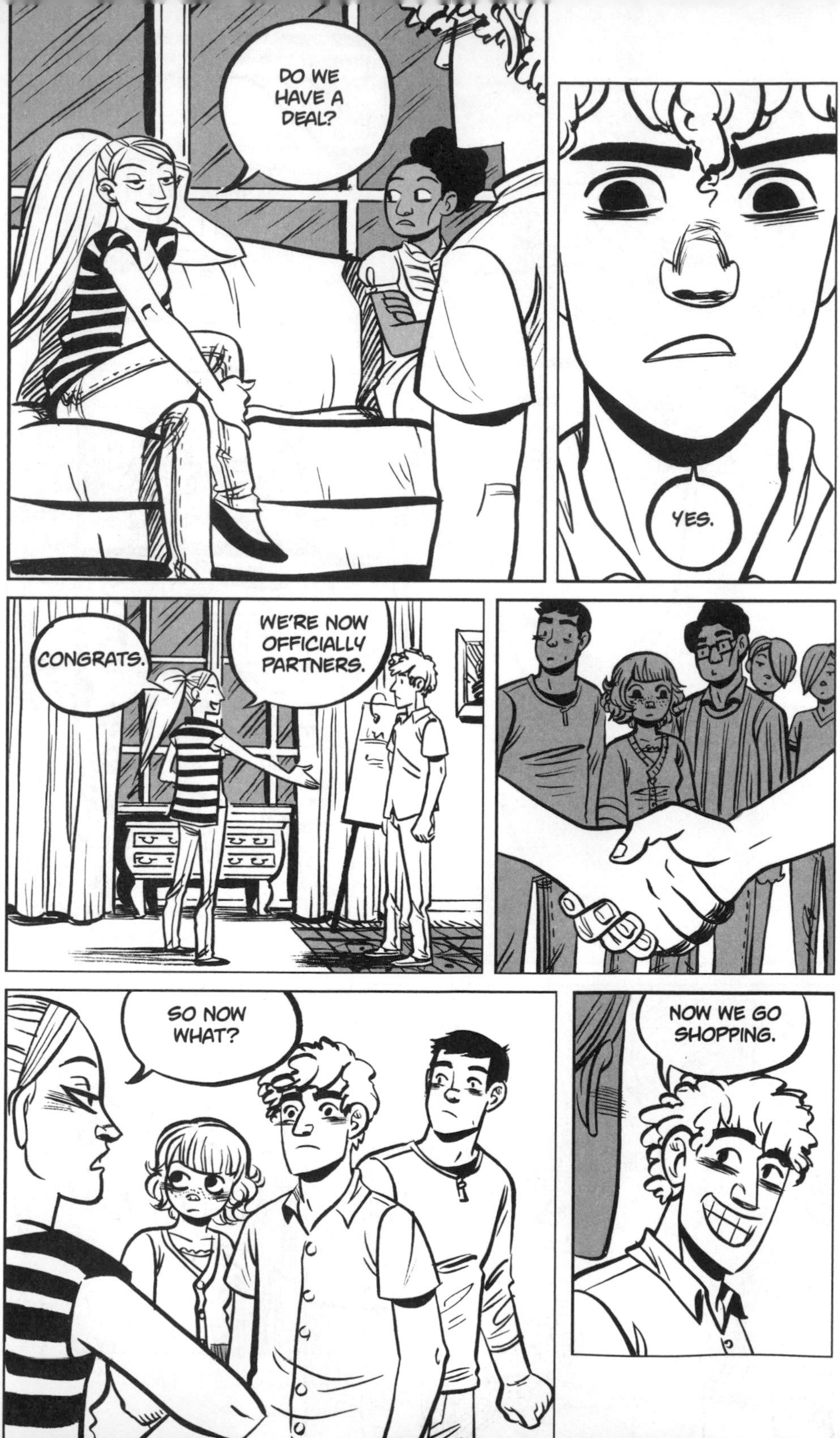
DO WE HAVE A DEAL?
YES.
CONGRATS.
WE'RE NOW OFFICIALLY PARTNERS.
SO NOW WHAT?
NOW WE GO SHOPPING.

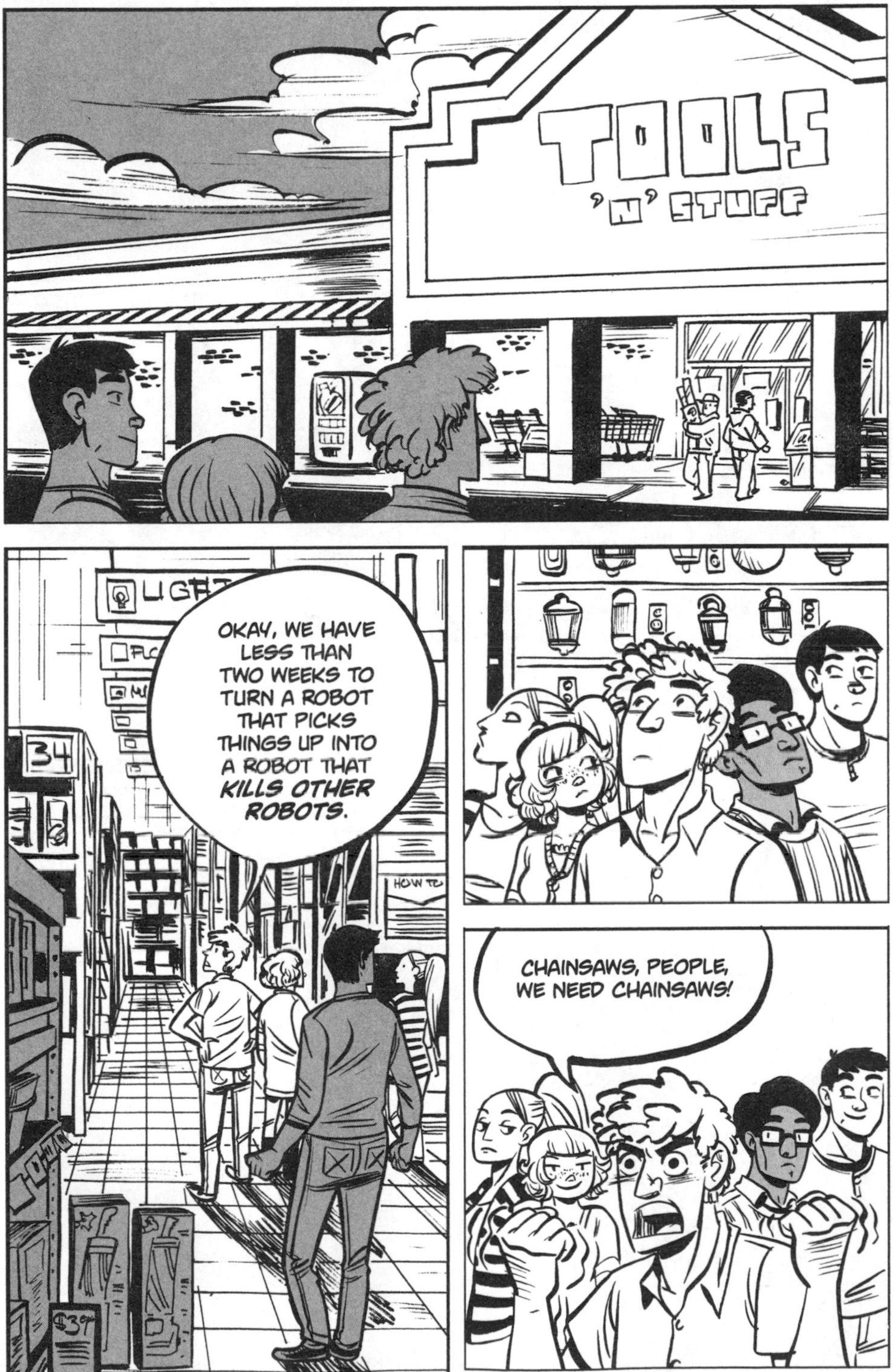
TOOLS 'N' STUFF
OKAY, WE HAVE LESS THAN TWO WEEKS TO TURN A ROBOT THAT PICKS THINGS UP INTO A ROBOT THAT *KILLS OTHER ROBOTS*.
CHAINSAWS, PEOPLE, WE NEED CHAINSAWS!

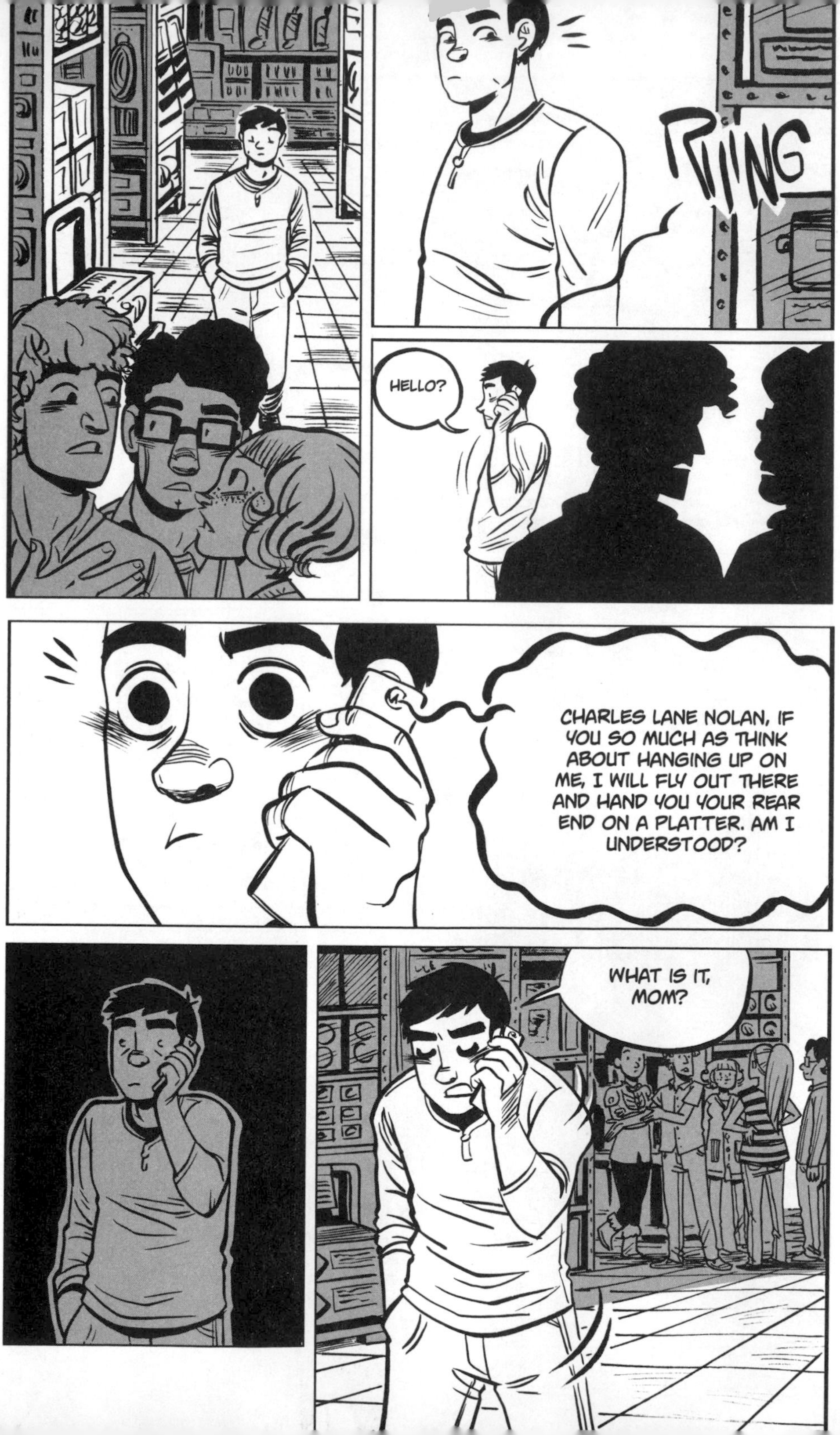
RIIING
HELLO?
CHARLES LANE NOLAN, IF YOU SO MUCH AS THINK ABOUT HANGING UP ON ME, I WILL FLY OUT THERE AND HAND YOU YOUR REAR END ON A PLATTER. AM I UNDERSTOOD?
WHAT IS IT, MOM?

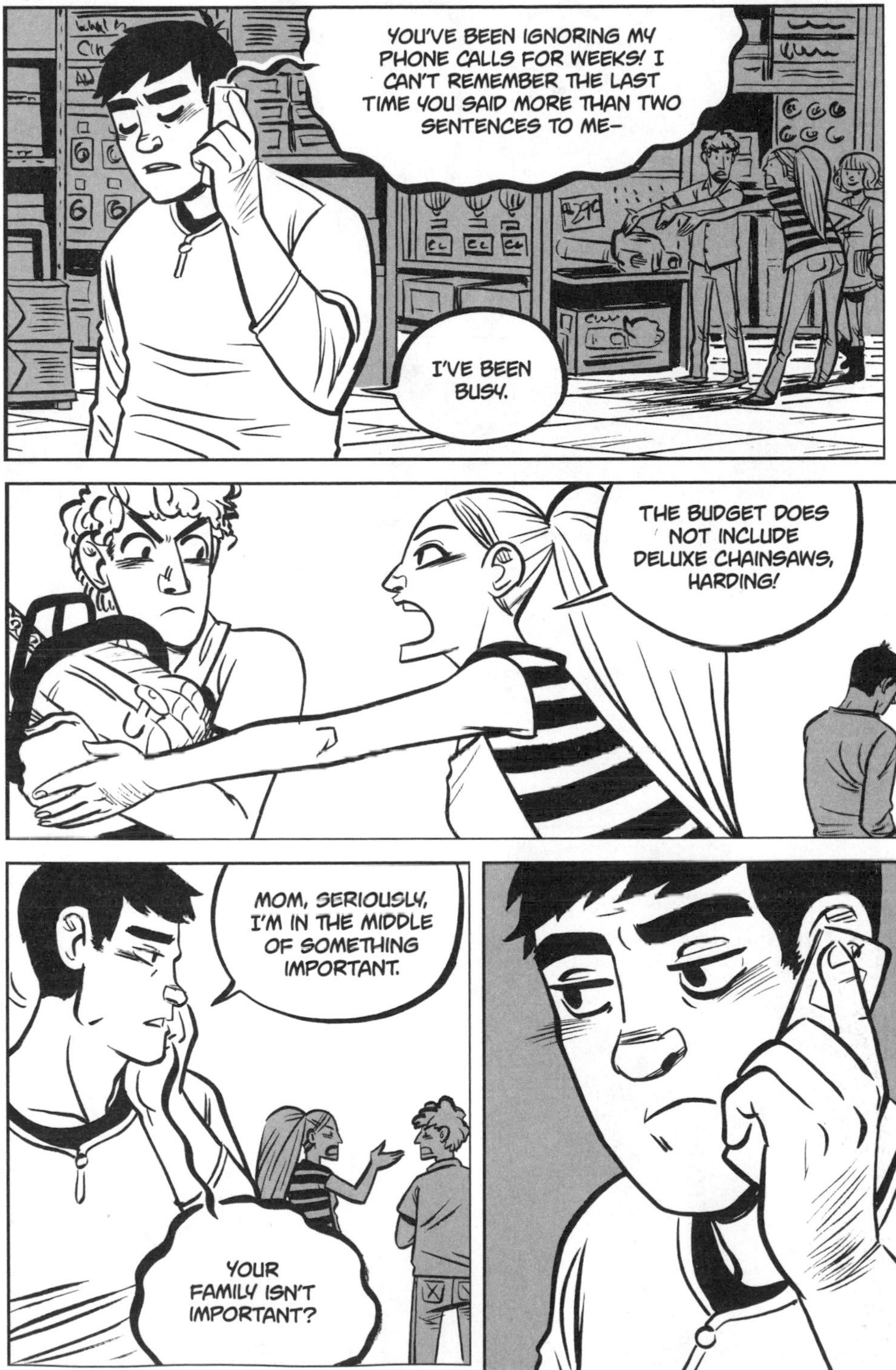
YOU'VE BEEN IGNORING MY PHONE CALLS FOR WEEKS! I CAN'T REMEMBER THE LAST TIME YOU SAID MORE THAN TWO SENTENCES TO ME–
I'VE BEEN BUSY.
THE BUDGET DOES NOT INCLUDE DELUXE CHAINSAWS, HARDING!
MOM, SERIOUSLY, I'M IN THE MIDDLE OF SOMETHING IMPORTANT.
YOUR FAMILY ISN'T IMPORTANT?

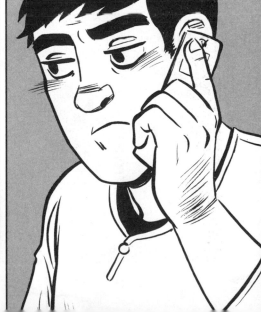

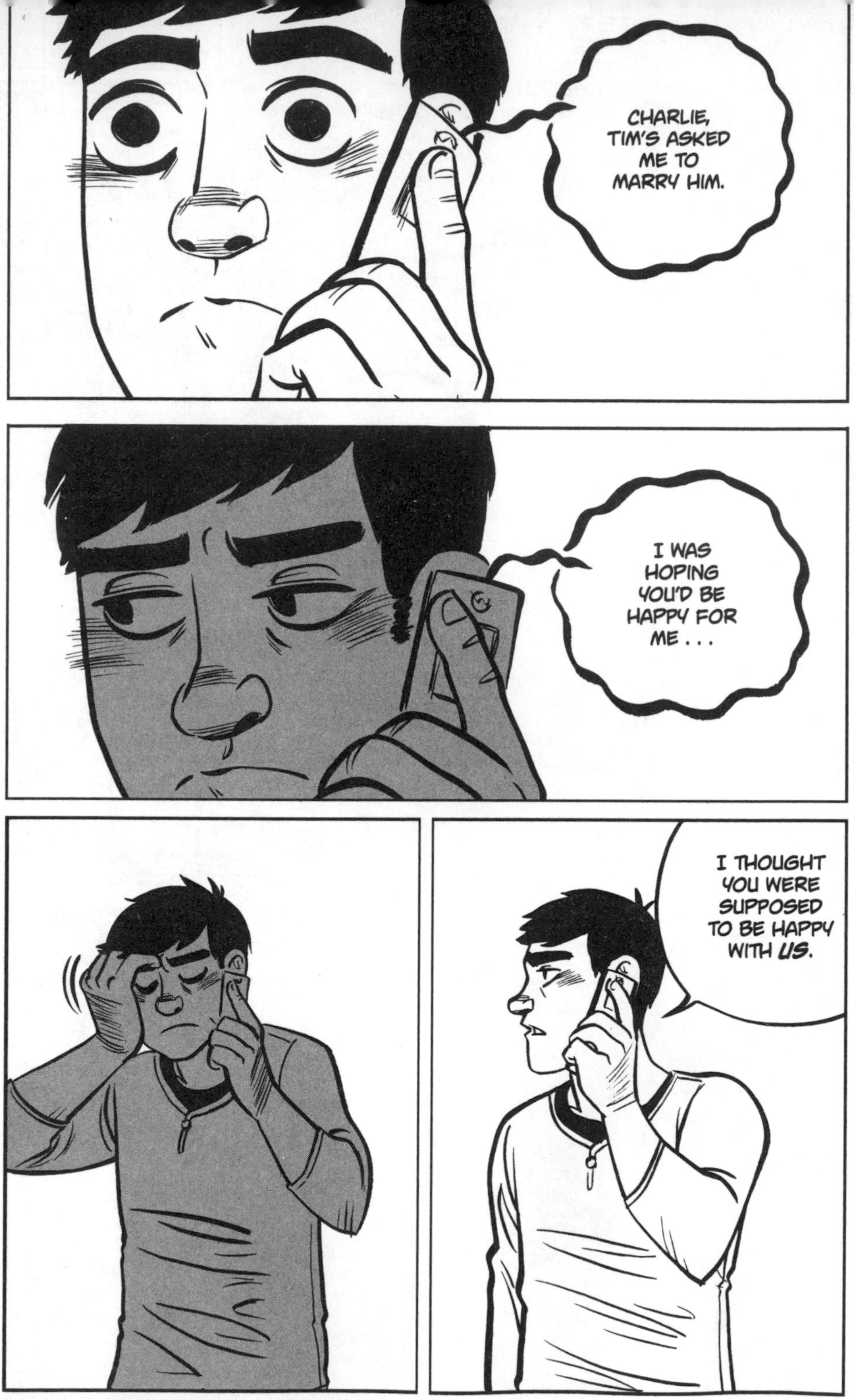
CHARLIE, TIM'S ASKED ME TO MARRY HIM.
I WAS HOPING YOU'D BE HAPPY FOR ME . . .
I THOUGHT YOU WERE SUPPOSED TO BE HAPPY WITH *US*.

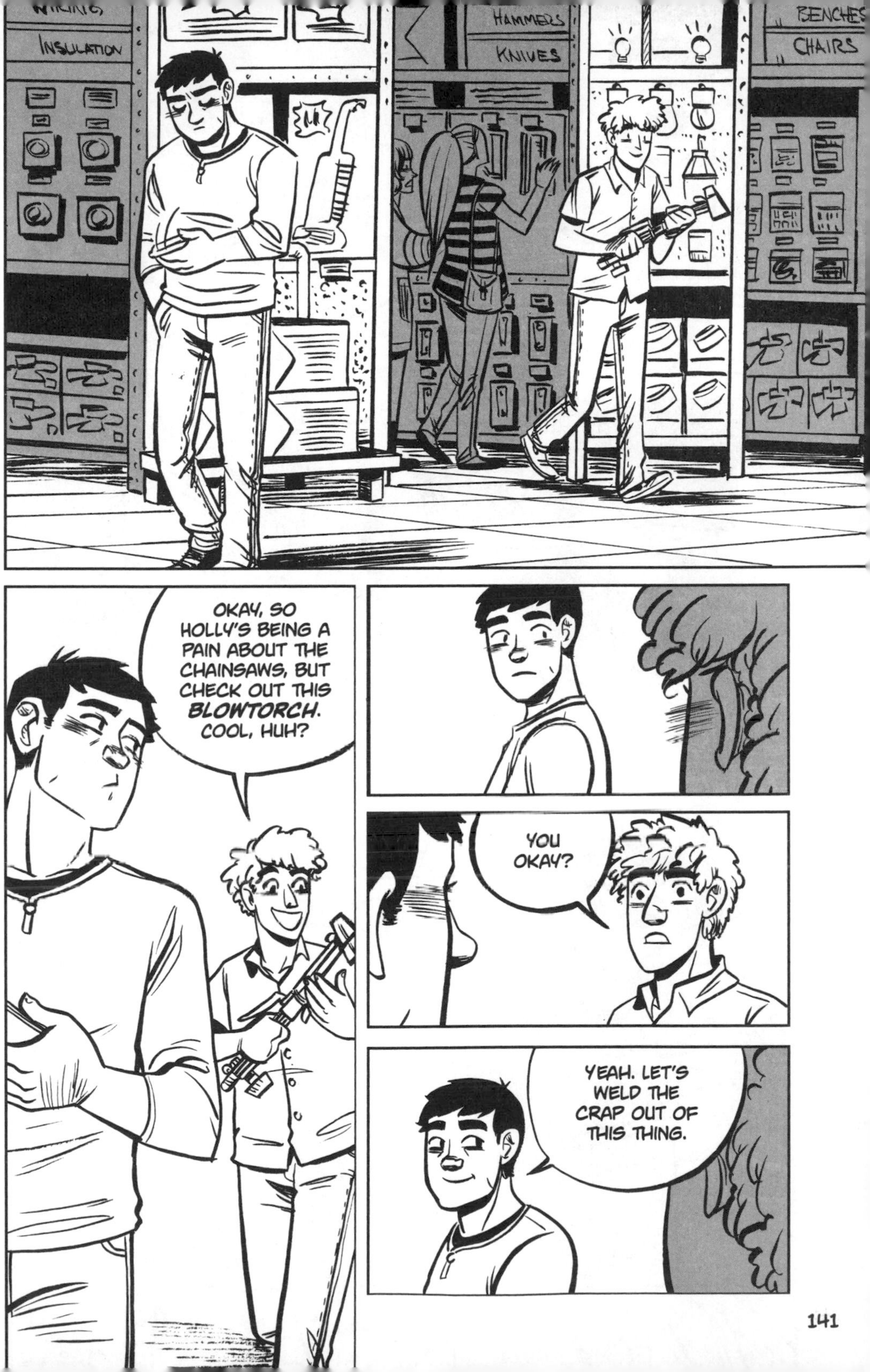
INSULATION
HAMMERS
KNIVES
BENCHES
CHAIRS
OKAY, SO HOLLY'S BEING A PAIN ABOUT THE CHAINSAWS, BUT CHECK OUT THIS **BLOWTORCH**. COOL, HUH?
YOU OKAY?
YEAH. LET'S WELD THE CRAP OUT OF THIS THING.

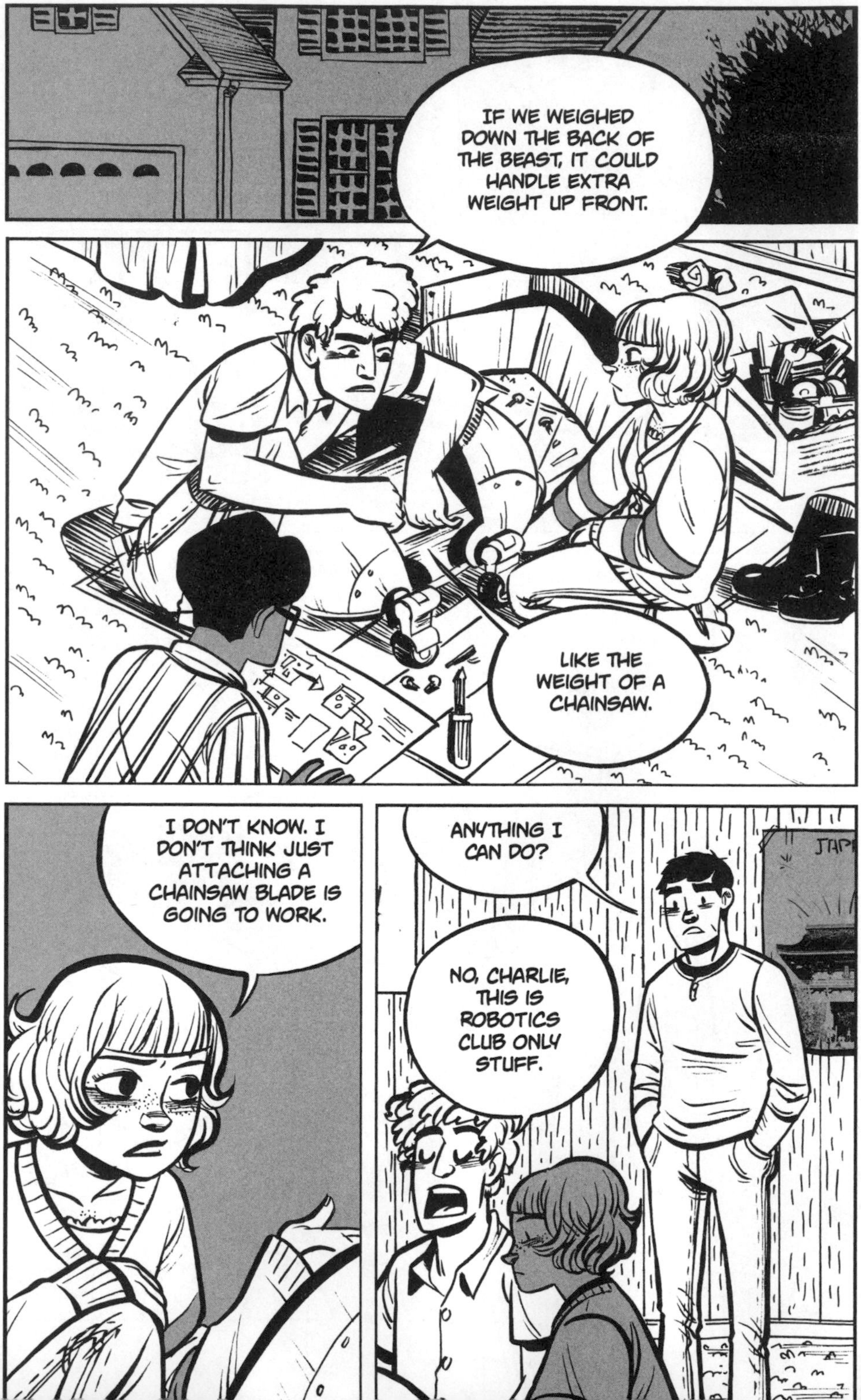
IF WE WEIGHED DOWN THE BACK OF THE BEAST, IT COULD HANDLE EXTRA WEIGHT UP FRONT.
LIKE THE WEIGHT OF A CHAINSAW.
I DON'T KNOW. I DON'T THINK JUST ATTACHING A CHAINSAW BLADE IS GOING TO WORK.
ANYTHING I CAN DO?
NO, CHARLIE, THIS IS ROBOTICS CLUB ONLY STUFF.

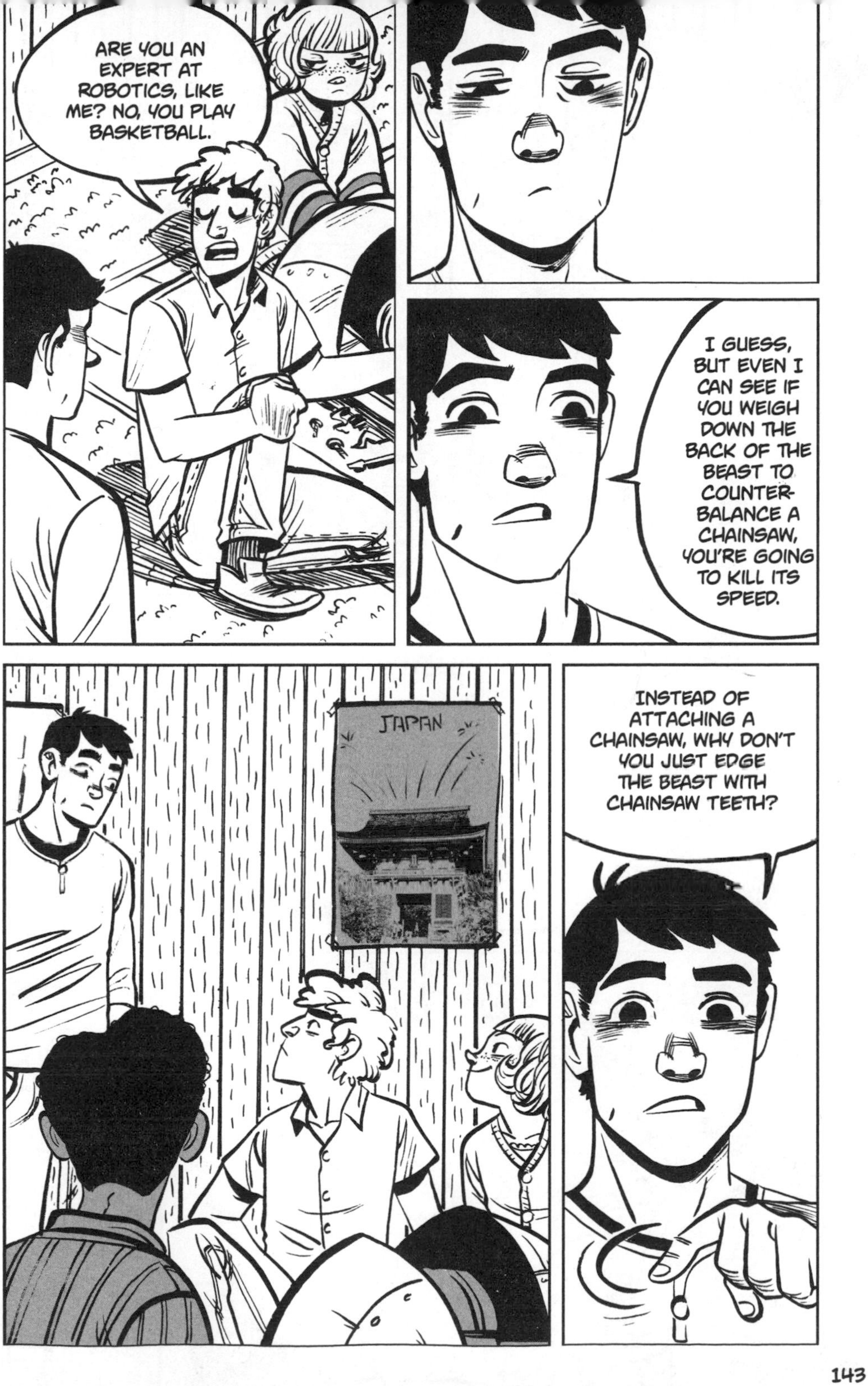
ARE YOU AN EXPERT AT ROBOTICS, LIKE ME? NO, YOU PLAY BASKETBALL.
I GUESS, BUT EVEN I CAN SEE IF YOU WEIGH DOWN THE BACK OF THE BEAST TO COUNTER-BALANCE A CHAINSAW, YOU'RE GOING TO KILL ITS SPEED.
JAPAN
INSTEAD OF ATTACHING A CHAINSAW, WHY DON'T YOU JUST EDGE THE BEAST WITH CHAINSAW TEETH?

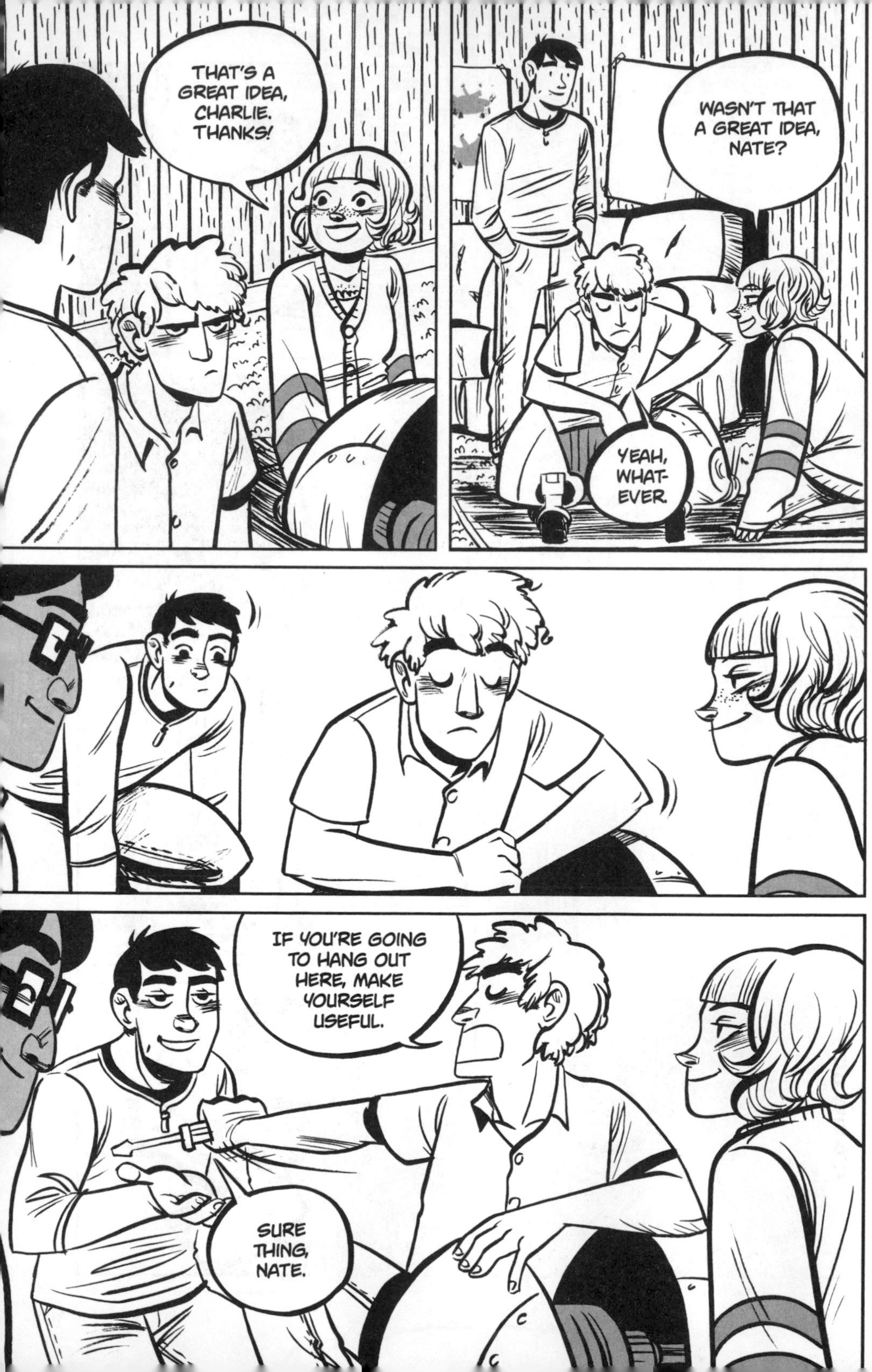
THAT'S A GREAT IDEA, CHARLIE. THANKS!
WASN'T THAT A GREAT IDEA, NATE?
YEAH, WHAT-EVER.
IF YOU'RE GOING TO HANG OUT HERE, MAKE YOURSELF USEFUL.
SURE THING, NATE.

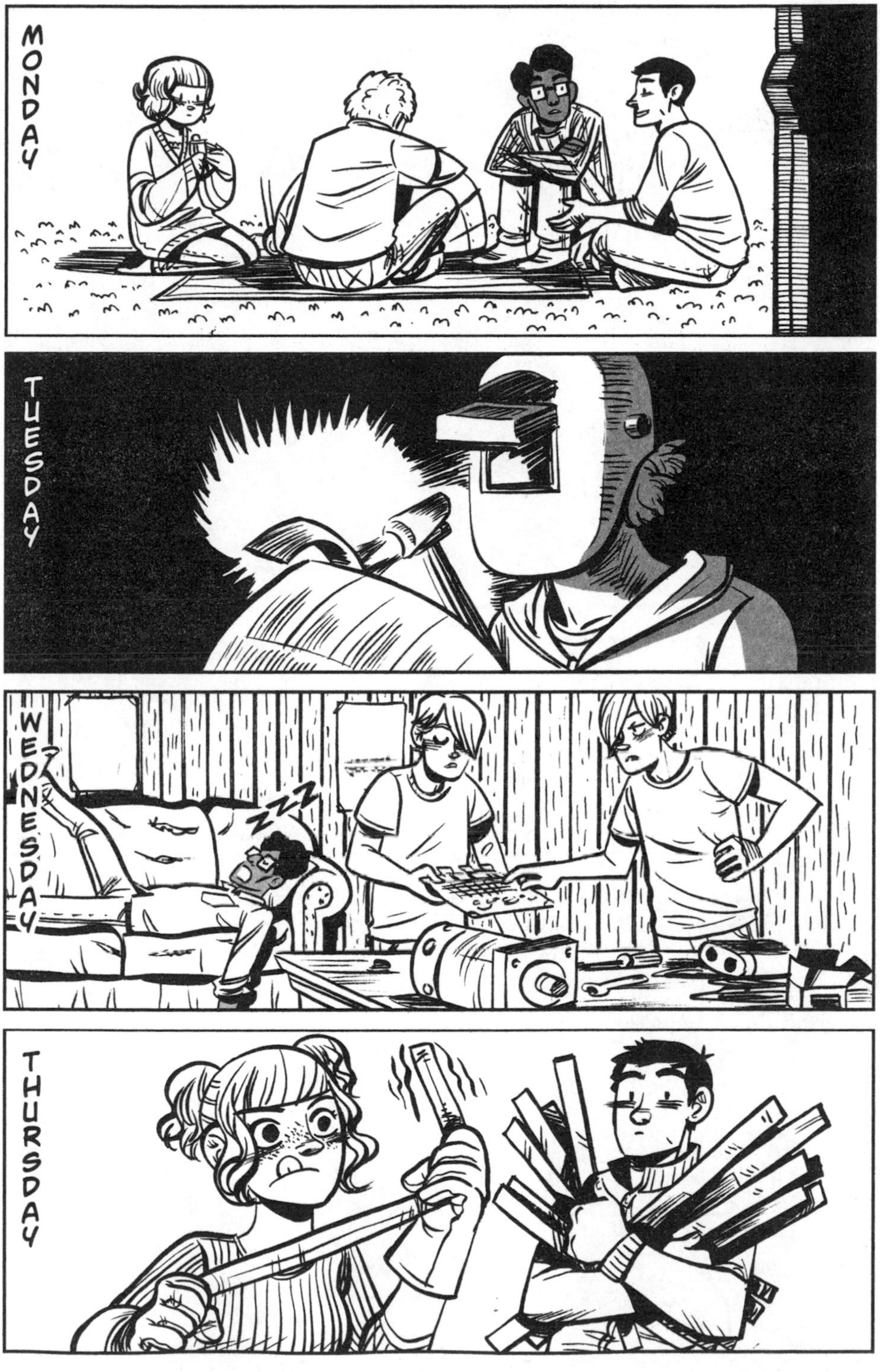
MONDAY
TUESDAY
WEDNESDAY
ZZZ
THURSDAY

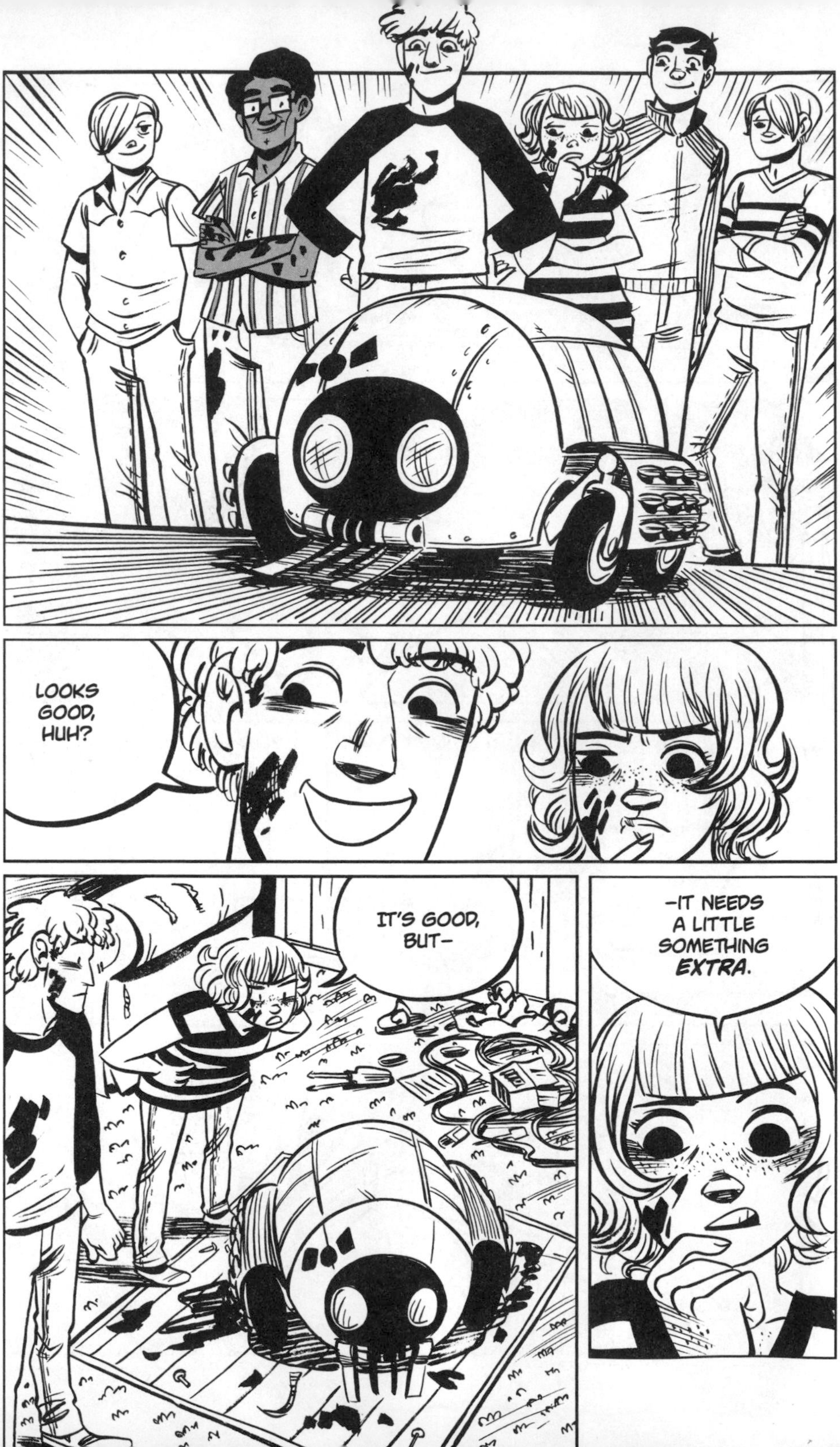
LOOKS GOOD, HUH?
IT'S GOOD, BUT–
–IT NEEDS A LITTLE SOMETHING *EXTRA*.

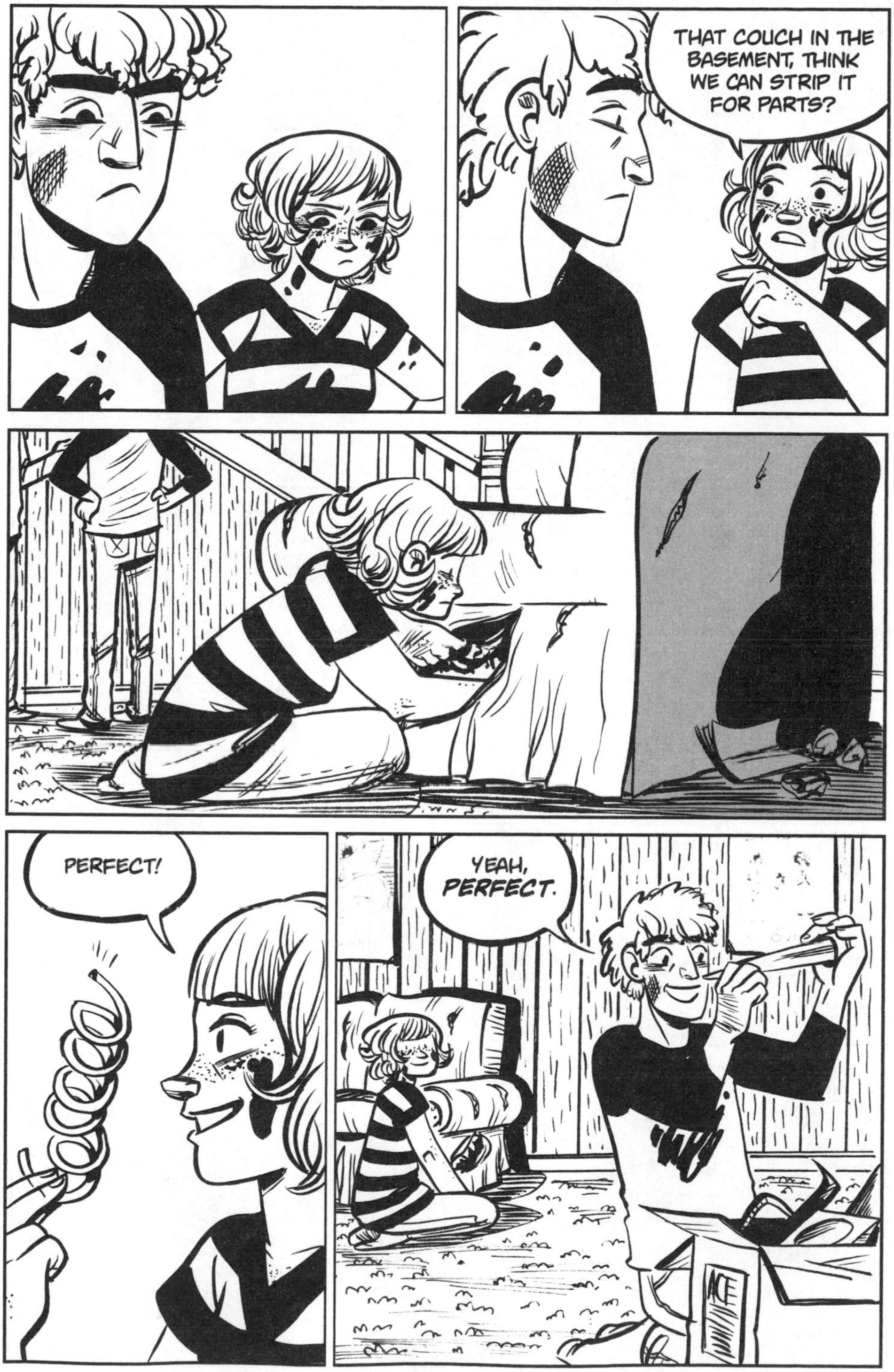
THAT COUCH IN THE BASEMENT, THINK WE CAN STRIP IT FOR PARTS?
PERFECT!
YEAH, PERFECT.
ACE

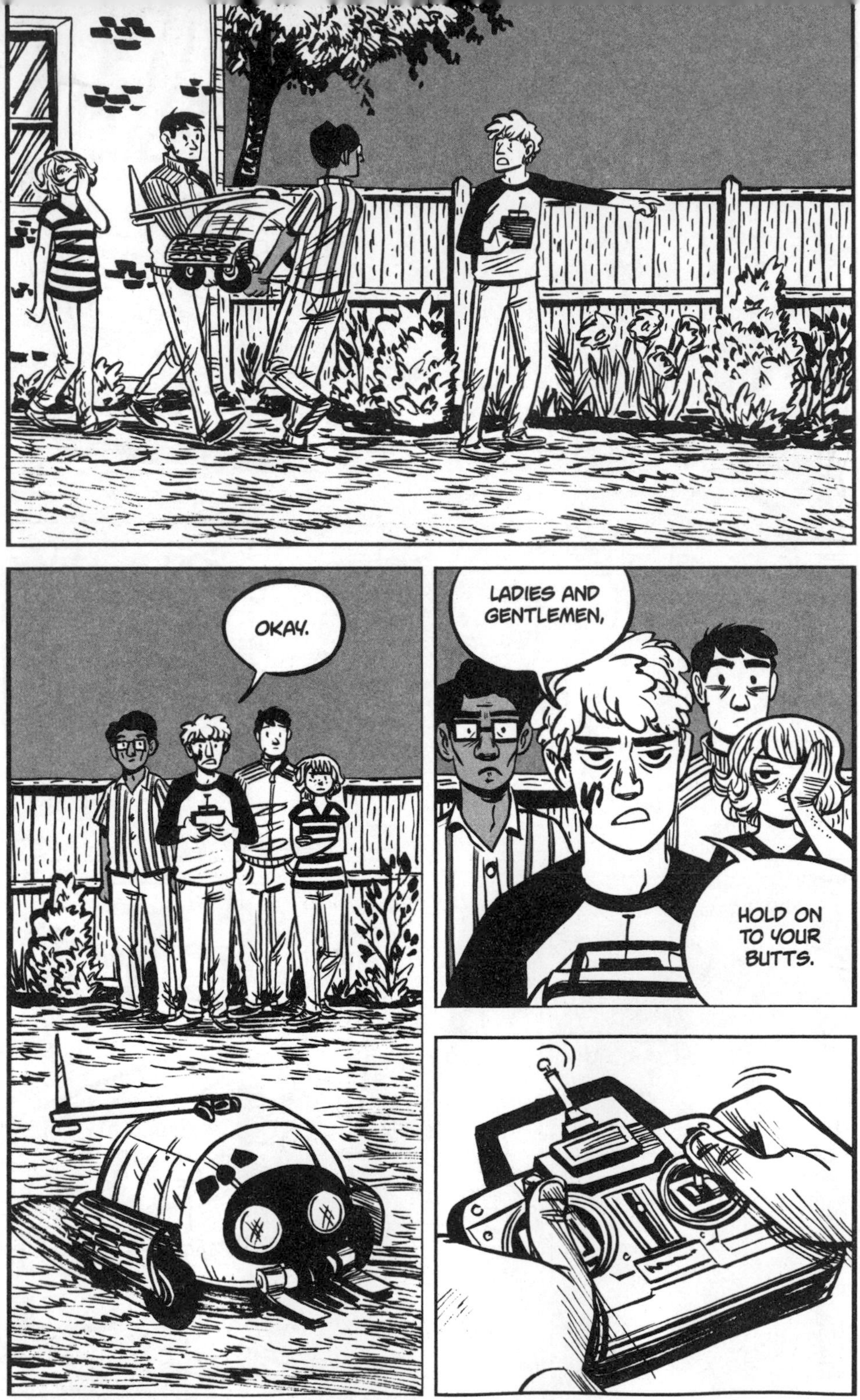
OKAY.
LADIES AND GENTLEMEN,
HOLD ON TO YOUR BUTTS.

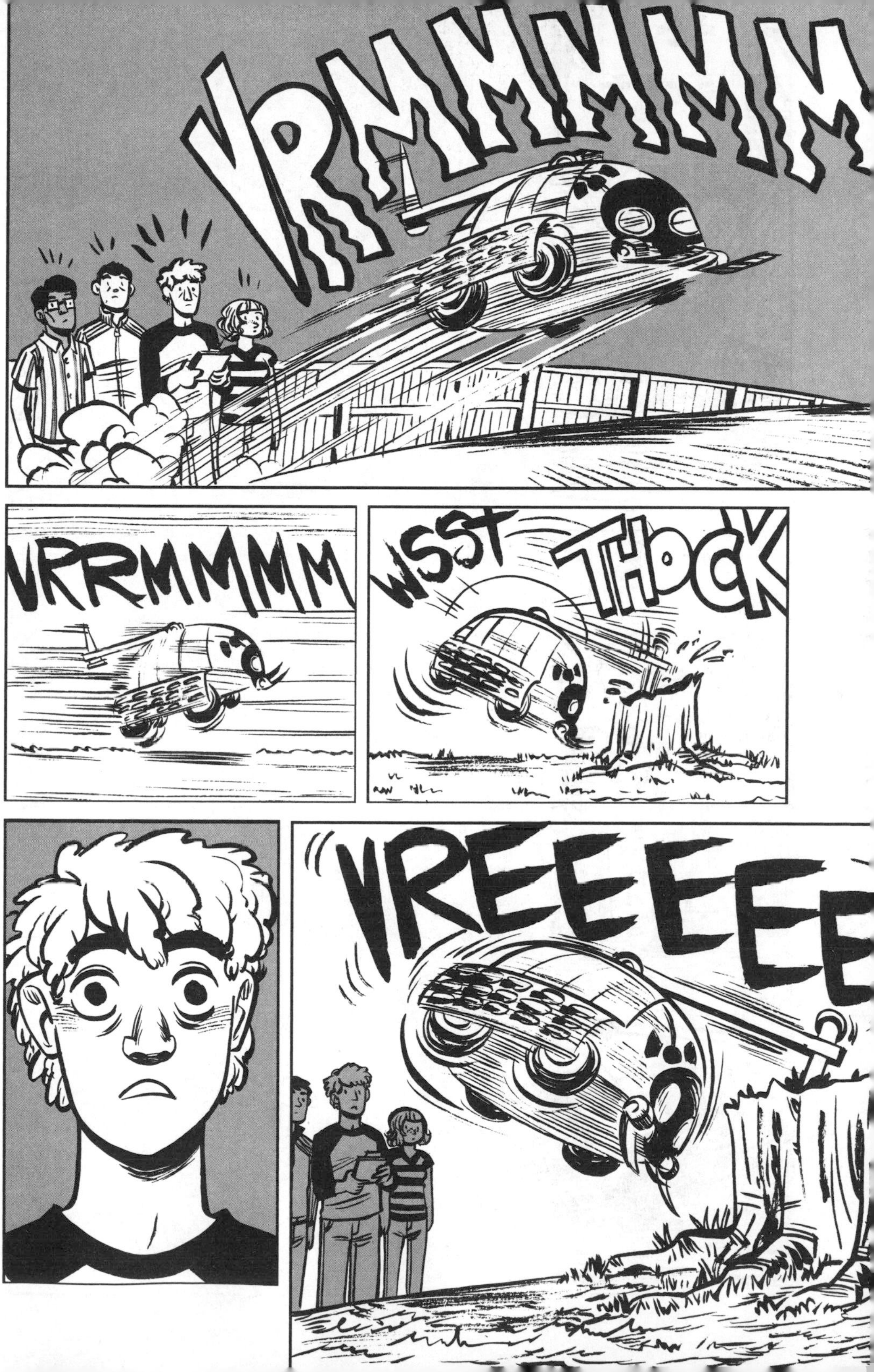
VRMMMMMM
VRRMMMMM
WSST
THOCK
VREEEEE

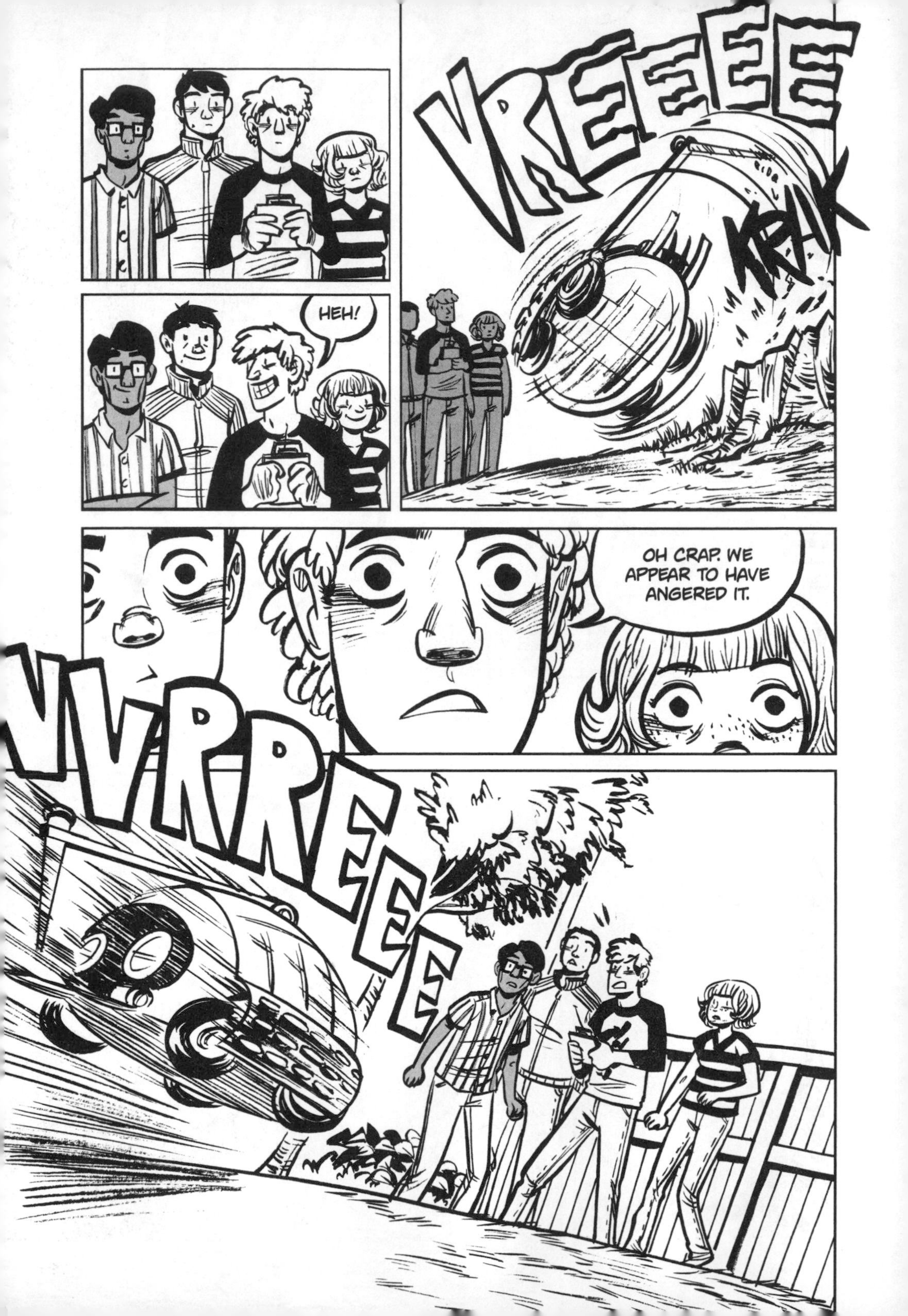
HEH!
VREEEEE
KRAK
OH CRAP. WE APPEAR TO HAVE ANGERED IT.
VVRREEEE

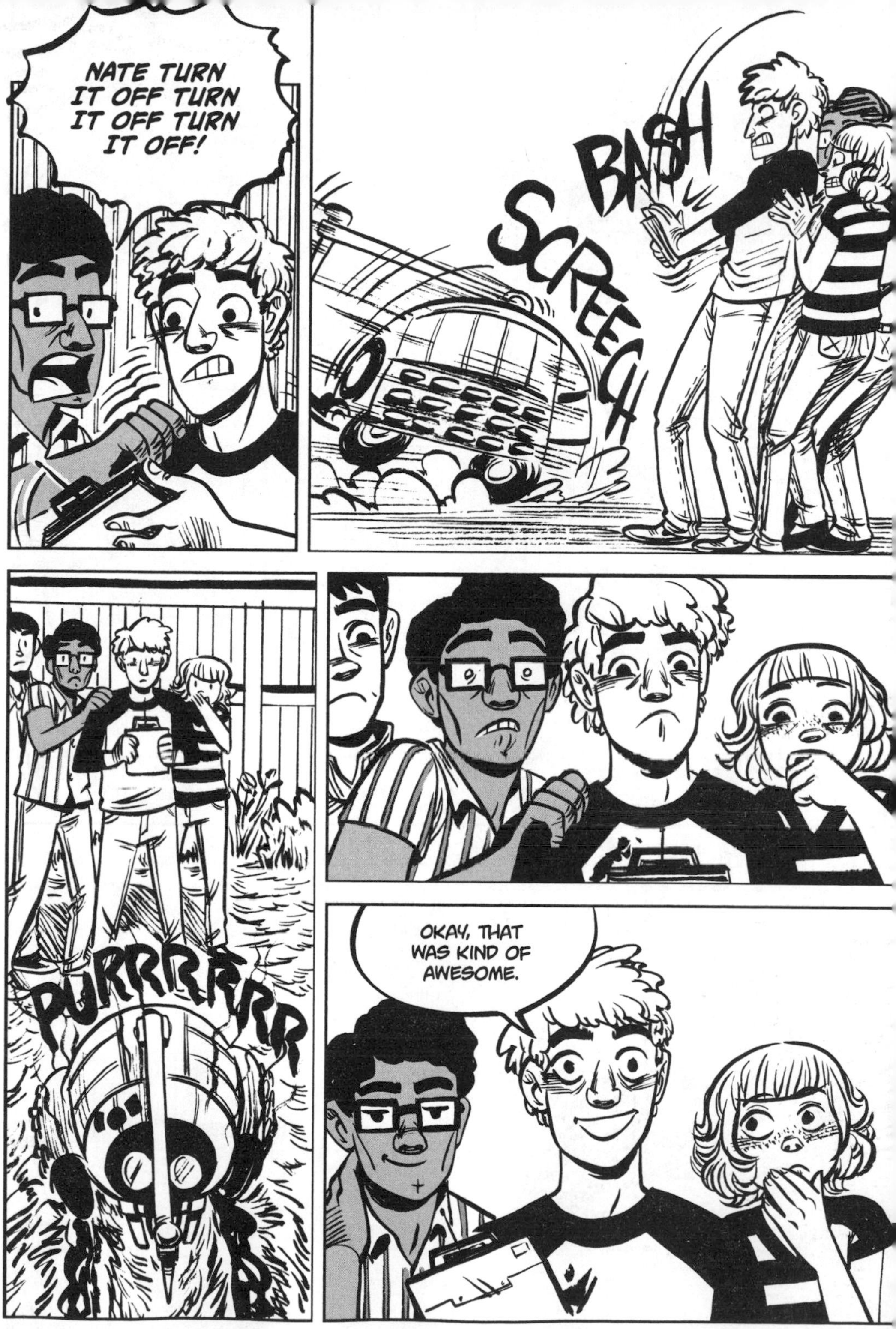
NATE TURN IT OFF TURN IT OFF TURN IT OFF!
BASH
SCREECH
PURRRRRRR
OKAY, THAT WAS KIND OF AWESOME.

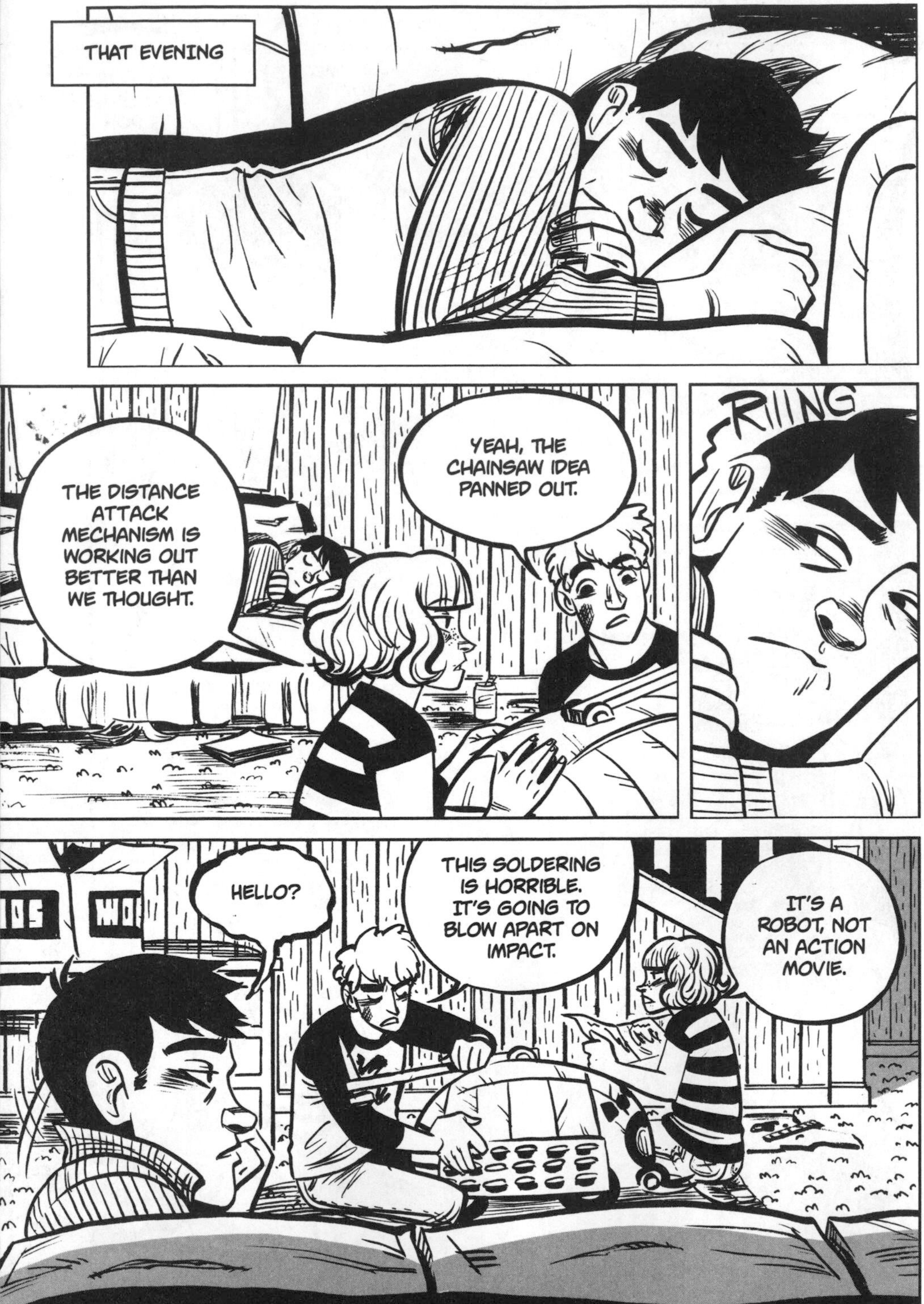
THAT EVENING
THE DISTANCE ATTACK MECHANISM IS WORKING OUT BETTER THAN WE THOUGHT.
YEAH, THE CHAINSAW IDEA PANNED OUT.
RING
HELLO?
THIS SOLDERING IS HORRIBLE. IT'S GOING TO BLOW APART ON IMPACT.
IT'S A ROBOT, NOT AN ACTION MOVIE.

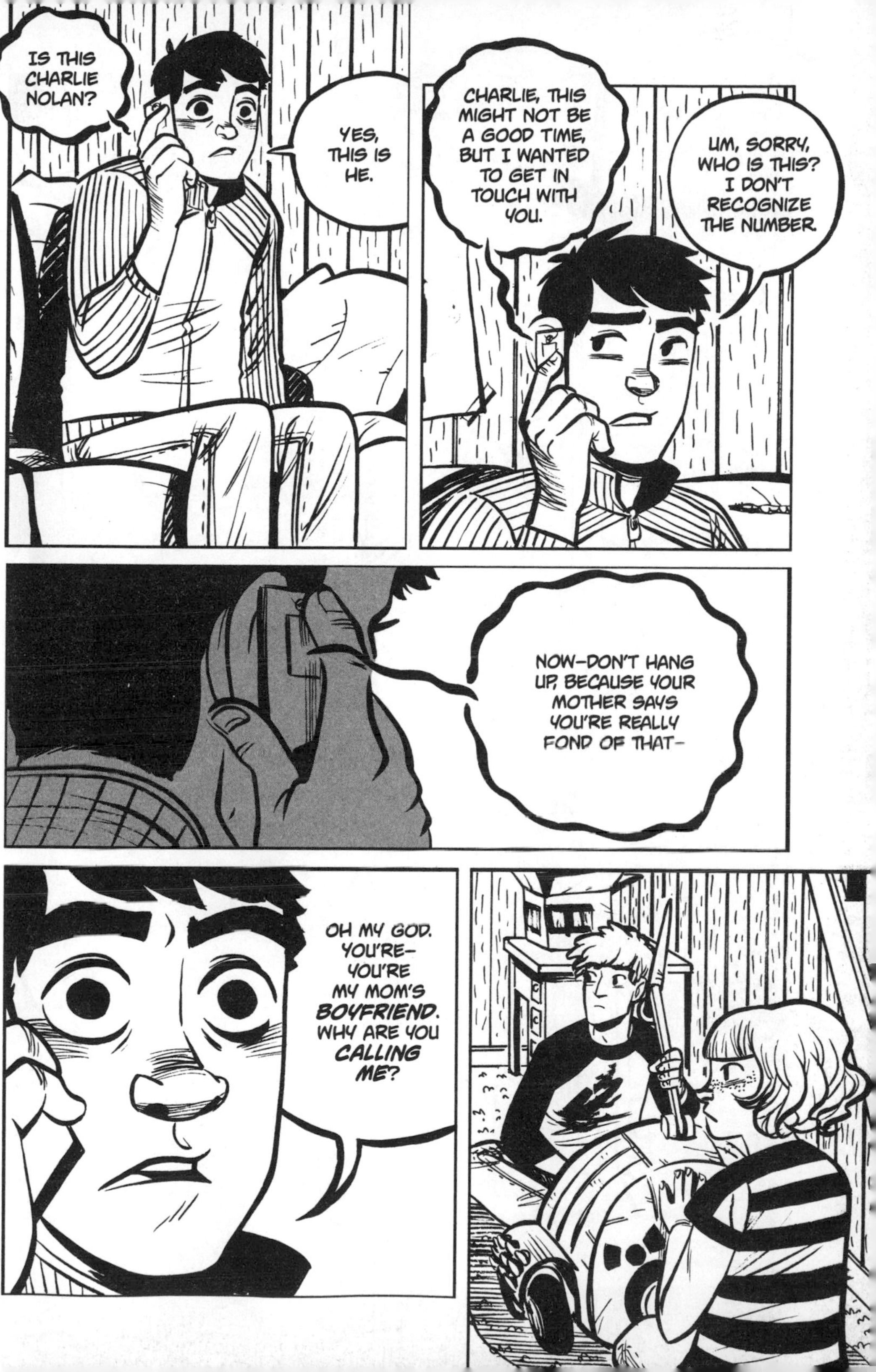
IS THIS CHARLIE NOLAN?
YES, THIS IS HE.
CHARLIE, THIS MIGHT NOT BE A GOOD TIME, BUT I WANTED TO GET IN TOUCH WITH YOU.
UM, SORRY, WHO IS THIS? I DON'T RECOGNIZE THE NUMBER.
NOW—DON'T HANG UP, BECAUSE YOUR MOTHER SAYS YOU'RE REALLY FOND OF THAT—
OH MY GOD. YOU'RE— YOU'RE MY MOM'S BOYFRIEND. WHY ARE YOU CALLING ME?

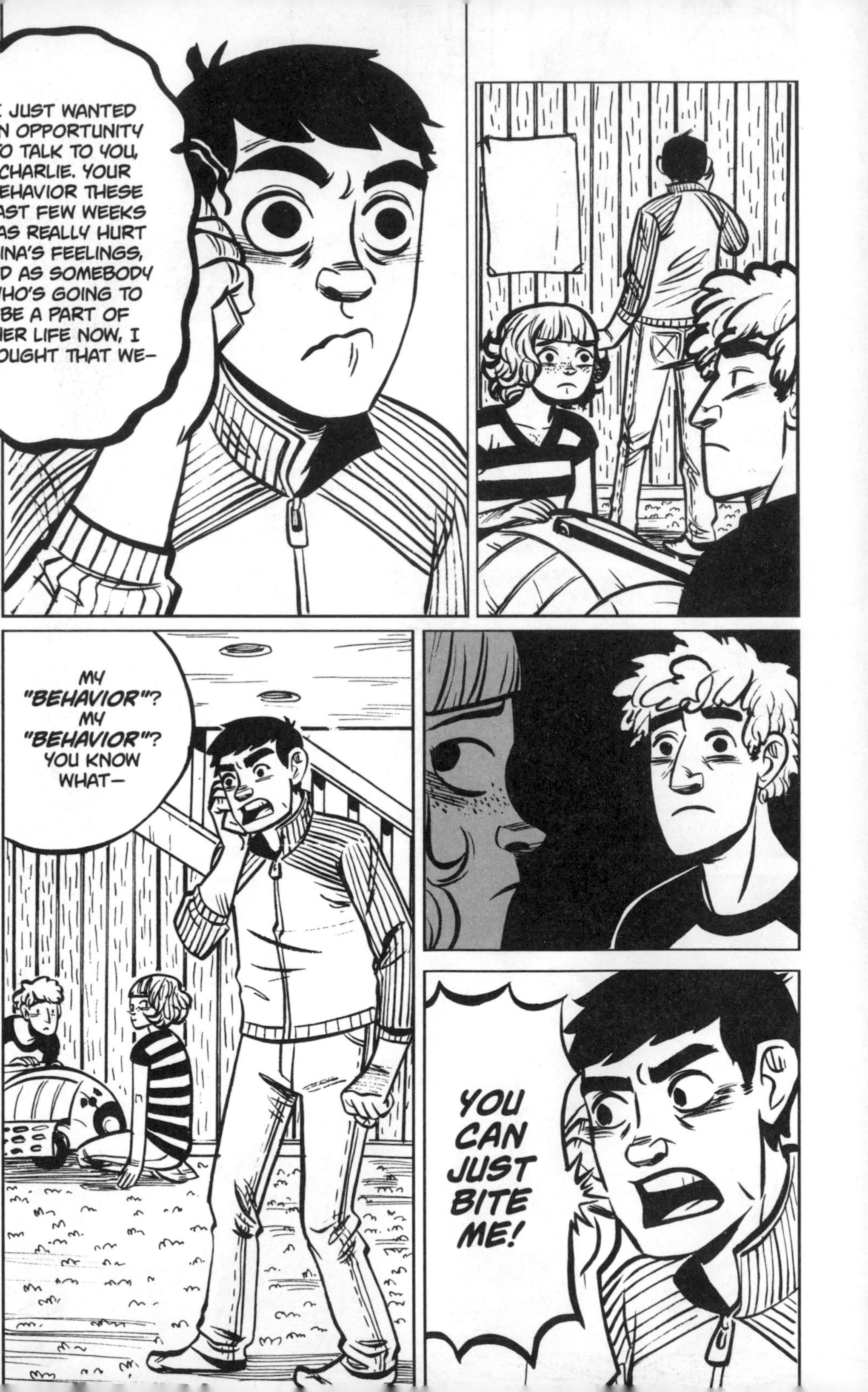
I JUST WANTED AN OPPORTUNITY TO TALK TO YOU, CHARLIE. YOUR BEHAVIOR THESE PAST FEW WEEKS HAS REALLY HURT GINA'S FEELINGS, AND AS SOMEBODY WHO'S GOING TO BE A PART OF HER LIFE NOW, I THOUGHT THAT WE–
MY "BEHAVIOR"? MY "BEHAVIOR"? YOU KNOW WHAT–
YOU CAN JUST BITE ME!

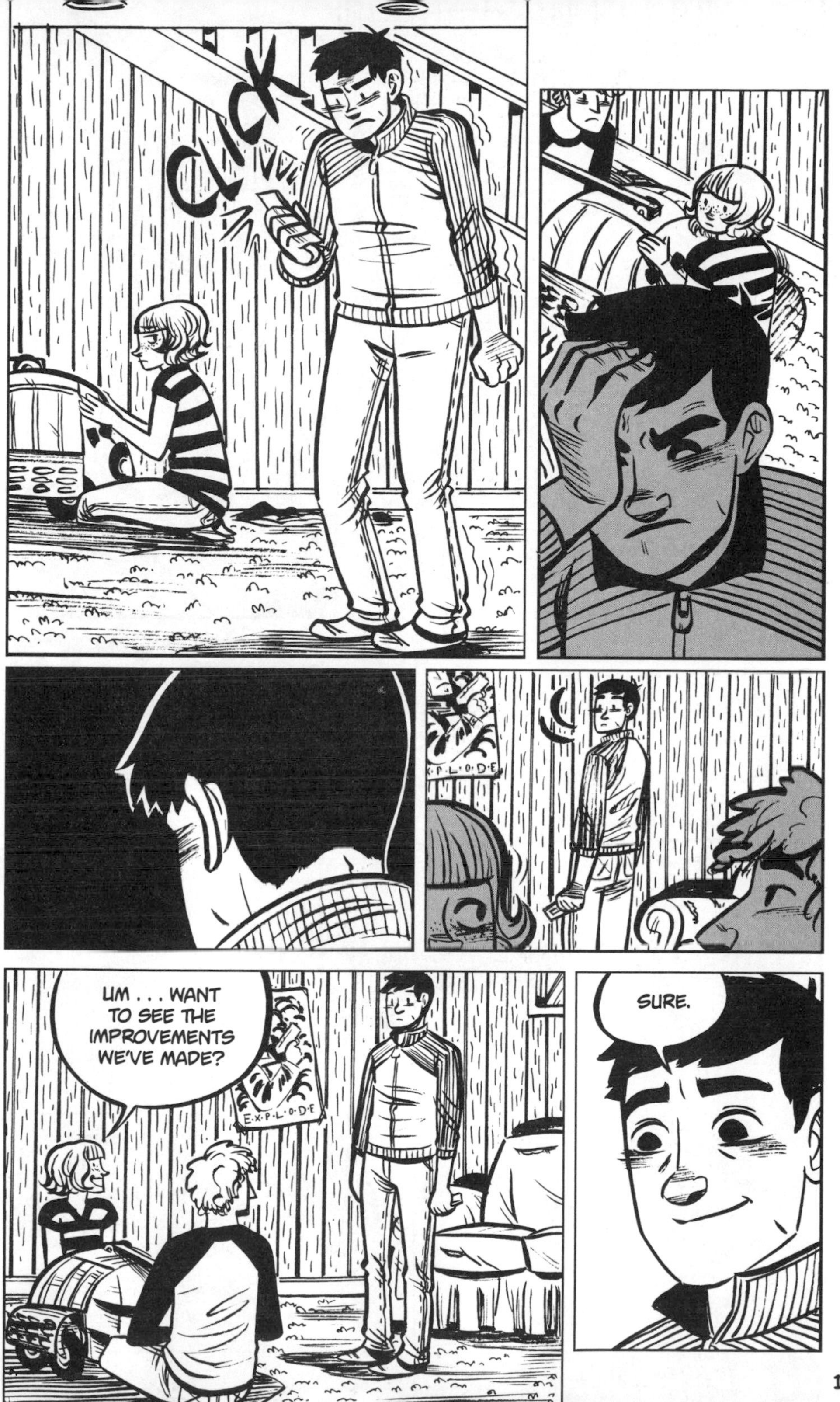
CLICK
E·X·P·L·O·D·E
UM . . . WANT TO SEE THE IMPROVEMENTS WE'VE MADE?
E·X·P·L·O·D·E
SURE.

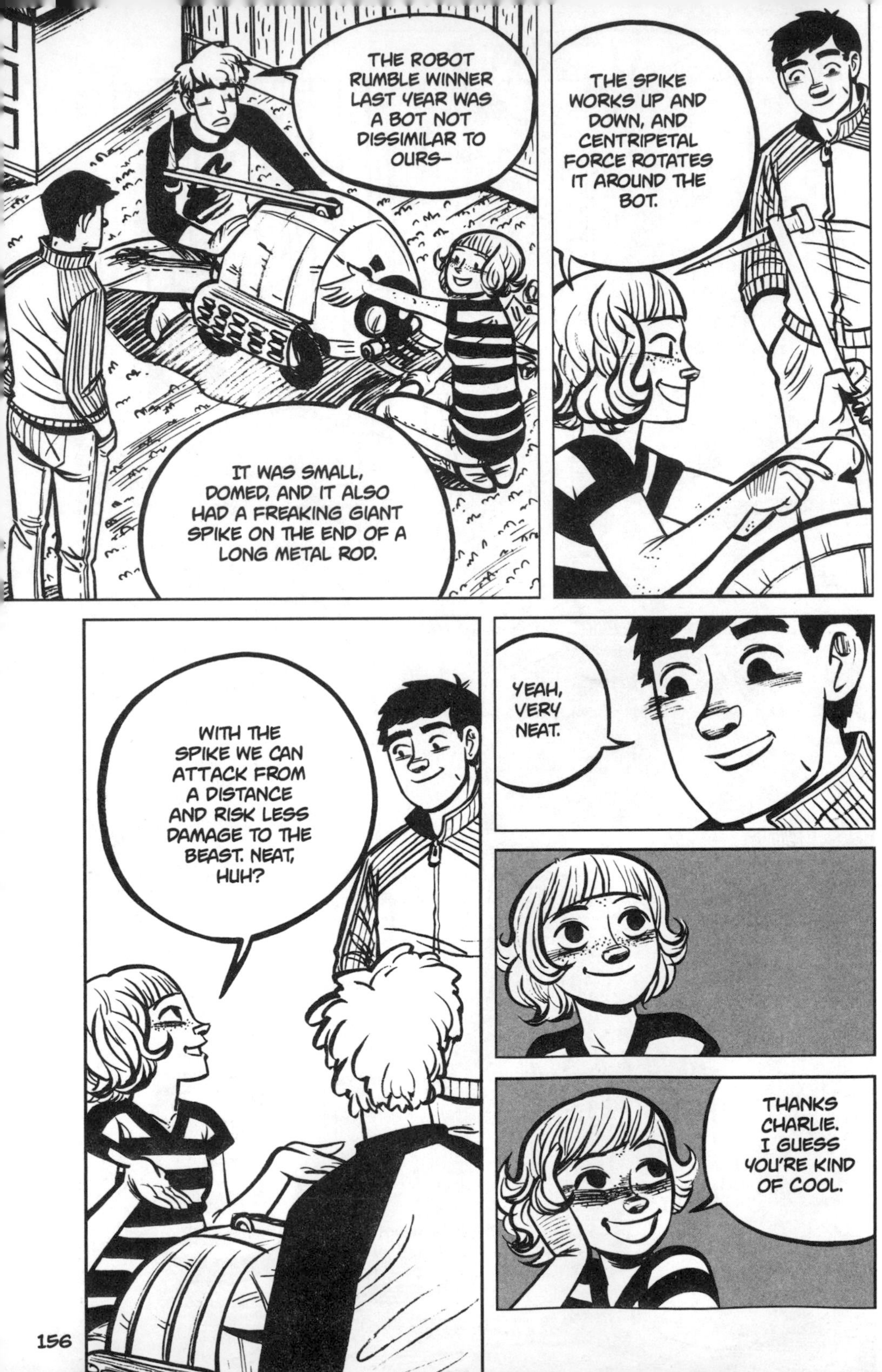
THE ROBOT RUMBLE WINNER LAST YEAR WAS A BOT NOT DISSIMILAR TO OURS–
IT WAS SMALL, DOMED, AND IT ALSO HAD A FREAKING GIANT SPIKE ON THE END OF A LONG METAL ROD.
THE SPIKE WORKS UP AND DOWN, AND CENTRIPETAL FORCE ROTATES IT AROUND THE BOT.
WITH THE SPIKE WE CAN ATTACK FROM A DISTANCE AND RISK LESS DAMAGE TO THE BEAST. NEAT, HUH?
YEAH, VERY NEAT.
THANKS CHARLIE. I GUESS YOU'RE KIND OF COOL.

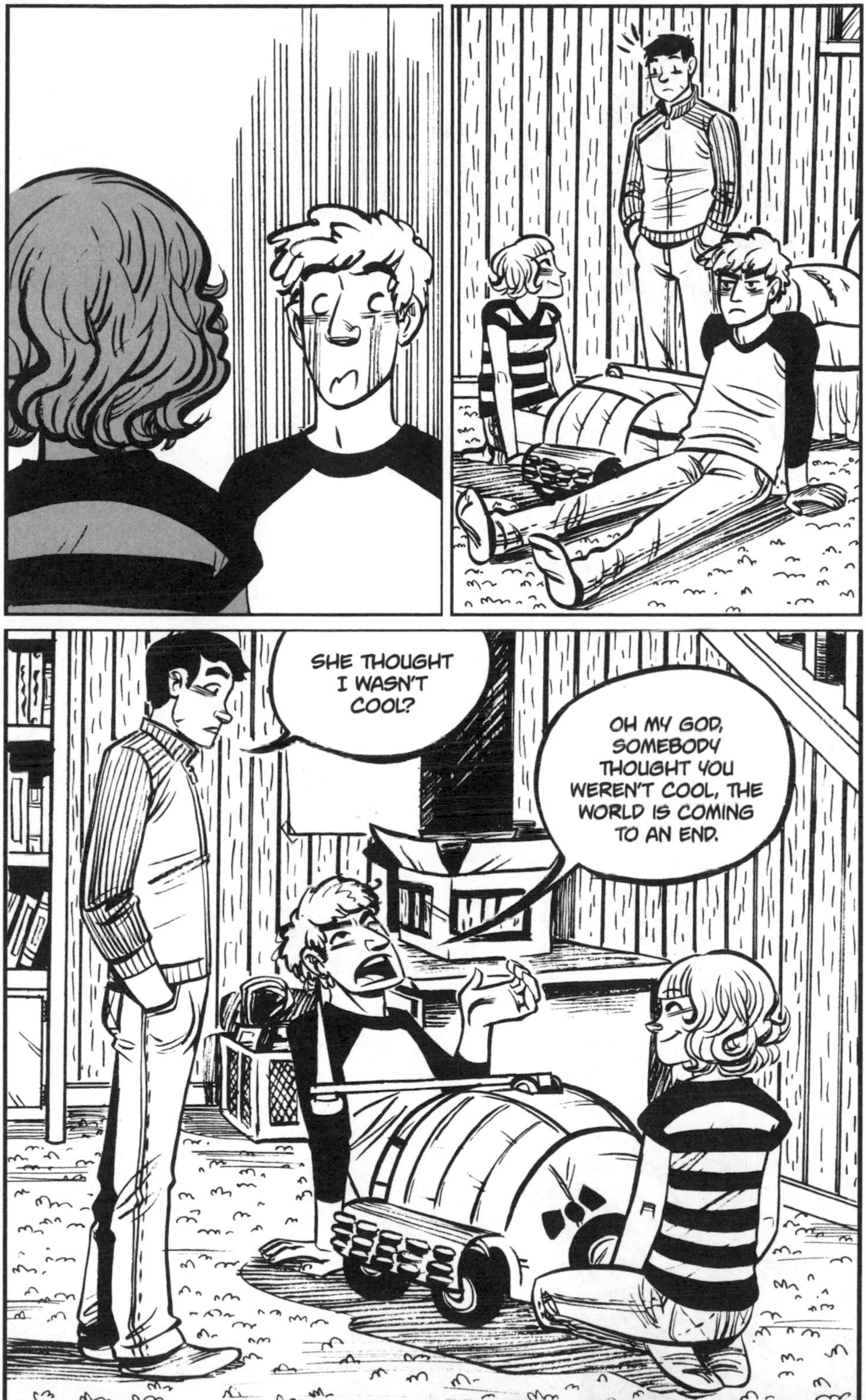
SHE THOUGHT I WASN'T COOL?
OH MY GOD, SOMEBODY THOUGHT YOU WEREN'T COOL, THE WORLD IS COMING TO AN END.

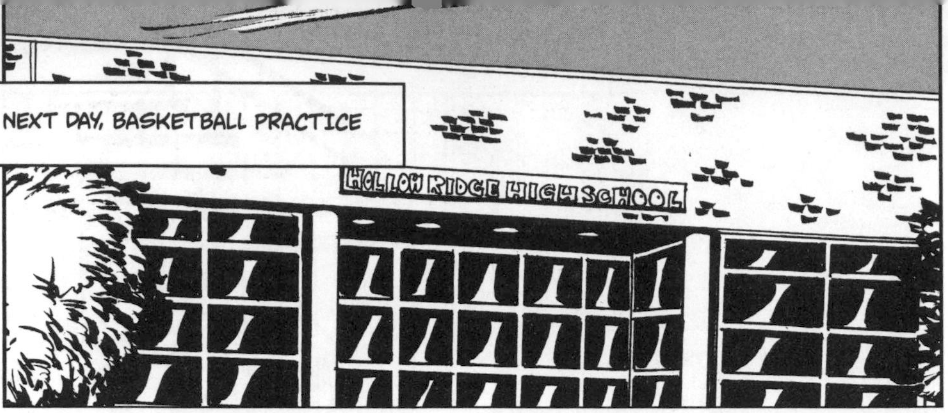
NEXT DAY, BASKETBALL PRACTICE
HOLLOW RIDGE HIGH SCHOOL

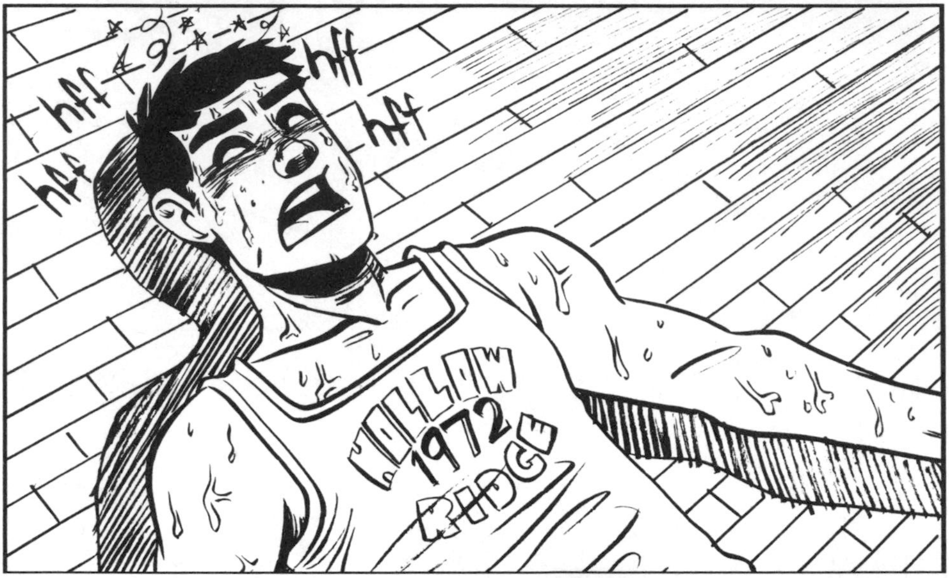
hff
hff
hff
hff
HOLLOW 1972 RIDGE

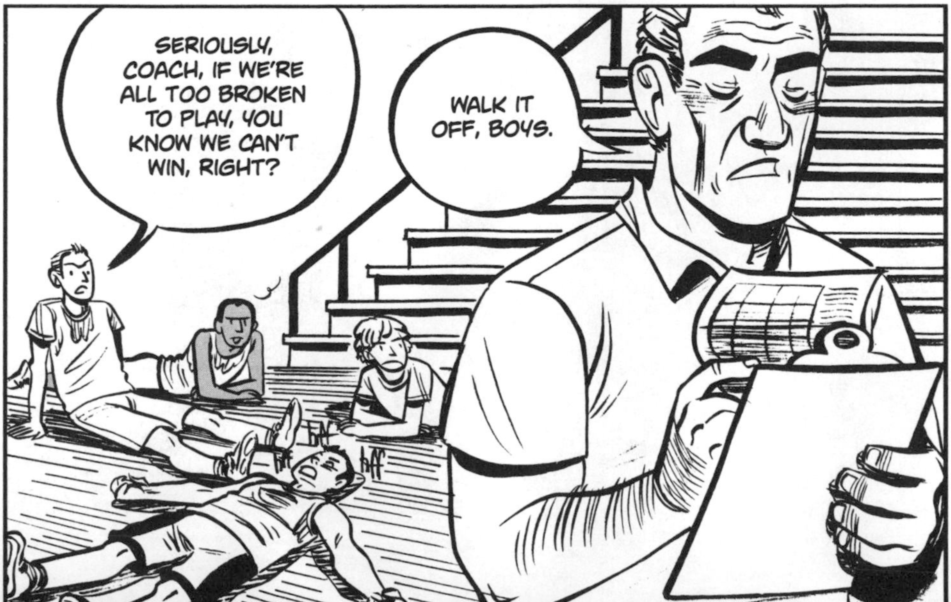
SERIOUSLY, COACH, IF WE'RE ALL TOO BROKEN TO PLAY, YOU KNOW WE CAN'T WIN, RIGHT?
WALK IT OFF, BOYS.

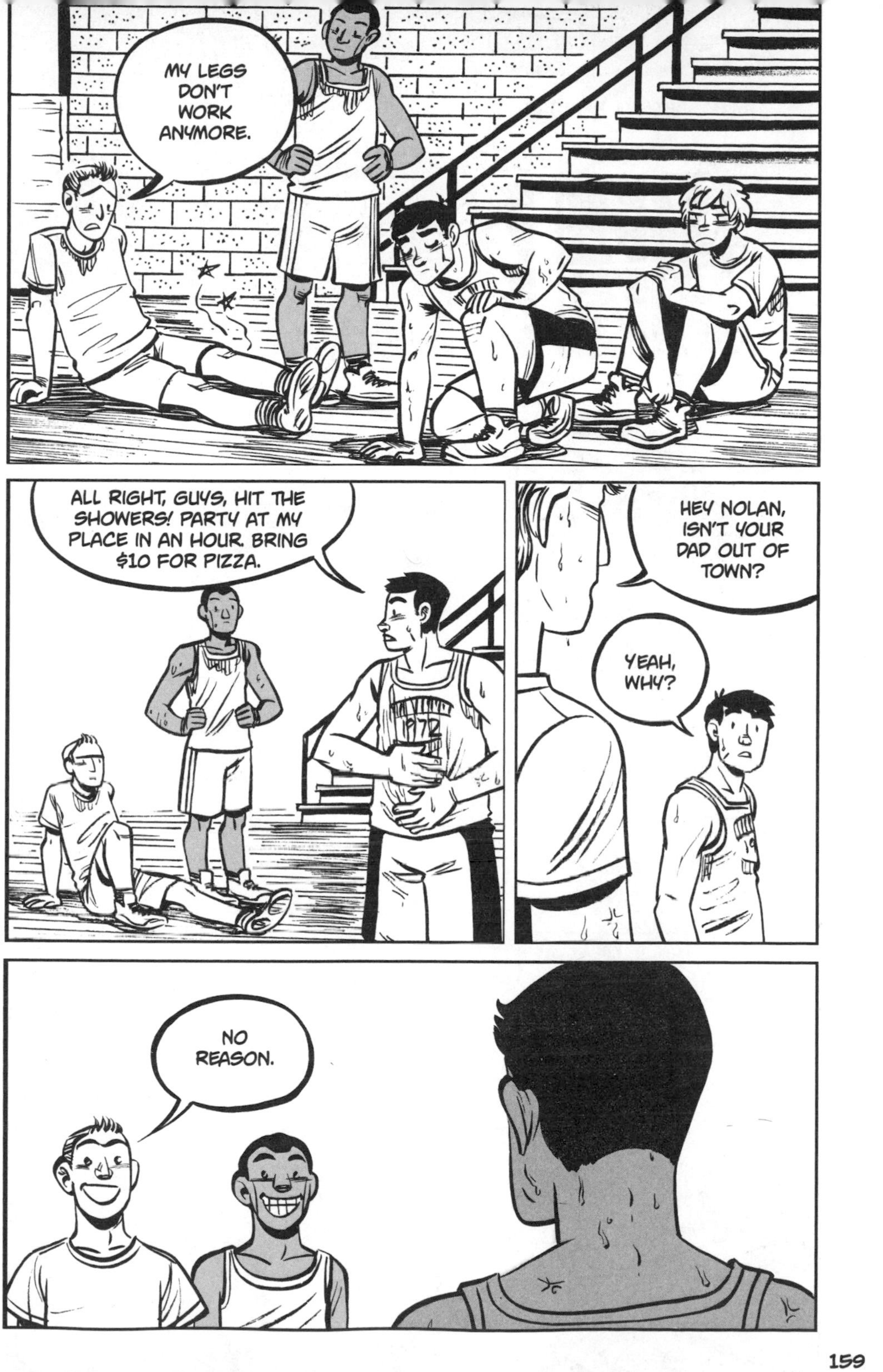
MY LEGS DON'T WORK ANYMORE.
ALL RIGHT, GUYS, HIT THE SHOWERS! PARTY AT MY PLACE IN AN HOUR. BRING $10 FOR PIZZA.
HEY NOLAN, ISN'T YOUR DAD OUT OF TOWN?
YEAH, WHY?
NO REASON.

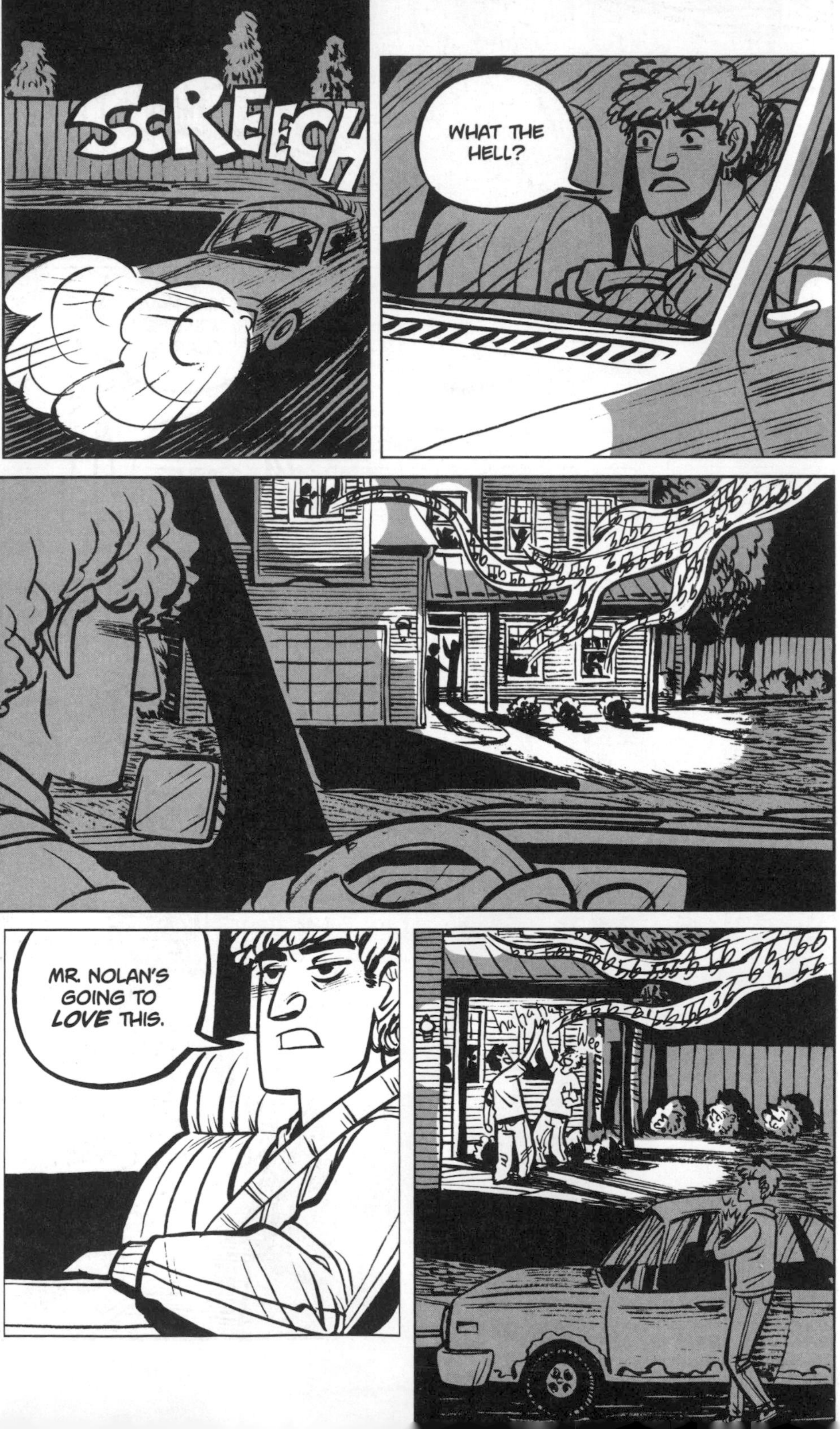
SCREECH
WHAT THE HELL?
MR. NOLAN'S GOING TO *LOVE* THIS.
Wee

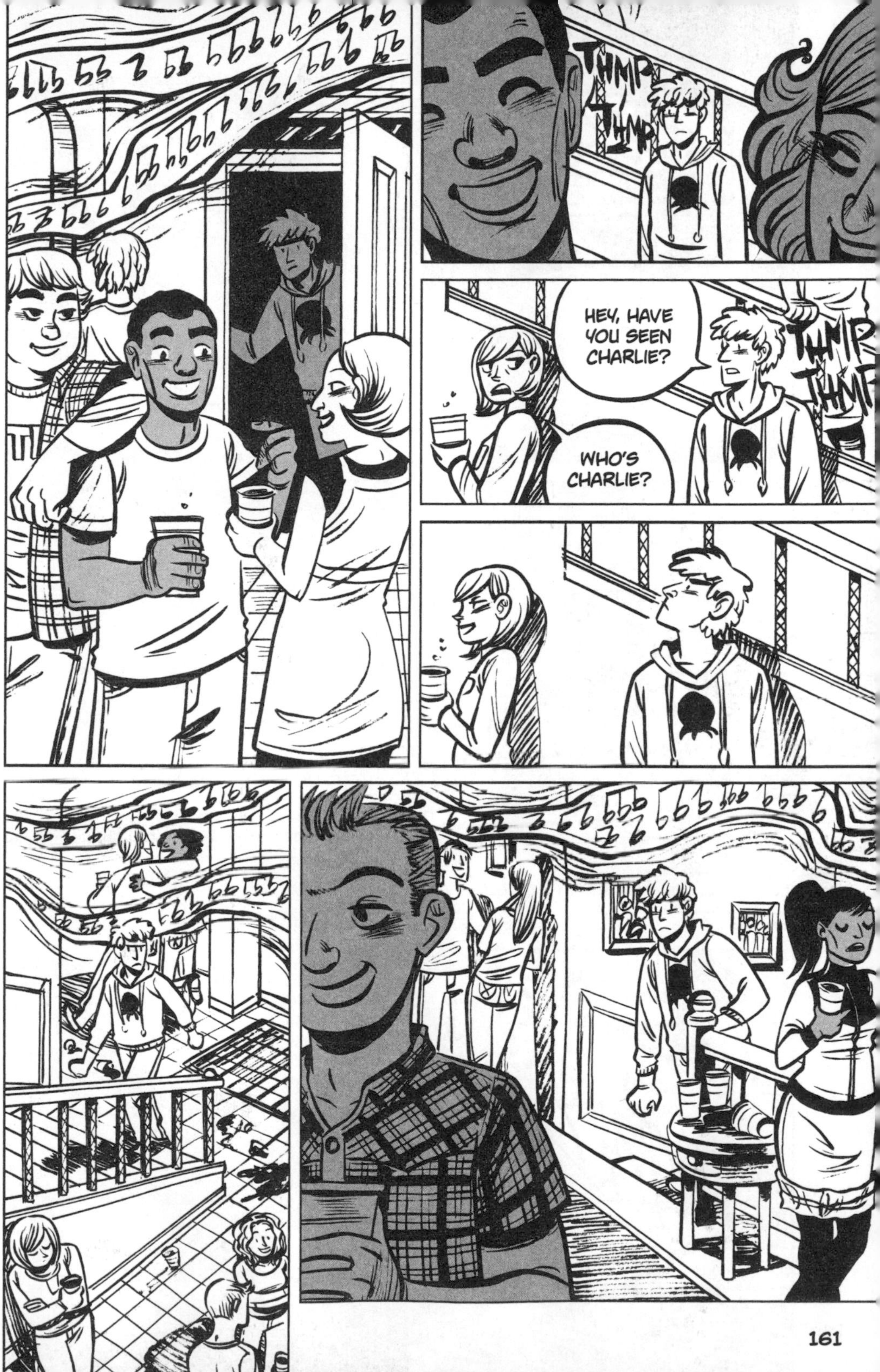
THMP
THMP
HEY, HAVE YOU SEEN CHARLIE?
WHO'S CHARLIE?
THMP
THMP

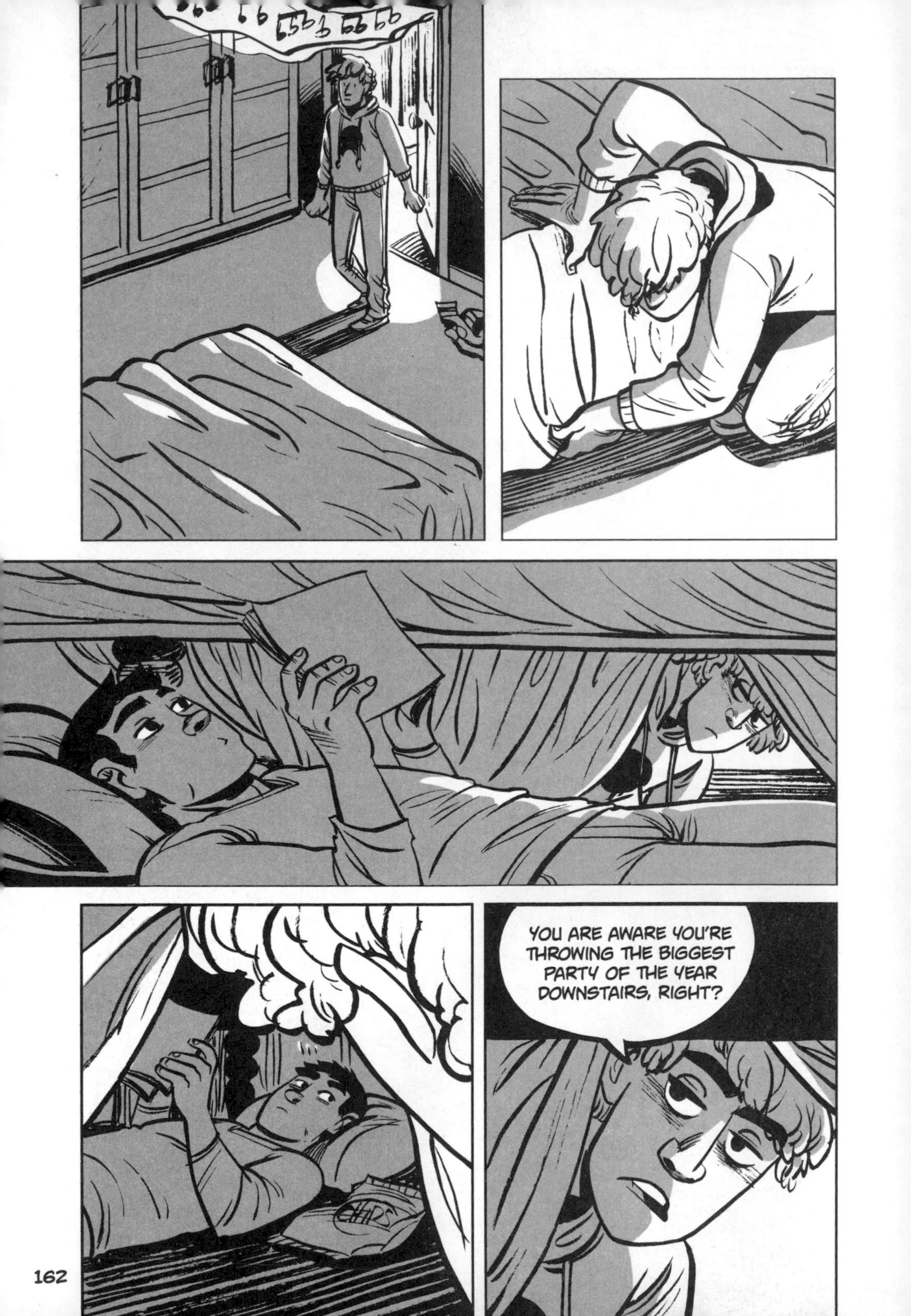
YOU ARE AWARE YOU'RE THROWING THE BIGGEST PARTY OF THE YEAR DOWNSTAIRS, RIGHT?

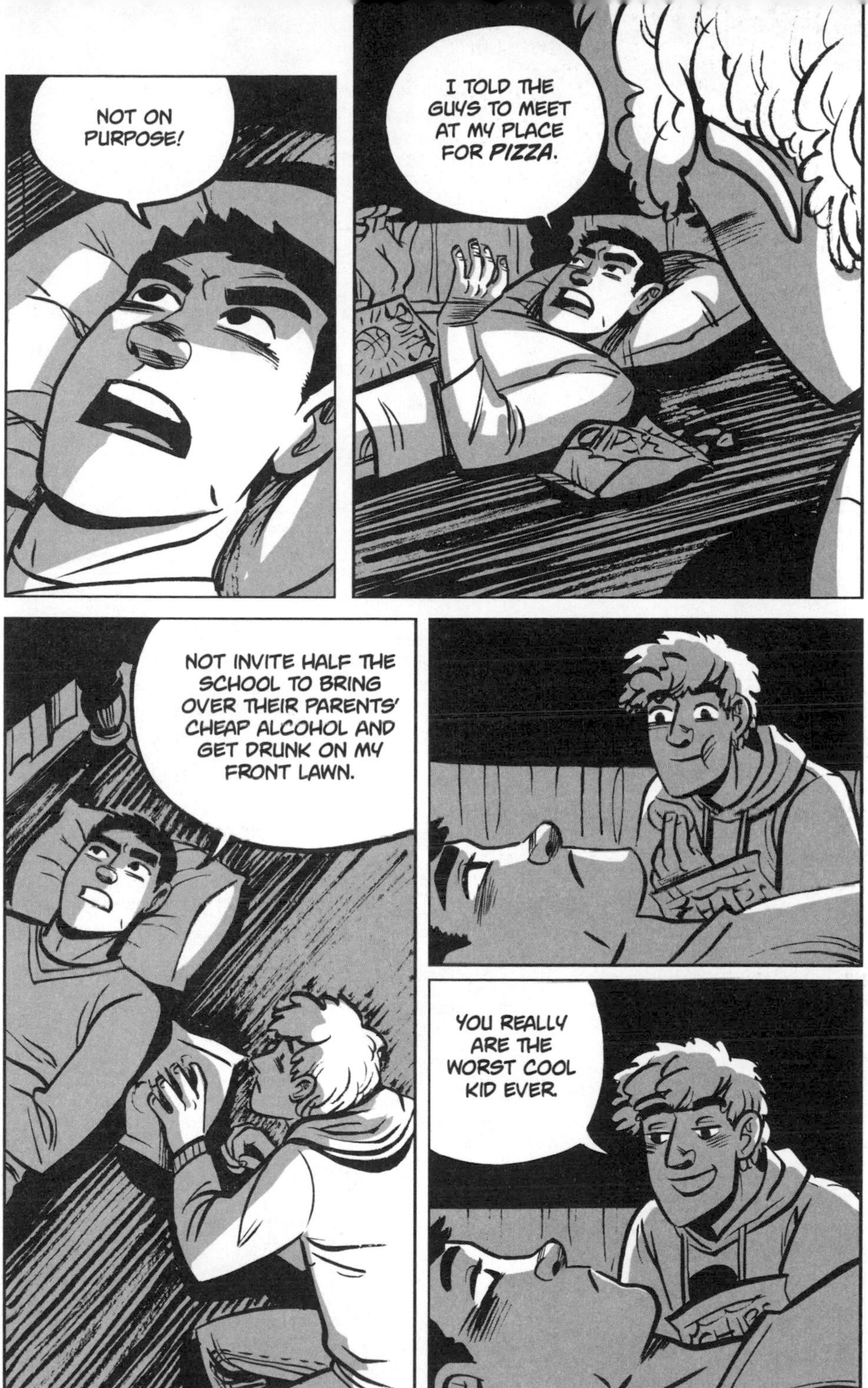
NOT ON PURPOSE!
I TOLD THE GUYS TO MEET AT MY PLACE FOR *PIZZA*.
NOT INVITE HALF THE SCHOOL TO BRING OVER THEIR PARENTS' CHEAP ALCOHOL AND GET DRUNK ON MY FRONT LAWN.
YOU REALLY ARE THE WORST COOL KID EVER.

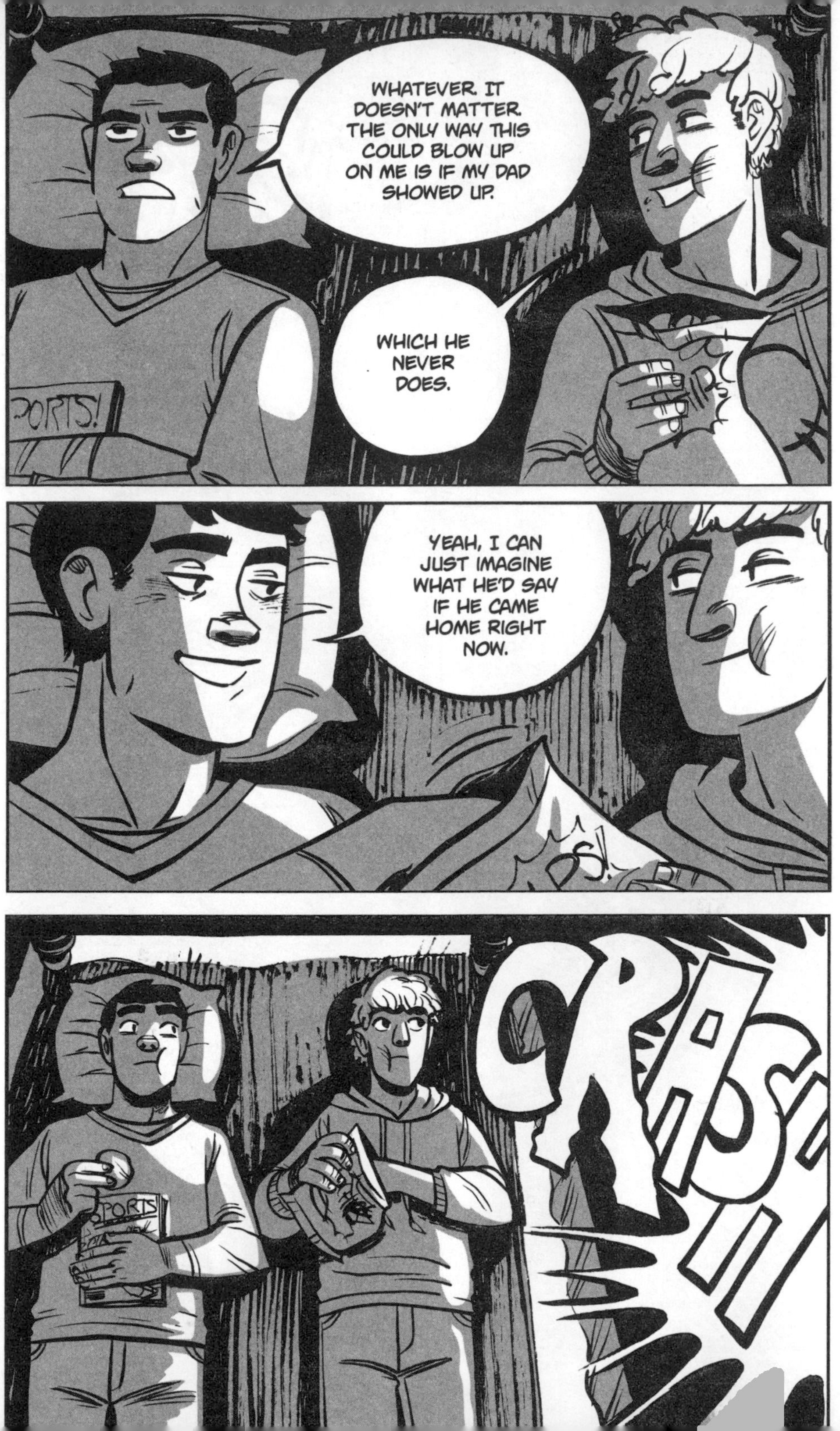
WHATEVER. IT DOESN'T MATTER. THE ONLY WAY THIS COULD BLOW UP ON ME IS IF MY DAD SHOWED UP.
WHICH HE NEVER DOES.
YEAH, I CAN JUST IMAGINE WHAT HE'D SAY IF HE CAME HOME RIGHT NOW.
CRASH!

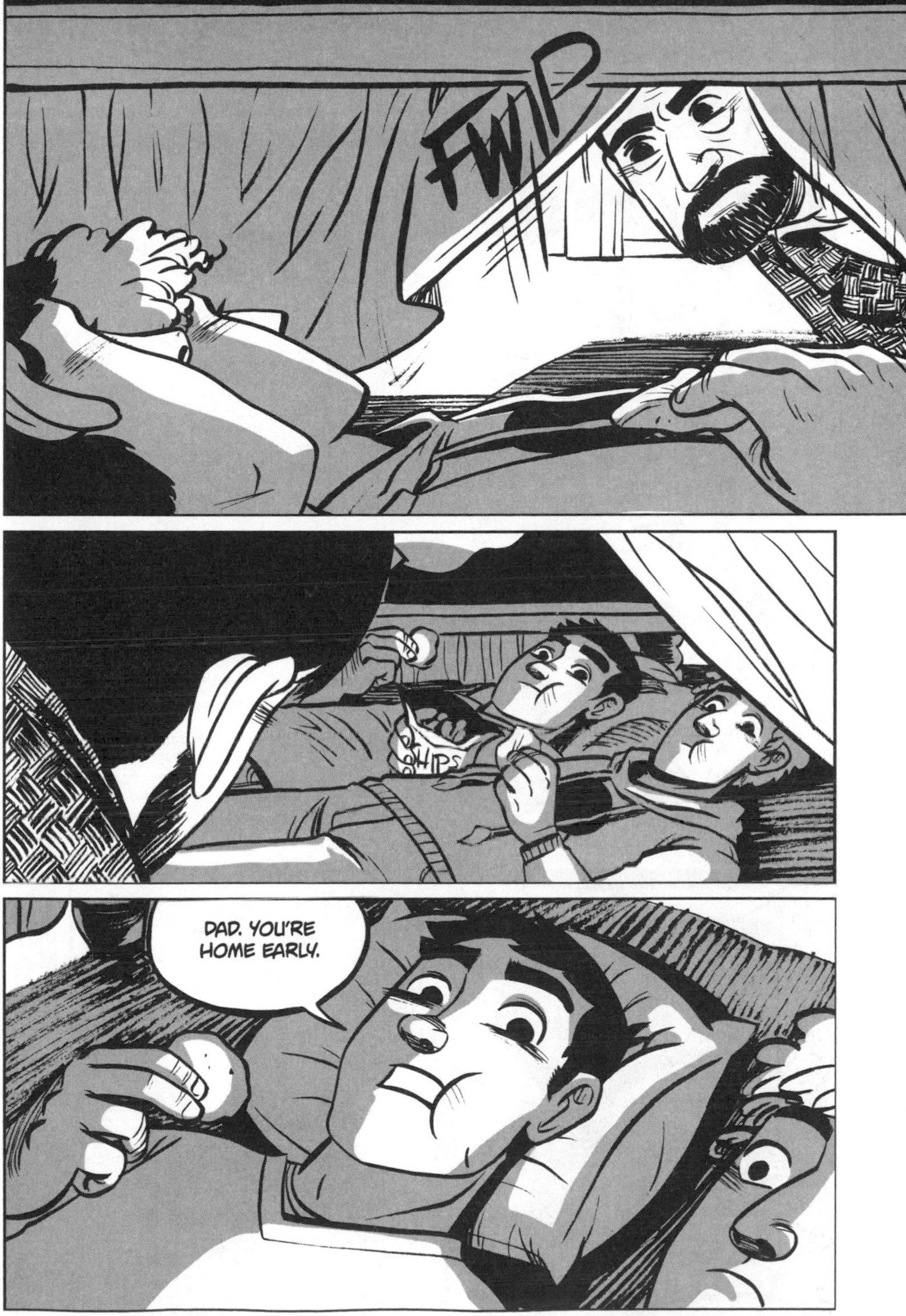
FWIP
CHIPS
DAD. YOU'RE HOME EARLY.

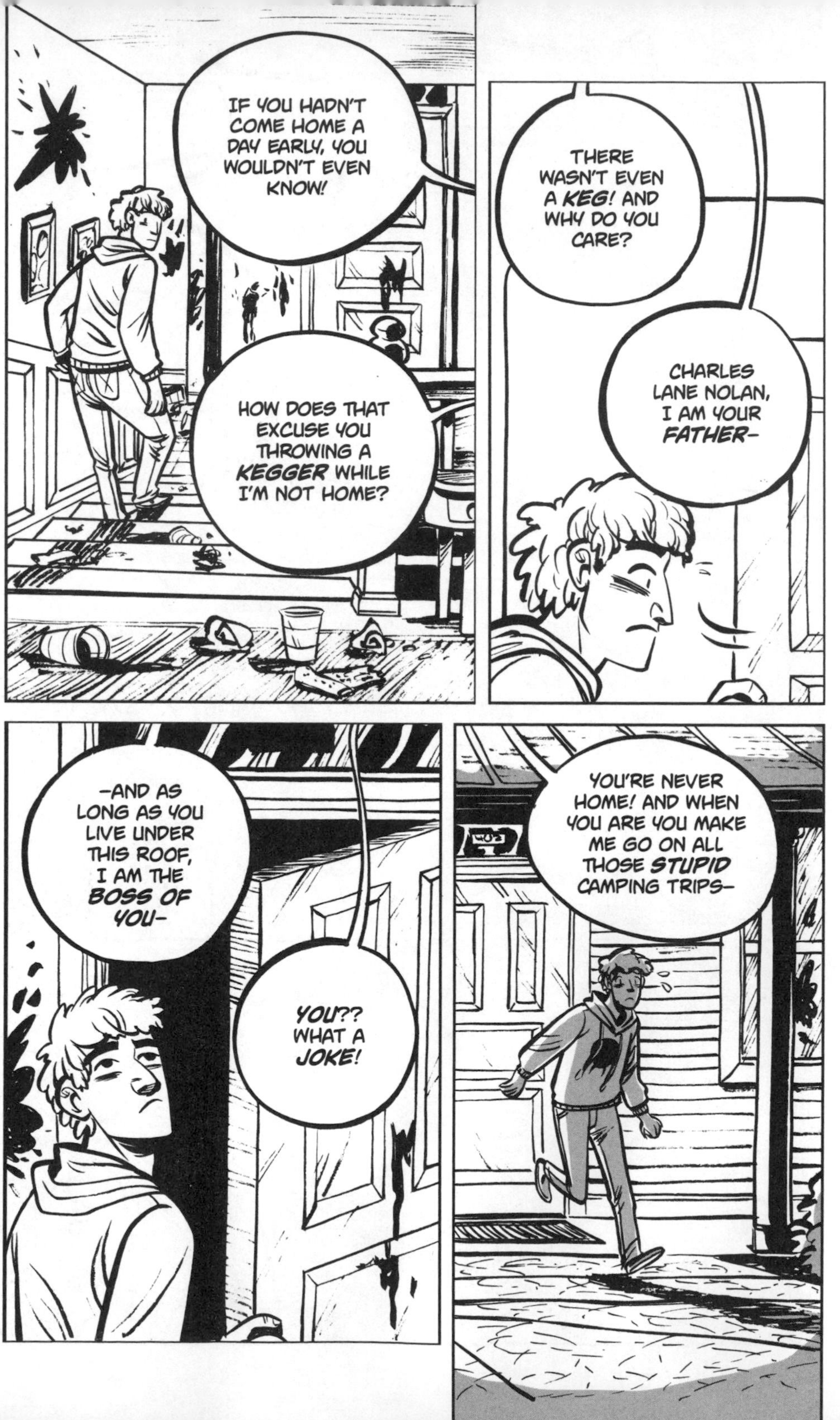
IF YOU HADN'T COME HOME A DAY EARLY, YOU WOULDN'T EVEN KNOW!
HOW DOES THAT EXCUSE YOU THROWING A KEGGER WHILE I'M NOT HOME?
THERE WASN'T EVEN A KEG! AND WHY DO YOU CARE?
CHARLES LANE NOLAN, I AM YOUR FATHER-
-AND AS LONG AS YOU LIVE UNDER THIS ROOF, I AM THE BOSS OF YOU-
YOU?? WHAT A JOKE!
YOU'RE NEVER HOME! AND WHEN YOU ARE YOU MAKE ME GO ON ALL THOSE STUPID CAMPING TRIPS-

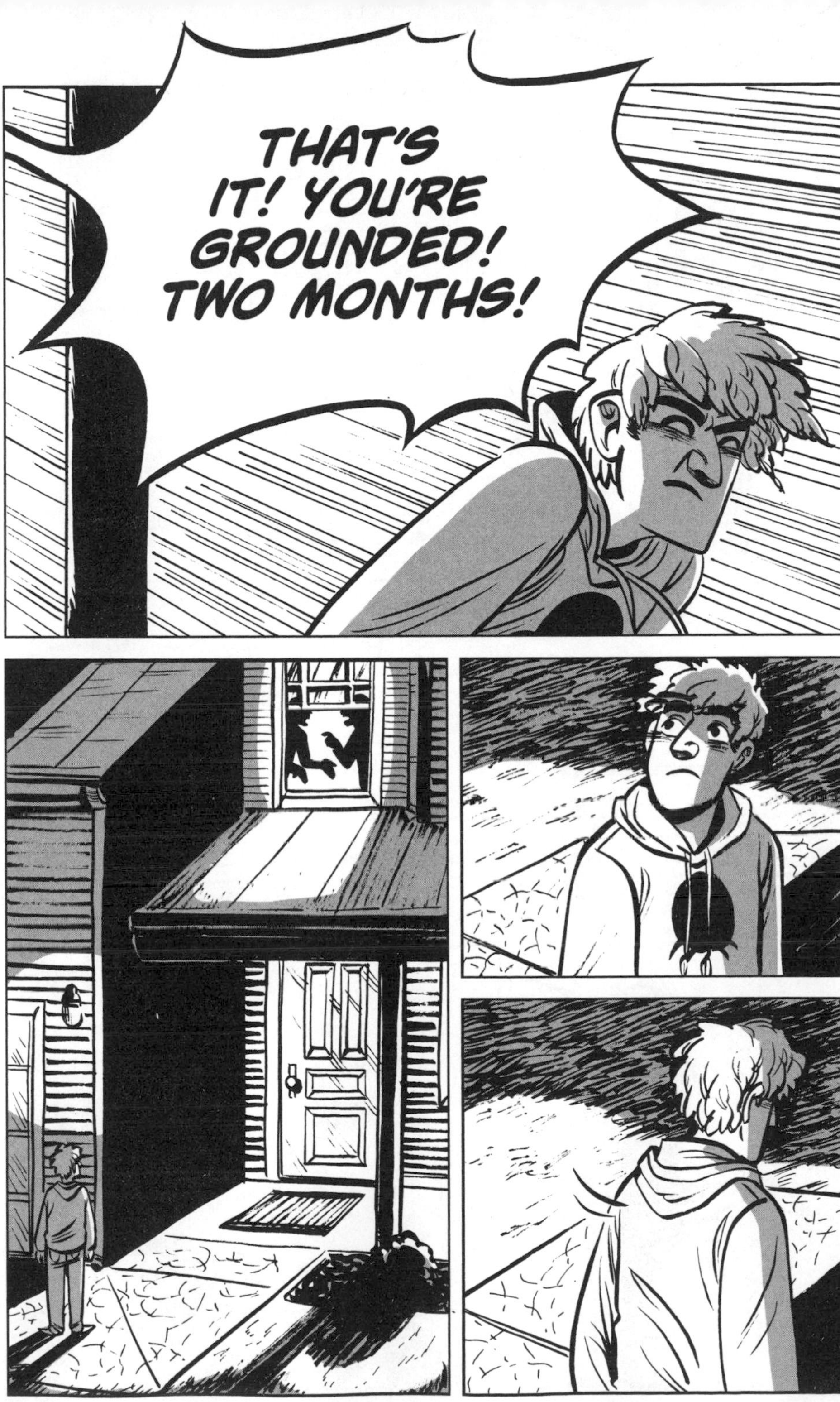
THAT'S IT! YOU'RE GROUNDED! TWO MONTHS!

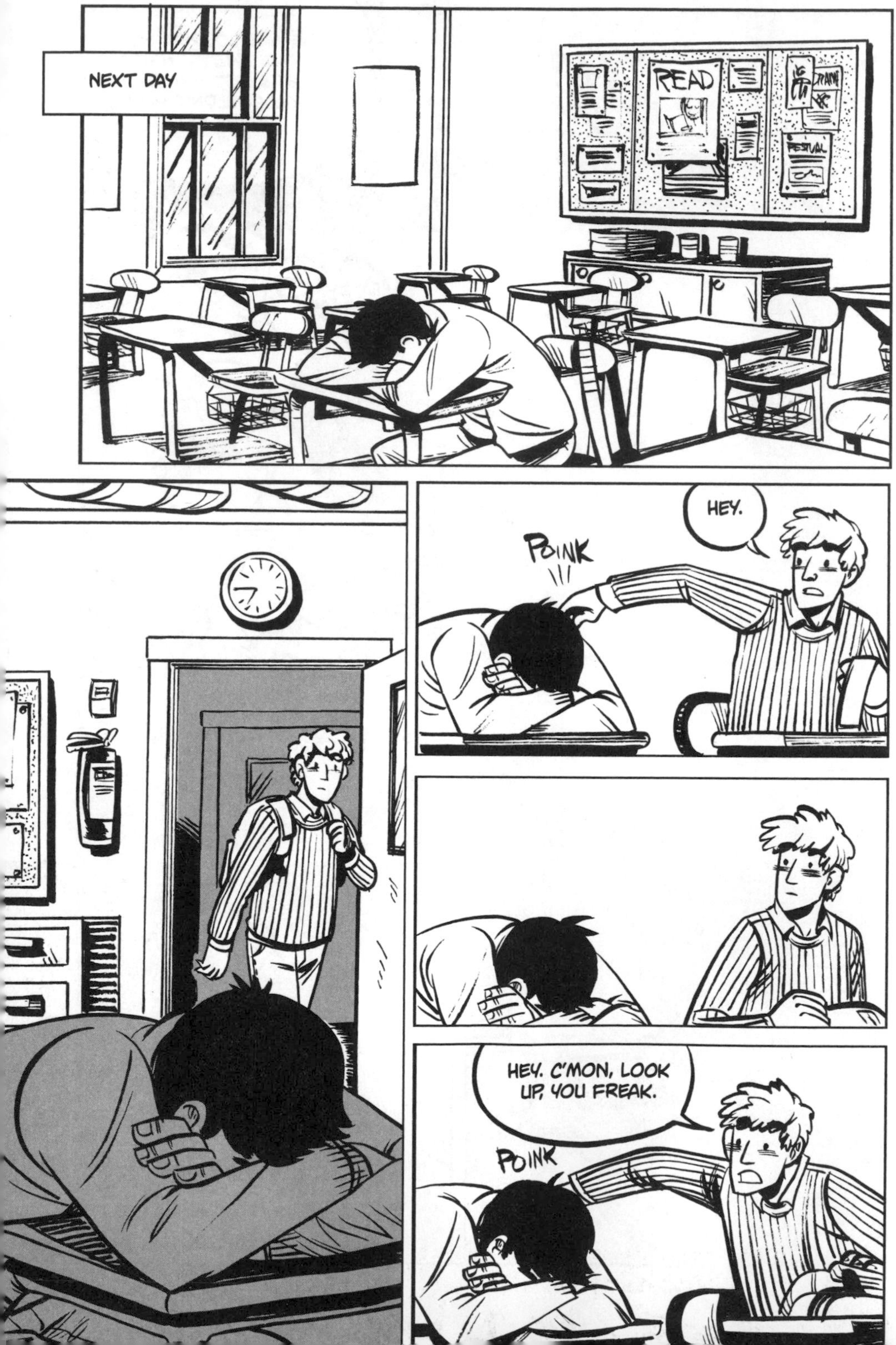
NEXT DAY
READ
FESTIVAL
HEY.
POINK
HEY. C'MON, LOOK UP, YOU FREAK.
POINK

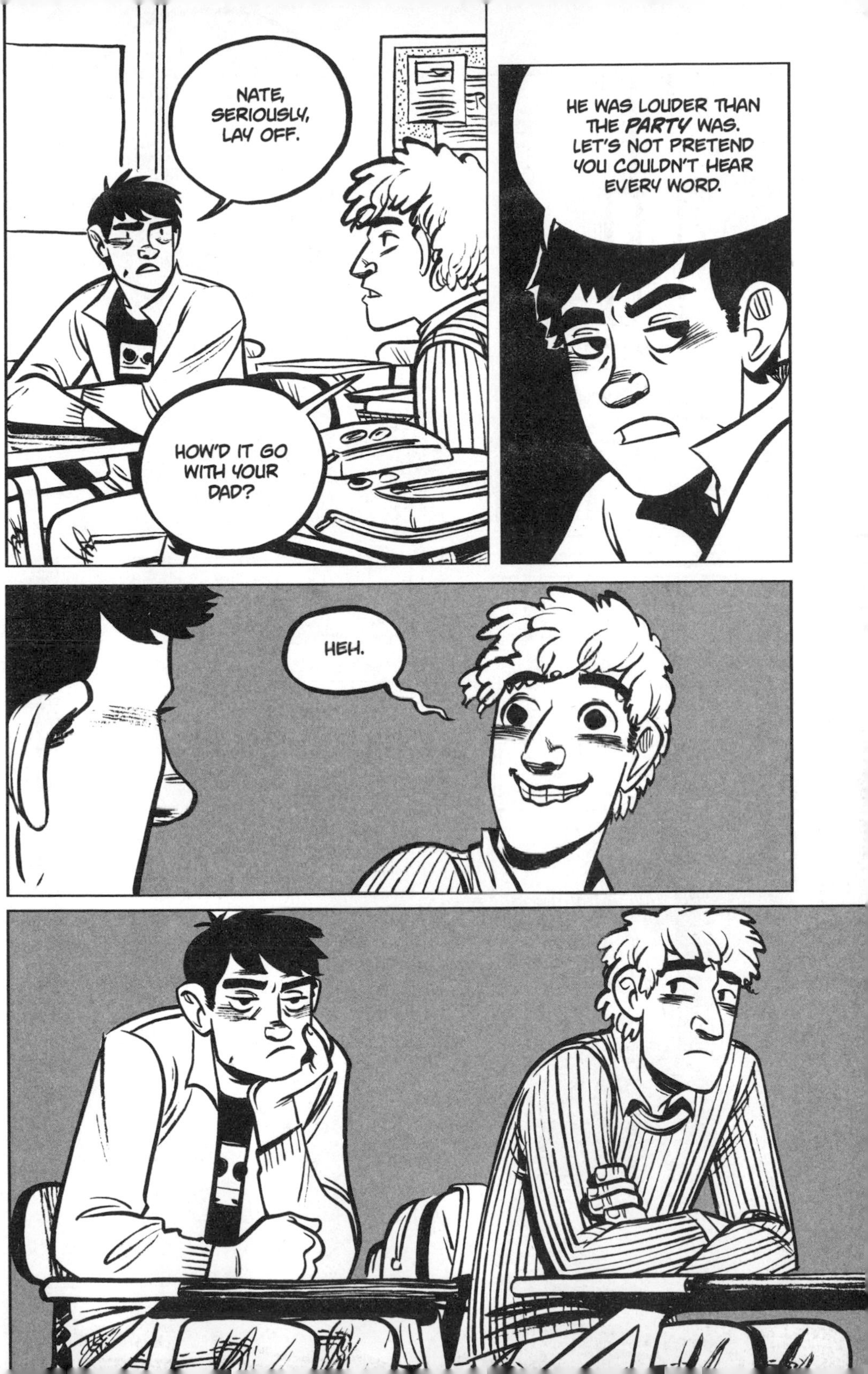
NATE, SERIOUSLY, LAY OFF.
HOW'D IT GO WITH YOUR DAD?
HE WAS LOUDER THAN THE *PARTY* WAS. LET'S NOT PRETEND YOU COULDN'T HEAR EVERY WORD.
HEH.

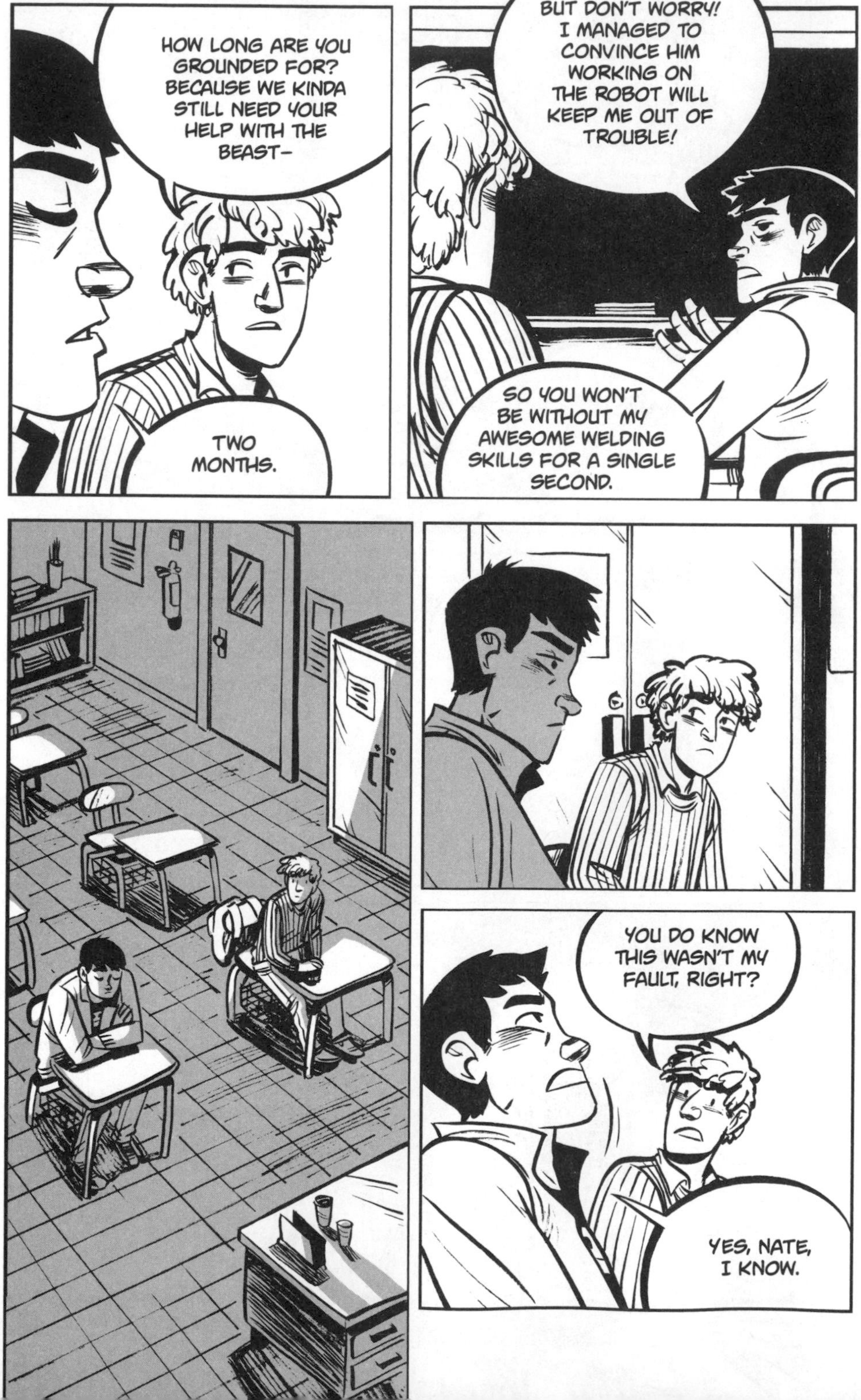
HOW LONG ARE YOU GROUNDED FOR? BECAUSE WE KINDA STILL NEED YOUR HELP WITH THE BEAST-
TWO MONTHS.
BUT DON'T WORRY! I MANAGED TO CONVINCE HIM WORKING ON THE ROBOT WILL KEEP ME OUT OF TROUBLE!
SO YOU WON'T BE WITHOUT MY AWESOME WELDING SKILLS FOR A SINGLE SECOND.
YOU DO KNOW THIS WASN'T MY FAULT, RIGHT?
YES, NATE, I KNOW.

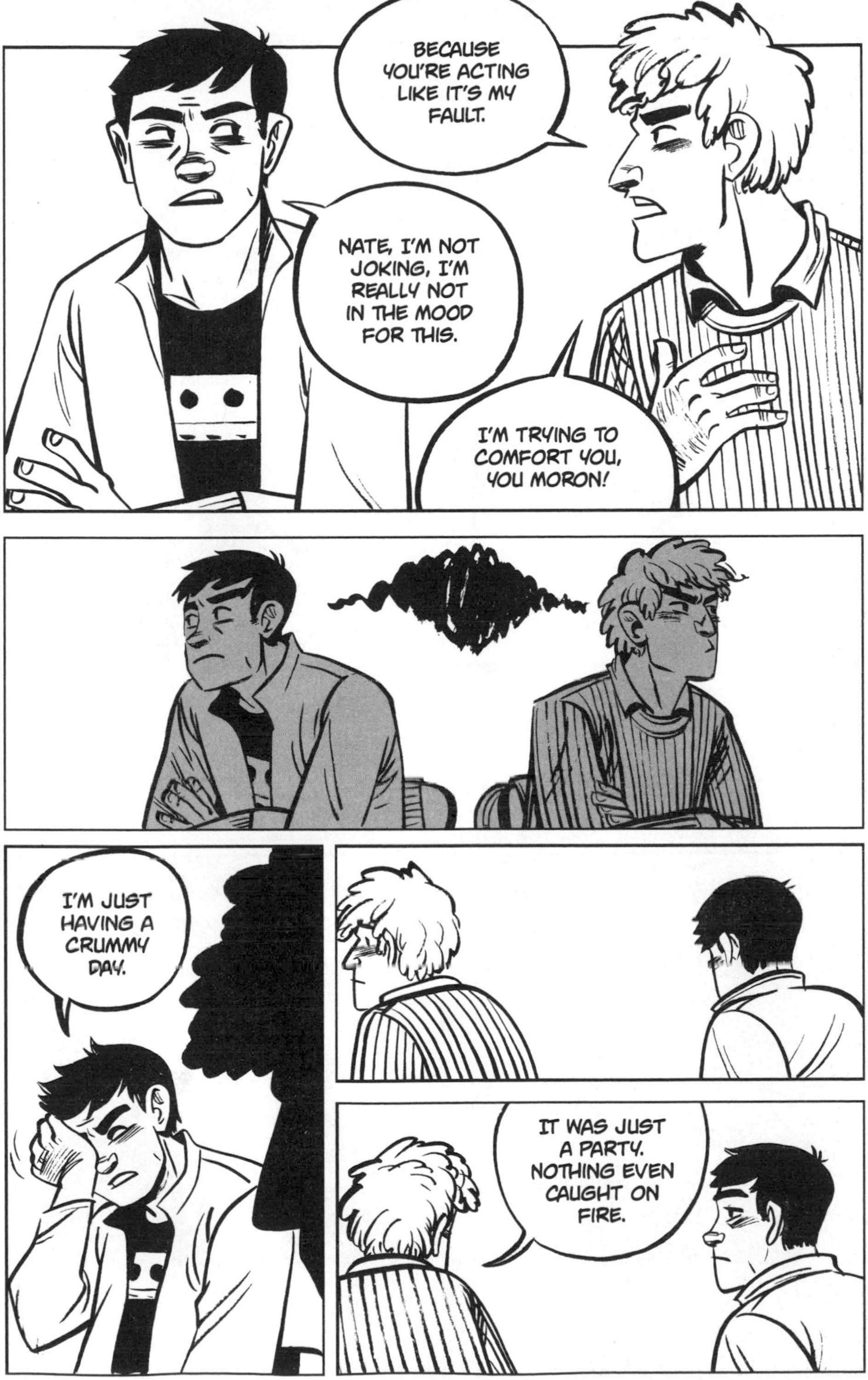
BECAUSE YOU'RE ACTING LIKE IT'S MY FAULT.
NATE, I'M NOT JOKING, I'M REALLY NOT IN THE MOOD FOR THIS.
I'M TRYING TO COMFORT YOU, YOU MORON!
I'M JUST HAVING A CRUMMY DAY.
IT WAS JUST A PARTY. NOTHING EVEN CAUGHT ON FIRE.

THE WEEK BEFORE THANKSGIVING

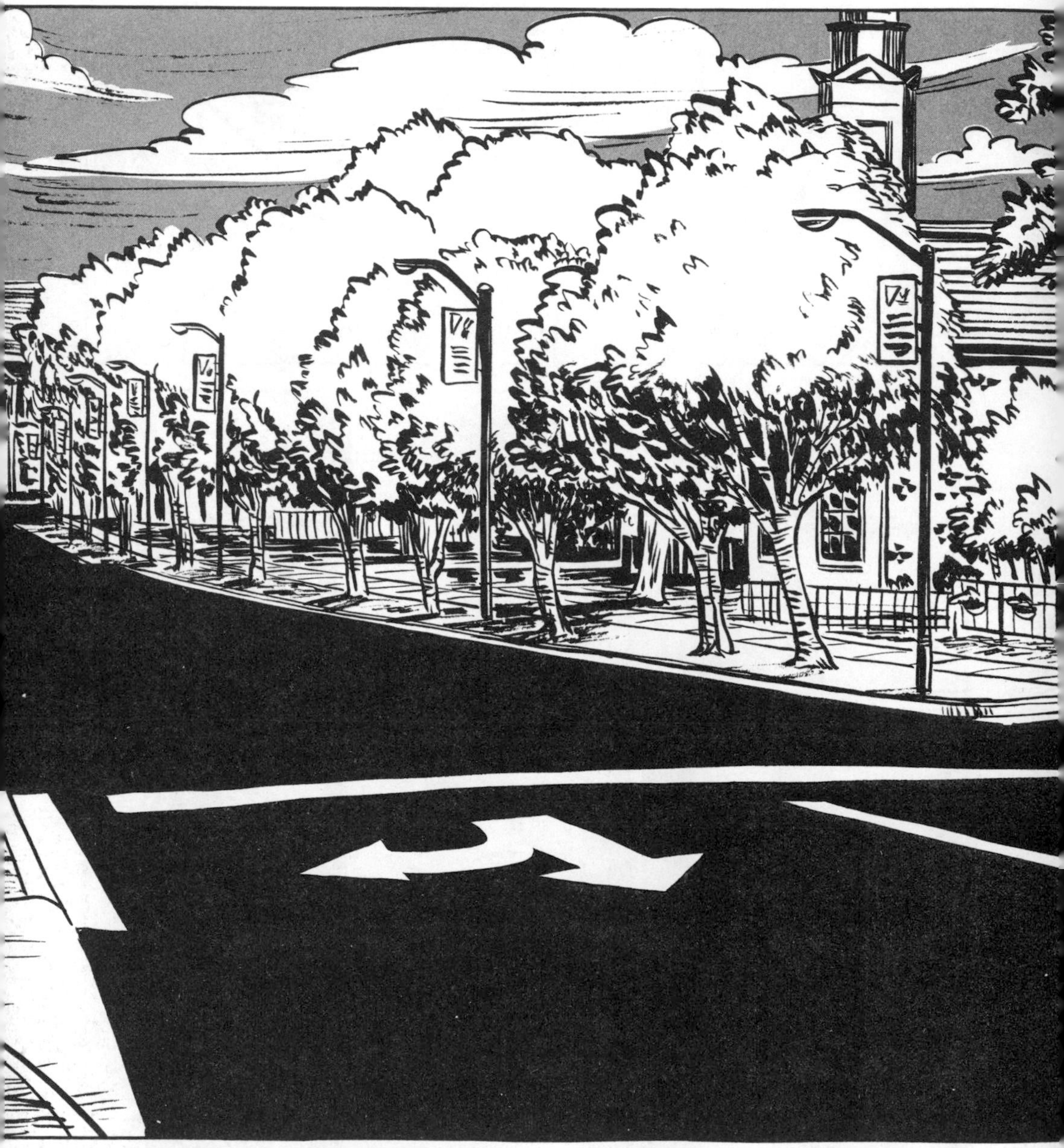

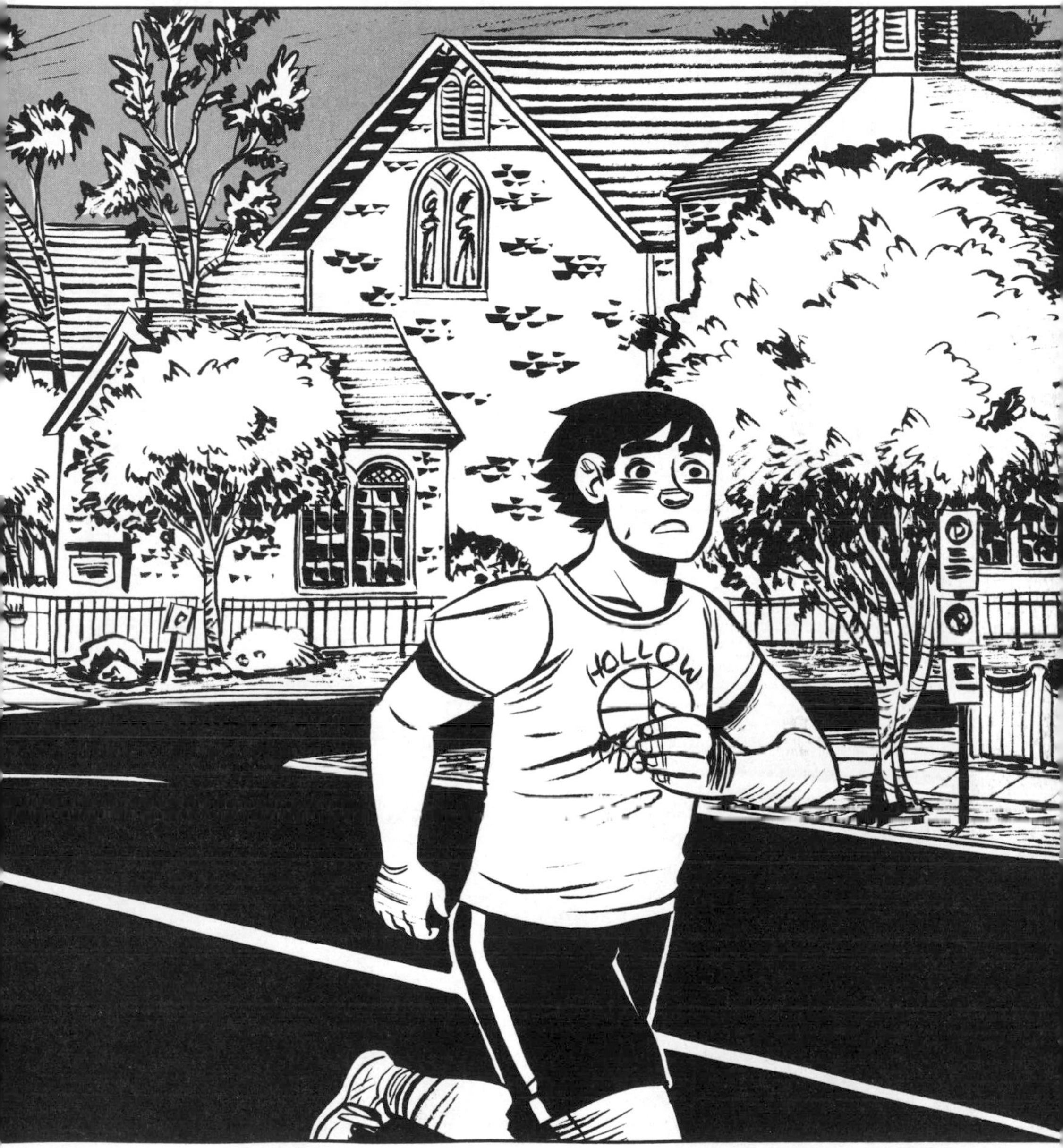
HOLLOW

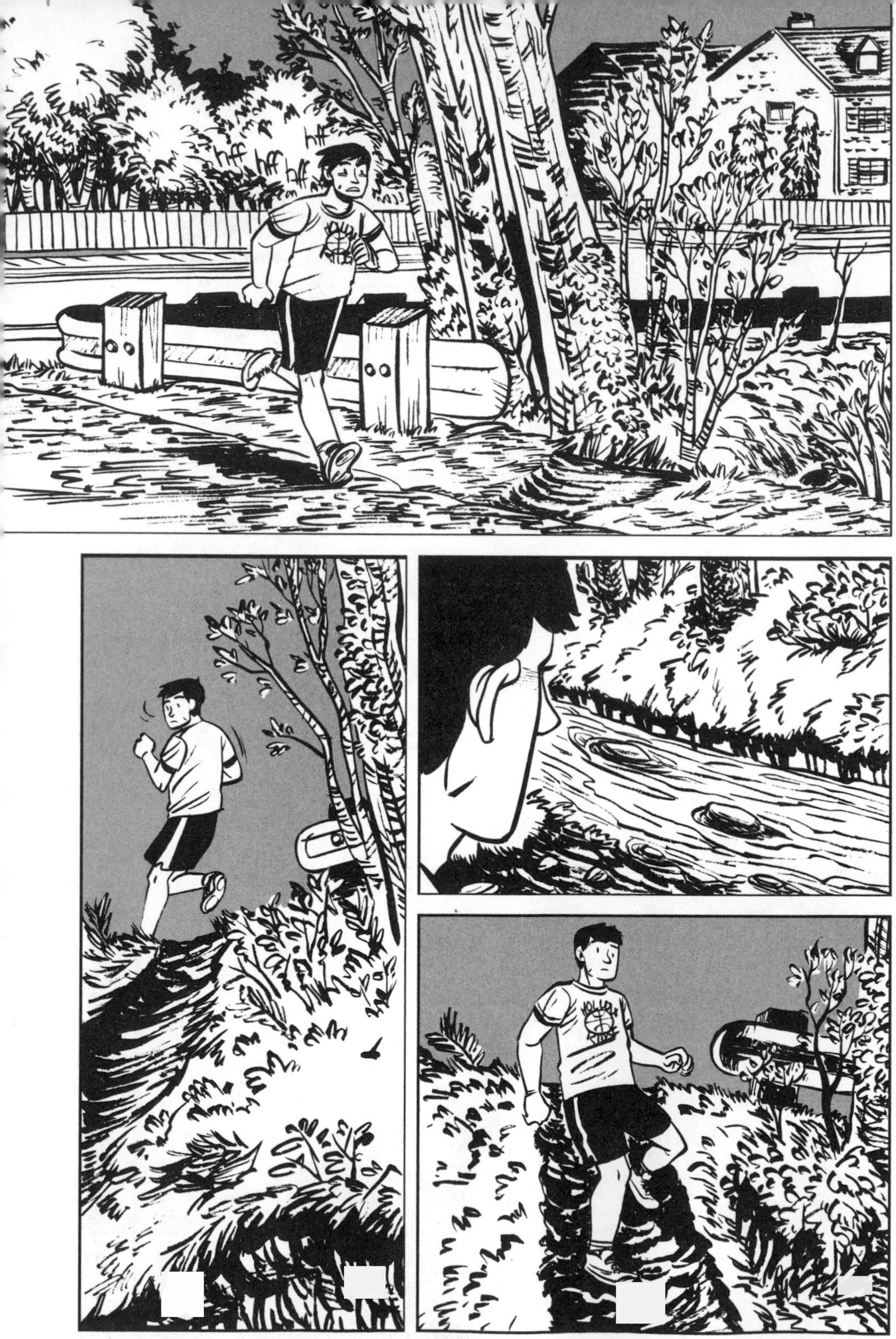
hff
hff
hff

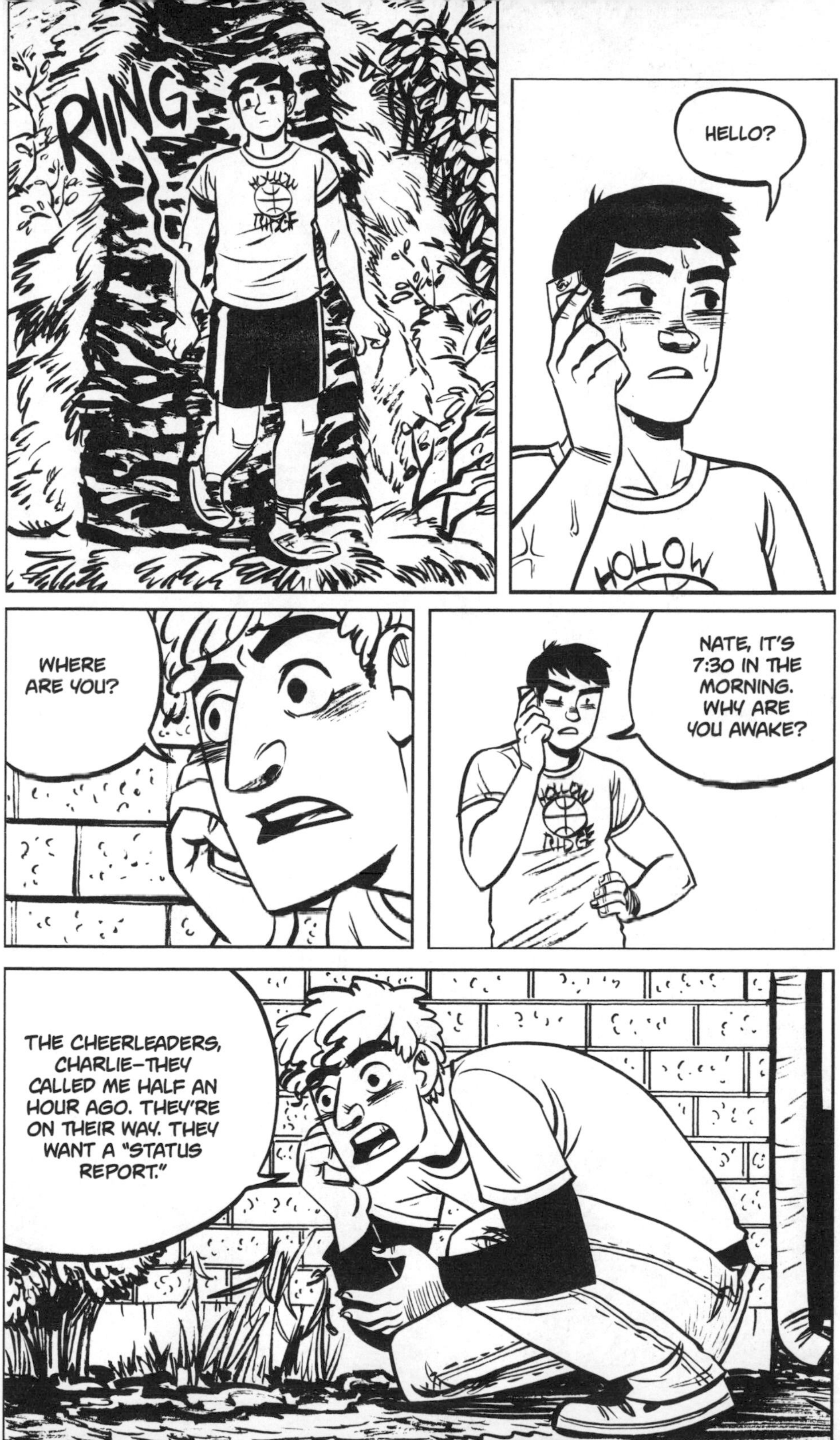
RING
HELLO?
WHERE ARE YOU?
NATE, IT'S 7:30 IN THE MORNING. WHY ARE YOU AWAKE?
THE CHEERLEADERS, CHARLIE—THEY CALLED ME HALF AN HOUR AGO. THEY'RE ON THEIR WAY. THEY WANT A "STATUS REPORT."

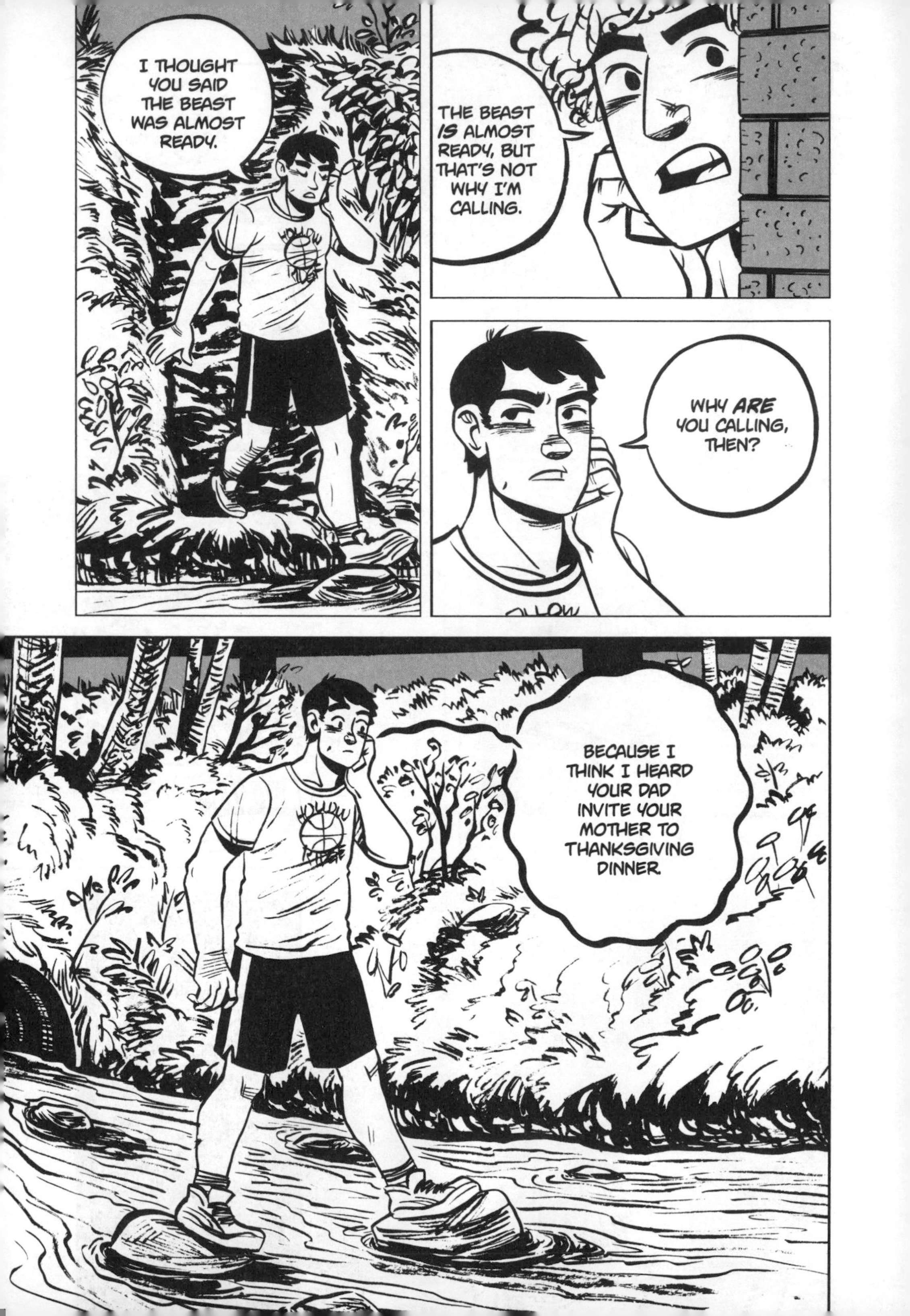
I THOUGHT YOU SAID THE BEAST WAS ALMOST READY.
THE BEAST *IS* ALMOST READY, BUT THAT'S NOT WHY I'M CALLING.
WHY *ARE* YOU CALLING, THEN?
BECAUSE I THINK I HEARD YOUR DAD INVITE YOUR MOTHER TO THANKSGIVING DINNER.

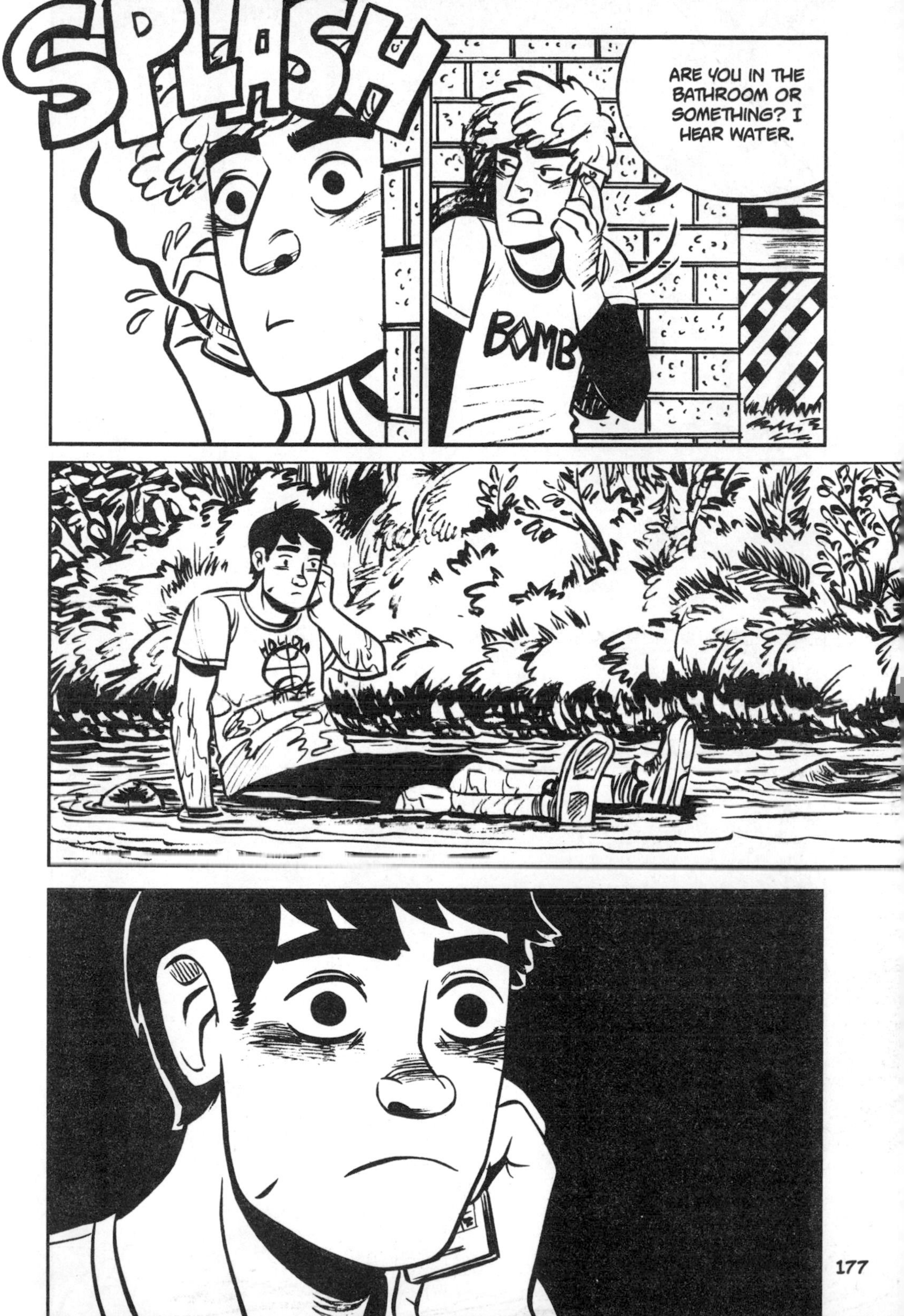
SPLASH
ARE YOU IN THE BATHROOM OR SOMETHING? I HEAR WATER.
BOMB
HOLLOW

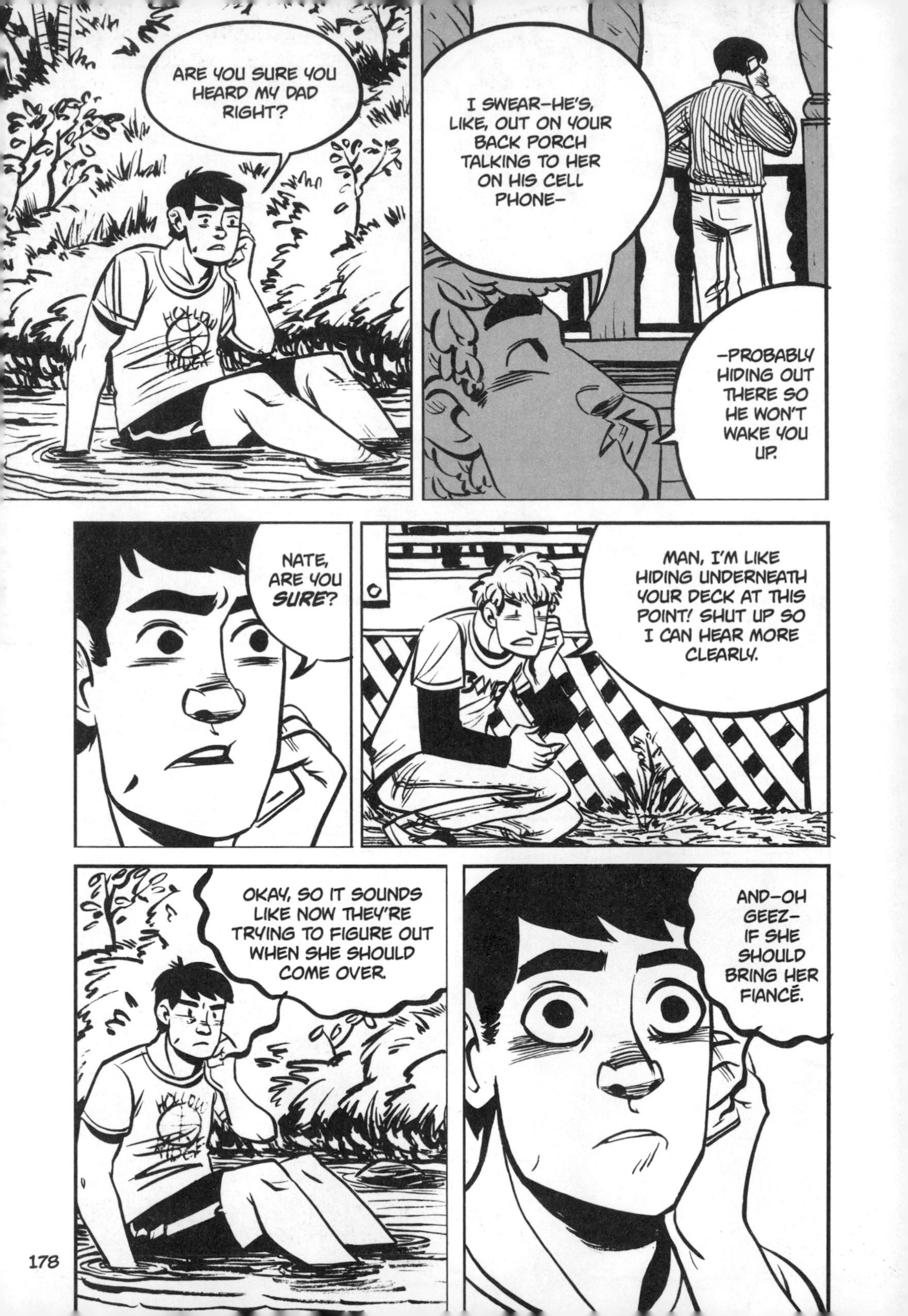
ARE YOU SURE YOU HEARD MY DAD RIGHT?
I SWEAR–HE'S, LIKE, OUT ON YOUR BACK PORCH TALKING TO HER ON HIS CELL PHONE–
–PROBABLY HIDING OUT THERE SO HE WON'T WAKE YOU UP.
NATE, ARE YOU *SURE*?
MAN, I'M LIKE HIDING UNDERNEATH YOUR DECK AT THIS POINT! SHUT UP SO I CAN HEAR MORE CLEARLY.
OKAY, SO IT SOUNDS LIKE NOW THEY'RE TRYING TO FIGURE OUT WHEN SHE SHOULD COME OVER.
AND–OH GEEZ– IF SHE SHOULD BRING HER FIANCÉ.

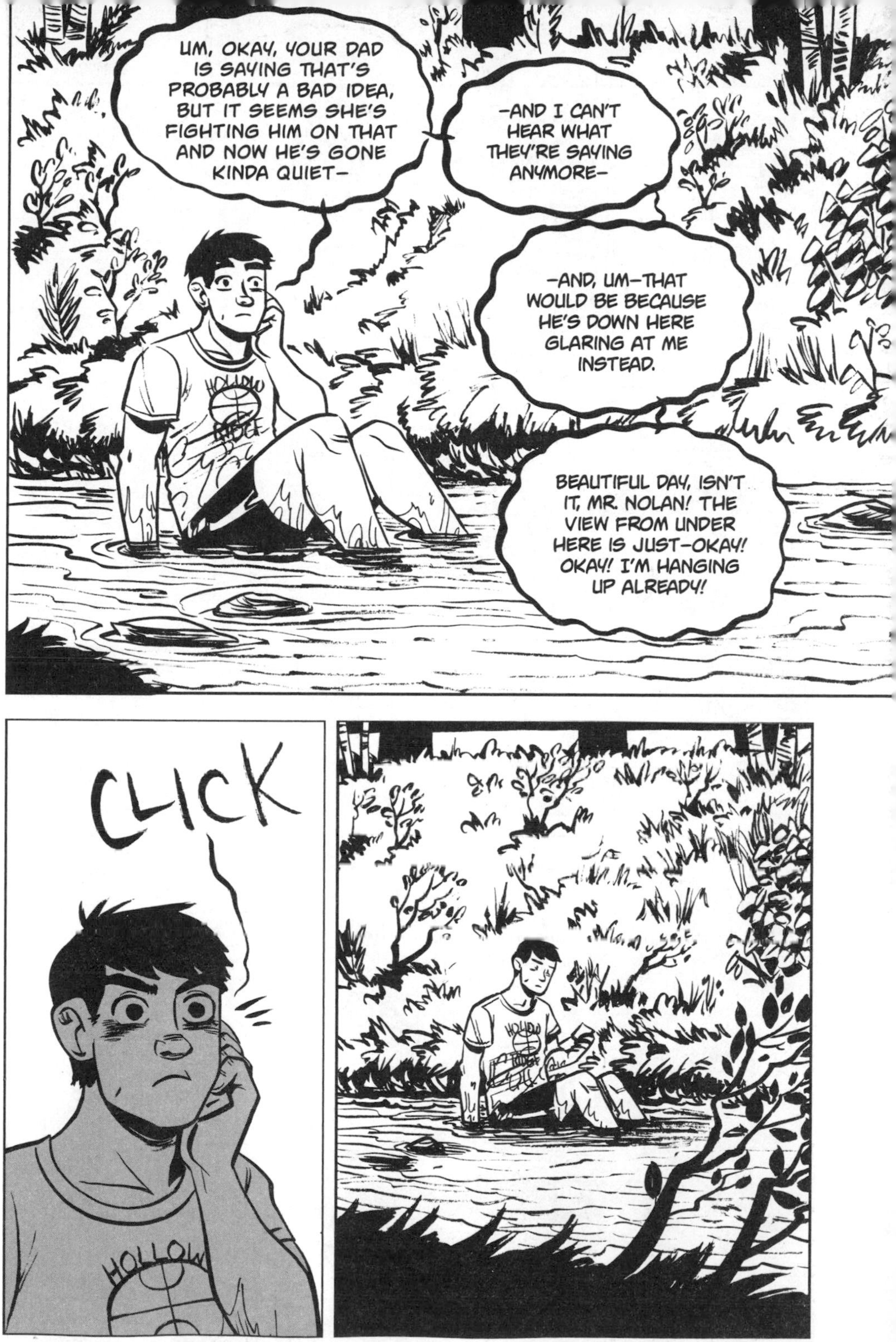
UM, OKAY, YOUR DAD IS SAYING THAT'S PROBABLY A BAD IDEA, BUT IT SEEMS SHE'S FIGHTING HIM ON THAT AND NOW HE'S GONE KINDA QUIET–
–AND I CAN'T HEAR WHAT THEY'RE SAYING ANYMORE–
–AND, UM–THAT WOULD BE BECAUSE HE'S DOWN HERE GLARING AT ME INSTEAD.
BEAUTIFUL DAY, ISN'T IT, MR. NOLAN! THE VIEW FROM UNDER HERE IS JUST–OKAY! OKAY! I'M HANGING UP ALREADY!
CLICK
HOLLOW RIDGE

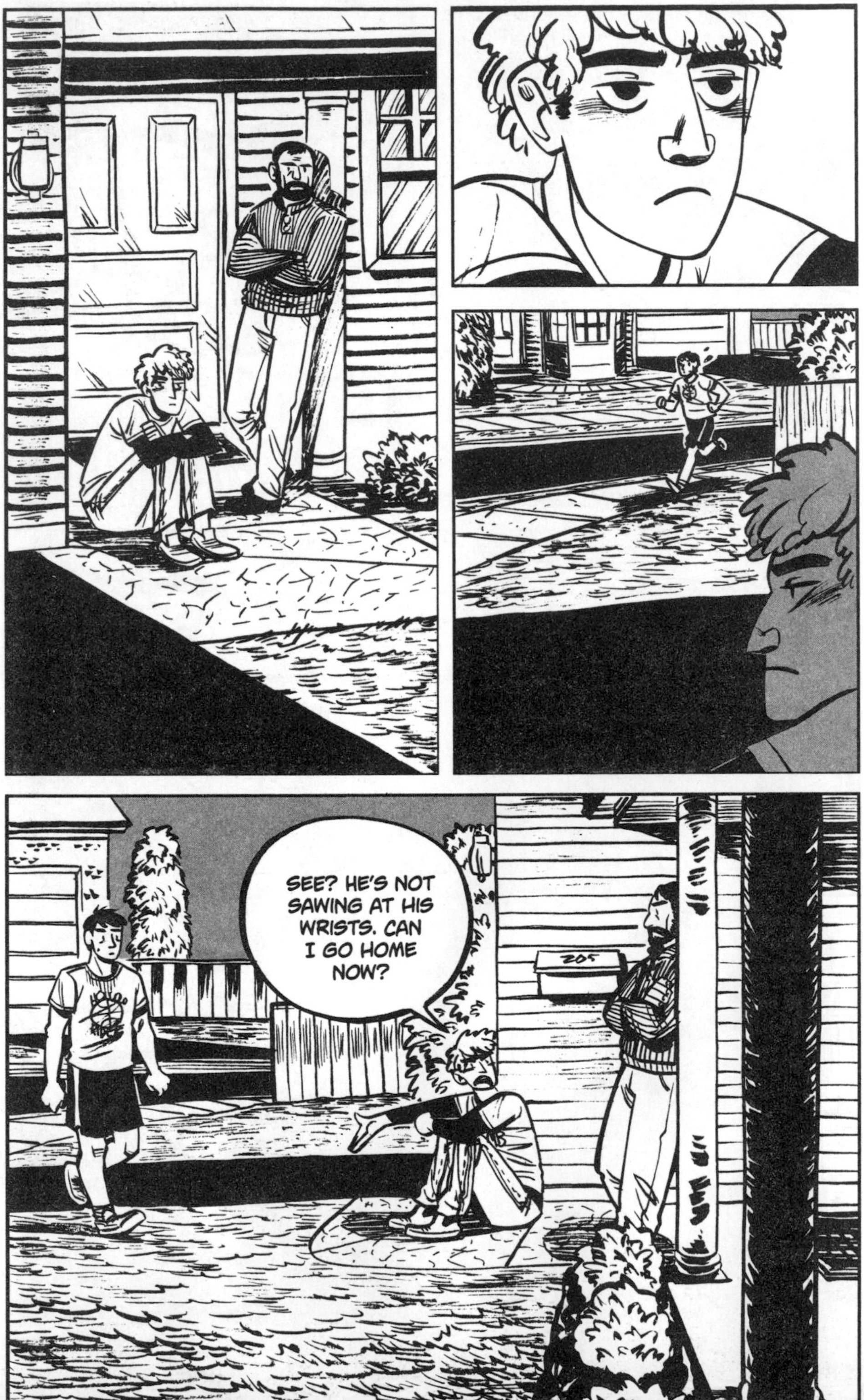
SEE? HE'S NOT SAWING AT HIS WRISTS. CAN I GO HOME NOW?
205

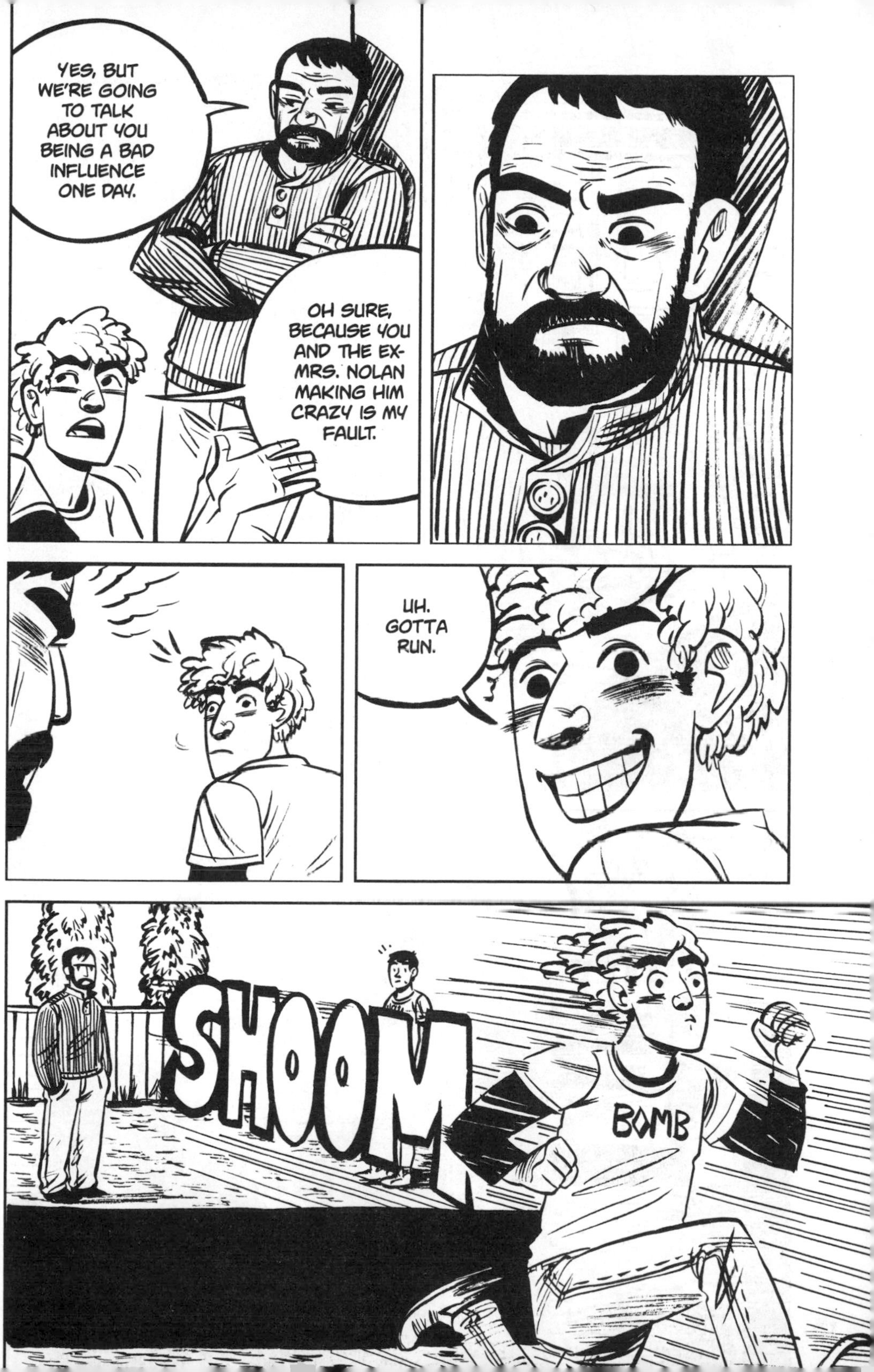
YES, BUT WE'RE GOING TO TALK ABOUT YOU BEING A BAD INFLUENCE ONE DAY.
OH SURE, BECAUSE YOU AND THE EX-MRS. NOLAN MAKING HIM CRAZY IS MY FAULT.
UH. GOTTA RUN.
SHOOM
BOMB

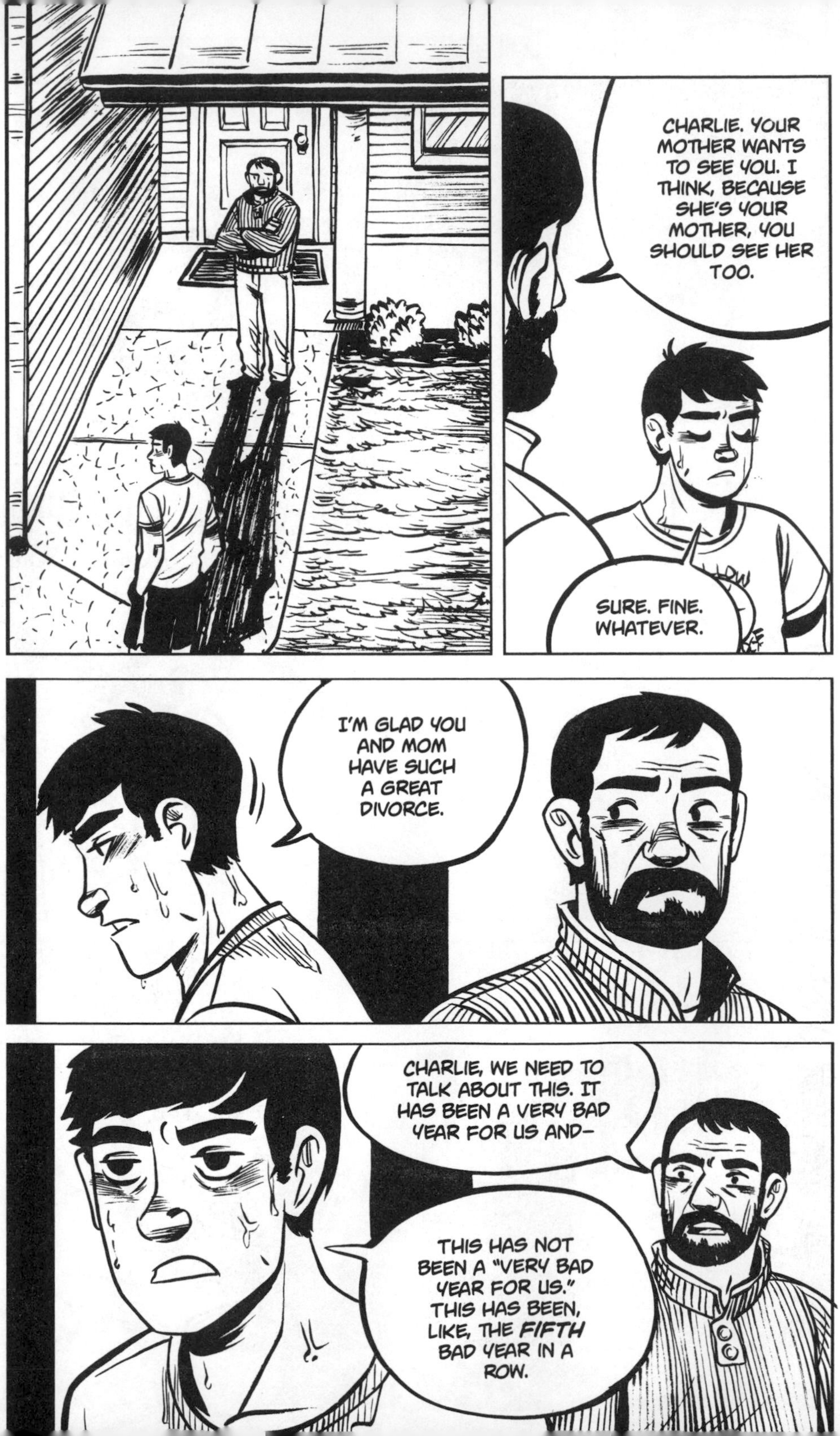
CHARLIE. YOUR MOTHER WANTS TO SEE YOU. I THINK, BECAUSE SHE'S YOUR MOTHER, YOU SHOULD SEE HER TOO.
SURE. FINE. WHATEVER.
I'M GLAD YOU AND MOM HAVE SUCH A GREAT DIVORCE.
CHARLIE, WE NEED TO TALK ABOUT THIS. IT HAS BEEN A VERY BAD YEAR FOR US AND–
THIS HAS NOT BEEN A "VERY BAD YEAR FOR US." THIS HAS BEEN, LIKE, THE *FIFTH* BAD YEAR IN A ROW.

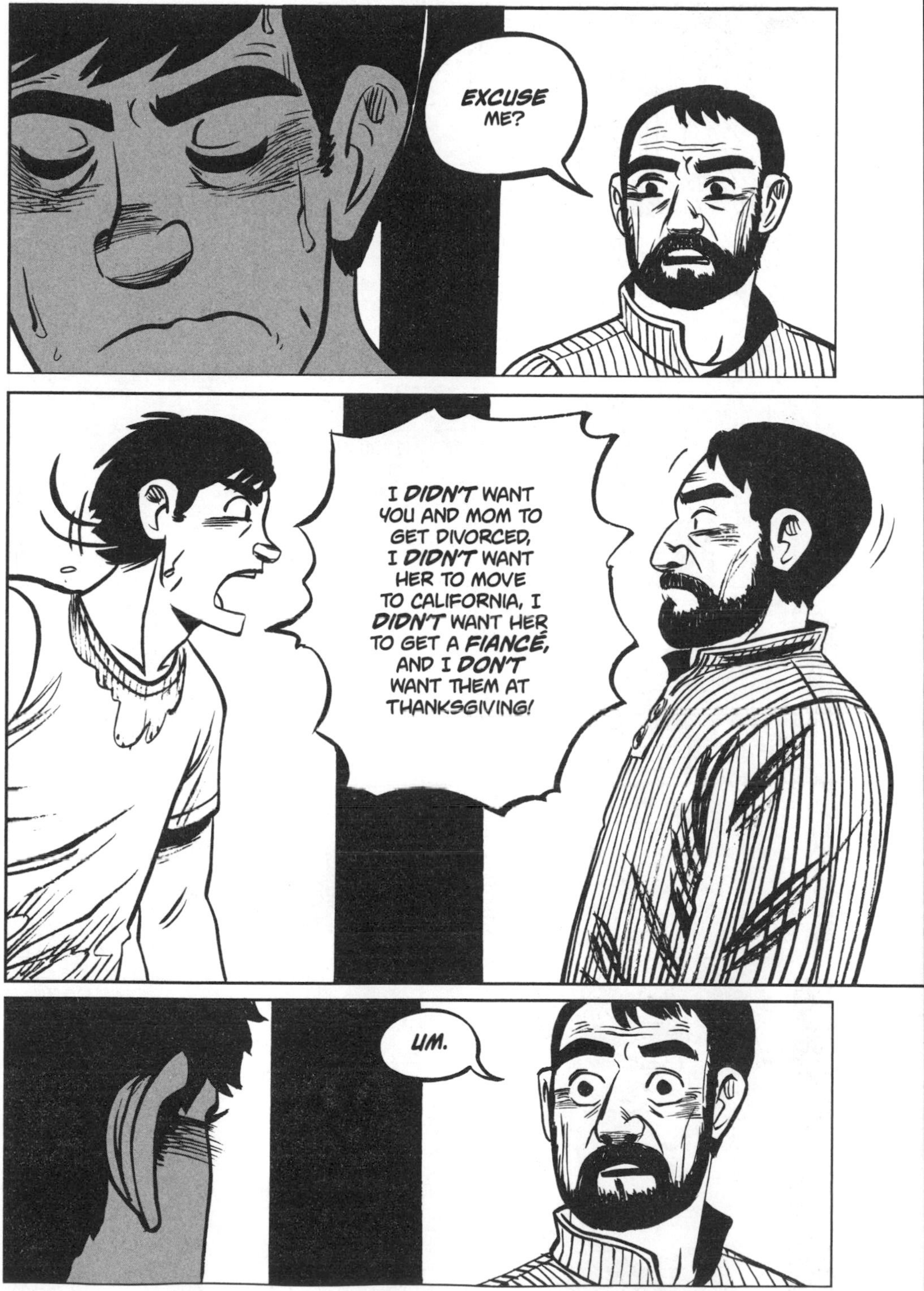
EXCUSE ME?
I DIDN'T WANT YOU AND MOM TO GET DIVORCED, I DIDN'T WANT HER TO MOVE TO CALIFORNIA, I DIDN'T WANT HER TO GET A FIANCÉ, AND I DON'T WANT THEM AT THANKSGIVING!
UM.

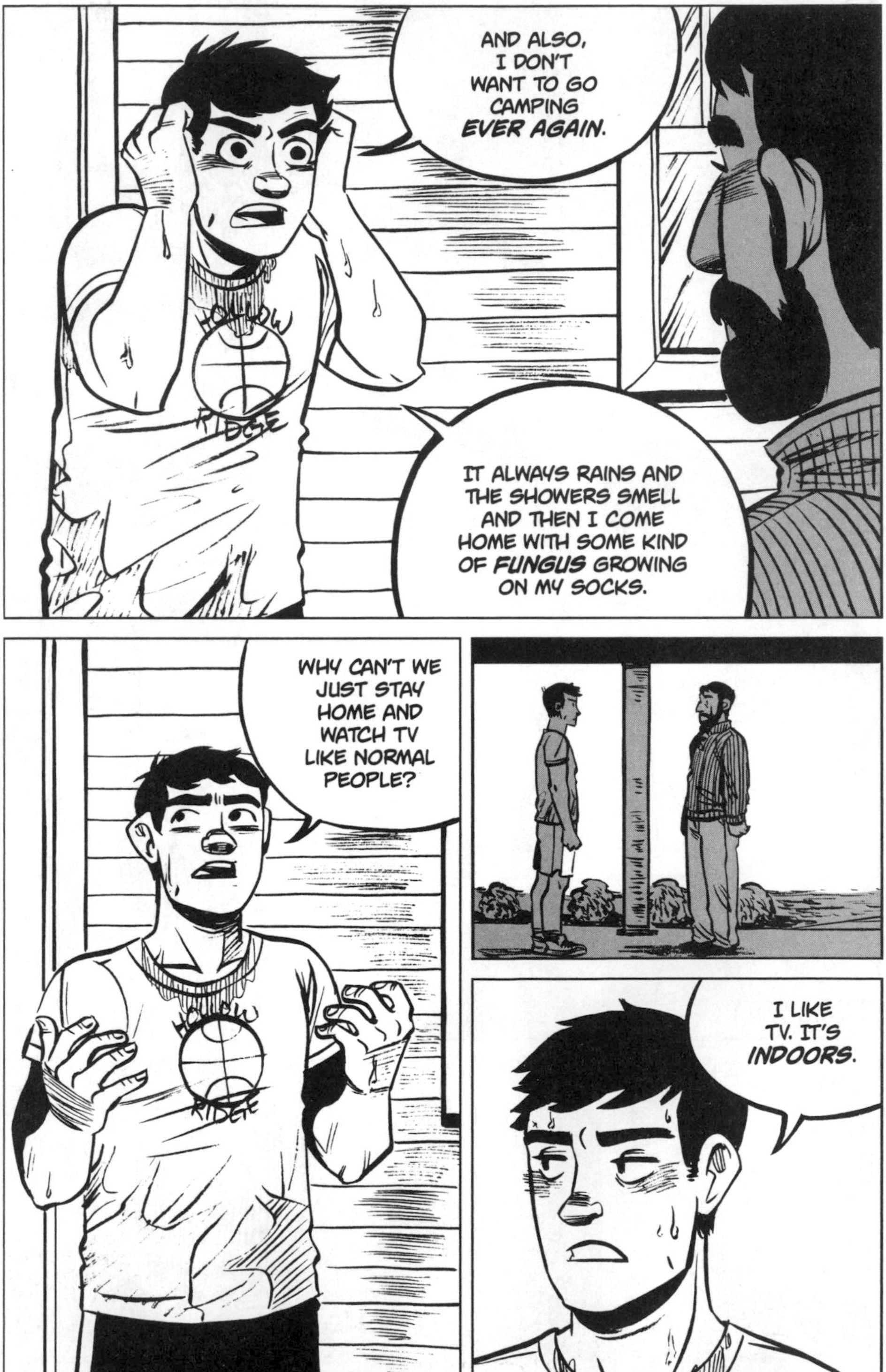
AND ALSO, I DON'T WANT TO GO CAMPING EVER AGAIN.
IT ALWAYS RAINS AND THE SHOWERS SMELL AND THEN I COME HOME WITH SOME KIND OF FUNGUS GROWING ON MY SOCKS.
WHY CAN'T WE JUST STAY HOME AND WATCH TV LIKE NORMAL PEOPLE?
I LIKE TV. IT'S INDOORS.

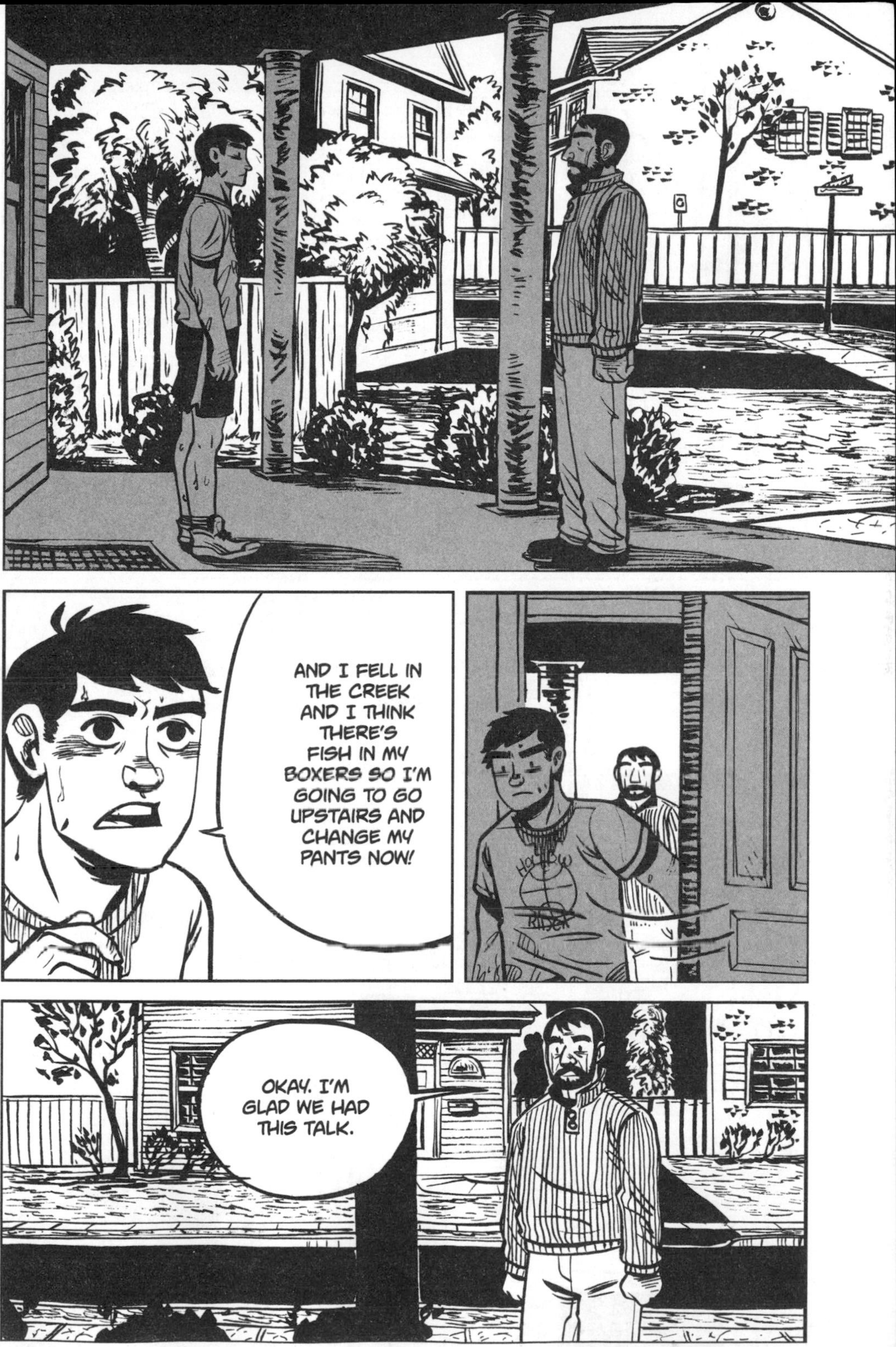
AND I FELL IN THE CREEK AND I THINK THERE'S FISH IN MY BOXERS SO I'M GOING TO GO UPSTAIRS AND CHANGE MY PANTS NOW!
OKAY. I'M GLAD WE HAD THIS TALK.

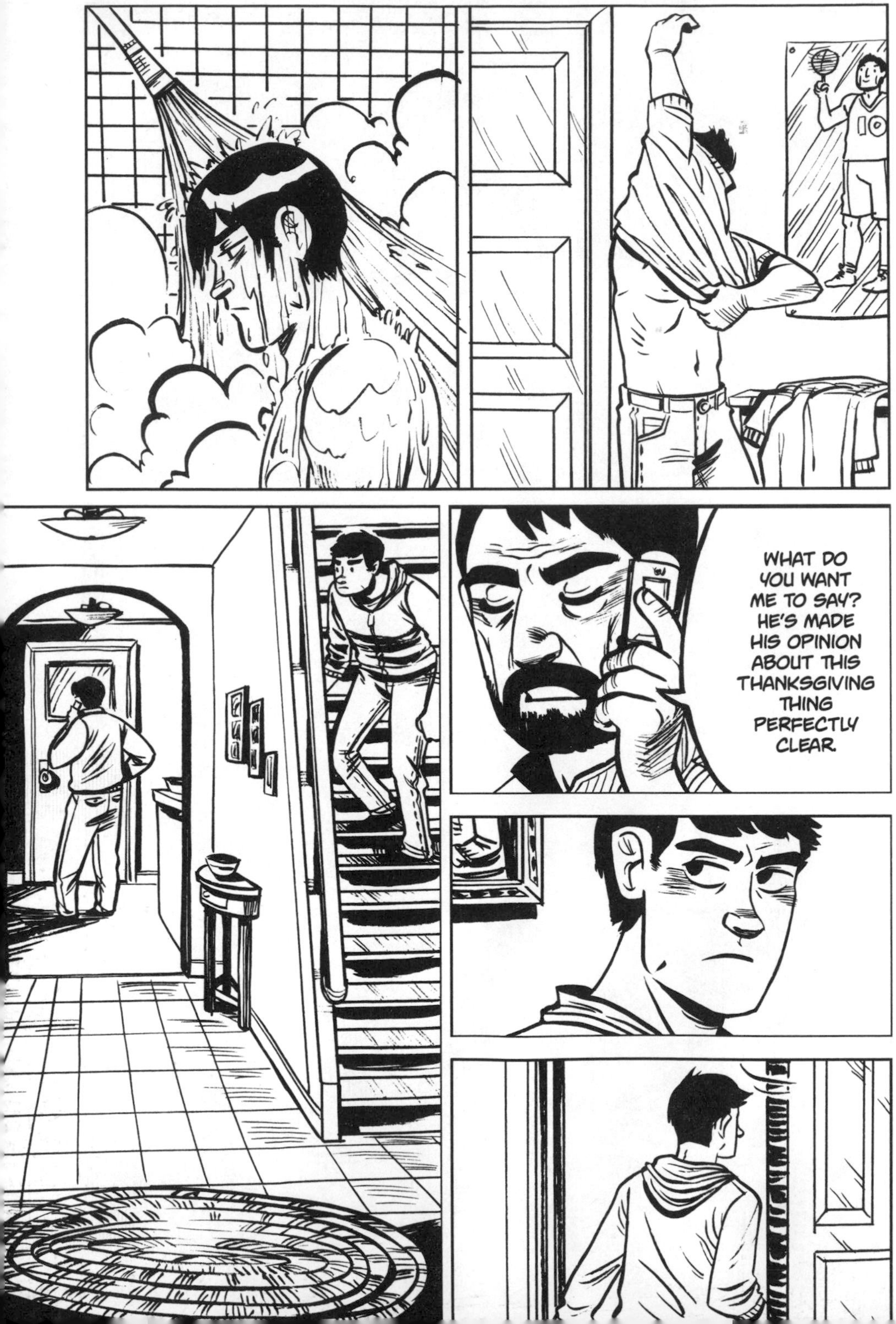
WHAT DO YOU WANT ME TO SAY? HE'S MADE HIS OPINION ABOUT THIS THANKSGIVING THING PERFECTLY CLEAR.

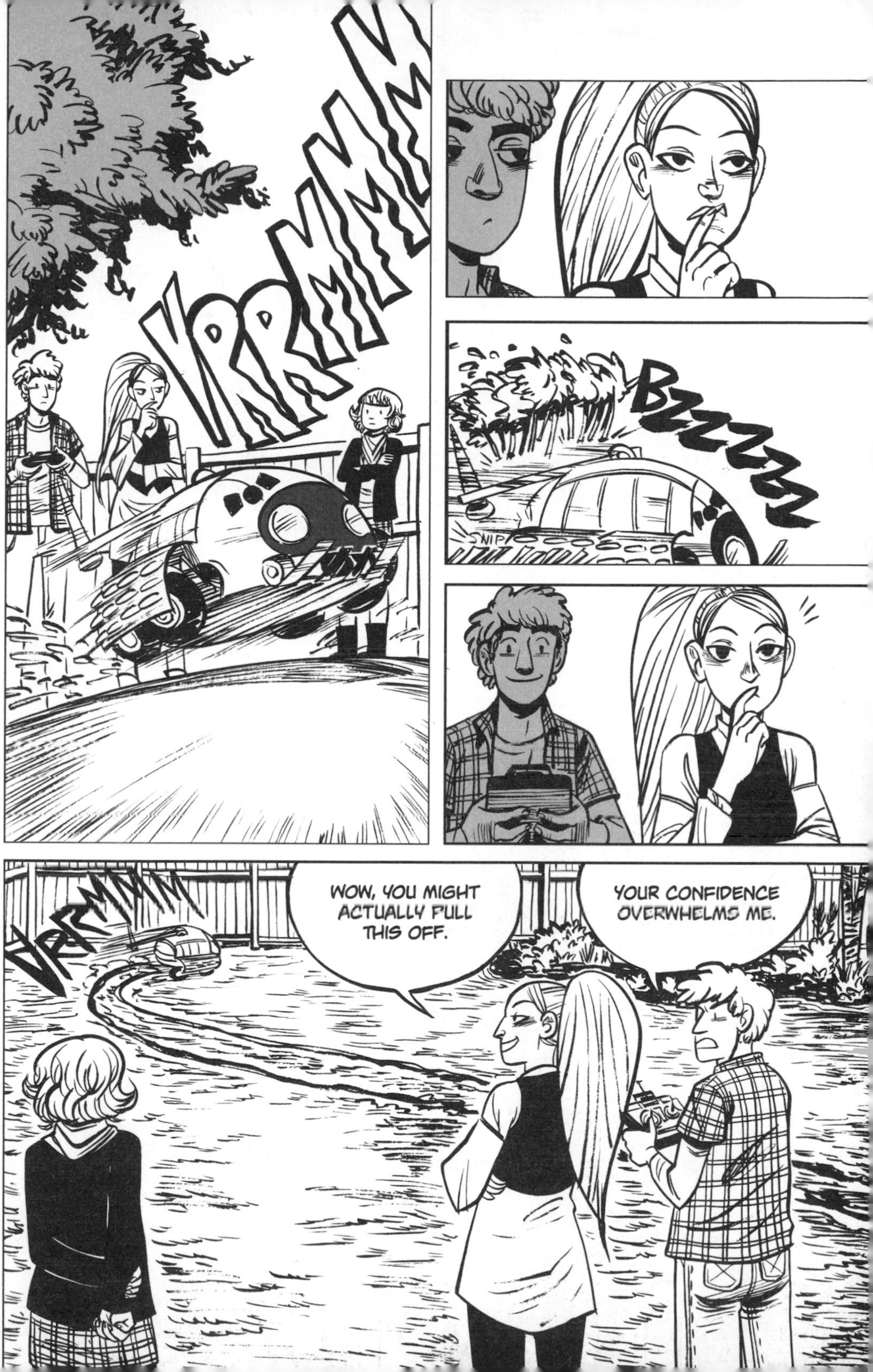
WOW, YOU MIGHT ACTUALLY PULL THIS OFF.
YOUR CONFIDENCE OVERWHELMS ME.

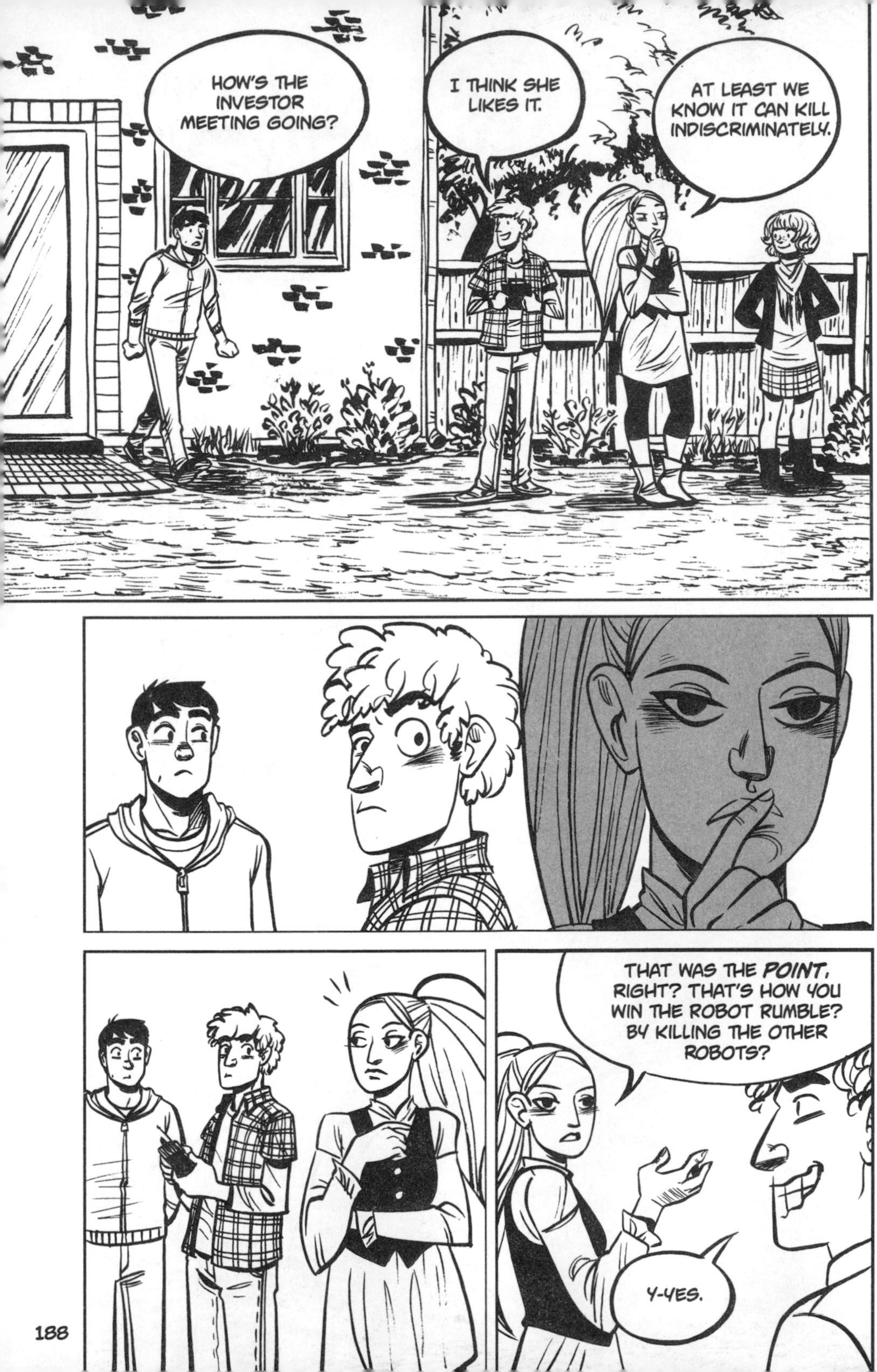
HOW'S THE INVESTOR MEETING GOING?
I THINK SHE LIKES IT.
AT LEAST WE KNOW IT CAN KILL INDISCRIMINATELY.
THAT WAS THE *POINT*, RIGHT? THAT'S HOW YOU WIN THE ROBOT RUMBLE? BY KILLING THE OTHER ROBOTS?
Y-YES.

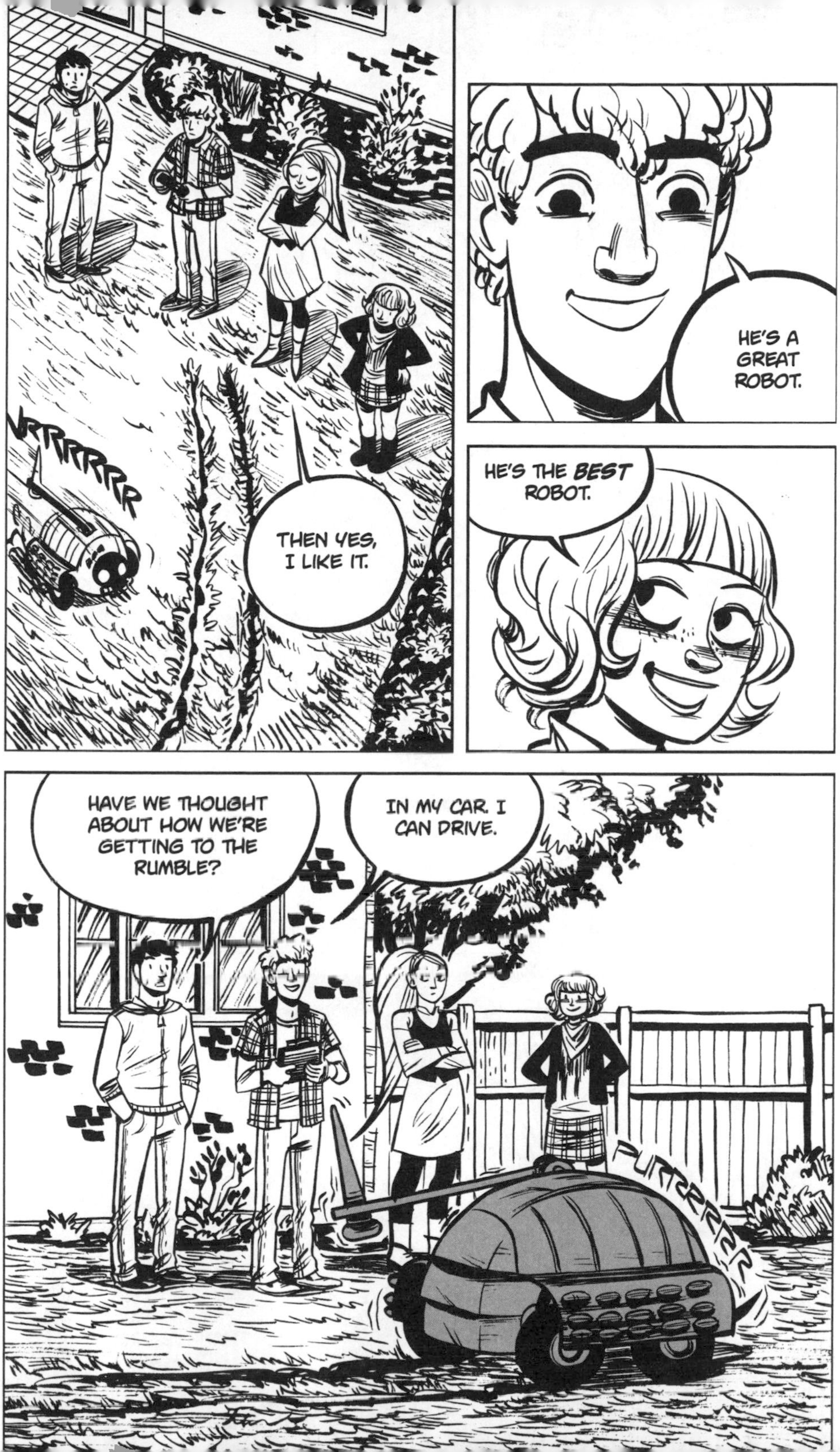
THEN YES, I LIKE IT.
HE'S A GREAT ROBOT.
HE'S THE *BEST* ROBOT.
HAVE WE THOUGHT ABOUT HOW WE'RE GETTING TO THE RUMBLE?
IN MY CAR. I CAN DRIVE.

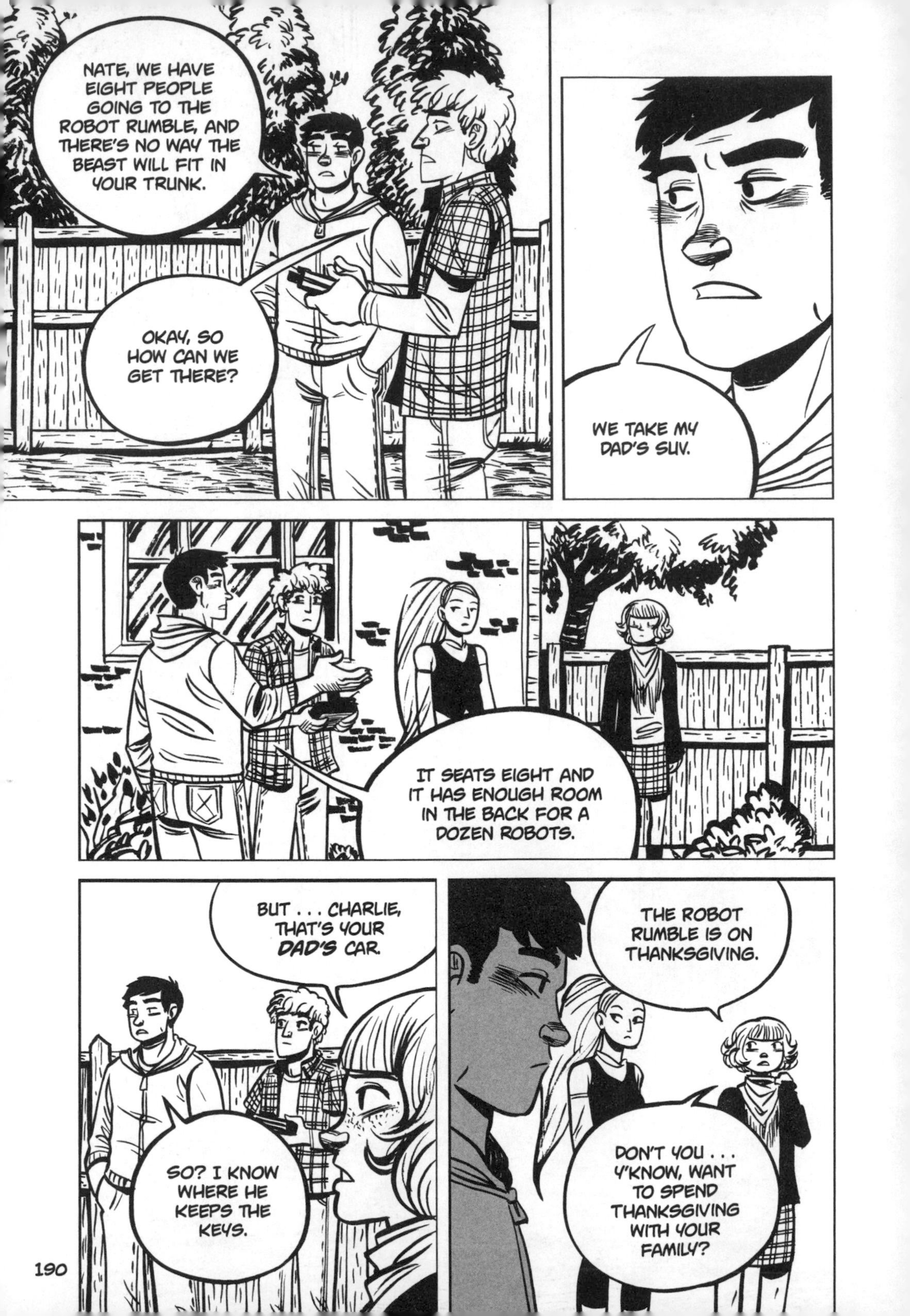

NATE, WE HAVE EIGHT PEOPLE GOING TO THE ROBOT RUMBLE, AND THERE'S NO WAY THE BEAST WILL FIT IN YOUR TRUNK.
OKAY, SO HOW CAN WE GET THERE?
WE TAKE MY DAD'S SUV.
IT SEATS EIGHT AND IT HAS ENOUGH ROOM IN THE BACK FOR A DOZEN ROBOTS.
BUT . . . CHARLIE, THAT'S YOUR *DAD'S* CAR.
SO? I KNOW WHERE HE KEEPS THE KEYS.
THE ROBOT RUMBLE IS ON THANKSGIVING.
DON'T YOU . . . Y'KNOW, WANT TO SPEND THANKSGIVING WITH YOUR FAMILY?

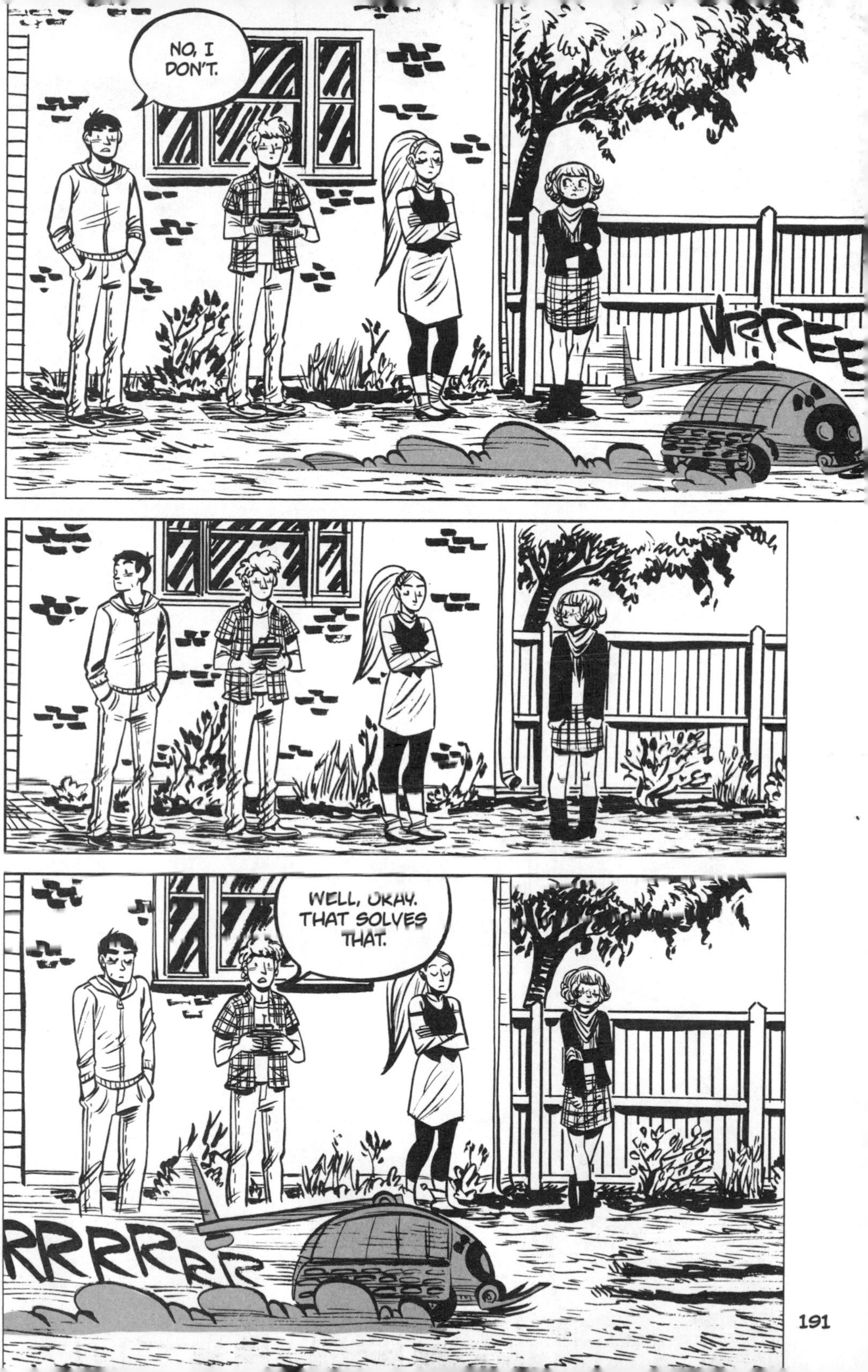
NO, I DON'T.
VRREE
WELL, OKAY. THAT SOLVES THAT.
RRRRRR

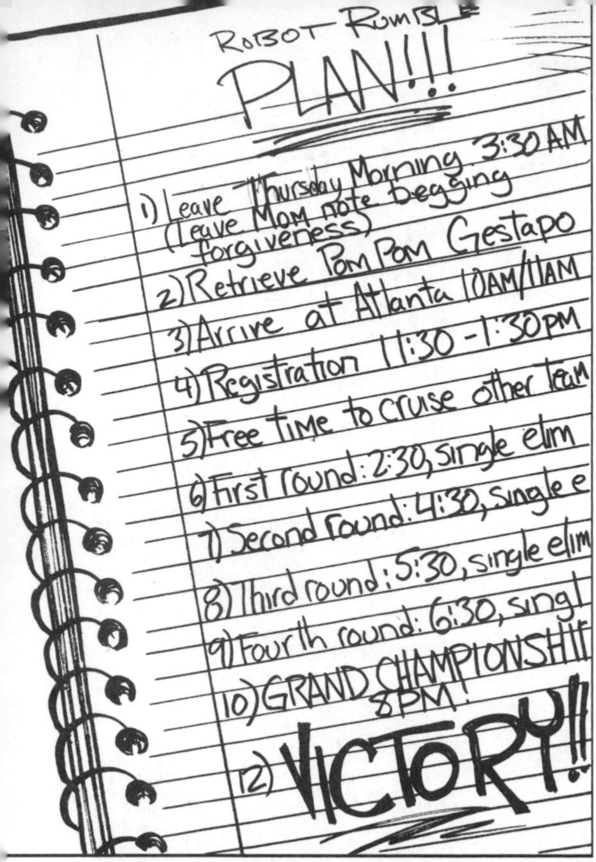
ROBOT RUMBLE
PLAN!!!
1) Leave Thursday Morning 3:30 AM
(Leave Mom note begging forgiveness)
2) Retrieve Pom Pom Gestapo
3) Arrive at Atlanta 10AM/11AM
4) Registration 11:30 - 1:30PM
5) Free time to cruise other team
6) First round: 2:30, single elim
7) Second round: 4:30, single e
8) Third round: 5:30, single elim
9) Fourth round: 6:30, singl
10) GRAND CHAMPIONSHI 8PM!
12) VICTORY!!

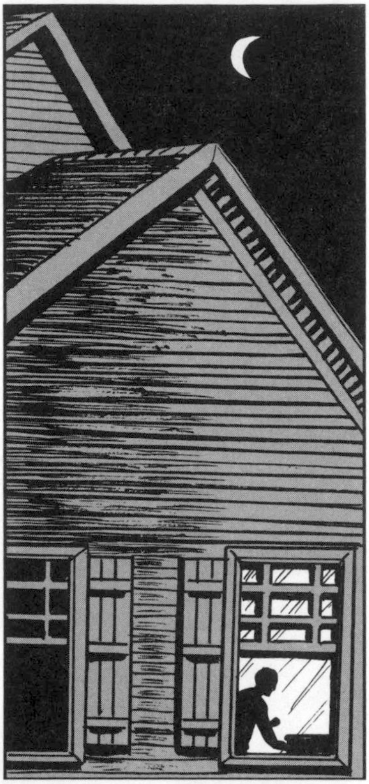

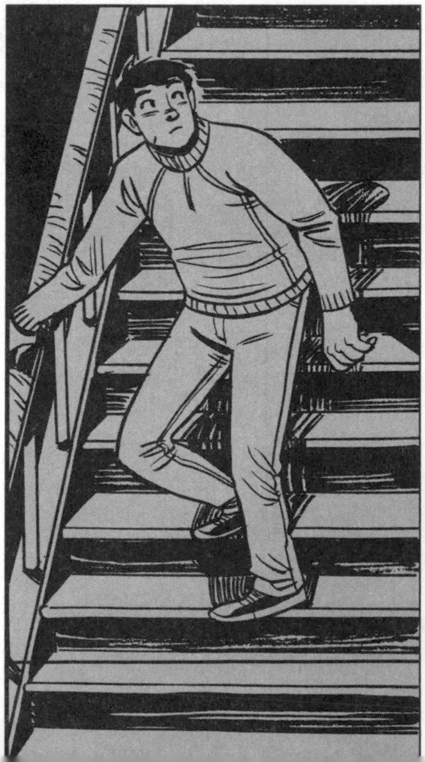

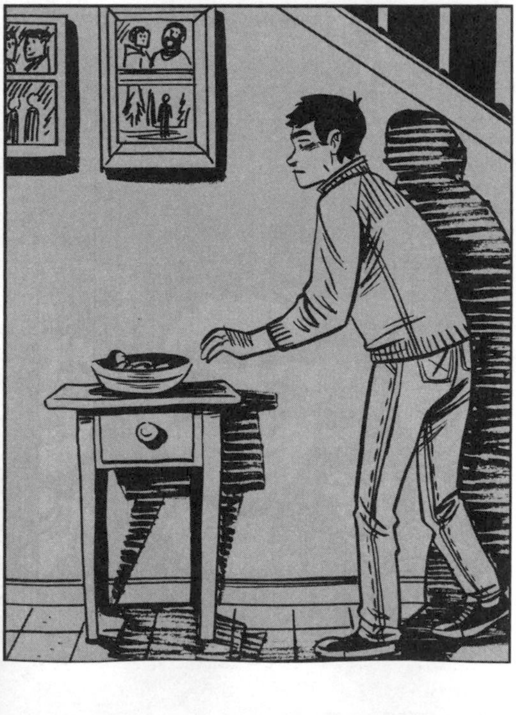

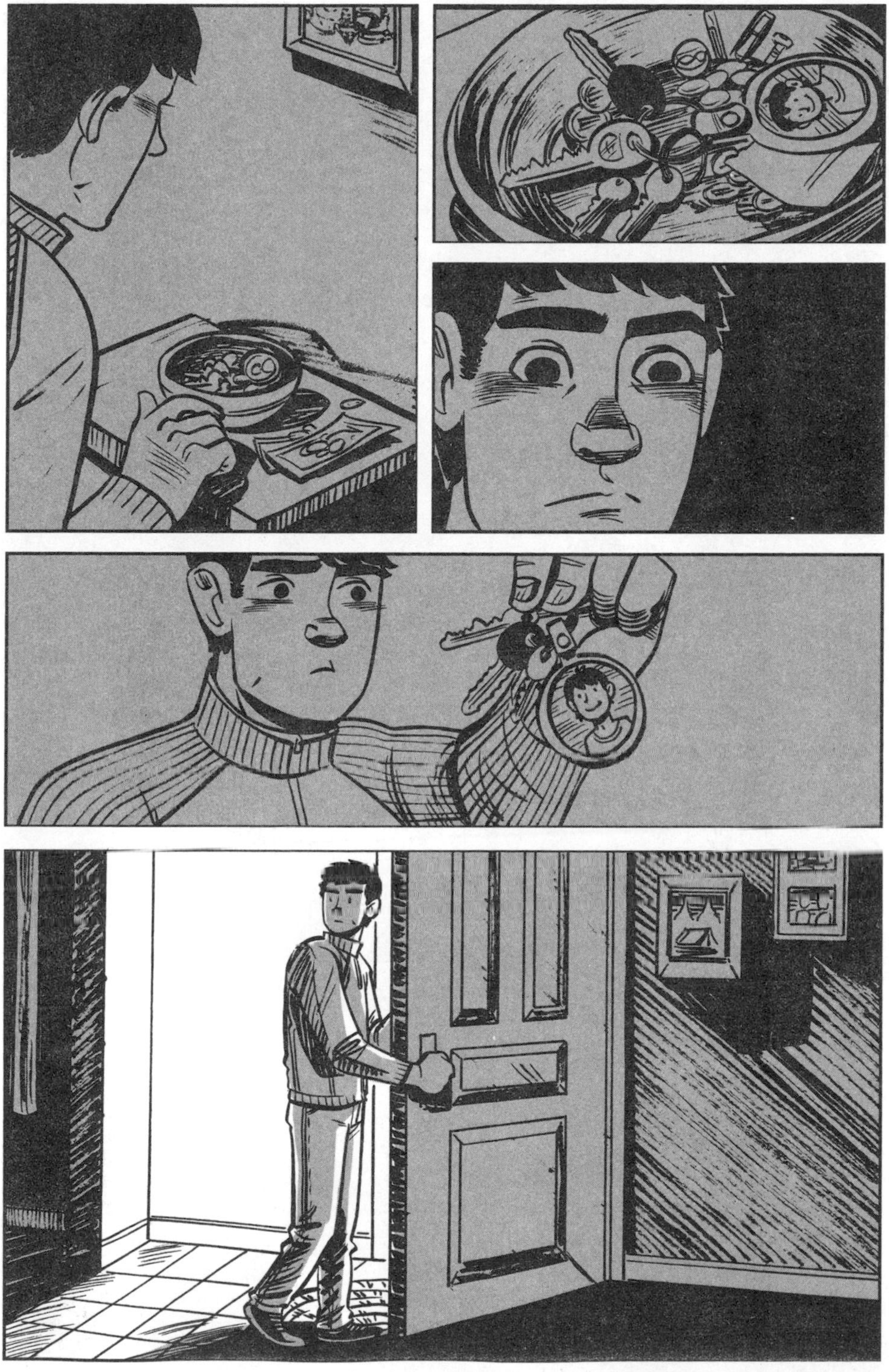

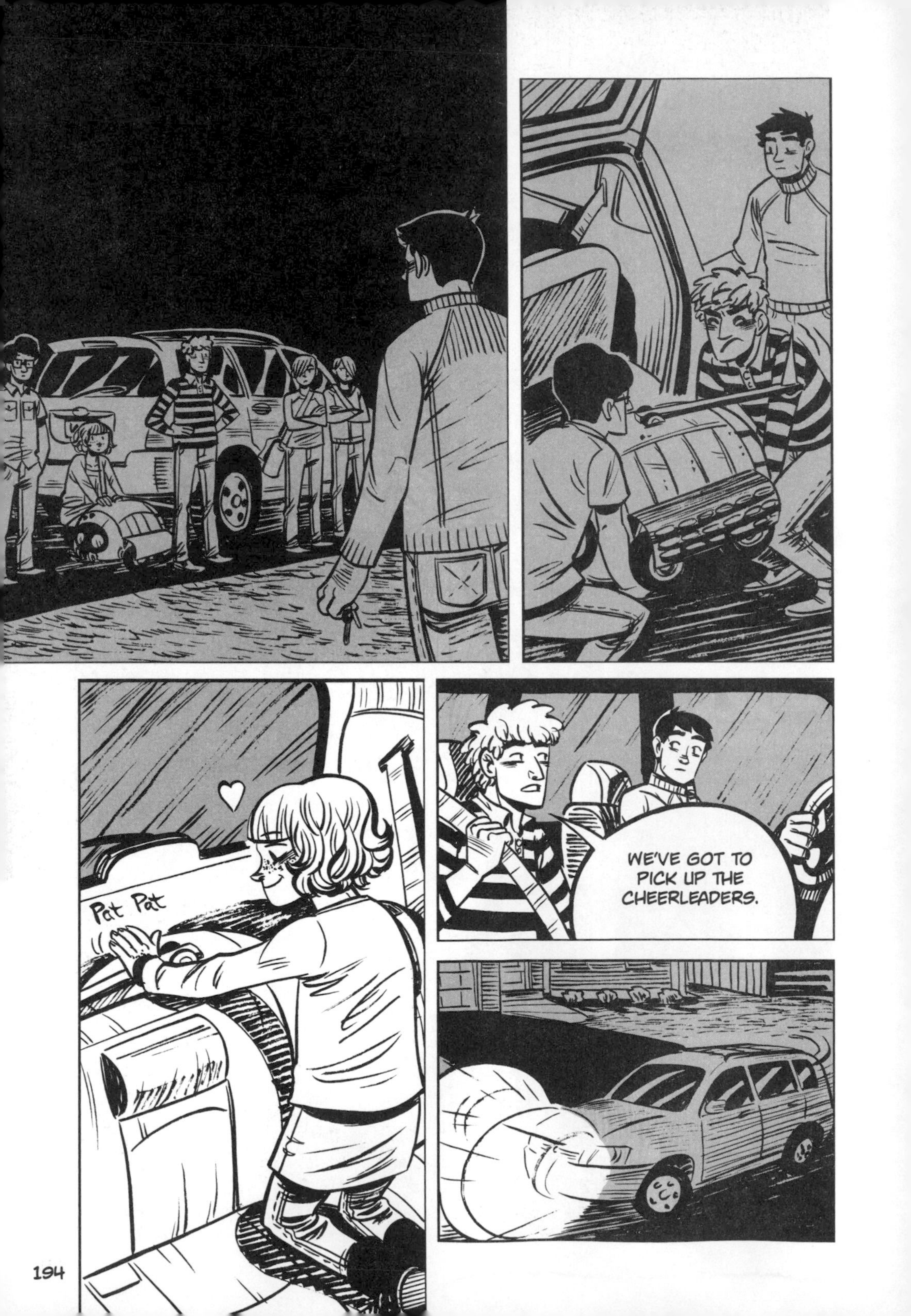
Pat Pat
WE'VE GOT TO PICK UP THE CHEERLEADERS.

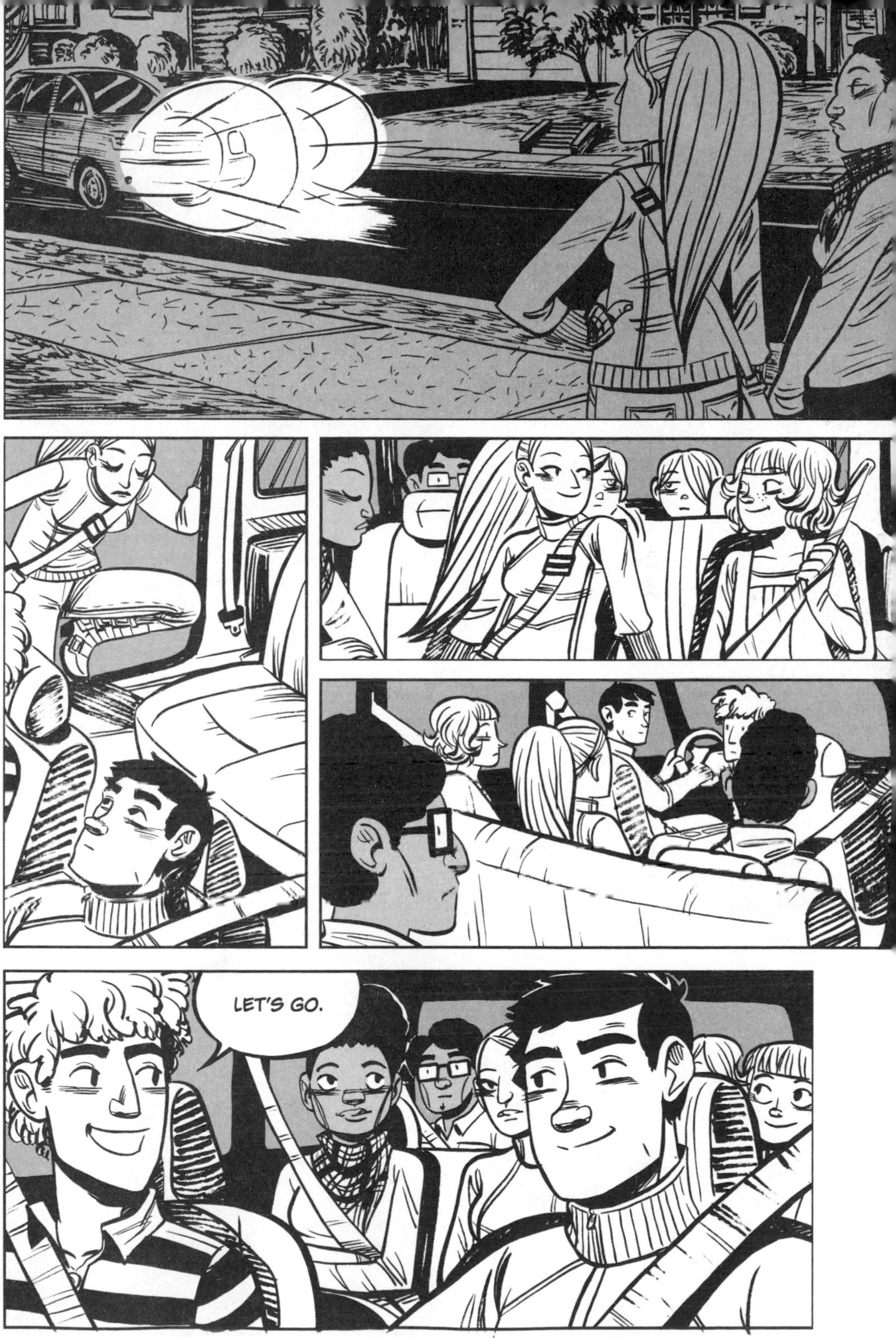
LET'S GO.

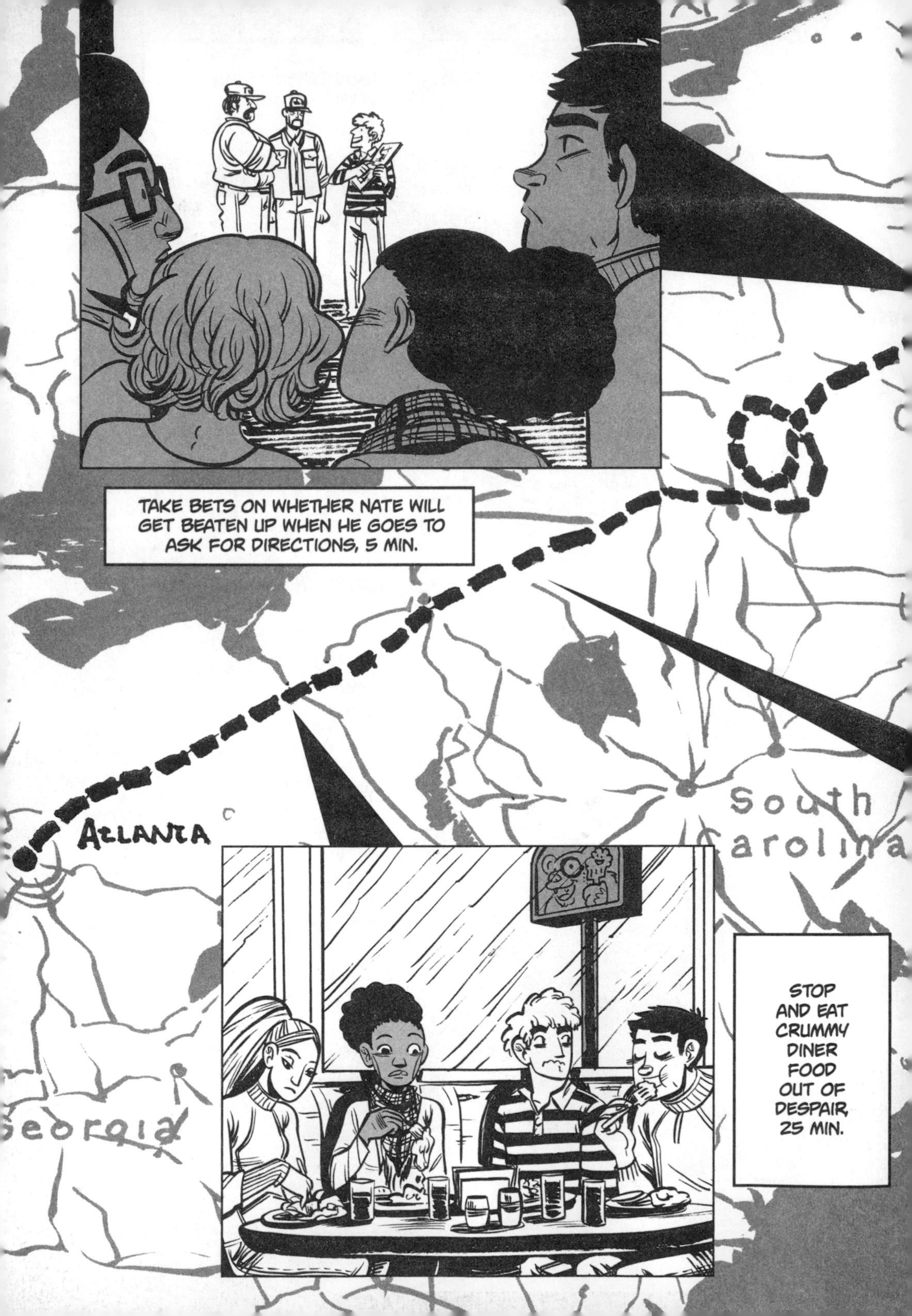

TAKE BETS ON WHETHER NATE WILL GET BEATEN UP WHEN HE GOES TO ASK FOR DIRECTIONS, 5 MIN.
ATLANTA
South Carolina
Georgia
STOP AND EAT CRUMMY DINER FOOD OUT OF DESPAIR, 25 MIN.

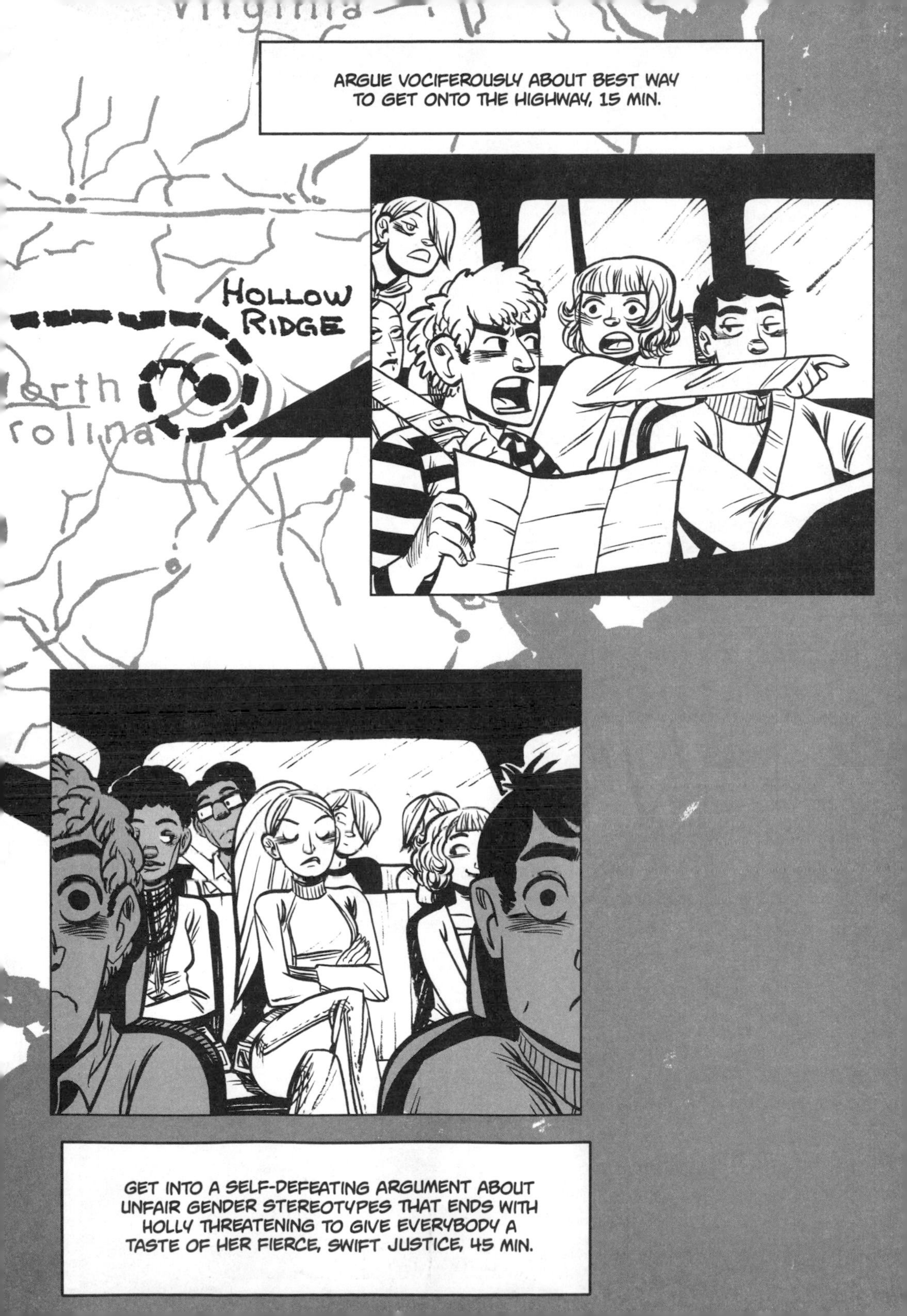
ARGUE VOCIFEROUSLY ABOUT BEST WAY TO GET ONTO THE HIGHWAY, 15 MIN.
HOLLOW RIDGE
GET INTO A SELF-DEFEATING ARGUMENT ABOUT UNFAIR GENDER STEREOTYPES THAT ENDS WITH HOLLY THREATENING TO GIVE EVERYBODY A TASTE OF HER FIERCE, SWIFT JUSTICE, 45 MIN.

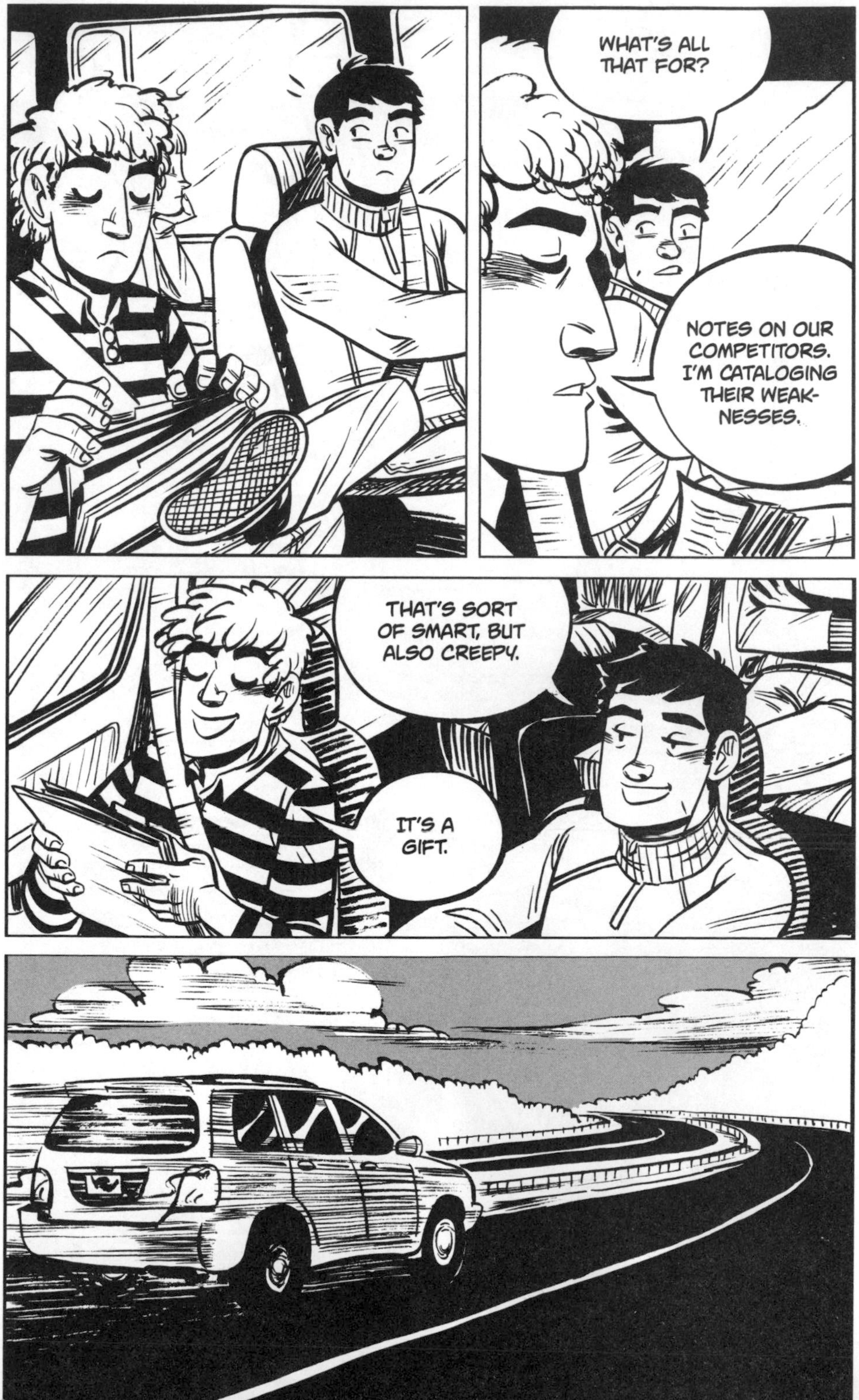
WHAT'S ALL THAT FOR?
NOTES ON OUR COMPETITORS. I'M CATALOGING THEIR WEAK-NESSES.
THAT'S SORT OF SMART, BUT ALSO CREEPY.
IT'S A GIFT.

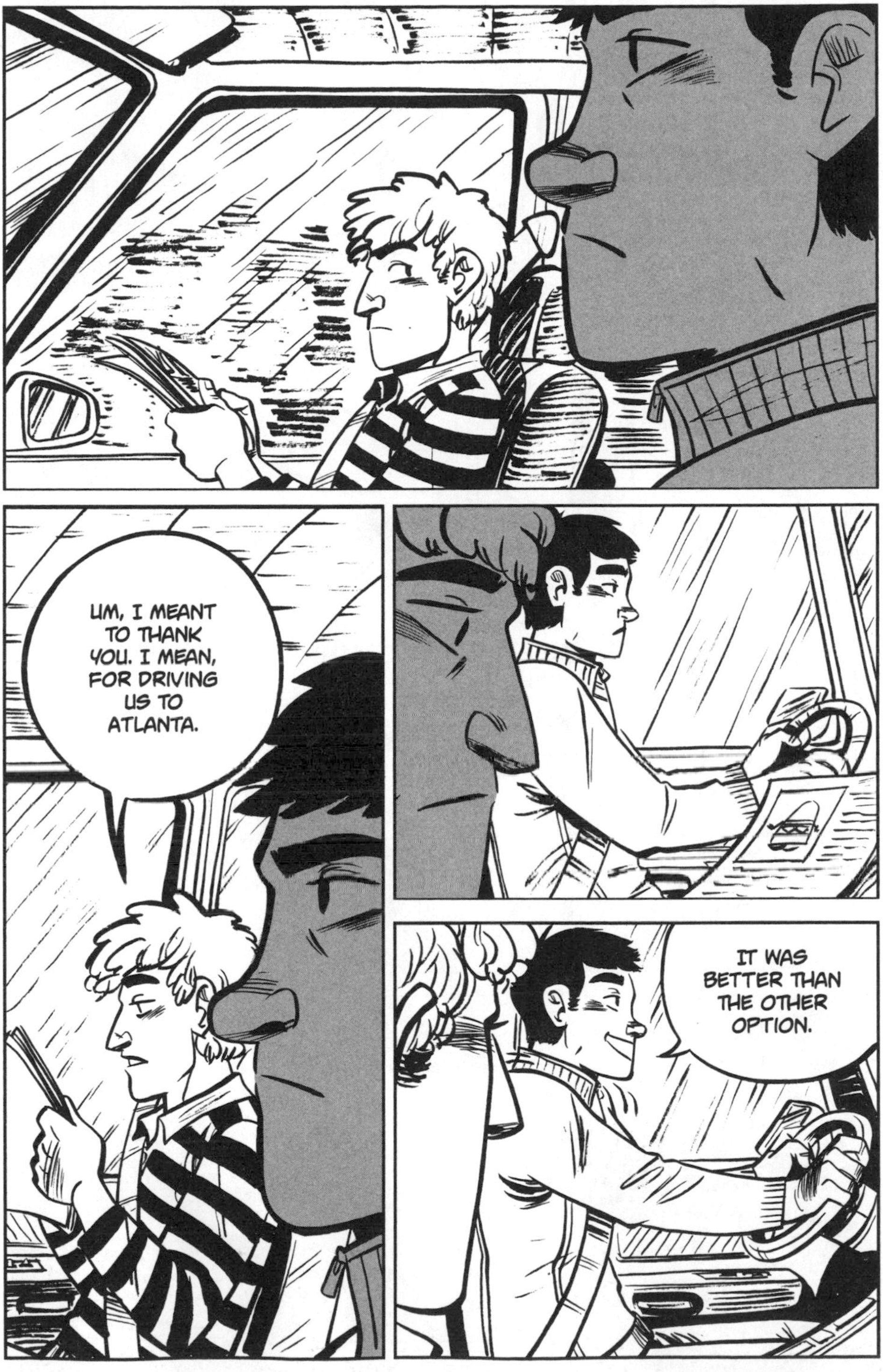
UM, I MEANT TO THANK YOU. I MEAN, FOR DRIVING US TO ATLANTA.
IT WAS BETTER THAN THE OTHER OPTION.

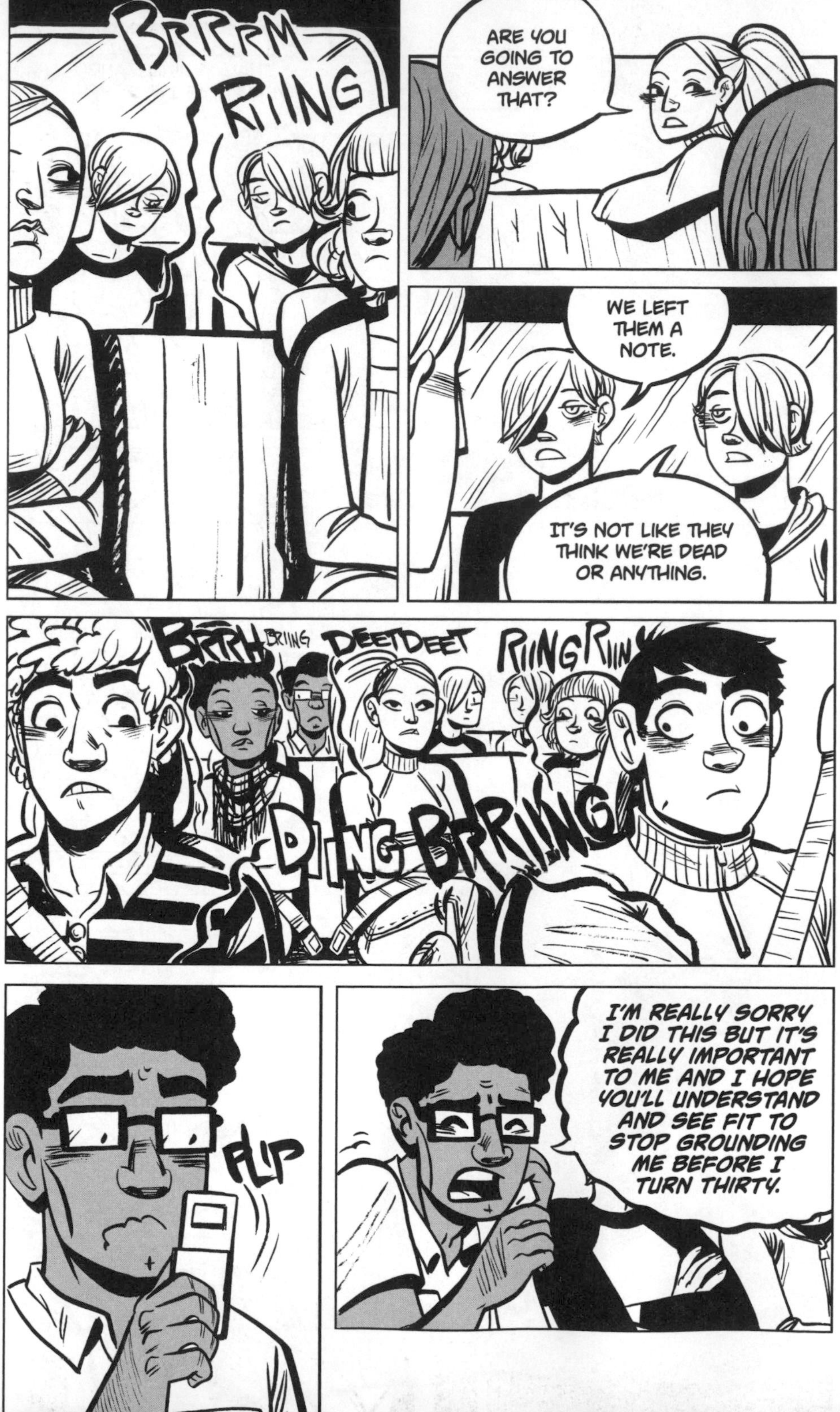
BRRRRM
RIIING
ARE YOU GOING TO ANSWER THAT?
WE LEFT THEM A NOTE.
IT'S NOT LIKE THEY THINK WE'RE DEAD OR ANYTHING.
BRRRH
BRIING
DEETDEET
RIINGRIIN
DIING
BRRIIING
FLIP
I'M REALLY SORRY I DID THIS BUT IT'S REALLY IMPORTANT TO ME AND I HOPE YOU'LL UNDERSTAND AND SEE FIT TO STOP GROUNDING ME BEFORE I TURN THIRTY.

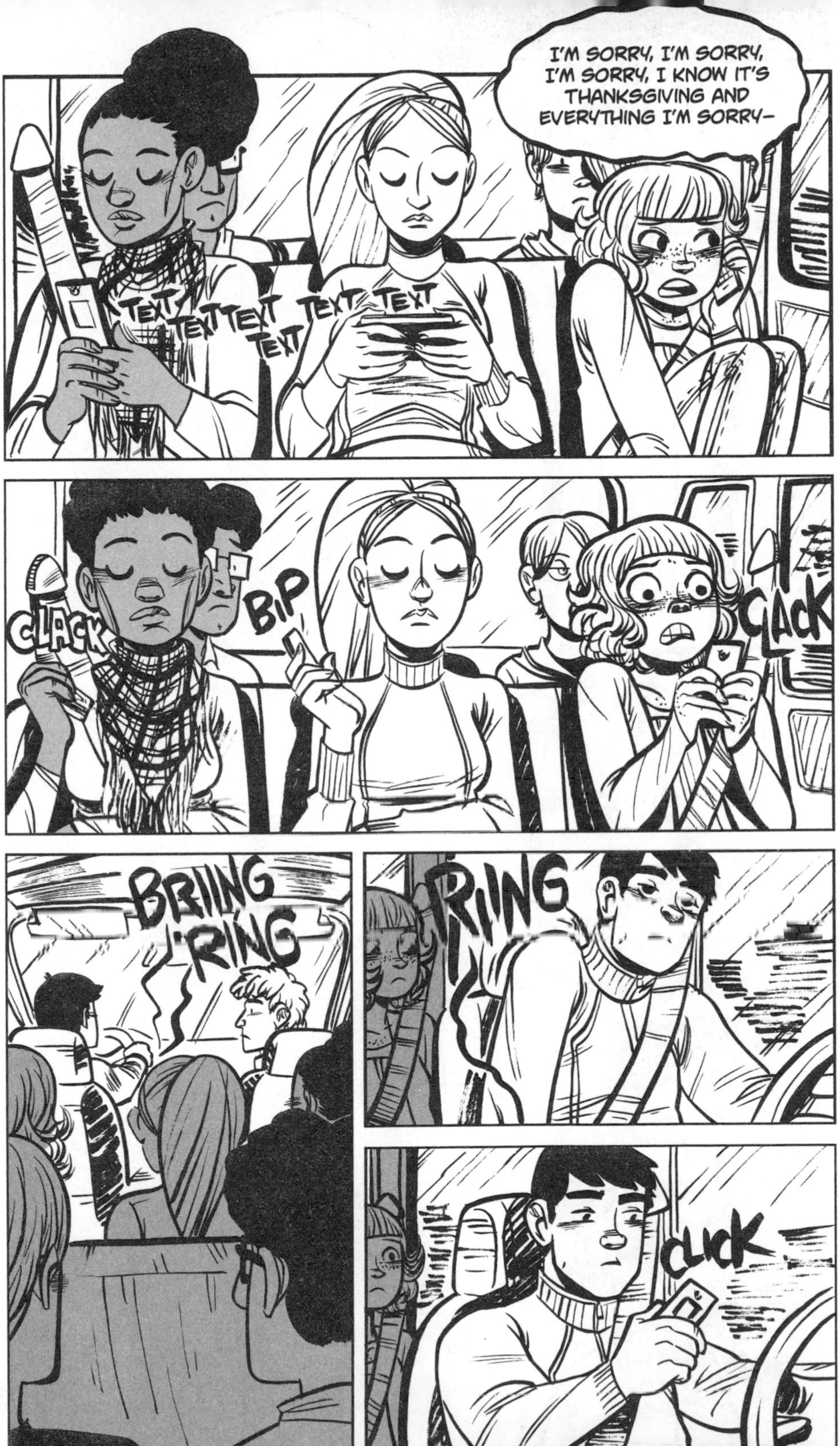

I'M SORRY, I'M SORRY, I'M SORRY, I KNOW IT'S THANKSGIVING AND EVERYTHING I'M SORRY–
TEXT TEXT TEXT TEXT TEXT TEXT TEXT
CLACK
BIP
CLACK
BRIING RING
RIING
CLICK

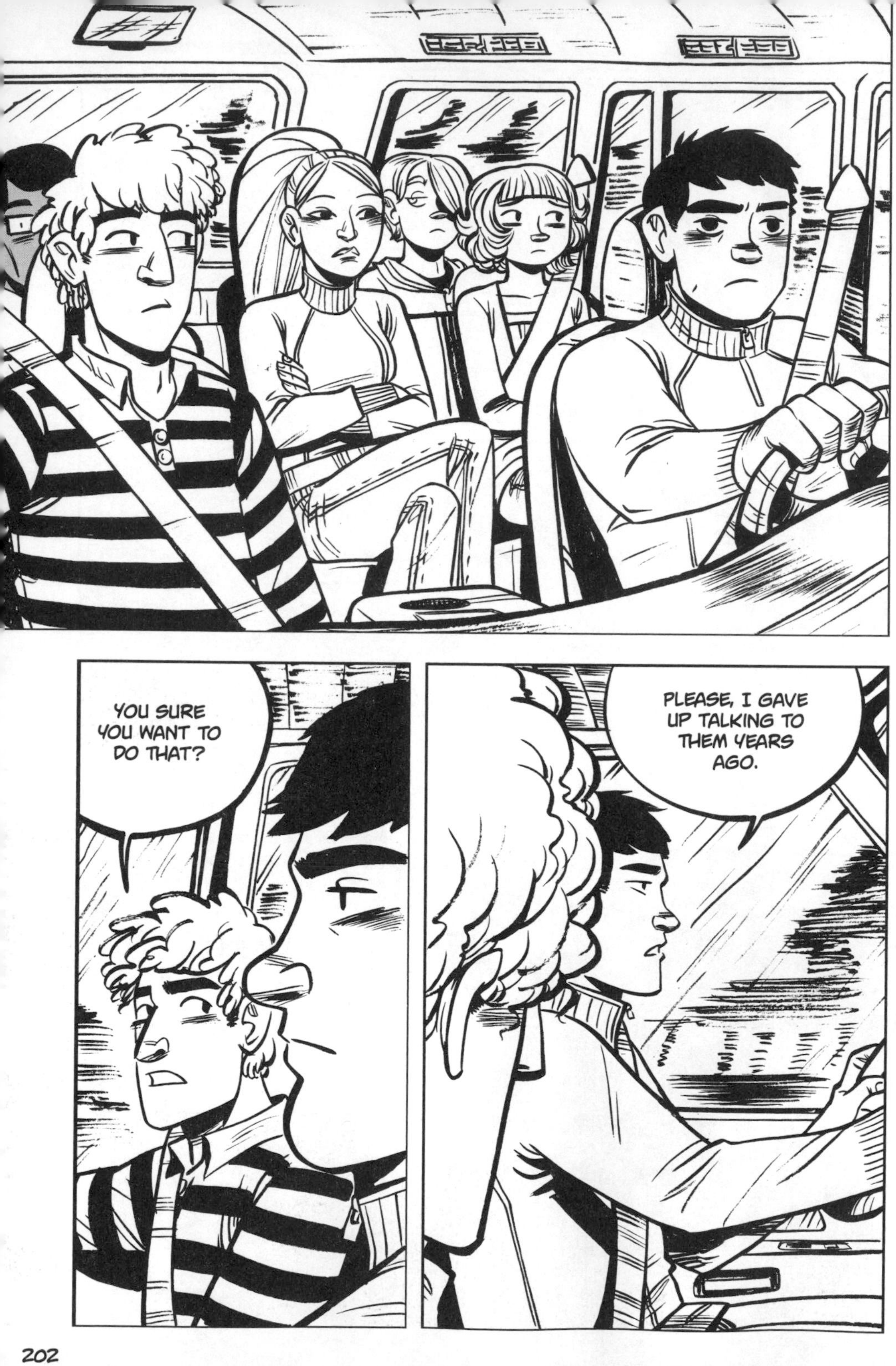
YOU SURE YOU WANT TO DO THAT?
PLEASE, I GAVE UP TALKING TO THEM YEARS AGO.

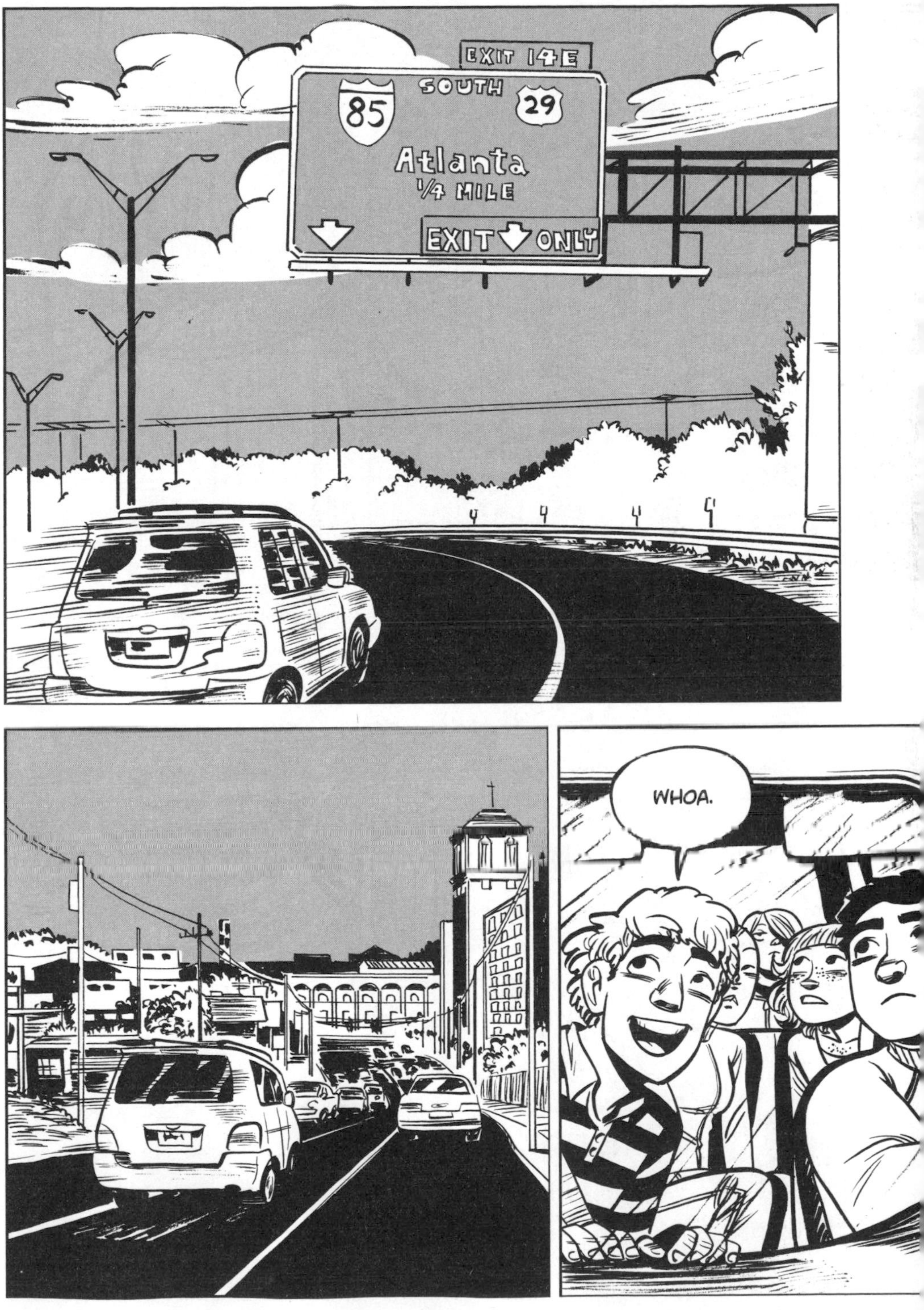
EXIT 14E
SOUTH
85
29
Atlanta
1/4 MILE
EXIT ONLY
WHOA.

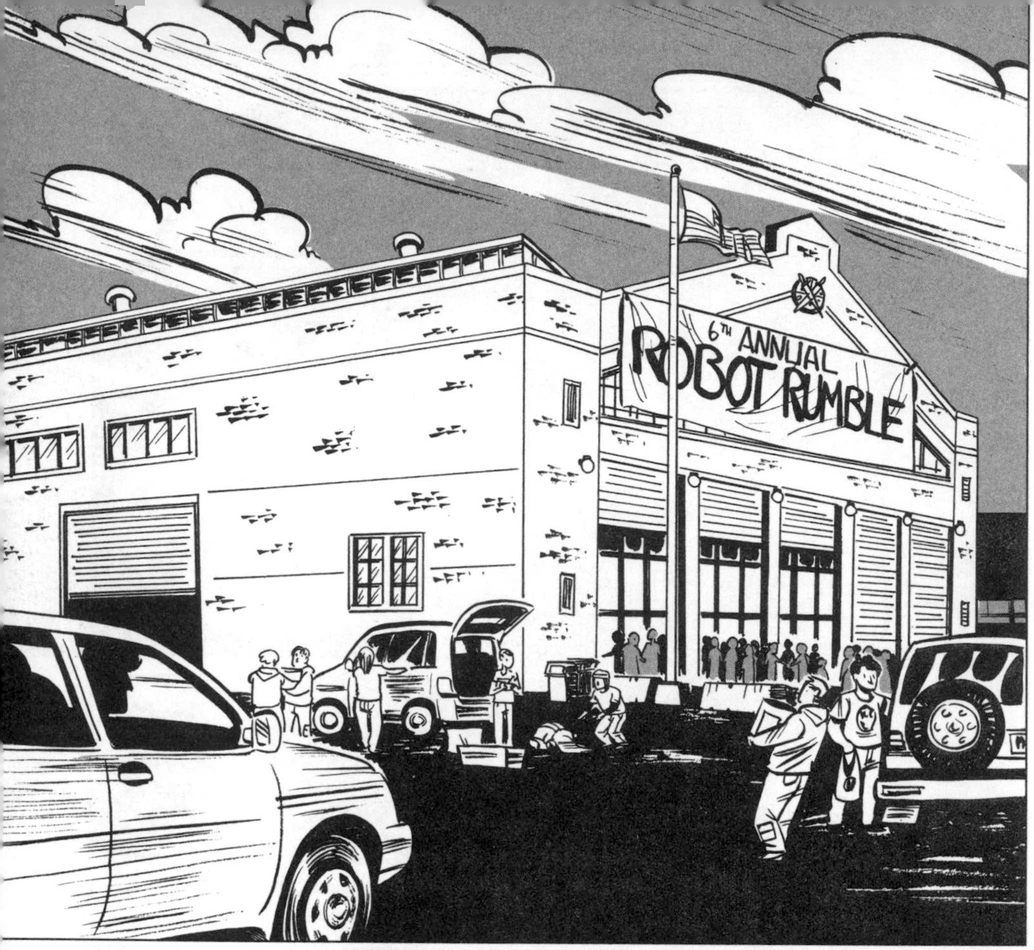
6TH ANNUAL
ROBOT RUMBLE

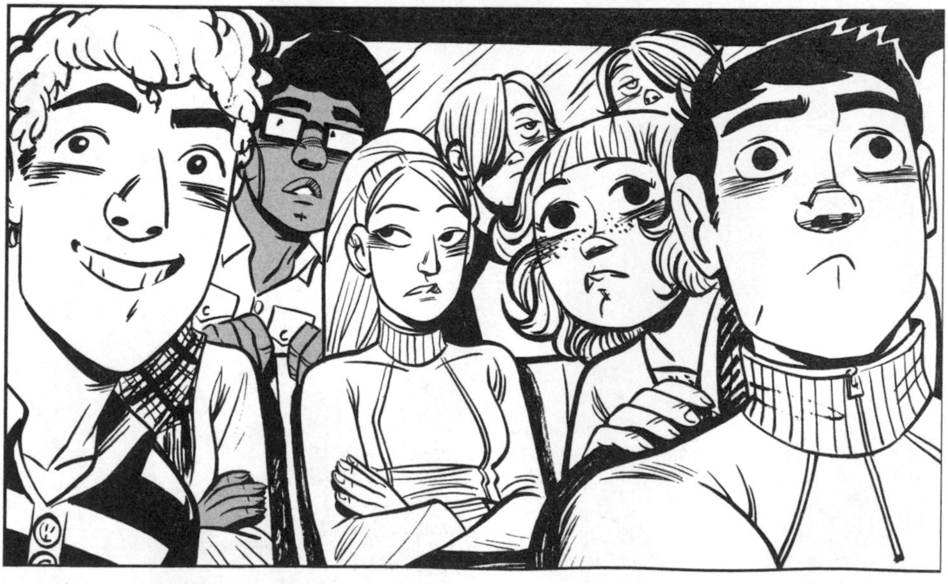

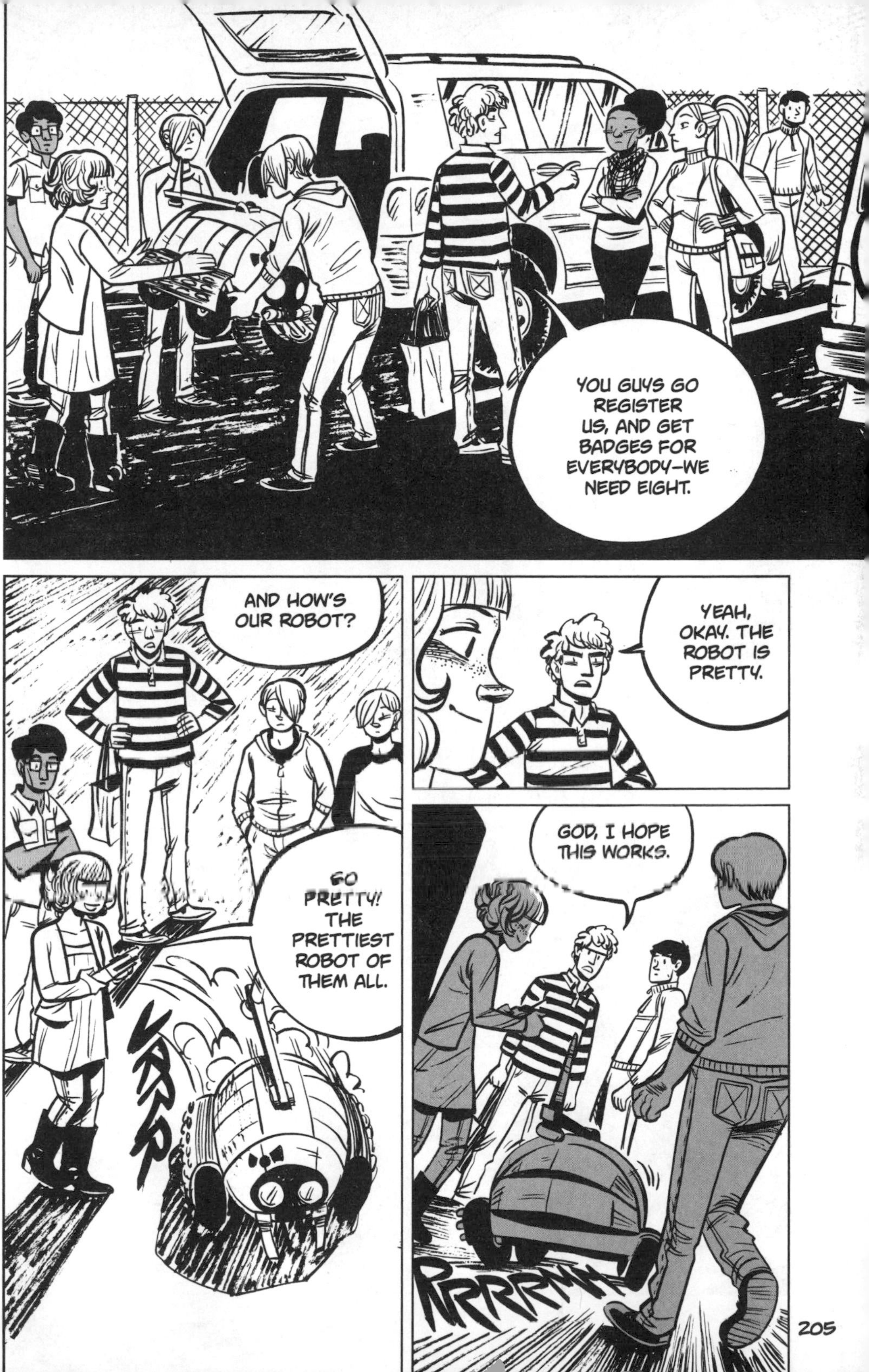
YOU GUYS GO REGISTER US, AND GET BADGES FOR EVERYBODY—WE NEED EIGHT.
AND HOW'S OUR ROBOT?
YEAH, OKAY. THE ROBOT IS PRETTY.
SO PRETTY! THE PRETTIEST ROBOT OF THEM ALL.
VRRP
GOD, I HOPE THIS WORKS.
RRRRMM

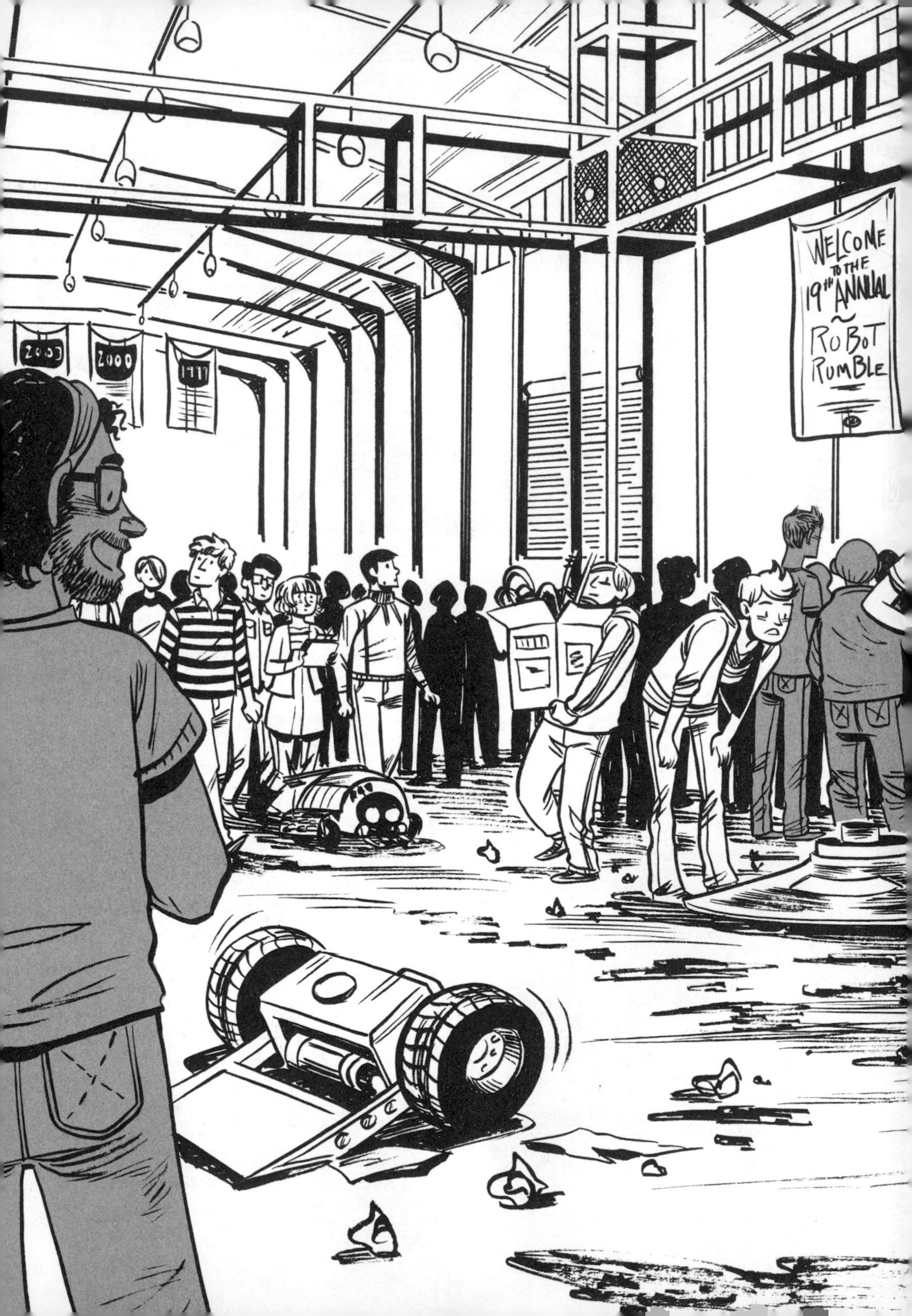
WELCOME TO THE 19TH ANNUAL ~ ROBOT RUMBLE
2000

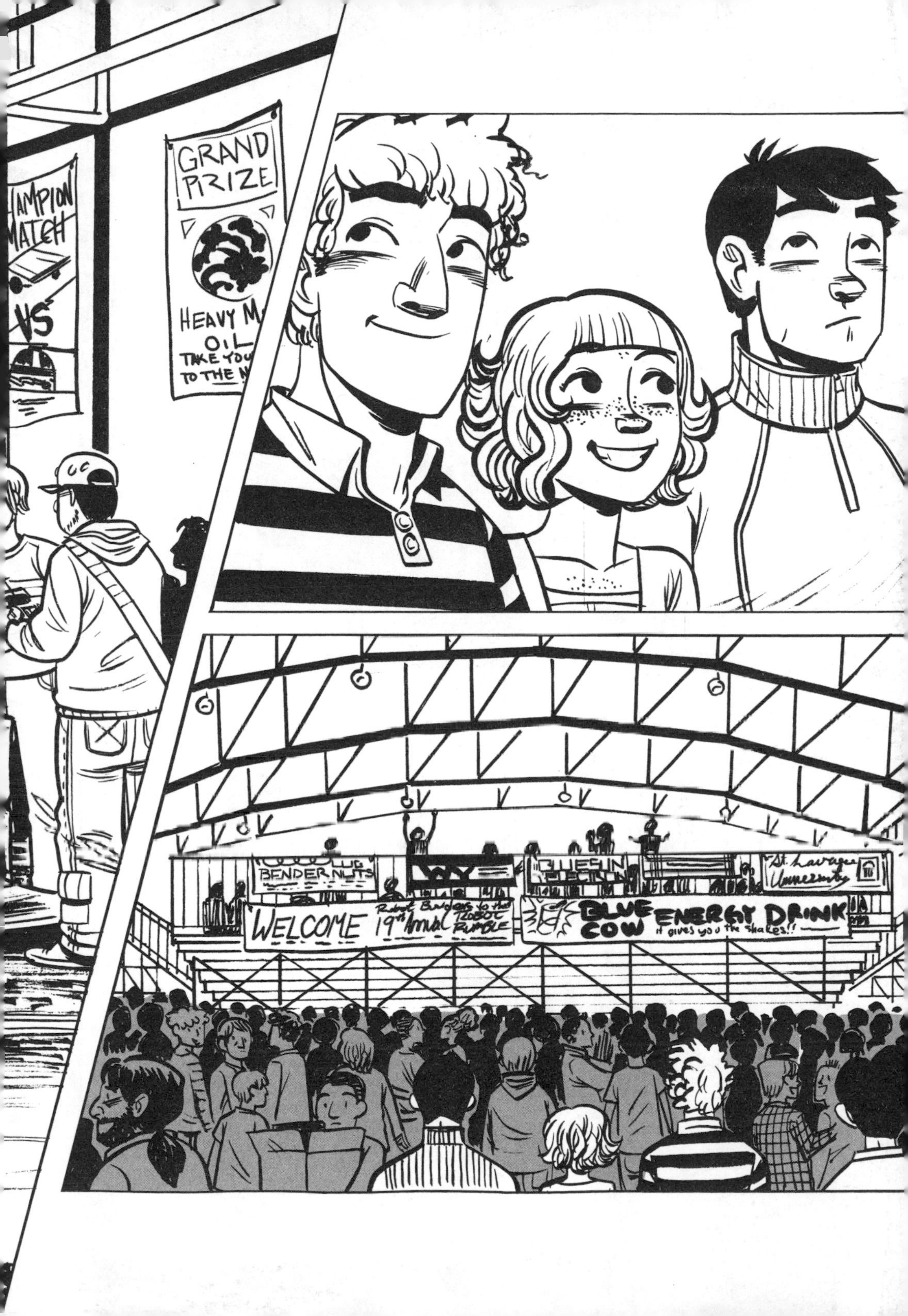
HAMPION
MATCH
VS
GRAND PRIZE
HEAVY M
OIL
WELCOME
Robot Builders to the 19th Annual ROBOT RUMBLE
BENDER NUTS
BLUE COW ENERGY DRINK
it gives you the shakes!!

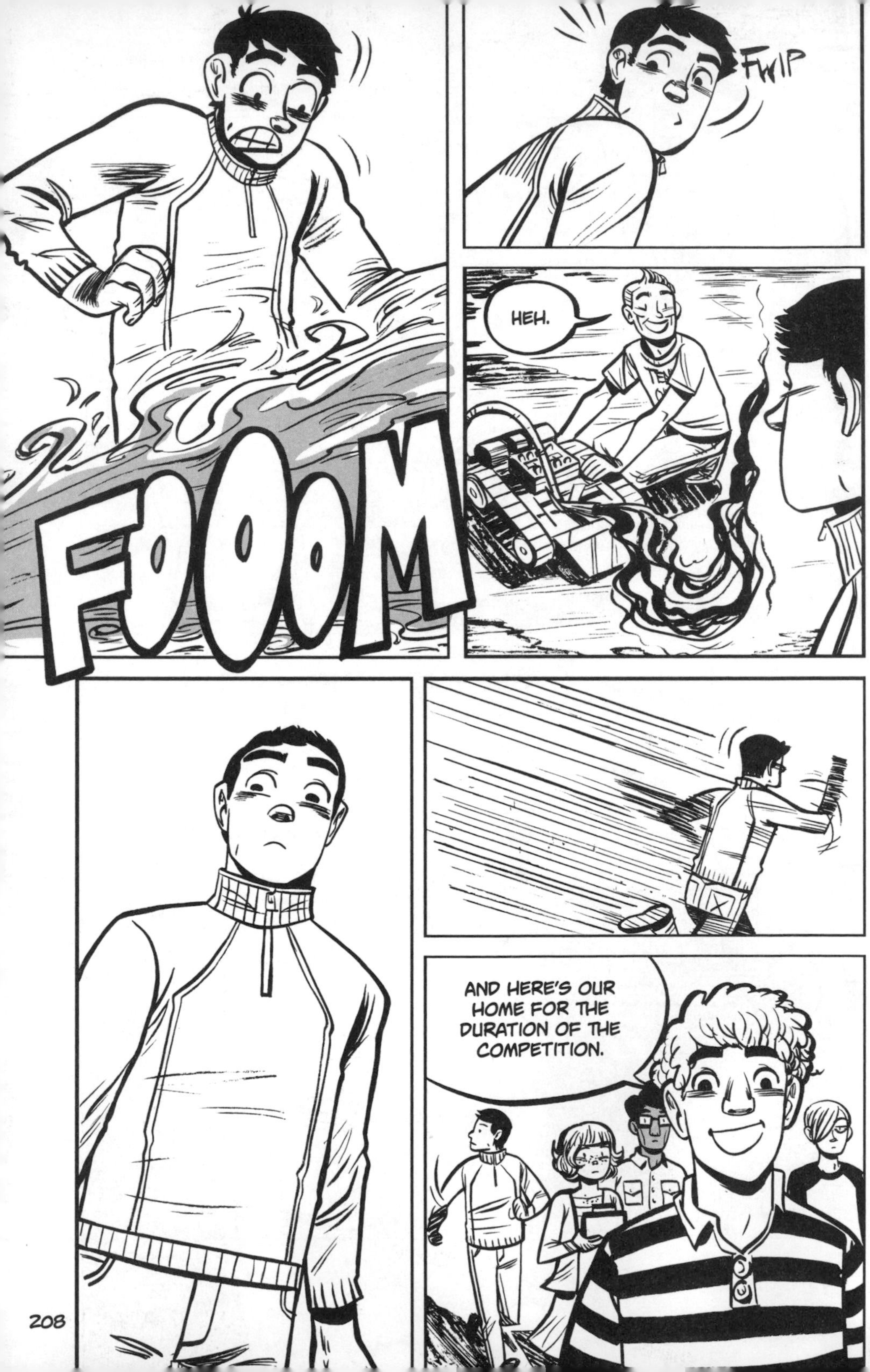
FWIP
FOOOM
HEH.
AND HERE'S OUR HOME FOR THE DURATION OF THE COMPETITION.

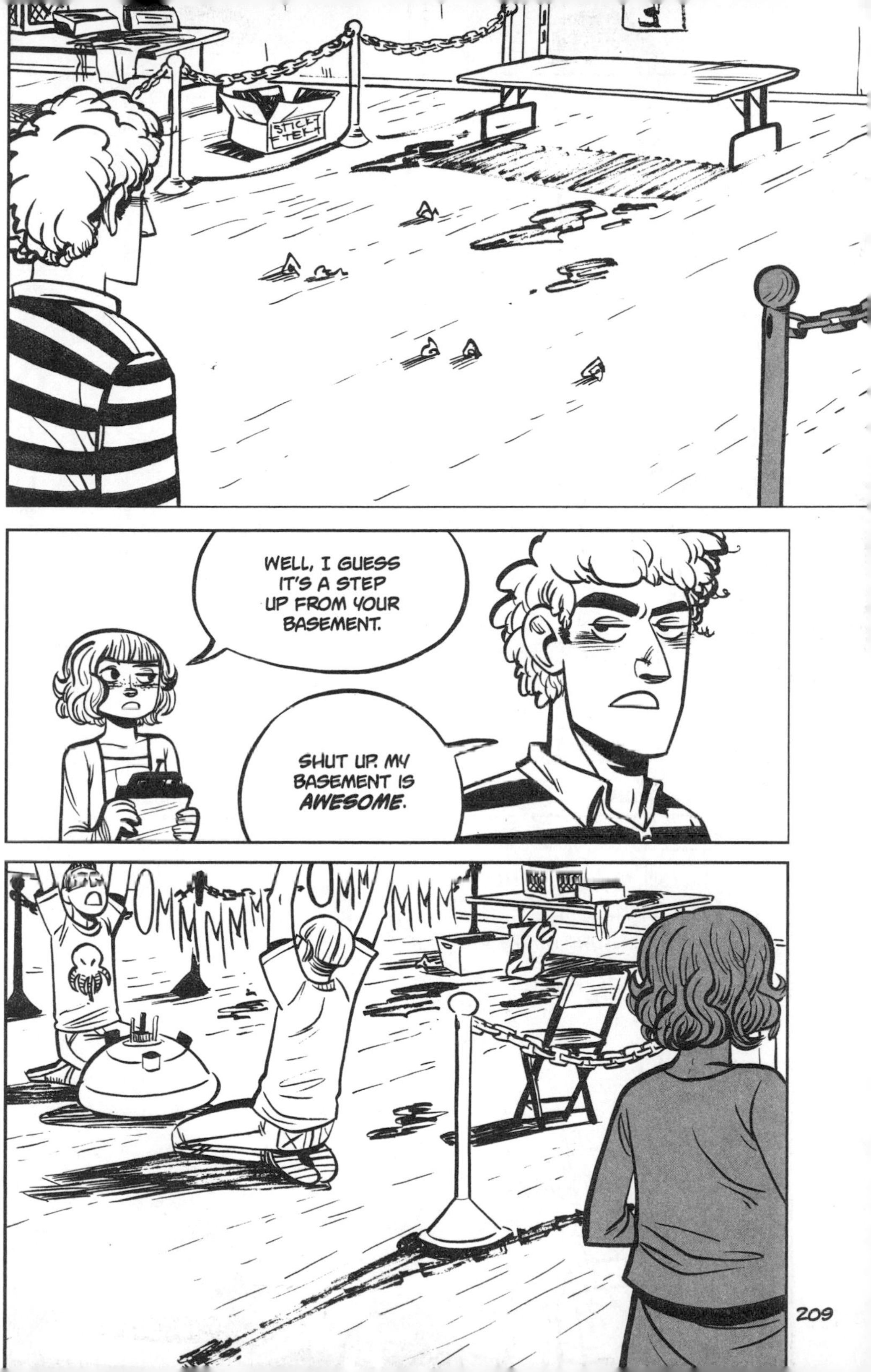
STICKY TEK
WELL, I GUESS IT'S A STEP UP FROM YOUR BASEMENT.
SHUT UP. MY BASEMENT IS *AWESOME*.
OMMMMMM
OMMMMM

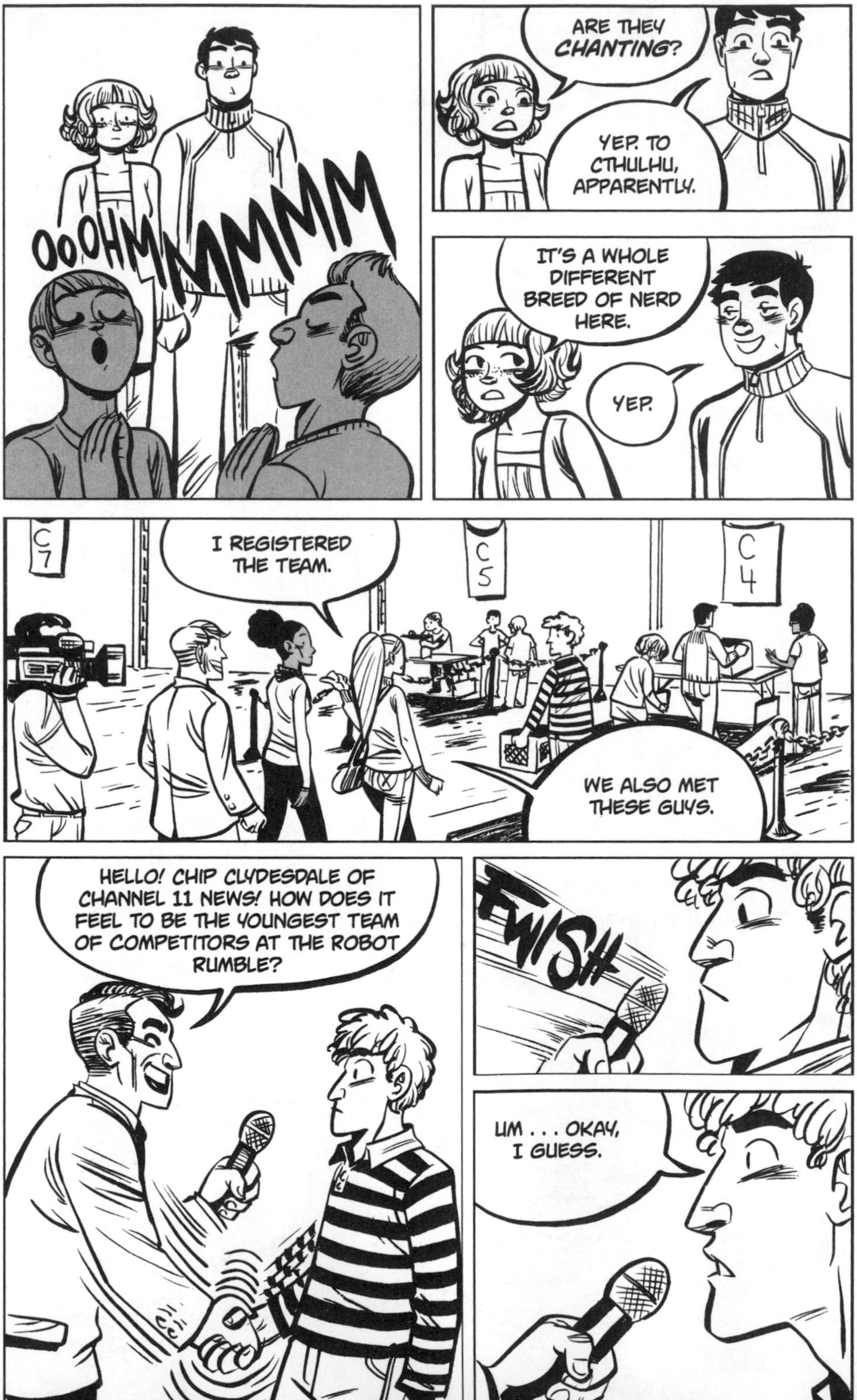
OOOHMMMMMM
ARE THEY CHANTING?
YEP. TO CTHULHU, APPARENTLY.
IT'S A WHOLE DIFFERENT BREED OF NERD HERE.
YEP.
C7
C5
C4
I REGISTERED THE TEAM.
WE ALSO MET THESE GUYS.
HELLO! CHIP CLYDESDALE OF CHANNEL 11 NEWS! HOW DOES IT FEEL TO BE THE YOUNGEST TEAM OF COMPETITORS AT THE ROBOT RUMBLE?
FWISH
UM . . . OKAY, I GUESS.

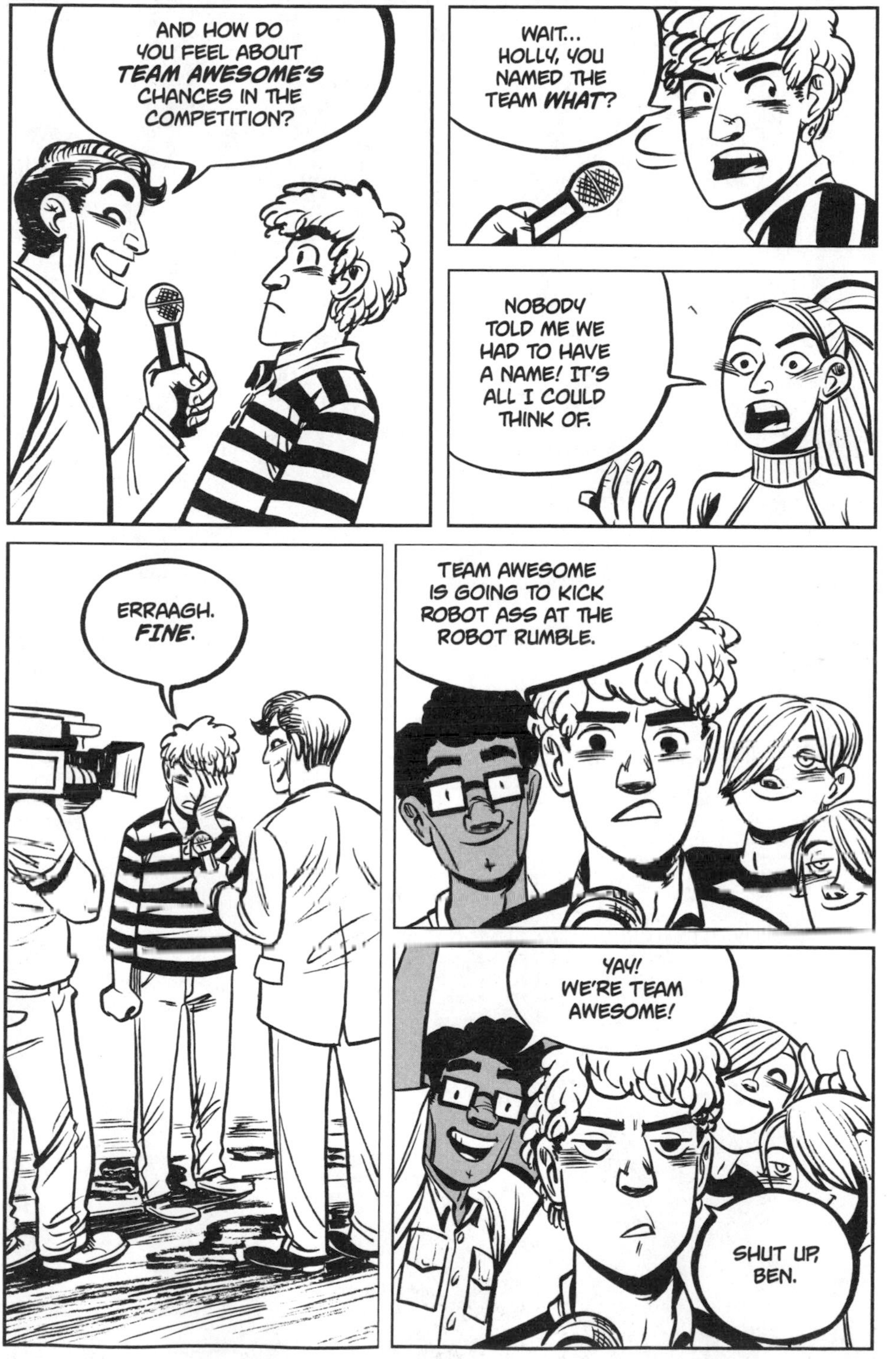

AND HOW DO YOU FEEL ABOUT ***TEAM AWESOME'S*** CHANCES IN THE COMPETITION?
WAIT... HOLLY, YOU NAMED THE TEAM ***WHAT***?
NOBODY TOLD ME WE HAD TO HAVE A NAME! IT'S ALL I COULD THINK OF.
ERRAAGH. ***FINE***.
TEAM AWESOME IS GOING TO KICK ROBOT ASS AT THE ROBOT RUMBLE.
YAY! WE'RE TEAM AWESOME!
SHUT UP, BEN.

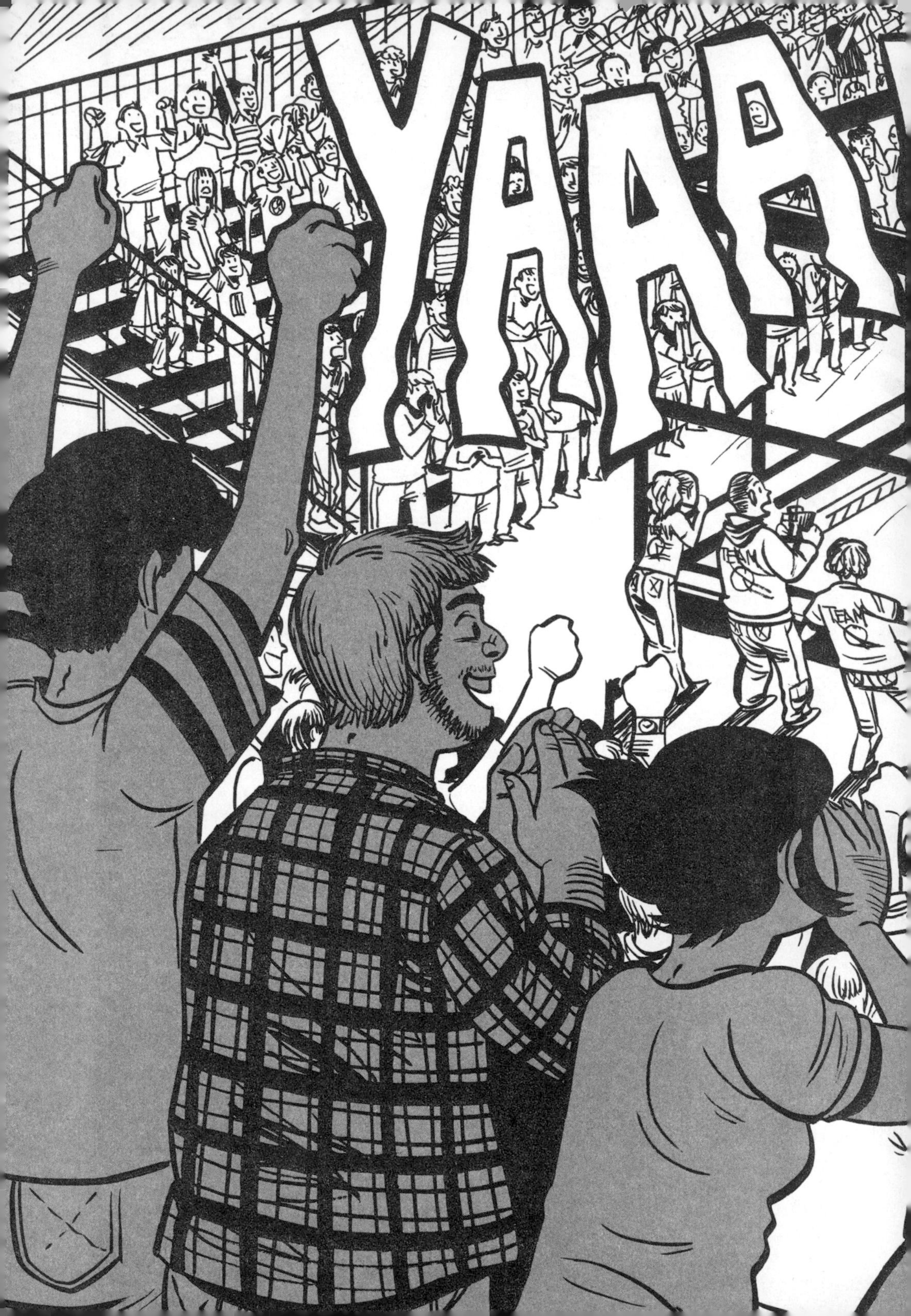
YAA
TEAM
TEAM

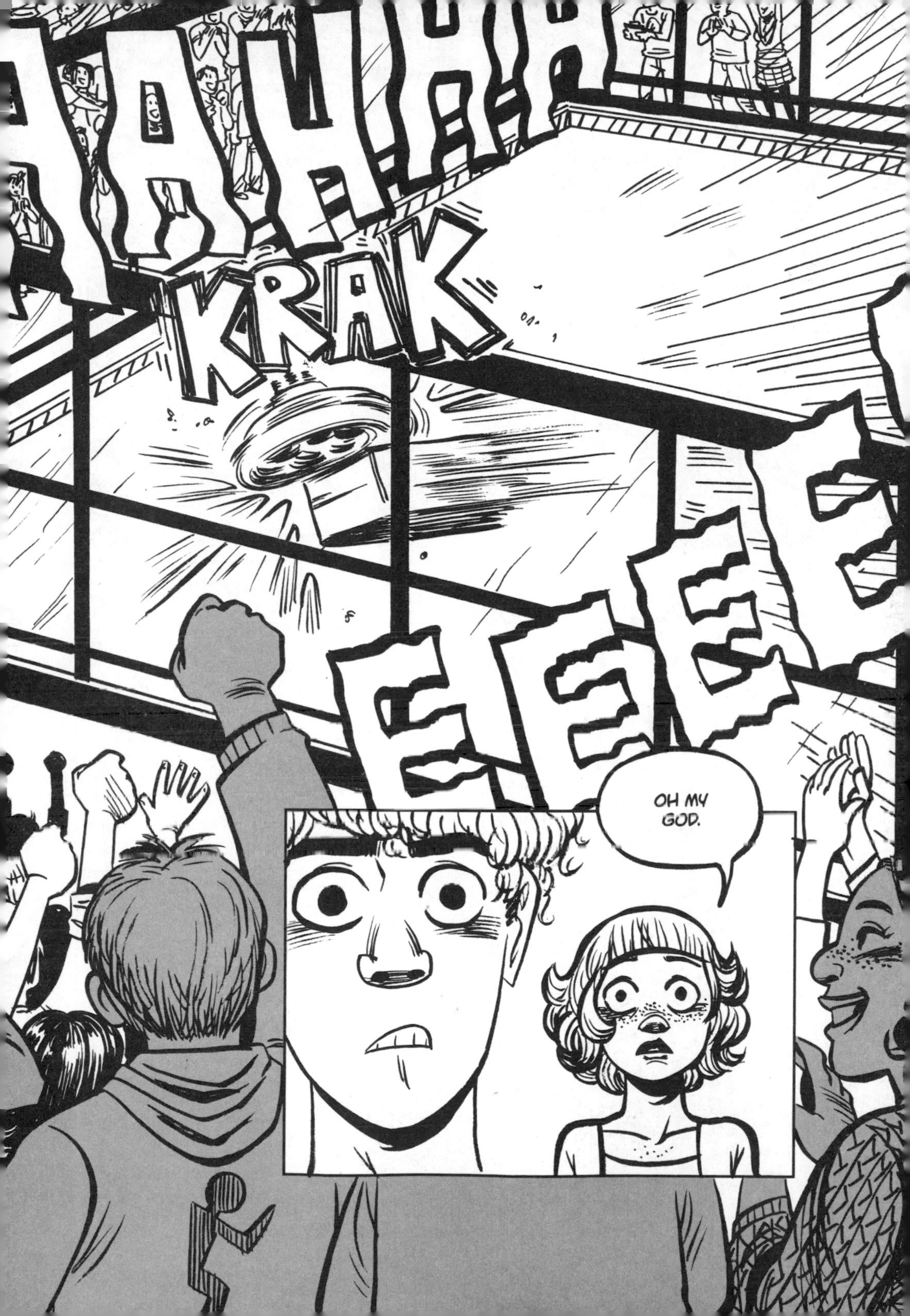

AAAHHH
KRAK
EEEE
OH MY GOD.

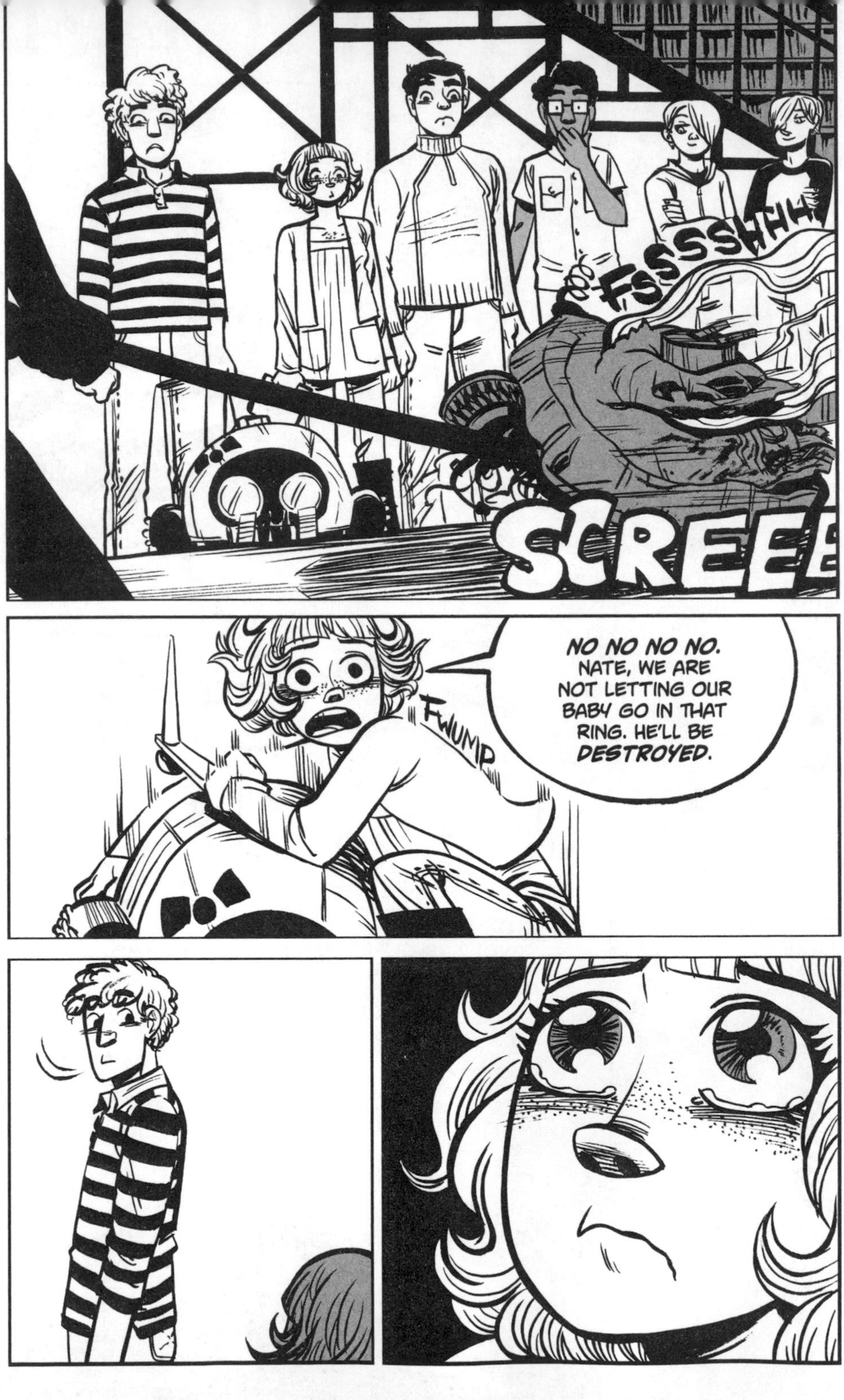
FSSSSHHH
SCREEE
NO NO NO NO. NATE, WE ARE NOT LETTING OUR BABY GO IN THAT RING. HE'LL BE DESTROYED.
FWUMP

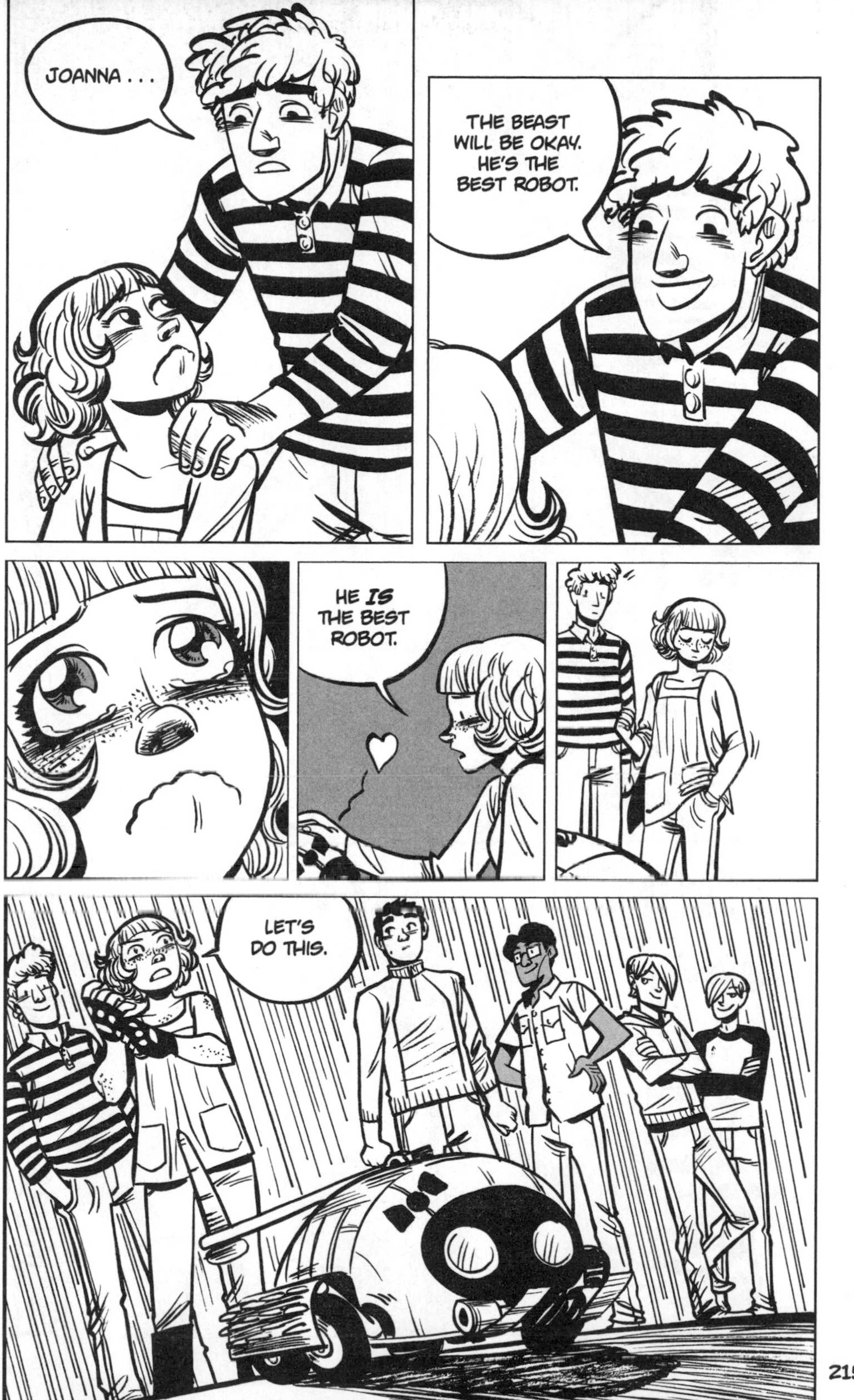
JOANNA . . .
THE BEAST WILL BE OKAY. HE'S THE BEST ROBOT.
HE *IS* THE BEST ROBOT.
LET'S DO THIS.

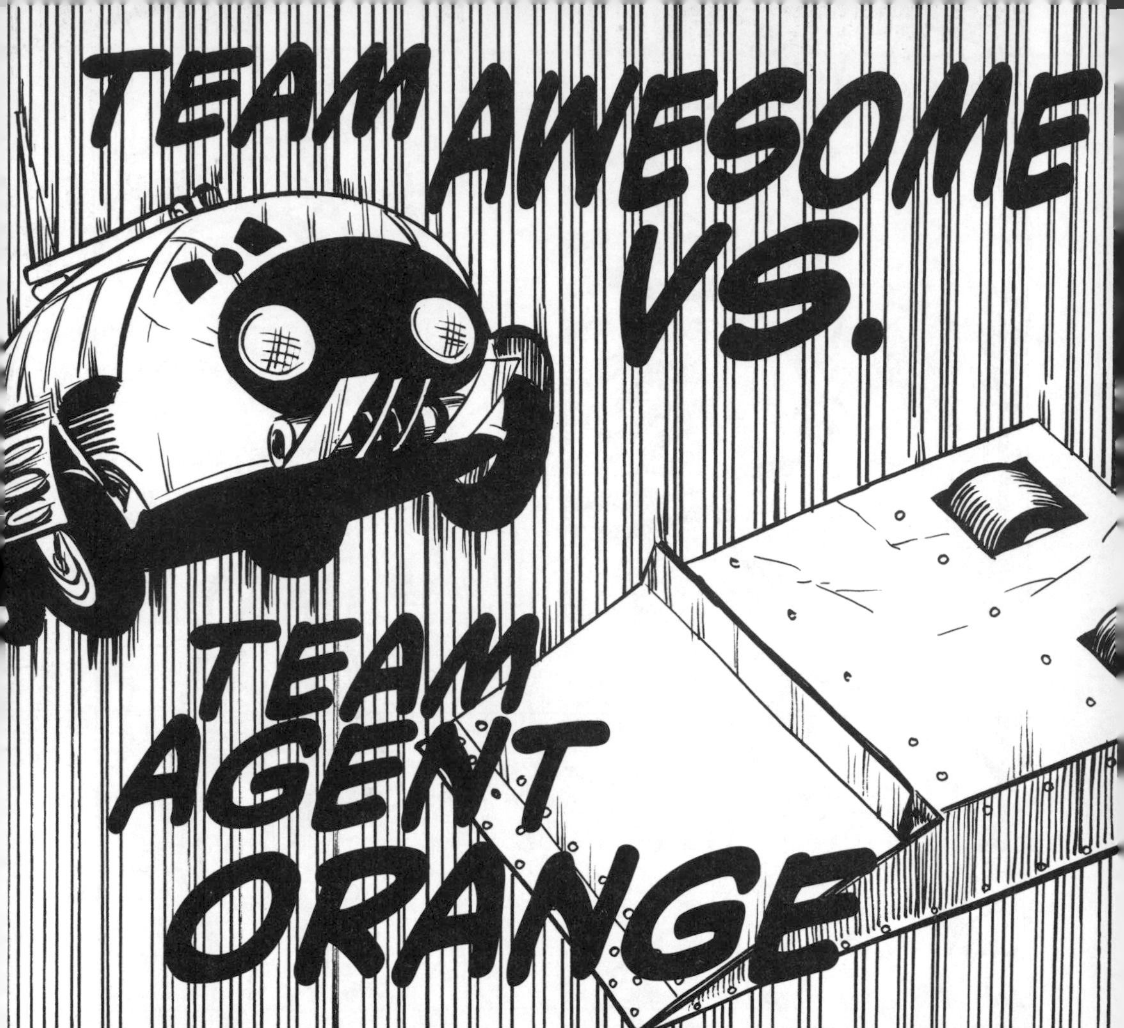
TEAM AWESOME
VS.
TEAM AGENT ORANGE

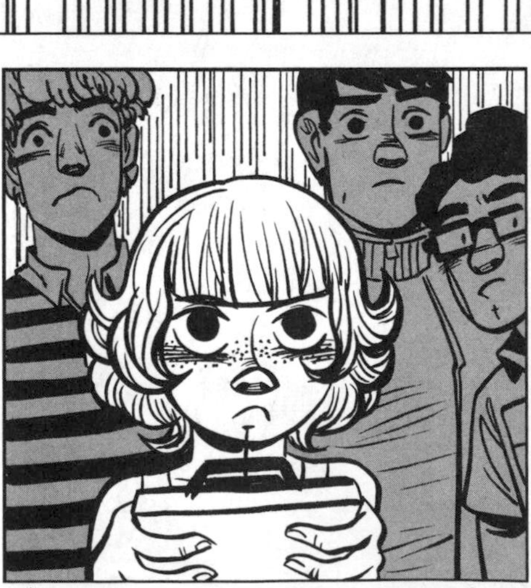

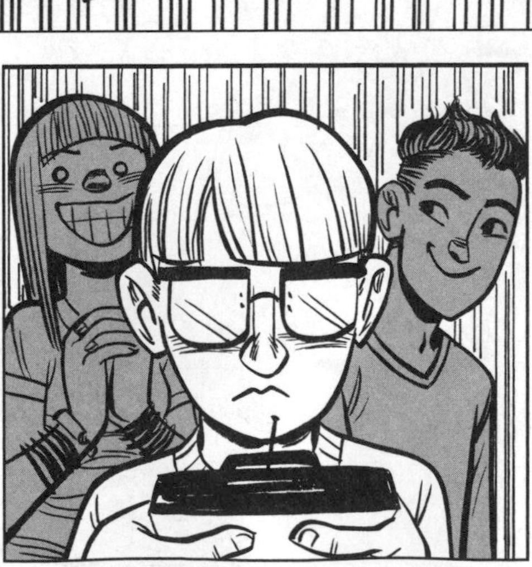

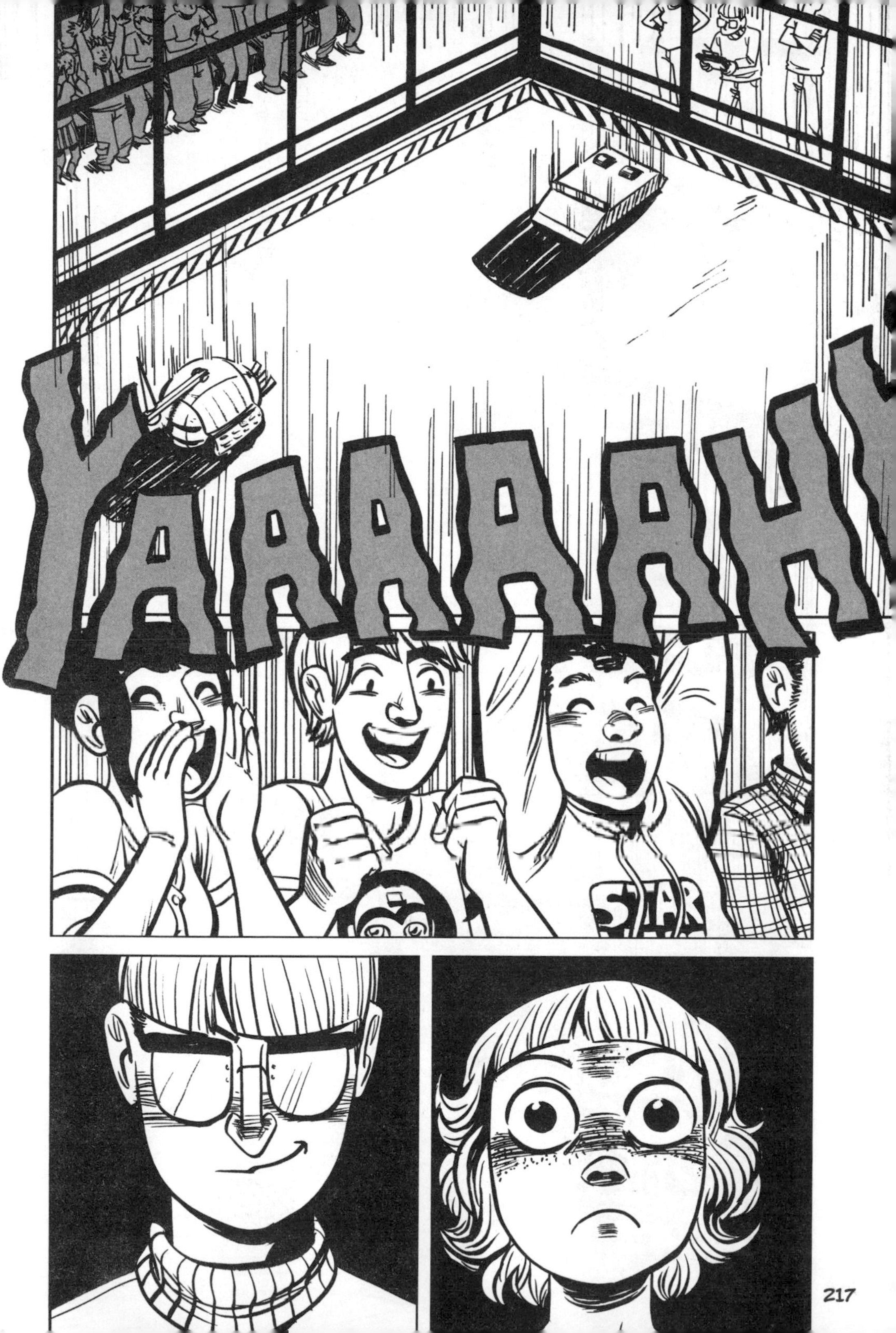
YAAAAH!
STAR

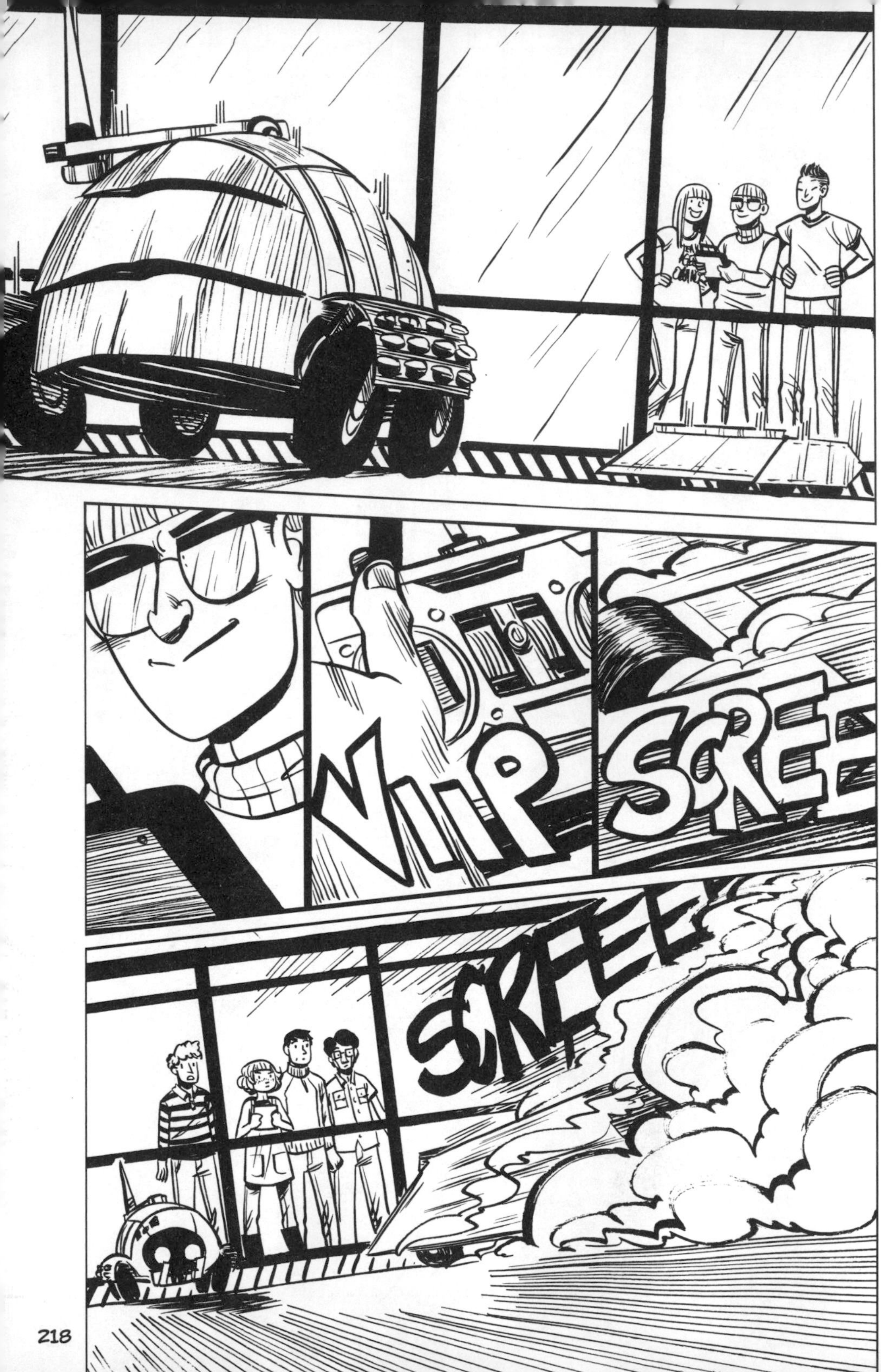
VIIP
SCREE
SCREEEE

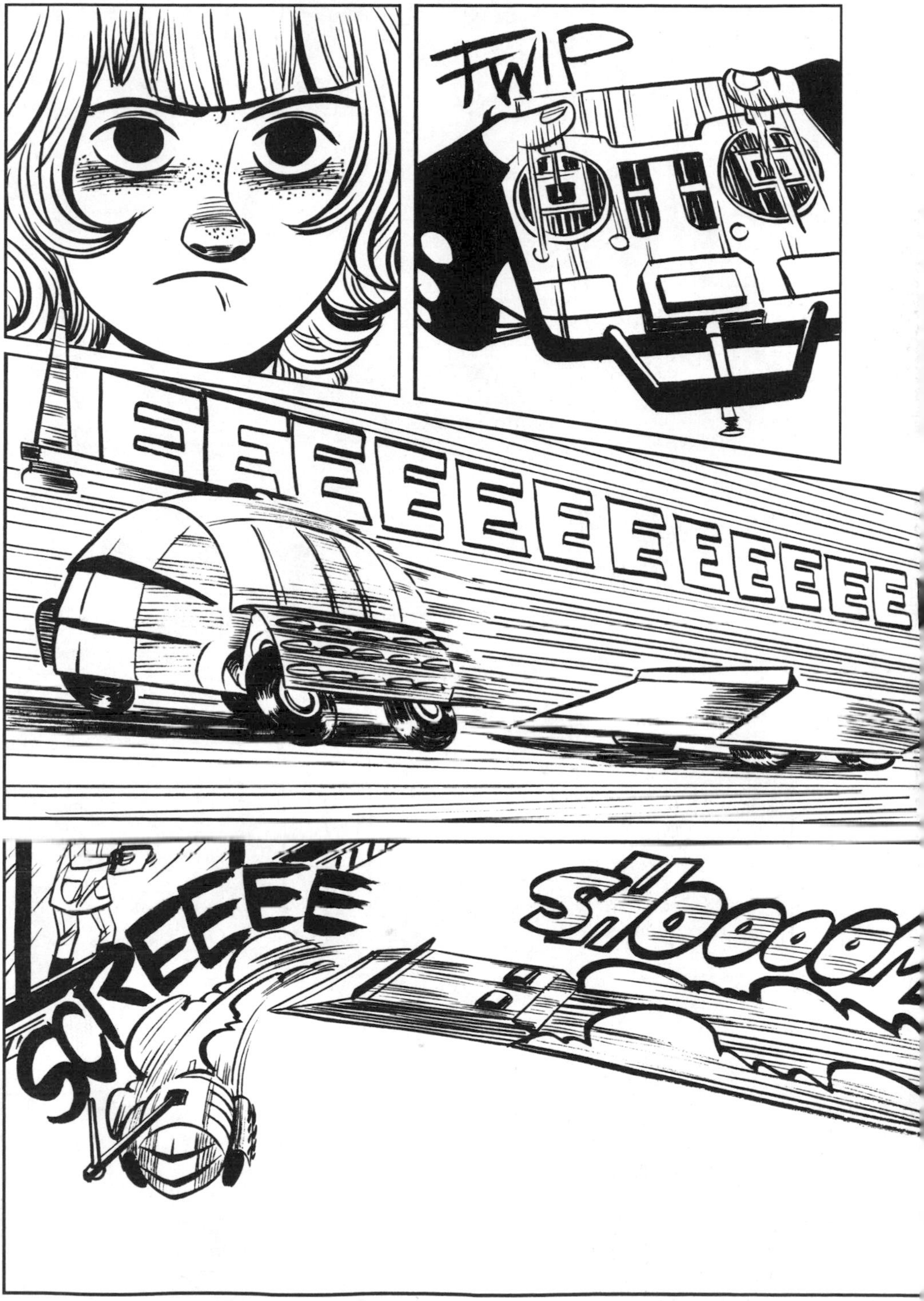
FWIP
EEEEEEEEEEEEEEEE
SCREEEE
SHOOOOM

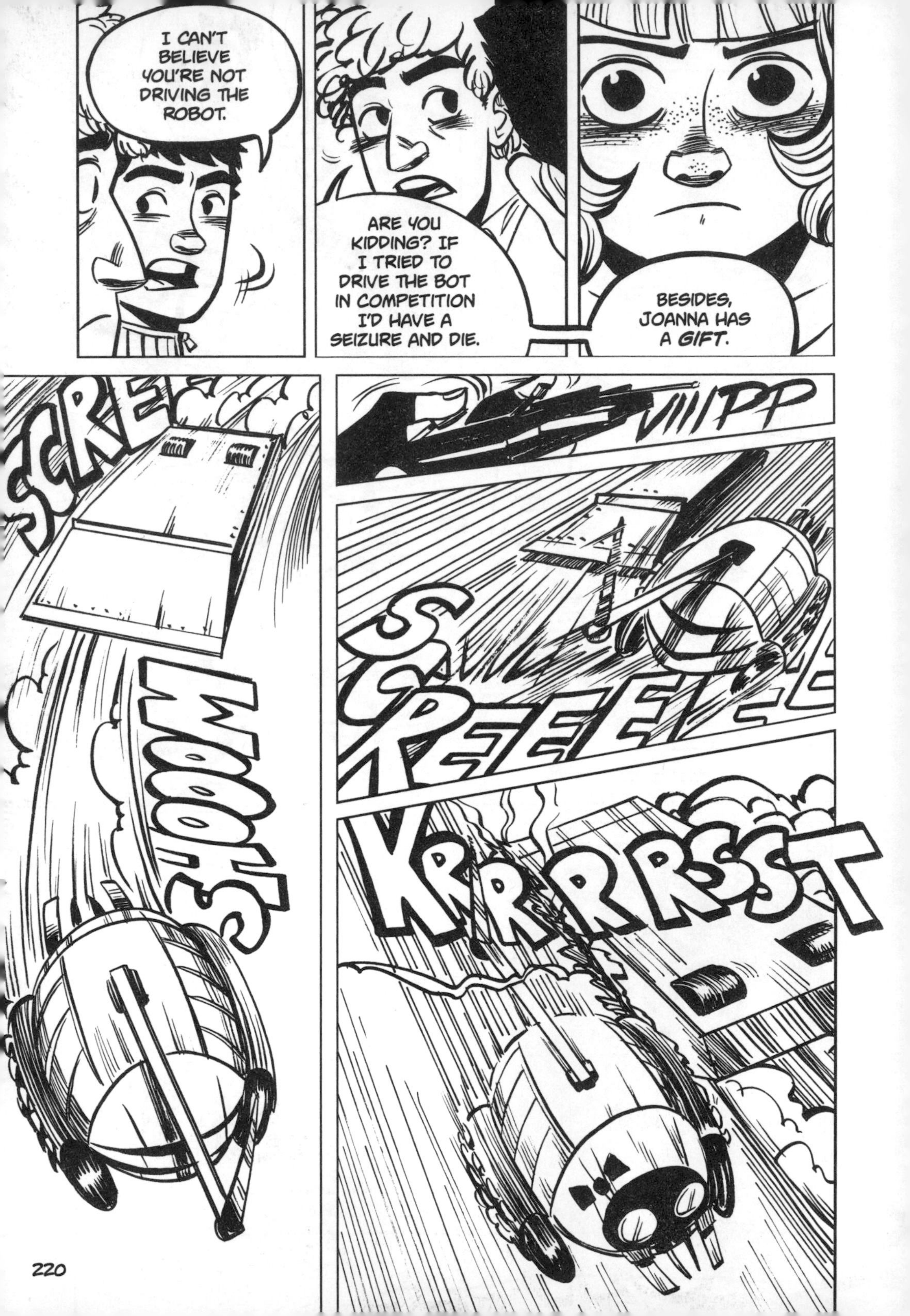
I CAN'T BELIEVE YOU'RE NOT DRIVING THE ROBOT.
ARE YOU KIDDING? IF I TRIED TO DRIVE THE BOT IN COMPETITION I'D HAVE A SEIZURE AND DIE.
BESIDES, JOANNA HAS A *GIFT*.
SCRE
SHOOOOM
VIIIPP
SKREEEE
KRRRRSST

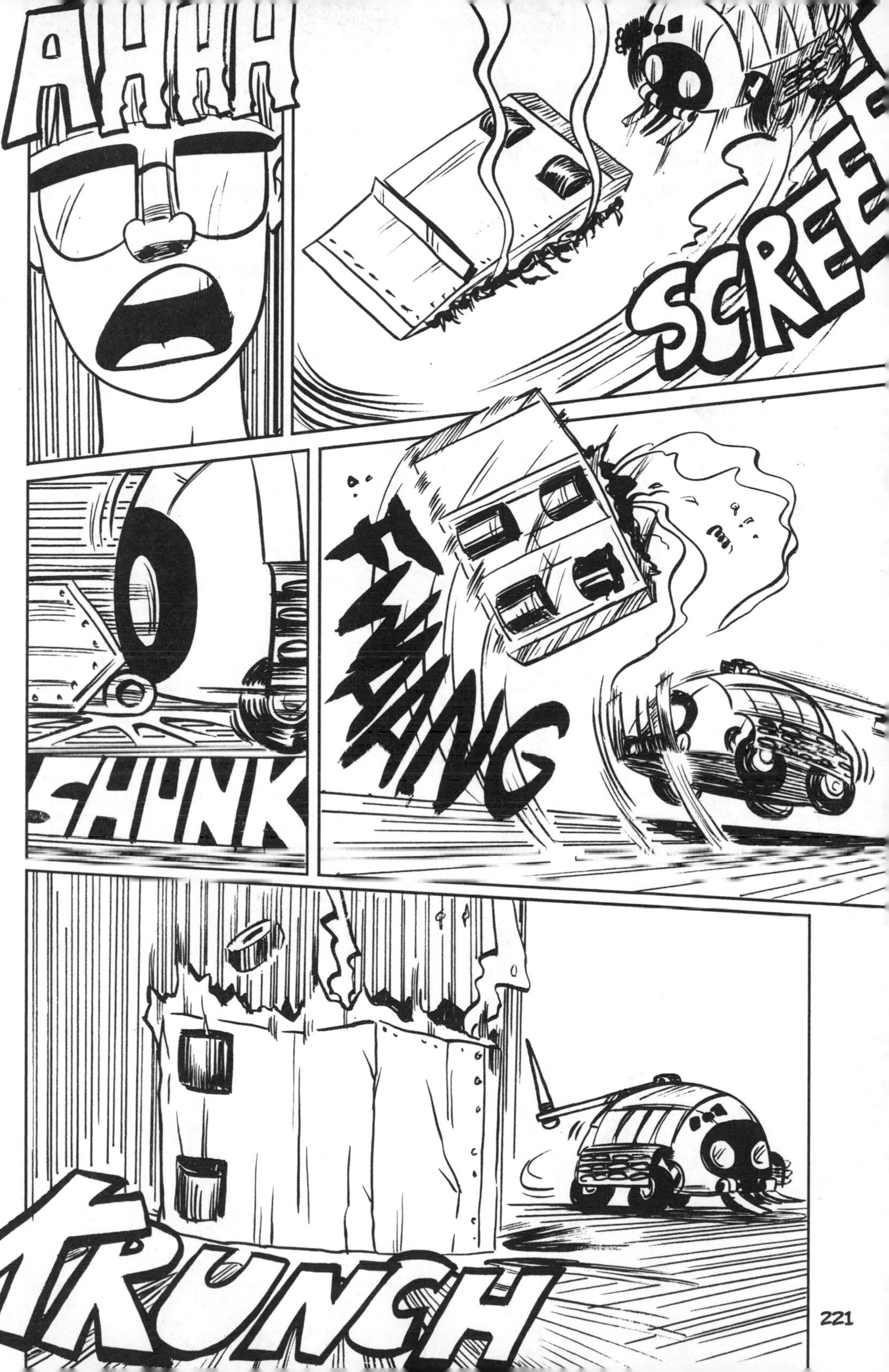
AHHH
SCREE
SHUNK
TWANG
KRUNCH

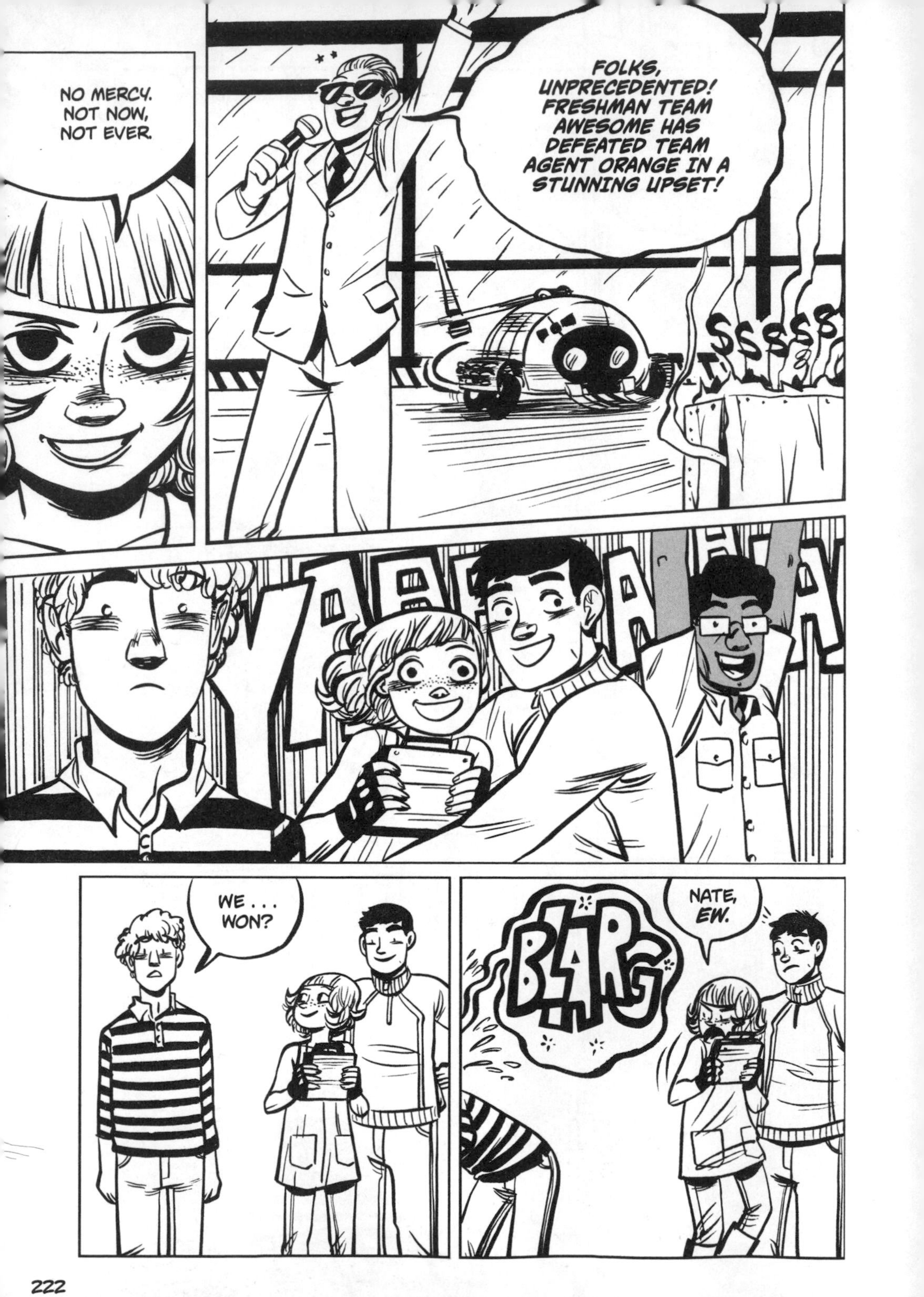
NO MERCY. NOT NOW, NOT EVER.
FOLKS, UNPRECEDENTED! FRESHMAN TEAM AWESOME HAS DEFEATED TEAM AGENT ORANGE IN A STUNNING UPSET!
SSSSS
WE . . . WON?
BLARG
NATE, EW.

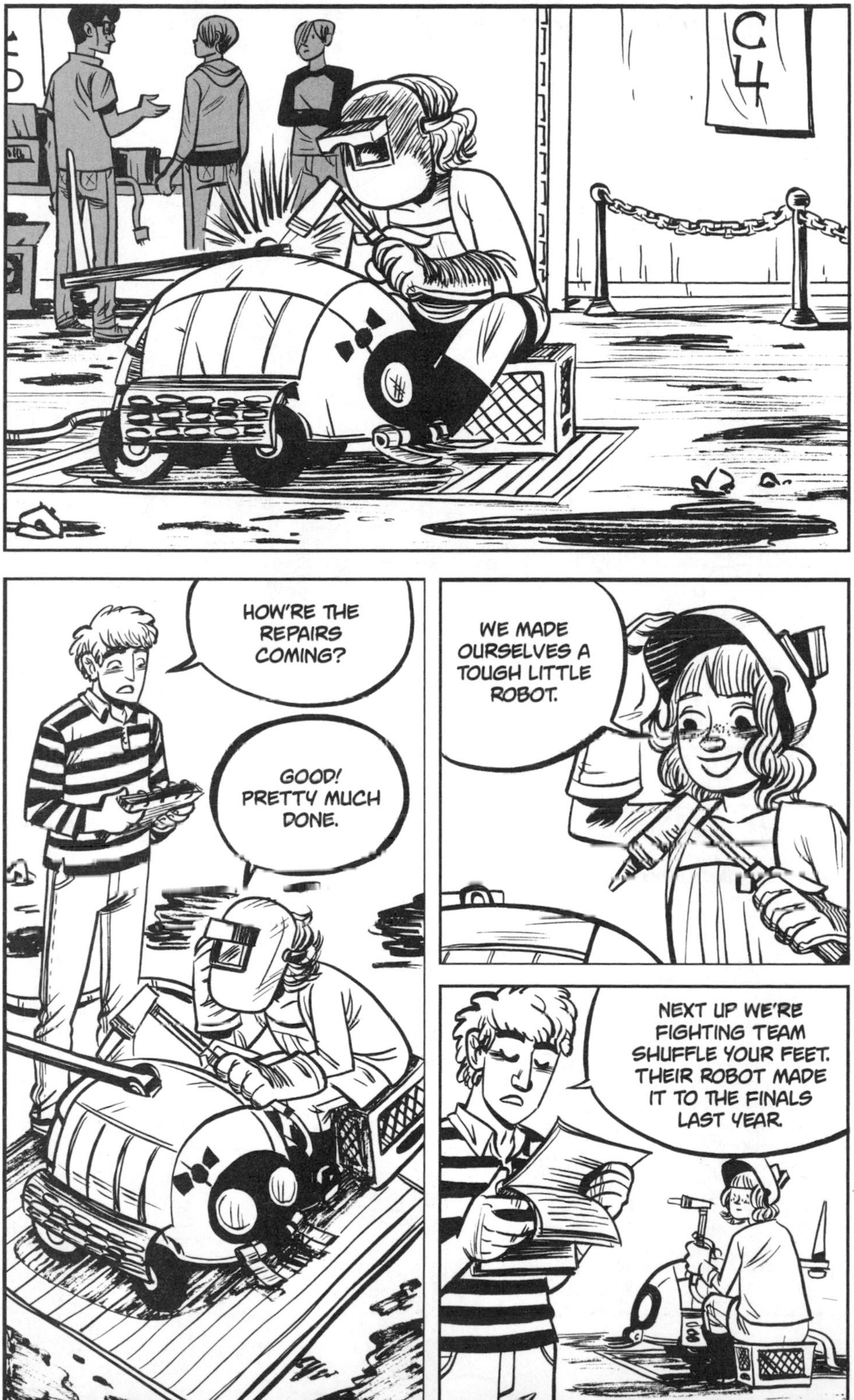
C4
HOW'RE THE REPAIRS COMING?
GOOD! PRETTY MUCH DONE.
WE MADE OURSELVES A TOUGH LITTLE ROBOT.
NEXT UP WE'RE FIGHTING TEAM SHUFFLE YOUR FEET. THEIR ROBOT MADE IT TO THE FINALS LAST YEAR.

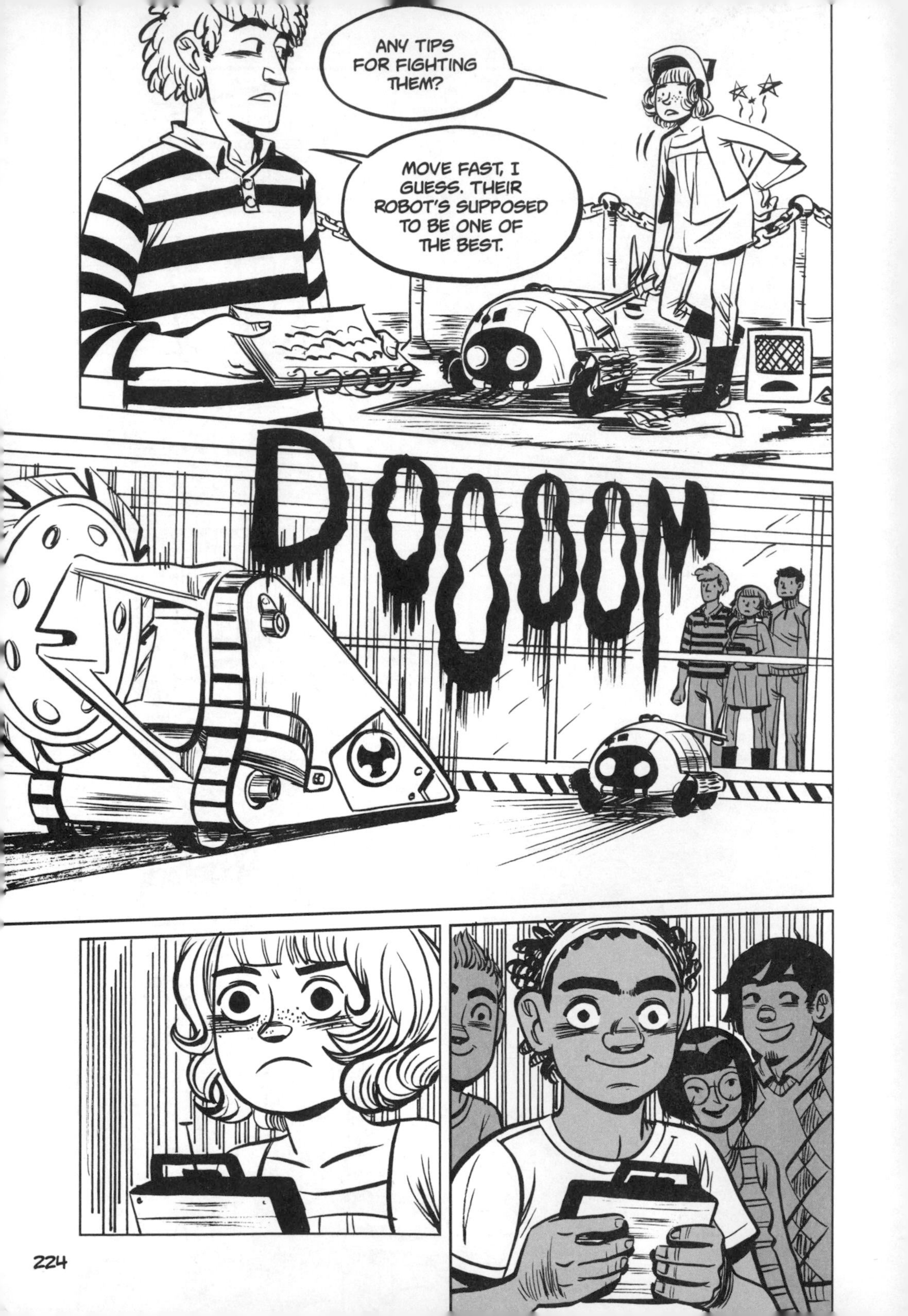
ANY TIPS FOR FIGHTING THEM?
MOVE FAST, I GUESS. THEIR ROBOT'S SUPPOSED TO BE ONE OF THE BEST.
DOOOOM

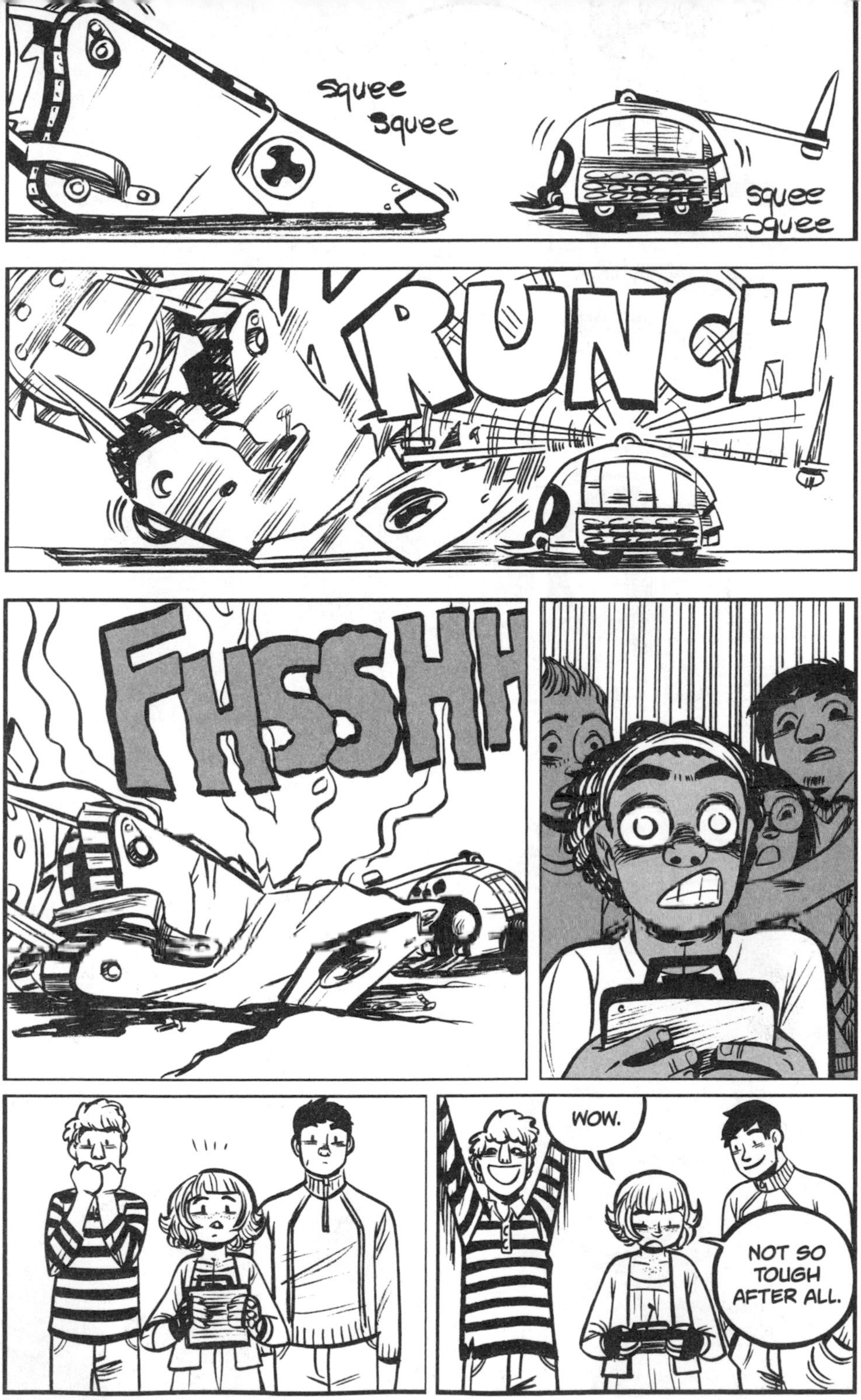
squee
squee
squee
squee
KRUNCH
FHSSHH
WOW.
NOT SO TOUGH AFTER ALL.

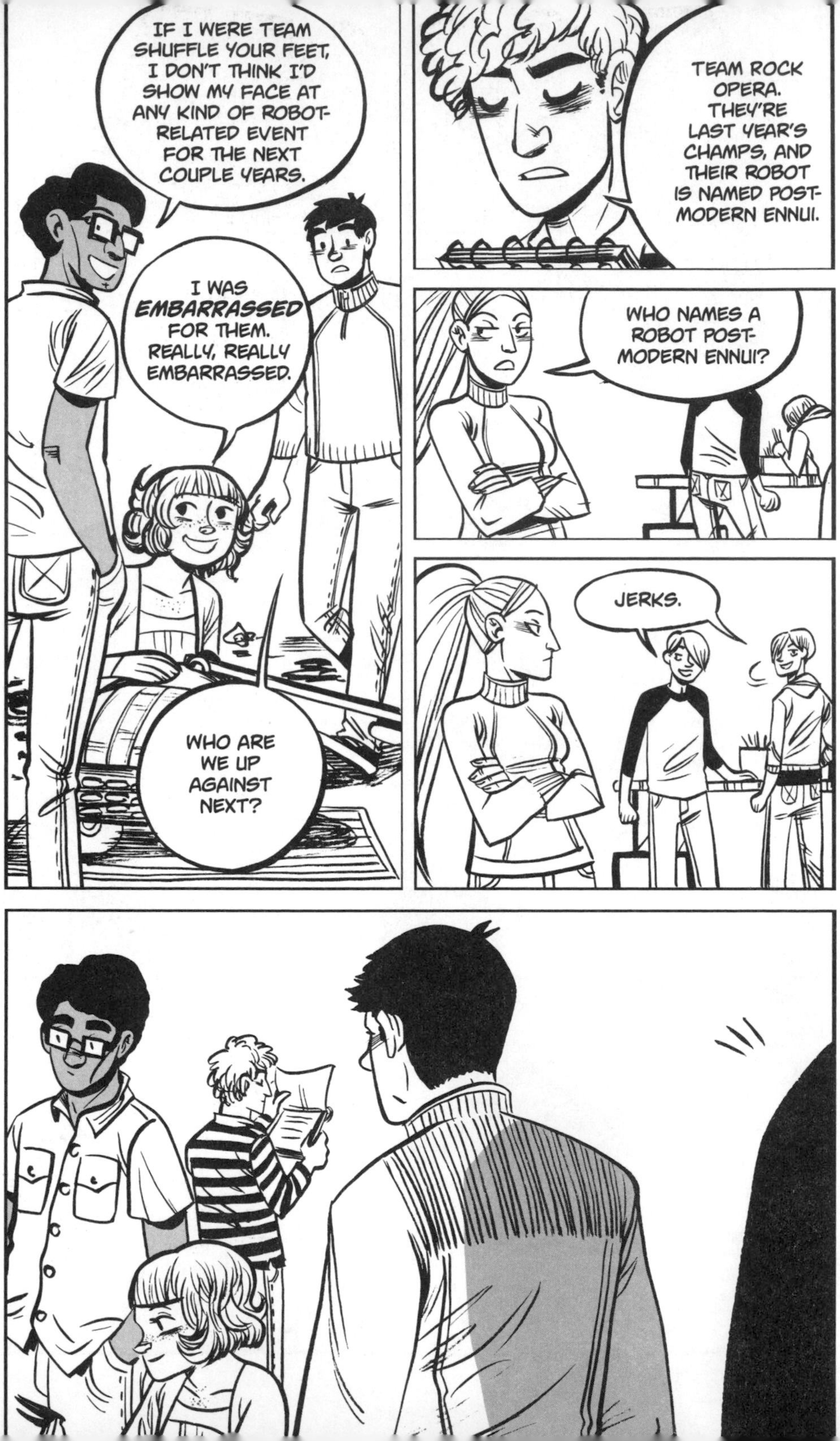
IF I WERE TEAM SHUFFLE YOUR FEET, I DON'T THINK I'D SHOW MY FACE AT ANY KIND OF ROBOT-RELATED EVENT FOR THE NEXT COUPLE YEARS.
I WAS ***EMBARRASSED*** FOR THEM. REALLY, REALLY EMBARRASSED.
WHO ARE WE UP AGAINST NEXT?
TEAM ROCK OPERA. THEY'RE LAST YEAR'S CHAMPS, AND THEIR ROBOT IS NAMED POST-MODERN ENNUI.
WHO NAMES A ROBOT POST-MODERN ENNUI?
JERKS.

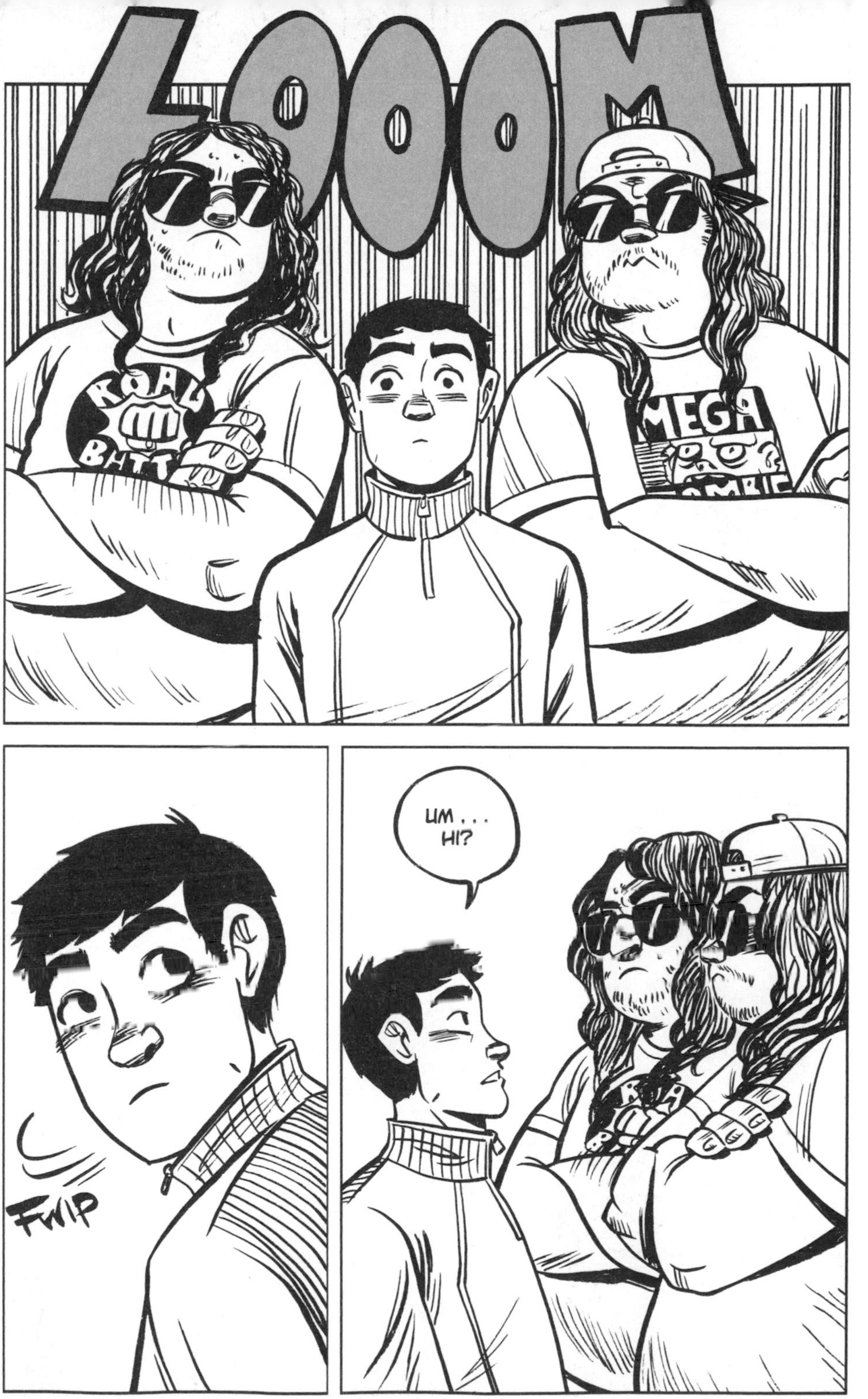
LOOOM
MEGA
FWIP
UM . . . HI?

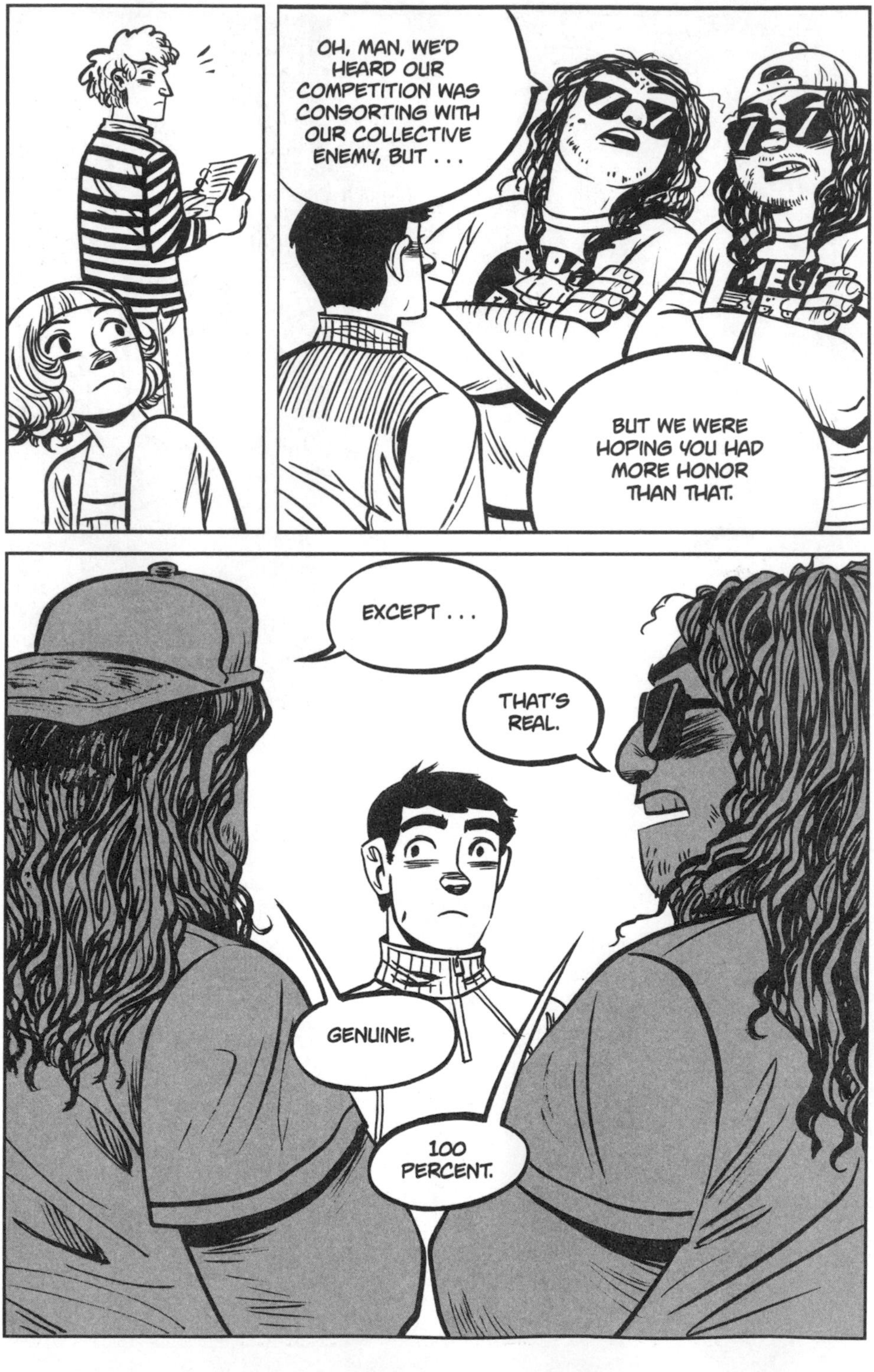
OH, MAN, WE'D HEARD OUR COMPETITION WAS CONSORTING WITH OUR COLLECTIVE ENEMY, BUT . . .
BUT WE WERE HOPING YOU HAD MORE HONOR THAN THAT.
EXCEPT . . .
THAT'S REAL.
GENUINE.
100 PERCENT.

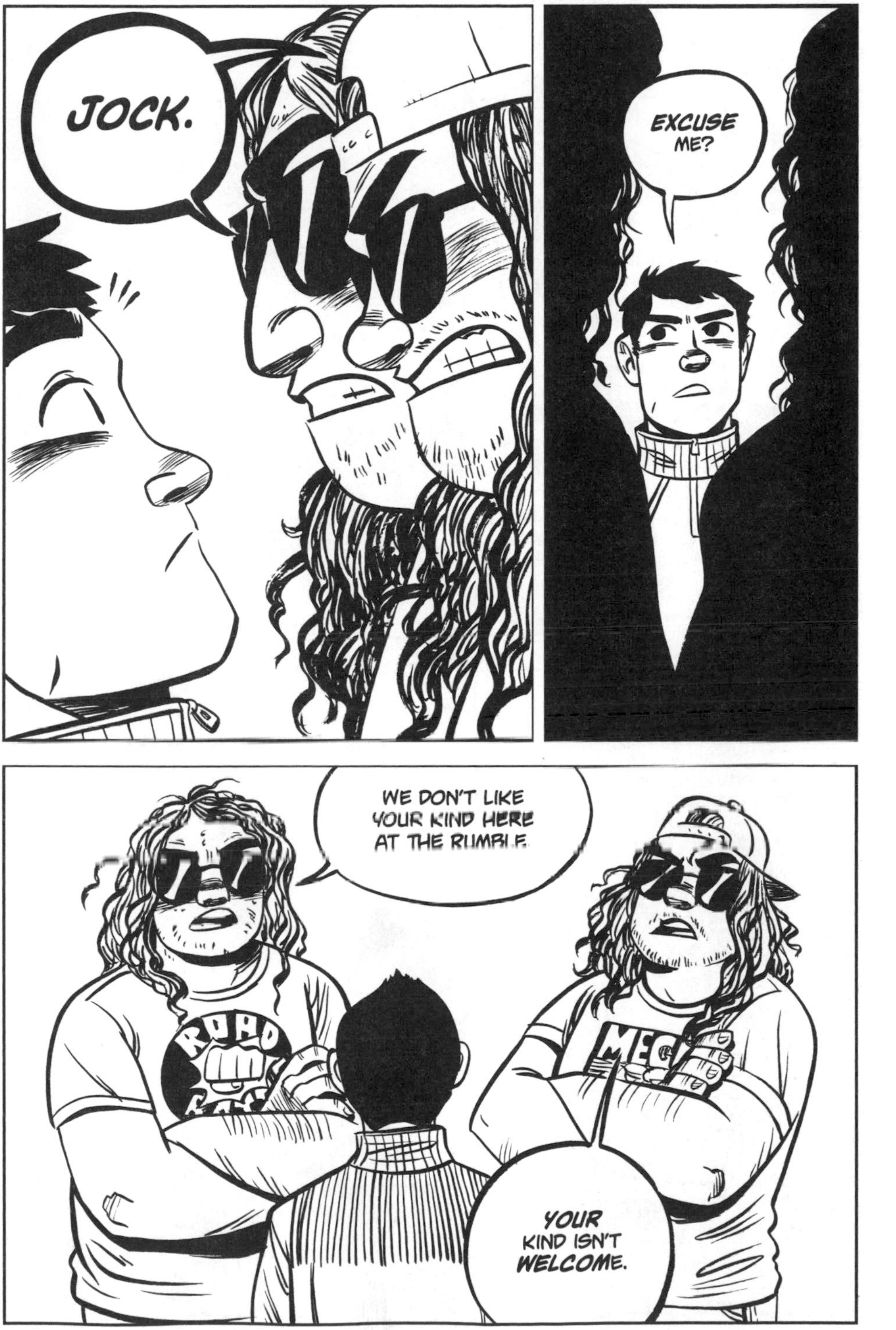
JOCK.
EXCUSE ME?
WE DON'T LIKE YOUR KIND HERE AT THE RUMBLE.
YOUR KIND ISN'T WELCOME.

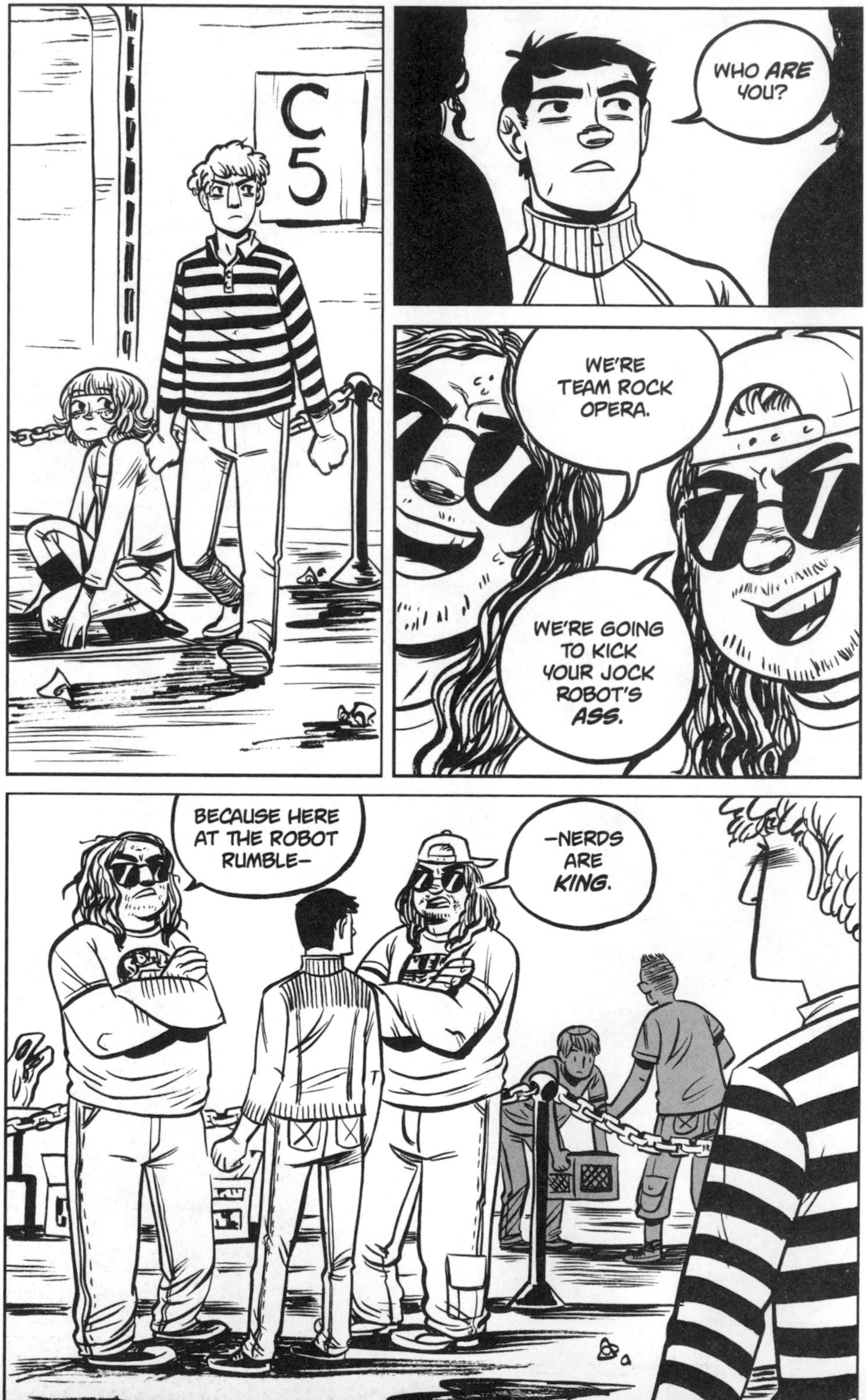
C5
WHO ARE YOU?
WE'RE TEAM ROCK OPERA.
WE'RE GOING TO KICK YOUR JOCK ROBOT'S ASS.
BECAUSE HERE AT THE ROBOT RUMBLE—
—NERDS ARE KING.

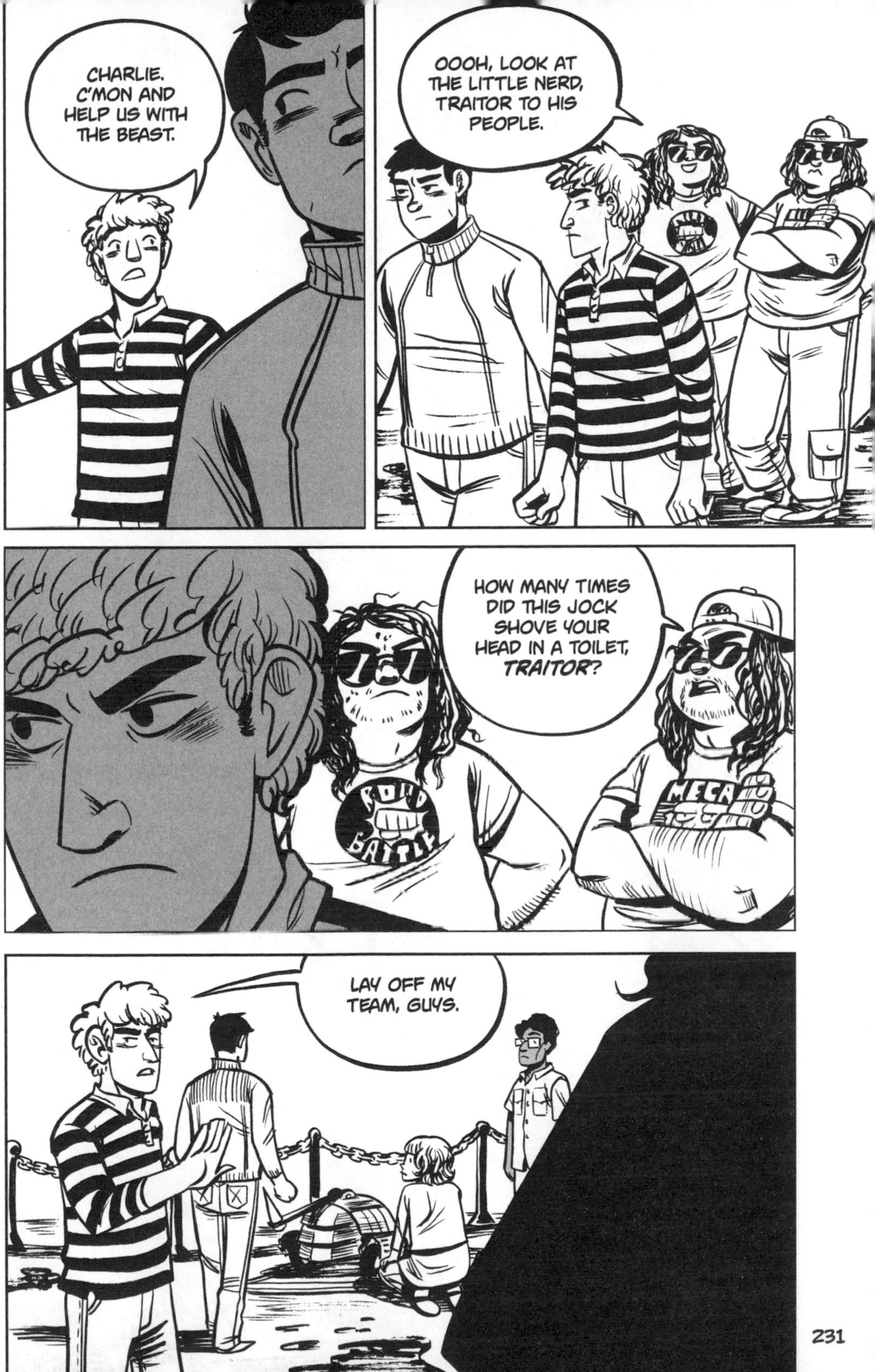
CHARLIE. C'MON AND HELP US WITH THE BEAST.
OOOH, LOOK AT THE LITTLE NERD, TRAITOR TO HIS PEOPLE.
HOW MANY TIMES DID THIS JOCK SHOVE YOUR HEAD IN A TOILET, *TRAITOR*?
MECA
LAY OFF MY TEAM, GUYS.

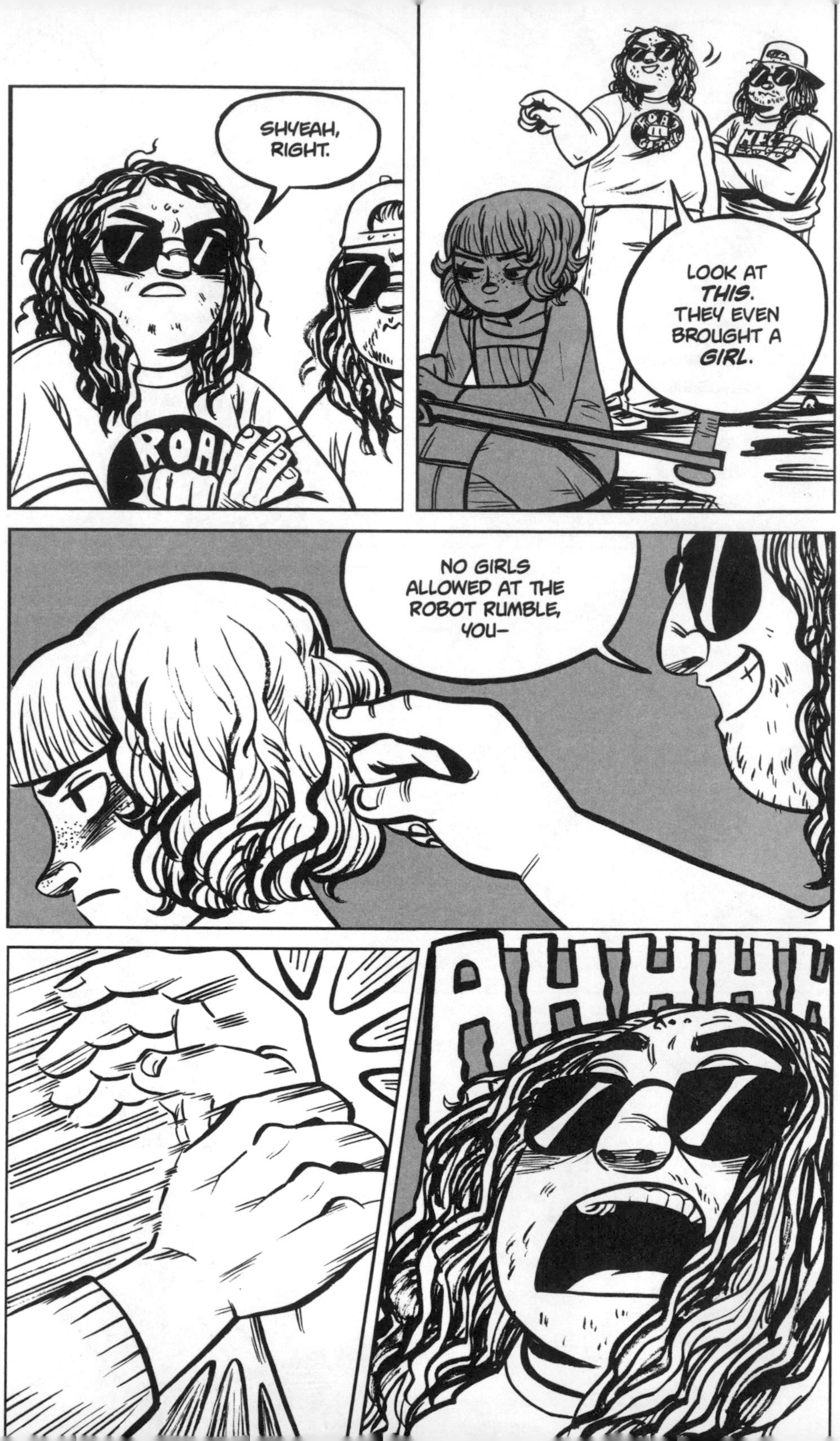
SHYEAH, RIGHT.
LOOK AT THIS. THEY EVEN BROUGHT A GIRL.
NO GIRLS ALLOWED AT THE ROBOT RUMBLE, YOU-
AHHHH

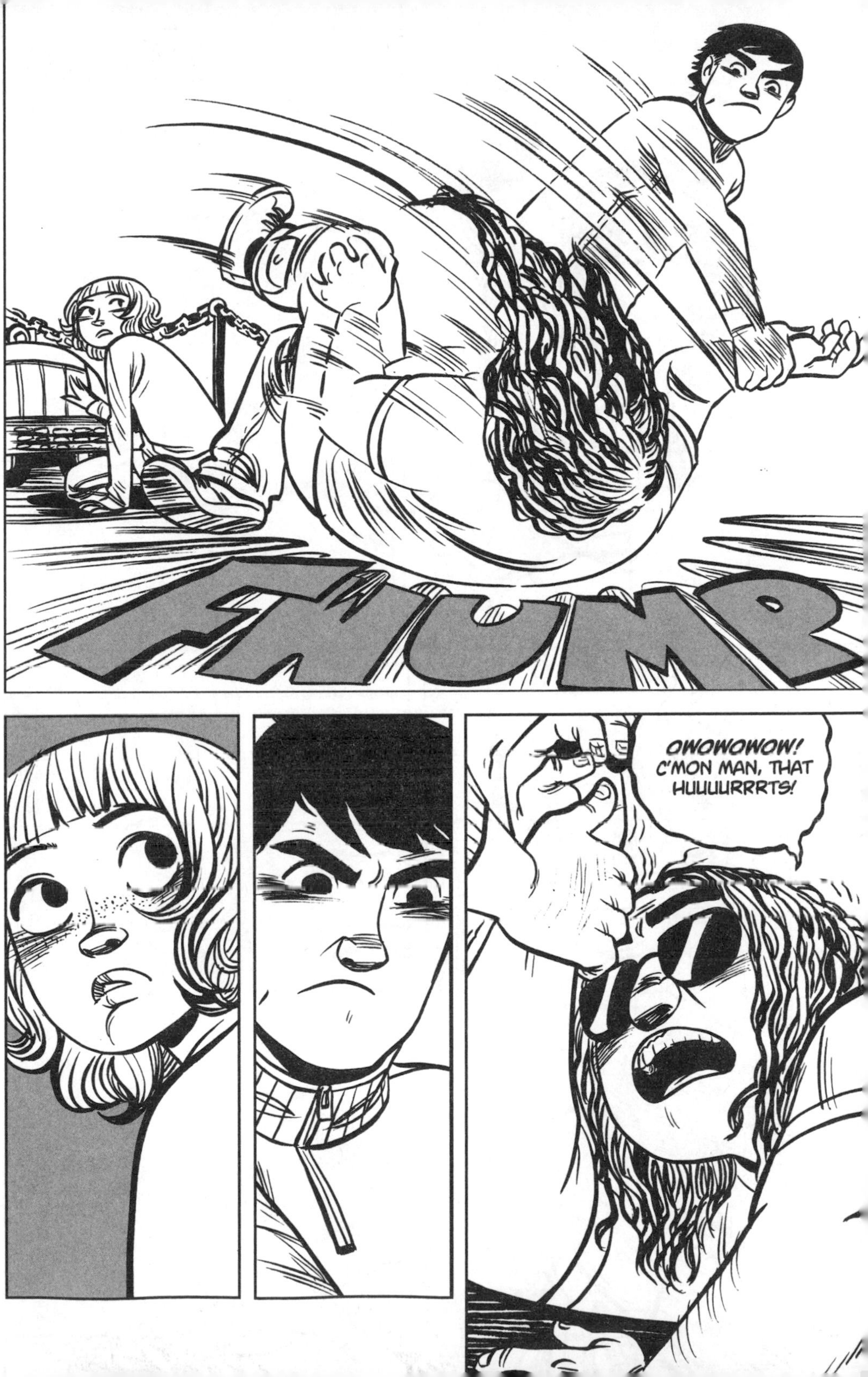
THUMP
OWOWOWOW! C'MON MAN, THAT HUUUURRRTS!

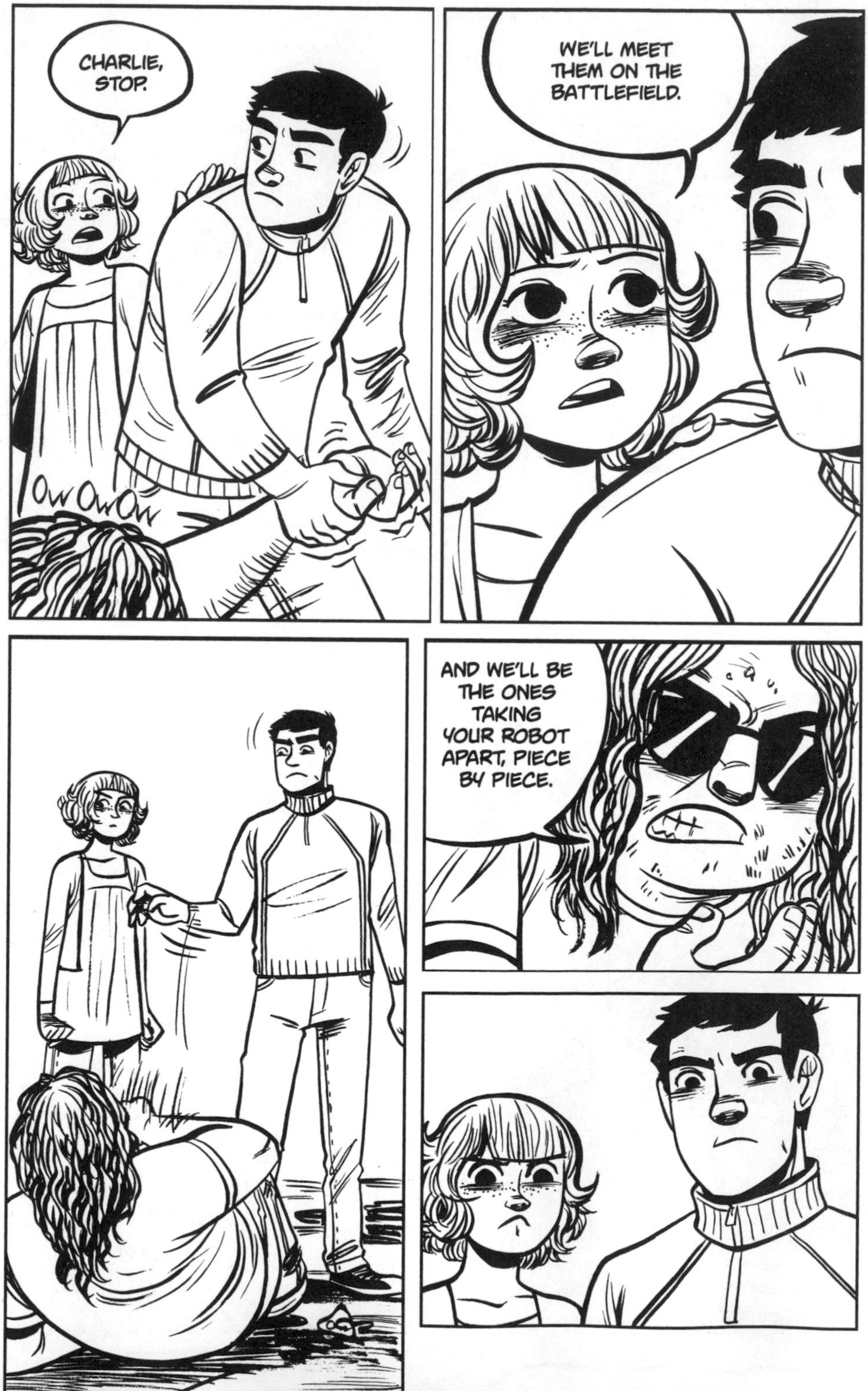
CHARLIE, STOP.
OW OW OW
WE'LL MEET THEM ON THE BATTLEFIELD.
AND WE'LL BE THE ONES TAKING YOUR ROBOT APART, PIECE BY PIECE.

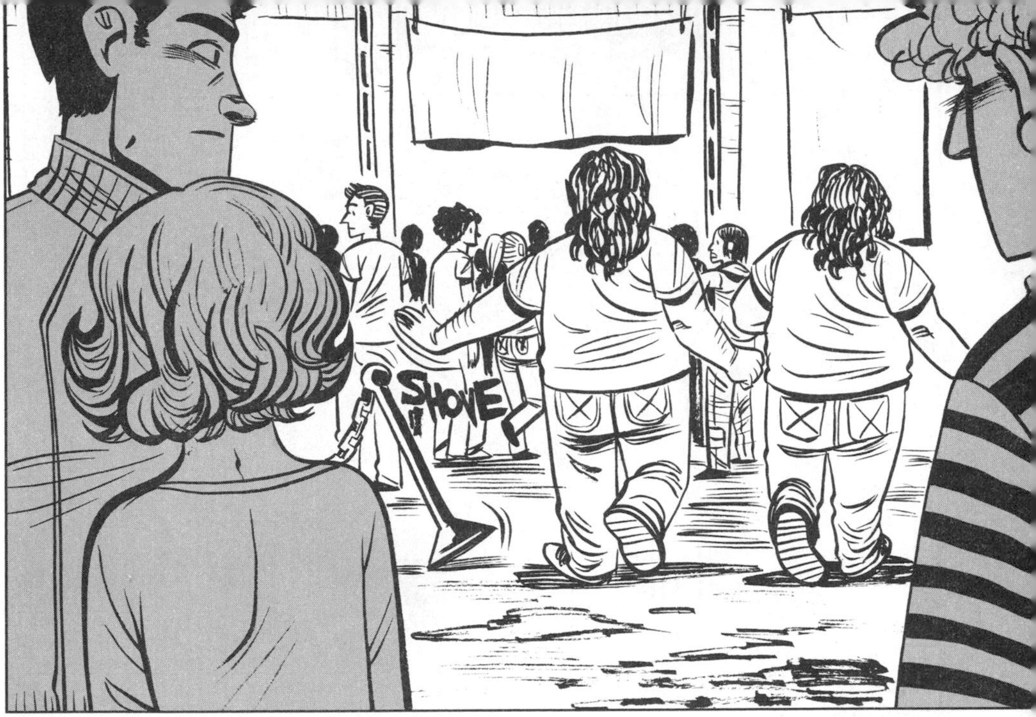
SHOVE

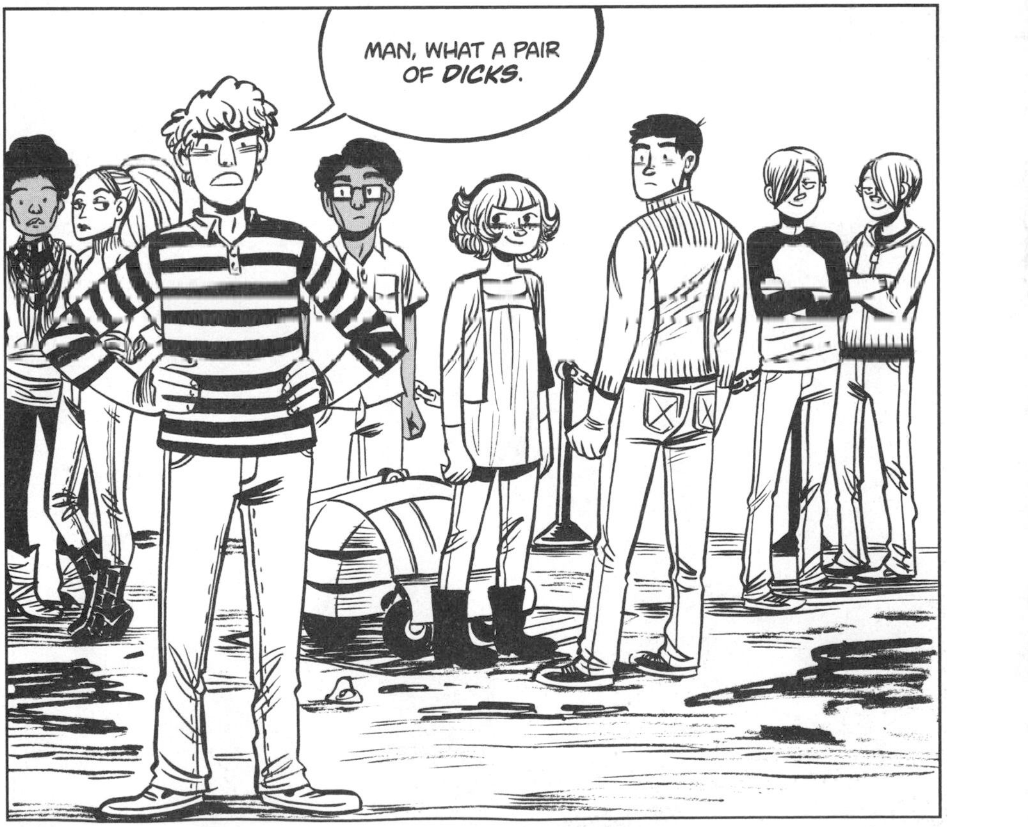
MAN, WHAT A PAIR OF *DICKS*.

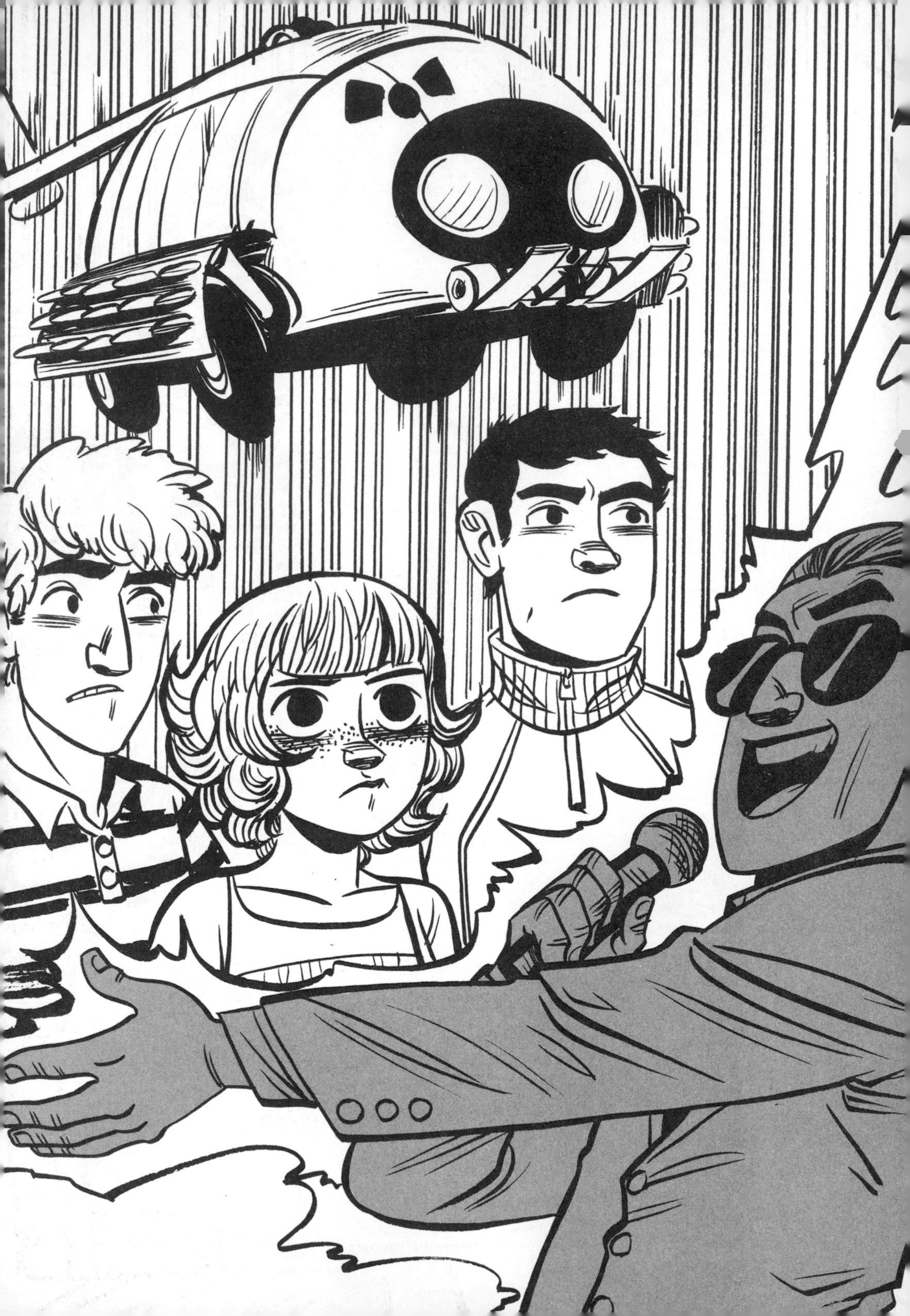

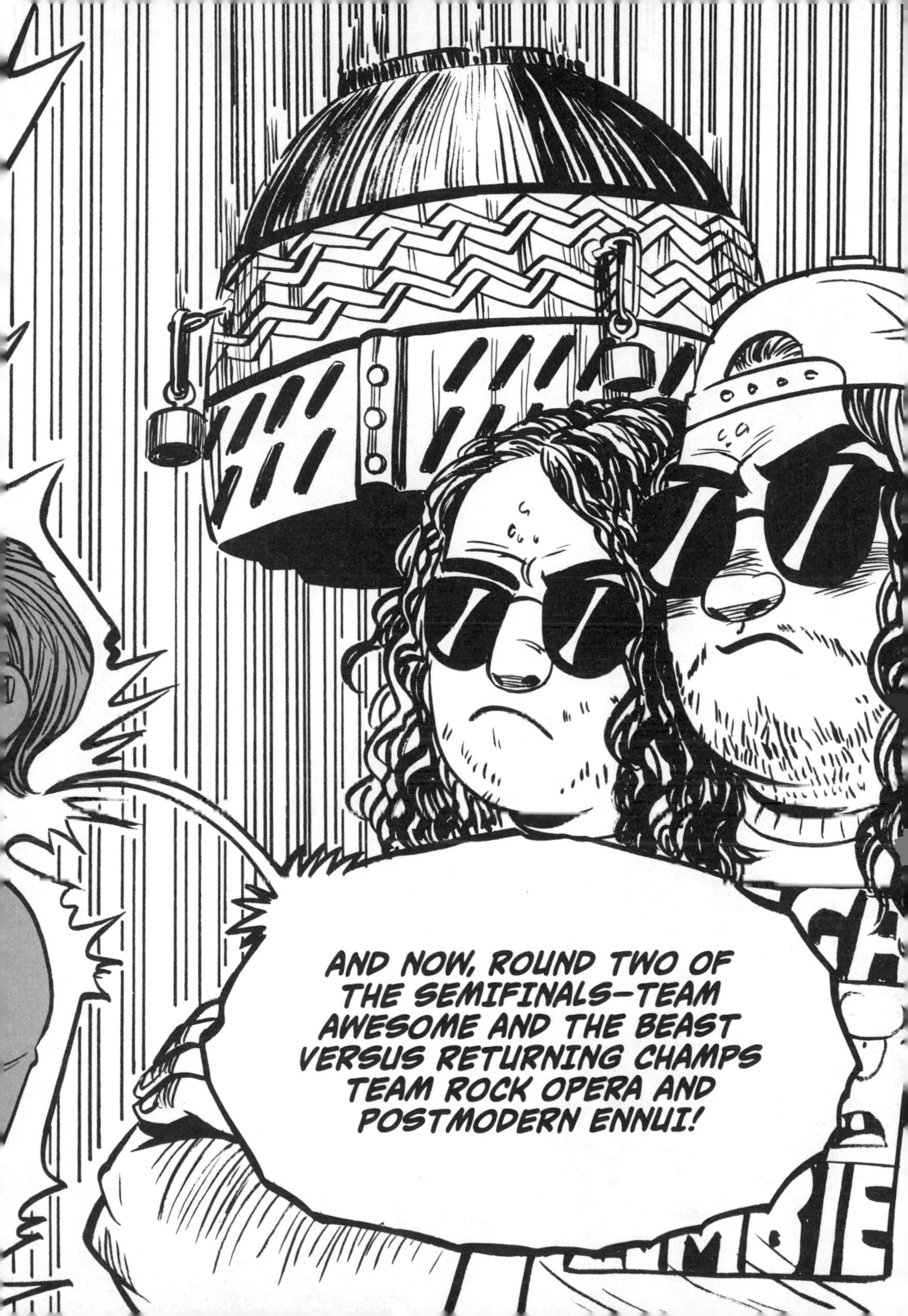
AND NOW, ROUND TWO OF THE SEMIFINALS—TEAM AWESOME AND THE BEAST VERSUS RETURNING CHAMPS TEAM ROCK OPERA AND POSTMODERN ENNUI!

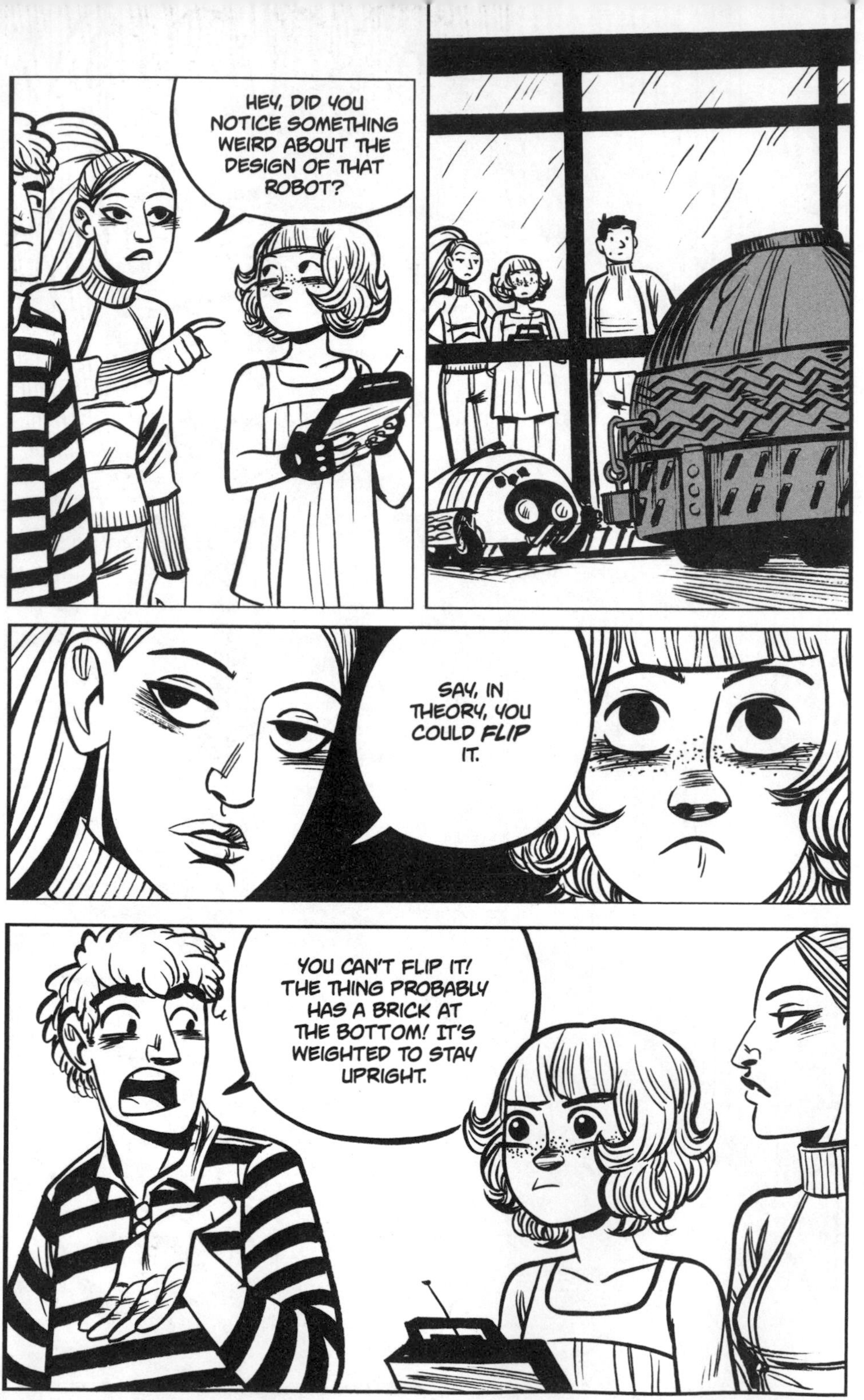
HEY, DID YOU NOTICE SOMETHING WEIRD ABOUT THE DESIGN OF THAT ROBOT?
SAY, IN THEORY, YOU COULD *FLIP* IT.
YOU CAN'T FLIP IT! THE THING PROBABLY HAS A BRICK AT THE BOTTOM! IT'S WEIGHTED TO STAY UPRIGHT.

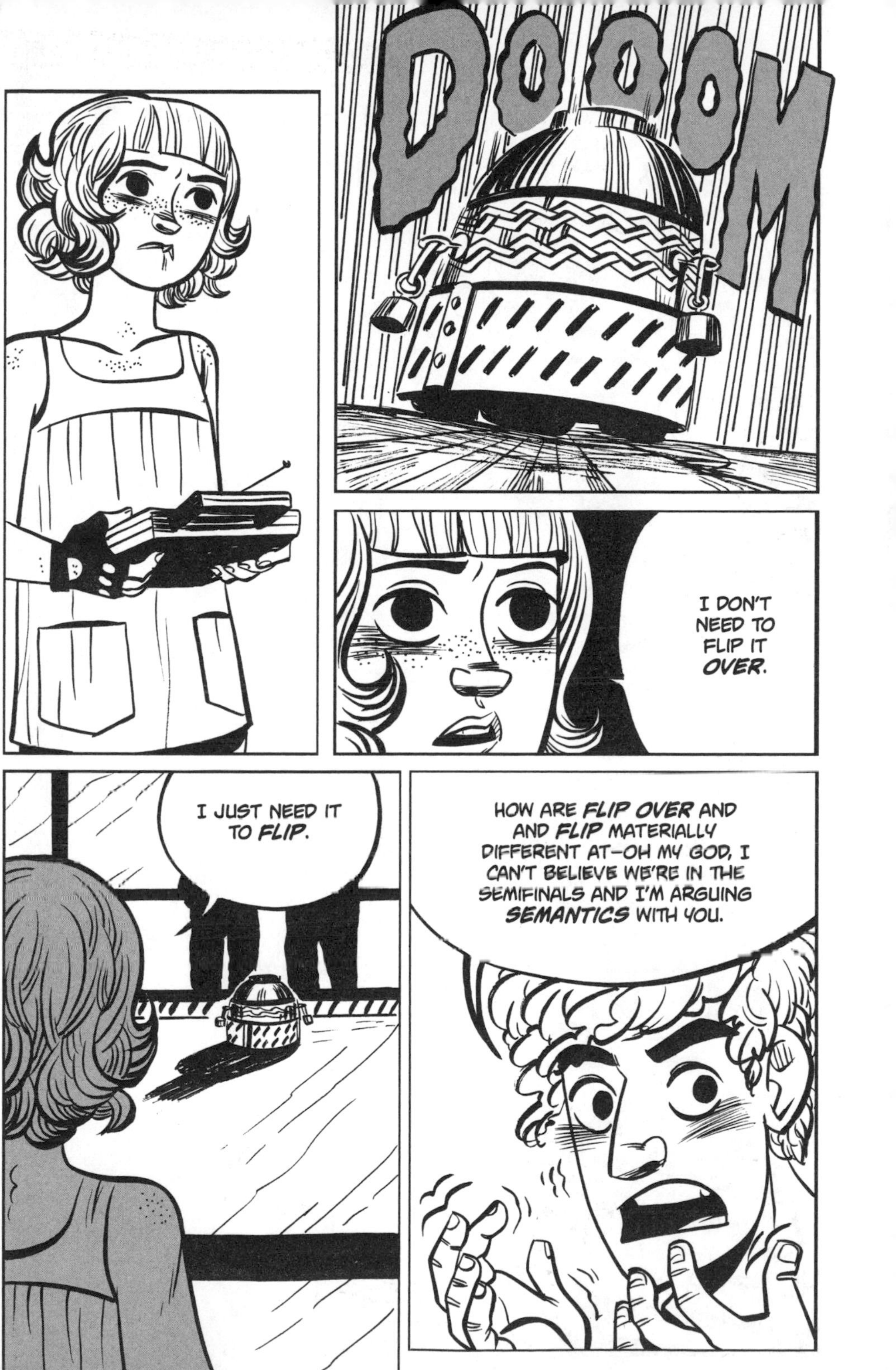
DOOOM
I DON'T NEED TO FLIP IT OVER.
I JUST NEED IT TO FLIP.
HOW ARE FLIP OVER AND AND FLIP MATERIALLY DIFFERENT AT—OH MY GOD, I CAN'T BELIEVE WE'RE IN THE SEMIFINALS AND I'M ARGUING SEMANTICS WITH YOU.

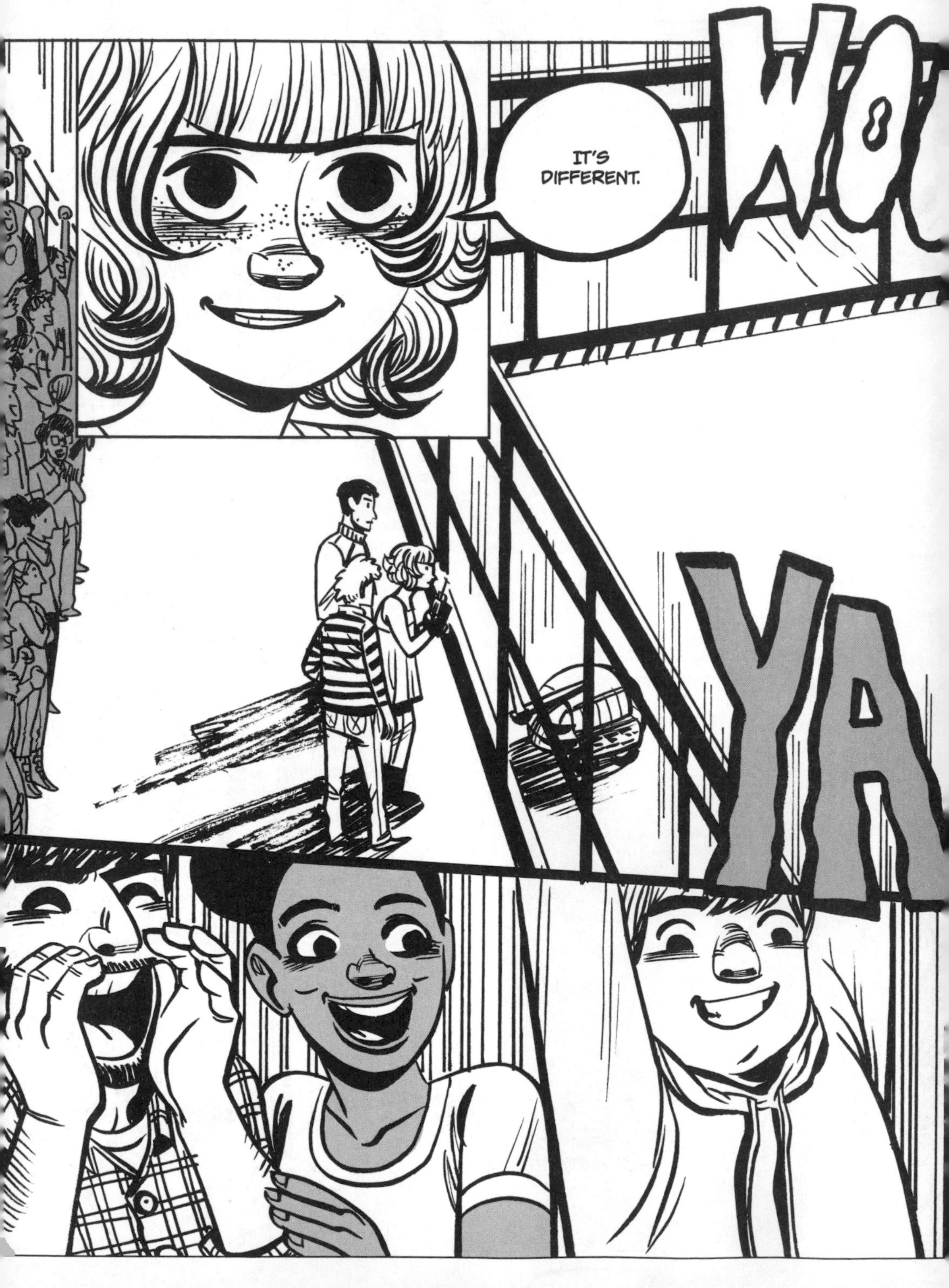
IT'S DIFFERENT.
WO
YA

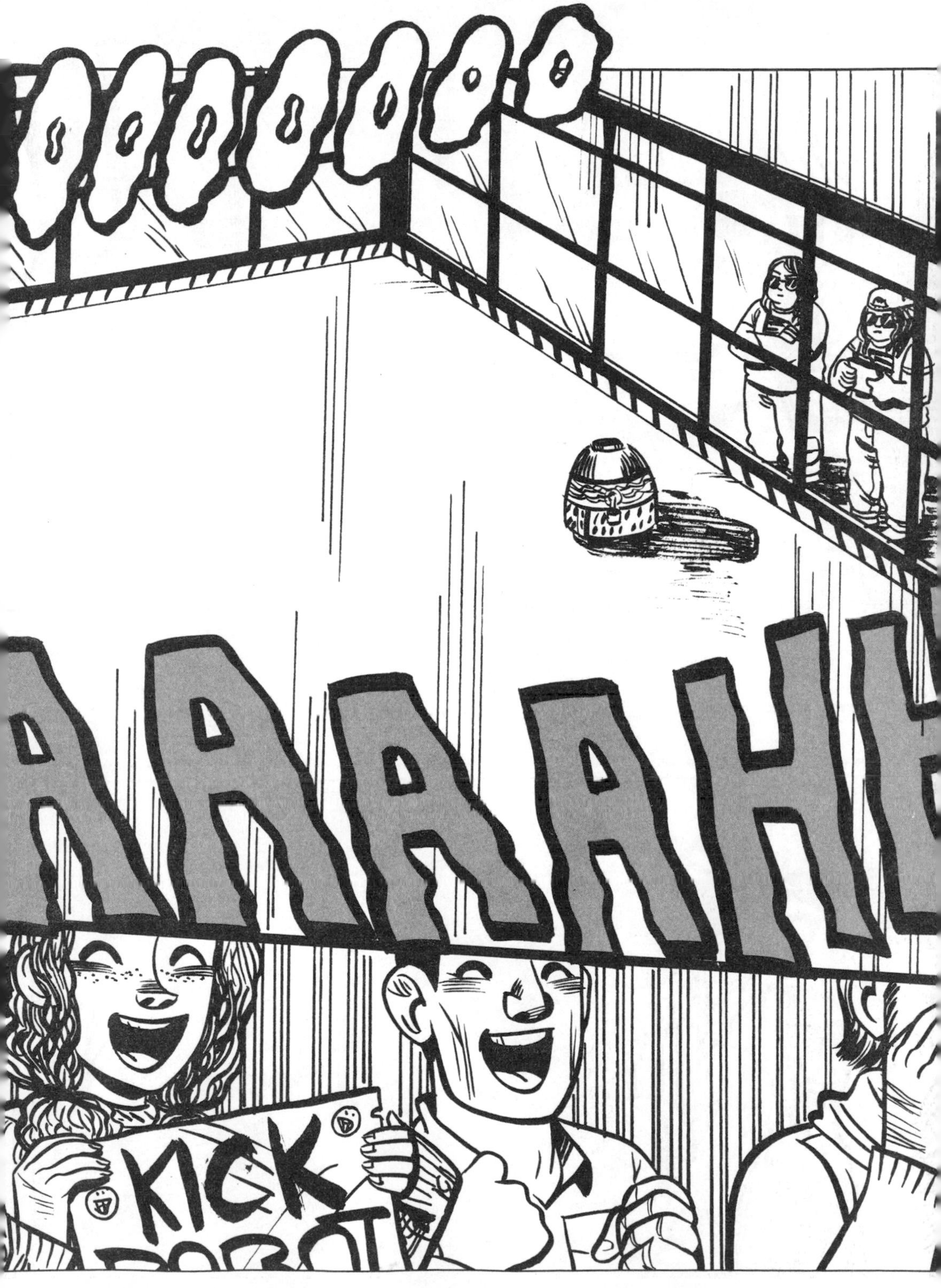
KICK

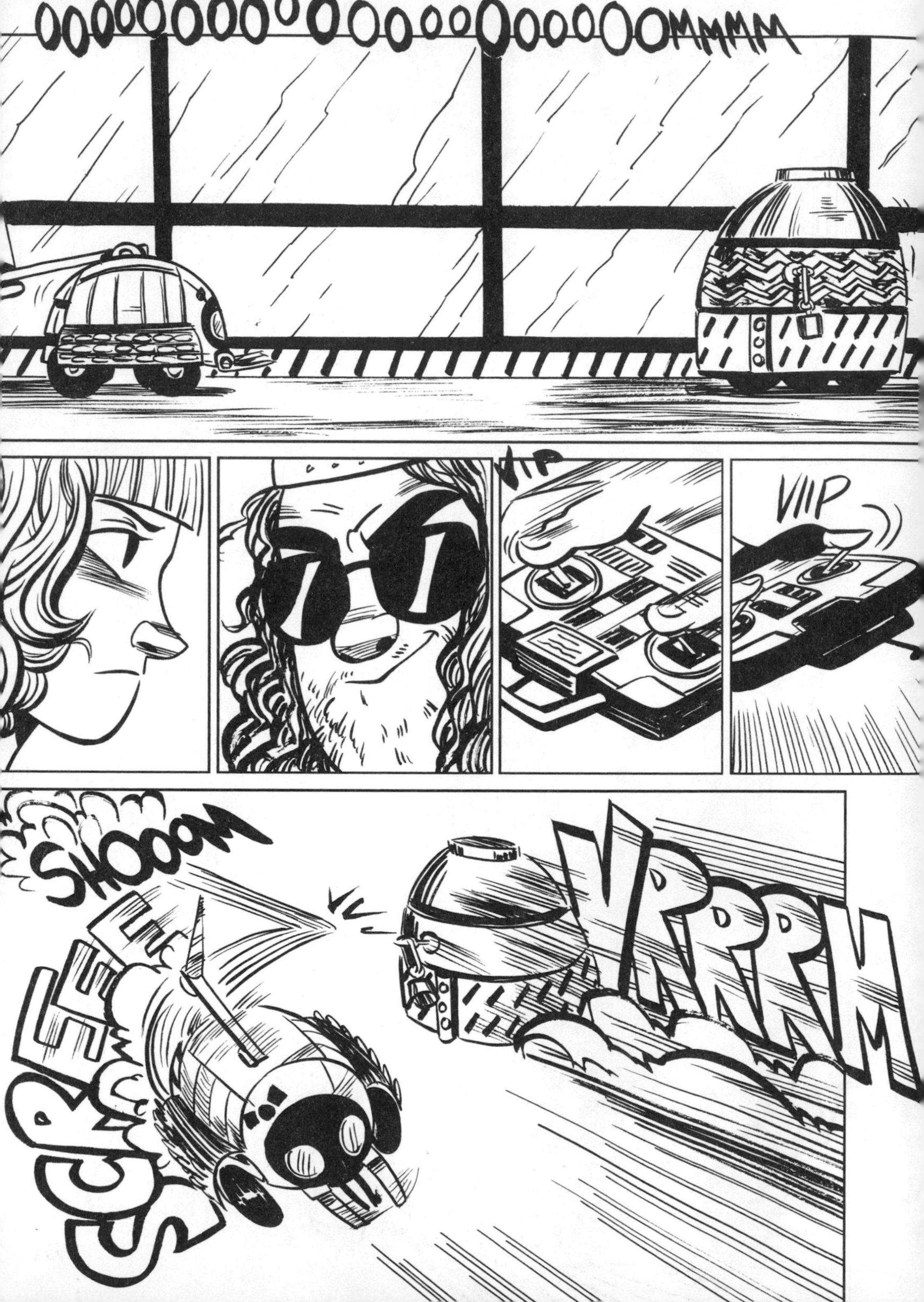
OOOOOOOOOOOOOOOOOOOOOOOMMMM
VIP
VIIP
SHOOOM
SCREEE
VRRRM

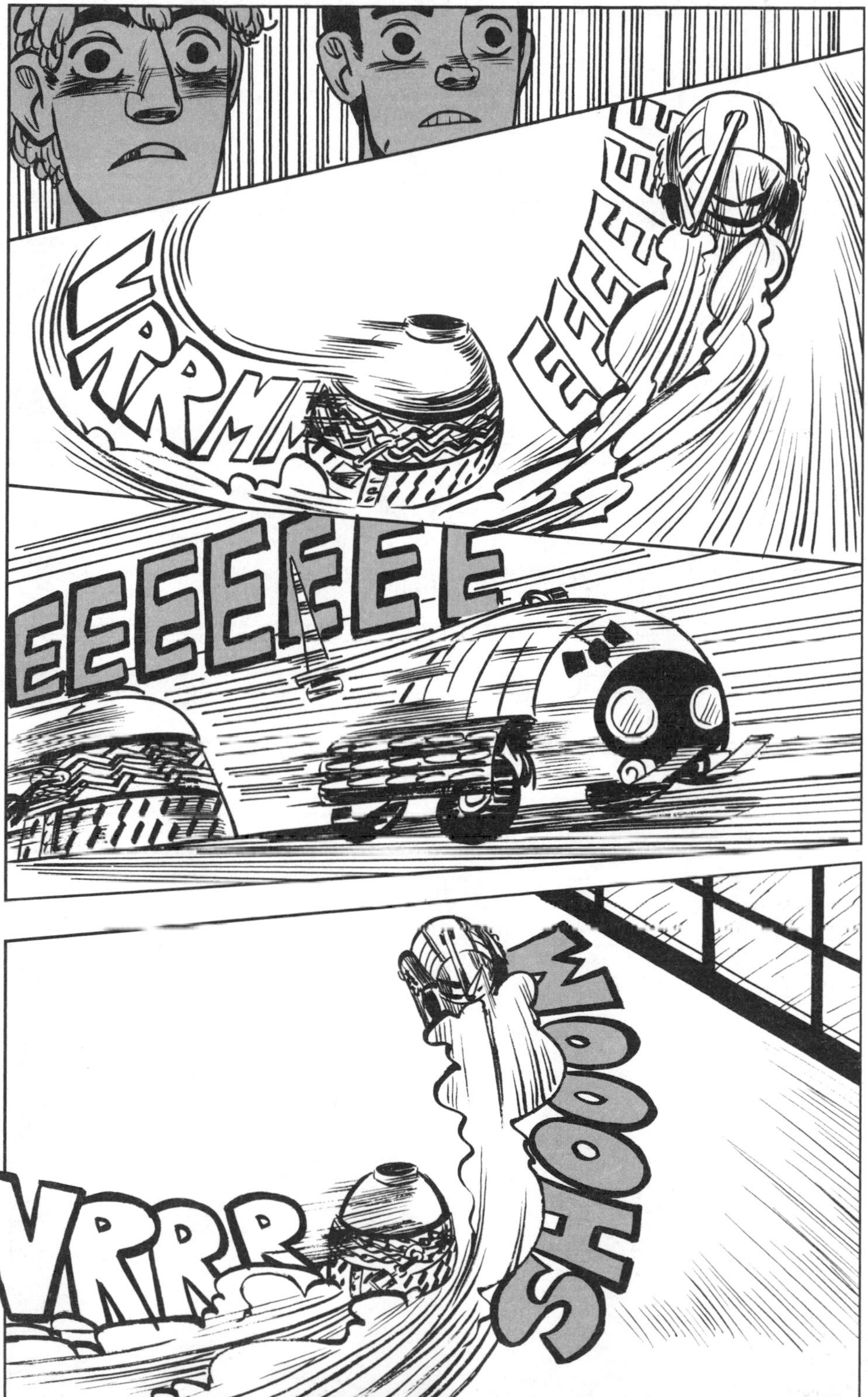
VRRMM
EEEEEE
EEEEEEEE
VRRR
SHOOOOOOM

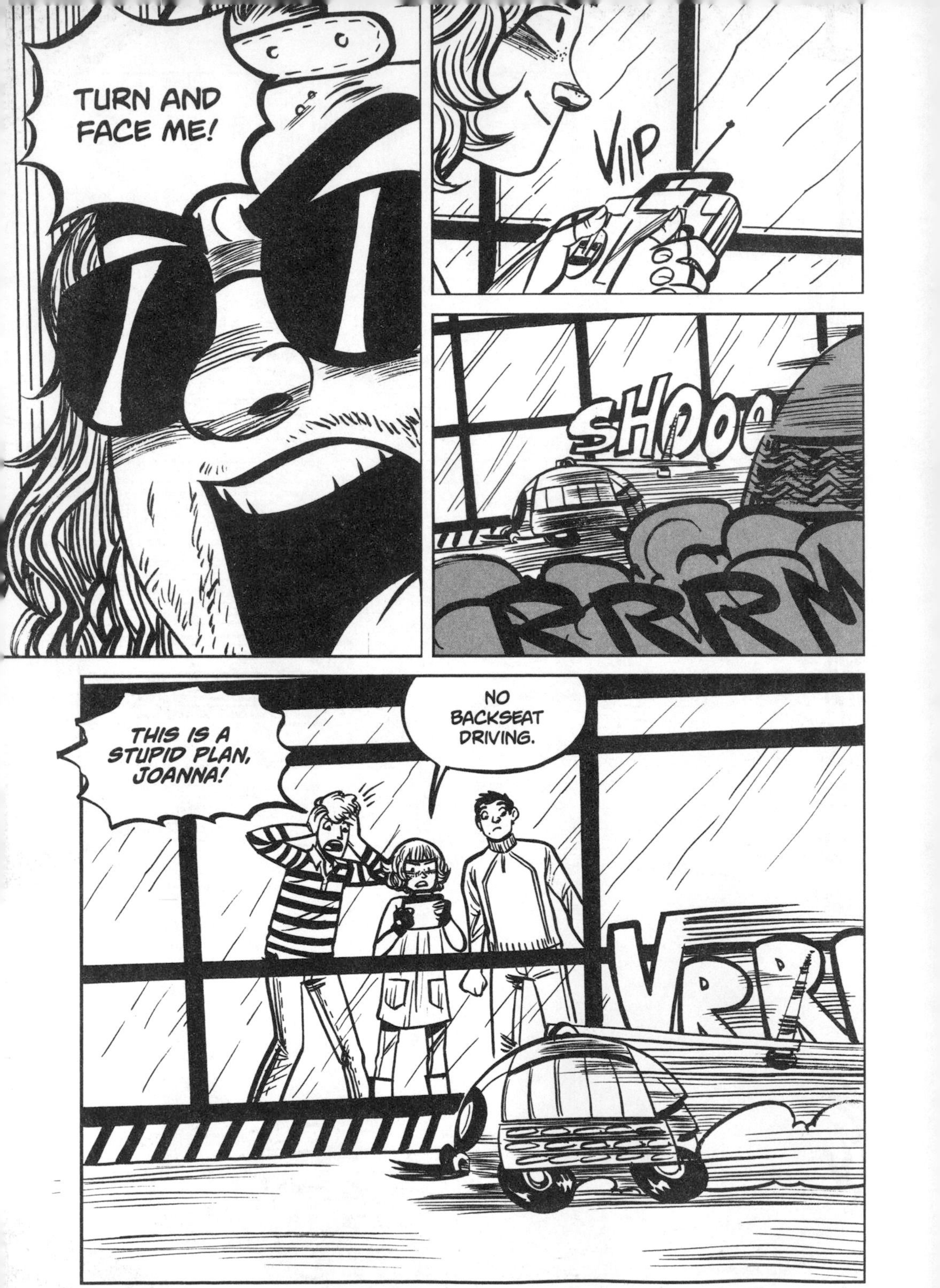
TURN AND FACE ME!
VIIP
SHOOO
RRRM
THIS IS A STUPID PLAN, JOANNA!
NO BACKSEAT DRIVING.
VRR

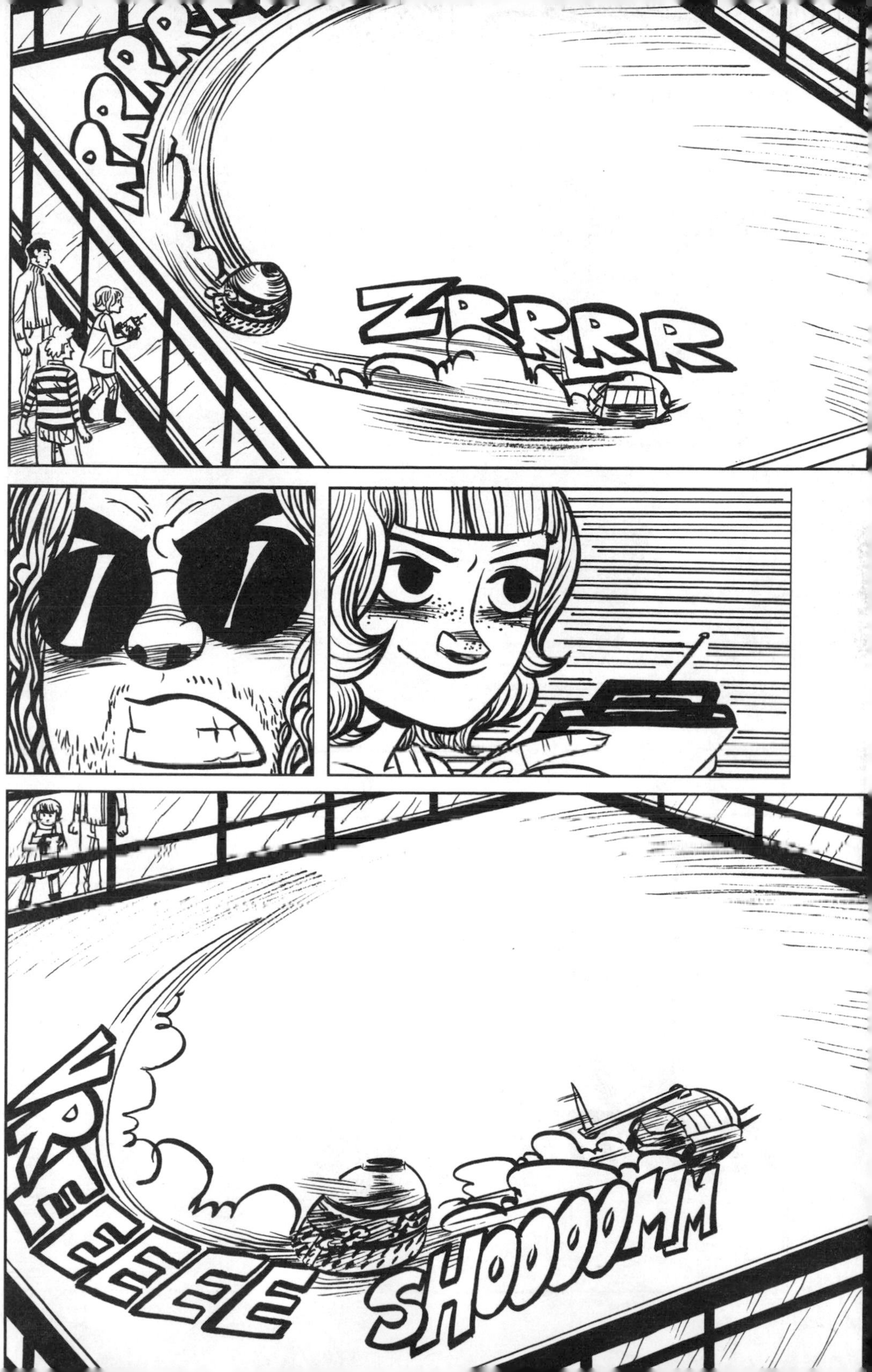
ZRRRR
VREEEEE
SHOOOOOMM

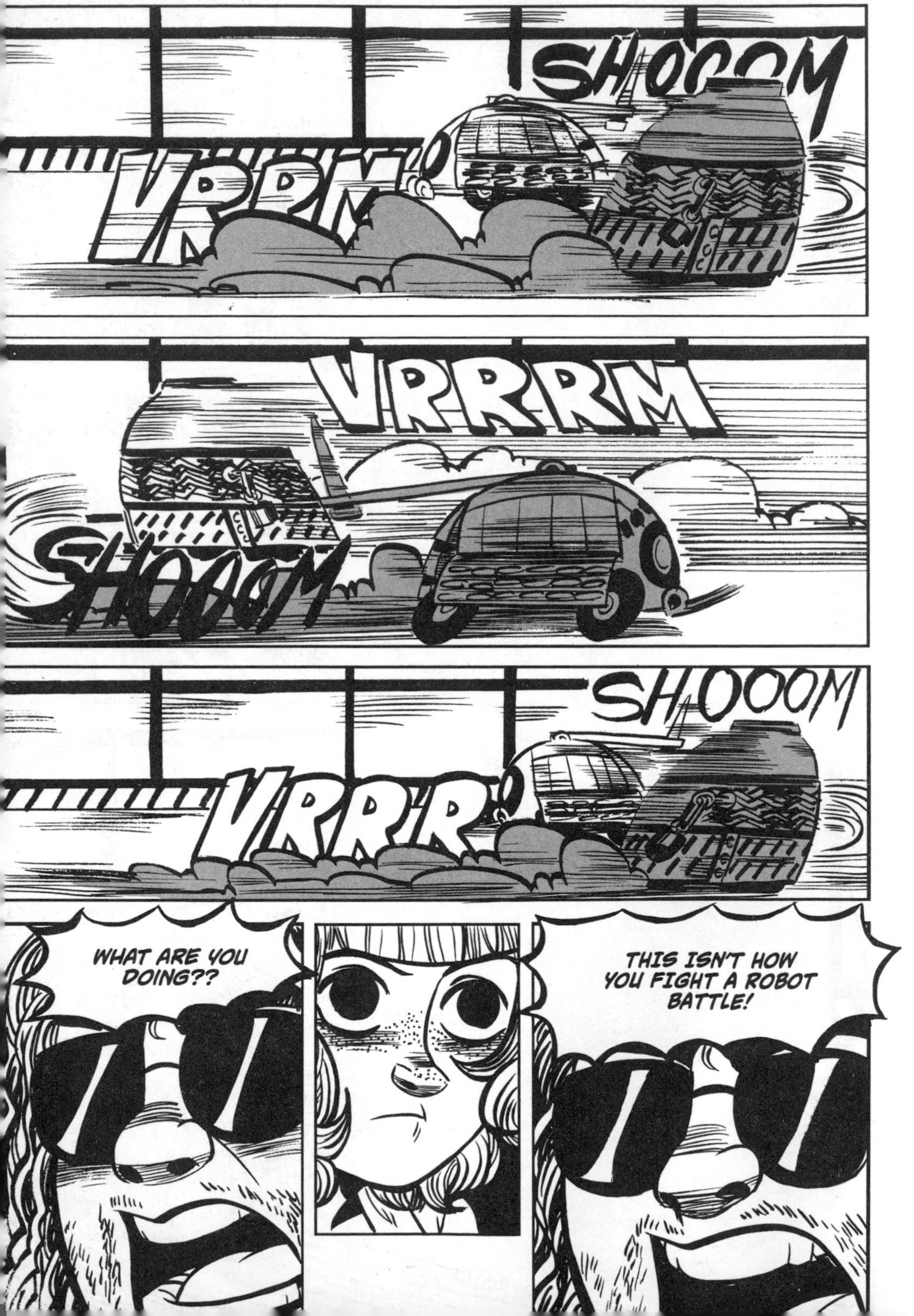
SHOOOM
VRRM
VRRRM
SHOOOM
SHOOOM
VRRR
WHAT ARE YOU DOING??
THIS ISN'T HOW YOU FIGHT A ROBOT BATTLE!

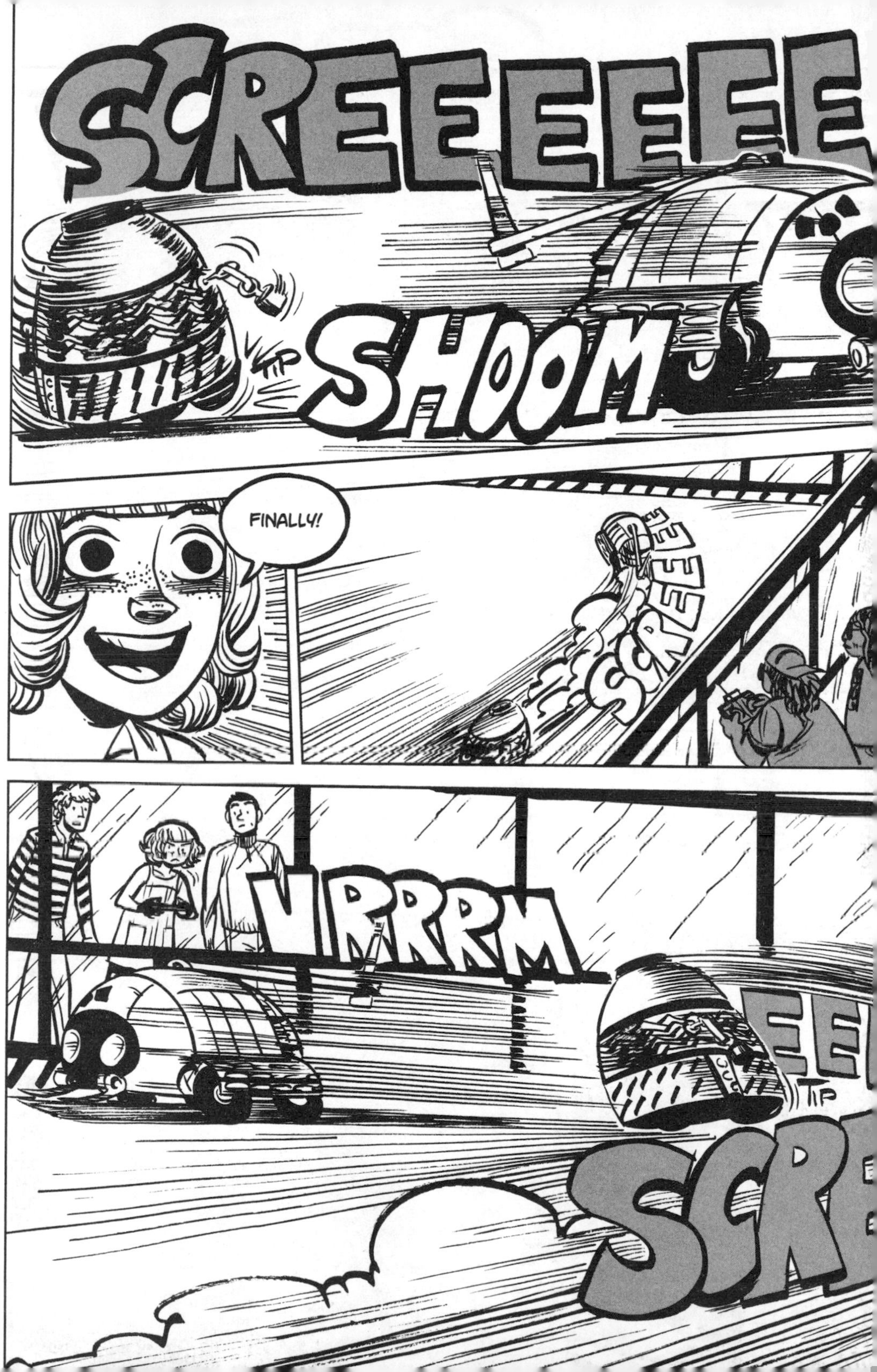
SCREEEEEE
TIP
SHOOM
FINALLY!
SCREEEEE
VRRRM
EE
TIP
SCRE

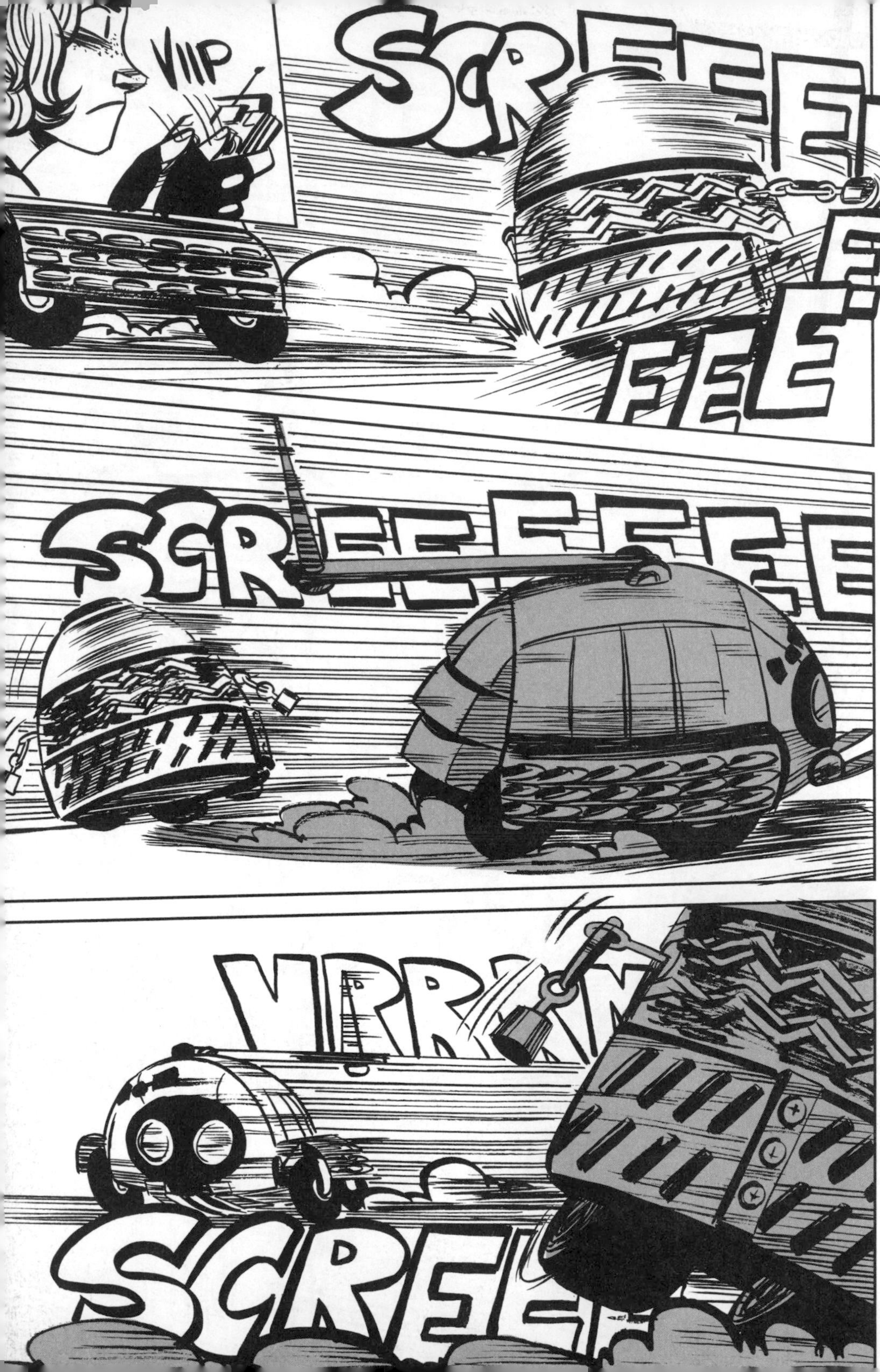
VIIP
SCREEEEEEEEE
SCREEEEEE
VRR
SCREE

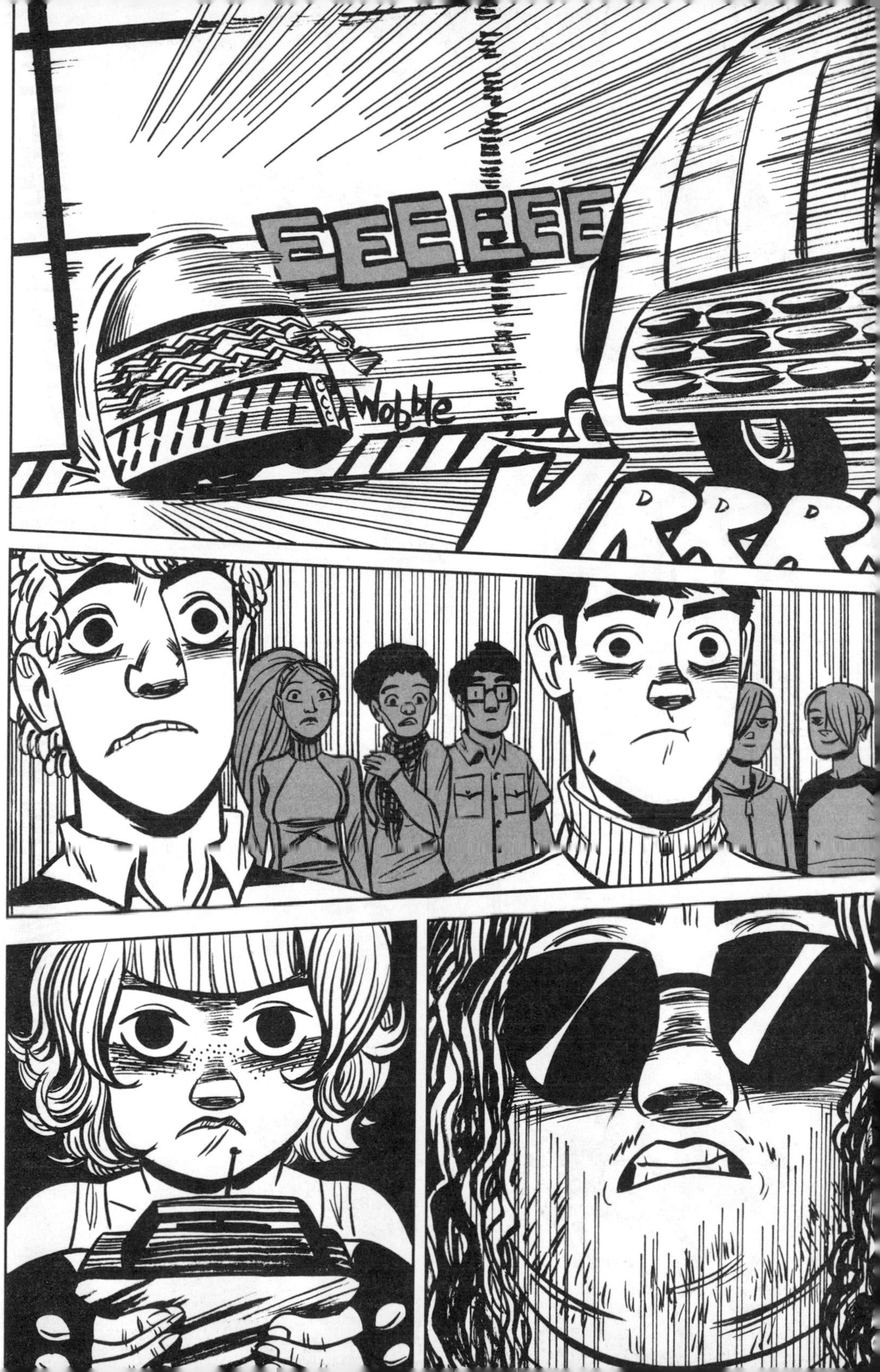

EEEEEE
Wobble
VRRR

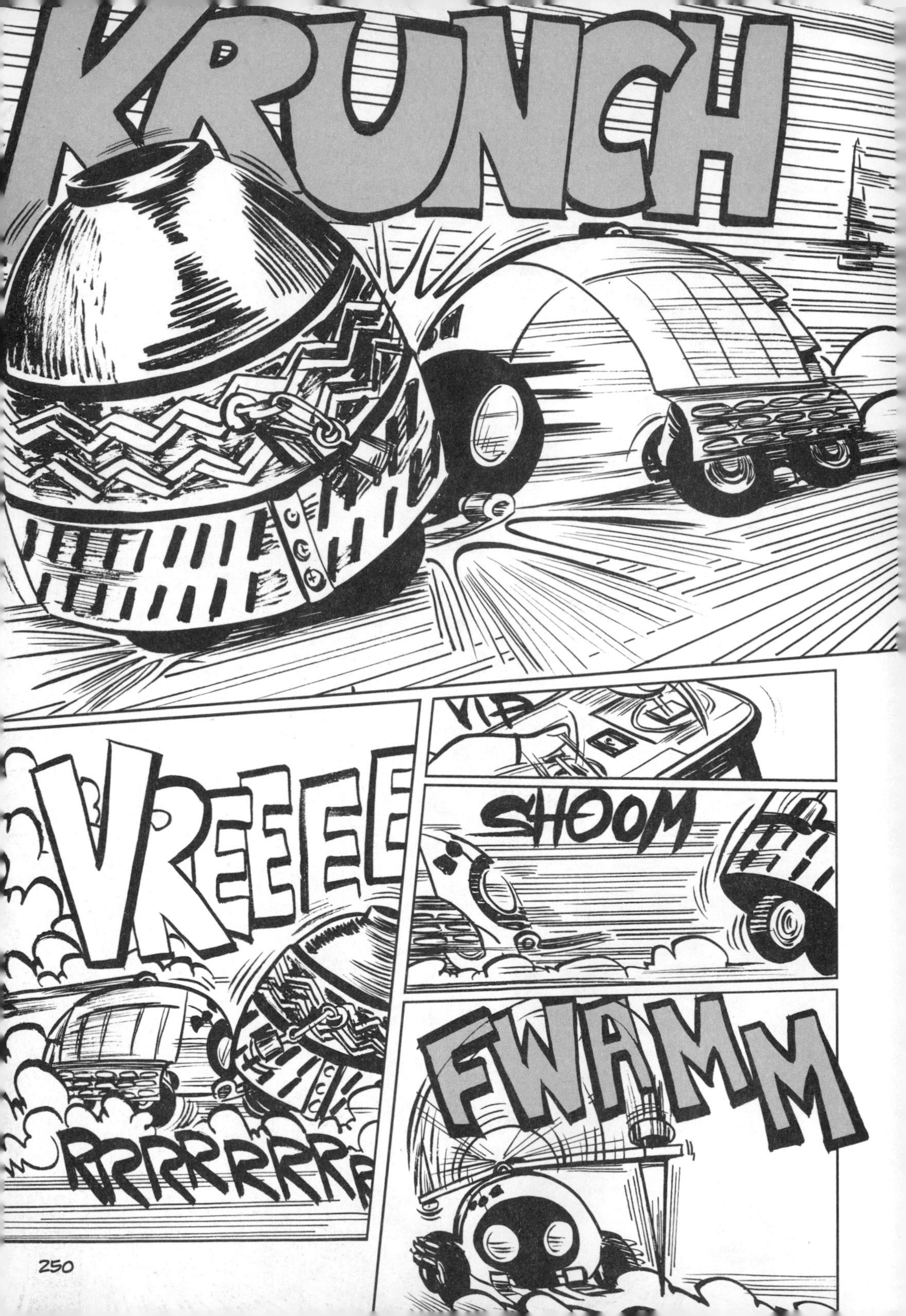
KRUNCH
VREEEE
RRRRRRRRR
SHOOM
FWAMM

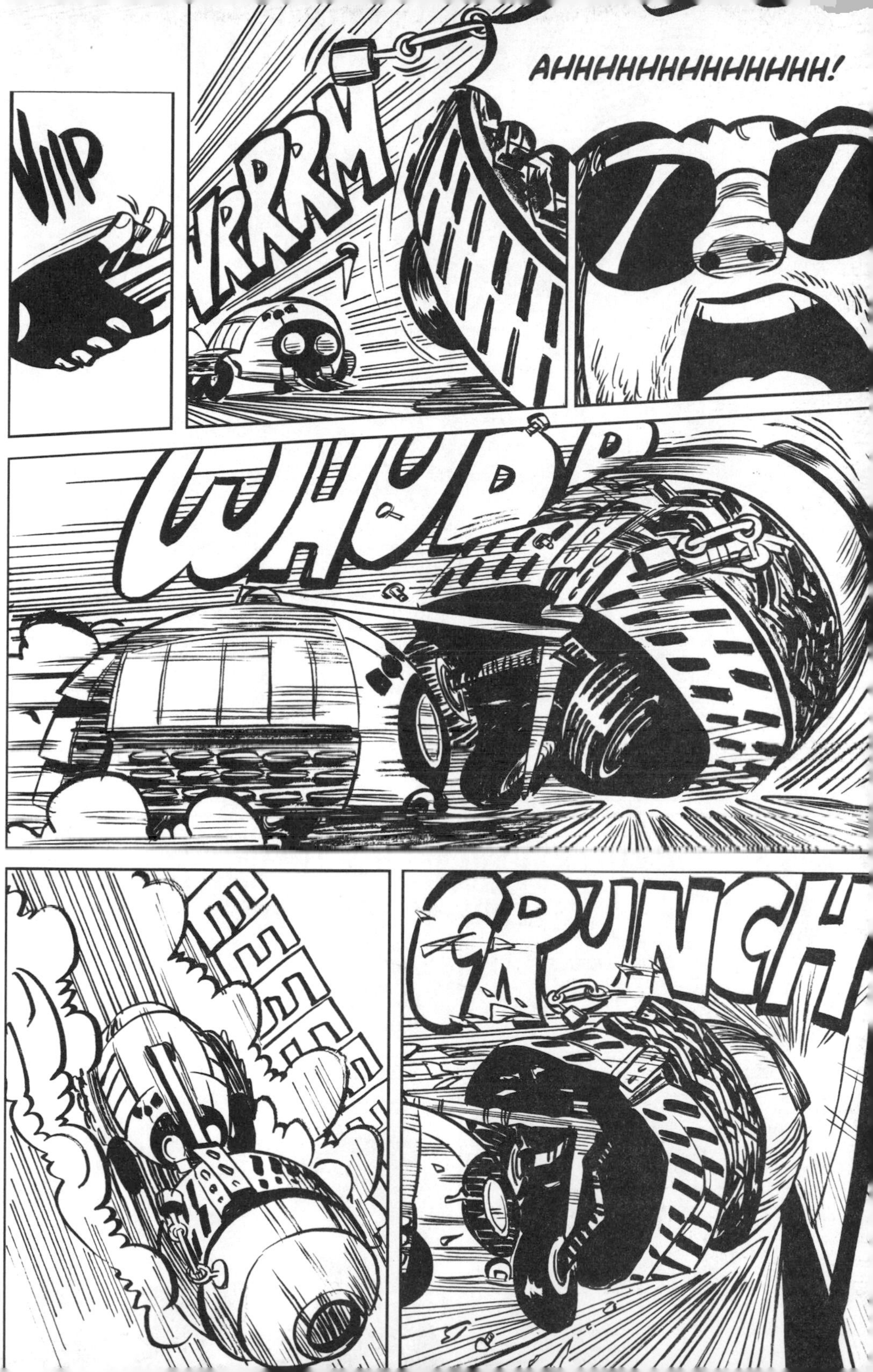
VIIP
VRRRM
AHHHHHHHHHHHHH!
WHUDP
EEEEEE
CRUNCH

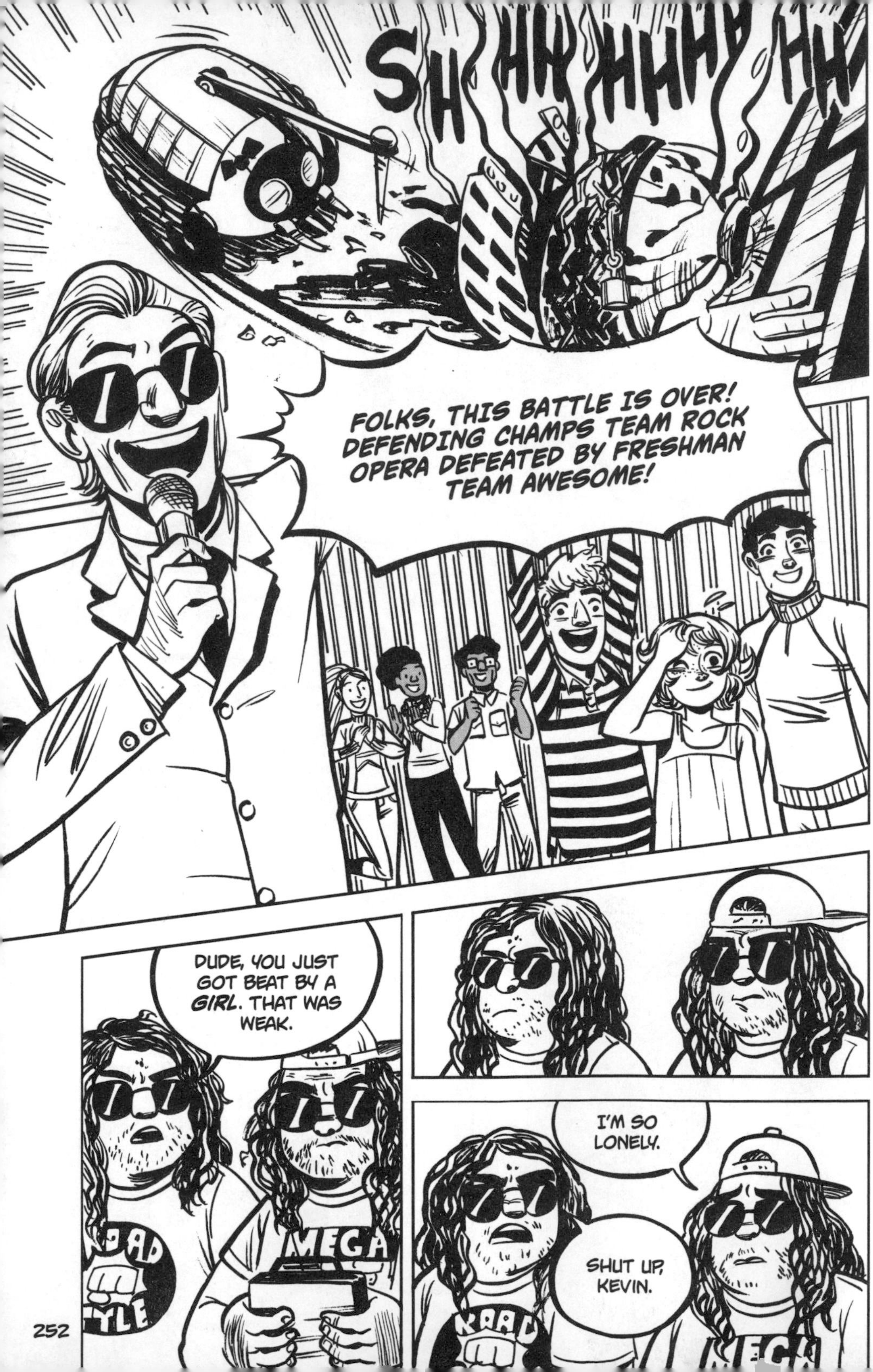
SHHHHHHHHH
FOLKS, THIS BATTLE IS OVER! DEFENDING CHAMPS TEAM ROCK OPERA DEFEATED BY FRESHMAN TEAM AWESOME!
DUDE, YOU JUST GOT BEAT BY A *GIRL*. THAT WAS WEAK.
MEGA
I'M SO LONELY.
SHUT UP, KEVIN.

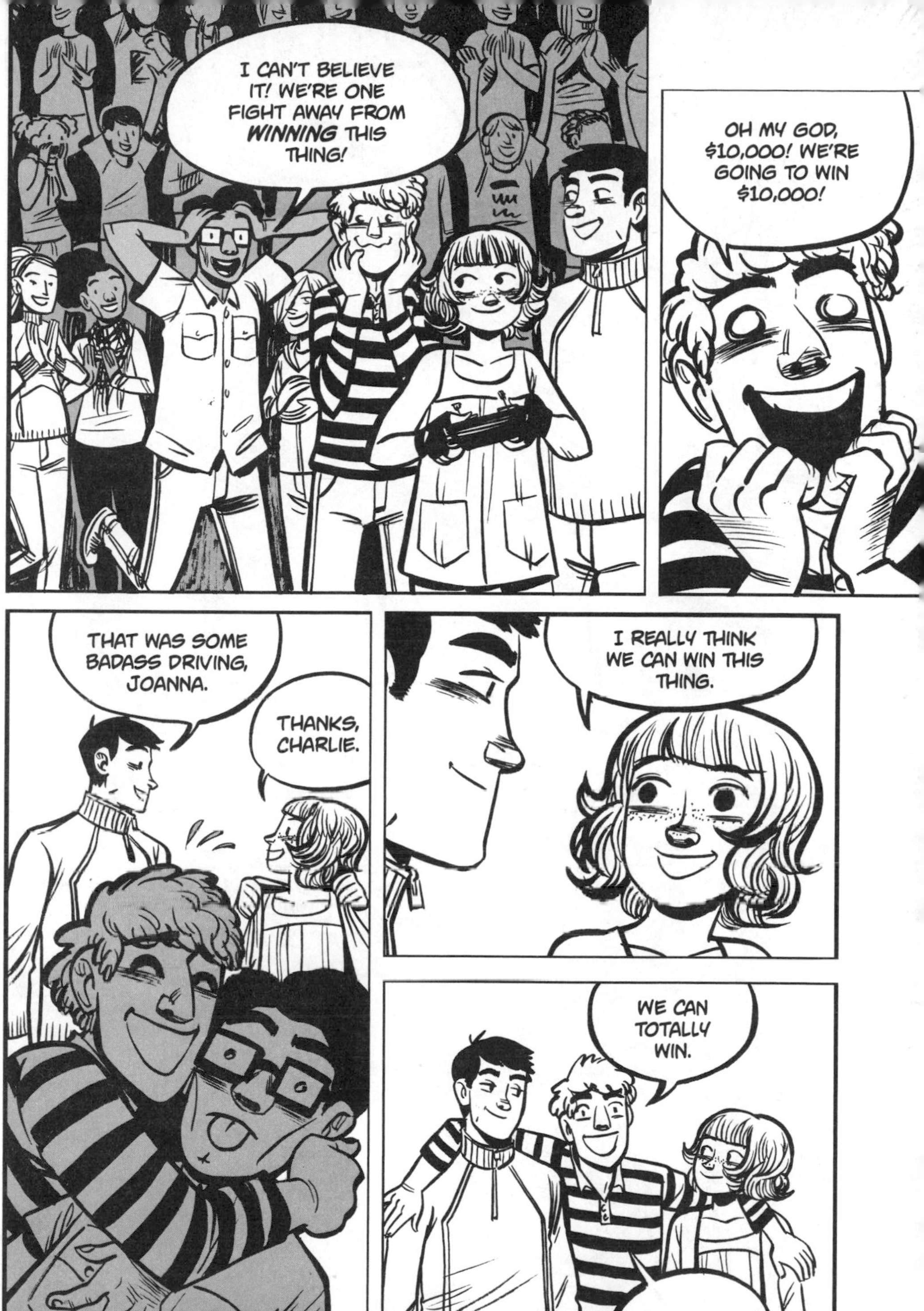
I CAN'T BELIEVE IT! WE'RE ONE FIGHT AWAY FROM WINNING THIS THING!
OH MY GOD, $10,000! WE'RE GOING TO WIN $10,000!
THAT WAS SOME BADASS DRIVING, JOANNA.
THANKS, CHARLIE.
I REALLY THINK WE CAN WIN THIS THING.
WE CAN TOTALLY WIN.
NOTHING CAN STOP US.

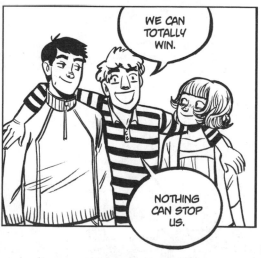

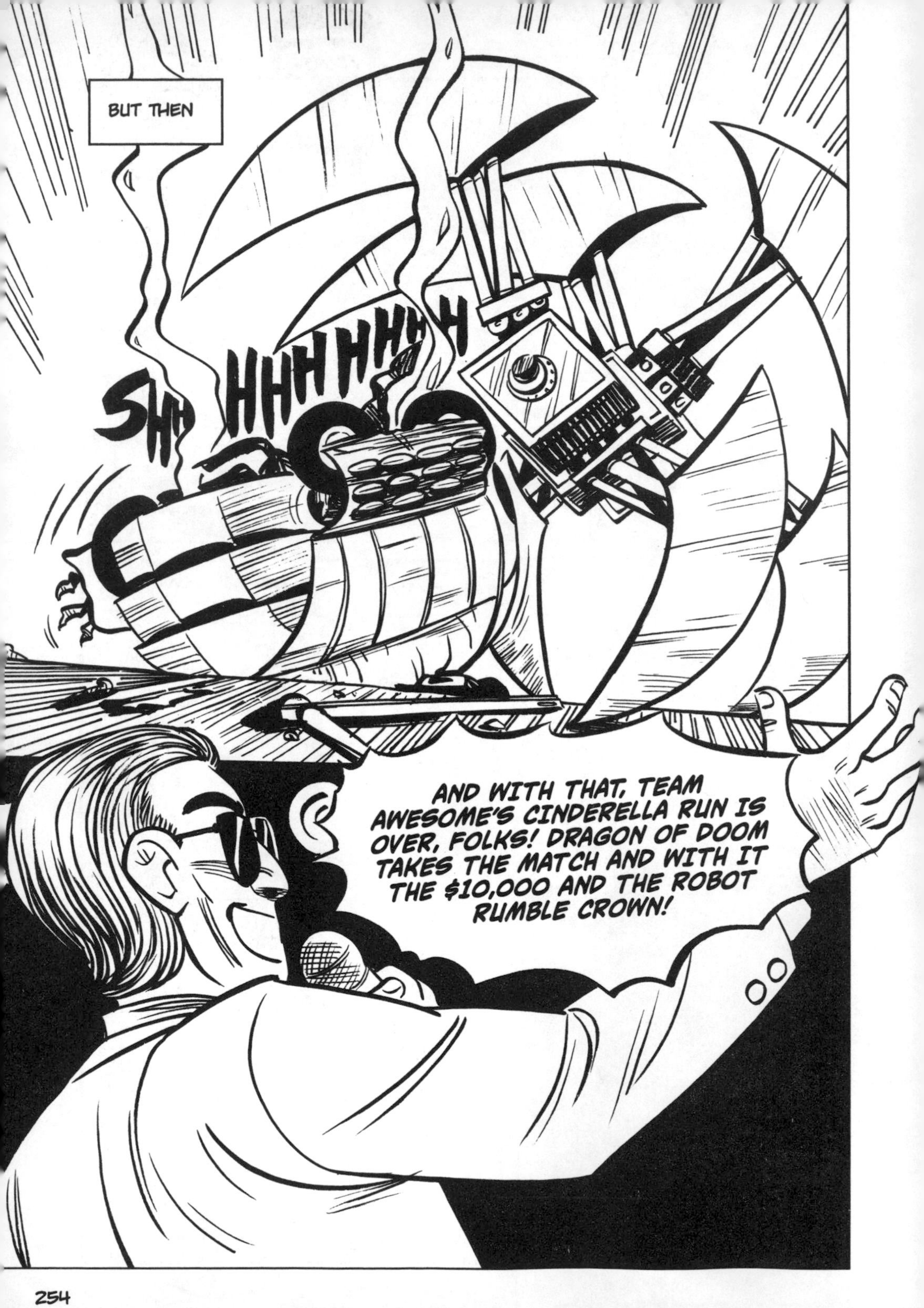
BUT THEN
SHHHHHHHHHHH
AND WITH THAT, TEAM AWESOME'S CINDERELLA RUN IS OVER, FOLKS! DRAGON OF DOOM TAKES THE MATCH AND WITH IT THE $10,000 AND THE ROBOT RUMBLE CROWN!

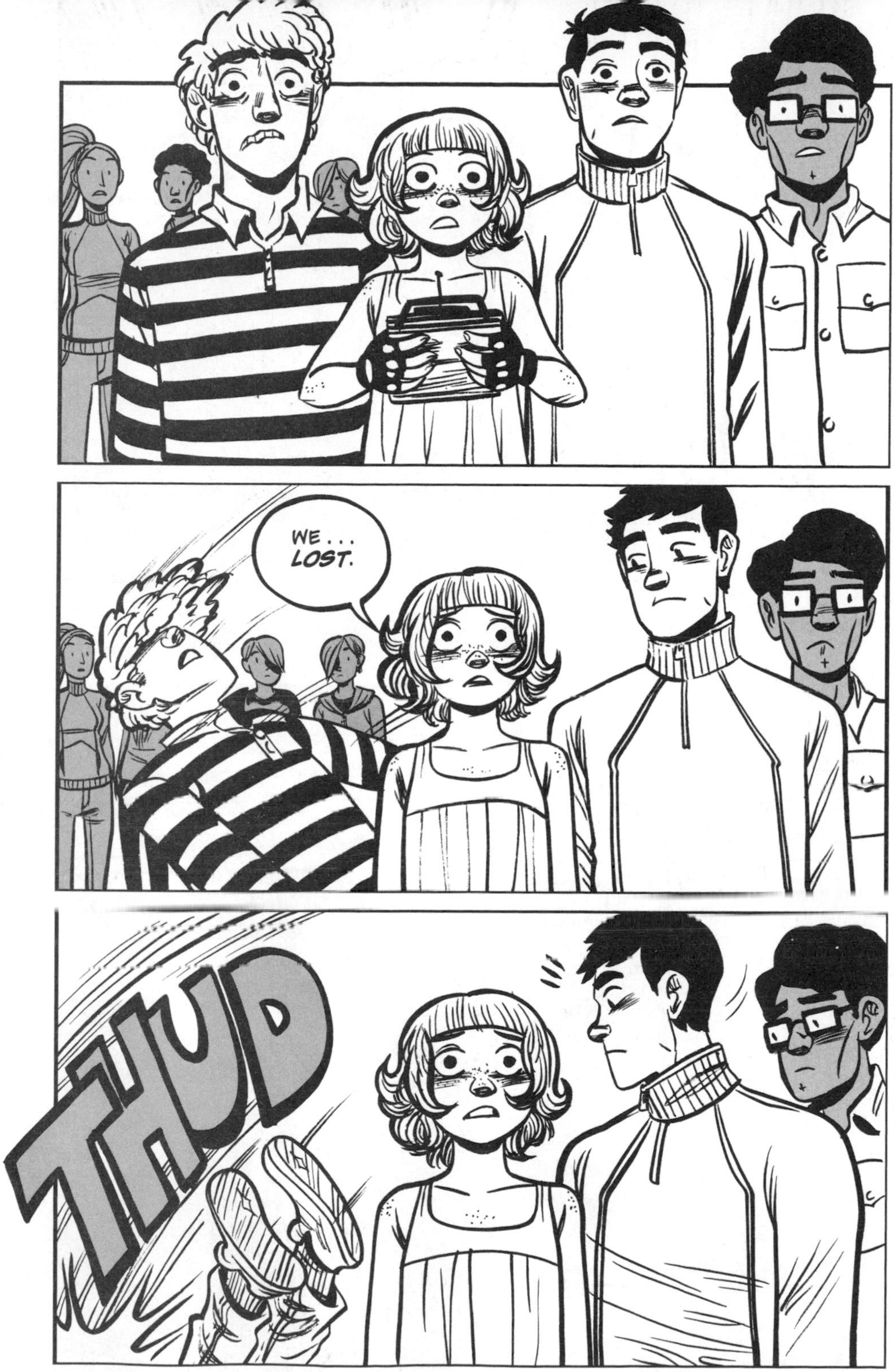
WE . . . LOST.
THUD

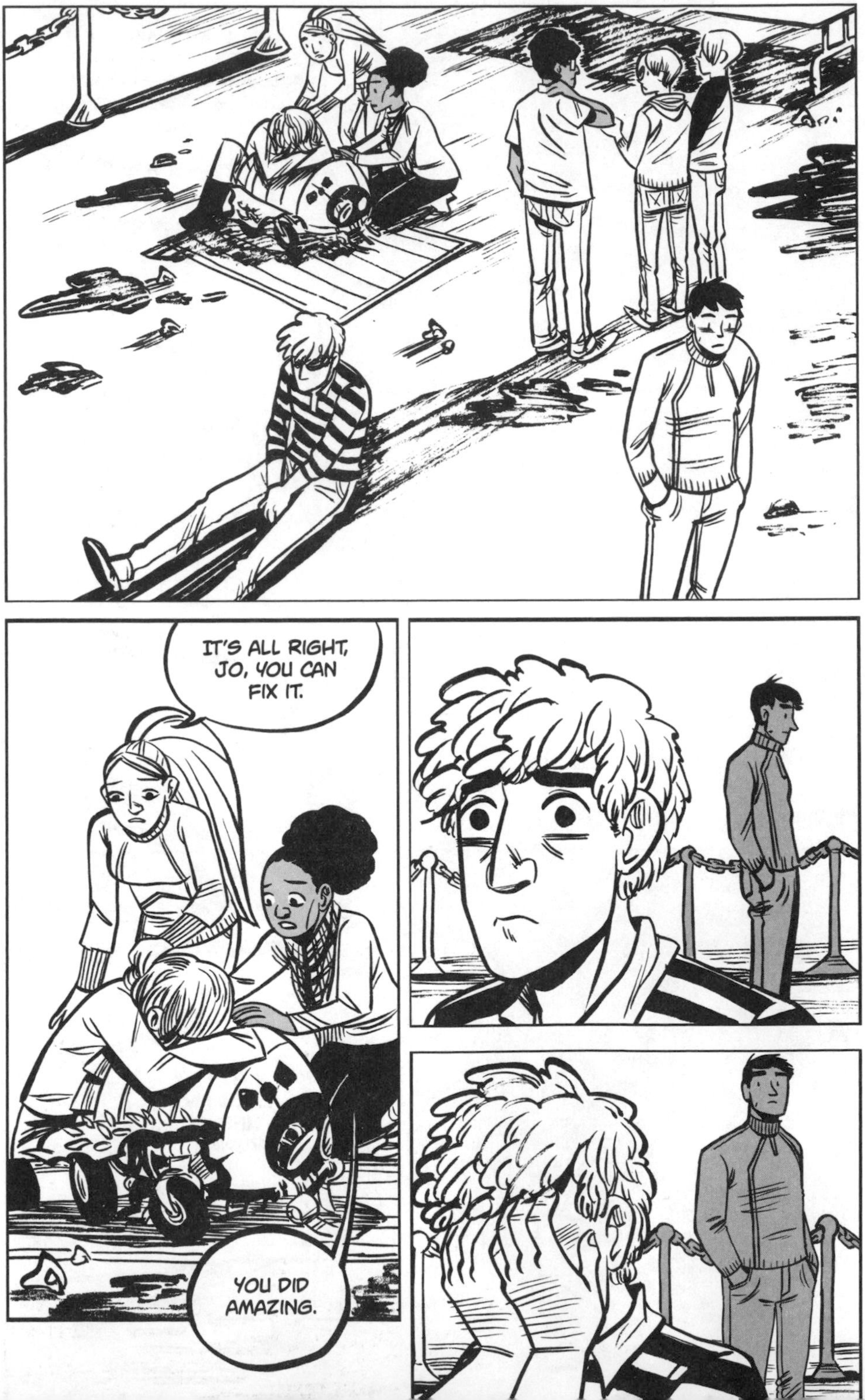
IT'S ALL RIGHT, JO, YOU CAN FIX IT.
YOU DID AMAZING.

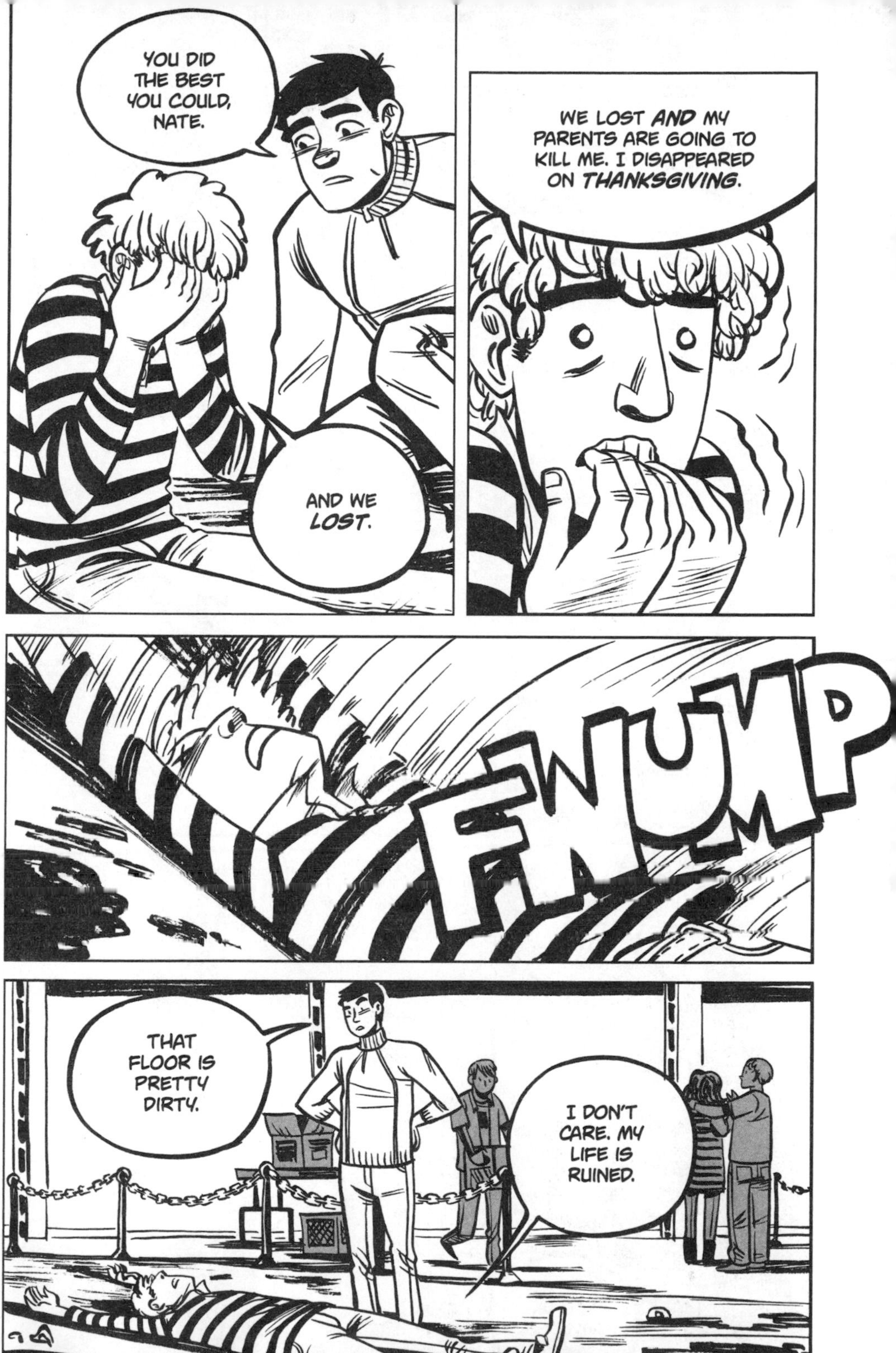
YOU DID THE BEST YOU COULD, NATE.
AND WE LOST.
WE LOST AND MY PARENTS ARE GOING TO KILL ME. I DISAPPEARED ON THANKSGIVING.
FWUMP
THAT FLOOR IS PRETTY DIRTY.
I DON'T CARE. MY LIFE IS RUINED.

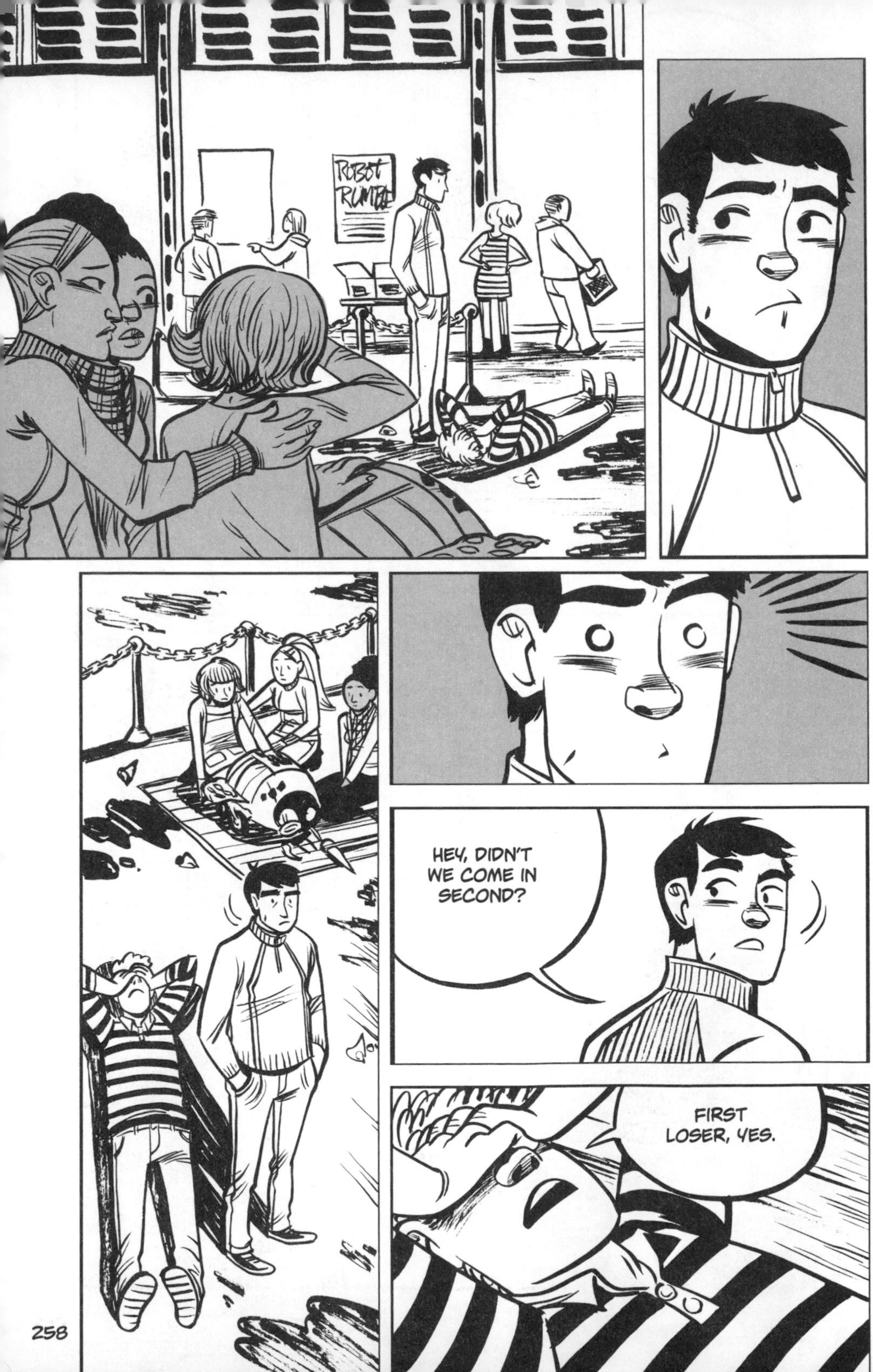
ROBOT RUMBLE
HEY, DIDN'T WE COME IN SECOND?
FIRST LOSER, YES.

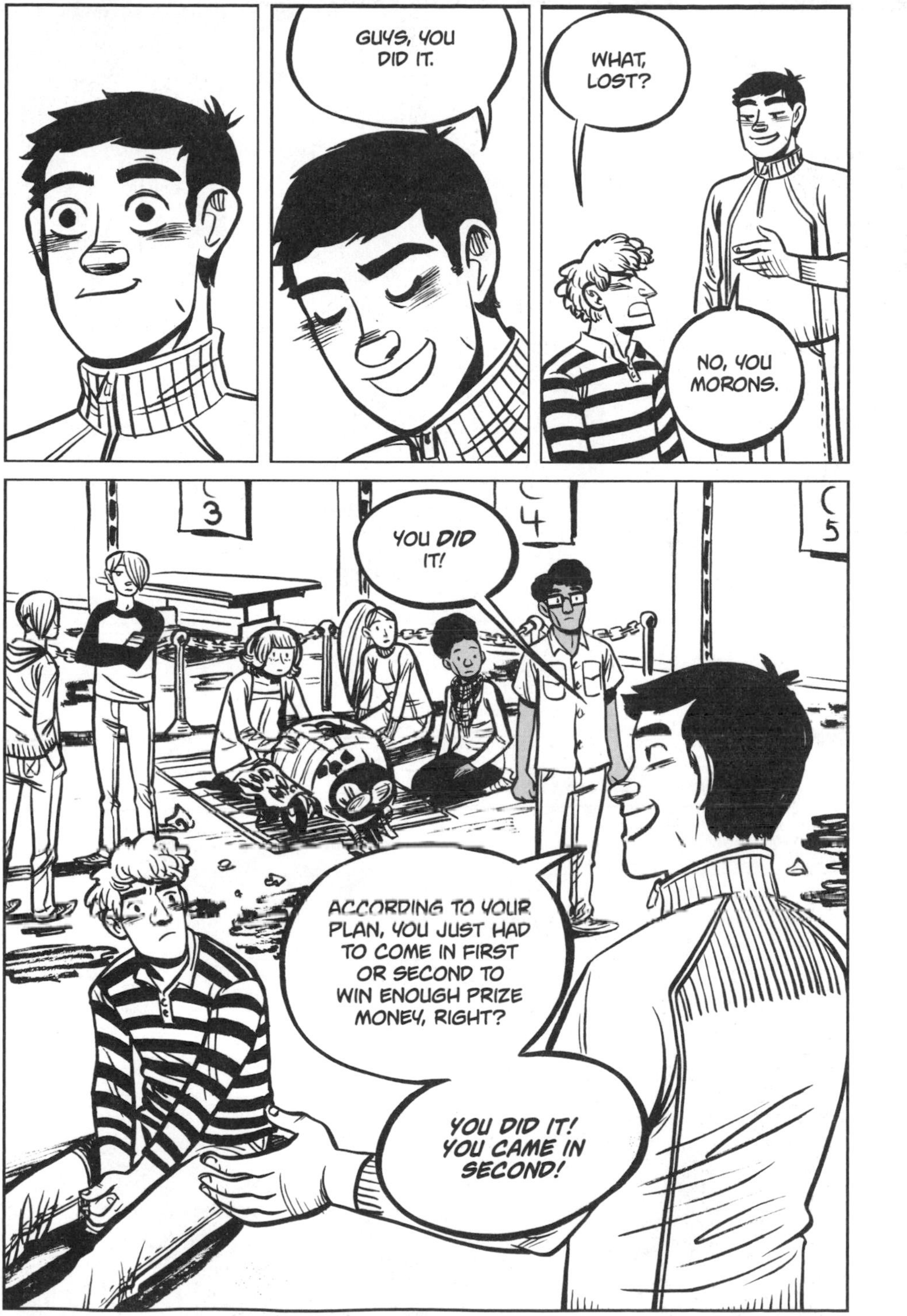
GUYS, YOU DID IT.
WHAT, LOST?
NO, YOU MORONS.
3
4
5
YOU DID IT!
ACCORDING TO YOUR PLAN, YOU JUST HAD TO COME IN FIRST OR SECOND TO WIN ENOUGH PRIZE MONEY, RIGHT?
YOU DID IT! YOU CAME IN SECOND!

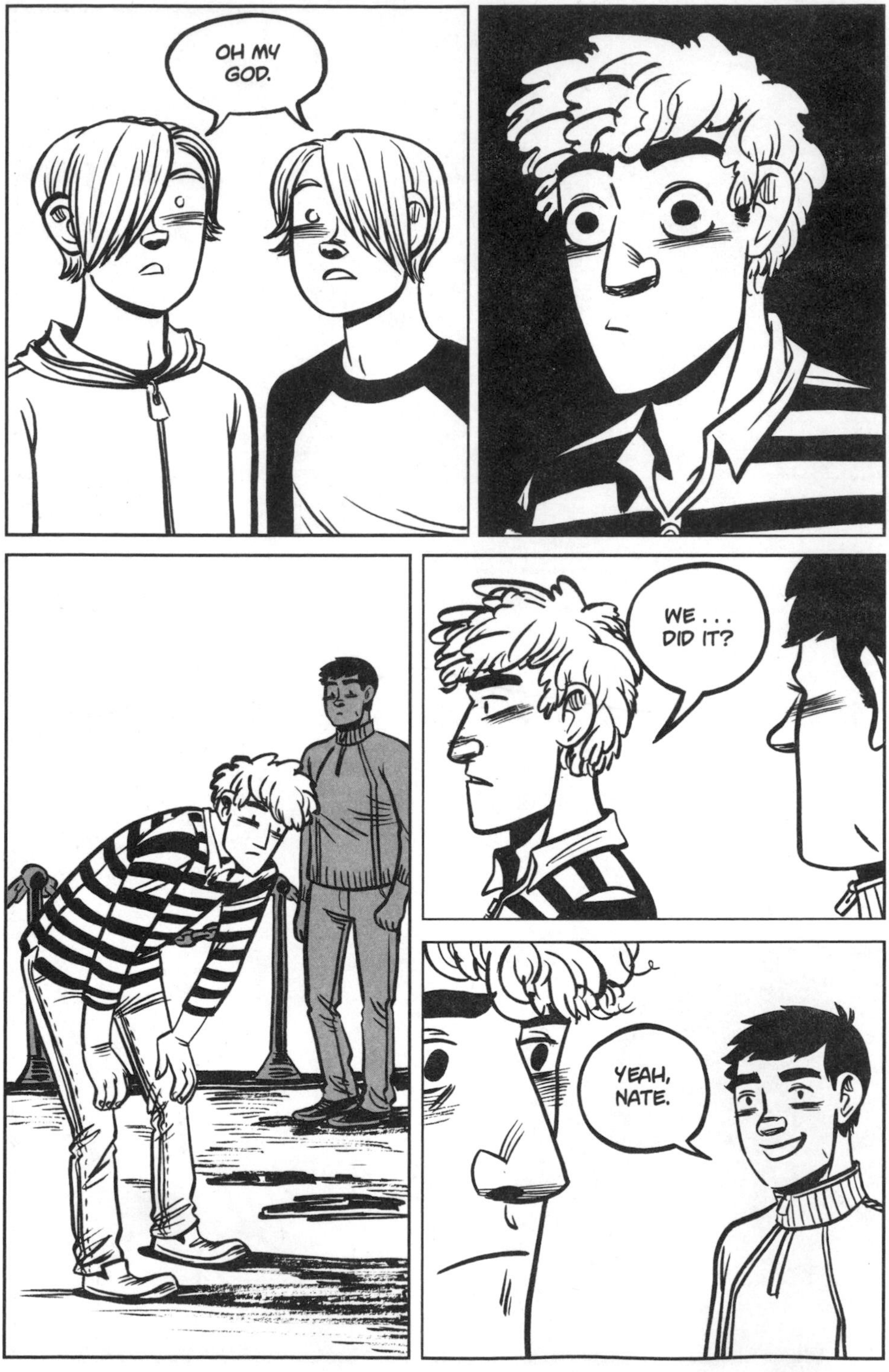
OH MY GOD.
WE . . . DID IT?
YEAH, NATE.

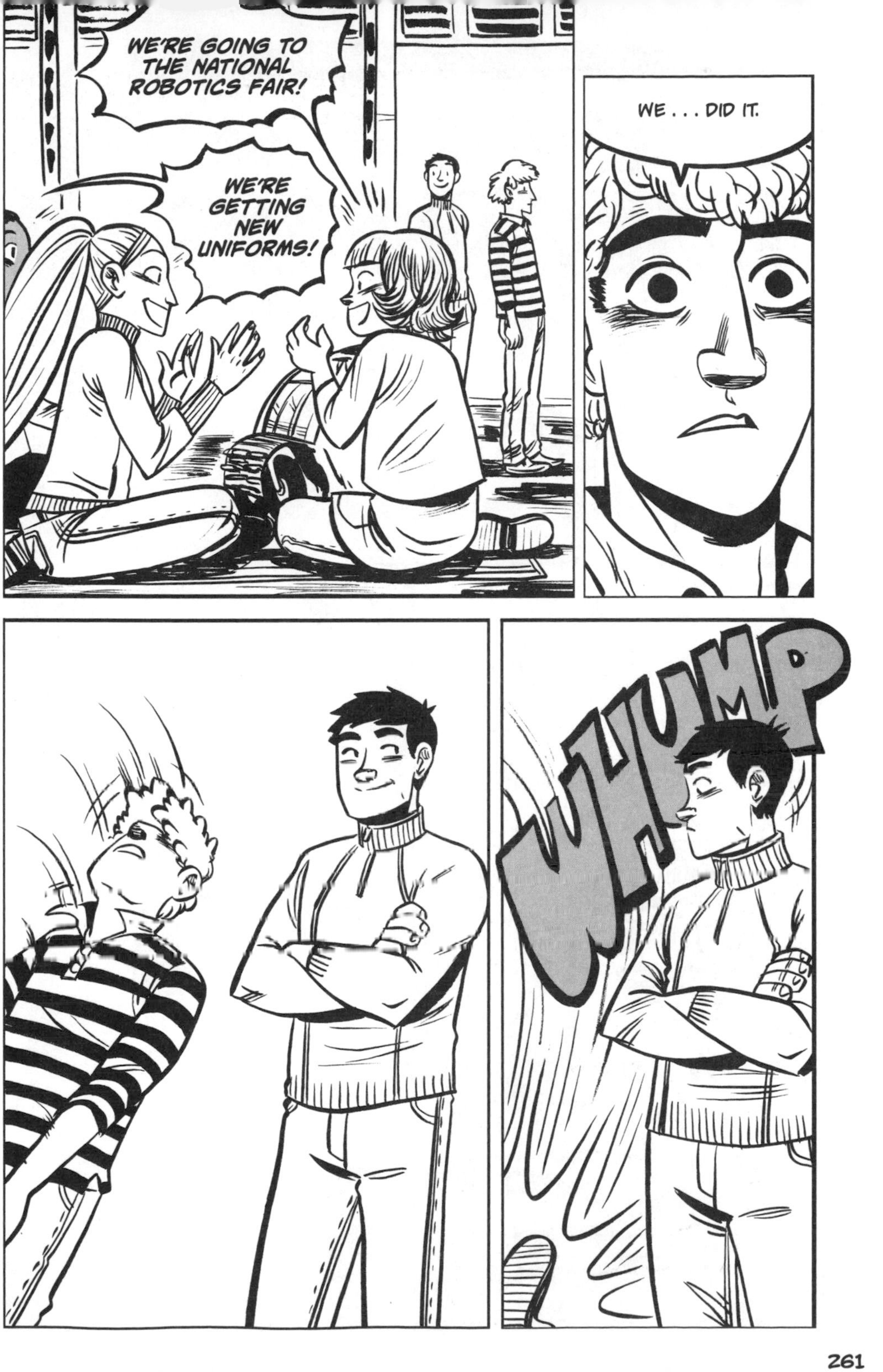
WE'RE GOING TO THE NATIONAL ROBOTICS FAIR!
WE'RE GETTING NEW UNIFORMS!
WE . . . DID IT.
WHUMP

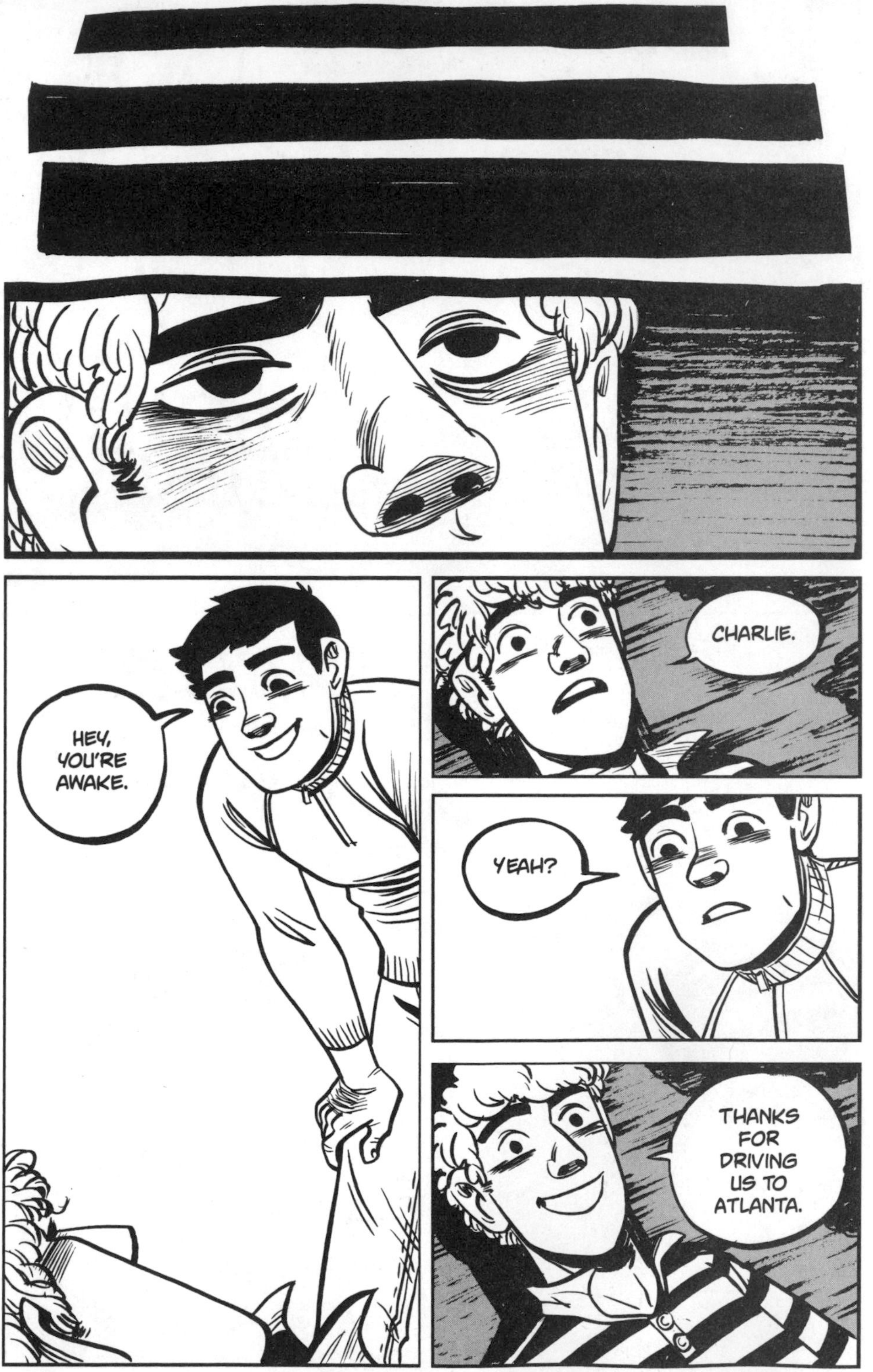
HEY, YOU'RE AWAKE.
CHARLIE.
YEAH?
THANKS FOR DRIVING US TO ATLANTA.

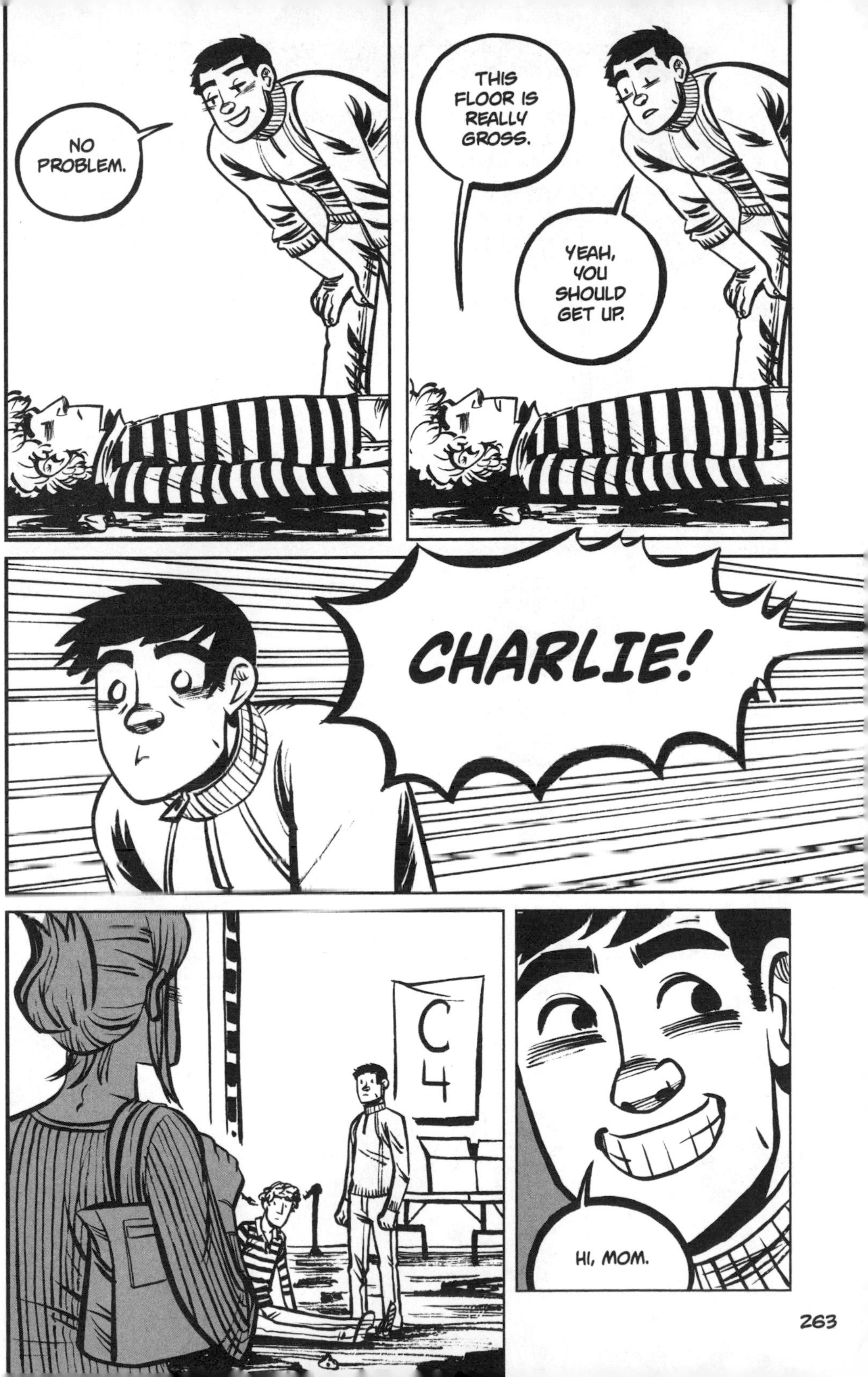
NO PROBLEM.
THIS FLOOR IS REALLY GROSS.
YEAH, YOU SHOULD GET UP.
CHARLIE!
C
4
HI, MOM.

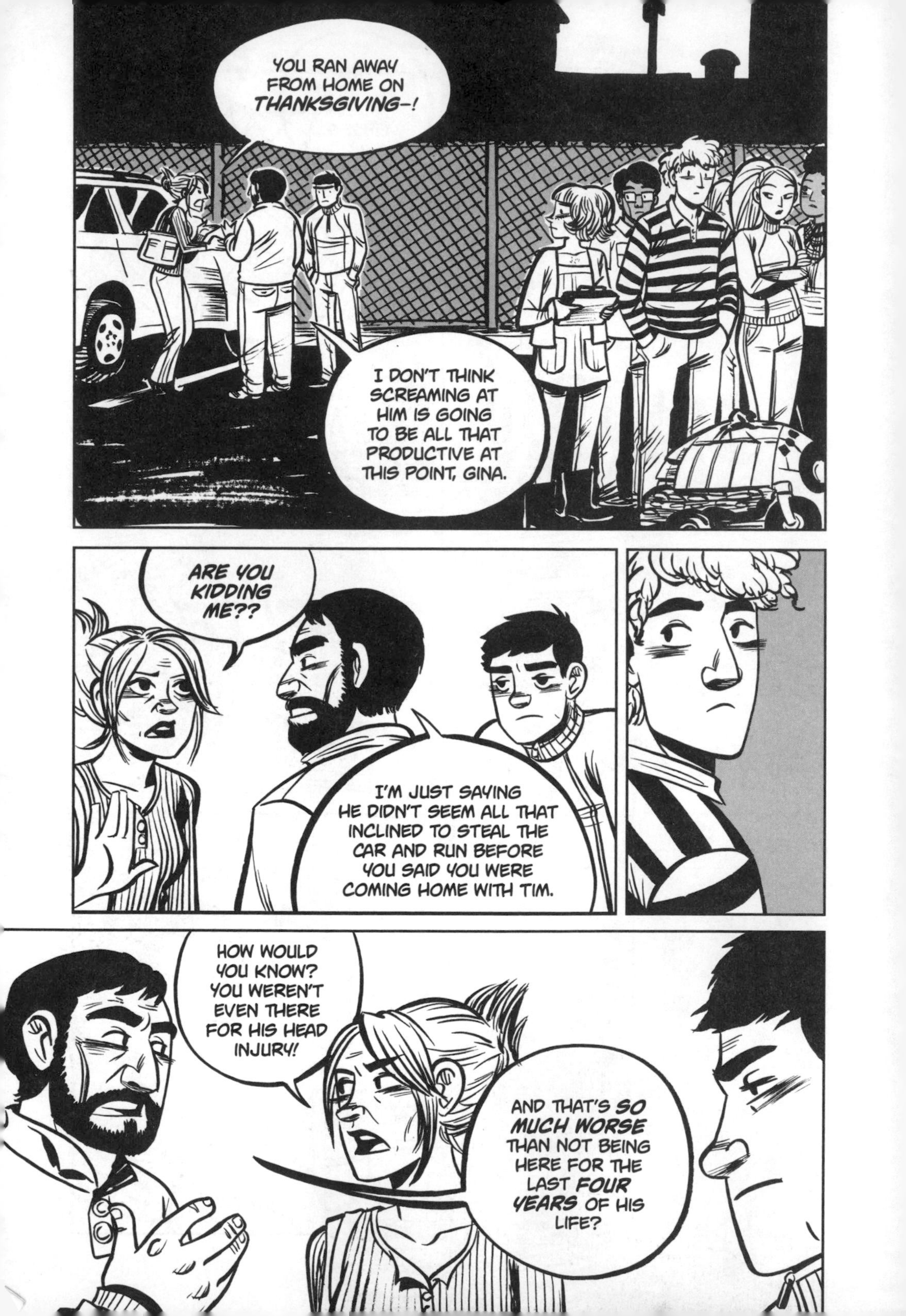
YOU RAN AWAY FROM HOME ON THANKSGIVING-!
I DON'T THINK SCREAMING AT HIM IS GOING TO BE ALL THAT PRODUCTIVE AT THIS POINT, GINA.
ARE YOU KIDDING ME??
I'M JUST SAYING HE DIDN'T SEEM ALL THAT INCLINED TO STEAL THE CAR AND RUN BEFORE YOU SAID YOU WERE COMING HOME WITH TIM.
HOW WOULD YOU KNOW? YOU WEREN'T EVEN THERE FOR HIS HEAD INJURY!
AND THAT'S SO MUCH WORSE THAN NOT BEING HERE FOR THE LAST FOUR YEARS OF HIS LIFE?

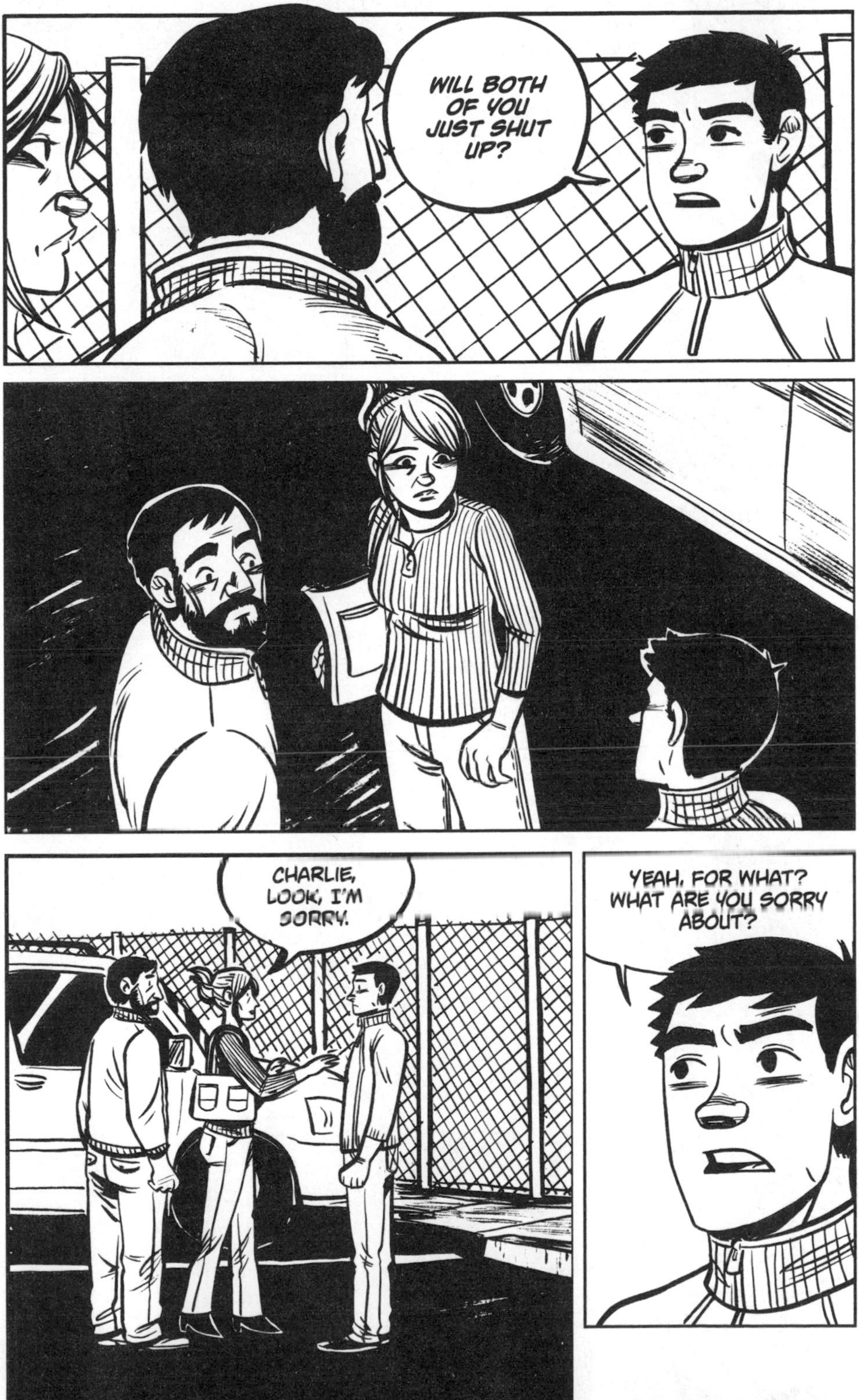
WILL BOTH OF YOU JUST SHUT UP?
CHARLIE, LOOK, I'M SORRY.
YEAH, FOR WHAT? WHAT ARE YOU SORRY ABOUT?

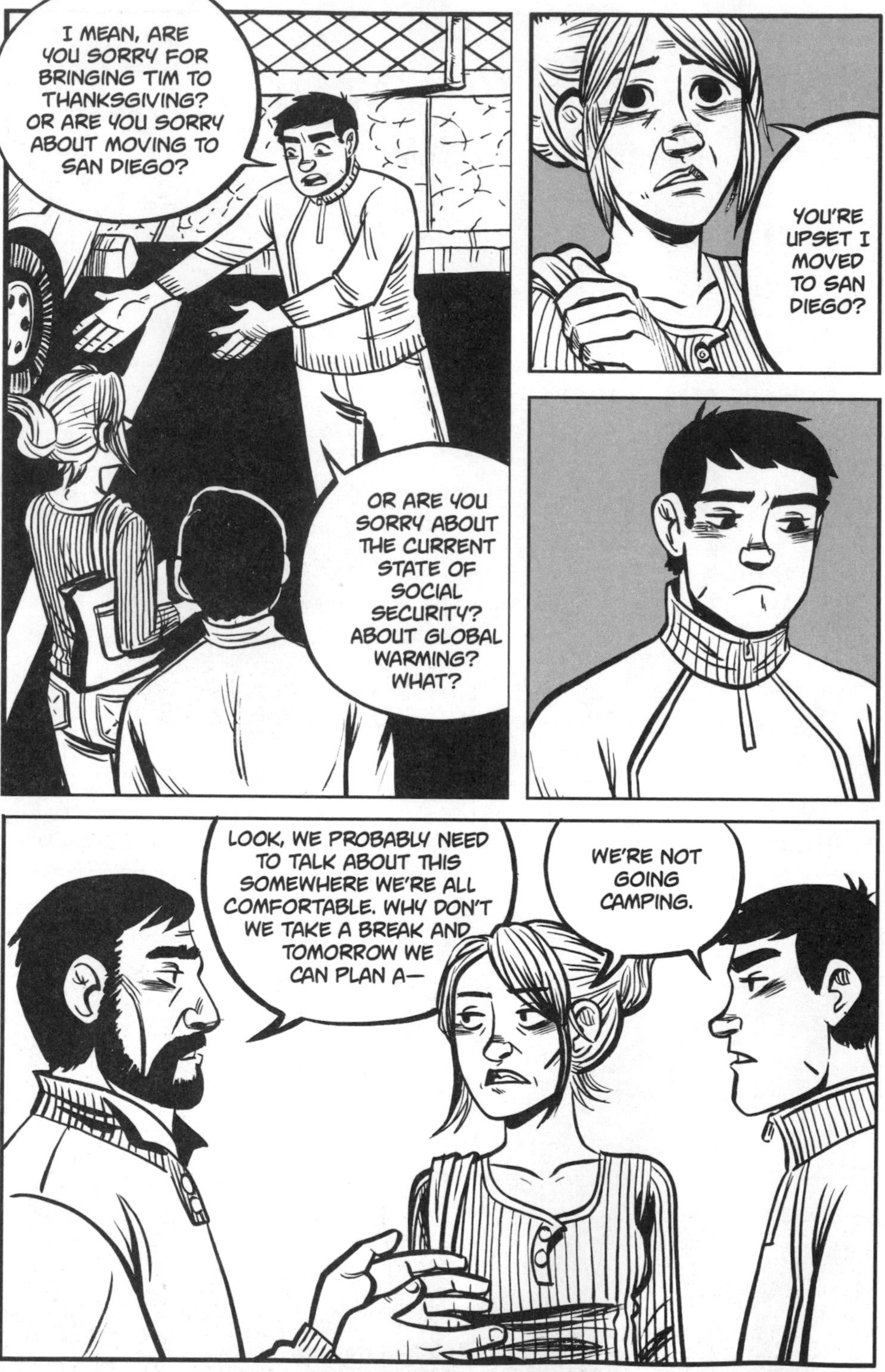
I MEAN, ARE YOU SORRY FOR BRINGING TIM TO THANKSGIVING? OR ARE YOU SORRY ABOUT MOVING TO SAN DIEGO?
OR ARE YOU SORRY ABOUT THE CURRENT STATE OF SOCIAL SECURITY? ABOUT GLOBAL WARMING? WHAT?
YOU'RE UPSET I MOVED TO SAN DIEGO?
LOOK, WE PROBABLY NEED TO TALK ABOUT THIS SOMEWHERE WE'RE ALL COMFORTABLE. WHY DON'T WE TAKE A BREAK AND TOMORROW WE CAN PLAN A—
WE'RE NOT GOING CAMPING.

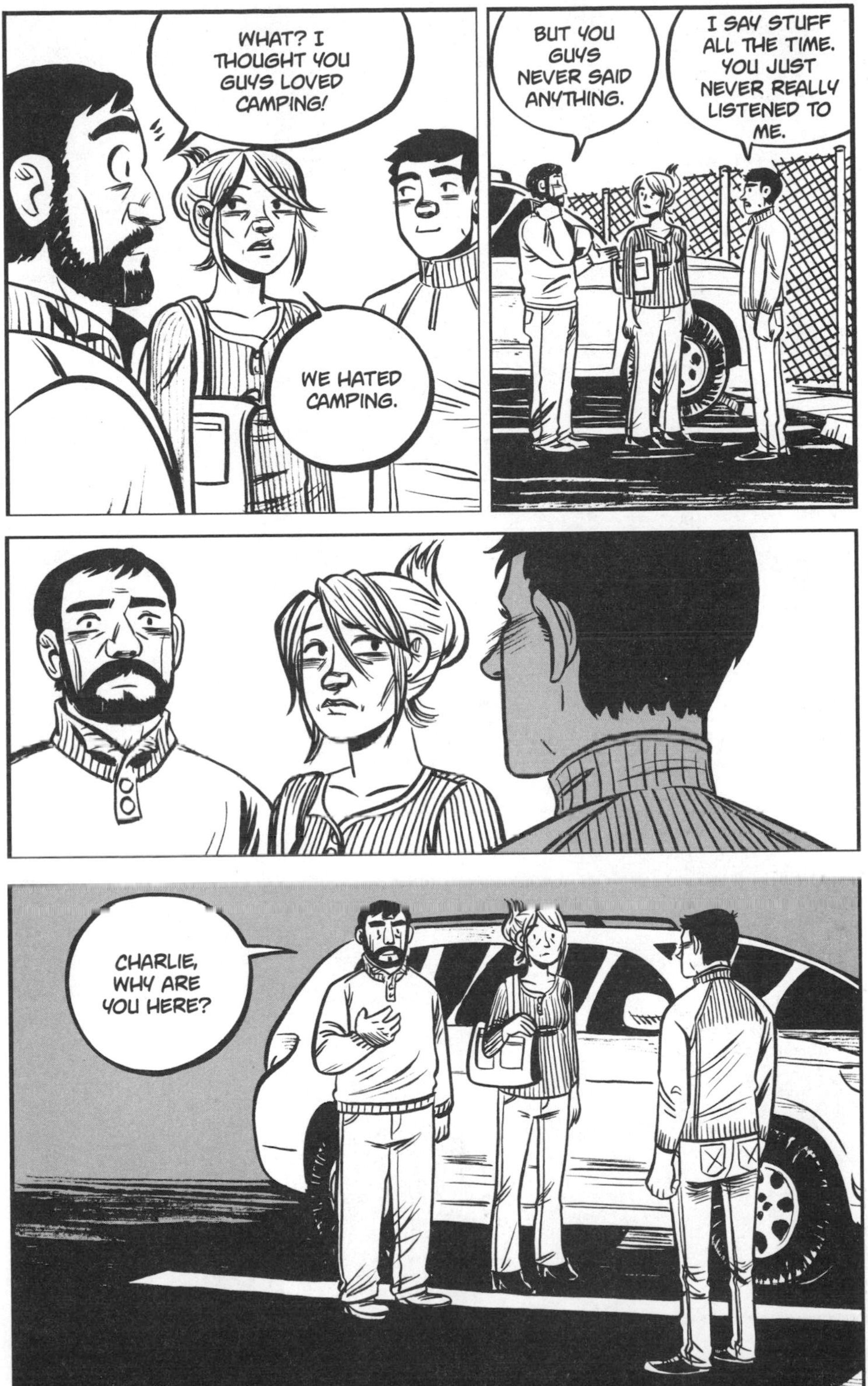
WHAT? I THOUGHT YOU GUYS LOVED CAMPING!
WE HATED CAMPING.
BUT YOU GUYS NEVER SAID ANYTHING.
I SAY STUFF ALL THE TIME. YOU JUST NEVER REALLY LISTENED TO ME.
CHARLIE, WHY ARE YOU HERE?

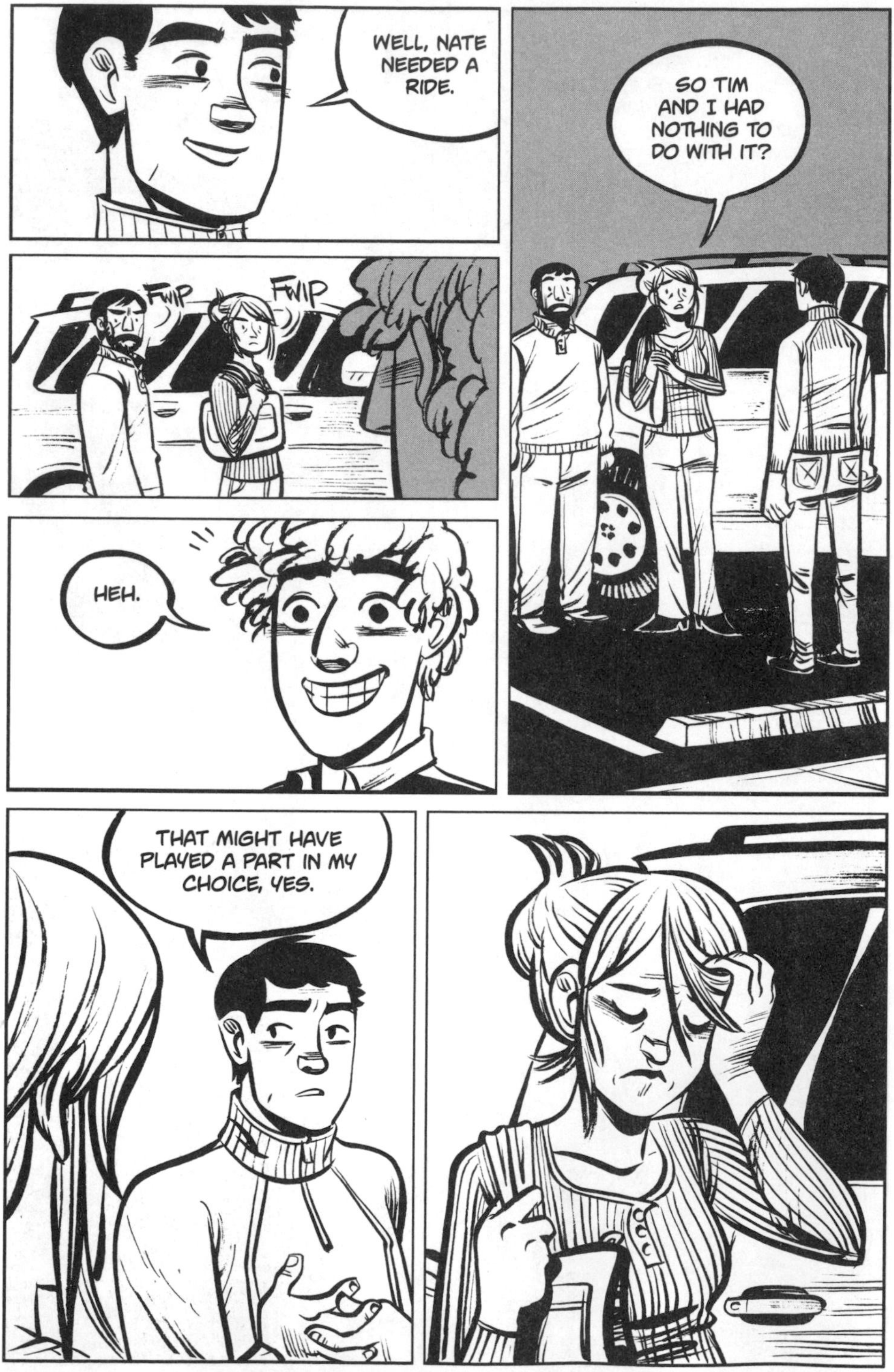
WELL, NATE NEEDED A RIDE.
SO TIM AND I HAD NOTHING TO DO WITH IT?
FWIP
FWIP
HEH.
THAT MIGHT HAVE PLAYED A PART IN MY CHOICE, YES.

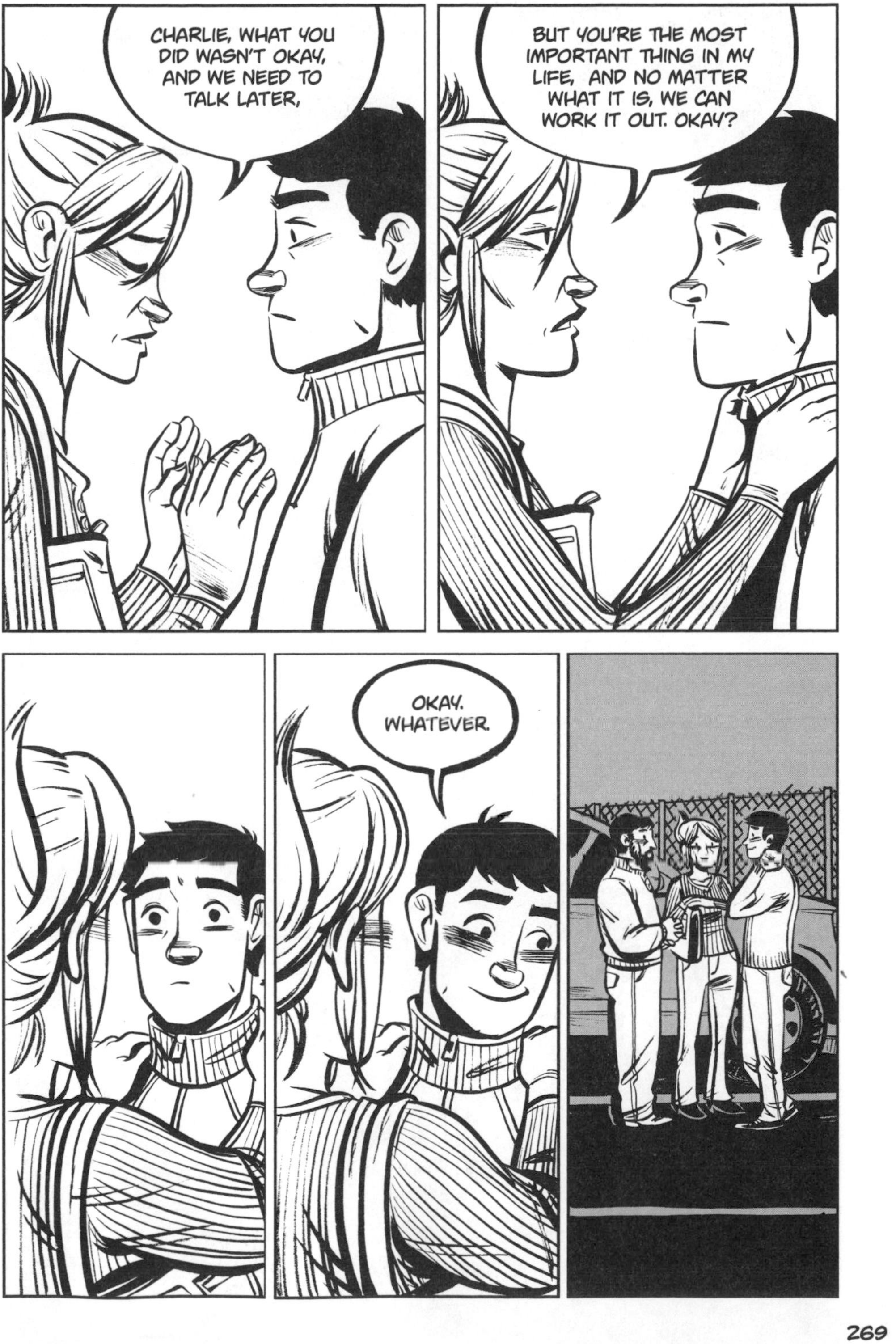
CHARLIE, WHAT YOU DID WASN'T OKAY, AND WE NEED TO TALK LATER,
BUT YOU'RE THE MOST IMPORTANT THING IN MY LIFE, AND NO MATTER WHAT IT IS, WE CAN WORK IT OUT. OKAY?
OKAY. WHATEVER.

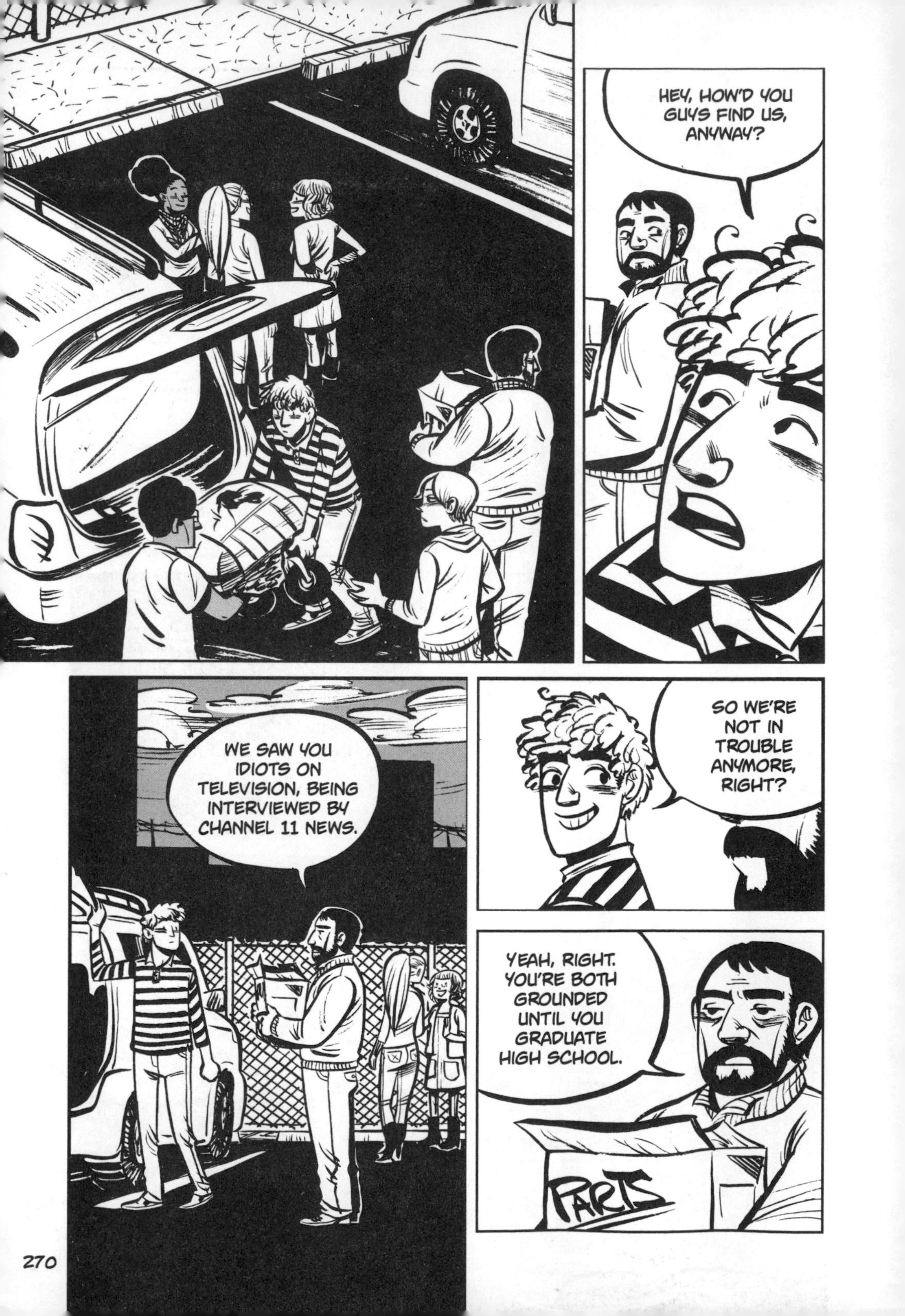
HEY, HOW'D YOU GUYS FIND US, ANYWAY?
WE SAW YOU IDIOTS ON TELEVISION, BEING INTERVIEWED BY CHANNEL 11 NEWS.
SO WE'RE NOT IN TROUBLE ANYMORE, RIGHT?
YEAH, RIGHT. YOU'RE BOTH GROUNDED UNTIL YOU GRADUATE HIGH SCHOOL.
PARTS

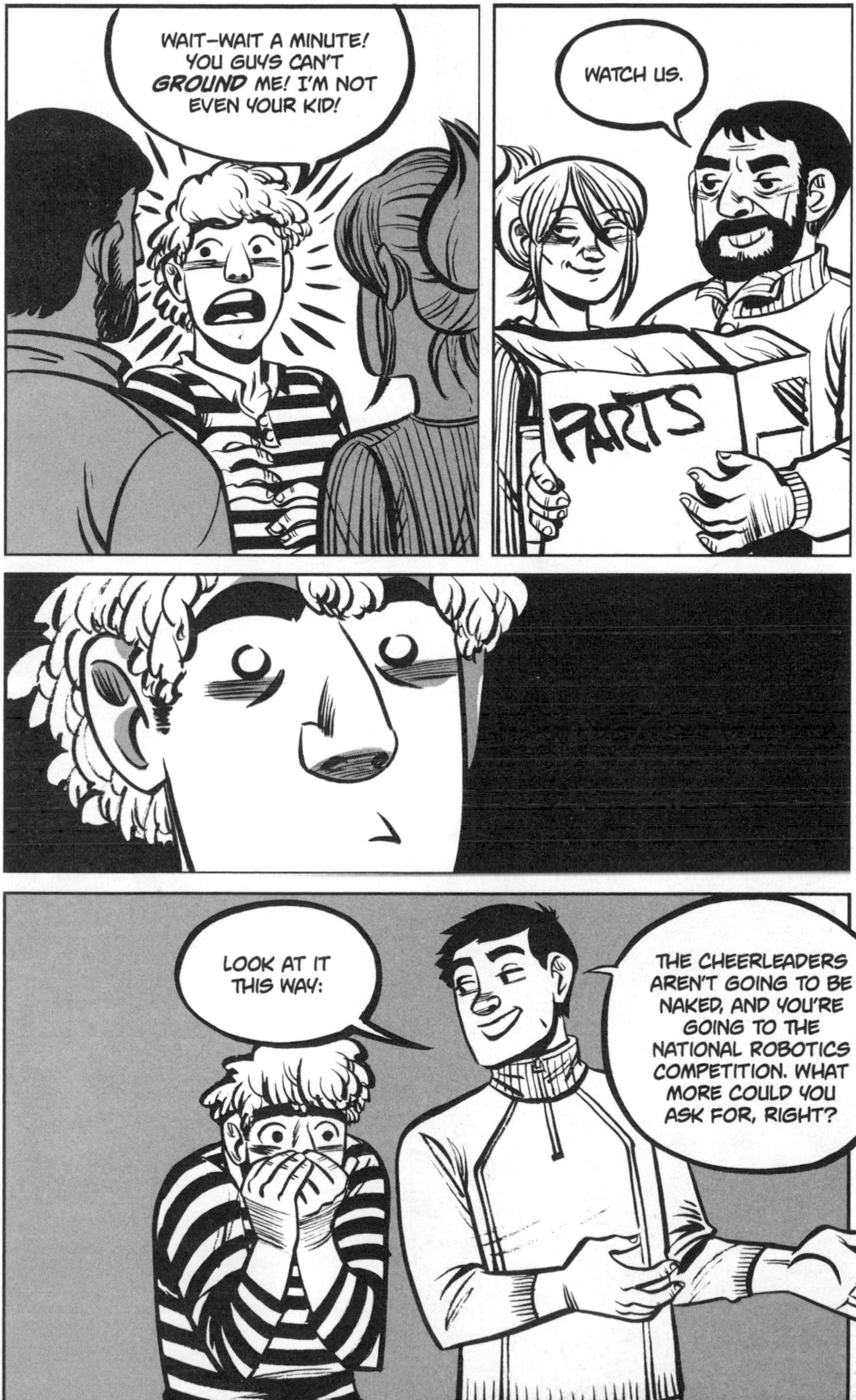
WAIT—WAIT A MINUTE! YOU GUYS CAN'T GROUND ME! I'M NOT EVEN YOUR KID!
WATCH US.
PARTS
LOOK AT IT THIS WAY:
THE CHEERLEADERS AREN'T GOING TO BE NAKED, AND YOU'RE GOING TO THE NATIONAL ROBOTICS COMPETITION. WHAT MORE COULD YOU ASK FOR, RIGHT?

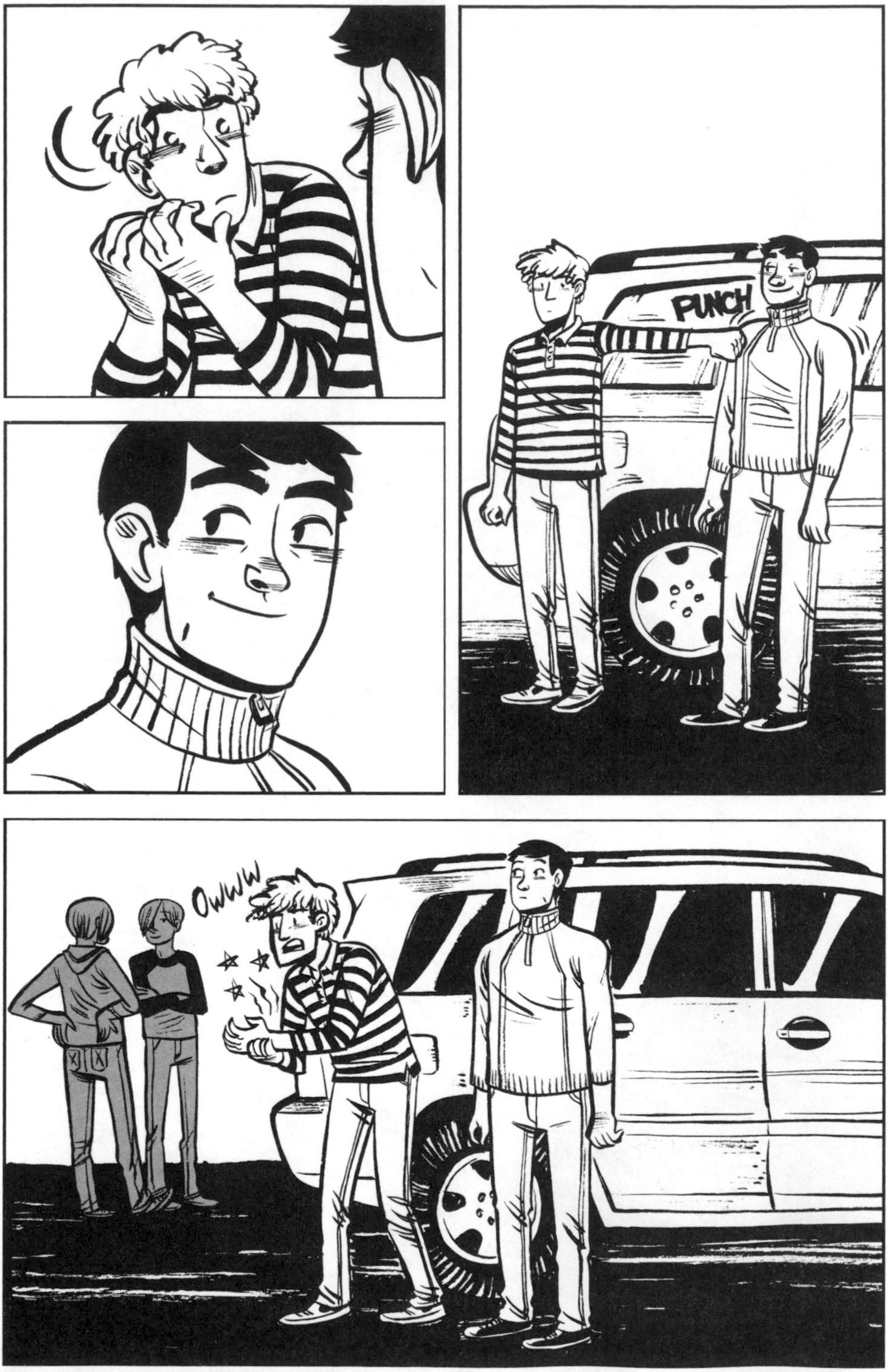
PUNCH
OWWW

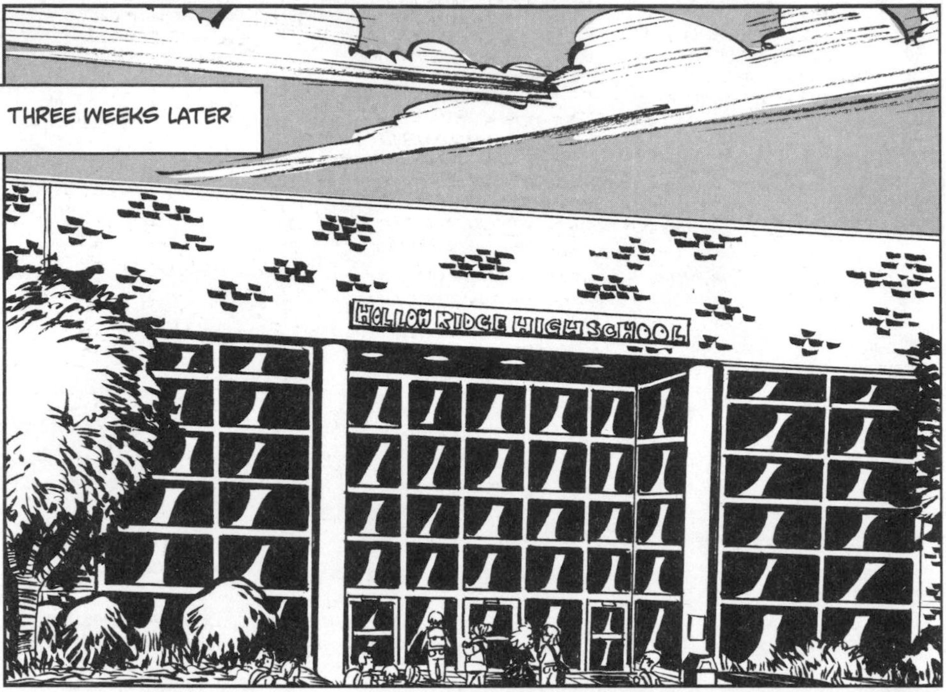
THREE WEEKS LATER
HOLLOW RIDGE HIGH SCHOOL

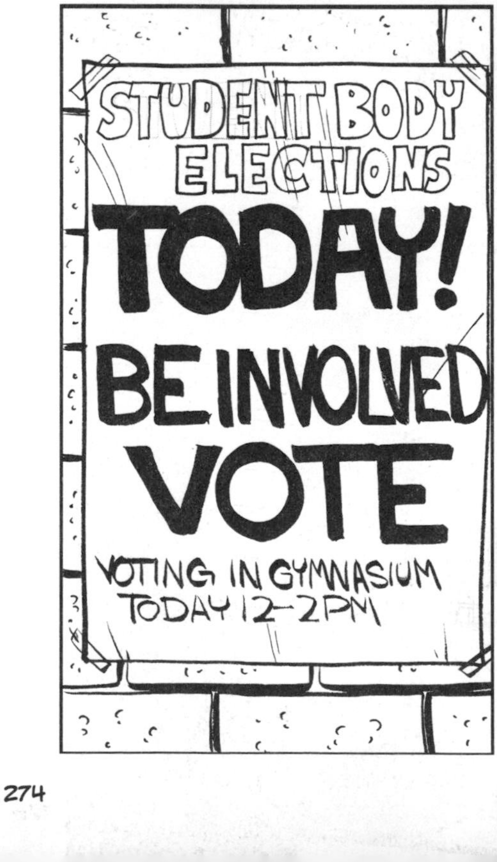
STUDENT BODY ELECTIONS
TODAY!
BE INVOLVED
VOTE
VOTING IN GYMNASIUM
TODAY 12-2PM

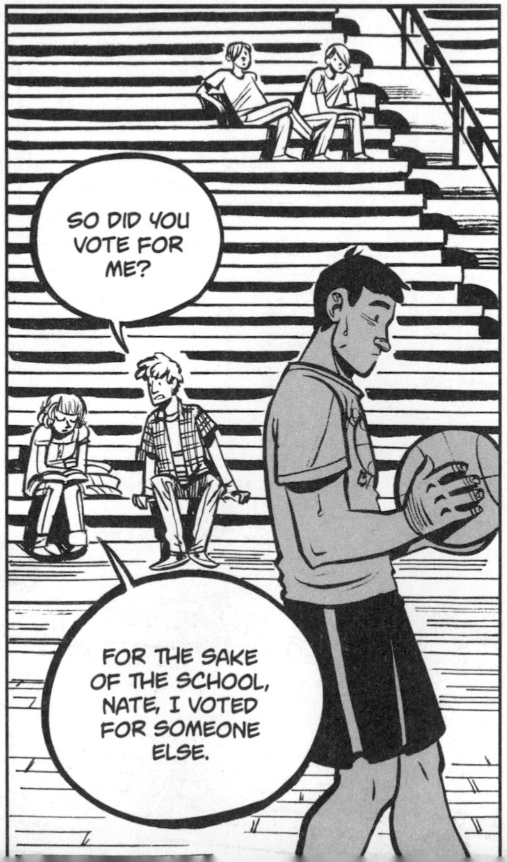
SO DID YOU VOTE FOR ME?
FOR THE SAKE OF THE SCHOOL, NATE, I VOTED FOR SOMEONE ELSE.

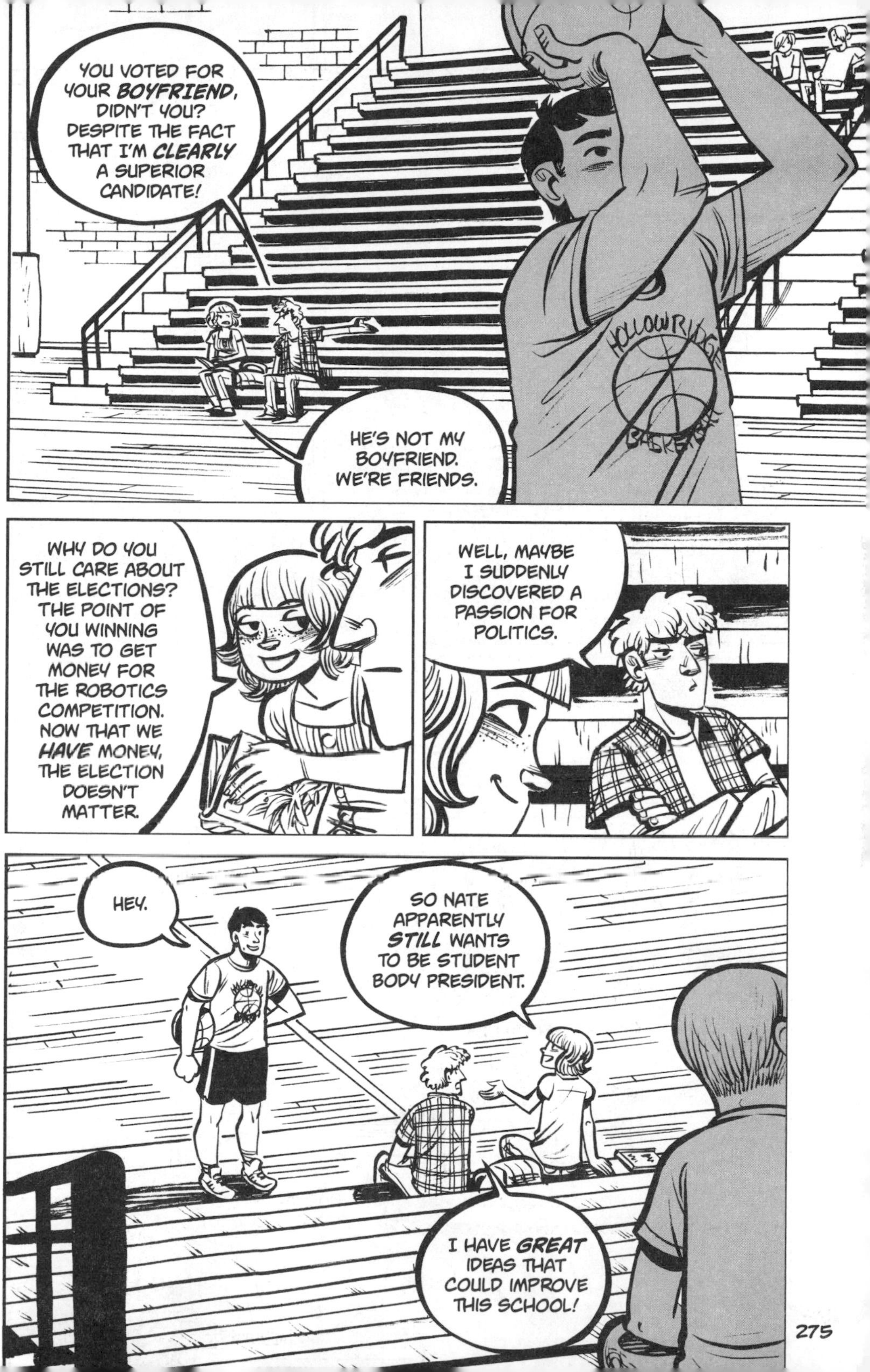
YOU VOTED FOR YOUR BOYFRIEND, DIDN'T YOU? DESPITE THE FACT THAT I'M CLEARLY A SUPERIOR CANDIDATE!
HOLLOW RIDGE BASKETBALL
HE'S NOT MY BOYFRIEND. WE'RE FRIENDS.
WHY DO YOU STILL CARE ABOUT THE ELECTIONS? THE POINT OF YOU WINNING WAS TO GET MONEY FOR THE ROBOTICS COMPETITION. NOW THAT WE HAVE MONEY, THE ELECTION DOESN'T MATTER.
WELL, MAYBE I SUDDENLY DISCOVERED A PASSION FOR POLITICS.
HEY.
SO NATE APPARENTLY STILL WANTS TO BE STUDENT BODY PRESIDENT.
I HAVE GREAT IDEAS THAT COULD IMPROVE THIS SCHOOL!

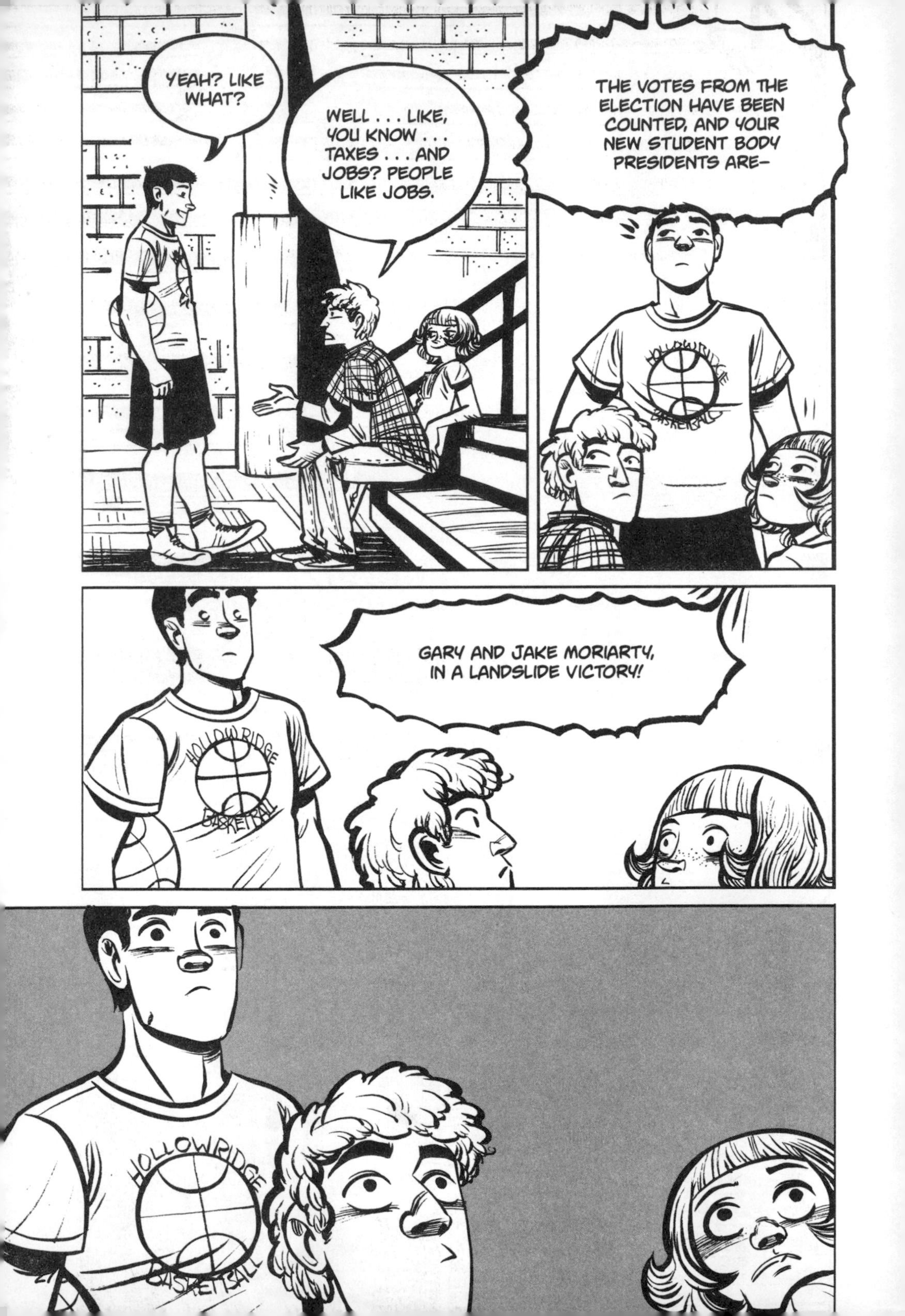
YEAH? LIKE WHAT?
WELL . . . LIKE, YOU KNOW . . . TAXES . . . AND JOBS? PEOPLE LIKE JOBS.
THE VOTES FROM THE ELECTION HAVE BEEN COUNTED, AND YOUR NEW STUDENT BODY PRESIDENTS ARE–
HOLLOWRIDGE BASKETBALL
GARY AND JAKE MORIARTY, IN A LANDSLIDE VICTORY!
HOLLOWRIDGE BASKETBALL
HOLLOWRIDGE BASKETBALL

EEX-CELLENT.

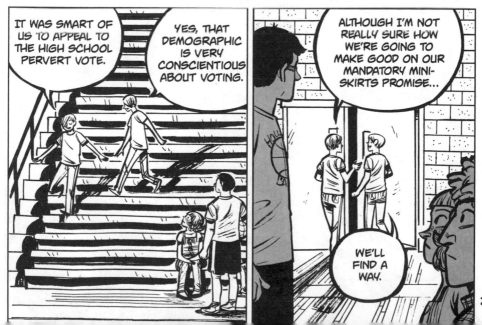

IT WAS SMART OF US TO APPEAL TO THE HIGH SCHOOL PERVERT VOTE.

YES, THAT DEMOGRAPHIC IS VERY CONSCIENTIOUS ABOUT VOTING.

ALTHOUGH I'M NOT REALLY SURE HOW WE'RE GOING TO MAKE GOOD ON OUR MANDATORY MINI-SKIRTS PROMISE...

WE'LL FIND A WAY.

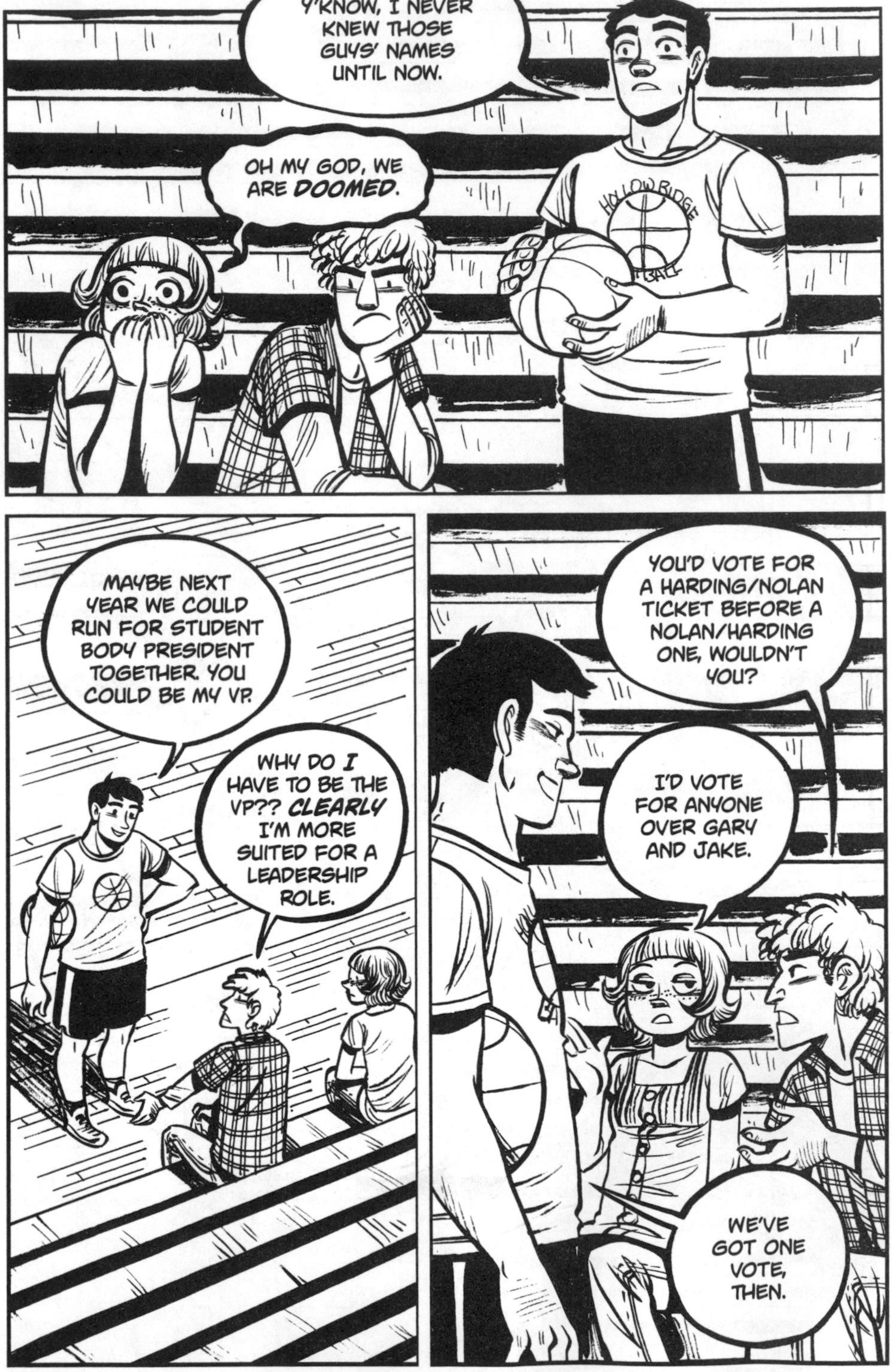

Y'KNOW, I NEVER KNEW THOSE GUYS' NAMES UNTIL NOW.
OH MY GOD, WE ARE *DOOMED*.
HOLLOW RIDGE
MAYBE NEXT YEAR WE COULD RUN FOR STUDENT BODY PRESIDENT TOGETHER. YOU COULD BE MY VP.
WHY DO *I* HAVE TO BE THE VP?? *CLEARLY* I'M MORE SUITED FOR A LEADERSHIP ROLE.
YOU'D VOTE FOR A HARDING/NOLAN TICKET BEFORE A NOLAN/HARDING ONE, WOULDN'T YOU?
I'D VOTE FOR ANYONE OVER GARY AND JAKE.
WE'VE GOT ONE VOTE, THEN.

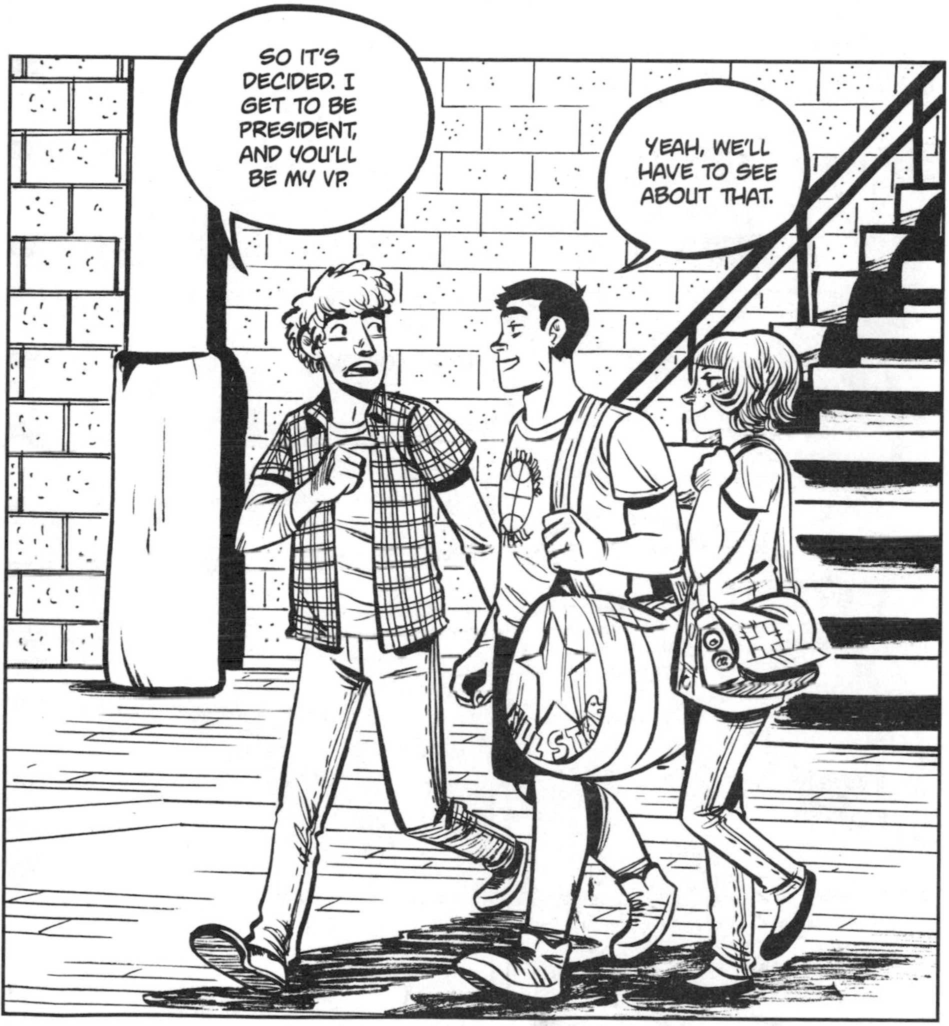
SO IT'S DECIDED. I GET TO BE PRESIDENT, AND YOU'LL BE MY VP.
YEAH, WE'LL HAVE TO SEE ABOUT THAT.

ACKNOWLEDGMENTS

Enormous thanks go to Diana Fox, who took a chance on me, as did Calista Brill, Gina Gagliano, and the rest of the talented crew at First Second. Also, there cannot be enough effusive adjectives for Faith, whose art breathed laughter into these characters.

Thanks also to my friends, who though spread across three continents in a multitude of countries, always had time for my panic attacks, thought experiments about driving sort-of-stolen SUVs, and routinely let me sleep on their couches.

Lastly, I am endlessly grateful to the poor souls who had the misfortune of teaching me through the years: Mrs. Thorsen, who let a twelve-year-old make mosaics; Mr. Dickerson, who proved me wrong about science fiction; and Mrs. Nelson, because when I told her I was going to law school, she laughed and said, "No, you're not. You're going to be a writer."

—Prudence Shen

As always, thanks to the First Second elite literary ninja squad: Calista Brill, Gina Gagliano, Colleen AF Venable, Mark Siegel; my awesome agent Bernadette; Prudence, for being totally cool with me transforming a word book into a picture book; the Saturday coffee shop sketch group: Noreen, Mitch, Miriam, Andrew, Ben, Joe, and Tony (sometimes); and Tim. 'Cause he's the best.

—Faith Erin Hicks